A Cornelius Calendar

The Michael Moorcock Collection

The Michael Moorcock Collection is the definitive library of acclaimed author Michael Moorcock's SF & fantasy, including the entirety of his Eternal Champion work. It is prepared and edited by John Davey, the author's long-time bibliographer and editor, and will be published, over the course of two years, in the following print omnibus editions by Gollancz, and as individual eBooks by the SF Gateway (see http://www.sfgateway.com/authors/m/moorcock-michael/ for a complete list of available eBooks).

ELRIC

Elric of Melniboné and Other Stories

Elric: The Fortress of the Pearl

Elric: The Sailor on the Seas of Fate

Elric: The Sleeping Sorceress

Elric: The Revenge of the Rose

Elric: Stormbringer!

Elric: The Moonbeam Roads
comprising –
Daughter of Dreams
Destiny's Brother
Son of the Wolf

CORUM

Corum: The Prince in the Scarlet Robe
comprising –
The Knight of the Swords
The Queen of the Swords
The King of the Swords

Corum: The Prince with the Silver Hand
comprising –
The Bull and the Spear
The Oak and the Ram
The Sword and the Stallion

HAWKMOON

Hawkmoon: The History of the Runestaff
comprising –
The Jewel in the Skull
The Mad God's Amulet
The Sword of the Dawn
The Runestaff

Hawkmoon: Count Brass
comprising –
Count Brass
The Champion of Garathorm
The Quest for Tanelorn

JERRY CORNELIUS

The Cornelius Quartet
comprising –
The Final Programme
A Cure for Cancer
The English Assassin
The Condition of Muzak

Jerry Cornelius: His Lives and His Times (short-fiction collection)

A Cornelius Calendar
comprising –
The Adventures of Una Persson and Catherine Cornelius in the Twentieth Century
The Entropy Tango
The Great Rock 'n' Roll Swindle
The Alchemist's Question
Firing the Cathedral/Modem Times 2.0

Von Bek
comprising –
The War Hound and the World's Pain
The City in the Autumn Stars

The Eternal Champion
comprising –
The Eternal Champion
Phoenix in Obsidian
The Dragon in the Sword

The Dancers at the End of Time
comprising –
An Alien Heat
The Hollow Lands
The End of all Songs

Kane of Old Mars
comprising –
Warriors of Mars
Blades of Mars
Barbarians of Mars

Moorcock's Multiverse
comprising –
The Sundered Worlds
The Winds of Limbo
The Shores of Death

The Nomad of Time
comprising –
The Warlord of the Air
The Land Leviathan
The Steel Tsar

Travelling to Utopia
comprising –
The Wrecks of Time
The Ice Schooner
The Black Corridor

The War Amongst the Angels
comprising –
Blood: A Southern Fantasy
Fabulous Harbours
The War Amongst the Angels

Tales from the End of Time
comprising –
Legends from the End of Time
Constant Fire
Elric at the End of Time

Behold the Man

Gloriana; or, The Unfulfill'd Queen

SHORT FICTION

My Experiences in the Third World War and Other Stories: The Best Short Fiction of Michael Moorcock Volume 1

The Brothel in Rosenstrasse and Other Stories: The Best Short Fiction of Michael Moorcock Volume 2

Breakfast in the Ruins and Other Stories: The Best Short Fiction of Michael Moorcock Volume 3

A Cornelius Calendar

The Adventures of Una Persson and Catherine Cornelius in the Twentieth Century

The Entropy Tango

The Great Rock 'n' Roll Swindle

The Alchemist's Question

Firing the Cathedral

Modem Times 2.0

MICHAEL MOORCOCK

Edited by John Davey

This edition published in Great Britain in 2014 by
Gollancz
An imprint of the Orion Publishing Group
Orion House, 5 Upper St Martin's Lane,
London WC2H 9EA
An Hachette UK Company

7 9 10 8 6

A CIP catalogue record for this book is available from the British Library

ISBN 978 1 473 20074 6

Typeset by Jouve (UK), Milton Keynes

Printed and bound in Great Britain by Clays Ltd, Elcograf S.p.A.

The Orion Publishing Group's policy is to use papers that are natural, renewable and recyclable products and made from wood grown in sustainable forests. The logging and manufacturing processes are expected to conform to the environmental regulations of the country of origin.

www.multiverse.org
www.sfgateway.com
www.gollancz.co.uk
www.orionbooks.co.uk

Introduction to *The Michael Moorcock Collection*

John Clute

He is now over 70, enough time for most careers to start and end in, enough time to fit in an occasional half-decade or so of silence to mark off the big years. Silence happens. I don't think I know an author who doesn't fear silence like the plague; most of us, if we live long enough, can remember a bad blank year or so, or more. Not Michael Moorcock. Except for some worrying surgery on his toes in recent years, he seems not to have taken time off to breathe the air of peace and panic. There has been no time to spare. The nearly 60 years of his active career seems to have been too short to fit everything in: the teenage comics; the editing jobs; the pulp fiction; the reinvented heroic fantasies; the Eternal Champion; the deep Jerry Cornelius riffs; New Worlds; the 1970s/1980s flow of stories and novels, dozens upon dozens of them in every category of modern fantastika; the tales of the dying Earth and the possessing of Jesus; the exercises in postmodernism that turned the world inside out before most of us had begun to guess we were living on the wrong side of things; the invention (more or less) of steampunk; the alternate histories; the *Mitteleuropean* tales of sexual terror; the deep-city London riffs: the turns and changes and returns and reconfigurations to which he has subjected his oeuvre over the years (he expects this new Collected Edition will fix these transformations in place for good); the late tales where he has been remodelling the intersecting worlds he created in the 1960s in terms of twenty-first-century physics: for starters. If you can't take the heat, I guess, stay out of the multiverse.

His life has been full and complicated, a life he has exposed and hidden (like many other prolific authors) throughout his work. In *Mother London* (1988), though, a nonfantastic novel published at what is now something like the midpoint of his career, it may be possible to find the key to all the other selves who made the 100 books. There are three protagonists in the tale, which is set from about 1940 to about 1988 in the suburbs and inner runnels of the vast metropolis of Charles Dickens and Robert Louis Stevenson. The oldest of these protagonists is Joseph Kiss, a flamboyant self-advertising fin-de-siècle figure of substantial girth and a fantasticating relationship to the world: he is Michael Moorcock, seen with genial bite as a kind of G.K. Chesterton without the wearying punch-line paradoxes. The youngest of the three is David Mummery, a haunted introspective half-insane denizen of a secret London of trials and runes and codes and magic: he too is Michael Moorcock, seen through a glass, darkly. And there is Mary Gasalee, a kind of holy-innocent and survivor, blessed with a luminous clarity of insight, so that in all her apparent ignorance of the onrushing secular world she is more deeply wise than other folk: she is also Michael Moorcock, Moorcock when young as viewed from the wry middle years of 1988. When we read the book, we are reading a book of instructions for the assembly of a London writer. The Moorcock we put together from this choice of portraits is amused and bemused at the vision of himself; he is a phenomenon of flamboyance and introspection, a poseur and a solitary, a dreamer and a doer, a multitude and a singleton. But only the three Moorcocks in this book, working together, could have written all the other books.

It all began – as it does for David Mummery in *Mother London* – in South London, in a subtopian stretch of villas called Mitcham, in 1939. In early childhood, he experienced the Blitz, and never forgot the extraordinariness of being a participant – however minute – in the great drama; all around him, as though the world were being dismantled nightly, darkness and blackout would descend, bombs fall, buildings and streets disappear; and in the morning, as though a new universe had taken over from the old one and the world had become portals, the sun would rise on glinting rubble, abandoned tricycles, men and women going about their daily tasks as though nothing had happened, strange shards of ruin poking into altered air. From a very early age, Michael Moorcock's security reposed in a sense that everything might change, in the blinking of an eye, and be *rejourneyed* the next day (or the next book). Though as a writer he has certainly elucidated the fears and alarums of life in Aftermath Britain, it does seem that his very early years were marked by the epiphanies of war, rather than the inflictions of despair and beclouding amnesia most adults necessarily experienced. After the war ended, his parents separated, and the young Moorcock began to attend a pretty wide variety of schools, several of which he seems to have been expelled from, and as soon as he could legally do so he began to work full time, up north in London's heart, which he only left when he moved to Texas (with intervals in Paris) in the early 1990s, from where (to jump briefly up the decades) he continues to cast a Martian eye: as with most exiles, Moorcock's intensest anatomies of his homeland date from after his cunning departure.

But back again to the beginning (just as though we were rimming a multiverse). Starting in the 1950s there was the comics and pulp work for Fleetway Publications; there was the first book (*Caribbean Crisis*, 1962) as by Desmond Reid, co-written with his early friend the artist James Cawthorn (1929–2008); there was marriage, with the writer Hilary Bailey (they divorced in 1978), three children, a heated existence in the Ladbroke Grove / Notting Hill Gate region of London he was later to populate with Jerry Cornelius and his vast family; there was the editing of NEW WORLDS, which began in 1964 and became the heartbeat of the British New Wave two years later as writers like Brian W. Aldiss and J.G. Ballard, reaching their early prime, made it into a tympanum, as young American writers like Thomas M. Disch, John T. Sladek, Norman Spinrad and Pamela Zoline found a home in London for material they could not publish in America, and new British writers like M. John Harrison and Charles Platt began their careers in its pages; but before that there was Elric. With *The Stealer of Souls* (1963) and

Stormbringer (1965), the multiverse began to flicker into view, and the Eternal Champion (whom Elric parodied and embodied) began properly to ransack the worlds in his fight against a greater Chaos than the great dance could sustain. There was also the first SF novel, *The Sundered Worlds* (1965), but in the 1960s SF was a difficult nut to demolish for Moorcock: he would bide his time.

We come to the heart of the matter. Jerry Cornelius, who first appears in *The Final Programme* (1968) – which assembles and coordinates material first published a few years earlier in NEW WORLDS – is a deliberate solarisation of the albino Elric, who was himself a mocking solarisation of Robert E. Howard's Conan, or rather of the mighty-thew-headed Conan created for profit by Howard epigones: Moorcock rarely mocks the true quill. Cornelius, who reaches his first and most telling apotheosis in the four novels comprising *The Cornelius Quartet*, remains his most distinctive and perhaps most original single creation: a wide boy, an agent, a *flaneur*, a bad musician, a shopper, a shapechanger, a trans, a spy in the house of London: a toxic palimpsest on whom and through whom the *zeitgeist* inscribes surreal conjugations of 'message'. Jerry Cornelius gives head to Elric.

The life continued apace. By 1970, with NEW WORLDS on its last legs, multiverse fantasies and experimental novels poured forth; Moorcock and Hilary Bailey began to live separately, though he moved, in fact, only around the corner, where he set up house with Jill Riches, who would become his second wife; there was a second home in Yorkshire, but London remained his central base. *The Condition of Muzak* (1977), which is the fourth Cornelius novel, and *Gloriana; or, The Unfulfill'd Queen* (1978), which transfigures the first Elizabeth into a kinked Astraea, marked perhaps the high point of his career as a writer of fiction whose font lay in genre or its mutations – marked perhaps the furthest bournes he could transgress while remaining within the perimeters of fantasy (though *within* those bournes vast stretches of territory remained and would, continually, be explored). During these years he sometimes wore a leather jacket constructed out of numerous patches of varicoloured material, and it sometimes seemed perfectly fitting that he bore the semblance, as his jacket flickered and fuzzed from across a room or road, of an illustrated man, a map, a thing of shreds and patches, a student fleshed from dreams. Like the stories he told, he seemed to be more than one thing. To use a term frequently applied (by me at least) to twenty-first-century fiction, he seemed equipoisal: which is to say that, through all his genre-hopping and genre-mixing and genre-transcending and genre-loyal returnings to old pitches, *he was never still*, because 'equipoise' is all about *making stories move*. As with his stories, he cannot be pinned down, because he is not in one place. In person and in his work, it has always been sink or swim: like a shark, or a dancer, or an equilibrist…

The marriage with Jill Riches came to an end. He married Linda Steele in 1983; they remain married. The Colonel Pyat books, *Byzantium Endures* (1981), *The Laughter of Carthage* (1984), *Jerusalem Commands* (1992) and *The Vengeance of Rome* (2006), dominated these years, along with *Mother London*. As these books, which are non-fantastic, are not included in the current *Michael Moorcock Collection*, it might be worth noting here that, in their insistence on the irreducible difficulty of gaining anything like true sight, they represent Moorcock's mature modernist take on what one might call the rag-and-bone shop of the world itself; and that the huge ornate postmodern edifice of his multiverse *loosens* us from that world, gives us room to breathe, to juggle our strategies for living – allows us ultimately to escape from prison (to use a phrase from a writer he does not respect, J.R.R. Tolkien, for whom the twentieth century was a prison train bound for hell). What Moorcock may best be remembered for in the end is the (perhaps unique) interplay between modernism and postmodernism in his work. (But a plethora of discordant understandings makes these terms hard to use; so enough of them.) In the end, one might just say that Moorcock's work as a whole represents an extraordinarily multifarious execution of the fantasist's main task: which is to *get us out of here*.

Recent decades saw a continuation of the multifarious, but with a more intensely applied methodology. The late volumes of the long Elric saga, and the Second Ether sequence of meta-fantasies – *Blood: A Southern Fantasy* (1995), *Fabulous Harbours* (1995) and *The War Amongst the Angels: An Autobiographical Story* (1996) – brood on the real world and the multiverse through the lens of Chaos Theory: the closer you get to the world, the less you describe it. *The Metatemporal Detective* (2007) – a narrative in the Steampunk mode Moorcock had previewed as long ago as *The Warlord of the Air* (1971) and *The Land Leviathan* (1974) – continues the process, sometimes dizzyingly: as though the reader inhabited the eye of a camera increasing its focus on a closely observed reality while its bogey simultaneously wheels it backwards from the desired rapport: an old Kurasawa trick here amplified into a tool of conspectus, fantasy eyed and (once again) rejourneyed, this time through the lens of SF.

We reach the second decade of the twenty-first century, time still to make things new, but also time to sort. There are dozens of titles in *The Michael Moorcock Collection* that have not been listed in this short space, much less trawled for tidbits. The various avatars of the Eternal Champion – Elric, Kane of Old Mars, Hawkmoon, Count Brass, Corum, Von Bek – differ vastly from one another. Hawkmoon is a bit of a berk; Corum is a steely solitary at the End of Time: the joys and doleurs of the interplays amongst them can only be experienced through immersion. And the Dancers at the End of Time books, and the Nomad of the Time Stream books, and the Karl Glogauer books, and all the others. They are here now, a 100 books that make up one book. They have been fixed for reading. It is time to enter the multiverse and see the world.

September 2012

Introduction to *The Michael Moorcock Collection*

Michael Moorcock

By 1964, after I had been editing New Worlds for some months and had published several science fiction and fantasy novels, including *Stormbringer*, I realised that my run as a writer was over. About the only new ideas I'd come up with were miniature computers, the multiverse and black holes, all very crudely realised, in *The Sundered Worlds*. No doubt I would have to return to journalism, writing features and editing. 'My career,' I told my friend J.G. Ballard, 'is finished.' He sympathised and told me he only had a few SF stories left in him, then he, too, wasn't sure what he'd do.

In January 1965, living in Colville Terrace, Notting Hill, then an infamous slum, best known for its race riots, I sat down at the typewriter in our kitchen-cum-bathroom and began a locally based book, designed to be accompanied by music and graphics. *The Final Programme* featured a character based on a young man I'd seen around the area and whom I named after a local greengrocer, Jerry Cornelius, 'Messiah to the Age of Science'. Jerry was as much a technique as a character. Not the 'spy' some critics described him as but an urban adventurer as interested in his psychic environment as the contemporary physical world. My influences were English and French absurdists, American noir novels. My inspiration was William Burroughs with whom I'd recently begun a correspondence. I also borrowed a few SF ideas, though I was adamant that I was not writing in any established genre. I felt I had at last found my own authentic voice.

I had already written a short novel, *The Golden Barge*, set in a nowhere, no-time world very much influenced by Peake and the surrealists, which I had not attempted to publish. An earlier autobiographical novel, *The Hungry Dreamers*, set in Soho, was eaten by rats in a Ladbroke Grove basement. I remained unsatisfied with my style and my technique. *The Final Programme* took nine days to complete (by 20 January, 1965) with my baby daughters sometimes cradled with their bottles while I typed on. This, I should say, is my memory of events; my then wife scoffed at this story when I recounted it. Whatever the truth, the fact is I only believed I might be a serious writer after I had finished that novel, with all its flaws. But Jerry Cornelius, probably my most successful sustained attempt at unconventional fiction, was born then and ever since has remained a useful means of telling complex stories. Associated with the 60s and 70s, he has been equally at home in all the following decades. Through novels and novellas I developed a means of carrying several narratives and viewpoints on what appeared to be a very light (but tight) structure which dispensed with some of the earlier methods of fiction. In the sense that it took for granted the understanding that the novel is among other things an internal dialogue and I did not feel the need to repeat by now commonly understood modernist conventions, this fiction was post-modern.

Not all my fiction looked for new forms for the new century. Like many 'revolutionaries' I looked back as well as forward. As George Meredith looked to the eighteenth century for inspiration for his experiments with narrative, I looked to Meredith, popular Edwardian realists like Pett Ridge and Zangwill and the writers of the *fin de siècle* for methods and inspiration. An almost obsessive interest in the Fabians, several of whom believed in the possibility of benign imperialism, ultimately led to my Bastable books which examined our enduring British notion that an empire could be essentially a force for good. The first was *The Warlord of the Air*.

I also wrote my *Dancers at the End of Time* stories and novels under the influence of Edwardian humourists and absurdists like Jerome or Firbank. Together with more conventional generic books like *The Ice Schooner* or *The Black Corridor*, most of that work was done in the 1960s and 70s when I wrote the Eternal Champion supernatural adventure novels which helped support my own and others' experiments via NEW WORLDS, allowing me also to keep a family while writing books in which action and fantastic invention were paramount. Though I did them quickly, I didn't write them cynically. I have always believed, somewhat puritanically, in giving the audience good value for money. I enjoyed writing them, tried to avoid repetition, and through each new one was able to develop a few more ideas. They also continued to teach me how to express myself through image and metaphor. My Everyman became the Eternal Champion, his dreams and ambitions represented by the multiverse. He could be an ordinary person struggling with familiar problems in a contemporary setting or he could be a swordsman fighting monsters on a far-away world.

Long before I wrote *Gloriana* (in four parts reflecting the seasons) I had learned to think in images and symbols through reading John Bunyan's *Pilgrim's Progress*, Milton and others, understanding early on that the visual could be the most important part of a book and was often in itself a story as, for instance, a famous personality could also, through everything associated with their name, function as narrative. I wanted to find ways of carrying as many stories as possible in one. From the cinema I also learned how to use images as connecting themes. Images, colours, music, and even popular magazine headlines can all add coherence to an apparently random story, underpinning it and giving the reader a sense of internal logic and a satisfactory resolution, dispensing with certain familiar literary conventions.

When the story required it, I also began writing neo-realist fiction exploring the interface of character and environment, especially the city, especially London. In some books I condensed, manipulated and randomised time to achieve what I wanted, but in others the sense of 'real time' as we all generally perceive it was more suitable and could best be achieved by traditional nineteenth-century means. For the Pyat books I first looked back to the great German classic, Grimmelshausen's *Simplicissimus* and other early picaresques. I then examined the roots of a certain kind of moral fiction from Defoe through Thackeray and Meredith then to modern times where the picaresque (or rogue tale) can take the form of a road movie, for instance. While it's probably fair to say that Pyat and *Byzantium Endures* precipitated the end of my second marriage (echoed to a degree in *The Brothel in Rosenstrasse*), the late 70s and the 80s were exhilarating times for me, with *Mother London* being perhaps my own favourite novel of that period. I wanted to write something celebratory.

By the 90s I was again attempting to unite several kinds of fiction in one novel with my Second Ether trilogy. With Mandelbrot, Chaos Theory and String Theory I felt, as I said at the time, as if I were being offered a chart of my own brain. That chart made it easier for me to develop the notion of the multiverse as representing both the internal and the external, as a metaphor and as a means of structuring and rationalising an outrageously inventive and quasi-realistic narrative. The worlds of the multiverse move up and down scales or 'planes' explained in terms of mass, allowing entire universes to exist in the 'same' space. The result of developing this idea was the *War Amongst the Angels* sequence which added absurdist elements also functioning as a kind of mythology and folklore for a world beginning to understand itself in terms of new metaphysics and theoretical physics. As the cosmos becomes denser and almost infinite before our eyes, with black holes and dark matter affecting our own reality, we can explore them and observe them as our ancestors explored our planet and observed the heavens.

At the end of the 90s I'd returned to realism, sometimes with a dash of fantasy, with *King of the City* and the stories collected in *London Bone*. I also wrote a new Elric / Eternal Champion sequence, beginning with *Daughter of Dreams*, which brought the fantasy worlds of Hawkmoon, Bastable and Co. in line with my realistic and autobiographical stories, another attempt to unify all my fiction, and also offer a way in which disparate genres could be reunited, through notions developed from the multiverse and the Eternal Champion, as one giant novel. At the time I was finishing the Pyat sequence which attempted to look at the roots of the Nazi Holocaust in our European, Middle Eastern and American cultures and to ground my strange survival guilt while at the same time examining my own cultural roots in the light of an enduring anti-Semitism.

By the 2000s I was exploring various conventional ways of story-telling in the last parts of *The Metatemporal Detective* and through other homages, comics, parodies and games. I also looked back at my earliest influences. I had reached retirement age and felt like a rest. I wrote a 'prequel' to the Elric series as a graphic novel with Walter Simonson, *The Making of a Sorcerer*, and did a little online editing with FANTASTIC METROPOLIS.

By 2010 I had written a novel featuring Doctor Who, *The Coming of the Terraphiles*, with a nod to P.G. Wodehouse (a boyhood favourite), continued to write short stories and novellas and to work on the beginning of a new sequence combining pure fantasy and straight autobiography called *The Whispering Swarm* while still writing more Cornelius stories trying to unite all the various genres and sub-genres into which contemporary fiction has fallen.

Throughout my career critics have announced that I'm 'abandoning' fantasy and concentrating on literary fiction. The truth is, however, that all my life, since I became a professional writer and editor at the age of 16, I've written in whatever mode suits a story best and where necessary created a new form if an old one didn't work for me. Certain ideas are best carried on a Jerry Cornelius story, others work better as realism and others as fantasy or science fiction. Some work best as a combination. I'm sure I'll write whatever I like and will continue to experiment with all the ways there are of telling stories and carrying as many themes as possible. Whether I write about a widow coping with loneliness in her cottage or a massive, universe-size sentient spaceship searching for her children, I'll no doubt die trying to tell them all. I hope you'll find at least some of them to your taste.

One thing a reader can be sure of about these new editions is that they would not have been possible without the tremendous and indispensable help of my old friend and bibliographer John Davey. John has ensured that these Gollancz editions are definitive. I am indebted to John for many things, including his work at

Moorcock's Miscellany, my website, but his work on this edition has been outstanding. As well as being an accomplished novelist in his own right John is an astonishingly good editor who has worked with Gollancz and myself to point out every error and flaw in all previous editions, some of them not corrected since their first publication, and has enabled me to correct or revise them. I couldn't have completed this project without him. Together, I think, Gollancz, John Davey and myself have produced what will be the best editions possible and I am very grateful to him, to Malcolm Edwards, Darren Nash and Marcus Gipps for all the considerable hard work they have done to make this edition what it is.

Michael Moorcock

Contents

The Adventures of Una Persson and Catherine Cornelius in the Twentieth Century 1

The Entropy Tango 249

The Great Rock 'n' Roll Swindle 413

The Alchemist's Question 509

The Final Programme Portfolio 677

Firing the Cathedral 693

Modem Times 2.0 785

Illustrated by Mark Reeve, Romain Slocombe
and Michael Moorcock

The New Nature of the Catastrophe

EDITED BY LANGDON JONES & MICHAEL MOORCOCK

THE APOCRYPHAL JERRY CORNELIUS STORIES BY BRIAN W. ALDISS, NORMAN SPINRAD, M. JOHN HARRISON, JAMES SALLIS, LANGDON JONES, SIMON INGS, MAXIM JAKUBOWSKI AND OTHERS INCLUDING MICHAEL MOORCOCK

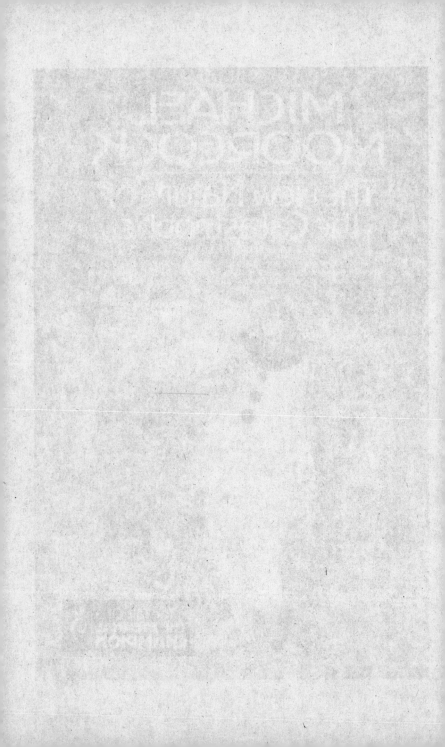

The Adventures of Una Persson and Catherine Cornelius in the Twentieth Century

A Romance

For
Miss C. Malone,
Aviatrix

I shall not say why and how I became, at the age of fifteen, the mistress of the Earl of Craven. Whether it was love, or the severity of my father, the depravity of my own heart, or the winning arts of the noble Lord, which induced me to leave my paternal roof and place myself under his protection, does not now much signify: or if it does, I am not in the humour to gratify curiosity in this matter.

– Harriette Wilson,
Memoirs

Introduction

A note concerning the principal characters and sources of this book

The unpublished memoirs of Miss Una Persson, the temporal adventuress, have been the chief source for the story which follows. These memoirs, entrusted to me some time ago and constantly added to and modified by Miss Persson, exist partly in the form of notes in her own hand, partly in the form of tape-recorded interviews between myself and Miss Persson, partly as notes taken by me after one of our many conversations. The memoirs, therefore, are discursive and unorganised, but are remarkably consistent in their details and I have used them indirectly in several novels where I have needed to write about the earlier years of this century or, indeed, the last years. Occasionally I have used them to check certain facts found in other published accounts concerning important moments in recent history and in all cases where there have been inconsistencies it has been proven that Miss Persson's record was the most objective, the most accurate.

Only when the subject of her method *of time travel is raised does Miss Persson become a little vague. That the time-travelling often works profound and subtle changes on her character is undeniable (and there are sometimes physical changes, too) but how she achieved the ability to move easily through the years and centuries and why the changes take place are mysteries I can only hope that one day she will choose to explain. There is no doubt that a few other people share her ability (she has described it as a 'talent') including at least three members of the ubiquitous Cornelius family, that stranger figure Karl Glogauer, Lord Jagged of Canaria, and the doomed Oswald Bastable (whom my grandfather knew so well) and it is fair to assume that she has been responsible for helping some of these develop the talent – Catherine Cornelius quite obviously learned the knack from Miss Persson, with whom she has had a close friendship since adolescence. Most of my knowledge of the Cornelius family comes from Miss*

Persson's accounts, received in turn from Miss Cornelius; most of my information about that peculiar period of the far future known as the Age at the End of Time also comes from Miss Persson.

Needless to say, I have often enquired about the reason for Miss Persson's rarely revealing her marvellous talent or, indeed, using it to obvious advantage, and again I have found her answers a trifle numinous; something to do with the creation of 'alternative' futures, with unwanted paradox and the tendency of Time itself to resist anachronistic events by 'spitting out' any time-traveller who might seek radically to change the course of history. This, I gather, is why a good psychic and physical disguise is necessary to the committed time-traveller; and the result is often a form of temporary amnesia where the traveller sinks so thoroughly into the spirit of the age that he or she forgets any other identity or having existed in any other period (indeed, Miss Persson has suggested to me that the ability to achieve this state might even be a crucial factor in the make-up of those who have found it possible to travel through time).

As for the question of 'alternative' versions of our history, I am afraid that I have neither the intelligence nor the information from which to speculate; I can merely repeat in good faith what Miss Persson has told me – that a very few people are also able to cross from one 'alternate' age to another and that few of those do so of their own volition (here I must cite the two volumes edited by my grandfather, published under the titles The Warlord of the Air *and* The Land Leviathan, *for anyone wishing to consider further evidence).*

One last point: the narrative which follows is fiction in so far as I have taken liberties of interpretation, organisation and speculation with Miss Persson's records, moreover the selection and therefore the bias is mine. My simple intention has been to make from the material entrusted to me an entertaining book which can be enjoyed as a work of fiction is enjoyed, and I hope that the reader will judge it in that light alone.

Michael Moorcock,
Ladbroke Grove,
London
November 1975

Part One

Depression Days: Taking It Easy

> This may be hard to believe … but when you're looking at this little sweetheart you're looking at Miss World. True enough, she hasn't got a proper crown – it's only an old cake decoration. And she is just eight months old. But her Mum, Pauline, will support little Layla's claim that she was born to be Miss World. That is largely on account of her Dad being Mr World … Well, a girl has to make the most of her assets.
>
> *Daily Mirror*, 3 November, 1975

I. In which we are introduced to our heroines and learn that, having rested and recovered sufficiently from the experiences of their previous adventures, they are prepared to embark upon a new series of excursions into the twentieth century

It was light at last.

Jars of cosmetics rattled and perfume bottles clinked on the dressing table, pushed back towards the white-framed oval mirror by Una Persson's breakfast tray, heavy and steaming, as in some relief she let go of the handles. She crossed to the wide bow windows and jerked a cord, sending the white-and-black art deco blind whizzing on its roller to reveal the sunlit shrubbery, the sloping lawn, the broad, shallow river and, beyond it, the green wooded Pocono Mountains. Two days ago the boy scouts had set up their camp on the far shore of the river. The camp was invisible from the house; Una could hear one of the scouts practising dawn bugle calls from somewhere behind the elms near the bend where the muddy Delaware was at its widest. The sun rose over the Poconos: another cloudless day. Naked, Una stretched her fine, strong arms and fluffed at her short chestnut hair, yawning. The bugle call faltered, became a series of brief, desperate discords, then collapsed and did not begin again. The birds resumed their interrupted chorus.

Una turned to look at Catherine Cornelius who was peacefully asleep in the midst of the white sheets and primrose pillows; she was undisturbed by the sunlight which fell on her fair skin, reflected in her gleaming, near-white hair, the silver filigree rings on the fingers of her exposed left hand.

Reflecting that she was pleased with the world this morning, Una concluded that she must be bored; then she smiled: she was becoming far too interested in the minute details of her momentary states of mind. She opened the windows and took a deep breath. The air was already very warm. In the bed Catherine stirred, drawing her hand under the sheets, awake but unwilling to wake up. Una went back to the breakfast tray, lifted it and carried it to the bed, placing it carefully near the edge, climbing back in, pulling a sheet up to her waist, reaching forward and taking the tray again to lower it onto her lap. She began to pour herself a cup of coffee, noticing how its smell blended so well with the smell of Catherine's skin. She unfolded the *Briggstown Examiner* and without glancing at the headlines turned at once to the funnies page.

By the time Una had read 'Krazy Kat' and 'The Katzenjammer Kids' Catherine was on one elbow glancing over her shoulder to see how Tarzan and Flash Gordon were doing (Una had known that this would draw Catherine out of her sleep – Tarzan and the smell of coffee).

'Coffee?'

Una smiled as she poured another cup. Catherine rubbed at her head and sighed, trying to focus her eyes on her favourite strip. She nodded and then kissed Una's shoulder before taking the offered coffee in an unsteady hand. The cup rattled in the saucer. Catherine sat up and began to drink, her large blue eyes staring bleakly at the window. The sheet fell away from her breasts. She opened her mouth in a wide yawn.

'Is it Tuesday?'

'Yes.' Una looked at her watch. 'It's early. Not seven.'

'Oh, shit.' The tone of despair was profound.

'You were asleep by eight,' said Una good-humouredly. 'You've had eleven hours.'

It took Catherine a short while to make sense of this statement but when she did understand it she was relieved. 'Oh, well…'

'You missed the boy scouts.'

Catherine licked her lips. 'What?'

'They were playing their bugles. Do you want the paper?'

Catherine accepted the *Examiner*. Her expression was rapt as she followed the adventure strips (she could only rarely see what was amusing about the joke strips). She sipped her coffee. She relaxed; she came to life. She finished the coffee and handed the paper back. 'That's better.'

Una folded the pages slowly, glancing at the news. 'They had a fire yesterday, in town. The general store. Not a lot of damage. There's a German rival to Ford. A popular car within the reach of everyone's pocket.'

'Bullshit,' said Catherine, and then, self-consciously, 'life's too bloody short for bullshit.'

Una had not really been listening. 'Go back to sleep, if you like. I've…'

'Sorry, but it is a bit early.' Catherine hugged her, kissed her cheek. Una scarcely flinched. She returned the kiss.

'Have you any plans for today?' Catherine swallowed the remains of her coffee.

'Not really. Maybe finish off the bit of writing I started.'

'Your "memoirs"?'

'And you?'

'I don't know. Read, I suppose. Lounge on the lawn. Improve my tan.' Catherine held her arms in front of her and inspected them. She was already very brown. 'Are you all right?'

'A trifle bored.'

'You're sure that's it?'

'Yes. Why?'

'You seem distant.'

'I am. But it's just boredom.'

'As long as you're not brooding. Proper holidays always are boring, of course. That's what they should be, shouldn't they?'

Una laughed. 'I know.' She was grateful for Catherine's common sense which so often saved her from her moods of morbid introspection. Una hugged her friend, this time with spontaneous affection. Catherine looked vaguely surprised, but she was pleased. She sighed.

As Una got up Catherine asked, 'Do you feel like another Adventure, then?'

'I suppose I do. I'm trying to curb the impulse. I swore I'd have a good long rest.' She opened the door to the landing. 'I'll see what a lukewarm shower does for me.'

The landing was bright with light from the huge window which ran almost from roof to floor on two levels of the big wooden house. The bathroom, pink, black and silver in a local decorator's idea of art deco, was comparatively dark. The plumbing began to groan as Una turned on the hot tap for the shower; a spurt of steaming hot water was immediately followed, as usual, by a gush of tepid, rusty liquid. Philosophically, Una stepped under it. The businessman who had originally bought the place as a summer retreat had crashed with all the others in 1929, before he could make the improvements he had planned. As his chief creditor, Una had inherited it and had left it pretty much as she had found it. If he hadn't made his thirty-storey jump a little ahead of the fashion Una would have given it back to him. She felt it was only right, therefore, not to make any radical changes. The poor man had no other monument.

She finished her shower and began to dry herself with a large brown bath-towel, singing a song which, in another of her rôles, she had made popular. This led her to wondering what had happened to her old lover and manager Sebastian Auchinek who, by now, must have become mixed up in the Zionist politics that would cause him so much anguish in the years to follow. She considered this mood of sympathy a dangerous one for her at the moment and tried to stop the process of association which brought memories of other lovers, other romantics, other victims. It would be much healthier, for one thing, if she considered herself a victim; after all, so many had betrayed her. On the other hand it was rather difficult to sustain that attitude of defensive bitterness, although it was an attitude which had enabled her to make her last escape to this haven. She must be in a healthy state of mind, of course, if she was thinking in these terms; it meant that the holiday had done what she had intended it to do – it had restored her sense of perspective. As yet, though, she was not sure that she welcomed the restoration. It would mean giving up that comfortable ambience of conspiracy which she had been sharing with Catherine, who had taken this holiday for the same reasons as herself – because she had become, as she put it, pissed off with men. It was probably more important for Catherine to maintain her cynicism, since there was far less of it in her character than was sometimes good for her. There again perhaps it was equally unhealthy to take towards Catherine an attitude of maternalism which surely indicated a lack of respect for Catherine's own identity. Checking herself before she went any deeper into such questions, Una burst again into song, this time a bawdy revolutionary ballad concerning the inadequate sexual proficiency of some soon-to-be-forgotten Mexican general. It never failed to make Catherine laugh and now, as Una swept grandly back into the bedroom, Catherine enthusiastically joined in the chorus with an accent which only Spaniards found charming. She was standing by the window, wrapped in a silk kimono tied around the waist with one of the ex-owner's yellow cravats. Una donned pants and bra with a flourish, climbed into a pair of jazzy lounging pyjamas, still singing, and strode to where the tray lay upon the bed. Picking up the tray she marched out of the room, down the curve of the stairs and through the long, wide living room to the kitchen, washing the dishes under the impetus of what remained of the final verse and was able to dry the last cup with an 'Olé' which was decidedly off-key.

Her notebook was on the kitchen table where she had left it the night before, having written a couple of pages after Catherine had gone to bed. She controlled the slight sense of panic she felt on realising that she had left the clasp unlocked. She went to the cupboard where she kept the key, took the key down and locked the book. Through the kitchen window she could see the dusty Duesenberg parked near the back door. The Duesenberg was also part of her inheritance. Later, in the nineteen-fifties, she would give it to Catherine's brother Jerry. She considered a drive in the hills, but the thought produced an agoraphobic twinge and she decided that it would not be a good idea. It was not really agoraphobia at all, she told herself, but an unwillingness to meet anyone, no matter how briefly; an encounter with one of the residents of this period and place would require a disguise and she still did not feel fit enough to relish such artificiality for its own sake. At this, she became reconciled to enjoying the rest of her retreat and she wandered back into the living room to take down one of the late-nineteenth-century bound volumes of *Life* magazine (in those days a sort of American *Punch*) and continue through the French windows, out onto the sweet-smelling lawn where butterflies were already at work on the bright assortment of roses, hollyhocks and sunflowers. There was a movement in the shrubbery: she caught a glimpse of a deer galloping through the broken fence and into the forest on the other side. And that, thought Una with satisfaction, was what 1933 had to offer that you wouldn't be able to get in 1983 (indeed, by 1980 this particular stretch of the valley would have been flooded to make a boating resort and nearby Briggstown itself would be under water). She sat down on the battered wrought-iron bench in the middle of the lawn. The bench's white paint was peeling to reveal a more durable layer of green. As she leafed through the dusty pages of *Life*, Una picked unconsciously at one of the larger blisters until the grass beneath was littered with little white spots, like confetti.

From inside the house came the sound of the pianola being pedalled, a Strauss waltz which lasted only a few bars before Catherine became bored. There was silence, then Una heard the familiar sounds of selections from *The Merry Widow*, Catherine's favourite. Una realised that she had left her cigarettes in the kitchen.

For some reason Una chose not to go back the way she had come and instead walked right round the house to the kitchen door, getting her cigarettes and lighter from the table and leaving again, passing the windows of the living room where Catherine, still in her kimono, sat with her knees pumping up and down at the pianola, her lips soundlessly forming the words of the song she was playing.

Life lay open on the bench, but she ignored both as she wandered on down to the riverbank, lighting a cigarette and looking to see if there were any signs of the scouts' tents, but they were well camouflaged. Save for a glimpse of khaki, they remained invisible. Something organic and tangled went past, drifting swiftly on the current. Una shivered and refused to look at it. She took a deep drag on the Sherman's and then threw the thin brown cigarette into the water. The music had stopped.

Turning, Una saw Catherine come wandering down the lawn towards her. So that Catherine should not catch sight of the disappearing refuse on the river, Una walked rapidly back, calling, 'Hello!' She said: 'I saw a deer!'

'Where did it go? Through the gap?'

'Yes.'

'Phew! I think it's going to be hotter than ever today, don't you?'

'Seems likely.'

'You picked a nice time, Una.'

'Thanks.'

Catherine frowned. 'Am I repeating myself?'

'I don't think so.'

Catherine sat down on the grass, pulling back the kimono to expose her legs. 'Can the boy scouts see us from here?'

'I haven't noticed a glint of field glasses.'

'I rather like the idea...' Catherine peeled off the kimono to reveal her shoulders and breasts. 'I wonder what American boy scouts are like. Even primmer than the British ones, I'd guess...'

'Very probably. But there's always the odd black sheep,' said Una. 'Or is it wolf?' She frowned, adding: 'Boy scouts, indeed! You're bored too, by the sound of it.'

'How long have we been here now?' Catherine stretched herself out in an attitude of crucifixion. 'A month?'

'A bit longer.'

'We said a month, didn't we?'

'Or two, we thought.' Una tried to keep her tone neutral.

'Where was it we jumped from? 1960 –?'

'1975.'

'That was a heavy year. For me, anyway. I thought next time I'd go back a bit, to somewhere nice and early, where there's not quite so much happening on what you'd call an international scale. Fewer people, too. 1910 or sometime like that. It would be a good way of leading into a new cycle – starting with a fairly easy period, you know…'

'A bit *too* dull for me, 1910. I'm not sure why. It depends, I suppose, on the place.' Una hoped that she wasn't manipulating Catherine. 'Russia might be all right.'

'There should be brochures,' said Catherine. 'Come to Sunny Bali in 1925, and so on.' Her eyes were shut against the glare. 'I'd like to see my rotten old mum again, anyway.'

'It takes all tastes.' Catherine's mother terrified Una. Catherine, however, had never lost affection for her.

'And Frank. And Jerry.'

Una raised her eyebrows, returning her attention to the river.

She did not have a lot of time for Catherine's family, though she suspected that this could be because she saw them as rivals. Catherine's boyfriends (those she had met, at any rate) did not arouse the slightest feelings of jealousy in her, merely dislike. She had once admitted to Catherine that she found her friend's taste in men bewildering.

The bundle in the river had disappeared.

'I've known some good, brave lads,' Catherine was saying, sentimentally.

'And a lot of cunts,' said Una, but she spoke affectionately.

'You're thinking what I'm thinking, aren't you?' Catherine sat up.

'What?'

Catherine laughed.

'Oh!' Una turned so that she could see their jetty, where the little white motor launch was moored. 'Yes.' With a sigh she went and sat down beside Catherine. She stroked Catherine's hair, picking out one or two pieces of grass which had stuck there.

'Christ,' said Catherine. 'It seems a long while since I heard some good rock music. I suppose it's a craving, really. I tried that book you recommended, but I'm not much into books, as you know. I liked the title. *The Amazing Marriage*.'

'There's no reason why you should enjoy it.' Una regretted what might have been taken for a note of condescension in her tone; she had meant exactly what she said. 'It would make a better film, probably. I'd love to play the part.' She was relieved and did not continue in this vein when Catherine seemed to accept the statement without interpretation. Catherine yawned; she shrugged off the kimono and rolled over to let the sun get at her back. Absently, Una stroked her bottom. A little later she heard soft snores and realised that her friend was asleep again.

Una now felt much more relaxed. She rose and entered the cool of the living room, replacing *Life*, then moving from bookshelf to bookshelf, finding little but children's books and adventure stories and obscure humorous novels from the previous century (whose humour, like that in *Life*, seemed almost wholly based on the fact that the characters spoke in thick dialect and did not understand very much about North American society). A few unbroken records in the electric phonograph's cabinet had been heard too often to be entertaining. She began to wish that it was lunchtime. She considered playing a practical joke on the boy scouts, but was unable to think of anything suitable.

She had become depressed. Perhaps she had been depressed all morning and had only now admitted it to herself; but then boredom easily led to depression. She wondered if her period was early.

She went upstairs and changed into a swimming costume. Instead of going immediately to the river she allowed herself to lie down on the unmade bed. She stared at the cracks in the ceiling, studying them as she might study the map of a familiar country. She chose part of the ceiling as a military objective and planned how best to move the troops and artillery along the cracks and visualised her forces so well that when a cockroach walked slowly across the ceiling she was shocked, seeing it as a grotesque monster which threatened to crush her tiny army underfoot.

Her spirits much improved, she swung herself off the bed, ran down the stairs, through the living room, through the French windows, down the lawn (jumping over a still sleeping Catherine) and into the river.

Deliberately, she chose to swim against the strong current, so that she would not be carried too far down. Slowly, with a patient breaststroke, she swam towards the far bank.

2. In which Catherine Cornelius and Una Persson receive a visitor and reach a decision

A young man in a soft brown hat was standing on the lawn at the side of the house when Una, having startled a party of paddling scouts, returned. The young man was quite good-looking, rather scrawny, dirty and shabby, and his red-rimmed eyes showed that he was either insane or had not had much sleep. He had not yet noticed Catherine, though he could now see Una as, dripping, she waded through weedy mud to the bank.

'Good morning,' said Una. The young man had some sort of haversack over his shoulder. 'Are you on the run?' she asked.

'Oh, no...' His grin of understanding was embarrassed. 'No, ma'am. The bum. I'm looking for work.'

'Work? Here?'

'What!' Catherine looked up suddenly. 'Ah!'

The young man saw her and he blushed. He lowered his head. 'Gee, I'm sorry. I'll be...'

'That's all right,' said Catherine. She stood up, tying the kimono round her body. 'I'm nearly burned as it is.'

'Oh, dear,' said the young man to himself and then, as he looked up, 'I can see I'm intruding. I'm not quite myself, you know. I forgot my manners. This house is the first I've seen all day and I hoped...'

'You're hungry?' Without thinking, Una put her hands on her hips. Catherine folded her arms under her breasts. They stared together at the young man.

'Hungry! You bet!' He sniggered. 'I'm on my way to California, to work for my uncle, I hope. I lost my job in New York about a month ago, so I decided that California was the place for me. Anyhow, I've been on the road a week...'

'A week?' Una calculated the distance.

'I'd gotten almost to Washington when I jumped a train which took me back to New York,' he explained. 'I guess I make a lousy hobo, don't I?'

'A what?' said Catherine.

'A tramp,' said Una.

'A what?' said the young man. He blushed again. 'Sorry.'

'I'll do you an omelette,' said Una. 'Will that be all right?'

'That'll be fine. I'll work for my bread, though. You must have some odd jobs you need doing. Although I suppose your husbands fix most things.'

'No,' said Una. 'We do everything ourselves.'

'Oh.'

'We haven't any husbands,' said Catherine. She winked at Una who grinned back.

'Ah.'

The two women advanced up the lawn. The young man seemed to consider bolting, but a combination of hunger and good manners made him hold his ground.

'Through the door, there.' Catherine pointed.

He went into the living room.

They followed. 'Sit down,' said Una.

He sat on a sofa covered in worn chintz. 'Oh, this is *very* comfortable,' he said. 'You have a nice home.'

'What would you like to drink?' Una asked.

'I'm not sure I –'

'With the omelette? Milk?'

'Milk! Oh, fine!' His laugh was hollow and it pained them both.

'Please relax,' said Una. 'It won't take a minute.'

Catherine sat down in an easy chair on one side of the sofa. She stretched her legs in front of her; she stretched her arms over her head.

'What do you do, Mr – um?'

'Bannermann – William Bannermann – Billy...' He added 'Junior' under his breath. 'I was working in this office – advertising agency. I wanted to be a copywriter. I've been there four years, since I was fifteen. I was working my way up.'

'What happened?'

He laughed at a joke he had evidently told a number of times. 'I was working my way up to the top of a scrap heap, as it turned out. The agency collapsed. We were all laid off. My uncle isn't doing bad. He's got a store in Berkeley there. I'm going to handle his publicity and displays – among other things. I've got plenty of ideas. And the weather's so good out there, isn't it?'

'I've never been there,' Catherine told him. 'This is really my first time in America.'

'Oh, it's great weather.'

Catherine was only half-aware of the effect she was having on Mr Bannermann. It had been so long since they had had visitors that she had become used to following her impulses. And while she had not set out to embarrass him, she couldn't help relishing his discomfort. He blushed as she crossed her legs.

'The weather's been very nice here,' she said.

'In New Jersey?'

'In Pennsylvania, I think. I'm sure this is Pennsylvania.' She was pleased to be able to name the hills. 'And those are the Appalachians!'

'Well, you'd know where you live, eh?' He drew a deep breath and looked at the books in the shelves. 'I've been travelling a bit erratically...'

'So have I,' she said.

'You've been travelling?'

'Until recently.'

He lifted his hand to his head and realised that he still wore his hat. He snatched it off. 'This is your home.'

'Not really. I live in England most of the time.'

'You're English?'

'Yes.'

'I wouldn't have guessed.'

'Don't I look English?'

'Not what I think of as English.' His neck reddened still more. 'I mean – you don't seem typical. I mean, I always think of English ladies as – I mean, well, you know, *English*.' He added, lamely, 'I *like* English people.'

'I like Americans. They're friendly. Easy-going.' She pushed her hair back from her cheek. 'Relaxed.'

'The English are very polite.' He struggled in the depths of the sofa, trying to sit closer to the edge.

'Thank you.'

'I used to read a lot of, you know, Jeeves.' He managed to get to the edge at last and sat there breathing heavily. In the *Saturday Evening Post*. Gee, I *am* tired.'

'What? Jeeves?'

'Right!'

Una came in with a tray. She had made a huge omelette and there was some salad left over from last night. She had put a glass of milk on the tray. As he reached for it he spilled it. He moaned helplessly while Catherine stifled a snort. Una put the tray on a table and went to get a cloth. Mr Bannermann took a dirty handkerchief from his pocket and began first to mop at the milk in his lap, then at the milk on the carpet.

'Don't worry about it,' said Catherine.

'Gee, I really am sorry. My reflexes aren't what they should be.'

'You're tired.'

'Yes sirree.'

Catherine got up and took the tray over to him. 'Eat it while it's hot, Mr Bannermann.'

He wolfed the omelette.

Una came in and cleaned up the milk.

'Best omelette I've ever eaten, ma'am.' He spoke with his mouth full; his eyes held a feral glint.

Una smiled. 'It's because you're hungry. Thank you.'

She glanced at Catherine and then glanced away again, smirking. They were both staving off a giggling fit and neither wanted to make the young man any more uncomfortable than he was. Indeed, Catherine felt sorry for him and was sure that Una did as well.

Carefully, Billy Bannermann picked up the fresh glass of milk and sipped it. His caution was so exaggerated, his hand so shaky, that Catherine gave up her efforts and, spluttering, ran from the room. The young man looked up in surprise and for an instant stared full into Una's grey eyes. He coughed and put down the glass of milk. Una said gravely: 'Bladder trouble.' She sat down in Catherine's place and stretched languorously.

'Oh, yes?'

'Would you like to bathe?'

'If it isn't any trouble.'

'The bathroom's upstairs, along the landing, second door on the left. The water's only warm.'

'Oh, anything, anything!'

He fled.

Catherine returned. 'We shouldn't laugh,' she said. 'He's tired and hungry and dazed. Isn't he delicious, though?'

'I wonder what he makes of us.' Una lit a cigarette. 'Just imagine his fantasies!'

'Oo-hoo,' said Catherine and uttered something very close to a belly laugh.

Una lifted a recent copy of *Vogue* from the floor and began to turn the pages. 'We must seem pretty glamorous to him. You're right. I was thinking of leaving tomorrow.'

'So was I. For 1910?'

'Or thereabouts.' Una studied an advertisement for riding boots. 'I thought 1917. Would that suit you?'

'Fine. If you could drop me off in London.'

'Of course.'

'Shall we ask Mr Bannermann to stay the night?'

'What do you mean?'

'Just to stay. Nothing else.'

'I suppose he could do with a rest and a bit of feeding up. All right. But I don't want to…'

'No. Neither do I.'

'I'm not sure it would do *him* any good.' Una grinned. 'You know how clinging lads like that can be.'

'Well, he couldn't very well follow us back to 1917.'

'You never know.'

'He's an antidote for boredom, anyway.'

'He wouldn't last very long.'

Catherine showed her teeth. 'Long enough.'

With pursed lips Una chuckled. 'We're being very childish, you know.'

'Why not?'

'Ah!' Una stretched once more. 'I feel so good all of a sudden.'

'Me too. Awake.'

Una was glad that her analysis seemed to have been correct. With the advent of Mr Bannermann and a break in what had become a monotonous routine her fears and her worries were gone, although she was still determined to leave, to get back into what she would have called 'real life'. It was dreadful, she thought, how one went round and round, experiencing the same succession of moods and never quite being able to do anything about them: did everyone have this almost schizoid cycle of intense activity followed by periods of equally intense lethargy? Most people, she supposed, were not free to experience the extremes: the more you had of what was called leisure, the more you were inclined to lose the centre. And was the centre worth holding? She had, in her time, made a virtue both of holding it and of leaving it behind. At this moment, however, she felt merely irresponsible – she would have used the word 'naughty' if it didn't have such awful associations with infantile sexual fantasy and the kind of rôle-playing whimsy she abhorred. And 'wicked' was far too strong. 'Irresponsible' would have to do. She winked at Catherine who appeared to be in an identical mood.

'It's silly really,' said Una. 'We're like a couple of excitable old maids, no matter how you look at it – no matter how innocent our intentions are.'

'I quite fancy him,' Catherine said, 'but he's not really my type. I prefer old foreigners, as you know.'

'You wouldn't have fancied him before we arrived here,' Una reminded her.

'You have to take what you're given,' said her friend.

'That's the sort of attitude which has got you into so much trouble,' said Una.

'You mean them knocking me about. Well, that could be my fault, couldn't it?'

'Don't let's go into that one. You blame yourself too much. Avoid people who make you feel guilty, that's my motto.'

'I seem to bring out the worst...'

'Stop it! You just happen to like childish, ego-bound, flashy little sods who always want more than anyone can give them. I'm not going to say it all again.'

'Don't,' said Catherine, 'because I might resent it, Una, at the moment. We all make mistakes.'

'True.' Una was anxious to avoid tension.

The two women fell silent, though it was a perfectly friendly silence, and when the spruced-up Mr Bannermann returned he found them both looking at him through sleepy, half-closed lids. Una thought he shivered so she said kindly: 'The shower's done you good.'

'It was very welcome.'

'We've a spare room, if you'd like to get some sleep.'

'Well...' The idea was attractive to him, but he was still nervous.

'Come on,' said Una rising, 'I'll show you where it is. Are there any sheets on the bed, Catherine?'

'I think so.'

Showing Mr Bannermann into the rather dark room on the opposite side of the landing to her own, Una resisted any further impulse to embarrass him. She looked in briefly, to make sure the bed was made. She smiled a neutral smile. 'There! Sleep as long as you like, Mr Bannermann. Sleep tight!'

'You're very kind...'

'These are bad times for everyone.' She found the conventional phrase useful now.

'Yes sirree!' He brightened at the familiar sound.

'I won't wake you, but if you should get up after we've gone to bed, help yourself to anything you find in the icebox.'

'You're very kind…'

'We've all got to pull together nowadays.'

'Yes, sir!'

Glad to have given the young man the reassurance of this Depression dialogue, that most comforting of all ideas, the idea of the 'common struggle', Una hummed to herself as she descended the stairs and rejoined Catherine in the living room.

'What are we going to give him for dinner?' asked Catherine. 'All we've got is a lettuce.'

'I hadn't thought. I'll go into town and get some meat. Or a chicken. What else, do you think?'

'I'll do the cooking, if you like. Shall I write out a list?'

'Okay.' Una was amused by the transformation in Catherine who, up until this moment, had been content to let her prepare the small amounts of food they had been eating. 'He might sleep on, past dinner.'

'We'll wake him up. I could do with a good feed myself,' Catherine pushed herself out of the chair. 'Perhaps we'll both go into town. I've only seen the place once, and that was at night.'

'What if Mr Bannermann is a thief?'

'What is there for him to steal?' Her eye swept the room.

'The boat. But it wouldn't do him much good.' Una smiled. 'You'd better dress carefully, if you're coming. Nothing out of period.'

'You should know me better!'

'Sorry.' Una swung her arms as she followed Catherine upstairs and into the bedroom.

'This is a bit too chic for Briggstown, I suppose,' said Catherine, holding up a blue-and-yellow Chanel tunic dress, 'also it's four or five years out of date, but maybe one offsets the other.'

'It'll do. Put it on.' Una donned an incongruous gingham over her bathing costume.

Catherine wriggled into her bra and pants. 'These do feel strange.' She pulled the dress over her head and straightened it on her body. 'There!'

'Fine.'

They found shoes for themselves and tottered downstairs and out to the Duesenberg. Catherine sat beside Una as she turned the engine over and put the car into gear. 'It's really falling to bits,' said Una. 'All it needs is a service. Maybe I'll book it for one while we're in town.'

'I thought we were leaving soon.'

'The car can't.'

The engine growled; the body lurched backwards as Una reversed; gravel crunched and spattered. Una hauled on the big steering wheel, changed, and drove down the path towards the iron gate which had hung by only one of its hinges since they had arrived. She was able to squeeze the car through the gap without Catherine having to get out to open the gate further, and then they were bumping down the track towards the road. 'I wouldn't like a car like this to rot,' Una said. 'I mean, think how much they're going to be worth in thirty years' time.'

'You sound like my brother.' Catherine sighed.

'I'll say that for him. Frank made himself a rich man by thinking ahead.'

'But who wants a family fortune based on old copies of the *Wizard* and *Hotspur*?' complained Catherine.

'He couldn't do much else. You know the dangers of people like us manipulating the stock market, or even buying gold. He kept a low profile. He invested in cheap, trashy comic books.'

'It's a bit vulgar, though, isn't it?'

They turned on to the Briggstown road; here the hills were gentler and unwooded; in drowsy fields cows and sheep panted and the countryside was broken only by the occasional Pennsylvania Dutch farmhouse or National Recovery billboard.

'It's very peaceful,' said Catherine as she brushed her hair. 'What a pity they don't have stereo yet.'

3. In which Mr William Bannermann comes into an unexpected inheritance

Catherine leaned towards the full-length mirror; she puckered her lips; she dabbed delicately with the lip-rouge brush; she fluttered mascara'd lashes. Una grinned. There was no response from Catherine, who was concentrating.

'The black chiffon, I see!' Una fingered it.

Catherine gave an affirmative grunt.

'Well, it always suited you better than me.'

Catherine had not heard her. She was stepping back from the mirror with a dissatisfied sigh, shaking her head. 'It doesn't take long to lose the knack, does it?'

Una shrugged and made a humorous face. She already had on her dark blue costume. 'You're really giving our guest the works,' she said. 'He might be shocked – by the make-up.'

'I'm doing it for the fun of it.' Catherine was defensive. 'I mean, it's been such a long time...'

'I'm only taking the piss.' Una lifted a calming hand. 'Can you take him in a cup of coffee and wake him while I go and look at the dinner?'

Absently, Catherine nodded, her attention drifting back towards the mirror. 'Are you sure this is all right?'

'It's simple and elegant.' Una patted Catherine's bare shoulder. 'You look lovely.'

'But do I look lovely *enough*?' With a snort of self-mockery, Catherine put her lip-rouge away. 'You know what a perfectionist I can be.'

'Poor Mr Bannermann's going to be overwhelmed. He saw a pair of scruffy slags and he wakes up to find us transformed into fancy harlots.'

'He seemed pretty overwhelmed to begin with!' They went out onto the landing, dropping their voices. 'Are you sure you don't want me to do my salad?'

'It isn't worth it. You be the hostess. I'll be the cook.'

'Don't tell me I've got the easiest job this time.'

They crept downstairs. In the kitchen Una opened the oven and looked at her chickens. Catherine smacked her lips. 'Oh, that really smells delicious. And all the trimmings, too. It's like Christmas. Did you have Christmas, Una, when you were a little girl?'

'Oh, yes.' Una carried the dishes to the table and began to baste the birds. 'Oh, yes. Trees and tinsel and so on.' She spoke vaguely, as if she could not really remember; as if it had occurred to her that her memories might be false, based on films she had seen and books she had read rather than on direct experience.

'Is that your amnesia?' Catherine asked tentatively. 'Can't you –?'

'Just a minute.' Una replaced the chickens in the oven. She took the lid off a saucepan and studied the contents. 'What did you say?'

Catherine heaped coffee into the filter pot; she filled it with cold water and put it on the stove. She lit the gas.

'What were you saying?' Una stepped aside.

'I was saying about your amnesia. You know – those areas of childhood you find hard to recall. You've told me about them...'

'Have I? Yes?'

'Christmas...'

'Oh. Yes, maybe you're right.' Una rinsed her basting spoon under the hot tap.

'Am I in your way?' asked Catherine.

Una kissed her. 'I hadn't thought about it, but, yes, you probably are.'

'You're feeling a bit solitary again, aren't you?'

'It's only temporary.'

Catherine wandered out of the kitchen and into the living room. She was whistling to herself as she stood looking through the windows; it was not yet sunset; a breeze had sprung up and was moving the tops of the elms; birds of some kind wheeled in a flock over the boy scout camp. Catherine fancied they were vultures and the boy scouts had all been wiped out by Indians, but a distant blaring assured her that at least some of the scouts had survived. Then she saw two canoes, filled with small green- and khaki-clad figures paddling hard against the current, come slowly round the bend, heading for the camp. All at once she felt self-conscious, as if she were wearing an imperfect disguise. She wondered if one only wore clothes for reasons of disguise not, as she usually thought, to emphasise one's 'personality'. She shrugged and moved away from the window, entering the small dining room where the table had already been laid. It would have been nice, she thought, to have had some good wine, but the California rosé wasn't all that bad. She was tempted to open a bottle and try some; instead she turned to the sideboard behind her and poured from a decanter half a glass of Madeira (the last of the businessman's supply). Feeling a little guilty, for she didn't like the Madeira very much and knew that it was supposed to be very good, she knocked it back. A snort of fine cocaine had the effect on her which others claimed for favourite wines. She resisted the temptation to pour herself another glass and returned to the kitchen where Una was bending over a salad, picking delicately at some cucumber and tomatoes. The water had boiled and Una had already turned the pot over. Catherine could hear the water dripping through the filter. She took a cup from its hook and put it in a saucer; she filled the cup, put it on a tray, found sugar and milk and placed them beside the cup.

'I'll take it up,' she said.

'Fine,' said Una without turning.

Catherine carried the coffee to the top of the stairs, pausing outside the spare room and balancing the tray on one hand while she knocked on the door. There was no answer, so she went inside. It took her a few moments to make out Mr Bannermann in the bed. His head lay awkwardly against the pillow; his mouth was open and he was snoring quietly. Catherine thought he looked more attractive now. She leaned forward and shook him gently by the shoulder. He grunted, opened his eyes, licked his lips.

'Coffee?' she said. She put it on the bedside table. 'Dinner's almost ready. We're making a special one. In your honour.'

Mr Bannermann's mouth moved, but he said nothing. His expression was almost ludicrously puzzled.

'Quarter of an hour,' said Catherine. 'For dinner?'

'Oh, right...'

'It's chicken.'

He began to wake up. 'Chicken!'

Pleased by his response Catherine left him with his coffee and his bewilderment.

When Mr Bannermann came down, his hair carefully combed, his eyes betraying an eager appetite, a neat tie at his throat, Catherine Cornelius was jigging about the living room to the scratchy strains of 'Livin' in the Sunlight, Lovin' in the Moonlight' by Paul Whiteman. Outside, the sky was spread with the oranges and purples of an Italian religious lithograph, almost incredibly lurid, and no lights burned indoors as yet. 'Feeling better, Mr Bannermann?' The chiffon swished. 'Can I get you a drink?'

'A beer, if you have it. You're very kind.'

'We all have our parts to play.' She swayed to the table where she had already laid out the drinks. 'Whisky?'

'Well, if...' He nodded.

'Soda?'

'To the top. I'm not really used...' He took note of her perfume as she handed him the glass. She saw his Adam's apple give a convulsive movement.

'Do you like Paul Whiteman?'

'He's the tops.'

'He is here,' she said mysteriously. She skipped a few more steps, doing a kind of modified jitterbug which was interrupted by the thump and click of the record ending. She lifted the lid, selecting another record. 'It's almost all Paul Whiteman. What about "My Suppressed Desire"?'

'Your –?'

'"Suppressed Desire". Bing Crosby vocals, too.'

'He's great. Have you seen any of the movies?'

'I might have done,' she replied vaguely. She had probably seen some on television.

Una entered as the record started. She lit a cigarette and smiled at Mr Bannermann. 'It's almost ready,' she said. She sank, with a sigh, onto the sofa. 'I hope you like fowl, Mr Bannermann.'

He leaned forward to show that he had not quite caught the remark.

'Fowl,' she hissed. He blushed.

'Do you dance, Mr Bannermann?' Catherine opened her arms.

He cleared his throat. 'Uh.'

Mockingly reproving Una said: 'Mr Bannermann's only just woken up, Catherine.'

'I'm a bit drunk.' Catherine excused herself. 'Oh, I feel smashing!' She continued to dance.

'Sit down for a second, Mr Bannermann.' Una patted the sofa. He obeyed, sipping his Scotch. 'You must forgive us if we seem rude,' continued Una. 'We haven't had a visitor here before. You can imagine, I'm sure, how a pair of spinsters, with only one another's company, can get a bit strange…'

'Oh, no! Miss –?'

'Persson. You see, we haven't even thought of introducing ourselves. I'm Una Persson and this is Catherine Cornelius.'

'It seems an odd place, ma'am, to find two English ladies living alone. Aren't you ever scared?'

'I think we can look after ourselves when we need to, Mr Bannermann. And there aren't many dangers to worry about in this part of the world, are there?'

'There are stories of roving gangs, looters, hobos…'

'I'm sure they're exaggerated.' She rose to her feet. 'I'll get dinner. Catherine, would you like to escort Mr Bannermann in?'

Catherine took Mr Bannermann's arm.

'It's through here.'

'My, that looks good,' said Mr Bannermann. He eyed the cucumber salad, the mushroom salad, the tuna fish salad, the dish of roast potatoes, the sweetcorn, the squash. He stared reverently at the chickens as Una carved. 'A real country meal.'

'Help yourself to some tuna fish salad,' said Una. 'I'm sorry there's no soup. Treat the tuna fish as an hors d'oeuvre. Pour Mr Bannermann some of that rosé, Catherine. Do you prefer breast or leg, Mr Bannermann?'

'As it comes, ma'am.'

'There you are.' She handed him the plate. He put down the spoon with which he had been about to take some tuna fish salad. He accepted the plate. 'Gravy's there,' she said, 'and cranberry sauce, if you like it. Have as many potatoes as you like. We don't eat them.'

'You must let me do some work around the house for you before I go,' he said. 'Just to repay your kindness.'

'We're better off than you, Mr Bannermann. It's our duty to do what we can,' said Catherine piously. She put out her fork and impaled two potatoes. 'Besides, we're leaving tomorrow.'

'Oh, which way are you heading?'

'We're going upriver,' said Una. 'I'm sorry we can't give you a lift.'

'It wasn't – I didn't mean...'

'You haven't had the cucumber yet.' Catherine handed him the dish. 'Take a lot. It's lovely.'

'Squash?' said Una.

'Well, if you don't mind...'

'You don't like it.' Catherine winked at him. 'Neither do I. I never did. Of course, we don't have it in England. Do we, Una?'

'No, not squash. Swedes.'

'Something like it,' said Catherine. 'Parsnips are okay, though.'

An expression akin to terror came and went in Mr Bannermann's mild brown eyes.

They fell silent as they ate.

'Phew!' said Mr Bannermann, after a while. He put down his knife and fork and sipped his wine. The alcohol had made him relax more; for the first time his smile was not nervous. 'I think this is the best dinner I've ever had.'

'It makes a nice change for us, too,' said Una. 'Would you like some more chicken?'

'Not just yet, ma'am, thank you.'

'Do you like the house, Mr Bannermann?' Una became thoughtful.

'Very much. And the country.'

'Do you drive?'

'Yes, ma'am.'

Catherine filled Mr Bannermann's glass to the brim. She touched his wrist as she steadied herself. Open-mouthed, he turned to look at her. He shut his mouth.

'There!' she said, settling back. She lifted her own glass. 'Here's to you, Mr Bannermann. To your improved fortune!'

'Well, I will drink to that, if you don't mind.' He grinned and clinked his glass against hers. Pink wine spilled on the cloth. He offered his glass to Una and she put down her own cutlery to join in the toast.

'To your improved fortune, Mr Bannermann.'

He downed the wine in one enormous swallow. 'This is so strange. It's like a dream. Like a story.' He became enthusiastic. 'You're like goddesses, both of you. Diana and Venus. I'm sorry. I'm drunk.'

'Carry on, Mr Bannermann!' This time Una filled his glass for him. 'It's lovely.' She glanced at Catherine who uttered a luxurious sigh. 'Who would have guessed you had a penchant for poetry.'

'You're making fun of me, ma'am.' He was flattered.

'Not at all,' Catherine told him.

Una frowned. 'We must get an early start.'

Catherine and Mr Bannermann stared at her without speaking.

'In the morning,' said Una.

'It can't be that late.' Catherine cast about for a clock. 'Can it?'

'Well.' Una smiled apologetically at Mr Bannermann. 'After dessert and coffee – that'll take us to eleven.' Having suddenly developed a lust for Catherine and seeing Mr Bannermann as a rival she was having a hard time controlling her manners. 'We ought to try to get as much sleep as possible.'

Catherine, who had taken a fancy to Mr Bannermann, felt that Una was being a bit of a killjoy. She considered making this observation directly to Una but contented herself with: 'You've had a tiring day, really, Una – and then doing all the cooking.'

'Actually, I feel very fresh.' Una was anxious to make it clear that she was motivated only by common sense. 'But we had agreed...'

Mr Bannermann, having taken another half glass, began to tell a joke about two Jewish stockbrokers which was not improved for Una by the fact that she had read that morning an almost identical story in an 1897 number of *Life*. She began to collect up plates. Catherine, unable to sustain as much interest in Mr Bannermann's joke as she would have liked, helped her. Una, with a slightly malicious wink at her friend, carried the plates to the kitchen.

Mr Bannermann finished his joke and began to laugh. Catherine did her best to join in and was very glad when Una returned with the dish of trifle. Mr Bannermann was also pleased. It had dawned on him that his story had not gone over well. Una felt that a relaxed Mr Bannermann lost much of his charm. She offered him the bowl and the serving spoon.

'I could trifle with some trifle, I think,' he said.

It surprised Una when Catherine found this amusing. Mr Bannermann winked at Catherine in recognition of her appreciation and Catherine added with drunken archness: 'I hope you're not *trifling* with my affections, Mr Bannermann, when I have entrusted you with the *custardy* of my heart.'

Una found it difficult to remain silent. She ate her own trifle with surly steadiness.

Becoming conscious of a change in the atmosphere but unable to identify its source Mr Bannermann complimented Una on the dessert. 'It's very sweet,' he said. 'I love sweet things.'

'You're very sweet, too, Mr Bannermann.' Catherine, giggling, helped herself to more wine. 'Isn't he, Una?'

'We're not being very polite, tonight, I'm afraid, Mr Bannermann.' Una put down her spoon.

Mr Bannermann half-rose, steadying himself with one hand on the table as he lifted his glass. A little indistinctly he said:

'Nonsense! I give a toast to the two most charming ladies in the whole US of A!'

Una's mood passed. She could see that Mr Bannermann was very drunk and she blamed herself. She should have realised that he had not eaten any proper food for days. She had overwhelmed him.

He staggered against the table and Catherine reached up to help him. He apologised. He blushed. He collapsed into his chair and began to cry. He said something to the effect that no-one had shown him such kindness since his mother had been prematurely taken from him. He said that he had given up hope of ever finding it but now his optimism was restored, that he could face life again, that if it had not been for them he might have followed the example of so many New Yorkers and ended it all. There had been times, he said, when he had been known far and wide for his cheerfulness, his ability to console others less fortunate than himself, but, when his own need for consolation had materialised, there had been no-one to offer that which he had given so freely and with such good will. Wasn't this, he asked them, always the way – or so he had thought until now.

The two women listened: Catherine with sympathy and Una with disapproval bordering on cynicism – until with a sudden sigh, like a locomotive reaching its destination after a long and difficult haul, he subsided. Catherine and Una began to clear away the dishes while Mr Bannermann toyed with his glass and murmured general apologies for his outburst.

'We're all a bit tired,' said Una kindly.

'I think we ought to get him to bed, don't you?' Catherine said when they were both in the kitchen.

'We?' Una lifted a nasty eyebrow.

'Oh, Una! You know what I mean. Don't you fancy him, though?'

'I think you've been too long away from masculine country.'

'You do sound bitchy!' Catherine laughed without much rancour. 'You're probably right. But he does make you want to mother him a bit.'

'That isn't quite the same thing as fancying him,' said Una. 'Or maybe, in your case, it is.'

'Off and on. Shall I wash?'

'Don't you want to continue mothering Mr Bannermann?'

'I'll ask him if he wants coffee.' Catherine departed.

By the time she returned Una had almost finished the dishes. 'He kissed me,' Catherine told her, 'and then he went to sleep.' She sighed as she picked up a cloth to dry a plate. 'Actually, I'll be glad to get away. Should we leave him there, or what?'

'We'll have some coffee and then see what he looks like.' Una felt dislike for herself as she detected in her tone an increased friendliness, now that Mr Bannermann was no longer a potential rival. She hated to detect signs of jealousy in her behaviour.

Catherine kissed her. 'Let's have a really nice time tonight,' she said.

Una brightened. She indicated a sealed envelope on the kitchen table. It had *Mr William Bannermann* written on it. 'I'm letting him have the house and a loan of the car,' she said. 'They might as well benefit somebody.'

'I thought you didn't like him much.'

'That's hardly the point.'

'You're genuinely good-hearted, Una. Much more than me. I'm so selfish, really.'

'I'm practical, that's all. And you have more to protect. Selfishness is just unrationalised instinct in your case.'

They sat in the kitchen and enjoyed a cup of coffee together.

Later, as they lay in each other's arms in the big bed, they heard Mr Bannermann stumbling up the stairs and they grinned, wondering what he would make of Una's letter when he woke up in the morning and found them gone.

4. In which our heroines give themselves up, once again, to the Tides of Time.

Una, with an expertise Catherine always admired, got the little white motor boat going and they began to move slowly out into the water. They picked up speed where the river widened at the bend. For the first time Catherine had a good view of the boy scouts. Some of them had come crawling from their tents at the sound of the engine. 'It's a pleasure to wake them up, for a change,' said Una. One or two of the scouts whistled and waved. Carefully, Catherine waved back. 'Take it easy, boys,' she called.

Una wished that she could get a better sight of Catherine, standing there with her hand on her hip, her scarf fluttering in the wind. Catherine looked at her most beautiful in the white dress with the red, green and blue embroidery. 'It's funny.' She gave the wheel a quarter turn. 'I don't feel like going at all now. Still, I expect I'll get into it.'

Catherine looked up at the sky. 'I know what you mean.' She added, 'Can you feel jaded, even when you've nothing, as it were, to be jaded about?'

'Is that how you feel?'

'Not now. I didn't like to bring it up before. It would have sounded as if I were complaining.'

'You're only talking about boredom again.' Una straightened the bottom of her khaki fatigue jacket, keeping one hand on the wheel. 'That's all.' The water began to run faster as they neared some easily negotiated rapids. The boat bounced. 'Are you sure 1917's okay?'

'Oh, yes. Fine.'

'At least you won't meet any rock-and-roll musicians there.'

Catherine considered this a bit unfair and she replied a little sharply. 'It doesn't matter where you go, Una – you'll always find politicians.'

'True.'

'God,' said Catherine. 'I really need to hear some good music.'

'Well, you're going to hear some in a minute,' said Una. 'Unfortunately.'

'They went past a poverty-stricken town which looked as if it had been deserted.

'Don't you get cravings for music, Una?'

'Not that kind. Music hall and musical comedy's my first love. It's a different sort of sentimentality.'

Catherine laughed. 'You couldn't call Mick Jagger sentimental.'

'Couldn't I just.' Una pursed her lips and concentrated on the rapids.

Catherine settled herself on the port-side seat, humming in time to the roar of the water, but the rhythm was too erratic and so she stopped. She yawned. It had been a long while since she had got up this early. She wondered if she were wise to go back as far as 1917, when really she would have preferred what she considered to be her own period, the mid-seventies. The hills on her right had become gentler and were giving way to blackened fields. In the distance, near the horizon, black smoke boiled. She stared, without curiosity, at the smoke until another stretch of forest obscured it. The boat entered calmer waters. Una removed the canvas cover from an instrument set close to the wheel. The instrument looked a bit like a large brass ship's chronometer; engraved on the dial, where the maker's name was usually found, were the words *Cornelius and Co., Ladbroke Grove, London W.* It was, in fact, the work of Catherine's brother and it would help them to get to the period they had selected.

'It's beautifully made, isn't it?' Catherine was proud of her brother's craftsmanship. 'You'd think it was a hundred years old.'

Una made adjustments to the controls just below the rim. 'I sometimes wish he could produce a machine to take us right back – say to the nineteenth century. It would save so much energy.'

'He did get to 1870 once.' Catherine was almost defensive. 'But he didn't like it. He always says he's a twentieth-century person at heart and he might as well accept it.'

'Well, I'm no conservative,' Una brought an outer dial into alignment with two of the inner ones, 'but I find that remark a bit prissy. I'd love to go back, say, to St Petersburg around 1890.'

'You couldn't leave well alone.'

'I agree, it is dangerous. It becomes harder and harder to acclimatise, too.' The motor boat's engine began to complain as the current flowed with increased pressure against the hull. Its note rose to a high whine. 'We're approaching the real rapids. Are you ready, dear?'

'Ready,' Catherine gripped the seat with both hands. The boat began to bounce dramatically, the water became white and up ahead she could see a wild, undulating spray. Gradually, the river began to shout.

Una had been through these rapids a hundred times, but she still liked the feeling of danger they gave her. A glance to her left showed her that Catherine was not enjoying the sensation at all. People sought different kinds of danger, physical or emotional, and Catherine tended to prefer emotional dangers which Una would go to almost any lengths to avoid. 'This is it!' she called. She felt an intense surge of love for her friend as she turned on the sound. The Deep Fix began to play their version of 'Dodgem Dude' at full volume (why had that bastard geared everything to cheap rock-and-roll vibrations, and his own rotten band, at that?). The boat plunged into the spray which gradually became a white, muffling mist.

'We'll give ourselves up to the darkness and danger…' began Catherine, quoting some popular song, but the rest was obscured by the echo of a nameless vowel.

Part Two

Going To The Front: Woman's Rôle In Wartime

> This girl has a mission in life … to kill. She is one of the women soldiers in a private army fighting a civil war. The battlefield is a street in Beirut … It is a bloody religious and political conflict tearing the country in half. On the one side are the right-wing Christians – to which the girl in the picture belongs. On the other are the left-wing Moslems, who include Palestinian guerillas … BEAUTY IN BATTLE: Two girls man a barricade while another takes up a strategic position.
>
> *Daily Mirror*, 3 November, 1975

> Bursts of small-arms fire and the intermittent explosion of mortars and rockets continued to paralyse Beirut's seafront hotel district today. The St George, Phoenicia, Holiday Inn, and Excelsior hotels remained in the hands of the right-wing Phalangist militia, despite mounting pressure from an array of left-wing groups who now control the Vendome and Palm Beach hotels.
>
> *Guardian*, 3 November, 1975

5. In which Miss Una Persson encounters a Hero of the Revolution

Una glanced down through the tall French window, through a broken pane, at the street. In the dusk a line of her former comrades was being marched along Lesnoye Prospekt towards the Finland Station. Dumpy and downcast, most of the women made no attempt at maintaining military step. Una had heard rumours of ill treatment after they had been captured during their defence of the Winter Palace on the previous day, but for the most part there were no signs that they had been so much as involved in the fighting; save for their rifles, they retained their uniforms, insignia and accoutrements, and the attitude of the Red Guards escorting them was humorous; kindly rather than brutal.

'Well,' said L. Trotsky from behind her. He was in a languid, sated mood. 'So much for the Women's Battalion of Death. I thought better of you, Una. A Kerenskyite. Oh, they won't be shot. Just disbanded quietly.'

'After they're raped?' The accusation came without force.

Trotsky spread his hands. 'Which do you think they'd prefer?'

He remained attractive, as relaxed and controlled as ever, but Una was disappointed by his attitude. One such piece of easy cynicism, she thought, and a revolution was as good as lost. One act of treachery (and there had already been many) and the ideals themselves became worthless. She felt in the pockets of her black greatcoat for her cigarettes and matches. Trotsky handed her one of his, yellow and long, a Latvian brand; she lit it herself, holding it gently between her teeth so that when she spoke her words were slightly slurred. 'It wasn't merely a propaganda stunt, you know. Those women wanted to fight for the revolution.'

'Yet they allowed themselves to be mobilised against it.'

'Against your counter-revolution. Can it last?'

'We've been very successful so far.'

'Because you've been prepared to sacrifice everything for the short term,' she said. 'How many allies have you?'

'Surprisingly, quite a few, if temporary.'

'Whom you intend to betray?'

Trotsky shrugged and sat down on one of the bare desks of the office. 'Anarchists, nihilists, opportunists, bandits...'

'Whom you'll sacrifice?'

'They're naïve. They'd betray *us*, many of them without realising it. We use them. We direct their energy.'

'They're innocent and naïve, at least. You're a much more depressing spectacle. You're depraved and naïve. You used to be so charming. In London. This revolution will last no longer than Kerensky's.'

He considered her criticism. 'I think you're wrong. You want a bourgeois utopia. Sweetness and light are no substitute for bread and cabbage, Una Persson. Perhaps it's the difference between weeping for the people and soiling one's hands for them. Between dying for them and killing for them. Committing their crimes for them. Taking the moral responsibility, if you like. Which is the bravest deed? Which is the hardest?'

Her smile was thin. 'All ego – a politician's logic. Very masculine and high-sounding. Very romantic, too. But one need neither die nor kill. The hardest thing to do is patiently to nurse the wounded. This war has made you as simple-minded as the rest.'

'Wars do that. But the war gave us the revolution!'

'Because it robbed us of our subtlety, our humanity. Look what a general you've become. Are you any different from Kornilov or Haig now? Where is your old voice, comrade? Do you ever listen to it these days?'

'This is merely rhetoric, Una. I'm disappointed. You're overtired. How much sleep have you had in the past few days? You must consider your nerves.' He paused. 'I must say you're not at all grateful. You could have been marching to the Pavlov Barracks with your friends.' He shook his head. 'I'd never have expected you to join anything so ludicrous.'

'I thought it had possibilities.'

'The daughters of merchants, armed with a few old rifles?'

Petersburg was dark. Electric lights burned in some buildings, others were lit by flames. The power supply to the Winter Palace had been restored. Occasionally a shot sounded or a motor truck or a horse-drawn cart would rush urgently through the street below.

'I'm letting you leave,' he said. 'For old times' sake.'

'I don't want to leave. I worked for this revolution.'

'No. You worked for the other revolution. The wrong revolution.' His dark eyes were sardonic.

'The same one you were working for until you thought it might fail.'

He laughed. 'Well, it did fail.'

'Do you think that if I stay I will try to sabotage what you're doing?'

'I hadn't considered that. You're not Russian, after all. We're facing purely domestic problems at present.'

'Your problems aren't even domestic any more, Leon. They're entirely personal.'

He scowled at this. 'I don't really need your criticisms, Una. Not on top of everything else. I *do* accept certain responsibilities, you know.'

'You saved me, because you needed my moral support?'

'Scarcely.'

'Because you wanted to make love to me?'

'You won't allow me any expression of altruism?'

'Is that it? Sentimentality. I'm not sure I like being free, if it's merely to let you salve your conscience a little.'

'Una, you're trying my patience.' He removed his spectacles. It was a threatening gesture. She refused to acknowledge it. 'It would be easy to make out a case for your being a foreign spy.'

'My record's too well known.'

'You overestimate the memory of the people.'

'Oh, maybe.' She had indeed had very little sleep in the past few days and felt too tired to continue this silly argument. 'I think

I should have stayed in 1936.' The scene before her began to flicker. She became alarmed.

'What?' he said.

'It doesn't matter.' The scene stabilised. 'Are you kicking me out of Peter, then?'

'Out of Russia,' he said.

'All my friends are here.' The words sounded feeble to her own ears.

'Cornelius and his sister?'

'And the others.'

'They're leaving, too, if they haven't gone already. The train should be on its way to Germany by now. I signed the safe-conduct papers myself.'

It was her turn for self-pity. 'After all I've done…'

'You can't change history,' he said.

He rang a bell.

6. In which Mrs and Miss Cornelius hear some news of the past

Mrs Cornelius was flustered, and the weight of her overloaded hat, with its feathers, ribbons, lace and imitation flowers, had caused sweat to gather on her broad, red forehead and run between her eyes and down her nose; but in spite of this she was able to set her features in the expression of prim disapproval she always reserved for her encounters with authority (in this category she included doctors, dentists, postmen and anyone employed by the town hall). Catherine was beginning to regret her impulse to visit home. She had found her mother in a state of unusual agitation, having that morning received a letter from Whitehall telling her that if she could call at the Ministry's offices she might learn something to her advantage.

'About bloody time,' Mrs Cornelius had said. 'You'd better come along, too, Caff.'

Catherine had said that she was tired and that, anyway, she hadn't been sent for. Secretly she knew that her mother wanted her moral support and refused to admit it.

'Yore comin', my gal.' Mrs Cornelius had insisted and, to make things worse, had found her an off-white old-fashioned linen frock with a sailor collar, a boater with a broad, faded ribbon (which looked and felt as if it had been cut from deckchair canvas) and a pair of brown boots which, with some polishing, looked fairly respectable. The underwear, stiff with starch, had not been worn for years, and she was sure to discover patches of red, rubbed skin when she took it off. The spring weather was bright, but hardly hot, and she shivered as she sat beside her mother in the waiting room. Mrs Cornelius had given her name to the uniformed man at the desk. Now they sat on a dark mahogany bench in a draughty green-tiled hall opposite the desk watching the uniformed man pretending to check a typewritten list while actually reading the racing page of the *Daily Sketch*.

Catherine, with her hair brushed back at her mother's insistence and pinned under her hat, remembered that she had felt a bit like this when she had appeared in court, several years before, when they had sent her to the Reform School. She had almost forgotten those days; she had run with an all-girl gang in Whitechapel until her mother had moved to Notting Dale. They had all worn more or less the same clothes in the gang – dark blue coats and skirts trimmed with red ribbon. They had worn grey in the Reform School. They had been training her to be a housemaid.

A messenger boy, with bright, silvery buttons securing his navy-blue serge, a pillbox cap precisely positioned on his brilliantined head, appeared from the far end of the hall.

'Mrs Cornelius?'

'And Miss Cornelius,' intoned her mother significantly. She rose like a cast-off airship. 'Come on, love.'

Mrs Cornelius kept a firm grip on Catherine as they followed the boy down another green-tiled passage, up a short flight of wooden stairs, along another passage, to arrive outside a plain green door at which the boy knocked.

A man of military bearing opened the door and smiled graciously at them. 'Good afternoon, ladies. I am Major Nye.'

Momentarily won over, Mrs Cornelius gave a kind of half curtsey.

'It was good of you to drop everything,' said Major Nye as he stepped aside to let them enter his office.

'Eh?' said Mrs Cornelius brightening. Her mask returned almost at once as she realised that no innuendo had been intended. 'Oh, yeah. See wot yer mean.'

Catherine was in an agony of embarrassment. Not only was her mother, true to form, putting the most vulgar interpretation on this man's statements but, worse, she was using her 'posh' voice: a grating tone that was nearly twice as loud as usual.

'Will, is it?' added Mrs Cornelius.

'Um.' He crossed back to his big desk, indicating a leather armchair and an ordinary chair with a basketwork bottom. Catherine took the ordinary chair. Her mother, with an expression of some satisfaction, settled herself in the leather one. Major Nye waited until they were both at ease before he sat down behind his desk and picked up a file with a smile. 'Well. It's um…' He paused, glancing, for no apparent reason, towards the window on his right. A little daylight showed between the dark green blind filling the top half of the window and the grey net curtaining at the bottom. He looked at the file.

'The procedure. Well, I'm going to follow the book – in so far as there is a book for this sort of occasion.' He smiled as if he had made a joke, noted their expressions, tapped the file and cleared his throat.

'If it *is* a will,' said Catherine's mother, 'you can skip all the 'ows and wherefores, major. We don't mind.'

'Well, there are formalities,' he said. He seemed to be ashamed of himself, thought Catherine. She studied him.

'Oh, netcherelly.' Mrs Cornelius drew her knees together and placed her handbag in her lap. 'Ai was only suggesting, in case…'

'Appreciated. Do you mind if I begin? I want to read something to you for a few minutes. It might seem a bit dull, but we think it might be important.'

The fact that her mother showed no impatience made it evident to Catherine that Mrs Cornelius found Major Nye attractive, that she was beginning to feel at ease in the office. Mrs Cornelius glanced at the picture of the king on the wall behind Major Nye, at the highly polished wooden filing cabinets near the door. She winked comfortably at Catherine and Catherine knew her mother had recognised the ceremony as Tradition. Tradition always cheered Mrs Cornelius up. 'Please continue, major,' she said in her poshest accent.

'This is a report.' Major Nye raised his voice a little. 'We've held it for some time. A bit dry, I'm afraid. Well, here we go, eh?' Major Nye began to read but Catherine did not catch the opening words because her mother was leaning over and whispering, as if they were at the theatre: "Asn't 'e got a lovely speakin' voice? Almost like music.'

Major Nye had not, apparently, heard. His head was bent over the report. '... Frederik George Brown. He was born in 1874. His father was, so he later claimed, an Irish merchant sea captain and his mother was Russian. After being educated in Petersburg on purely Russian lines he obtained what appears to have been his first post with the Compagnie de Navigation Est-Asiatique. He seems to have acquitted himself well so that in 1900 he was appointed the chief agent for the company at Port Arthur. He remained in Port Arthur for four years, evidently familiarising himself with political conditions in the Far East and obtaining a degree of personal influence and connection which, in a few years' time, was to be of the greatest use to himself and to the Russian government.'

Mrs Cornelius blew her nose. She might have been at a funeral.

'In 1904 he returned to St Petersburg, appointed to a good post with the house of Mendrochovitch and Count Tchubbersky at 5 Place de la Cathedrale de Kazan. This house was, of course, the most important Russian firm of naval contractors and, in the Russian capital, also represented the great Hamburg firm of Bluhm unt Voss. At the conclusion of the Russo-Japanese War, Bluhm unt Voss acted as agents for the Russian government in the repatriation of Russian prisoners in Japan and, in this connection, the experience and personal influence of Frederik Brown made his services invaluable, much enhancing his reputation in Russian official circles. More than this, he was able to use the influence he had gained with the Russian government to place with Bluhm unt Voss large orders in connection with the restoration of the Russian Navy, on which that nation was then engaged. It may be assumed that his commission was large...'

Mrs Cornelius looked up from where she had been inspecting the quality of the leather on the armchair, but since it was evident that Major Nye had not yet finished she nodded and gave her attention back to the chair.

'Except for two or three very intimate friends,' said Major Nye, frowning as he read, 'Brown never entertained at his own home. Hardly anyone could boast of being his friend. Always a little sombre; serious, elegant, Frederik Brown was greatly admired at St Petersburg but, naturally enough, the mystery in which he shrouded his personal affairs made him the subject of innumerable whispered stories and rumours.'

Major Nye rubbed his left eye. He had a plain gold ring on his left hand. 'On his passport he was described as a British subject, but he neither knew nor cared for the English colony there. Russians regarded him as an Englishman who had become to all intents and purposes Russian. He was known in a dozen European capitals and was everywhere at home. He wrote and spoke English, Russian and German irreproachably, but each one, it was remarked, with an accent equally foreign.

'In 1909, the year of the greatest exploits of the brothers Wilbur and Orville Wright, some of the leading spirits of Petersburg decided to launch an Aeronautical Club. A committee was formed and the club, *Les Ailles*, came into being. Then, following a general council meeting of all its members, a letter was addressed to Frederik Brown, asking him to join them. Frederik Brown consented, joined them as a respected and much admired active member, and very soon had become the leading spirit of the club, flying his own aeroplane. For the next two years all his activities seemed engrossed in *Les Ailles*. He was recognised, we gather, as a loyal friend, a good companion and as a man who dominated his company.'

Catherine thought that the account sounded like a private report, probably requested by the Ministry from one of its contacts in the business world. She had no idea who Brown might be or why her mother, who was plainly unaware of the man's relevance to her own affairs, was being read to from the report. 'In the year of the foundation of *Les Ailles*,' said Major Nye, and then, looking up, 'I really must apologise for the style. It isn't mine.' Another smile, with no response from either Catherine or her mother.

'In that year he was appointed to the council of his old firm, the Compagnie de Navigation Est-Asiatique. By this time he was recognised as one of the leading figures in the Russian business world, and circumstances were soon to provide a field for his talents in commercial diplomacy. This was his position and reputation when in 1914 war broke out between Russia and Germany.

'There came a demand for munitions to which he, more perhaps than any other man in Russia, was in a position to attend. He immediately proceeded to Japan to place contracts for military equipment in the name of the Banque Russe-Asiatique. From Japan he went to America and placed large orders with the chief engineering firms there. During this period he returned twice to Petersburg but was in America when news arrived that the revolution had broken out, that Russia's continuance of hostilities was unlikely and that, in any case, her need for munitions had come to a sudden stop.

'Brown seems to have been at a loose end. There was nothing left for him to do in America and little purpose in his returning to Russia. The orders which he had placed in America were taken over by the British government and he himself came to England to put his services at the disposal of his father's country. His particular value to the British Intelligence Department became immediately obvious. Evidently a man of the greatest courage and resource, he had the added advantages of flying experience and perfect mastery of the German language, and in a very short space of time he had become one of those who undertook the difficult and hazardous task of entering Germany (usually by aeroplane via the front line) in quest of military information. His services in this direction were of undoubted value and his exploits in Germany have become legendary, so much so indeed that it is practically impossible to sift the true from the false in what has been told of his adventures there. He certainly made a number of trips to Germany and brought back information of the greatest value to the Allies and, with the complete breakdown of Russia and the working there of influences inimical to the Allies, he was sent to Petersburg to work against the German agents in Russia. Shortly thereafter, he disappeared.'

Major Nye closed the file. Catherine, who had become

absorbed in the story, felt disappointment. The major was looking expectantly at Mrs Cornelius.

Mrs Cornelius looked from him to her daughter. 'Oh, yes?' she said vaguely.

'These details are, by and large, familiar to you, I suppose, Mrs Cornelius?' Major Nye stroked the file with two fingers.

'What?' Mrs Cornelius glanced furtively about, seeking, as if by occult means, the right answer, but she failed and gave up, asking weakly: 'Whatcher want me ter say?'

Major Nye frowned. 'That is your husband, is it not?'

A sly, conspiratorial look crossed her face. Then her expression changed to one of cool appraisal. Catherine shivered with embarrassment. Her mother pursed her lips. 'Well,' she began, 'it could be, couldn't it?' Mrs Cornelius thought she had scented money. Major Nye, leaning across the desk, showed her a photograph. Catherine did not recognise the rather heavily built, sombrely dressed man. Mrs Cornelius, however, grinned in relief. 'Blimey!' Her recognition was genuine. 'That's my 'ubby orl right! Wot yer say 'e's bin up ter?'

'Didn't you hear anything at all, Mum?'

With the knuckle of his right index finger Major Nye smoothed his moustache away from his upper lip. 'Is that the name you knew him by, Mrs Cornelius? Brown?'

'Nar!' She found this outrageously amusing. 'Cornelius 'e was corled. Obviously.' She stopped grinning and became horrified. 'Blimey! Don't say we wasn't legally married! There's free kids!'

Major Nye was sympathetic. 'You seem to be properly married, Mrs Cornelius.'

'Phew!' Turning to Catherine her mother raised a relieved brow.

'For all we know,' said Major Nye, 'his real name is Cornelius. What I have read to you is everything we could find out about him. When we were considering employing him for the work in Russia. There were no lady friends, if that reassures you. No personal friends at all, so far as we could discover. There is, however, evidence that he had several names, indeed that he worked for several governments. He might, it emerges, have been Dutch, his mother not Russian but part-Chinese or Javanese. There is a little evidence that he was of Greek-Albanian extraction. There are many conflicting stories.'

''E was a bit on the dark side,' confirmed Mrs Cornelius. ''E's not dead, is 'e?' She was trying to disguise the urgency in her tone. She was eager to know if she was in for some money. She had been speculating on the amount since she had received the letter.

'That's what we're trying to discover,' said Major Nye. 'It's more likely he changed sides – and changed his name. When was the last time he visited you?'

'It'd be a while back now,' she said. 'Ten years?'

Catherine could not remember anyone visiting them who had looked like the man in the photograph but, aged eleven, she hadn't been in very much.

'You can't be exact?' Major Nye was coaxing Mrs Cornelius.

'Year o' the Corernation?'

'1910?'

'Sounds right. 'E said 'e'd be gettin' me an 'ouse, aht Peckham way, but nuffink come of it. Is this abaht me entitlements?' She had lost patience at last.

Major Nye glanced at Catherine, as if for an interpretation. 'Your –?'

Catherine was fairly certain that she must be blushing. She gathered her courage. 'Money,' she murmured.

'Money,' said her mother warmly. 'Was you 'is boss, then?'

'We worked for the same department for a while. I'm afraid there's no pension, Mrs Cornelius. And, indeed, we've no idea of your husband's private assets, though they must have been considerable.'

'But you said "to my advantage" in the letter!' Mrs Cornelius reminded him. Even Catherine felt the pathos.

'Yes.' Major Nye drew an envelope from the file. 'I'm sorry it's opened. We had to, you see. I'm afraid it was mislaid here and only recently came to light. That's how we were able to contact you.' He passed the envelope to her. She withdrew a sheet of yellowed paper. Attached to it by a pin were two large white five-pound notes. She folded them back so that she could let Catherine see the letter as she read it.

Dear H,

Sorry I couldn't make it Friday after all. Just passing through. Back next week and hope to look in then. In the meantime, here's a little present for you and the kids. Get yourselves something nice.

Lots of love,

J.

'When did 'e write this?' asked Mrs Cornelius.

'We think 1914.' Major Nye cleared his throat. 'He asked someone in the office to post it. They put it in the file by mistake.'

'Cor!' said Mrs Cornelius feelingly. 'I could 'ave done with a tenner in nineteen bloody fourteen!' She put the note and the money in her bag. 'An' that's orl, then?'

Major Nye stroked his small moustache with the tips of the fingers of his right hand. 'We'd appreciate hearing from you if he turned up again, Mrs Cornelius.'

''E done somefink?'

Major Nye drew a deep breath, but did not speak.

'Y'wan' me ter turn 'im in?'

'We're not the police. There are no criminal charges involved.'

'A wife can't testify against 'er 'usband,' she reminded him gravely. 'Y'know that, doncha?'

'Quite.'

'An' Caffy 'ere wouldn't know 'im if she saw 'im!'

Suddenly Catherine became aware of the major's own embarrassment. It was much more intense than hers. She caressed her lower lip with her front teeth, studying him again. She thought he might be reddening. She almost smiled. She lowered her eyes and studied her hands which rested in her lap.

'Of course,' said Major Nye. 'But you are legally entitled to demand maintenance from him. It could be back-dated, if necessary. He was, as I said, a rich man.'

'I've managed to keep them kids on me own, wivaht an 'usband...' Mrs Cornelius began proudly.

Catherine was not as impressed by this as the major. It was not her father who had married bigamously. Her mother was rising awkwardly to her feet. 'Oops!' She steadied herself. 'I'll be off, major, if yer don't mind. If there's nuffink else...'

'I cannot keep you, Mrs Cornelius. I can only say that there might be money in it – a sort of reward – services to your country. Something of that kind.'

'Yeah?' Mrs Cornelius straightened her hat, considering, reasonably, what he said. Then she shook her head, 'Nah. I couldn't. I advise *you* ter keep a sharp eye aht fer 'im, though. An' if y'find 'im, let *me* know. I wouldn't mind 'avin' a word or two wiv 'im.' She laughed, her confidence returning now that the end of the interview was in sight and the pubs were about to open. 'Still, that's life, innit?'

He moved across the room and opened the door for her.

'Come on, Caffy, dear.'

Obediently, Catherine followed her mother from the room.

'Thank you, Mrs Cornelius. At least you've cleared up one mystery,' said Major Nye. 'I regret, um...'

Her mother had paused so that Catherine had to stop directly in front of Major Nye. She studied his neck. It was a definite pink. She resisted the urge to touch the sleeve of his tweed jacket. She loved the sensation of tweed against the palm of her hand, although she couldn't wear wool herself.

'Mystery?' said her mother.

Major Nye laughed. 'Goodbye, ladies.'

They moved forward, into the passage. The boy was waiting for them. The door closed.

'I 'ope I didn't say anyfink to incriminate 'im,' whispered Mrs Cornelius as they walked behind the boy.

'I don't think so, Mum.'

''E was a funny bloke. I wonder if 'is real name was Brown.'

'He was a bastard, whatever his name was,' said Catherine feelingly.

'Wotch yer language, gel.' Mrs Cornelius nodded primly at the back of the messenger.

'He was stinking rich,' said Catherine. 'And what did we have? Three rooms in Whitechapel! Frank getting TB. Jerry...'

'Oh, well.' Her mother hadn't heard her. She patted her bag. 'We made a tenner aht of it, anyway.'

7. In which Miss Una Persson begins to witness the first signs of World Anarchy, the inevitable result of the Bolshevik Revolution

The sea was rising; there were black clouds gathering to eastward; the ship swayed rather than rolled; a big liner, she was fitted with the latest stabilisers. Una drew her chiffon scarf tighter about her face and turned up the collar of her coat. Her companion's hands tightened a little on the rail of the first-class recreation deck, but the movement of this ship did not interrupt him.

'To see them wilt before the brute power of the proletariat,' he continued enthusiastically, 'to see their authority snatched from them as a strong animal snatches meat from a weaker one – to hear the loud authoritative voice, used to being obeyed, falter and grow mute before the demoralising silence of the mob – oh, there is my relish, Una Persson.' He spoke in Russian although a moment ago he had begun in French.

They had come aboard at Marseilles and were going all the way to New York. From the ballroom below came the faint strains of a dance band. 'Well, you should have a good time in America.' She was feeling pleasantly melancholic; the grey sky and the broad grey sea always had this effect, particularly if, as now, the wind was gentle and cold.

'We.' His eyes were intense behind his spectacles. 'We can be married formally in America.'

She was amused. 'Your principles…'

'I thought you'd be pleased. Women need these evidences of security.'

'Men don't?'

She was flattered by the notion but, of course, she had no intention of marrying him. When they reached America, she would tell him. There was no point in spoiling his voyage when he was enjoying himself so much. Also, she could not face a cross-examination. Let her leaving him, in Chicago or San Francisco (she had not quite made up her mind at what stage of his lecture tour she would abandon him), be his first and smallest disappointment. There would be worse to come.

'I am unworthy of you,' she told him. It is what he would think, in a month or two. He would think the same of the United States for that matter.

'No. If anyone is unworthy…'

A slim finger on his lips silenced him. He looked sheepish. This expression was so rare these days that she had almost forgotten it. When he had worn it often she had been most in love with him. When he had been a revolutionist without a revolution. Responsibilities ruined an idealist so. Power might make men attractive to some women, but it made rotten lovers of them. She recalled him when he had been hesitant, gentle, when his words had seemed more like poetry than rhetoric, when Utopia would be achieved through good will and self-discipline, when the reins of power would be taken gently but firmly from the hands of the misguided ruling classes. He had seemed impotent then, his dreams so unrealistic as to be no more than fairy tales to which she would listen, dismissing her dim, disturbing memories of the future, of filth, blood and the rationalisation of brutality.

'Is it too cold for you out here?' he asked.

She shook her head. 'Not yet.'

'I was going to make some notes this evening.'

'You go to the cabin. I'll join you soon.'

'I can't leave you here.'

'I'm not likely to be washed overboard.' She smiled. 'Make your notes, my dear.'

'I'll stay.'

She accepted this, though she knew that he would soon condemn her for keeping him from his work. This knowledge made the melancholia all the sweeter. She felt guilty. 'Well, perhaps I'll come down now.'

'You're sure? If...'

'It is getting cold,' she agreed. 'Could we possibly have a hot drink brought to the cabin?'

'Why not? It's all paid for by the Americans.' He grinned, happy that she had decided to go with him, although she knew that once he had begun to write he would be disturbed by the slightest movement she might make, that she would have to find some dreadful novel from the ship's library and pretend to read it. If she did not, he would decide that her restlessness was a sign that she wanted attention from him. She linked her arm in his as they crossed to the companionway. She hoped that he would decide to practise one of his lectures aloud to her; it would be preferable, certainly, to the novels. She sighed to herself. In a situation of this kind it was so hard for her not to fall back on easy cynicism. After all, she had agreed cheerfully enough when, in Paris, he had suggested they make the trip together, that his expenses allowed him to bring his wife. It was a way out of the plague ghetto, where she had been working as an auxiliary nurse and where, as a result, she had been confined when the Commune voted to quarantine the area.

As they entered the warmer air of the corridor she began to cough. An officer saluted them, speaking English. 'Good evening, madam. Evening, sir.' They nodded to acknowledge him. He turned the handle of the cabin door. 'I can never tell if they're using English or German,' he complained. 'I'm so rusty on languages. I'll have to improve. You must give me lessons, Una.'

'Your lectures sound all right.'

'The accent is good?' He turned a light switch. The cabin was untidy, scattered with his clothes and papers. Apart from a few cosmetics on the tiny dressing table there was hardly any sign that she also occupied the room.

'Well, perhaps you could do with a refresher course in pronunciation.'

'I want them to understand every word.'

'They will.'

He was nervous of America. It seemed that he was anxious to

win the approval of the workers there, more than anywhere else. He regarded them as more sophisticated, more articulate, more politically educated than workers in any other country. 'To win America,' he murmured to himself. Here was a return to the unrealistic idealism which had first attracted her to him when she had met him at the International before the war, in London. 'They want me. They have sent for me. Oh, I know I am one of many speakers contracted by the agency, but if they didn't wish to hear me, they wouldn't pay, would they?'

Una nodded. She peered through the porthole at the ocean; the horizon moved upwards and disappeared. She drew the tiny curtains.

Una awoke at dawn. She was cold. There was fresh, sharp air in her nostrils and she thought at first that the porthole had come open; then she wondered if the book, crushed between her body and the side of the bunk, had been the cause of her early waking. The book's edges were pressing into her ribs. She moved it, leaning over to place it on the floor. In the opposite bunk he was asleep, half-dressed, one leg hanging free, characteristically. She was about to turn on her side and go back to sleep when she realised that what had actually disturbed her was a series of loud noises, shouts, thumps, possibly gunshots. She rose, went to the porthole and looked out. The sea had vanished. In its place was the side of another vessel, painted a creamy white but covered in large patches of rust where the paint had peeled. Craning her neck she looked up. She could see the ship's rails and parts of her superstructure. She appeared to be a battleship.

The sea was very calm now. If there had been a storm then it had passed in the night. She went to the wardrobe and took out a slightly crumpled morning frock in green silk. As she dressed she listened, trying to interpret the sounds. It seemed as if the ship was being commandeered, possibly for provisions, as sometimes happened in wartime. She was not aware of any international war taking place at that moment. She had unpacked very few of her clothes, since they had to appear in public only once or twice on the voyage. Thoughtfully, she put everything into her suitcase. Experience told her that it was as well to be ready for flight in this sort of situation. Another shot: clearly identifiable. It was closer. It had probably come from one of the nearby passages.

Men in heavy boots could be heard running along companionways towards the cabins. There were more shouts: orders. She heard angry voices, exclamations, banging doors. The passengers. There came a rap on her own door. He stirred in his sleep, feeling for his spectacles even before he awakened. Una lit a cigarette while the knock was repeated. She heard a man say in Spanish: 'Give me the passenger list.' A moment later she heard the same man laugh.

She opened the door.

He was swarthy, looking Jewish rather than Spanish, and the barefooted sailors grinning behind him were mainly negroes, some very black, some quite pale. His uniform was of the same cream colour as his ship and the jacket and the left leg of his trousers had large brown bloodstains on them, like rust. It was almost as if the similarities between ship and uniform were deliberate. He was very tall, his head almost touching the ceiling. He saluted cheerfully. 'Good morning, Comrade Persson. There was a rumour that you were aboard. And this comrade, also.'

He was grumbling, sitting on the edge of his bed and rubbing at himself. 'Are we sinking?'

'Your ship is perfectly seaworthy, if that's what you mean, comrade. If you are speaking symbolically…'

'Get out,' he growled. 'What do you want?'

'We are requisitioning stores and personnel for the use of our navy,' replied the tall man.

He was buttoning up his shirt. Now he recognised the voice of the newcomer. He looked up. 'Good God! Petroff! I thought you were dead.'

'I know that my services were no longer useful to your particular struggle, comrade.' Petroff handed him his tie. 'However, I am now employed in another cause and seem to be appreciated better.' He spoke, Una guessed, not without bitterness. Petroff had been regarded as something of an opportunist in Moscow, but she had always thought him nothing more than a well-intentioned realist. She was as surprised as her companion to discover that Petroff was alive.

'Your own cause, eh, comrade?' Polishing his glasses he glared at the intruder. 'What is it? Simple piracy? How do you dignify it?'

'I support the principles of World Revolution and I am presently representing the Cuban Revolutionary Council. I am an officer in the CRC Navy. I hold the rank of Commander.'

'You will hardly get British recognition for your council,' he said, 'by committing acts of piracy against her civilian shipping.'

'We aren't interested in British recognition,' Petroff told him frankly. 'We want your food and your women.'

'What?'

'You're kidnapping the women?' Una felt a stir of interest at last.

'The young and the beautiful only.' He bowed to her.

'For ransom?'

He smiled. 'Certainly not. For pleasure.'

From over Una's shoulder there came a braying laugh. 'Thieves and rapists! Well, Petroff, you are revealed in your true colours. You are one of those who uses the vocabulary of revolution to justify acts of the grossest criminality…'

Petroff sighed, saluted again, but addressed Una. 'You will come with us willingly, comrade?'

'You intend to take Mademoiselle Persson? This is ridiculous. She is a comrade. An important and respected worker…'

'She is young and very beautiful.' Petroff drew a long-barrelled Colt revolver from the holster at his belt. 'We have orders to shoot anyone who resists. We have already shot fourteen members of the crew and five passengers.'

'I am horrified.' Vigorously he knotted his tie. 'We executed men for less during the revolution.'

'Perhaps that is where you went wrong, comrade. Cuba is primarily a Catholic country. Rather than learn to be puritans, renouncing our humanity, we intend to follow our instincts and achieve, as a result, a healthy and vital revolution. We are seizing only the first-class passengers and taking food intended for the first-class galley.'

'Your logic is ludicrous. If there is no food for the first-class passengers, the other food will be shared.'

'Requisitioned from the less fortunate. Exactly. An excellent moral lesson. Thus we sow the seeds of World Revolution.'

He turned away in disgust.

'I'll get my bag,' said Una.

'I'll die before they'll take you!' He moved to put himself between Una and Petroff.

Una kissed him. 'Your work is too important,' she told him. 'You must go to America. You know what it means to you – what it could mean to the American workers. The revolution is more important than the feelings of a couple of individuals.'

He hesitated. 'But I love you, Una.'

'And I love you, Fred.' She whispered: 'I will find you again, as I have found you before.' She picked up her suitcase.

This satisfied him. With an expression of contempt, he watched the sailors escort her from the cabin.

Petroff was the last to leave, casually waving the revolver. 'I suspect, Comrade "Brown", that it was you who signed the order for my liquidation. Happily for you, I am proud of the fact that I am not a vengeful man. Besides, to shoot you would carry no weight. Much better that I should take the only human being for whom you have any natural affection.'

'Brown' screamed at him. Quickly, Petroff closed the door. He seemed upset.

Una joined the other women in the line in the corridor. One or two of them were in shock but the others (about ten) appeared to be either amused or angry; most of them were in nightclothes and dressing gowns but a few had managed to do their hair and make-up. Not one resisted as the party was herded on deck, into the mild dawn air. There were only a few bodies in evidence. A crane had been swung out from the pirate battleship and jutted over the liner's bottom deck, where they were now gathered.

From the crane ran a heavy chain attached to a makeshift wooden platform which was lowered to the deck as they emerged.

In pantomime the sailors indicated that the ladies should step onto the platform. Nervously, they complied. Una settled her suitcase on it and turned as she heard a scuffling near the rail. They had the captain, a small, round-featured Irishman. There was a flesh wound in his left arm. He had been handcuffed. 'Piracy,' he was saying with an almost romantic relish. 'Nothing but old-fashioned piracy!'

Petroff approached him and saluted, offering him a piece of paper which he accepted with both hands, wincing at his wound. Petroff explained. 'It is your receipt, captain. The cases of food have been itemised. The fourteen passengers have also been itemised. There will, of course, be no compensation.'

The captain raised his head to stare at Petroff. 'Hum.'

'Your company is insured against acts of piracy, presumably,' said Petroff.

'I don't know…'

'It would be wise of you to remind them, when you get to New York.'

'Yes.' It was obvious to Una that the captain was only dimly aware of what was happening. The platform swayed as the crane began to crank it up and swing it over the side. One dark-haired girl of eighteen cried out as her little bag fell off the edge.

'I think it would be better if we were all seated.' They accepted Una's suggestion and the platform steadied itself. Looking down, Una caught the captain's astonished eye. She waved.

Una noted that grappling lines had been secured between the ships. Already the pirates were using these to cross back to their own vessel while their comrades, at the battleship's rails, brandished light machine guns and rifles, covering them. Though all the pirates adopted a style of rakish villainy there was amongst them an almost childish good-humoured ambience, as if they knew they were being bad. Una saw that Petroff remained on the liner's deck, chatting to the captain until the last of his men had returned, then he holstered his revolver, took hold of a grappling line and clambered, hand over hand, to his ship. As the crane began to lower the women to the battleship's deck the grappling lines were cast off. Petroff jumped from the rail, ran to his bridge and disappeared. A moment later the ironclad's engines began to turn and its big guns moved to menace the passenger vessel. 'Oh, goodness,' breathlessly murmured a young American girl, as the liner receded. Shouldering their weapons, the crew gathered round the platform to inspect their prizes.

Petroff reappeared above. 'Mrs Persson,' he called in English. 'Would you join me, yes?'

Leaving her luggage on the platform Una stepped off, pushing through the hot bodies to climb up to the bridge. Petroff awaited her. He was pleased with himself. 'Do you really intend to rape us?' she asked.

He smiled, enjoying the idea for a moment. 'Certainly not. The women may pick anyone they choose to be their husband. I shall marry them myself. We think in the long term, you see. It is the children we want. Good stock, wouldn't you agree? Some of the finest blood from the Old and New World.'

'And who am I to marry?'

'The choice is yours. You are free to decide. We are democrats, of course.' He offered her a cheroot which she accepted.

As he lit the cheroot for her she said: 'I was just congratulating myself that I'd avoided one suitor with minimum embarrassment to both parties.' The cheroot began to smoulder. He blew out the match. 'Still,' she continued, 'I suppose this is a much healthier situation, though I'd be happier if there was less talk of freedom of choice, comrade.'

Petroff was amused. 'I take your point. But you are right. We are running a very healthy revolution, as I told "Brown".'

'How much time are you giving me to decide?' Through her thin dress the morning sun had begun to warm her skin.

'As long as you like. In the meantime, I invite you to join us. I can have a uniform modified for you.'

'You're disappointing me. Now I'm being offered a job.'

'An enjoyable job. Look how happy we all are! You would also receive a big pistol, like mine.'

'I have my own weapons, in my luggage.'

He folded his arms on the rail, sighing with pleasure, looking to starboard where the SS *Queen Victoria* could still be seen, her four funnels smoking, on the horizon. 'The sooner we return to Havana the better. They will repair their wireless shortly and the American war-fleet will be chasing us. I hope you'll consider me, by the way, Una. We would have beautiful children.' He tilted his cap to shade his eyes.

'I'm not sure it's possible for me to have children,' she said speculatively. 'It might cause all sorts of trouble. "Browns" are very,' she smiled to herself, '"unstable".'

'That would be a shame.' He had only taken note of the first remark.

'Yes,' she said. She watched as the women, in their expensive négligées, were taken to their quarters. The men were excessively, if sardonically, polite. She envied the women the simplicity of their situation. 'It's odd, isn't it? There are so many ways of losing a revolution.'

8. In which Catherine Cornelius takes part in a union of two nations

'They're gonna fink yore th' bleedin' delivery boy!' Mrs Cornelius floundered up from the dip in the iron bed, casting off some half a dozen blankets and an emerald-green quilt. The bed shook and creaked. Catherine felt the vibrations on the floor beneath her feet as she stood at the door. ''And me me 'arscoat, love.'

Catherine crossed quickly to the chair on which her mother's many garments were piled. She selected the stained and faded man's woollen dressing gown and the Savage Club tie and passed them over. Mrs Cornelius, in musty liberty bodice and drawers, began to pull the dressing gown around her, securing it with the tie. 'You 'ad such lovely 'air, an' all.'

Catherine stroked the back of her naked neck. 'Don't make me feel embarrassed, Mum. There's lots of girls have Eton crops now. Lots of society people, and actresses and that.'

'Yeah...' said Mrs Cornelius darkly. With only the remains of yesterday's make-up her face had a pale, pitted look, a dignity not normally distinguishable. She began to sip the cup of lukewarm tea Catherine had left on the littered bamboo table beside the bed. 'Well, there's 'ores wearin' more than yore wearin'. It don't mean everyone's gotta start 'angin' abaht Piccadilly, does it?' She cast a cold eye over the beige rayon frock, copied by Catherine from an original Molyneaux she had seen in last month's *Vogue*. 'Yer show it all, gel, and there's nuffink left ter offer 'em.'

'What,' said Catherine mockingly, 'the customers at the flower shop?'

'And where *is* th' flah shop?' Her mother matched her tone, bettered it. 'Eh? In Shepherd's bleedin' Market! When I arsked

Edna ter give yer the job I also bloody arsked 'er ter keep a bloody eye on yer, an' all! Y'should 'ear the stories she's told *me*!'

'I have, Mum. Don't worry. I'm not the only girl in the world wearing short frocks these days.'

Mrs Cornelius began her morning cough. 'Yaaaah! Kar! Kar! Yaaaaah! Kar, kar, kar!' Catherine called goodbye and ran down the stairs, out onto the damp, bright pavements of Blenheim Crescent. She pulled on her coat as she walked to the corner, turning up Kensington Park Road, past Sammy's pie shop (not yet open), keeping pace with two totters' carts which had emerged from the mews running behind the Cornelius flat, where all the rag-and-bone merchants had their stables. Catherine was barely aware of the strong smell of mildew and manure the carts bore with them, for she had known the smell ever since her family had moved here at the end of the Great War. The carts turned off at Elgin Crescent, heading towards the richer parts of Bayswater, and she hurried on up the hill to Notting Hill Gate, to catch the tram which would take her to Mayfair.

Although her Auntie Edna (not a blood relation) was already opening the shop when Catherine arrived no mention was made of her lateness. Monday mornings were normally fairly slow and gave the staff a chance to assess and arrange the stock, ordered that morning by Edna Bowman and delivered from Covent Garden. All along the paved court of the Market other shopkeepers were opening up. 'Lovely day, dear, isn't it? Spring's 'ere, at last.' Auntie Edna was a tiny, cheerful woman, rather heavily made up, who had known her mother since the early days in Whitechapel. Edna had done quite a bit better for herself than had Mrs Cornelius; she had received the capital for her shop from an admirer, long since dead, of whom she had been particularly fond. As Catherine went to the back of the shop to hang up her coat, Edna called: 'You're the first to arrive. Nellie 'asn't turned up. Get Ted to 'elp you with them boxes. Like your 'airdo.'

'Glad someone does.' Catherine put her coat on the only hanger. 'Mum thought someone would take me for Ted.'

Edna shouted with laughter. Ted himself appeared, wheeling his big black delivery bike through the court. He wore a fresh apron, a striped blazer and moleskin knickerbockers. Although only fourteen, he was nearly five foot ten, fat and ruddy, with a faint black moustache and a permanently morose expression belying a sharp sense of humour.

'Morning, Ted,' said Auntie Edna, still laughing.

'Morning, Mrs Bowman.' His large eyes regarded her with considerable gravity. 'You really shouldn't start before they open, you know. It's bad for the liver.'

'Cheeky blighter,' said Auntie Edna affectionately. 'Give Cath an 'and with the big boxes will yer. Nellie's not 'ere yet.'

'Probably married 'Is Lordship over the weekend,' suggested Ted, letting down the bike's iron stand with a clang. It was a familiar joke. Mr Stopes, the dignified butler from the Cannings' house in South Audley Street and popularly known in the Market as His Lordship, was sweet on Nellie, who thought a butler beneath her. Nellie was not merely an assistant in the shop. She was, she said, a Floral Artiste. Sometimes she would go to customers' houses and arrange their flowers for them. As a result she had seen how the other half lived and had set her sights on having nothing less than the best for herself.

Catherine and Ted began to carry the cardboard boxes of irises into the shop. Outside, Auntie Edna passed the time of day with the owner of the ironmonger's next door. They were talking about a man who had assassinated somebody in Germany and who was now on trial for murder. The ironmonger, apparently, had known the murderer when he had been a prisoner of war in England. ''E was a meek little blighter, too.'

When all the boxes were empty and the flowers transferred to pots and vases Catherine, now in a green overall, began to arrange them. Auntie Edna finished her conversation and came in. 'You've got a knack for it, Cath – better than Nellie, really. That's a very tasteful arrangement.' She moved a daffodil, thought better of it, replaced it where Catherine had originally put it. 'Where could that silly girl 'ave got to?' A customer entered. It was the old lady who looked after the Member of Parliament whose flat was in Curzon Street. 'Good morning, Mrs Clarke.' Auntie Edna raised her voice a fraction. 'Lovely, isn't it?'

'He's coming up from his constituency today, you see.' Mrs Clarke frowned, staring hard at Catherine as if trying to determine her sex. Catherine snapped a stalk too short and sighed. 'So I thought I'd get him a bunch or two of nice spring flowers. What have you done to your hair, dear?'

'It's the Eton crop,' said Auntie Edna, 'isn't it, Cath? The latest fashion.'

Catherine became conscious of a slight flush on the back of her freshly shaved neck. She continued to arrange the flowers.

'Well I never,' said Mrs Clarke. 'How much are the daffs?'

'Sixpence a bunch this morning, I'm afraid.' Auntie Edna shook them in their vase and removed a few to show her.

'Give us two, love,' said Mrs Clarke.

As Mrs Clarke left and Auntie Edna put the shilling in the till Catherine glanced through the shop's window and saw someone looking in, his face partially obscured by the broad leaves of the aspidistra and the feathery foliage of the ferns used for display. She knew, by the way he began to study the tulips, that he had been looking at her. She started to move towards the back of the shop, wondering if Mrs Clarke was outside soliciting opinions about recent hair fashions. The man remained at the window. Then he was gone. He stood in the entrance to the shop, the light behind him. He was good-looking, middle-aged, dark. He was dressed in formal but slightly old-fashioned clothes: grey frock-coat and trousers, grey waistcoat, grey homburg. He had a wing-collar and a yellow cravat with an amber pin in the shape of a moth. He carried a black, silver-headed stick and, as he entered the shop, she saw that he wore light tan shoes with spats. He had the air of a foreigner who had spent some years in England. Catherine had never seen him before but Auntie Edna recognised him with pleasure. 'Oh, good morning, Mr K! Just back in London, are you?'

'From my island retreat, yes. I returned recently.' He had a deep, soft voice, with an accent. 'You have no orchids today?'

'I'm afraid not. I could order you some for tomorrow.'

'If you would, Mrs Bowman.'

Because he did not look in her direction Catherine became convinced that he was probably aware of her attention. She turned her back and began to clip the ends off some irises. 'There's not a very big selection at this time of the year, really,' Auntie Edna was saying. 'They had some roses in the market, but I didn't fancy them. Forced flowers never last, do they?'

'No, indeed. Then let us have a great many beautiful English spring flowers, Mrs Bowman. Give me three bunches of everything. I shall turn my apartment into a celebration of the season.'

'Your flat'll be more like Kew Gardens, Mr K!' Auntie Edna giggled. 'When shall I have them sent round?'

'This afternoon. About three o'clock. And I will need somebody to arrange them for me.'

'Oh dear. Well, Nellie's off today. She might be in later, but...' Auntie Edna called: 'Miss Cornelius!'

Catherine was forced to face her aunt and the foreigner. 'Yes, Mrs Bowman.' They were always formal in front of this kind of customer.

'D'you think you're up to arranging some flowers for Mr K?'

'Well, if Nellie can't do it...'

'She's got a lovely touch,' said Auntie Edna to Mr K. 'I think you'll be satisfied. Can you go round with Ted at three, love?'

'Of course, Mrs Bowman.' She continued to be embarrassed. She made herself lift her chin, to look back at him, but luckily he was already turning, smiling at Auntie Edna.

'Thank you.' He raised his hat as he left, causing Auntie Edna to stare fondly after him. 'He's very gentlemanly, that Mr K. Ever so polite, Cath. And one of our best customers.'

'What does he do?'

'He's Greek. Owns a lot of ships and stuff. He's got flats all over the world, but he prefers to live in London most of the time. It's his favourite city, he reckons. They say he's a millionaire. You'll do well this afternoon. Nellie once got a quid for arranging his flowers for him. He loves flowers. Has fresh ones every day he's in London. I could keep going on his custom alone when he's here, but, of course, he has to travel a lot. I think he's got a wife in Paris, but he never brings her with him. Maybe they're divorced. He took a fancy to you, you could tell. Kept looking at you while you were arranging them irises. He might tip you more than a quid, who knows?'

'He seemed very nice.' She thought she flushed again, though Auntie Edna didn't seem to notice. The back of her head felt so vulnerable since she had had her hair cut.

'You'd better do his flowers as soon as you've had your lunch, Cath. Three bunches of everything.'

'All right, Auntie Edna.' She wished that Nellie were here, to do the arranging. Nellie had a brashness, a self-assurance which could carry her through a situation. Besides, Nellie relished intense stares from dark-eyed millionaires: her hopes for the future depended on them. Mr K. did not seem a bad sort and she was sure he had no real interest in her – he had probably also been trying to guess if she were a girl or a boy in her short hair and overall – but she was afraid that she would be awkward if he was there when she was arranging the flowers, that she might let Auntie Edna down. She tried to stop worrying; after all, the odds were that he wouldn't want to hang around while she was working. He probably had too much to do.

By lunchtime she felt better, was even amused by her own nervousness, but when she and Ted set off for Hertford Street she was abstracted and hardly heard what Ted was telling her about his dad's having gone for a job as a baker only to find, when he got there, that the bakery was kosher. Ted was balancing the flower boxes on his bike and she was carrying four big cellophane-wrapped bunches in her arms, wishing that she had remembered to wear her overall, or at least her coat, for she could feel water running down her right knee.

Ted stopped outside a house with a black door. The paint looked fresh. There was a brass plate on the wall beside the door: *Koutrouboussis and Son*. 'Is that Mr K?' she asked. 'Kou-trou-bou-ssis.'

'Bit of a mouthful, eh?' said Ted. 'I think the old man's dead or gone back to Greece. This is his son.'

A maid opened the door at Ted's ring. 'Ah, the flowers.' She was small and Chinese. Catherine thought she had never seen a more beautiful girl. She was dressed conventionally, in a black-and-white uniform. 'We go upstairs, please.' Catherine and Ted followed the maid up a fairly narrow staircase. Judging from the look of the doors on the ground floor, Mr Koutrouboussis's business was conducted there. The maid came to a door at the top of the stairs. She opened it and led them into a wide hall. The hall was furnished opulently with slightly unfashionable Chinoiserie, although the preponderance of lacquered wood and black-framed mirrors was not overpowering and, against this setting, the maid no longer seemed incongruous.

'Isn't it lovely,' whispered Catherine.

It was not to Ted's taste. He said nothing as he wiped his boots on the mat. They followed the maid into a large sitting room, also furnished in a mixture of oriental styles and art nouveau, again giving an impression of lightness. Catherine thought it was probably more like a Japanese room than a Chinese one, though she could not have defined the difference. It was odd to see, through the large French windows which opened onto a balcony, the familiar Mayfair street.

The maid handed something to Ted as soon as he had set his boxes down. 'This is for you, thank you.'

'Thanks very much, love,' said Ted. He lumbered from the room. 'See you in a little while, Cath.'

'Yes. Cheerio, Ted.' Her voice sounded feeble in her own ears. She looked helplessly at the maid. 'Where do you want me to begin? In here? Are there some vases?'

With Ted gone the maid's manner seemed to change. She was no longer brisk. Her voice became at once more intimate and virtually inaudible. 'I will fetch pots, miss.'

Alone in the sitting room, Catherine bent and removed the lid from the nearest box. It was full of daffodils. She began to look for suitable surfaces on which to place the vases, wishing that she had some idea of Mr Koutrouboussis's preferences. The door opposite opened. He was smiling, wearing a dark brown quilted smoking jacket over the waistcoat and trousers he had worn when he had come to the shop. He was smoking a cigarette in a holder. 'Ah, the little girl from Mrs Bowman's. What shall I call you, my dear?'

'My name's Catherine Cornelius, sir.' She suppressed a strong satirical urge to lisp and curtsey and wondered almost with horror where such a notion could have come from, particularly since she felt so nervous. For his part he bowed, with an air of light mockery. 'I am honoured to make your acquaintance, Miss Cornelius. Your beauty outshines the beauty of the flowers you bring me.' His tone had the effect of relaxing her almost too much. She smiled in return as he held out his hand for hers. His soft lips, his moustache, touched her knuckles. She became gay. 'Where would you like me to start, Mr Koutrouboussis?'

He was evidently pleased that she had pronounced his full name. 'There is a large vase which the maid will bring. I think a selection of all the flowers could go in that, on top of that cabinet there, where they will catch the light. What do you think? Women have a better sense of these things.'

'I think it would look very well there,' she said. She was flattered. The maid came in, carrying the large fan-shaped vase. 'Thank you,' said Mr Koutrouboussis. 'Put it on the cabinet, please.' As the maid left to fetch another vase he said, 'You think it unusual, a Chinese girl for a maid?'

'Unusual in these parts, sir.'

'I brought her with me from Hong Kong. I love feminine things, you see. And Chinese women are the quintessence of femininity. I celebrate femininity where most men, particularly men of business, try to banish it. We are born of women. I refuse to deny my mother's blood.'

For a moment Catherine wondered if he were trying to tell her that he was a pansy, so that she should not be afraid of being in the room alone with him, but he continued:

'These days everyone is trying to stop women being women. It was the war, I suppose. Or perhaps it is fear of emancipation. If women are to have the vote, they say, then let us force them to become masculine – then we shall not be afraid of them.'

Catherine was now certain that he disapproved of her hair. She became confused again. 'I'm not at all sure, Mr Koutrouboussis.' His laughter calmed her. 'Oh, I am sorry, Miss Cornelius. I am not referring to your delicious hairstyle. It is lovely. It displays an exquisite neck, draws attention to a perfect face, a delightful figure. Your femininity, I assure you, is emphasised. Your presence gladdens my heart. You must come to arrange my flowers every day.' The scent of the anemones she had been holding now seemed very heady and she wondered if the room itself were perfumed. Perhaps, being foreign, he was wearing perfume himself. A thought came to her, that it was his praise which made her feel so dizzy, but she decided it was, after all, the anemones. 'Thank you,' she said.

The maid returned with two tall vases on a tray. At her master's instructions she placed the vases on a small table standing before the French windows. She seemed to be smiling, although her eyes remained directed downwards. 'I will fetch more pots,' she said.

'I'd better be getting on with my job, sir,' said Catherine easily. 'Mrs Bowman's a bit short-handed today.'

'Of course.' He waved her towards the large vase. 'Will it embarrass you if I watch? I admire skill, particularly those skills at which women excel.'

She smiled. 'I'll probably make a terrible job of it now. It's my first time, you see. In a house, I mean. I've only done the arrangements in the shop up to now.'

'If it seems to me that I am making you shy I will leave, I promise you.'

She drew a deep breath and nodded. 'All right, sir. It's a bargain.'

He seated himself in an armchair with a padded oval back. He drew a small table with an ashtray on it towards him.

Although she felt self-conscious, his flattery had given her confidence. She felt rather like a dancer who knows she has an appreciative audience, and the ambience in the apartment, cool, comfortable and slightly erotic, also helped to put her at her ease. As she worked she was hardly aware of his presence. The arrangement came easily and was finished quickly. 'There. Will that do?'

'You are an artist, Miss Cornelius.' He rose to admire the display. 'You have studied this sort of thing?'

'Studied?'

'Flower-arranging. In Japan…'

'Oh, no. I like doing it. It's what I enjoy most about working for Mrs Bowman?'

'And what do you do, other than working for Mrs Bowman?'

She selected some more flowers and approached the first of the tall vases. The maid entered, carrying a round, pewter vase, decorated with semi-naked ladies wearing flowing drapery which, with the stylised lilies and water-lilies, made up the main design. 'Well, nothing really,' she replied.

'You do not paint?'

Catherine was amused. 'I never thought of it. I haven't any talent.'

'Oh, I think you have talent. You should go to art school.'

She smiled, saying nothing. She snipped some of the longer stems of the tulips. The maid left the room again. He walked to the window and looked out. 'What a beautiful day it is. Will you dine with me tonight, Miss Cornelius?' She was taken aback and yet at the same time the question came as an inevitable one so she answered 'Yes' without thinking, then she hesitated, the scissors in one hand, the tulips in the other. 'I'm not sure. I mean…'

'I suppose it is the springtime,' he said gently. 'But I would be honoured.' He turned to regard her. 'Not a question one should ask a respectable young English lady, really. But I do not regret the impulse. And you said "Yes" before you began to change your mind. Why not follow your first impulse?'

'Well, there's my mother,' said Catherine lamely.

'She has warned you about rich men who would rob you of your virtue and leave you with nothing.' He made a quiet joke of it. 'I promise you, Miss Cornelius, that I value your virtue quite as highly as your mother would.'

'And I've nothing to wear,' she added.

'You look exquisite in what you are wearing now. The frock is absolutely *à la mode*. Wear that. We shall dine in my apartment.'

'I couldn't...'

'The maid will remain here.'

'Oh dear.'

'I can see that you want to accept. Are you afraid of me?'

She wet her lower lip with her tongue. 'It would probably be better if I were, Mr Koutrouboussis.'

'Please accept.'

She told herself that she did not wish to anger him. Indeed, she very much wanted to win his approval. She had to think of Auntie Edna's business. Mr K. was her best customer. It would, however, mean lying to her mother. It would not be the first time, of course. 'When shall I come?'

'About seven. I like to dine fairly early.'

She knew that he intended to seduce her and she began to feel a heady excitement. He bowed. 'I will see you at seven.' He touched her shoulder. He inclined his head; his eyes were serious. He left the room.

She worked automatically, filling vase after vase with flowers. Some of the vases were removed by the little Chinese girl and taken to other rooms. As soon as he had gone she had begun trying to consider how she might release herself from the agreement she had made, but she could think of nothing. If she left without giving him a good excuse as to why she could not come back that evening there would be no way of escaping without angering him. She imagined that he would be very angry if she let him down – not heated, but cold, possibly vengeful. And yet, even out of loyalty to her mother's friend, could she commit herself to the bargain? She had to consider it: he could ruin her. Unless, of course, Mr Koutrouboussis were to marry her. It was possible that he might have fallen in love with her when he had seen her in the flower shop. No, he was already married. She sensed, however, that he would be loyal, whatever happened. She knew a moment's humour – perhaps he would set her up in a flower shop.

After she had left the flat, and during the rest of her day at the shop, on the tram home, she continued to debate with herself not about the wisdom of seeing him that night (she knew that she had reached that decision the moment he had asked her) but whether he would look after her if she did get into trouble. He seemed a sentimental man and he had demonstrated his kindness. He was also very attractive, the sort of man who had always attracted her. Sophisticated, free, original – a modern bandit-king, in a way. And certainly she had never felt more feminine than when she had been at his flat. As the tram approached Notting Hill Gate she glanced at the clock over the watchmaker's shop. It was already a quarter past six. She would be late.

She ran all the way home and was so out of breath when she reached the front door of the house that she had to pause for a moment before going upstairs and letting herself into the flat. 'Mum?' To her relief her mother was out, probably still working at Sammy's pie shop where she helped part-time. Sammy himself had been Mrs Cornelius's boyfriend of some years' standing. Catherine wrote a note saying that she was going to a dance with Nellie and might stay at Nellie's overnight. She knew that her mother would be suspicious but it was better to invent a simple and conventional excuse than a complicated one which her mother would resent as insulting both her intelligence and her sense of decorum. She put on a little make-up, took her best coat from the cupboard, pulled her new cloche over her head, filled her tiny evening bag with a few necessities, all the while hoping desperately that her mother would not arrive back before she could leave, and then she fled down the stairs again, out into the darkening street, past the pie shop, retracing her steps to the tram stop, seeing from the watchmaker's clock that it was ten to seven. She would only be about five minutes late, with luck.

When she returned to Hertford Street she realised that she did not know the number of the house. Almost all the doors looked alike to her, but eventually she found the one with the brass plate. She rang the bell. The Chinese maid opened the door. This time the girl's smile was direct and friendly and her eyes were appraising. 'Good evening, miss…'

'Good evening. Mr Koutrouboussis is…'

'He said to show you up, miss.' For a second time that day the maid led Catherine to the apartment, took her coat in the hall (now filled with flowers) and showed her into the sitting room. She was surprised at how fine her arrangements had been; they were certainly the best she had ever done. As before the other door opened and Mr Koutrouboussis emerged. He wore a different smoking jacket, dark green, with dark red lapels. It was longer than the one he had worn that afternoon, almost a dressing gown. 'My dear.' He seemed innocently delighted. 'You see, I, too, am informally dressed. You do not mind?' She shook her head. He crossed to a cabinet of decanters and glasses. 'What would you like to drink?'

'Dry sherry?'

'I think you will like this one. It is very light.'

'I'm sorry if I'm a bit late,' she said. 'I had to go home and tell my mum.'

'That you were coming here?' He handed her the sherry and indicated a place for her on the lacquered ottoman with the woven-cane back. She sat down. She decided not to answer his question directly.

'I left her a note,' she said. She sipped the sherry. He had the art of making her feel at once sophisticated and vulnerable. She enjoyed the sensation, but now that she knew that she was to be seduced she no longer had the same reservations about offending him. 'This is lovely sherry. What's it called?' He told her a name in Spanish. She decided to look at the bottle later, then she glanced across and remembered that he had poured the sherry from a decanter. He had drawn the heavy curtains over the French windows and the room had a luxurious, tranquil atmosphere; she felt safe in it.

The maid came in. 'The soup,' she said.

Catherine had finished her sherry. He took the glass from her and helped her rise. 'You are such a graceful creature. You are like a faun.'

She had not been listening. 'Fun?'

'That is how you would pronounce it?' He was politely interested as he led her across the hall and into the dining room with its electric flambeaux on the walls which were papered with a raised flock pattern showing Chinese horses and soldiers. This room, although in the same style as the others, had a much more masculine air to it. The dining table and the chairs were heavier. Even the tableware was of heavy porcelain and silver. She had felt completely at ease in the sitting room but here she felt like an interloper; like a child taking its first meal with its parents. After a moment's bafflement she selected a large soup spoon from the array of cutlery. She ate in silence, for he made no attempt at conversation. The soup was delicious, light and faintly fishy, with more than a hint of the sherry she had been drinking earlier. The maid cleared away the bowls and brought the main course, some sort of cutlet in breadcrumbs. 'I hope you will forgive a very simple meal, my dear.' With the cutlet were thin fried potatoes, spinach and some kind of vegetable she had never tasted before and which she didn't like very much; similar to sliced, cooked cucumber. Expecting a great deal from the meal she ate slowly, savouring it, sipping the wine he poured for her. The whole effect on her was to make her feel more alive to sensation than at any time since her first experience of puberty. It seemed to her that her skin tingled at the lightest touch – her napkin against her wrist, her arm against a glass – and a sense of well-being filled her so that, when the maid brought flaming crêpes suzettes, she could do little more than taste a morsel, enjoying for the first time that exquisite combination of bitterness and sweetness. Finally the Chinese girl came in with the cheese, and Catherine sampled something pungent, foreign and soft. Then at last there was a tiny glass of port, which warmed her through.

'We shall have coffee in the sitting room,' he told the maid, and he had touched Catherine's arm as he helped her from the chair. She was a little dizzy, but not unpleasantly so. He escorted her back to the sitting room, back to the ottoman. The room was full of floral scent, but she was not sure if it came from the flowers themselves. A small table had been placed near the ottoman. There were a pot of coffee, some brown sugar, a jug of cream, two small porcelain cups. The tray, art nouveau silver like the big vase she had filled that afternoon, matched the coffee things. 'I suppose all this looks a little old-fashioned to you,' he said.

'Oh, no! I've always liked it. I liked it before it came back.'

'Came back?'

Something unwanted was emerging in her mind. She dismissed it successfully. He was stroking her neck. 'You are very young. Are you afraid of me?'

'I could be.'

'Yes. How old are you, Catherine?'

'Twenty-nine?'

He smiled. 'If I knocked about thirteen years away would I be closer?'

'To what?'

'To your age.'

'Maybe.' She might have shrugged.

'You are very delicate.' He stroked the line of her jaw. It was wonderful. 'Utterly feminine. You are everything a young girl should be and so rarely is. You know that I intend to possess you.' She nodded as his dark eyes came towards her own and she felt first his moustache touch her upper lip, then his lips touch both of hers at first softly and then aggressively until his tongue was pushing through, parting her teeth, to touch her tongue, and she had closed her eyes as his body pressed against her soft breasts and her thigh and his arms grasped her about her shoulders and her waist, and then he had gently bitten her lip and she was sure that she tasted her own blood, but it was not pain she felt; it was an electric sensation that passed through her entire body and it was followed by another of possibly greater intensity as his thumbnail seemed to make a tiny incision in the back of her neck. She had probably gasped, for he withdrew his tongue, leaned back from her and with his other hand gently touched first one breast and then the other. 'Will you come with me?'

'Yes.'

He led her through the door by which he had first entered the room. His bed was the largest, the most opulent she had seen. The sheets were of dark blue silk, the cover was of a lighter blue embroidered with a single Chinese motif. There were candles burning in a candelabrum and it was these which gave off the floral scent, heavier and more erotic here. 'Undress,' he said. 'I will join you in a moment.' He went through another door, presumably into his dressing room.

She took off her frock, her underclothes, her stockings, putting them neatly on a nearby chair. She drew back the sheets and climbed into the softness of the bed; it became the universe. She had never felt more naked. She turned her head at a sound and he was standing beside the bed. The hair on his chest was almost grey, his belly was slightly rounded, seeming to shade his genitals as he moved in the candlelight. After he had got into the bed he did not immediately touch her but lay for a moment looking at her. Then his hand stroked her face. She kissed it. He stroked her neck and her shoulders, her waist, her stomach and he touched her pubic hair only for a moment before he withdrew and stroked her breasts. And then his hand was firm on her waist and he had rolled towards her so that his body touched hers and she thought she could feel his soft penis against her thigh while he kissed her forehead and her ears and her neck and her shoulders, then her breasts and her waist and her thigh, his right hand still firmly holding her waist. She wanted his whole body against hers. She moved towards him but he held her back and with his sharp-nailed thumb stroked her pelvis. She tried to move her vagina towards the thumb, but again he held her, his thumb stroking more gently. He moved his hand quite suddenly so that she rolled hard against him and his nails slid down her back and were like tiny knives moving across the flesh of her bottom, her inner thighs and the backs of her legs, behind her knees so that she forgot her immediate sexual needs, giving herself up to his cruel and gentle fingers, lying now on her stomach as he continued to caress her.

Gradually, perceptibly, the touch of his fingertips, scarcely felt, profoundly sensed, was replaced by the lightest pressure of his fingernails on her shoulders, neck and back so that she anticipated and welcomed the pain when it began to come, when he drew her onto her back, stroking and scratching her waist, breasts, stomach and groin until her sexuality was completely sublimated and she wished only for greater pain, for catharsis by means of his subtle and relentless cruelty, and she moaned very faintly, unable either to speak or to cry out, even as she became aware of another presence in the room, of his parting from her, of a soft body moving into the bed beside her, kissing her delicately upon her cheeks and her lips and her breasts, caressing her waist and her pelvis, touching the lips of her vagina, her clitoris, so that she lay completely still while the Chinese girl murmured to her, pressing her small, rounded breasts to her own, taking her hand and placing it against a vulva that was, to her surprise, completely hairless, like a child's, parting her legs a little, kissing her chin and her stomach and, finally, her vagina, her tongue firm and controlled as it licked her clitoris. Then Catherine's hands found the Chinese girl's head and grasped it as she tried to bring the girl up to her so that she might kiss her in turn, but at first the girl resisted, only gradually acquiescing, kissing her navel and her breasts again until at last her lips were on Catherine's and her tongue was in Catherine's mouth and her hairless pubis was hard against Catherine's vagina, moving with a rhythm that was at once gentle and demanding, and to which Catherine responded, shuddering as she felt the beginnings of orgasm. She felt him move, felt a quick hand on her body, on the girl's, an awkward movement, a break in the rhythm which she could not tolerate, then it was gone and the girl was kissing her again, one leg across Catherine's leg, and Catherine could no longer tell if the moans were her own or the girl's, for she identified the girl almost completely with herself. Without altering her rhythm, the Chinese girl moved her hand and it held something that was cold, smooth and hard. Catherine was afraid. Still on top of her the Chinese girl put the thing to the lips of Catherine's vagina and began slowly to move it inside. Now the cathartic pain and the orgasm were coming simultaneously. Catherine screamed as she was ripped; it was as if her entire body had been torn in two; from feet to head a cold fire ran through her again and again and she was sobbing, sinking, only partly aware that the girl had moved to join the man and, in turn, was crying as he took her.

By the time Mr Koutrouboussis had begun to push his flesh into her dry, painful vagina, she was wholly abstracted, noting the areas of his body where he was hard or where age betrayed itself in softness, listening with a kind of distant affection to his grunts as he rapidly reached orgasm and flung himself away from her. She felt liquid cooling between her legs and took a corner of the sheet to wipe it from her, peering through the candlelit darkness for the Chinese girl. The girl smiled at her from the doorway, blowing her a shy kiss before she vanished. Mr Koutrouboussis seemed already asleep. In a moment, Catherine slept, too. She was awakened by the Chinese girl, wearing a silk robe, bringing her a cup of tea. Mr Koutrouboussis was not in the bedroom. 'Gone out,' said the Chinese girl. 'Business.' She bent and kissed Catherine on the forehead. 'Feel good today?'

Catherine winced as she moved. 'I never felt better.'

The Chinese girl drew back the sheet and stroked Catherine's body. 'Shall I bring more tea? We drink together?'

'Oh, yes.' She began to sit up, arranging the many pillows for herself and the girl. She took the cup from the table and sipped the scented tea. She could not tell what the time was, for the room was still dark. The Chinese girl came back with her own teacup and got into bed with a sigh of pleasure. She had her hairbrush with her and, after a moment, began to brush her long, straight black hair. Wordlessly, Catherine took the brush from her and combed it through her hair, arranging it almost as, yesterday, she had arranged the flowers in the sitting room. 'Thank you,' said the girl. 'You are beautiful.'

'You're beautiful.' Catherine parted the girl's gown and stroked her pubis. This morning it did not seem quite so smooth; it was faintly bristly. 'Do you shave there?'

'He likes it.' The girl giggled. 'I like it, too. But it itch, you know. Have to do every day.'

'Will he want me to do that?'

'Oh, yes. Later I do.'

'Does it hurt?'

'Little bit.' The Chinese girl turned on her side so that she was facing Catherine.

'What's the time?' asked Catherine.

Again the girl giggled. 'No time here.'

'I've got to go to work.'

'Work?'

'To the flower shop.'

'Oh, yes.'

'Does he want me to come back? Tonight?'

'You want to come?'

'To see you.'

'Nice. Yes.'

'Then I'll have to send a postcard to my mum so that she'll get it this evening.' Catherine looked for her clothes. They were no longer on the chair. 'My frock?'

'Look. He said to wear that.' She indicated a silk kimono, similar to her own. Catherine laughed. 'I can't go to work in that.' She got up. Her legs were a little stiff and she had a pain under her ribs on the left, and in her back, like the beginnings of a period. She groaned and straightened. 'Goodness, I do feel well. I shouldn't. Should I?'

'Always feel good next day.' The Chinese girl moved like a cat in the bed. She watched Catherine with affectionate amusement.

'It doesn't seem wrong,' said Catherine. 'I feel guilty about not feeling guilty. Do you know what I mean?' She opened a cabinet and found her clothes neatly folded on one of the shelves. The cabinet was full of women's clothes, including underwear that had not been in vogue for thirty years. She closed the doors. There was a hand-basin in one corner of the room. It was of black marble. The taps were jade-green. She began to wash. 'Are you sure you don't know what the time is?'

'Early. You not stay with me today?'

'I'd love to, but if I don't go into work the lady at the shop will get in touch with my mum.'

The Chinese girl understood. 'You have large family?'

'No. There's just my mum and two brothers. I don't see my brothers much at the moment.'

'No sisters?'

'No.' Catherine got into her underclothes, pulled up her stockings and secured them. 'Can I borrow your brush?'

'Here.' The girl came across and with a few quick movements brushed out Catherine's crop.

'Will he be angry that I've gone?'

'Mr Koutrouboussis probably be out all day. I am sad. You stay.'

Catherine guessed that the girl was capable of better English but knew that her simplified syntax was attractive. She kissed the girl. 'Can you meet me for lunch? I only get half an hour.'

The girl shook her head. 'I must stay.'

'I'll nip round, then, to see you.'

The girl smiled. 'Nice.' She became grave as she took Catherine's face in her hands and kissed her on the lips. 'You promise.'

Catherine laughed. She was full of well-being. Her body felt lighter, more her own. She felt beautiful. 'I promise. If Mr Koutrouboussis comes back before I do, tell him I'm sorry. Tell him why I had to go.' She left the flat. The street was warm and sunny. Her body ached but there was a spring in her step. She had never been more aware of her body, nor more pleased with it. She turned the corner, entering Shepherd's Market. To her surprise it was earlier than she had guessed. Auntie Edna hadn't arrived yet. She would have to get a watch.

'Well,' said Edna Bowman, turning up five minutes later to unlock the shop, 'you're looking lovelier than ever, my girl. What is it? A touch of spring? You in love?'

Catherine grinned at her, wishing she could tell her what had happened. 'Maybe.'

'Nice young feller, is he?'

'Oh, Auntie Edna...' She averted her eyes.

Auntie Edna chuckled. 'Sorry, girl. You keep smiling like that and we'll double our profits. It's amazing how good a smile is for trade.'

At lunchtime Catherine ran round to Hertford Street. The girl answered the door. She was in her uniform again. She took her by the hand. 'He back,' she whispered, 'but not for long.'

'Does he want to see me?' She had hoped not to meet him. She had come to see her new friend.

'He going out.' They entered the sitting room. He was standing with his back to them, looking at her flower arrangement. It was only with an effort that she could believe that she had known the flat for less than twenty-four hours. As the Chinese girl closed the door Catherine immediately relaxed, became euphoric with a sense of safety. He turned, reached out for her and took her by the back of the neck. 'You are happy, I can see. Tell me, have the orchids arrived at the shop?'

'This afternoon.'

'Bring them on your way home – as it were. Tell your aunt I saw you in the street and asked you to come at five. That means you will be able to leave early. I will be back at seven. It will give you some time alone together.' He smiled fondly at both of them. 'My two little girls. I want you to think of us as the father and the sister you do not have.'

He was dressed in black, for business. He took a gold hunter from his waistcoat. 'I waited to see you, but now I must go. You wish to be with me tonight again?'

She lowered her eyes and nodded.

'Good. It is a shame that I must work in the world.' He looked about the room. 'But it makes this private world so much sweeter.'

'Your business is shipping, isn't it?' said Catherine on impulse, thinking she should respond. 'I love ships.' She hated them. She was always seasick.

'Oh, ships are involved.' He laughed as if he guessed that she had lied. 'I am an import–export specialist, you know. Well, that is the conventional term in my trade.' He placed his hat on his head and stroked her hair. 'I am, my dear, an old-fashioned war-profiteer. An exploiter of conflicts.' He ran his thumbnail down her spine.

9. In which Miss Una Persson returns to Europe in her efforts to discover the exact Nature of the Catastrophe and the Rôle of Women in the Revolution

In the Via Veneto the crowds were still marching, having tried to set fire to several buildings, including the American Embassy and Thomas Cook's. The noise was not much louder than that which could normally be heard at this hour, from taxi drivers, drunks and harlots. Una was grateful that the water was still hot as she turned the heavy chrome taps of the great white tub and used the shower attachment to rinse her short chestnut hair. She was alone in a vast bathroom, full of mirrors and Egyptianate metal, in her suite at the Albergo Ambasciatori, still in her opinion the best hotel in Rome and a fitting headquarters for the Provisional Government. When the phone rang from the other room she was already wrapping heavy white towels around her head and body; she walked without haste from the bathroom, sat down on the double bed and picked up the receiver.

'Did I wake you, Una?'

'Who's that?'

'Petroff. I just got in.' He was excited, unashamed. 'They said you might be asleep.'

'But you rang anyway.' It was typical of him.

'The phone never wakes you when you're really asleep, Una. Nothing does. Too much gunfire, eh?' He was in a friendly mood. She had absolutely no desire for a sentimental reunion, particularly after his wretched compromising of the San Francisco situation which lost them their foothold on mainland USA and resulted in a complete if temporary victory for the Philadelphians.

'What are you doing in Rome?' She was cool.

'Aren't you pleased to hear from me? I came in my official capacity – for the discussions. And to join in the celebrations, of course. (Have you a beau, currently?) You have won. Aren't you pleased?'

She rarely relished victory. 'There's a lot of work to do, yet. There have been repercussions, you know, over that Vatican business.'

He was plainly making an effort to sound sober. 'Yes. My people were not happy to hear about it. It was unnecessary brutality. Unfortunate.'

'Well, I might see you later. I'm going to sleep now.'

'You won't be at dinner, tonight?'

'Perhaps.'

'It's your duty to be there, surely?'

'I'm notorious for my moods. But I'll probably see you in the bar, just before dinner.' She immediately regretted relenting, but Petroff's charm had already had its usual effect. She would have to avoid him. She began to dress, furious with him for putting her in this position. She had intended to go out, to visit Lobkowitz who had arrived yesterday. He was too late to be given accommodation in the Ambasciatori and was staying two blocks up, in the St James, a flashy, recently erected place where most of the Balkan delegates had been quartered. Now, unless she wanted to risk bumping into Petroff downstairs, she would have to ring and invite Lobkowitz to her suite when she would have preferred to have met her old friend on neutral ground, in the bar or in a restaurant. She was not sure of his attitude towards her: he might misinterpret her invitation on both political and personal grounds. Already her life was getting far too complicated. One action produced a dozen permutations. The previous day, making her speech in the Coliseum, she was sure that she had seen Jerry Cornelius, Catherine's brother, moving through the audience holding a scrawny stray black-and-white cat, and she knew that he would not be here without a good reason. There were far too many ambiguities in Rome on this particular May Day. In her view they were prematurely celebrating their settlement with the Neapolitans over the Vatican issue.

By the time she had dressed in her Chanel pleated skirt and matching grey pullover she felt much better. Before putting through the call to Lobkowitz she decided to have another look at her notes. She sat down beside her desk, unlocked the drawer and withdrew a fat folder. The notes were even more confused than she remembered; some of them she could not understand at all; some of them referred to events which, she was sure, had not happened anywhere and could not possibly happen in the future. She dismissed, for instance, the whole idea of the Neapolitan royalists taking either Rome or Genoa under their idiot king Alfredo, and it seemed unlikely that they would raise money by selling Capri and Ischia to the Germans and, as a result, receive tacit German military support in their campaign.

The Vatican business was unfortunate, yet she could sympathise with Costagliola's impulse to eradicate the problem at a stroke, even if it had meant an awful lot of Michelangelo and Leonardo going down the drain. It certainly showed that Costagliola meant business and had created a good deal of useful confusion in Naples, as well as Venice, Florence and Turin (whose governments were relatively sympathetic to Rome) and throughout the whole Catholic world. Costagliola had also received a considerable amount of secret support since then; some from quite unlikely sources and, as he had calculated, there were now between ten and fifteen self-elected popes in Italy alone. She had heard there were at least three in France, one in Ireland, two in America and two in Spain. Greece had a couple of contenders in the field, as did Ethiopia. As yet, there was no news either from Constantinople or Avignon. Already fighting had broken out in Brindisi and Cosenza between supporters of rival popes. There was, incidentally, a thriving trade in art fakes which the dealers alleged had been salvaged from the ruins of St Peter's.

Perhaps, after all, the Roman situation was sufficiently stable for her to consider moving on. She certainly wanted to convince herself that it was stable: she had had enough of Italy for the moment, though it remained her favourite European country, and it looked as if something interesting was happening in Dalmatia, which was why she particularly wanted to see Lobkowitz, whose election to the Central Committee as Chairman in a free poll throughout Bohemia in the previous year had been one of the most surprising events in an astonishing (and heartening, she thought) pattern. Lobkowitz was probably the only aristocrat holding any authority in Central Europe and had calmly continued to use his title. At one point there had been a movement to ban him from the conference but Una and many others had been vociferous in demanding that he came. If the main Salzburg–Rome line had not been blown up he would have been here two days earlier.

She decided to phone his hotel.

After picking up the receiver she had to wait for several minutes before someone answered, took the number and told her that there would be a delay for perhaps a quarter of an hour before a line would be free. Patiently, she replaced the phone and returned to her notes. Petroff's arrival had affected her nerves. That and the glimpse of Cornelius had succeeded in confusing her more than it should have done. Both men were unpredictable, both could possibly make claims on her, as ex-lovers. Cornelius might even be trying to alter the balance of power, working some crazy scheme of his own. She wanted to give all her attention to Lobkowitz and then leave Italy as quickly as possible. It was an effort to maintain her resolve. As it was, she had already allowed Petroff to affect her plans.

The phone rang almost immediately. She picked it up quickly and then regretted her action – it could be Petroff or even Cornelius on the line. But they were calling Lobkowitz's hotel. She asked for him, heard a click, thought she had been cut off, and then it was his voice: 'Prinz Lobkowitz.'

'Good evening, your highness,' she said.

'Ah, Una! I called earlier, but you were asleep. Can we meet?' He was eager.

'I wonder if you would mind coming here, to my rooms.

Someone has arrived and I don't want to see them yet. You have a pass?'

'They gave me one a few minutes ago.'

'You'll come?'

'You're alone? Myself, I'm in no mood for general conversation.'

'I'm alone. It's on the second floor. Use the back staircase if you can. The lifts aren't working too well. Number 220.'

'I'll come now, yes?'

'That would be excellent. Again, I'm sorry...'

'Of course.' He rang off.

As she rose to go to her bedroom there was a tap on the door. 'Who is it?'

'Message, madam.'

Reluctantly she opened the door. It was one of the young waiters from the restaurant. He held a large envelope out to her. He had probably been tipped to bring it, so she gave him nothing, particularly since she disapproved of the necessity. She thanked him and closed the door, opening the envelope to find a fresh red rose inside. As she removed it, one of the thorns pricked her finger. How on earth had Petroff found such a thing in Rome at this time? Or had Petroff sent it? There was no message. She sighed and dropped the rose on top of her folder of notes, continuing into the bedroom to tidy her hair and dab a little eau de Cologne on her neck and forehead. She took a deep breath and felt more relaxed. Another knock. She was more cautious as she opened the door.

Lobkowitz looked older. His hair was completely grey. His familiar quiet smile gladdened her. He was tall, stooped, gentle. He had not changed.

'Oh, how lovely to see you.' She admitted him. She kissed him lightly on the cheek. 'You're looking so well. Your journey doesn't seem to have tired you at all.'

'I enjoyed it. I have a superstition about train trips. If the ride is trouble-free then something awful will happen when one arrives. You know the sort of thing. You, too, are looking extraordinarily well, Una. What's your secret of eternal youth?'

'You'd never believe me.'

He removed his soft felt hat and unbuttoned his ulster. 'It's raining. It's hot in Rome now! Have you been downstairs lately? So many people! So many old comrades!' He gave her his hat and coat and she hung it in her wardrobe. 'What a lovely room.'

'I gather yours is not very good.'

'I anticipated worse. And we have no right to demand luxury, have we?'

'I suspect it's the last we'll have in Rome. I'm making the most of it. Would you like some whisky?' She took the bottle from the drawer in her desk.

'A little one. Thank you.'

'How are things in Bohemia?' She poured some whisky into glasses. 'I'm sorry there's no mineral water. You'll have to drink it as it comes.'

'We seem to be coping.' He sipped the drink. 'I don't know what will happen after the honeymoon.' He shrugged. 'I don't expect to last more than one term.'

'You have popular support.' Una was surprised by his pessimism. 'They wouldn't dare get rid of you!'

'I shan't stay if the rest of the Committee is dissatisfied. It would be pointless.'

'Yes. I see what you mean.'

'I suppose you do, Una.' A small smile. 'I was surprised at you, in Albania, refusing the presidency after all your good work.'

She rubbed her forehead, amused. 'I'm an international troublemaker, not a national one. I like to move on.'

'You've accepted no position here in Rome?'

'Nothing permanent. It's one of the reasons I wanted to see you alone. I was wondering what you thought about Dalmatia.'

He wrinkled his nose. 'You're going there next?'

'Probably. If they can use me.'

'There are very few people wouldn't give you a job, Una. Your experience is legendary.' He unbuttoned his military jacket, pulled up his trousers and sat on the edge of the bed. From the street the sound of the crowds had dissipated so that it was possible to hear the noise from the hotel's ground floor: laughter, shouts, sudden bursts of clapping. 'But you won't accept leadership, will you? Is that the feminine part of you?'

She considered this. 'I know many men who feel as I feel. I gave up Albania for the same reasons that I gave up the stage when I became successful. It doesn't suit me to be on the winning side, I suppose. I'm embarrassed by lack of criticism. Could that be it?'

'You haven't thought of it before?'

'I've reached no conclusions. Besides, I felt sorry for Zog.'

'You see!' He was not wholly serious. 'You are a woman! You could argue, couldn't you, that femininity is the essence of radicalism? You must be in opposition or you are not happy. You must feel that the force to which you are opposed is more powerful than you.'

'Are you talking about women in general?'

'Yes.' He frowned, smiling to himself. 'Well, perhaps I'm not talking about Queen Victoria. Unless her petulance was the direct result of her resenting the responsibility she was told she had. Don't all successful revolutionaries similarly resent the power they are given? Is that why they will often invent new enemies, when their original enemy is defeated? Why they never realise that they have ceased to become the least powerful force and have come to be the most powerful one?'

Una lit a cigarette and immediately felt a pain in her chest. She put the cigarette down but did not extinguish it. 'What about Dalmatia?'

'I'm sorry if I seemed condescending, Una.'

'It's not that. Frankly, the discussion bores me. I've had it so often, you see.'

'Yes. Forgive me, anyway.'

'Do you think they have a good chance in Dalmatia?'

'It depends on the Turks. If they give support to the existing régime then any revolution will be difficult. You could help there, of course. You know the Turkish mind.'

'Hardly. I've known a Turk or two, that's all.'

'Well, it would help. Could I have a little more whisky?'

She poured it into the glass he held out. She was glad that his hand was steady. She had seen too many shaking hands in the past few days. 'So you'd think I'd be useful?'

'Of course.'

'And they wouldn't resent me?'

'Certainly not.'

'Then I'll go. Another couple of days. As soon as the conference is over.

'It's a relief to know you'll attend the conference at any rate.'

'Are you laughing at me, Prinz Lobkowitz?' She was not annoyed.

'Oh, I don't think so. If you detect anything hidden then it's my admiration.'

'You'll make me self-conscious.'

'Indeed? You should be beyond such feelings now, surely? Perhaps you identify this shyness with your idealism. You are still afraid, I suppose, of becoming cynical.'

'But I am a cynic. I'm trying to change the world. I'm altering history, or think I am.'

'Is that cynicism? If so, it isn't what I meant.'

'You think it would do me good to accept responsibility?'

'Well...' He gestured.

'I'm too immature.'

'Ah, yes, we are all that.'

'I haven't enough faith in my own convictions. I can't retain a conviction, not in detail. I'm exactly the same as I was as a child. I believe in love and justice. Free will, free speech, enlightenment, kindness. It's as general and as simplistic as that. One act of inhumanity shocks me. It still shocks me, Prinz Lobkowitz. I have killed people myself. I have inadvertently caused the deaths of many innocents. Perhaps I feel too guilty to accept power.'

He scratched his head. 'Perhaps you are too innocent to be offered it.'

'Now you are certainly condescending.'

'I apologise again. I can think of no-one nobler than you, Una. That nobility could destroy you. It has destroyed others like you.'

'Is this flattery?' She rounded on him, smiling, but she felt very awkward. 'I assure you I'm not always in this mood. Seeing you has plunged me into it. It's your own nobility you're discussing, not mine.'

He laughed. 'Oh, yes, perhaps. I'm a very noble person. I am aware of it sometimes. And it disgusts me. I am not flattering you, Una.'

'That's something.' She finished her drink. The smell of the whisky was offensive to her. 'I'm very bewildered today. The man I wanted to avoid is Petroff. You remember him? From the Spanish Main? The Barbary Coast? I wasn't expecting him.'

'I thought he was completely *persona non grata* here.'

'Apparently not. And I think I saw Cornelius yesterday.'

'Frank?'

'No, the other one.'

'Is that surprising?'

'He's my personal omen of disaster. I think he was nicknamed the Raven once. Like Sam Houston. Well, he's my raven.'

'And what disaster do you fear?'

'I don't know. Do you want another drink?'

'Thank you.'

Again she poured the whisky into his offered glass. 'I said personal, and it is personal. Perhaps I feel my identity threatened.'

'And that's why you're so nervous tonight?'

She had not known that he had been aware of it. 'Yes.'

He got up and walked across the room. 'Is this the bathroom?'

She nodded. He went inside and locked the door. She heard him pissing, then listened as he pulled the chain and washed his hands. 'At least you have a toilet which works,' he said as he came out. 'Perhaps the news about Mr "Brown" has disturbed you?'

'What's "Brown" doing?'

'Oh.' Lobkowitz looked at his hands. He said softly: 'He died.'

'Was he killed?' She had expected it.

'Suicide.'

'The fool.' She sat down heavily in her chair by the desk. 'The bloody fool. He was married, wasn't he?'

'With a couple of children. But they were living apart, I gather. It was in New York. He left a note – a very confused note. The authorities had limited his movements a great deal, you know, in the past year. He had nothing to do. He was writing rubbish. He had no close friends left. So he killed himself.'

Her sense of guilt was suddenly so intense she had to force herself to be rational: the effort produced in her a coldness, something very close to a clinical state of shock. 'What a waste,' she said.

Seating himself on the arm of the chair Lobkowitz gripped her shoulder. 'It happened over a month ago,' he said. 'Were you still fond of him?'

She nodded, wishing that she would cry, wondering at her own callousness when she found that she could not. 'Of course. I haven't seen any newspapers – only the one we produced towards the end of the fighting. He was my first lover, you know.'

'Oh, Una, how thoughtless of me. I am sorry.' The words were so conventional that they succeeded in comforting her. She began, at last, to cry, conscious of the hand which still held her shoulder. And as she cried it seemed that all the tension of the past two days washed out of her so that she wondered if Lobkowitz had deliberately given her the news of 'Brown's' suicide at that moment, knowing that this was how she would respond. She tried to apologise. He murmured to her. He helped her from the chair and made her lie down on the couch. She kissed the hand that stroked her face.

'Poor "Brown",' she said, 'poor bloody "Brown".' She sniffed. He gave her his large white handkerchief. She blew her nose. 'I'm sorry.'

He sighed. 'Don't try to pull yourself together yet, Una. Not yet.'

'I hate losing my self-control. You must be tired. It's a burden…'

'On the contrary, I find your response very satisfying.'

'What?'

'I feel much better when I see you reacting naturally. You were very tense when I came in. I have never seen you so bad. Perhaps you should go back to England for a while? It is very orderly over there. Or Sweden? Even better. You need to rest, to be away from violence and politics.'

'I can't rest very often. It's not in my nature. I feel so guilty, even about going to sleep, unless I am completely exhausted. What did the papers say about him?'

'Most of them were kind. I saw the obituary in the London *Times*. They said he was a brilliant political theorist but a confused practical politician.'

'Yes. He killed all the wrong people!' She tried to laugh but began to sob again and now the sobs seemed to come from the deepest parts of her body. She could scarcely breathe. 'Why couldn't they leave him alone? He was doing no harm!'

'Words seem to mean more to an American than to most Europeans, Una. It is the large peasant population. They have a greater faith in the magic of language. Perhaps they had more reason, therefore, to be afraid of him.'

'Oh, what bastards they are!'

'He chose to live there.'

'He always picked the wrong countries. Germany. England. America. Those horrible Teutons.'

Lobkowitz chuckled. 'Like you and me, Una?'

'Exactly,' she said. Her throat and chest were very painful now and her nose felt sore. 'I think I've got a cold. Oh, shit!' She blew her nose on his handkerchief. 'Why must it always happen when I've got a speech to make? My Italian's bad enough as it is.' She began to cough.

'I think you'd better go to bed,' he said. 'Can you get food served in your room?'

'Usually, though it takes them ages to bring it.'

'Shall we dine here, together?'

'That would be lovely. I won't bother to go down tonight. But haven't you any appointments?'

'Nothing important.'

'There's a menu on that little table,' she said. 'They don't give you a very wide choice and the chances are that there's only one main course available. I'll have the soup to start. This is very good of you.'

He reached for the menu. 'I am acting entirely from self-interest,

I assure you.' He looked at the card. 'What do you want? Minestrone or stracciatella?'

'Stracciatella, please. It won't be very hot.'

'Do you care what you have?'

'Something light. Veal, if possible. Or chicken.'

He picked up the telephone, waited, then spoke softly, in English. 'We should like to order a meal in our room. Madame is sick. Just a cold. Thank you. Yes, we will have stracciatella for two. Veal cutlets... Roast chicken? Fine. Oh, yes, cheese and so on. And coffee. Of course. Thank you.' He replaced the receiver and turned back to her. 'There! They were very concerned. You are as popular here as you are everywhere.'

'Not quite everywhere.' She began to weep again. 'This is stupid. It's self-pity. Nothing to do with "Brown".'

The phone rang. She tried to answer it, but he blocked her, answering it himself. 'Prinz Lobkowitz. I am afraid that Miss Persson is indisposed at present.'

Una giggled through her tears.

'She has a touch of influenza, that is all. Yes. I don't know.' He put his hand over the mouthpiece. 'Did you receive a gift, Una, just recently?'

'No.' She glanced at the desk. 'He means the rose.' She hesitated. 'Say, no.'

'I am sorry,' he said, 'she says...'

Una thought of the bribed waiter. Petroff could be vengeful in small matters. 'Say I received a flower.'

'She received a flower. Yes. I will tell her. Goodbye.'

'What a splendid protector you are, Prinz Lobkowitz.' She blew her nose again. 'You are corrupting me, you know, with your terrible avuncularity. Is it what you want to do?'

'Oh, secretly, I suppose.'

'What did he say?'

'On the phone? Just that he was passing through and might see you in Madrid.'

'Madrid?'

'He's going there tonight, he says, if he can make a connection in Milan.'

'Why is he going to Milan?'

'He didn't say.'

'He only arrived an hour or two ago.'

'It wasn't Petroff,' said Prinz Lobkowitz as he removed his jacket, 'it was Cornelius.'

She looked across at the rose and began to laugh, careless of her own hysteria. 'That gives an entirely different complexion to the message. Put the rose in some water, would you, my dear?' She stretched her arms wide on her cushions. 'Good old Cornelius. Gone. On the way to Madrid. Splendid! I feel a new woman already.' She got up and began to march round the room, singing in Spanish, '*Comrades, to the barricades, for honour and justice are ours!*'

Prinz Lobkowitz watched her expressionlessly for a few minutes, then he stepped quickly towards her and seized her by her arm.

Una screamed. His mouth was hot on her streaming eyes.

10. In which Catherine Cornelius continues to explore the promises of Eastern wisdom

'Lovely here, isn't it?' Ahmed leaned on the pole and the punt surged forward on the current. Catherine's heart sank.

'Mm,' she said. She was dressed all in white. Her frock was an original Hartnell, very simple, with the natural waistline. She wore two strings of pearls. Her strap-over shoes were white. Her Gainsborough hat was white, with a white ribbon; even her little bag was white. Her gloves and her stockings were white. As Ahmed had helped her into the punt he had said how virginal she looked. He had, as she had hoped, been much impressed. He had met her from the station in the taxi which took them directly to the river where his punt was waiting. When he had invited her to Oxford she told him that she had always wanted to go in a punt on the Isis. And here she was. Unless, she thought, it was the Cherwell.

'Is it as nice as you expected?' He smiled down at her. He was looking very nifty himself in his striped blazer, straw hat, creamy Oxford bags and soft off-white shoes. He had eager, handsome features.

'Oh, yes, it's lovely.'

He gave the pole a further shove. 'You're not disappointed?'

'Not at all.' She looked dutifully at the willows, the shrubs and the lawns. Sunlight rippled on the water. Another punt went by, filled with cackling youths; they were sweating.

'This is my favourite stretch,' said Ahmed. 'For punting, at least.'

'Mm.'

'You look so perfect.' His dark eyes were fond. 'Like an old-fashioned picture. You're beautiful, Catherine.'

She smiled.

'Is anything wrong?' he said.

'Oh, no.' She had known her period had started when she got into the taxi, but she had not had the presence of mind to ask him to stop before they reached the river.

'You're tired,' he was saying. 'Perhaps we should have had a cup of tea first. Never mind. You relax there. I'll do all the work.'

'You look very handsome,' she said. She had been looking forward to this for three weeks, ever since she had met him at the party in London. She was a sucker for dark foreigners, particularly Greeks or Indians. It had seemed such a stroke of good luck, meeting him two days after Mrs Goldmann had caught her and Mr Goldmann in his private office out at the studios (he had got her a job as a trainee script-girl) and had made Mr Goldmann fire her on the spot. She had enough money saved for at least six months if she lived at home, and could think of no nicer way of spending her holiday than with Ahmed, who had a rented house in North Oxford where, he had said, she could stay whenever she liked. She had promised him that she would come down for today, to go on the river and look round his college (the vacation had begun so there was little danger in bumping into the two old boyfriends who were also at his college).

'You're flattering me.' It was evident, though, that he agreed with her.

She tried to be amused by her situation, knowing that her nervousness was exaggerating the sensation of seepage. She had tried to spread her dress so that she would not be sitting on it. She could not help glancing down, expecting to feel the dampness at any moment. She stretched the material of the dress away from her as best she could. There was so much of it.

'How is London?' He guided the punt away from the bank. 'You've given up working for that film producer? You told me.'

'Yes.'

'My father was thinking of investing some money in talkies. Not here, though. In America. Someone's starting a new company in Hollywood. Maybe I could use my influence to get you a job?'

'That would be nice.' Carefully, she shifted her position on the padded seat. Her sanitary gear was in her bag. She wondered how she could get him to stop the punt.

'I *am* thirsty,' she said. 'It would be nice to have a cup of tea. Is there somewhere you know, by the river?'

'Oh, yes. But let's go a bit further first.'

'All right.'

She leaned back, closing her eyes, pretending to doze.

'Look,' he said, 'you can see my college from here.'

She opened her eyes. Beyond the trees were some Gothic buildings.

'The dreaming spires.' She became inane.

'Yes.'

They went under a bridge.

As they passed back into sunlight he withdrew the pole letting the punt drift, and climbed over the central seats to reach her. 'I have to kiss you now,' he said romantically. He pushed his face forward and the punt rocked. He kissed her cheeks. She did her best to smile at him. 'I've embarrassed you,' he said.

'Oh, no. I'm sorry.'

He stroked a lock of her hair. 'Why "sorry"? You think I'm forward, don't you?'

'It's not that,' she said. She couldn't tell him the truth. 'I'm just a bit self-conscious. There are so many people about.'

'Of course.' He returned to his end of the punt and retrieved the pole. He seemed angry.

'Don't be cross,' she said.

'No, no.' He plunged the pole into the water and almost overbalanced. It seemed that he swore in his own language. The punt jerked and she had to grip the sides to keep her position. Desperation dominated all other considerations. 'I really would like to stop soon.'

'You're not well?' He was brusque.

'Um...'

'Another ten minutes or so and there's a marvellous little place where we can have some tea.' He looked at his watch. 'And there's somewhere I'd like to take you for lunch. It *is* almost lunchtime. If you could wait...'

'No, just a cup of tea. I...'

'Very well.'

She was fed up. She had anticipated an idyllic day and now she was spoiling it. She tried to explain. 'I'm feeling a bit faint, you see.'

'Quite.' He poled in silence. He scowled. She realised that he thought he had made a fool of himself.

She tried to laugh. 'I'm really not playing hard to get, Ahmed.'

'No, no. It was my fault. Bad manners.'

'Your manners are perfect!' To herself it sounded as if she protested too much. 'Perfect.'

'You're very kind.'

Her tension increased. Harry Goldmann had at least been easy-going. She had forgotten how touchy young men could be. An older man might have guessed what the matter was.

'I've been so looking forward to seeing you.' She tried to start afresh.

'Yes.' He, too, made an effort. 'It seems such a long time ago, doesn't it? Only nineteen days since that awful party. You know Jamie well, don't you?'

'I know Yvette. She's an old friend. You weren't at the wedding.'

'No. I had to go home for a couple of months. My mother was ill.'

'I'm sorry.'

'She's better now. Incidentally, I told my father that we would meet him. He rang this morning to say that he was coming down. He's in London at the moment. Some business. I couldn't make it another day and it was too late to get in touch with you.'

'I'd like to meet him,' she said courageously. She was actually curious about Ahmed's father. Yvette had told her that he was one of the richest men in the Near East. Apparently he also held some sort of religious title.

'I wanted to make this our day.' He was almost accusatory.

Absently, she said: 'I'm sure I'll feel better later.'

'Oh, I didn't mean that.' It seemed that he had.

She became depressed and began to look forward to getting the train home. She had been vague about the train she planned to take back to London, preferring to leave her options open, but now it was obvious that there was no point in her staying. All she could hope to do was keep him interested until she could see him again.

'Here,' he said. She turned. There was a small building ahead. A few tables were scattered on the lawn beside the river. She tried to see if there was a lavatory. All the tables were unoccupied. Ahmed pushed the punt towards the little wooden jetty, jumped out with the line and tied up. Carefully she rose, swaying. She could feel no dampness against her legs. He helped her disembark. They walked along the gravel path to the tea shop. A man in shirtsleeves was sitting outside; he was adding figures in a small black notebook. He glanced at them as they approached, then pointedly looked down at his book.

'Good morning.' Ahmed was polite. 'Are you open?'

'Open again at three.' The man wrote something in the notebook. 'Sorry.'

Ahmed became ingratiating. 'You couldn't get this lady a cup of tea, I suppose? She's not feeling very well.'

'Sorry. The wife's off.' He continued to write. He seemed deliberately rude.

Ahmed controlled his temper. 'It wouldn't take a moment, surely, to make a cup of tea? That's what you sell, don't you?'

'The wife's off.'

Ahmed's voice became a falsetto. 'If you were a gentleman, sir, you would...'

'Well, I ain't.' The man sounded as if he was glad of it.

'Oh, come on,' whispered Catherine. This was unbearable. 'Let's try somewhere else.' She couldn't see a lavatory and could not, now, ask.

'So you won't serve us,' said Ahmed grimly.

'Nothing to serve you *with*,' the man told him. He indicated the 'Closed' notice on the door. 'The wife's got the key. I couldn't get in if I wanted to.'

'You're not a very good representative of your country,' said Ahmed contentiously.

'Never said I was.' The man yawned, frowning at Catherine as if to ask her what she was doing with this black man, anyway. He got up from the bench and put his notebook in his back pocket. He began to walk around the building.

'I should punch his nose for him,' said Ahmed. She was tugging at his arm.

'Let's go, Ahmed.'

'And you know what you'd get if you tried.' The man calmly watched them return to the punt. 'Don't you?'

'I'll never come here again!' Ahmed helped Catherine embark and untied the line.

'Just as well,' the man called happily. 'Good riddance.'

'You know why he was so rude, don't you?' Ahmed's voice was still shrill a few minutes later as they continued downriver. 'He didn't like a white girl and an Asian together. You know that?'

'Oh, he's probably rude to everybody.'

'No. You learn to recognise it.' He scowled again.

At least, thought Catherine with relief, he was no longer furious with her, or, if he was, he was turning all his anger against the man at the tea shop. 'My father could buy and sell the whole of Oxford.' Ahmed glared at the trees and the fields. 'If he knew who I was, he wouldn't have dared to be so insolent.'

'There's lots of people in England just like that,' she said. 'And they're all running tea shops. They want your money but they hate serving you. They resent you.'

'How I loathe this country sometimes.'

'I know what you mean.' She was glad that she was able to support him. 'English people can be so bloody bogus.'

'A nation of damned hypocrites.' He echoed her swearing.

'Absolutely.'

'What a rotten thing to happen, though. I wanted to give you the loveliest day you've ever had.' He sighed.

'Don't think about it. The river's wonderful. I'm enjoying myself.'

'You don't feel ill any more?' Concern.

She was desperate enough, at this point, to hurl herself willy-nilly into the water. 'Well, I would like to stop, actually. When we get the chance.' She was sure she heard him groan. She looked about her. On the other side of the river was a spinney. If she could somehow get a moment to herself, she might be able to fix it. 'What a pretty wood. Perhaps we could lie in the shade for a while. Would you mind?'

He seemed pleased. 'Not at all.' With a couple of brisk shoves he got the punt across, took hold of an overhanging branch and drew them in to the bank. 'Can you get out by yourself?'

'Oh, easily.' She clambered ashore. The smell of the leaves and the earth was delicious. The wood was dark and thick. She had her opportunity. 'This is lovely.' Pretending to be entranced, she ran into the trees. 'Wait there for me, Ahmed. Wait on the bank. I shan't be long.'

He was laughing. 'Can't I come?'

'No.'

Carefully, lifting her dress, she stepped over the roots and fallen branches until she reached a large oak whose trunk was big enough to hide her. As quickly as she could she took the apparatus from her bag, unwrapped it, pulled up her skirt, pulled her pants to her knees and began adjusting the napkin, fumbling with and almost dropping the pins.

'Catherine!' He was coming through the wood.

'Just a minute!'

He laughed. 'What a mysterious young dryad you are!'

Her pants snagged and in her haste to get them up she almost broke the elastic, but at last it was done and she was able to smooth her dress down, snap her handbag shut with an enormous sigh of relief, and cry: 'Come and find me, Ahmed!'

He must have been close; he reached her almost at once. 'You look radiant,' he said. He was puzzled. 'A moment ago you were so pale. Perhaps the motion of the water doesn't agree with you.'

'Maybe. I've always been a bit prone to seasickness. That's why I can't bear the idea of going abroad.' She smiled and held out her arms. 'Hello, Ahmed.'

Bewildered, he approached. 'You are as whimsical as the English climate.' He embraced her, kissing her gently on the lips. 'You're so beautiful. I think I love you, Catherine.'

Her laughter was forced. 'This is a bit sudden!'

'No more sudden than your change of mood.' He released her. He was almost wistful.

She kissed him back. 'Ahmed, I promise I won't be difficult from now on.'

He nodded slowly. 'You must have heard many people proclaim their love for you.'

'Not very many.' She stroked his dark head. 'Let's sit down for a minute. Have you got a gasper?'

From the inside pocket of his blazer he took a gold case, from his trousers he took an automatic lighter, displaying them. 'You'll get your dress dirty,' he said. 'Wait. I'll fetch the cushion things from the boat.' He had become cheerful and eager again. She was glad her risk had been worthwhile.

He came running back from the punt with the corduroy cushions in his arms. He spread them under the tree. 'That's thoughtful of you, Ahmed.' She seated herself demurely. He sat down beside her, leaning on his elbow, one leg crooked, offering her the open case. She selected a Turkish cigarette, thought better of it, but it was too late: he had snapped the case shut, replacing it in his pocket. He clicked the lighter and she accepted the flame. Immediately she inhaled she felt sick. She coughed. 'Oh, it's a bit strong.'

'You'd rather have a Virginia?'

'I think so. It's silly of me.'

'Not at all. I prefer Virginia myself.' Again he proffered the open case.

She let him light the next one as he had lit the first but the smell of the Turkish tobacco was still in her throat. She held the cigarette in the fingers of her left hand, unsmoked, taking a deep breath of the sweet air. 'Ah, alone at last!'

'Yes.' He picked a twig from her hair. 'I've been rushing you about rather, haven't I? You must think me an awful boor.'

'Don't be silly. I'm sorry that I spoiled it all. I really feel a hundred times better now.'

'It wasn't anything to do with me?'

'Of course not! I've been looking forward to coming ever since you asked.'

'You are a most beautiful girl!'

She was cheerful. 'And you're a most handsome man.'

'I'm serious, Catherine.' His voice was low. His black eyes studied her face. He stroked her arm. 'I love you.'

'You don't know me. I'm a terrible person.'

'I don't care if you have other boyfriends.'

'That's not actually what I meant.' She was tender. 'As it happens, there isn't anyone else.'

'Would you be mine? I mean, just mine?'

'I'm not really a flirt, Ahmed. If it works out, there won't be anyone else, honestly.' She wondered why she was giving him such assurances. It was not like her. 'But we don't know one another very well, do we? Look at the trouble I've caused you so far.'

'That wasn't your fault.'

'It might have been.'

'No!' He was emphatic.

'Well, it might have been…'

Again, without even attempting to draw her to him, he lunged awkwardly, clumsily kissing her on the cheek. It had not occurred to her before that he might not be very experienced. Now she put her arms round him and kissed him firmly on the lips. He moaned. She released him, conscious of the cigarette in her left hand. She took a puff.

His eyes were anxious. 'I'm going too fast for you…'

'Why don't we just lie here and relax for a moment?'

He was upset again. 'All right.' Resting his back against the tree he lit a cigarette for himself. There were always more cigarettes than embraces in these situations, Catherine thought with some amusement. She was beginning to feel hungry.

'I fell in love with you the moment I saw you come into that awful room,' he was saying. 'I wrote some poetry.'

'Have you got it with you?'

'No. It's at the house. I was afraid of losing it.'

'Will you let me read it later?'

'Oh, I want you to.' He turned towards her.

'I'm looking forward to it.' She did her best to put as much warmth as possible into her voice. Actually, the reaction had just come and she would have been glad now to be lying in the relative comfort of the punt, able to enjoy the day. 'What year are you in, then, at your college?'

'Third starts after the vac.'

'And what do you want to be, when you've finished?'

'Well, I'm reading English, you know. I had some thought of becoming a writer, but I'm not sure. My father is keen to take me into the business.'

'But you'd rather write?'

'Oh, I could probably do both. There are public responsibilities, you see, being my father's eldest son, as well as private ones. A man is expected to live and behave in a certain way, in my own country.'

'Quite.' She had only a vague idea of his meaning but, as usual, she found herself attracted to the idea of a man with slightly mysterious responsibilities. They were probably religious duties, she thought romantically. She extinguished her cigarette in the moss. 'Well, perhaps we'd better be moving along, eh?'

'Oh, no. It's lovely here.' He also put out his cigarette, stroking her hair again. She decided to make the best of it and reached to take him by the back of the neck, gathering him in. His body was firm against hers. She could feel his stiffening penis on her thigh. He was half on top of her.

'Oh, Catherine!' One of his hands was trapped behind her. The other began to squeeze her left breast which, as usual, had become sore with the advent of her period. She ignored the pain, tried to get some pleasure from the sensation, kissed him as passionately as she could. His hand stopped squeezing her breast and moved inexpertly down to her groin. Careful not to startle him, she moved the hand back to her breast.

'Catherine, please...'

'Not here, Ahmed.'

'At my house? We could go there now.' His voice was muffled.

'Later. Honestly. I'll explain.'

He continued to slide his penis against her thigh. She moved her own body, hoping to make him come, hoping that that, at least, would satisfy him for the time being. His grip was painful on her swollen nipple. She tried to goad him to a faster rhythm. 'Oh, darling,' she murmured. 'Oh, Ahmed.'

'C-c...'

His grip tightened. He jerked. She could hear his teeth scraping. He hissed. She kissed him.

His eyes were glazed as he looked down at her. He seemed about to ask a question. She hoped that she seemed receptive. 'Would you like another cigarette?' he asked.

'Yes please.'

He fumbled his case and lighter from his pockets, put two Virginia cigarettes between his lips and lit them, handing her one.

'Thanks.'

He was staring through the trees at the river. Suddenly he got to his feet. 'Oh, good God, I'm sorry.'

She was surprised. 'Sorry?'

'You must be disgusted with me.'

'Don't be silly. I'm only sorry I couldn't...'

'Please! It's me! It's me!'

'Ahmed...'

'I love you, Catherine. Really.'

She struggled up, brushing leaves and bracken from her frock. 'Look, this is stupid. I wanted you to – well, you know...'

With an expression of agony he began to pick up the cushions. He seemed about to cry.

'Ahmed, dear.' She approached him. He avoided her, stumbling towards the river. He dropped a cushion. He swore and picked it up again. 'I've made a fool of myself. You can't have any respect for me, Catherine. I behaved like a complete outsider.'

She began to run after him. He reached the punt and flung the cushions into it. He would not look at her. 'Ahmed. It's all right. I'm trying to explain!'

'Why should you have to? I thought you wanted… I couldn't…'

'Ahmed. Let's forget about it.' She sat down heavily. The punt rocked and he almost overbalanced into the water. 'We'll have some lunch. You'll feel better, then.'

'If you still want to spend the day with me…'

'Of course I do.'

He seemed more at ease, but he handled the pole with far less assurance than previously, turning the boat against the current.

'We'll lunch at The Mitre,' he said.

By the time they were eating she had lost her appetite and was regretting that she had ordered such heavy food. She left most of her whitebait and spent the main course trying to make her game pie as small as possible. She drank nearly a bottle of wine and it improved her spirits, though she began to feel sick. When he asked her whether she had to go home that day she said that she had to be home fairly early because her mother was alone and unwell. He received the news with a kind of sinister resignation which made her feel that she should have remained and let him find out about her period for himself. There was every chance, of course, that he wouldn't know, even when confronted with the bulky evidence. He was making her feel inexplicably guilty and at the same time kept behaving as if his few spasms in the wood had filled him with an ineradicable sense of shame. She was reconciled. It was not the first time she had expected to be swept off her feet by a remorseless despot only to find herself saddled with a confused, miserable and self-punishing tyro. Petulantly, she recognised the re-emergence of her maternal instincts as she did her best to cheer him up with promises of pleasure to come.

There was a tense and depressing walk through the almost deserted streets of Oxford until they passed through an enormous, ancient arch and entered the quadrangle of his college. He had his hands in his pockets and was taking an interest in the gravel. 'You can be very cruel,' he was saying. He had said similar familiar things during lunch. 'Don't you realise what you're doing to me? I'm only human. I hate ambiguity, you know. Why can't women be more direct?'

'I am being direct,' she said, but she had no taste for the ritual. 'If I was more direct, Ahmed, I'd shock you.'

'Is it because of my race, the fact that I'm an Asian? Is it because I'm different?'

She laughed. 'Different?'

'You ought to admit it, you know. To yourself, if not to me.' They were climbing some steps. 'This is the oldest part of the building.'

She pushed her lower lip out, to show interest. She found one old stone building much like another and she had made the college trek before, in Cambridge. There didn't seem a lot to choose between the two establishments. 'I'd rather go out with an Asian boy any day,' she said. She felt ridiculous. His accusations were making her say silly defensive things.

'Oh, you're too kind!'

She had anticipated that response. 'I find you sexually attractive, Ahmed.'

He looked nervously up and down the passage. They walked on.

'You see,' she said as they struck some cloisters, 'I've shocked you. You'll think me forward now.'

'No. I think girls should speak their minds. It makes things easier for everyone. But there's such a thing as a time and place, isn't there?'

'I see.' She controlled her impulse to tickle him or to kick his shins or to grab his balls from behind. 'I'm having a period. That's why I've been a bit strange.'

'I've heard that one before,' he said bitterly.

'It has been a bit abused,' she admitted, 'as a face-saver. Well,

I've said it. You'll have to take it for what it's worth.' She knew that she must still be drunk. Ahmed certainly was.

He stopped and inspected his watch. 'Try and pull yourself together before my father gets here. He's rather old-fashioned, you know.'

She tugged at his arm. 'Ahmed. Don't be boorish.'

'I am what I am.'

Her laughter was unforced. 'Ahmed! Let's calm down.'

'I am perfectly calm.'

She was sure that her hair and her dress needed attention and thought of asking him where she could go to prepare herself for meeting his father, but then she decided that she did not care.

'We'd better go this way,' said Ahmed. He guided her through another portico. 'This part was constructed in Henry the Eighth's reign, I believe.'

'Ho, ho,' she said. 'What for?' She winked at him. In this sort of situation she found that she could easily fall back into an imitation of her mother. She felt comfortable in the rôle. 'Did he keep all eight of 'em here?'

'He had six wives,' said Ahmed, 'at different times in his life.'

'Yes,' said Catherine. 'I forgot.'

They walked back through the quadrangle. As they reached the pavement of the street a red-and-yellow Rolls-Royce pulled up at the kerb. Ahmed smiled, forgetting all conflicts. 'It's the dad!' He became excited. 'He's a bit early. Oh, that's terrific!' He waved at the car. A shadow waved back. With his hand on her elbow, Ahmed drew her towards the limousine, opening the door. 'Hello, Father! This is Catherine Cornelius, the girl I mentioned.'

His father was heavier than Ahmed. He had jowls, a thick-lipped, self-indulgent mouth, a prominent nose, an intelligent eye. He was wearing a white European suit and a panama hat. There were a great many rings on his chubby fingers. Catherine fell for him immediately.

'I'm very pleased to meet you,' she said.

'How do you do, my dear.' He addressed his son. 'Shall we use the car to go somewhere?'

'Good idea,' said Ahmed. 'Hop in, Catherine.' She hopped, sitting beside the older man while Ahmed used one of the collapsible seats opposite.

'What a beautiful young woman you are,' said Ahmed's father. 'Ahmed is very lucky.'

'Thank you,' said Catherine.

Ahmed suggested that the car drive out of Oxford so that they could have tea beside the river. He winked at Catherine, but she did not catch the significance. Winding down the glass panel, he instructed the chauffeur where to go.

Ahmed's father, Catherine began to realise, was embarrassed by her presence. She had the impression that he had come to Oxford for a specific reason and wished to be away as soon as possible. The car drew up outside a fenced area. A number of people were seated in the open, enjoying their tea at tables set on a lawn which ran down to the river. Catherine didn't recognise the place at first. It was only when she saw a man, now in a white coat, serving a family near the river that she understood Ahmed's wink. He had deliberately returned to the scene of their morning encounter. Ahmed instructed the driver to take the car right up to the gate, then he wound down the side window and called to the white-coated man as he walked towards the building. 'Hi! I say, have you a table free?'

The man turned, inspected his territory, pointed to a table that was evidently vacant, and continued to set out places for the customers he was serving. He had not recognised Ahmed, neither had he been impressed by the large motor car, but Ahmed was undismayed. He stepped from the Rolls-Royce, helping first Catherine and then his father to the ground. He led them through the gate to the table. They all sat awkwardly on the benches. Ahmed's father had the amused expression of one who was joining in a children's party. He beamed at everyone. 'This *is* jolly,' he said.

The man arrived to take their order and it was then that he remembered Ahmed. He stared Ahmed directly in the eye. 'And what can I do for you?' he asked blandly. 'Set tea for three suit you?'

'Have you strawberries and cream?' said Ahmed staring back.

'Strawberries and cream for three?' The man made a note on his pad. 'And the set tea?'

'That would be lovely,' Catherine said anxiously.

'Cornelius.' Ahmed's father spoke suddenly. 'Any relation to the *Barber of Baghdad* Cornelius?'

'Barber?'

'The comic opera, you know. German. Last century. A great favourite of mine when I was a student.'

'I'm afraid my family's very ordinary,' she said.

He patted her hand. 'People always say that about their families. They always think it's true, I suppose. Are you of Dutch or of German origin?'

'English,' Catherine told him apologetically. She had the feeling she was being pumped. Perhaps Ahmed's father wondered if her intentions towards his son were honourable.

'I didn't know Cornelius was also an English name.' He seemed disappointed, perhaps with himself, for displaying ignorance.

Ahmed was still glaring after the man who had taken their order. 'He is being deliberately rude,' he muttered.

'I think it's natural to him.' She tried to lighten the atmosphere. 'Ahmed says you're thinking of investing some money in a talkie company.'

'Oh, I'd thought of it. My advisors keep telling me that one should invest in restaurants, couturiers and mass entertainment during times of economic decline. Bread *and* circuses, in fact. Possibly they are right.'

'Oh, I think so. I was working for a film company until recently…'

'Aha! You are an actress!' This seemed to relieve and enlighten him.

'No,' she said, 'just a lowly script-girl, I'm afraid. I worked behind the scenes.'

'Forgive me.' He spoke as if he had insulted her. She seemed to be able to make both father and son feel guilty at the drop of a hat. However, she was getting the picture. Ahmed's father was probably already working out how much she was to cost him when it came to a pay-off.

'That's all right,' she said. 'I'm not a gold-digger from Broadway – or Shepherd's Bush.' She spoke casually, as if she had not interpreted the implications of his questions. 'Anyway, as I was saying, the film company couldn't *help* making money, no matter how bad the films were, as long as they were talkies, of course.'

Evidently he had not seriously considered investing in films. She had not held his attention, although he pretended to be listening. She began to feel self-conscious, wondering if she were still drunk. He took a watch from his fob pocket. 'I hope they will bring the tea soon,' he said. 'I don't want to use any more of your time than necessary.' He stared hard at Ahmed and then seemed to reach a decision, taking an envelope from his jacket. 'This is what I told you about, my boy. I have spoken to Samiyah's father. It is all arranged for next year, when you return.'

Catherine pretended to be interested in the river.

'Oh, thanks,' murmured Ahmed. He put the envelope in his own pocket.

They ate their tea and chatted about how green the English countryside was. When they departed Ahmed left an enormous tip on the table and waved, in a lordly way, to the waiter who watched them go, pocketing the money casually as if it was no more than his due. They all got back into the car.

'Well, I must be returning to London,' said Ahmed's father. 'Where can I drop you?'

'What's the time?' asked Catherine.

'Catherine's going back to London, too,' Ahmed told him.

'Oh, perhaps…' He made the offer reluctantly.

'I'm going on the train,' she said. 'I've a return ticket. I think there's a fast train at five past five.'

Again he withdrew his watch. 'It's almost that now. Are you sure I can't –?'

'Yes thanks.' She would have liked nothing better than to be driven back to London in a comfortable Rolls, but she wanted at least a few moments alone with Ahmed, to try to save something from the situation. Moreover she was conscious of having come between them and she felt sorry for the older man. Doubtless he had wished to see his son alone. On the other hand she had the impression that Ahmed himself was glad of her presence, that he had wished to avoid a heart-to-heart with his father.

'You'd better drop us at the station.' Ahmed sounded miserable. He said something to his father in his native language. His father replied. The name Samiyah was used several times. Ahmed scowled and his father laughed and patted his knee. The car entered the station forecourt.

'Forgive me,' said Ahmed's father. 'It is the worst possible bad manners, to babble away in one's own language like that.'

'Not at all,' said Catherine. She wanted very much to make a good impression on him, though she did not know why. 'It is a beautiful language. It was like listening to music.'

'Oh! Ha, ha!' He clapped his hands together. 'Very fine. Ahmed is extremely lucky! Well, goodbye, Miss Cornelius. I hope we shall meet again.'

'I hope so, too.'

As the Rolls drove away from the station Catherine waved. Ahmed saluted. 'I'm dreadfully sorry about that. It really put the finish on a perfect bloody day, eh?'

She shrugged. 'Not to worry. I expect there'll be other days.'

'I can phone you?'

'We're not on the phone at home. But write. Drop me a postcard.'

'Yes. I'll copy out those poems.'

They walked into the station and looked at the timetable. There was a train to Paddington in three minutes' time. 'That's lucky,' she said.

They found the platform and sat down together on a bench.

'I'm afraid I made the most awful ass of myself,' he said.

'Don't be silly.'

'You're probably used to more sophisticated men, eh?'

'Both you and your father seem to have me firmly placed as a *femme fatale*!' She took hold of his hand, smiling. 'You should see where I live!'

'Oh, no!' He was eager. 'Oh, certainly not. Father might have made that mistake, but he didn't get the impression from me. Honestly, Catherine. I told you. I love you.'

'Oh, all right.'

'I'll send you those poems.'

'That would be lovely.' She kissed his cheek. The train was coming. She got up. 'Well…'

'You'll write back?'

'Of course I shall. And I'll see you again, very soon.'

'I hope so,' he said.

'By the way.' The train had drawn into the station. A few people got out. She headed for a second-class carriage. 'Who is Samiyah? Your sister?'

He became evasive. He opened the compartment door for her. Catherine began to laugh and a huge sense of relief swept through her. She knew. 'She's the girl you're going to marry! Your father's just finished the negotiations!'

His expression of alarm made her laugh still harder. She sat down in a corner seat.

'It's nothing to do with me,' he said. 'Really, Catherine. It's something my father arranged with Samiyah's father years ago. In my country…'

'It's all right.' She closed the door and opened the window, leaning out so that she could kiss him on his worried forehead. 'I'll see you soon, Ahmed. Send me those poems!'

'Yes.' He was doubtful. 'You're not upset?'

'Oh, a little.' She thought she had better say that in order to save his feelings. She waved her hand to him as the train trembled and pulled away from the platform. She had quite enjoyed herself, now she reviewed the day. The lady in the opposite corner stared at her in dismay as Catherine began to sing:

> 'There was I, waitin' at the church,
> Waitin' at the church, waitin' at the church,
> When I guessed he'd left me in the lurch,
> Lor, 'ow it did upset me!
> Then all at once he sent me round a note,
> 'Ere's the very note, this is what he wrote,
> Can't get away to marry you today –
> My wife won't let me.'

'You can't beat the old ones, can you dear?' warily remarked the lady in the opposite corner.

11. In which Miss Persson attends a meeting of veterans

A fly, one of the last survivors of the season, buzzed wearily about her face. Down below, in the thickly wooded valley, a wounded airship sank towards the waters of the Rhine. She heard the distant echo of a roar, primeval: she might at that moment have fancied herself some Parsifal, her quest Arthurian. It was the autumn of 1933. Although the afternoon sunlight was misty, each detail of the landscape was sharply defined in greens, browns and golds, with the sky a sharp blue-grey above.

She had arrived too late to witness the battle, bound to be decisive, between the tanks and the airships, but now, as she stepped deliberately into the middle of a wide unpaved forest track of churned orange mud, she came upon a camouflaged tank. There was every indication that the machine had been abandoned; its cannon pointed towards the tops of the pines, its engines were silent, a beam of dusty sunshine illuminated a section of its tracks like a delicate searchlight. The tank bore no markings, but seemed to be of a familiar Bavarian type; it was probably, therefore, part of the victorious fleet, unless it had been requisitioned by an enemy.

From within the tank there was a creak of metal. The hatch of the turret began to open. Una Persson cocked her Lee-Enfield and raised it to her shoulder, sighting on the hatch.

As if squeezed from a blackhead a yellow face slid into view. A frightened, bloodshot eye regarded her weapon.

'Oh.' Una lowered the rifle a trifle. 'It's you, you little wanker.'

Jerry Cornelius offered her a weak wink and then, as his confidence increased, raised his shoulders above the level of the hatch. Again, he hesitated. 'Um…' He was wondering if she were friend or foe.

'How did you manage to get out of this one?' she asked severely. To have reached his present position he would have to have left the battle early. The odds were that he had not even taken part in the fighting. 'Another breakdown?'

'Oh, come on!' He was getting cocky now. 'I survive, Una.' He pulled his mean body into the soft daylight and began to slide down the dented armour of his tank until his feet touched the thick pile of pine needles raised by his vehicle's tracks. He glanced at his flashy watch. 'Have you seen Frank?'

'It was probably him I shot,' she said. 'I thought it was you. He ran away.' She pointed towards the barbed wire, visible through the trees, the remains of some earlier and forgotten battle. 'He must have left a good deal of himself behind. I've never seen anyone go through wire so fast.'

'You're on foot?'

'My motorbike ran out of petrol about three kilometres back.'

'So you missed it?'

'Yes. Frank wasn't on our side, was he?'

She could tell by the way that he leaned his back against his tank, with folded arms and crossed legs, that she had frightened him. She knew very well that Frank was with the North Germans and she had not for a moment doubted his identity: Jerry had an entirely different way of panicking. She uncocked her rifle and slung it over her shoulder, approaching him. He was still nervous, but passive.

'Cheer up, Jerry,' she said. 'The war's almost over.'

'It's never fucking over,' he declared moodily. 'I'm getting tired of it, what with one thing and another. I deserve a rest.'

'It must be your monumental self-concern which makes you so charming.' She licked her handkerchief and began to dab at the dirt on his face. 'When you go to pieces, Jerry, you really go to pieces.'

'It's shell shock,' he said defensively, but his spirits were already improving. 'Did you see our attack? It was a classic.'

'Actually,' she told him. 'I was looking for Petroff. Isn't he with you?'

'If he is, we're really scraping the bottom of the barrel.'

She was offended. She put her handkerchief away. 'You don't like him? I thought you had a lot in common.'

'Bloody hell! Anyway, he's calling himself 'Craven' these days, for obvious reasons. You haven't got any time for him either, have you?'

She resisted the urge to defend Petroff, contenting herself with, 'He seems okay to me. Now.'

'Poncing about. He only joined for the uniform.' Jerry began to dust at his own leather combat jacket.

'You've got a scrawny little spirit, Jerry.' Her remark was somewhat hypocritical since she had had exactly the same thought about Petroff. 'Has Petroff stolen your glory, then?'

Jerry yawned and shook his head. 'I don't think so. It's about all he hasn't pinched. In return, I got his crabs.' Reminiscently he scratched his crotch. Una experienced a sympathetic twinge (at least, she hoped it was only sympathetic). She became depressed.

'So you haven't seen Petroff?'

'Didn't expect to. You'll find him at headquarters, if anywhere. Sucking up to any general who happens to be available. He's lost his style, has Petroff.'

'No,' she said to the first part of his remark, 'I radioed.'

'Then he's gone over to the Prussians. Temperamentally, he should have been with them all along. Christ!' He became enthusiastic. 'You didn't see any of them go up, I suppose? We were using incendiary shells as a matter of policy, but we didn't expect them to be using hydrogen. Boom! Boom!'

She sniffed and lit a cigarette. 'You sound like that horrible little friend of yours, Collier. He's not with you today?'

Jerry frowned, consulting his dodgy memory. 'He got left behind during the Shift, didn't he? It's a shame. This is just the sort of fighting he likes best. Better than shooting HTA stuff. Those airships take ages to come down, even when the whole gasbag's burning. What a shame it can't last.'

'So you were actually in the battle?'

'I broke ranks, chasing one of the last of the ships. Her engines had conked out and she was drifting on the wind. I thought I'd be able to pot her, but I only got one shot in before I lost her behind the trees.'

'She's down,' said Una. 'If it's the one I saw a few minutes ago. She was making for the river. Hadn't you better rejoin your squadron?'

He scratched his ear. 'Was there anyone with Frank?'

'Not that I saw.'

'A little bloke, looks a bit like Charlie Chaplin. Toothbrush moustache? Used to be on the Bavarian side?'

'Come off it, Jerry!'

'I'm serious,' he said. 'Frank's trying one of his lone-hand stunts again.'

'There's no possible way he could…'

'Frank's an optimist.'

She rubbed her lip. 'So was Petroff. I wonder if they're working together.'

'No. Petroff would have been too frightened. His nerve has gone completely.'

'I wish you'd stop crediting Petroff with your own cowardice.'

'Why shouldn't I? He was my replacement, wasn't he? After Prague?'

'So that's what it's about,' she said. 'I'll never believe the heights of egotism men can rise to.'

'Speak for yourself,' he said. 'After all, Frank's only trying to put things back the way he remembers. It's you who's changing the rules, Una.'

'There aren't any rules,' she told him.

'That's women for you.' He grinned his cheap triumph.

She became impatient. 'Do you think Frank will…?'

'We'll know soon enough, if he has any success. You prefer little wars, don't you? Civil wars.'

'I suppose I do. It keeps things tidier. World wars change things too much, too quickly. They're hard for me to identify with.'

'Personally,' he said, 'I'd like to see one big one get it all over with for good. It's all right for you, you always take the glamorous jobs.'

'Nonsense.' She knocked a piece of dried mud off one of the tracks. 'You're frighteningly simple-minded sometimes, Jerry.'

'*Aquila non capit muscas.*' He shrugged. He was back on form and twice as aggravating. 'Come on. I'll give you a lift.' He helped her climb up the side of the tank and down into the stuffy interior. It stank of disinfectant and aftershave. 'I was sick,' he apologised. 'It's the vibrations. All that bouncing about.'

'I think I'd better drive.' She handed him her Lee-Enfield and seated herself at the controls, squinting into the periscope. 'Is this reverse?'

12. In which Catherine Cornelius is confronted by the Horrors of War

'When the 'ell you gonna get married, Caff,' said Mrs Cornelius absently as Catherine pulled on the jacket of her suit, buttoned it up and tugged it into place over her hips.

'There's no-one *to* marry, is there, Mum?'

Mrs Cornelius folded the wet newspaper around the crumbs and vegetable scraps and hesitated before she took the lid off the waste bin and threw the bundle in. 'Ask Sammy if 'e got that bit of pork for me, will yer, Caff? On yer way ter work'll do.'

'All right, Mum.'

It was impossible to tell how Mrs Cornelius leapt from one association to another. 'Still, ya always come 'ome in the end, doncher?'

'Yes, Mum.' She was trying on the turban she had just bought with the last of her coupons.

'More'n ya c'n say for them two.' She meant Catherine's brothers. 'But Frank's doin' well, I 'ear, these days.'

'In the army?'

Mrs Cornelius guffawed. 'Wot d'*you* fink?'

'I thought he was called up.'

'Well, yeah, but 'e left, didn't 'e? I suppose that's why 'e didn't come 'ome. There was some chaps from the army come rahnd. You know, arskin' after 'im.'

'When was this?'

'Baht a monf ago.' Mrs Cornelius chewed at a piece of pastry. 'When did you git back?'

'Week before last.'

'That's it, then. A monf.'

'And Jerry?'

'Come off it!' Mrs Cornelius spluttered with mirth. 'Probly

workin' for the bloody Germans.' There was a certain pride in her tone. 'I *told* yer all this, Caff.'

Catherine's memory had become very hazy of late. 'Oh, yes. I remember.'

Mrs Cornelius gave the suit her appraisal. 'Not bad. *Very* up to date. We don't age much in our family, do we?'

'I suppose we don't.' It was hard to see anything in the long frameless fly-specked mirror. She shook out her perm and patted at it. 'That's better.'

Mrs Cornelius was rooting about in the junk on her mantelpiece. 'There was a postcard from Jerry. From France.'

'What, recently?'

'Nah! Two years ago! 'E'll turn up, jest like you. When the war's over. Wiv nowhere ter stay but 'ere.' Mrs Cornelius abandoned the search. 'It was a nice pee-see, though.' She sighed and waddled to her chair. 'Cor! It takes it aht o' yer, dunnit?'

'What?' Catherine carefully turned her lipstick a fraction of an inch above the case and began to apply it.

Mrs Cornelius shrugged. 'Life.' She began to leaf through a copy of *Lilliput*, looking at the pictures. 'Blimey! It's disgustin'. Feel like puttin' the kettle on fer a cuppa, Caff?'

'Yes, all right.'

Catherine finished making up and went to fill the kettle. Through the dusty window she could see all the way across to the ruins on the corner of Ladbroke Grove and Elgin Crescent, where the bomb had landed. 'What's disgusting?'

'These nude pitchers.' Mrs Cornelius dropped the magazine to the pile beside the chair. She yawned. ''Ow's it goin', then? Up at the pub?'

'Not bad.'

'Must see a lot of fellers in there, eh?'

'They're mostly old, Mum. There's a war on, you know.' Catherine lit the gas and put the kettle on the ring.

'Soljers on leave, though.'

'Some. I don't fancy soldiers.'

'You're not like me there. I never could resist the buggers.' Mrs Cornelius fidgeted in the chair.

'They go off and get killed, don't they?'

'Well, some of 'em do, yeah.'

'So there's no point in marrying one, is there?'

'Didn't say there was.'

'Oh, I thought that was what it was all about.'

'You ought ter fink abaht it, though, Caff.' Mrs Cornelius was serious. 'I was first married at sixteen.'

'And deserted by the time you were eighteen. With three kids.'

Her mother smiled reminiscently.

Catherine looked at her wristwatch. It was half past ten. She was due at the pub just before eleven. She preferred the lunchtime hours. It was busier, but much less confused. Sammy had got her the job last week. The pub was just across the road from his pie shop. Over the years Sammy had found employment for all the Cornelius family in the district, but none of the jobs had ever lasted long and some of them had turned out to be decidedly dodgy. But he had given Frank his first real start, selling imperfect clockwork toys off a stall in the Portobello market. From that Frank had gone on to cut-price frocks and invested his profits in stolen booze to re-label and sell to the posh pubs around South Ken. The army must have interrupted a steady upward movement in his career. He would be in the black market by now. A spiv. It was funny that someone as doggedly honest as Sammy had so many contacts in what you might call the benter side of the wholesale–retail trade. Poor old Sammy, she thought. She heated the teapot over the steam from the kettle, warming the leaves that were still in there. Tea was short. Her mother rarely benefited from Frank's business ventures. She half-filled the pot and stirred the brew round. She put the lid on the pot.

'There you are, Mum. I'll let it stand a bit, shall I?'

'Better.' Mrs Cornelius was leaning over the arm of her grease-spotted chair, searching amongst her magazines for one that was not completely read through. She extracted a yellowed copy of

Red Letter and began to look at the first story, rubbing at a flea bite on her neck as she concentrated.

'I don't know how you can tell those stories apart,' said her daughter. 'The plots are all the same.'

Mrs Cornelius grunted, turned two pages rapidly and set the *Red Letter* aside. 'I've read it,' she said. 'Wot?'

'Shall I get you another on my way home?'

'Book?'

'What d'you want?'

'*Peg's Paper*'ll do.'

'They're not printing it any more.'

'Bloody war.' Many of Mrs Cornelius's favourite weeklies had disappeared because of the paper shortage. 'Well, get me wot you can, Caff.' She considered this. 'Don't get me nuffink like *Picture Post*, though. I've 'ad enough o' the war. All they seem ter do…'

'I'm with you there,' said Catherine. 'You want to forget about it, don't you? While you can.'

'We could all go up tomorrer.' Mrs Cornelius spoke with some satisfaction. 'I might drop in for 'alf a pint, if I go aht. If I do, I'll get me own book.'

'Okay.'

'But arsk Sammy abaht that pork.'

'If you come in, I'll go straight on from work,' said Catherine.

'Where ya goin'?'

'West End. Pictures.'

'You be careful. Wot's on?'

'Some comedy. With Cary Grant.'

'Good, is 'e?'

'He's all right.'

'Goin' on yer own?'

'No.' She was deliberately mysterious.

'So you *'ave* got a feller!'

'No!'

''Oo yer goin' wiv, then?'

'Girl friend.'

'Oh. Do I know 'er?'

'No.'

'Where d'ya know 'er from?'

'I met her up the labour exchange. You know – just after I got back.'

'So she's local.'

'Portland Road.'

'Wot's 'er name?'

'Rebecca.'

'Rebecca wot?'

'You're not really interested, Mum.'

'I am. Honest.'

'Her name's Rebecca Ash.'

'Maybe she's got a boyfriend – 'oo's got a friend.'

'Her boyfriend was killed. He was in the RAF. Battle of Britain.'

'Oh. Poor fing.'

'So you can see why I don't want anything to do with anyone who's in the war.'

'Were they engaged?'

'Due to get married. He was shot down a week before the wedding.

'Oh, dear!' Mrs Cornelius was fascinated. Her eyes gleamed. It seemed to Catherine (and perhaps it was unfair of her) that this story was a good substitute for *Peg's Paper*. Maybe that was why so many fiction magazines died during a war. There was plenty of drama going on in real life. 'Were they young?'

'That's enough, Mum. I don't like to talk about it. Neither does Rebecca. She's had a lot of tragedies. She's got relatives in Germany. In the concentration camps.' Catherine wished she hadn't offered this information. It was whetting her mother's appetite.

'She Jewish, then?'

'Her mother was. Her father was Polish. He got wounded in the Spanish Civil War.' Catherine was proud of her new friend's romantic ancestry and she continued in spite of her better judgement. 'He was in Russia during the revolution, but he escaped.'

'An aristocrat?'

'They had a castle and land in Poland. They lost everything. Her real name's something like Aserinski, but they changed it when they settled in England.'

Mrs Cornelius had come to life. 'You ought to bring 'er rahnd. Poor kid. What 'appened to 'er mother?'

'She died of TB.'

'Tut-tut,' said Mrs Cornelius sympathetically, avidly. 'And 'er dad?'

'He started getting these dizzy spells. He was run over by a bus.'

'Poor *fing*.'

Catherine adjusted her turban on her head and ran her tongue round her red lips. 'Must go, Mum. Shall I pour you a cup?'

'There's a love…'

Catherine took one of the new Woolworth's cups she had bought and measured milk and sugar into it before she poured the tea on top. 'There you are.'

'Fanks, Caff.' Her mother stirred the tea. 'Probably murdered, eh?'

'Who?'

'Yore friend's dad.'

'Why?'

'Russians. They never let anyone go.'

Catherine shook her head. 'Likely. Or maybe it was the bus company found out he hadn't paid his fare from Shepherd's Bush.'

'Don't joke about it, Caff. Ya never know.' Mrs Cornelius relaxed with her tea, her mind full of fantasy. ''Ow terrible though…'

Catherine Cornelius left her mother with her dreams. She had now made it completely impossible for Rebecca Ash ever to meet her mother. It would be altogether too embarrassing.

When she got to the corner of Blenheim Crescent and Kensington Park Road she saw that Sammy's shutters were still up and there were no fresh smells of cooking, though the stale ones lingered. She banged on the door. 'Sam!' She still had plenty of time to get to work for the pub was a couple of seconds away, on the opposite corner. The Blenheim Arms. The day was cool and grey. She wished that she had brought her mac. She heard a sound from the back of the shop.

'Sammy!'

Carpet slippers shuffled on the tiles of the floor. The blind was raised. Sammy stood behind the glass. He was wearing his apron already, over a roll-neck pullover and corduroy trousers. He smiled at her. ''Ullo, young Cathy.' He unbolted the door at top and bottom, turned the key. 'Wot can I do fer you?'

'Morning, Sammy. Mum wondered about the pork.'

He tapped the side of his nose. 'Don't worry. 'Nuff said, eh? I'll drop it round. Or shall I pop it across to you at the pub?' He wiped a fat, greasy forehead which had been tanned by years of exposure to his pans and his gas-jets. 'An' I'll bring you over a fresh pork pie, eh?'

'Well,' she said, 'I might not be going home after I leave work.'

'Fair enough. I'll get the lad to take it down. 'Ow you keepin', Cathy? The job okay?'

'Fine thanks, Sam.'

'You ought to be doin' better, though,' he said, as if he had failed her. 'Receptionist or secretary or somethin'. What'd they say up the Labour?'

'It's war work mostly. Factory jobs.'

'Oh, you're too good for that.'

'I'd do it if I had to,' said Catherine, 'but the job at the pub gives me free afternoons. That's something.' She glanced across the street. 'Well, they're opening up. See you, Sammy.'

'Take it easy, Cath.' He shut his door and drew down the blind.

Mrs Hawkins was already behind the bar. 'Cold enough for you?' she said as Catherine came in.

'Not half,' said Catherine. 'Where do you want me today?'

'Better stay in the private bar, love. I'm sorry about last night.'

'He was drunk,' said Catherine. 'He didn't mean any harm.'

'The way he grabbed you! Filthy old devil.'

Catherine grinned. 'He wasn't really up to much else, was he?'

Mrs Hawkins folded her thin arms under her breasts and

roared. She was a pleasant, sensitive woman. Mr Hawkins was inclined to be as drunk as his best customers by the end of an evening and she was used to helping him to bed, often before the pub shut. He was a sweet-natured man and Mrs Hawkins didn't seem to resent his habits. 'Want a little something to warm you up, love?'

'I'd better not,' said Catherine. 'It never does me much good during the day.'

'I know what you mean.' Mrs Hawkins raised the hinged section of the bar to allow Catherine through. 'I don't think he'll show up for a day or two, though. Not after what you gave 'im!' She roared again. 'A real touch of the Knees Up Mother Browns, eh?'

Perhaps because of last night's trouble the pub was not as busy as it normally was and Catherine spent most of her time polishing glasses and, when her mum came in at about half past one, chatting.

''Ad ter get a *Woman's Weekly* in the end,' said Mrs Cornelius, settling herself on a stool at the corner of the private bar and sipping her half of bitter. 'There's only a few stories in that. Mostly it's 'ints.'

'How to make a pie out of two bits of gristle and some mouldy turnips,' said Mrs Hawkins, coming through to get some bottles of light ale for the public bar. 'It makes you laugh, doesn't it, Mrs C?'

'Not 'alf.' Mrs Cornelius drained her mug. 'Or 'ow ter get the caviar stains out o' yer mink stole!'

They all enjoyed this joke.

'All right!' called Mrs Hawkins, detecting a murmur of impatience from the public bar, 'just coming.' She winked at Catherine and her mother and left with an armful of light.

'Give us anuvver, Caff,' said Mrs Cornelius holding out her glass mug.

As Catherine pulled the handle of the beer pump, her mother said: 'I saw Sammy. 'E reckons we can both go rahnd to 'im fer Chris'mas. Watcher fink?'

'Nice.' She put the half-pint on the bar. 'Only I might not be home over the whole of Christmas.'

'Wot? Workin' 'ere?'

'No. I sort of partly promised Rebecca that I'd spend Christmas with her. At her flat.'

'Oh.'

'She'll be on her own, you see.'

'Yeah.' Mrs Cornelius reached for her drink. 'So will I be, won't I?'

'Not if you're with Sammy.'

'Well, Sammy's not family, is 'e? Not really.'

'Maybe Frank'll turn up. Or Jerry?'

'Some 'opes. Ah, well.' Mrs Cornelius was genuinely trying to hide her disappointment with the result that Catherine, in turn, felt genuinely guilty.

'The only family she's got is probably in Germany, you see, Mum. In a concentration camp. They might not be alive at all. So...'

'Oh, yeah. I can see that. Well, that's the time for charity, innit? Chris'mas. So you won't be arahnd fer Chris'mas dinner, even?'

'Well, I'll try to get over.'

'Wish y'd told me a bit earlier.'

'It's not December yet, Mum.'

'No, but there's all the arrangements. Y'know 'ow it creeps up on yer.'

'There is time to change the arrangements.'

'Yeah.' Her mother finished the beer and began to slide her bulk from the stool. She buttoned up her moulting fur collar. 'Okay, then, Caff. See yer later. Cheerio.'

'Cheerio, Mum.'

Catherine felt depressed after her mother had left. She would have been glad of a few more customers to serve, to take her mind off her guilt. Instead Mrs Hawkins came back at a quarter past two.

'You might as well get off now, Cath, if you like. Still going to the pictures?'

'Yes.'

''Ope it's a good 'un.'

'Cary Grant,' said Catherine.

'Is 'e the one with the moustache? *Gone with the Wind*? Or the other one?'

'The other one,' said Catherine. 'Thanks, Mrs Hawkins.' She would go straight to Rebecca's, even though it had begun to drizzle outside. She couldn't face going home to pick up her coat. She got her bag from where she kept it under the bar and swung the strap over her shoulder. 'Well, bye-bye, then. See you this evening.'

'Bye-bye, love.' Mrs Hawkins winked at her. She probably thought Catherine was going to meet a boyfriend.

Catherine walked hurriedly down Blenheim Crescent, crossed Ladbroke Grove, went down the rest of Blenheim Crescent, the posher bit with its big trees and front gardens, into Clarendon Road and then round into Portland Road. Rebecca actually owned the little terraced house and had done it up beautifully, with the number in brass figures, 189, on an apple-green door. The area railings were also painted apple-green and the window frames were a sort of peach colour. Rebecca lived on the ground floor and basement and rented the rest to a couple, both musicians with the Royal Philharmonic Orchestra, who had two children. Rebecca had inherited the house from her parents.

Catherine rang Rebecca's bell.

'You're a bit early.' Rebecca opened the door. She was wearing a long pink quilted housecoat. 'Come in.' She had thick black curly hair and large black eyes. Her eyebrows were high and plucked thin. She had a long face, with full lips and a large, broad nose. She often described her features as horsey, but Catherine insisted that she had the classical beauty of an ancient Greek goddess. She looked a little bleary, as if she had just woken up. She had been, until recently, a cellist in a string quartet, until the two male members had been conscripted for war work in the pits. Now she sometimes filled in for another cellist who lived in the country and couldn't always get to London.

Rebecca led the way down to the basement. Originally it had been two separate rooms, but now about a third of it was a kitchen and the other two thirds were a sort of bedsitter. She scarcely ever used the two rooms upstairs, unless she was practising.

A record was playing softly on the big cabinet electric gramophone. It was piano music. Catherine thought it was probably Mozart, who was her favourite composer. She sat down on the wide divan opposite the gramophone. 'That's beautiful. Is it Mozart?' She felt diffident about music in Rebecca's company.

Rebecca nodded. 'Coffee? It's fresh.'

'Thanks.'

Rebecca took the aluminium coffee-maker off the stove and placed two large breakfast cups on the table. The flat was as neat as usual. Even the divan, which was also her bed, had been made up. 'I had a job last night,' said Rebecca. 'Filling in for Stephen, as usual. So I was late getting in.' She yawned, as if to emphasise her remark. 'How are you, dear?'

Catherine found that she was also yawning. 'I was all right up to about an hour ago. Then my mum came into the pub.'

Rebecca was sympathetic. She brought the coffee over and sat down with Catherine. 'That's the new suit, is it? It's smart.' She fingered the material of the skirt. 'Oh, it's lovely.' She kissed Catherine on the cheek, adding softly, 'Nice to see you, love.'

Catherine squeezed her arm. 'I've missed you. It's been two days.'

'Seems a lot longer.' Rebecca stretched and put her coffee on the Indian rug at her feet. 'What was the row about? With your mum.'

'Oh, nothing. It wasn't really a row…'

'Didn't she want you to go out?'

'No. It's all right.' Catherine didn't want to make Rebecca feel as guilty as she had felt. 'If you still want to go to the pictures I thought that Cary Grant would be nice.'

'Well, let's think about it,' said Rebecca. She seemed distracted.

'Are you okay, Rebecca? There's nothing wrong?'

'No!' Rebecca patted her knee. 'No, I've just woken up, that's all.'

'D'you want to try the suit on, before you get dressed? You said you wanted to, remember?'

'That's a good idea.' The record finished. Rebecca went to the gramophone and removed the big twelve-inch disc. 'Is there anything you'd like to hear?'

'Whatever you want.'

'I won't put anything else on for the moment.'

'Right-ho.' Catherine reached out to take Rebecca's hand. 'Come here and give me a proper kiss. Oh, I've missed you such a lot!' Rebecca fell onto the bed beside her and Catherine hugged her, kissing her on the mouth. 'Oh, Rebecca.' They had become lovers almost as soon as they had met. Catherine had seduced Rebecca here after they had got drunk one night at a club, when two airmen had tried to pick them up. As Rebecca had said, a little self-consciously, the following morning, at least you could be fairly certain that if you fell in love with a girl you weren't likely to worry about her being called up.

'I love you very much,' Rebecca said. 'I always will, Catherine.' Her big eyes were full of tears. Her face was intensely serious. They kissed again. 'It's wonderful. It never for a moment felt strange. It happened so naturally.' Catherine smiled and stroked her friend's cheek. The words were familiar but she always relished hearing them. 'Shall we just stay in, then, this afternoon?' she suggested.

'I'd like to go to bed,' said Rebecca, 'and have a cosy day together.'

'I'd like that, too.' Catherine lay back on the divan and pushed her shoes off her feet. 'That's better!'

'The marvellous thing is,' said Rebecca, 'that we'll always be friends, no matter what happens to us.'

'Yes,' agreed Catherine. She unbuttoned her jacket and began to fiddle with the hooks and eyes of her skirt. She clambered out of the suit. 'That's better.' In underclothes, stockings and suspenders, she padded across the floor to put the suit on a chair. 'There you are, when you want to try it.' She undid her suspenders and carefully rolled her stockings down her legs. It was hard enough getting any kind of stockings, these days. She took off her girdle. 'Phew! I'm putting on weight, I think.'

'I like you a little bit dumpy,' said Rebecca. 'It makes me feel better. That lovely pink skin. I'm jealous. We're like Snow White and Rose Red, one as dark as dark can be and the other the fairest of the fair!'

Wearing her slip, Catherine came back to the bed. She got into it with a sigh. 'This is the most comfortable bed I've ever slept in.'

Rebecca drew the heavy red curtains. 'It's foggy outside now. Was it foggy on your way here?'

'No. There's no point in going to the West End. We'd never get home.'

Rebecca took off her housecoat. She had large, pendulous breasts. They were the only thing about her that Catherine didn't like; she had always preferred small, rounded breasts like her own. 'Move over,' said Rebecca. 'You're on my side.'

Catherine shifted towards the wall.

'You're not too cold, are you?' Rebecca asked. 'The radiators went off in the night.' She had a delicious, musty smell to her.

'Oh, no. Warm as toast. I'm just a bit tired. Tireder than I realised. To tell you the truth, I'm a bit nervy. It must have been Mum.'

'What did she say?'

Catherine did not want to mention Christmas. 'Just the usual stuff. She started off by telling me I ought to get married. I told her this wasn't exactly the right time to be thinking of the future, something like that. Then I said I was seeing you and she asked a lot of questions.'

'You think...?'

'Nothing like that. She just wanted to know what you did and who your parents were. She got very interested when I said you were half-Jewish and half-Polish.'

Rebecca was amused. 'Why? Is she anti-Semitic?'

'No. There's more than a drop of Jewish blood in our family, anyway. Mum's not like that. But she hasn't much to occupy her mind, so she takes an interest in other people's business. You know the sort of thing.'

Rebecca nodded. 'And that was all?'

'Yes, really.'

'Why don't you turn over and let me massage your back for a bit. It'll help you relax.'

'Would you mind? I'd love that.'

'Turn over, then.'

Catherine pulled away her cushions and settled herself with her arms at the sides of her head. Rebecca began to stroke her body. 'Is that nice?'

'Perfect.'

Rebecca massaged her shoulder blades.

'Are you sure that job at the pub's right for you?'

'It's all there is, apart from helping with the war effort.'

'It's not so much the work as the people you have to deal with. That must be a strain.'

'It's not too bad. Last night there was a bit of trouble. An old bloke took a shine to me. I'd been ever so nice to him. I thought he was harmless. Just before closing time I was on the other side of the bar and he made a grab for me. Hands everywhere. You know. Without thinking I gave him one where it hurts most.'

Rebecca said: 'You poor thing. But that's what I meant, really.'

'That's the only time it's happened. Oh! Smashing! Ah!' Her muscles seemed to be expanding under Rebecca's hands. Rebecca moved her body closer so that her pelvis was resting gently against Catherine's hip. The massage continued.

'I wish there was something you wanted to do,' said Rebecca.

'I'm not trained for anything. I left school at fourteen.'

'You ought to go to art school, or apply for RADA or something. You've got plenty of talent for anything.'

'You're not the first to tell me that. Only I can't paint, I can't act, I can't write. My talent seems to be for making people think I've got talent. My brother Frank's got a talent for making money. My brother Jerry's got a talent for causing trouble…'

'Is Jerry the one you…'

'Yes.'

The pressure of Rebecca's vagina on her thigh became a touch harder. Catherine turned her head so that she could see her friend. 'That excites you, doesn't it? The idea of me and my brother.'

Rebecca nodded.

'It's only the idea that makes it any different,' said Catherine. 'Once you get used to it, it's no different at all. Like everything else. Except maybe more friendly.'

'Like us.'

Catherine didn't reply. 'As I was saying – all our family are thought to be talented, but we haven't a real success amongst us. No education for one thing, of course. No will to improve ourselves, I suppose. Frank's an artist when it comes to thinking up shady deals. Jerry's quite a good guitar player. Jazz and that, though. I don't know what we'd have been good at, if things had been a bit easier for Mum.'

'Your dad went off?'

'My mum must be the most deserted woman in the world. *She's* got a talent for losing husbands!'

'That was Cornelius.'

'That's what he called himself. Apparently he used the name "Brown", too. Maybe that was why Mum was so interested in you. My dad was supposed to be Russian, or half-Russian. I can't remember. She's got a lot of different stories – probably all from him! Oh, that feels so good.' She fell silent as Rebecca massaged her just below the ribs.

Rebecca began to kiss her head and ears.

'Just a minute,' said Catherine. 'I'll take my slip off.'

When she had removed the last of her clothes, she lay on her back while Rebecca kissed her body. The kisses were delicate, fluttering against her skin and arousing her only very slowly. She knew that Rebecca was already very much aroused and this also had the effect of increasing her desire, but she was enjoying the sense of anticipation and happily could have spent the best part of the afternoon in quiet love-play if she had not been aware that she had to be back at work in just over two hours. She glanced at her watch. It was almost three o'clock. She decided to concentrate on helping Rebecca reach orgasm, stroking her, whispering to her, scratching her lightly, then reaching down past Rebecca's bottom and touching her at the base of her vagina. Rebecca began to push herself against Catherine's thigh, moving rapidly up and down and from side to side, gasping, her wet mouth against Catherine's ear and cheek, calling out as she came.

Rebecca's orgasm had aroused Catherine more than she had anticipated. Kissing her friend, she rolled again onto her stomach and began to masturbate. In a moment, Rebecca started to stroke her again. The orgasm was short and intense; it left her feeling edgy. She turned on her side and they embraced. 'That was terrific,' said Rebecca. 'Are you okay?'

'Oh, yes. Fine.'

'You're not, though, are you?'

'It can't work every time.'

'Is there anything...?'

'No. Maybe another massage if I don't relax. I'm sorry.'

'It wasn't anything I was doing wrong?'

'Don't be daft. My mum really got me worked up. I'm sure that's it.'

'Are you sure she doesn't think anything?'

'No. She was a bit disappointed when I told her I'd be spending Christmas here.'

'Oh.' Rebecca seemed startled.

'You asked me to. If...'

'I want to spend Christmas with you, Cathy. I couldn't want anything more. But there's a chance I won't be here now. So if it means a nasty scene with your mum...'

Catherine could not understand. 'You didn't say anything about going away.'

'I hadn't made up my mind, then.'

'You were so keen on us being together over Christmas.'

'I know. I still am.'

'What hadn't you made up your mind about?'

'I didn't tell you. I didn't want to be talked out of it. And you would have talked me out of it. I knew you would. It's silly. It's all mixed up with Robert and self-denial, and guilt about his being killed, but it seemed the right thing to do.'

'Do what?'

'I applied to join the WAAFs.' Rebecca began to cry. 'I got my letter yesterday. I've been accepted.'

'Oh, Christ!'

'So I don't know where I'll be at Christmas, you see. But if they let me come home, of course, I want to be with you.'

'Oh, fuck!'

'If it wasn't for the war…'

At this rate, thought Catherine, just before depression engulfed her, people are going to start handing me white feathers.

It seemed that everybody she knew was marching off to war.

13. In which Captain Una Persson considers questions of comfort

It was not uncommon for Una Persson to experience the sensation of déjà vu; but here, in the ruins of Oxford, with a discoloured mist rising from the damp ground, it overwhelmed her; she felt it as another might feel vertigo. She became dizzy, her identity began to fall away from her; she panicked. The ruins readjusted themselves, shifting their proportions: a building which had been almost whole now vanished, another was partially resurrected. Then they were stable again. Una thought she felt her clothes writhing on her body as they, too, were rearranged.

'Some sod's up to something.' She spoke aloud. The sound of her voice brought her back to sanity. 'But then,' she added, 'some sod's always up to something.' She took deep, regular breaths to slow down her heart-rate. She leaned heavily against the balustrade of the broken bridge where she had been standing studying the river. The river had scarcely altered: thick green weed grew in it. There was slime; a strong stench of stagnation.

The bomb which had taken out Magdalen College had also destroyed a fair amount of the bridge's superstructure, but it still functioned. Una looked at one of her watches, wondering if she had actually agreed to meet someone here. She could not remember making the arrangement or with whom she had made it. She turned up the collar of her black trench coat and put her bare, cold-reddened hands into her pockets which were filled with pieces of paper, rags and unspent cartridges. From curiosity she removed one of the pieces of paper. It was folded several times, was grey with dirt and tattered. She opened it. The letter was written in Cyrillic and at first she assumed it was from a Russian, then she realised that the letter was in Greek. It was headed Hydra, Monday, and referred to recent disastrous events in Athens. Substantially it was a love letter but the signature had been on a subsequent page. She searched through her pockets for the missing page without success. A creased visiting card from Naomi Jacobsen, 77 Blvde St-Michel, Paris, rang a bell. She turned the card over. Something had been written on it in pencil and was now almost completely obscured save for the words 'Cornelius' and 'relationship'. She pushed the stuff back into her pocket.

She began to wonder about the date. The ruins were not new; they could be up to a hundred years old. She considered the possibility of an overshoot, which would also explain the sensation she had first felt upon arrival. She decided to wait no more than five minutes longer. She strode to the other side of the bridge, noticing how silent everything was, how still, as if all life had ceased to exist in the area.

It had begun to rain. The drizzle either stank as forcefully as the river or it brought out more of the existing smell. She wished that she had a hat. She heard a footfall. A man came out of some trees by the riverbank and climbed carefully towards the bridge, slipping in the wet moss and grass. He reached the bridge, tested a piece of stone before using it to lever himself up and stand coughing into a large white handkerchief. He wore grey flannels, a tweed jacket with leather patches at the elbows; a dark green polo-neck sweater, a woollen scarf. His hair was turning grey. He also wore hornrimmed glasses. Una suspected the outfit. It was too typical of a don, she thought, to be anything other than a disguise. He stopped coughing. 'Miss Persson, of course?' His voice was without vibrancy: English middle class. 'Or should I say Captain?' He seemed friendly. 'I'm Chapman. We have met, actually, but you probably don't remember.'

'Munich?'

He laughed. 'Hardly! It was just after the last war. In Geneva.'

Una did not remember. She was not sure, at that point, where Geneva was. She nodded, offering her hand.

He hesitated, now, before taking it, but more from surprise, she guessed, than reluctance. The shake was hearty, unspontaneous, like an Englishman trying the flamenco. She began to dislike him.

'Well, Mr Chapman.' She rubbed her hands together. 'Where to now?'

'The child's in my rooms, of course. I left her there for safety. Did you bring any transport of your own?'

'None.'

'Wise, really. But it will take a little while to arrange from our end. You'll stay to lunch, I hope.'

'Thank you.'

'Good. You were dropped in, yes?'

She ignored the question. 'What sort of transport can you offer?'

'We've still got a couple of autogyros that are airworthy. One of those should get you to London.'

'Fine.' She now knew her destination, but was still unclear about her mission. Chapman seemed to sense this.

'They did brief you all right?'

'There wasn't much time. If you could outline the basic stuff again I'd be grateful.'

'Of course. We go this way.' He pointed through the dark, unhealthy trees in the direction from which he had come. 'You'd better let me be first. We can't afford to do anything about improving the roads. Oxford is supposed to be completely deserted, so we're a bit nervous of advertising.'

They slid down the slimy bank. He led her along a squelching path through the trees and bushes. 'We're lucky that the School's still operating in any way. Makes you value learning a bit more, eh? When I look back! Nothing more ludicrous, is there, than a middle-class Marxist English don.' He chuckled. 'Still, by and large we manage to keep ourselves pretty comfortable here. And there are a few traditions worth preserving.'

'I never knew one,' murmured Una.

'What? Aha! Yes, of course.' He seemed nervous of her, anxious for her good opinion. What sort of authority was she representing?

A bramble snagged the skirt of her coat. She stopped to pull free. He waited for her, his breath steaming, his eyes shifting. His insecurity seemed to increase whenever they were in the open. He led her across a marshy lawn. The drizzle had almost stopped and in the distance she could see that two wings of a college were still intact, though surrounded by ruins. She thought she detected a dim light in one of the grease-papered windows. It was even more overcast than it had been when she arrived. She wondered if it were, after all, twilight. Then she remembered that Chapman had mentioned lunch.

'The cloud's very low,' she said.

'Yes,' he replied in some relief. 'Yes.' Blocks of rubble began to appear in the soft ground. They reached a plateau of broken brick; they climbed over fractured granite until they could look down at a door. Some of the wreckage had been cleared, enough to make it convenient to enter and leave through the door. He slid down and knocked on the iron-bound oak. 'This was blown straight off its hinges,' he said with pride, 'but was otherwise completely unharmed. Good wood, eh? It stood up to Cromwell, too.'

The door was opened by a middle-aged woman holding a candle. She had pleasant, frightened features. She had darted a smile at Una before she had gone back into the shadows. Una wondered what sort of enemies induced such behaviour. She became melancholic.

'This is Miss Moon,' said Chapman, closing the door behind them. 'Ah! Safe and sound again, Eunice.'

'Would you like a cup of tea?' asked Eunice Moon. She wore a crumpled tweed skirt, a grey cardigan and a darned maroon sweater. The strength of her features was obscured by folds of coarse skin as if she had been at one time much fatter. There were pronounced bags under her mild grey eyes.

'I'd love one,' said Una, anxious to respond as comfortingly as possible, at least until she had worked out what she was supposed to be doing here.

Eunice Moon held the candle above her head, leading the way

up stone steps covered with threadbare coconut matting. They reached a gallery. She held the candle over the carved balustrade. 'That was the hall,' she said. 'We don't use it now. It's impossible to heat, for one thing.' Una thought she heard the movement of rats in the darkness below. They ascended another stairway. The flagstones of the next passage were also covered with worn carpeting. Eunice Moon stopped at the third door on her right and opened it. 'Here we are.'

The room had a small fire in it, burning some sort of smokeless fuel. The fireplace was surrounded by a large fender which had brass and leather seats at either end. The woodwork was dark and highly polished. There were photographs on the walls and mantelpiece, books on the shelves set into alcoves on both sides of the fireplace. The room seemed to Una to be a self-conscious reproduction of a late-Victorian study. There were a couple of pieces of blue china on a sideboard opposite the fire. There were leather, high-backed armchairs. The room was lit by oil lamps. There was a kettle on a stand over the fire. She could see neither fork, toast nor crumpets. Chapman took her coat and, in her long divided skirt, riding boots, leather shirt, she sat down in the chair he indicated, leaning forward to warm her hands. The kettle began to boil.

Eunice Moon removed the kettle and made tea in a large earthenware pot. 'It's Earl Grey, I'm afraid. It's all we have.'

'My favourite,' said Una. It was not, but she had always thought her preference for ordinary Indian popular brands of tea to be a bit vulgar.

Eunice Moon poured the tea and handed her the cup, which was pink Willow Pattern. 'There's no sugar or milk at the moment. And, of course, no lemon.'

'I don't take them.' Another lie. 'This is just what I need.' She smiled at Miss Moon. The woman's voice was tragic; it seemed to contain the fragments of a different voice, one that had been animated.

'And nothing to offer you to eat, until lunchtime,' Chapman said, standing to one side of the fire and accepting his own cup. 'Thanks, Eunice.'

'Actually,' said Eunice Moon very shyly, as she pulled her cardigan about her, 'we were told that they might send some supplies down with you.'

'They said nothing to me. I'm sorry.'

'Oh, we can manage.' Chapman was cheerful. Unlike the woman he seemed to enjoy the actual inconveniences of the life they were leading. 'Normally there's fresh bread, you know. I go to Aylesbury, where there's a baker. I should have gone today. And we had some Rich Tea biscuits up until yesterday. I must remember to ask for some. I don't know where Mr Whiting gets them from, do you, Eunice? He's a wonder.'

She nodded at him, pouring her own tea.

'Actually, we take a bit of a risk,' Chapman continued. 'If it wasn't for the people's good will we'd be scotched, of course. But we give a good service in exchange for the little luxuries. They send their children to us for whatever education we can give them. There isn't a school in Aylesbury now. In a roundabout way that's how we came across the girl – through one of her friends saying something to Eunice.'

'How did you get her here?' asked Una, for want of anything else to say.

'Well, of course, that's why I sent to London for the gold. 'Not for myself. You hadn't heard?'

'Gold? You're bribing her?'

Even Eunice Moon smiled at this and Chapman laughed aloud. 'Not her, Miss Persson. You must be unfamiliar with what's going on in these parts. I thought the same state of affairs existed in London – and Birmingham's notorious – or was. No, no. We bought the girl. It was the only way to get her. The farmer who had her wouldn't let her go. We couldn't make an enemy of him or bang would go our cover and our heads would be bound to roll.'

'She was working for the farmer? A slave?'

'In a manner of speaking.'

Una wondered why the child had been purchased. Her dislike for Chapman had increased.

'Wait till you see her,' chuckled Chapman, 'and you'll see why she was so expensive. I must say...' Eunice Moon caught his eye and he became embarrassed. 'Sorry, Eunice.'

'Of course,' began Miss Moon, 'she'll hardly...'

'You'll have to think up some sort of story in London,' Chapman said. His cup clacked against his saucer. 'To cover what's been going on. Luckily, the farmer didn't know who she was.'

'I can't think how she ever turned up in this part of the world.' Miss Moon shook her head. 'I'd heard that she had been killed with the other child, near Salisbury, wasn't it?'

'Salisbury,' confirmed Chapman. 'There were certainly two children in the photographs, though badly burned. They were buried in the Cathedral, when the FKA were pushed back for a while. Then, of course, the Cathedral got a direct hit when the FKA recovered, so...'

'So there was no real proof, apart from those photographs,' said Eunice Moon. 'Anyway, I don't think there'll be much doubt about her identity. She was very reticent before she learned we were friends. After that, everything she said confirmed who she was. Physically, there's no question.'

'She's nervous, naturally,' continued Chapman, placing his cup and saucer on the mantelpiece beside a photograph of himself in a black gown and mortarboard. 'But she knows she'll be safe as soon as you get her to London.'

'And she's heard of you, which helps,' added Eunice Moon. She sighed and collected up the cups, putting them on a brass Chinese tray.

The woman left with the tea things. Chapman sat down in the other chair. 'It's been a very nerve-racking time for her,' he explained. 'You can imagine.'

'Quite,' said Una.

'We didn't leave Oxford with everyone else and we managed, as it happened, to live quite well. It's isolated. Nobody takes an interest in the place. We get along. Eunice didn't want to be involved in this business and it seemed odd that I, with my political convictions, should be the one to discover the girl and decide to tell London. But there you are.' He sat back in the chair. 'I thought it was for the good of the country. Anything's better than this sort of anarchy, isn't it? And your people should be able to control her.'

'Oh, certainly.' Una was beginning to recover her memory. There were images, now, of the group in London, but they were unspecific.

'We'll be glad to have her off our hands.' Chapman grinned. His pale features seemed to stretch in abnormal lines. He waved his hands, his fingers spread. 'Still, a bit of excitement stops you getting stale, as I told Eunice.'

'Yes,' said Una. She hoped that when she finally met the girl her amnesia would lift. It was the worst attack she had had for a long while, she thought. Carefully, she suppressed that particular line of contemplation.

'There's some hope now, at any rate, of order being restored throughout the country, of Oxford being rebuilt, of proper university life beginning again. I suppose that's what I'm chiefly hoping for, to be frank. Call it self-interest.'

Una could not resist a random and vicious question. 'You're not worried, then, about knowing the child's secret?'

Chapman frowned. 'What do you mean?'

'Well, I'm sure it isn't worth considering, but if you and Miss Moon are the only ones to know what was going on. With the farmer...'

He was still puzzled. Perhaps she had misjudged the importance of what he had told her.

'You don't think,' she continued, 'that there'll be an attempt to silence you both?'

'Kill us, you mean?'

'Or keep you locked up. There are, after all, medieval precedents. And we do seem to have returned to the conditions of the Middle Ages.'

'Not in our *thinking*, surely?' He stroked his upper lip where once, she was sure, a moustache had grown. 'Not in our judgements?'

She pretended to shrug off the problems she had herself raised. 'Some believe we've never really left the Middle Ages.' As she spoke, she received an inkling of the girl's identity or, at least, her political importance.

He took out his handkerchief and blew his nose. 'Well, I hope you inform London that it's certainly not in our interest to say anything.'

'I will.' She affected a comforting tone. 'Of course I shall. They'll see that.'

'It would be most unfair if…'

'Don't worry, Mr Chapman. Justice will triumph.'

'All I want to see is Oxford restored. And the other great universities, too, of course. Cambridge, at any rate.'

'If the population merits it,' she said.

'Get the country running properly again and we'll soon have the population.' He seemed glad to return to what were obviously familiar opinions. 'A constitutional monarchy is better than the kind of fascism, whether it's from left or right, that we've been experiencing. England could do worse than to start from scratch. Back to 1660. A genuine Restoration, in more senses than one.'

Una's mirth was spontaneous. 'And you a Marxist!'

'There's nothing really strange about it, if you accept that societies must experience certain stages in their development towards a state of true Socialism. You see, England's trouble is that she was the first nation to begin the experiment, just as she was the first nation to experience the industrial revolution – there are obvious disadvantages to being the first. You create a structure containing too many of the old factors and as a result you get far worse confusion than, say, in France or America – and they were confused enough.'

'You're confusing me!' Una spoke good-naturedly. 'Don't bother to explain, Mr Chapman. It's hard enough for any of us, these days, to rationalise our instincts with our politics. Miltonian ideals are probably more suitable than Marxist ones, at this time.'

'I'm perfectly serious,' he said.

'I respect your opinions.'

'Can't you see what I'm getting at, though? We've got a fresh start, a new chance. Everything's broken down. We can rebuild it properly.'

'If there are enough optimists of your persuasion we might.'

'You think I'm foolish. You could be right. But being in London can also make you cynical, you know.'

'I know.' She began to warm to him a little more. 'So can hiding in Oxford make you cynical. You could argue that. In more fundamental ways. You would have dismissed your own statements as being thoroughly reactionary a few years ago, wouldn't you?'

'I'd argue now that we have to go back a bit before we can press on forward. It's a respectable argument.'

'And a conservative one.'

He shrugged. 'Circumstances shape one's political opinions. The circumstances are a bit different today from those of even two years ago. I welcomed the FKA at first. They had some good men, but most of those were killed in the early fighting, and the brutes that followed them were nothing less than bandits.'

'Bandits often make the most successful revolutionaries. Certainly they are very good at preparing the way. Robin Hood, Pancho Villa, Makhno.'

'Makhno was hardly a bandit.'

'"Trotsky" thought he was.'

'He was simply naïve. A martyr.'

'You've made my point.'

He accepted this with a stiff, ironical smile. 'All right. But you'd put Cornelius in the same category, would you?'

She sighed.

'Well?'

'Cornelius?' She had been taken off-guard. 'The leader of the FKA?' A guess.

'In actuality, for all he calls himself an advisor. Does he see himself as a responsible revolutionary, do you think?'

'He's very complex.'

'You knew him, didn't you?'

'I've had some dealings with him, yes.'

'I didn't mean to suggest...'

'No, no. That's all right. I'd call him something of an agent provocateur, with few discernible goals – a renegade, if you like. That is, the goals are probably private, half-conscious. And yet his heart's often in the right place and certainly he's been known to support some unlikely and unfashionable causes for apparently excellent reasons.

'Well, as far as I'm concerned, he's a bandit – an assassin – and all you've done is describe a bandit, Miss Persson. Or would you prefer to dignify him with a more romantic title – soldier of fortune, perhaps?' He was becoming aggressive. Una brightened. 'God! Women will always fall for these flashy buccaneer-types!'

'I wouldn't call him that...'

'He works for himself,' Chapman went on, 'and not for any cause. That's a bandit.'

'All right.' She had discussed the Cornelius brothers' motives too often for the subject to hold any interest, but she liked Chapman better when he rose to her baiting, so she continued: 'He's done a lot of good for a great many of the poor devils abandoned by their previous leaders.' She had no idea what this would mean to Chapman.

'Really? You'd admit that he was entirely responsible for the Sack of Birmingham, wouldn't you?'

'He never liked Birmingham.'

'And Leicester? And Rugby? And Lincoln? Another cathedral...'

'He wasn't very fond of the Midlands at all.'

'Eunice's mother died when they levelled Wolverhampton. There's no sanity in killing innocent old women or kids. You're not serious, Miss Persson?'

Una wondered why Jerry always did take it out on Birmingham. It had to be personal.

'I didn't say he was sane,' she said.

'Just a disenchanted idealist?' Again the constipated grin. His irony.

'Aren't we all that?'

'Not me, Miss Persson. Not you, either, or you wouldn't be here.'

'I suppose not. Sometimes I think, however, that Jerry Cornelius is the only one who isn't disenchanted. He manages to enjoy life, in a desperate sort of way.'

'You could say the same for me,' said Chapman. 'And I've nobody's blood on my hands. Of course, I'm not exactly Douglas Fairbanks, either...'

'It was you who made the remark about circumstances.' She was still being deliberately contentious.

'Well,' said Chapman with satisfaction, 'it'll certainly put his nose out of joint when you get back to London with your charge.'

Una was probably even more pleased by the thought than Chapman, but she said: 'He could win her over, perhaps, to his side.'

'Or go over to hers, more likely.'

'You wouldn't like that?'

'It would make my efforts meaningless.'

'Yes. I'm sorry, Mr Chapman.' She felt that she had probably gone too far. 'It is a factor, however, they'll have to consider in London. Little girls always liked Cornelius.'

'I think this particular little girl has had enough of men, however charming.'

'Exactly.' She had become alarmed by Chapman's change of colour. There were red, puffy blotches under his eyes.

'I know you were only joking, Miss Persson. I'm a bit on edge. It's been a strain. And I was trying to do my duty.'

'You've done it marvellously, Mr Chapman. Oxford will soon be a thriving university again. And I shouldn't be surprised if they don't make you Chancellor or something.'

'Oh, all I want is the old life back.' The prospect attracted him, although he did not seem willing to admit it to himself. He looked at the clock on the mantelpiece. It was half past twelve. 'Time for lunch. Would you like a glass of Madeira? We've run out of sherry, I'm afraid.'

'Madeira would be excellent.'

'You don't mind if she – the girl – lunches with us?'

'It would be a good idea to have a chat with her, to reassure her before I take her back to London.'

'Quite.' He poured three glasses of Madeira, draining the bottle. 'Ah, well, that's that. Another link with civilisation broken.' He brought her the drink, sipping his own. 'Enjoy it while you can, eh?'

'Shouldn't we toast the future?' Half-mockingly Una raised her glass.

'Or the queen,' he said, joining in the joke. 'The future's been pretty thoroughly toasted, wouldn't you say?'

She took his meaning.

Eunice Moon entered. She had brought the girl. She was nine or ten years old, with a creamy skin, blonde hair to her shoulders, and wide blue eyes. Una could see why she had cost London so much gold. Una wondered if the farmer or Chapman had dressed her up in the green silk Alice in Wonderland dress with the white ankle socks and the patent leather shoes. Una began to rise. Chapman was already bowing, the glass still in his hand so that a little of the contents spilled. 'Your Majesty,' he said.

Una could see that already the child was no stranger to power.

14. Innocents at home: in which the Cornelius family celebrates a reunion

'Oo-er, look at 'er face!' Mrs Cornelius shrieked with excitement. 'Covered in pimples. *And* she's got a case o' dandrufft!' She fell back onto the off-white plastic upholstery of her new settee. 'Oh, Gawd!' Her cheeks glowed under their rouge; tears fell into her powder, like rain on the desert.

'Well,' said Sammy patiently, 'is that good enough for ya?'

'It'll do, honestly, Sammy,' said Catherine over her shoulder. She was arranging mixed nuts in two glass bowls on the tawny sideboard. The sideboard was also relatively new, in the 'contemporary' style of the other furniture. Only her mother's armchair remained. Mrs Cornelius had refused to have it removed or recovered. Frank had brought her the furniture from the warehouse he was running. He was in the HP business. Everything was of light wood and imitation brass, white plastic; distemper dashes in three colours on the walls, jazzy red, brown, blue and yellow carpet. The spirit of the Festival of Britain recaptured in Blenheim Crescent. And here was Sammy with the TV he had hired for the week so they could watch the Coronation. The problem was that the portable aerial didn't give a very good picture, so he had added a length of cable and hung the whole thing out of the window. The picture was moderately better.

'I'll 'ave to go up on the roof,' said Sammy. He plucked at his shirt, where it stuck under his arms. 'I'll need an 'and, Jerry.'

Jerry was trying to crack a nut with his teeth. He sat in his mum's old chair; there was a half-finished glass of pale ale on the arm beside his left hand. He wore a grey two-piece suit with narrow velvet-trimmed lapels and drainpipe trousers. His yellow paisley waistcoat was of satin. He had thick crêpe-soled shoes on his feet; they were brown suède. When questioned about his appearance he would argue that he was ahead of his time.

'What can I do?' Jerry remained seated.

'I'll lower the cable down from the roof. All you 'ave to do is plug it in an' then tell me when the picture looks right. Okay?'

'Okay.' Jerry abandoned the nut and jumped to his feet. Sammy disappeared through the door onto the landing and began to climb the ladder which went through the loft and up to the roof. Jerry opened the window and stuck his well-greased head out. 'Ready when you are, Sammo!'

Catherine heard a catcall or two from the street, as if in response to her brother's shout.

'Why's it gone off?' said Mrs Cornelius. She had only just realised that the picture had vanished altogether. The screen hissed, and agitated black and white dots fluttered all over it.

'They're fixing the aerial, Mum.'

'We didn't 'ave this trouble with the wireless.'

'You need a more powerful one for a telly, Mum.'

''Ardly seems worf it.' Mrs Cornelius reached behind her for a nut, her eyes still on the screen. 'It 'asn't broken dahn, 'as it, Caff?'

'No, Mum.' Her brother was holding on to the window frame and sitting on the sill, looking up at Sammy. 'You be careful, Jerry.'

'Oh, I'm all right,' said her brother. 'Down she comes, Sam. Ow! Watch it!' He slid back into the room, rubbing his eyes, holding the cable. He began carefully to dust grime off his sleeve.

Sammy's distant voice came from above. 'Plugged in?'

'Give us a minute.' Jerry found the socket behind the set and plugged it in. The sound came on, very loud – a posh, plummy voice talking about uniforms and horses.

'There they are!' cried Mrs Cornelius. Jerry came round to inspect the picture.

'Not bad,' said her son. 'That'll do, eh, Cath?'

'That's lovely.' Catherine stood behind the settee and watched the Horse Guards.

'Well!' Sammy was aggrieved. ''Ow is it?'

Jerry leaned out of the window again. Immediately there was

another chorus of catcalls from the street. 'That's great, Sam. Leave it like that.'

'I'll do me best. It's stuck in the bloody chimney at the moment.'

Jerry gave his attention to the kids below. 'Ignorant little bleeders! Piss off!'

Catherine laughed. 'Don't pander to them, Jerry.'

Jerry seemed pleased with his sally. He swaggered over to the sideboard and selected a brazil nut. 'When's the actual Coronation?'

'Should be on shortly.' Catherine winked at him. 'Did you only come over for that? Mum's been worrying.'

'I didn't know about it till I arrived,' he said. 'Did I?' He leaned on the sideboard, one hand in the slit pocket of his drainpipes.

'What you been doing?' she asked him. She liked his clothes. She liked to see him feeling confident. Most of his spots had cleared up and he looked, in his sullen, dark way, quite handsome.

'This an' that,' he said. He picked a tooth with a fingernail. 'You?'

'Much the same.'

For the first time, he looked her up and down. She was wearing her pink sweater and the full, blue ballerina skirt which reached down to just below her calves. 'You're looking your usual sexy self.' He grinned. He returned her wink.

'There she is!' Mrs Cornelius hugged herself, swaying on the settee, just as Sammy, covered in dust, returned from the roof. 'Oo! Look, Sammy! There's the coach!'

'That's not 'er,' said Sammy, 'is it?' He wiped his face and arms with a cloth from his pocket. 'Nah! That's not the State Coach!'

'Then why's she wavin'?'

Sammy's interest in the screen was technical. ''Orizontal 'old's a bit dodgy.' He moved to adjust it. 'There. Any better?'

The grey, poorly defined picture warped vividly for a moment and then was steady again.

'Didn't know it was snowing up West,' said Jerry in a deadpan voice. Catherine dug him in the ribs. She enjoyed her brother's dry wit.

Sammy sat himself beside Mrs C. 'That's not *snow*,' he said. 'It's the screen.'

'Oh,' said Jerry.

She felt his hand on her bottom. He gave both cheeks a squeeze. With her long fingernails she pinched his leg.

'Stop fidgeting, you two,' said their mum. 'If Frank don't 'urry up, 'e'll miss it.'

Catherine trod on Jerry's foot. In retaliation he goosed her. She gasped.

'Sit *dahn*!' said Mrs Cornelius. 'Cor blimey! You're as bad as you ever was!' There were pictures, now, from inside Westminster Abbey. Mrs Cornelius moaned with joy. A choir was singing. Men and women in heavy, ermine-trimmed robes stood stoically about.

'They ought to start a roof fund,' said Jerry. 'It's snowing inside, too.'

'Bloody shut up!' said his mother.

Giving Catherine one last squeeze Jerry swaggered round the settee and slumped into the chair, picking up his glass of flat beer. 'You seen one coronation you seen 'em all,' he said. His knowing look disturbed Catherine. She followed him, sitting on the arm of the chair, leaning her hip against his padded shoulder. They watched in dutiful silence, touching one another from time to time, exchanging exaggerated expressions of lust. It was very hard for her not to giggle.

The ceremony over, Sammy turned down the sound on the set. A woman, looking not unlike the queen, replaced the picture of the Abbey. She wore long earrings.

'D'yer fink they're real diamonds?' said Mrs Cornelius.

'Not allowed to wear 'em on telly,' Sammy told her. 'They'd glitter too much. Well, wot about a drink?' He wiped sweat from his neck with the heel of his hand. 'Eh? To celebrate. The pub'll be open.'

Jerry held tight to her elbow. It was a familiar signal. She let him reply. 'I haven't seen Cathy for quite a while. Maybe we'll follow on later.'

'Yes,' she said, 'we'd like a bit of a chat.'

'You 'aven't seen yore mum for a good long time, either,' said Mrs Cornelius. 'Where's me bag?' She found it on the floor at her feet. 'Oh, okay. I could do with a Guinness after that. Come on, Sammy.'

'See you, then, Mum,' said Jerry.

'Yer'll be dahn, then?'

'Yeah. Soon, most likely.'

'Okay.' In her damp red-and-blue print dress she made painfully for the door. 'Cor! Me legs. Sittin' on that fing don't do 'em no good.' She resented Frank's reorganisation of the premises. He was now threatening to move her to a ground-floor flat – a basement. She guessed, as well as anybody, that he had designs on this place.

'See ya,' said Sammy, getting into the jacket of his best black suit. He was wearing a Union Jack in the buttonhole. He waved at them. The door closed. Catherine listened as they went downstairs. Her brother stroked her knee.

'Shall we go into my room?' she suggested.

'Why not?' He stood up and walked ahead of her, opening the door on the left of the new sideboard. 'Well, it's nice to see you haven't changed your bit much.'

'I like to keep it familiar. I didn't half tear Mum off a strip when she said she'd told Frank he could decorate in here.' She closed the door of her room, locking it behind her. He put his hands on her narrow waist, squeezing her as he looked her over. 'I'm so glad to see you, Jerry.' She kissed his nose.

The room had the old aspidistra in it. The dark green leaves obscured much of the light from the small window, but they helped to produce the atmosphere she liked. There were heavy, old-fashioned red velvet curtains, too, and she had covered her bed with a blue velvet canopy, and put red velvet on the top of her tallboy and dressing table. There were big Turkish cushions on the bed and Afghan carpets on the floor, Japanese, Chinese and Indian prints on the dark walls. 'A proper little scene of oriental opulence.' Jerry let go of her waist. 'It never dates, though, does it?'

'It never will,' she said.

'I heard you were living with some bloke over in Hampstead. An actor or something. Well known.'

'That's over.'

He took a Japanese book from the shelf and began to flip through it. 'What happened there, then?'

'Oh, you know.' She stretched her body on the bed, her back supported by the big pillows. 'He had another girlfriend, as well as his wife. He couldn't keep it up, poor bugger, without something snapping. I got out before he turned on me.' She leaned to light a scented candle.

'Didn't he mind?' Jerry picked up two of her coloured bottles and held them to the candlelight. He was disappointed to find them empty.

'What do you think? Anyway, I don't care.' She was eager to tell him her more recent news. There was nobody else she was able to tell.

'Was he Greek?'

'The actor? As a matter of fact,' she admitted, 'he was. My fifth, I think. I'm running out of them.'

'What are you doing now, then?' Jerry finished his inspection and sat down beside her at last. He smiled affectionately. 'Eh?' He remained a little distant. Perhaps he was shy.

She fiddled with her wristwatch. 'Something a bit naughty, I suppose.' The raspberry scent of the candle filled her nostrils.

Not unselfconsciously Jerry hugged her. 'Let's hear it, Cath. You're dying to tell me.'

'It's embarrassing.' She wanted him to coax her.

'Now I'm really interested.' He licked her ear. 'Is it a bloke? Or a lady?'

'Well, a bloke, mainly.' Absently, she licked him back.

'Up to your three-card tricks, are you? Ho, ho…' He squeezed her nipple through her bra.

'Not exactly.' She stroked his neck. 'We could put a record on.' She indicated her new Dansette record player.

'Who is he?' He squeezed her other nipple. 'Is he rich and famous, too?'

'He's a Member of Parliament.' She blushed. She was pleased with herself.

'Conservative?' His hand massaged her groin through her skirt.

'Absolutely.' She shifted her position.

'Ho, ho, ho,' said Jerry again. Carefully he removed his drape jacket, hanging it over the chair next to her bed. 'It's a change from Greeks, anyway.'

'His grandparents were Spanish.' She was almost defensive. 'Jewish probably.'

'Where did you meet him?'

'At his office. I was doing temporary typing for a while, when I last got home.'

'And he asked you round to his place to do some extra confidential work.'

'You are corny!' She kissed him. 'He's got this flat. You know, not his home. It's a pied-à-terre.'

'Or screwing gaff, as it's called in Frank's circles.' Jerry made himself more comfortable. 'Go on.'

'He's a right little creep, really,' she said, 'but I think that's part of the appeal. Know what I mean?'

'Not really. I'm a romantic.' He licked her wrist. 'Tasty.'

'I'm not going to tell you, if you make a joke of it.'

'Sorry.' He put his hand under her skirt and ran a finger over her nyloned knee. She moved closer to him.

'It's not a lot to do with sex,' she went on. 'At least, not for me. It might be for him. I can't tell.'

'What's he doing, then? Watching? Making you watch?'

'No…' She couldn't tell him. Instead she turned so that she was lying face down on the bed with one eye still on her brother. Her body felt heavy and her voice was slurred and muffled. 'Have a look for yourself.'

She felt him lift her skirt. He pulled down her panties. He said, 'Blimey,' as he touched the marks on her bottom. 'Are you like that all over?'

'Those are the most recent,' she said.

'And you enjoy it?'

'I love it. And it makes me feel great the next day. I've never felt better.'

'Blimey. Are those his initials?'

'Mm.'

'Bloody hell, Cathy. Are you sure you know what you're doing?'

'Not really. I don't care.'

'He could be a maniac.'

'No. I could easily handle him if I wanted to. That's what I mean about his appeal. He's not very strong.'

'Strong enough. What's he use? A razor?'

'He's got this special little gold knife. It doesn't hurt much.' She felt his lips on her bottom. 'It's all right, Jerry. I thought you'd – well, you know. I didn't mean to worry, you.' She looked up. He was pale. 'You're a man of the world, aren't you? Done and seen everything?'

'It's a bit hard to take, Cath. You are my sister, after all.'

She couldn't stop the laughter. 'Oh, Jerry. You sound so pompous. You'll make me feel guilty. I thought you'd like it.'

'Like it? How d'you mean?'

'I thought you might like to have a go yourself.'

'Not a chance!' He pulled her skirt back.

'No, I don't mean with a knife, Jerry. Just the whip. I'm supposed to. He won't mind that. I bought one from that second-hand shop – you know, with the hunting gear in it – up Pembridge Road. It's a riding crop. They're the best ones to use.'

He pushed the hair away from her ears and tickled her under the jaw. His initial shock had passed. His eyes were hot. 'You know me, I'm game for anything you want to do, Cathy.' He sucked his lower lip. 'So, if this is what you feel like, I don't mind having a – bash...' His voice tailed off. 'Hurting you, though...'

'It's lovely.' She put her hand on his heart. 'You're the only man I'll ever really trust, Jerry. I love you. Are you all right now?'

'Sure.' He glanced about him. 'Where's this whip, then?'

'Under the bed.' She wriggled over to the edge and felt for where she had lodged the riding crop between the mattress and the frame. 'Here it is.' She put it into his hands.

'You're corrupting me, young woman.' He swished the whip through the air.

'You don't have to.' She became confused. 'I'll understand. I don't want to spoil anything.'

'You couldn't. We're too close. We're almost the same person. I'll tell you what, though.' He grinned. 'Will you do it to me, after I've done it to you?' He always wanted to share her experiences, if he could.

'All right,' she said. 'You'll love it. I know you will.'

Jerry began to strip off his waistcoat. He unlaced his heavy crêpe-soled shoes. He drew off his bright orange ankle socks. Finally he removed his shirt and his narrow trousers and hung them with his jacket on the chair. He stood on the cream, red and green Afghan rug in his Y-fronts and his identity chain, his pale, skinny body tensed, the crop held uncertainly in his hand. 'D'you want to get undressed, too?'

'Okay.' She threw her clothes down on the floor.

'You have got a lovely body, Cath.' He fondled her. 'All right. Where do you want 'em and how many?'

'Just do three on my bum. Really, you shouldn't ask me – you should *tell* me. Warn me first, though.' She prepared herself for ecstasy.

His first stroke struck her at the base of the spine and she yelled. His second hit her just above the knees and she shouted 'Ouch' and began to turn over. But before she could stop him, he had sworn and struck again, this time landing squarely on her bottom.

'I was a bit off target,' he said. 'Was that all right?'

She did her best to sound pleased. 'Oh, yes. It was beautiful.'

'You need to practise,' he said. 'I didn't realise. That isn't half a horrible welt on your legs – and I think that's a bruise on your back. It is okay, then, is it?'

'Yes. Really.' She glanced up at him. He was scratching his balls with the end of the riding crop, scratching his head with his free hand.

'And that's it, then is it?' He frowned. 'I could see how you could get into it.' He reached a decision. 'Right! Now you do it to me. Let's see what this is all about, shall we?'

Resignedly, she took the whip. She straightened her wounded back as he removed his pants and lay down on the bed. 'I'm ready,' he said encouragingly. His poor little white bottom wriggled as he made himself comfortable. 'Give it all you've got!'

'Are you sure you want me to?' She had never whipped anyone herself, not in earnest. Somehow it went against the grain; but she did want him to feel something of what she felt, and this was the only way.

'If you like it, Cath, I'll like it, won't I? You ought to know that by now.'

'Maybe we should leave it until later.'

'No. Come on.' His voice tried to reassure her. 'Beat me! Beat me!'

She lifted the riding crop high in the air but somehow, as it descended, it lost impetus and the stroke when it connected with his flesh was feeble. She followed that one with two more, equally feeble. She felt miserable. She dropped the whip.

'Well,' he said when she had finished, 'I suppose you have to be in the mood, really.' He sat up, rubbing his backside, fondling his cock. 'Yeah. I can see what it's all about. Yeah.'

'You didn't enjoy it, did you?' She was close to tears. 'I'm sorry. Maybe we're too close, you know. Too friendly.'

'We couldn't be much closer. Let's give it another try later.' He looked at her hesitantly.

'What?' she said.

His expression became appealing. His cock was erect. He seemed bashful. 'What about a quick wank to be going on with?' he suggested.

She winced as she knelt before him.

15. In which Una Persson confronts the final decay of capitalism

Frank Cornelius was changing when Una Persson left the vestry and entered the dressing room, tracing him by means of the tinny tune issuing from his transistor. She watched him as he rapidly zipped his trousers.

'I enjoyed the sermon,' she said. 'You've found your vocation at last.'

'I didn't know you were about.' He did up his cufflinks. 'They said you were in some Poland or other. No wonder it's all breaking up.'

'It's the Conjunction of the Million Spheres,' she said.

He rubbed his blue chin. 'Don't be funny. There's a time and a place for mysticism.'

'Really I was looking for Jerry.'

'Do you think he came to listen to the sermon, too?'

'No, but my information was that you were working together.'

'Forget it!' He began, lovingly, to knot his tie, peering into the mirror of his locker. 'What are you after, Mrs Persson?'

'I'm a journalist. I'm on a job. I was supposed to cover the witchcraft stuff. You ought to know something about that. You performed the exorcism. Did you also take part in the rites?'

'Has Miss Brunner been talking to you?'

'Now she *is* a more likely candidate. Have you got her address?'

'It shouldn't take one witch long to find another.' He fingered the edges of his blazer.

'What about your sister?'

'Me and my sister don't get on. Anyway, she isn't about, these days. I don't think she exists any more. Jerry sent her to sleep, don't you remember?'

'No?' She was curious.

'Well, give the disc another spin. It might all come back to you.'

'Is this really all you do, nowadays?'

'Yeah. And I open bazaars, fêtes, sports days. I do weddings, christenings, funerals, exorcisms.'

'It's the exorcisms take up the most time, I suppose.'

'These days, yes. We live in a very superstitious age, Mrs Persson. Why try to swim against the tide?'

'You don't have to stay here, any more than I do.'

'Then why are you here, if you don't like it?'

'I'm trying to help.'

'So am I.' He smirked, smoothing back his hair. 'You're a bit short of charity, aren't you, Mrs Persson? I don't sit in judgement on people. That's the difference between us.'

'You can't afford to, can you?'

'You sound tired.' He rounded on her.

'So do you, Frank.'

'Do me a favour!' He put away his vestments. 'I've never been fitter.'

'Where do you think I might find Jerry?'

'Try the hospitals. Or the loony bins. He wouldn't let me treat him. I should think he's in one of his comas by now.'

'Copping out again.'

'See what I mean about judging people?'

'You could be right.' She drew her S&W from her pocket. 'I'll do a bit of self-analysis tonight. In the meantime, it won't stop me executing you, Frank.'

'You can't kill me. They can't kill any of us.'

'Effectively, I can kill you. I can take you out of all this. You might go somewhere nasty.'

'Jerry's staying at our mum's. Blenheim Crescent. Know where it is? He's resting.'

'In London.'

He contemplated her revolver. 'He knows I can't touch him there. It's a sort of sanctuary for us.'

'And Catherine?'

'Probably there with him. They always get together when they can.' He sounded petulant, resentful. 'What are you trying on, Mrs Persson? Still hoping to find a world you can change? You've no chance here. Or is it just the Truth you're after?'

'It hasn't occurred to you that all this was created by my manipulation of events?'

'Don't kid yourself!' He was amused. 'I shouldn't have thought it would suit you.'

'Things have to go through stages,' she said.

'And they never work out the way you expect.'

She put the gun away.

He cackled. He was enlightened. 'You're calling them all in, aren't you? You're worried. You think we *might* have fucked things up. Why?'

'Can you always remember everything you've done?'

'Of course not. But I don't feel guilty... No – of course not...'

'Can you remember now?'

'Yes.' He became alarmed.

'Work it out, then. I can remember, too. Almost everything. Clearly. Is that normal?'

He sniffed, playing with his tie. 'Jesus Christ!'

'I think there's time to get clear before the disintegration really hits,' she told him. 'You can have that information for nothing, though you deserve whatever happens to you. You've seen what *can* happen, haven't you? To people like you and me.'

'All right! That'll do.' He wiped his mouth.

She headed back through the arch. 'If I don't see you again...'

'You're just trying to fuck things up for me here, aren't you?'

'I wouldn't do that. I'm not interested in individuals one way or another. Maybe that's my trouble. You ought to know that, at least, by now.'

'Bloody puritanical bitch!'

She entered the cold air of the churchyard. She buttoned up her coat. The last of the congregation were getting into their cars. Those who had come on foot were plodding up the asphalted road towards the village. Una caught a whiff of charred flesh. She avoided a second sight of the stake and the corpse. The afternoon light was already fading. The sky was red behind the hill on which the village stood. A dog barked as its owner unlocked the door of his car. 'Good boy. Good boy.' An engine started. 'See you tomorrow, Harry.' Someone got on a bicycle, saluting a limousine. 'Bright and early, sir.'

Una could never get used to the alienating sights and sounds of the rural Home Counties. She controlled her fear, making for her helicopter. At least she had the information she was looking for. The sun sank. Getting into the chopper she looked back at the church. Candles were flickering in two of the windows. She thought she heard Frank chanting. She was pleased. At least he was more frightened than she was. The same could be said for the whole congregation. She strapped herself into her seat and started the rotors, lifting towards the first stars and the comfort of the darkness, of hatred divorced from its object. She flew over hard fields and stiff little towns, over mean rivers and petty hillocks and the pathetic remains of forests. All that was really left of the forest, she thought, was the stake and the black corpse hanging from it, for the inhabitants of this world seemed to have a profound will towards preserving only the worst aspects of their way of life and banishing the best. Was there any point at all to her trying to save them from their inhuman destiny?

She pulled herself together. Frank had been right. She was tired and, because of that, she was getting the usual delusions of grandeur. It was lack of sleep which destroyed many a promising revolution. She recalled the faces of all those many friends who had failed. She saw their red-rimmed eyes, the lines: the intense stares of those denied the security of their dreams. And it was their efforts to find those dreams, to create them from the objective world, that brought doom to their endeavours and terror to millions. But was it possible, any longer, to distinguish between the dream and the reality? She had seen so many futures, so many ruins.

She yawned. The sooner she got to sleep herself, the better.

She would not bother to visit Blenheim Crescent tonight but would leave it until the morning, when she could cope with the Cornelius family, particularly the mother, who would almost certainly deny that her children were at home.

It would not be the first time Mrs Cornelius would try, in her blind mistrust of reason, to stem the tide of history.

16. In which Miss Catherine Cornelius finds Fresh Romance

Jerry was laughing at his little mate Shakey Mo Collier. 'It's a complicated number, all right. Four bloody chords, Mo!' They leaned in the shadows of the alcove at the back of the stage, trying through a small practice amplifier at their feet to get their guitars in tune. The alcove was of grimy, bare brick. Catherine thought the whole back of the club was more like a disused railway tunnel than anything else.

Catherine was confused and self-conscious, feeling like an interloper as, around her, young men in Italian suits humped electrical gear about, apparently at random, and exchanged mysterious jokes.

There were four groups playing tonight, Jerry had told her, and his group, the Blues Ensemble, was on third. They would go on stage at about midnight. It was now eight o'clock. Only Jerry and Mo had so far turned up. The drummer and the bass guitarist were coming together in the drummer's dad's van. Jerry was friends with The Moochers who were top of the bill and they had agreed to lend the Ensemble their amplifiers because they were going on last to play their second set which, if they were in good form, wouldn't finish until about four.

Two men, middle-aged and heavily built, also wearing Italian suits, came out of the darkness at the side of the stage. By their distinctive, menacing swaggers, Catherine guessed that they must be coppers. Her mouth went dry as she saw one of them put a hand on Jerry's shoulder and whisper in his ear. She was surprised that Jerry didn't go with them. Instead he stayed where he was and nodded seriously. Their mission finished, the two men sauntered back the way they had come.

'Who was that?' she said.

'Manager,' Jerry told her. 'They want us to do a longer set, to spin it out a bit. The Yellow Dogs can't make it.' He shrugged. 'There's an extra fiver in it.'

'That's not bad,' said Mo Collier. 'Over a quid each. That's about six quid for everybody. Blimey!' He was impressed.

'If we get paid,' said Jerry.

'They're all right here.' Mo was confident. 'They're straight. Johnny said so.' Johnny Gunn had fixed up the gig for them. He liked to call himself their manager and they paid him ten per cent of every gig he arranged. This was their first in Central London. Mo paused. 'Have we got enough material rehearsed?'

'We'll just jam the standards a bit longer,' Jerry said. 'Like everybody else.'

'Oh, good.' Mo preferred jamming. He began to play the chords of 'Bo Diddley'. He and Jerry were fanatical Chuck Berry and Bo Diddley fans.

Catherine felt cold and it seemed to her that grease was settling on her bare arms. She was wearing a cotton jumper and slacks. She wished that she had brought her chunky sweater.

'You bored, Cath?' Jerry asked.

'Oh, no. It's very interesting.'

'You could go through to the bar and get a coffee if you wanted to,' said Mo. 'They'll be open now.' Unplugging the lead of his guitar he walked to the side of the stage and pushed back the filthy curtain to look through into the hall. 'Yeah. It's open.'

'I think I will, then. Does anyone else want one?'

'No, thanks.' Jerry pulled a bottle from his pocket. It contained Coca-Cola mixed with whisky (the club had no liquor licence). 'This'll do me. Did you manage to get the other stuff, Mo?'

'Naturally!' Mo drew a manila envelope out of the top of his pullover. 'I got twenty.'

'Twenty what?' asked Catherine.

'Purple hearts. They're lovely.' Mo smacked his lips.

Catherine walked to the curtains, peering nervously through. There were about fifty people scattered about the hall. Nobody was dancing to the record playing through the loudspeakers. The sound was so distorted it was impossible to tell what the record was. As she went down the steps at the side of the stage everyone looked at her. She thought they must be wondering what she was doing here and she felt a bit shaky as she crossed to the far side of the hall to the little bar selling espresso coffee, Wall's hot-dogs, hamburgers and Coca-Cola. The hall was painted a bright yellow all over. On the walls were pictures of various jazz musicians; until recently, this had been a modern jazz club.

'White coffee, please,' she said to the girl at the counter. The girl had dyed red hair and heavy, fantastic make-up. She looked worn out. She pulled the handle of her machine, holding the Pyrex cup under it. She put the cup in a Pyrex saucer. 'Shilling, love.'

'Cor!' said Catherine, taking the money from the purse in her left hand. 'And it's half foam!'

'Don't tell *me* about it.' The girl was friendly. 'You with one of the groups?'

'My brother's the Blues Ensemble.'

'Good, are they?'

'Not bad.'

'You heard The Moochers?'

'Not live. I saw them that time on TV.'

'They're really too much. Really groovy, you know. Fabulous!' The girl became confiding, leaning on the bar. It was the first time that Catherine had heard this sort of slang used naturally, without a hint of irony or embarrassment. 'Oh, good,' she said.

'D'you know any of them?' the girl wanted to know. 'D'you know Paul?'

'Is he the tall one?'

'Yeah! All the scrubbers hang around him.'

'I've met him once. I've only just come back to London, you see.'

'Where've you been?'

'Carlisle. Liverpool.'

'Liverpool! That's fantastic. The Cavern an' that?'

Catherine began to feel ashamed that she hadn't visited the Cavern, seen The Beatles or Billy J. Kramer or Gerry & the Pacemakers. 'I was just working there,' she said. 'I didn't get out much in the evenings.' Gerard had been jealous of her going out on her own and he hated popular music. 'Oh, I've been there a few times.'

'That's my ambition,' the girl said, 'to go to Liverpool. But I suppose it's not the same now.'

'Not really,' agreed Catherine. That, at least, was bound to be true. 'Well...' She picked up her coffee cup and began the long walk back to the stage. 'See you, then.'

'See you.' There was admiration in the girl's voice. Catherine hadn't realised quite how much respect one got from being associated with beat groups. She grinned to herself, no longer bothered by the stares, as she pushed her way through the curtain.

Jerry and Mo had disappeared. She felt abandoned. A thickset young man went past. 'Looking for Jerry? 'E's in the dressing room.' He pointed over his shoulder with his thumb. Jerry's group hadn't merited the dressing room which was technically reserved for the main attraction. She approached the dark door in the wall and opened it. The lights were brighter in here. The room was roughly eight feet long by five feet wide. There were about ten people in it, including two girls in short plastic skirts and waistcoats who were made up like the girl at the bar. Catherine couldn't help thinking how much like young prostitutes they looked. Were these 'scrubbers'? Jerry was leaning against a tiled fireplace. The dressing room had long ago been lived in, it seemed. There were fragments of rotting carpet on the floor and two steel-framed chairs with torn plastic seats. As Catherine entered, one of the girls sat down, glancing curiously at her. Neither of the girls was speaking to anyone and yet they both seemed to take a keen interest in what the men were saying. Their language was as strange as the girl's at the bar.

'I dunno how he kept that riff going so long.'

'Put Black Diamonds on and see if they're any better.'

'Roy put them on his acoustic and pulled the whole bloody belly off!' They were laughing, enthusiastic, friendly with each other. Catherine thought she had never seen her brother looking more cheerful. This atmosphere seemed to bring out all that was best and most idealistic in him. 'Or it could be the pick-ups,' Jerry was saying. 'You could move them apart a bit more, couldn't you?'

'Not on my guitar, mate. What d'you think it is, a fucking Fender?'

Jerry passed his bottle round. With some dismay, she saw him put a couple of pinkish pills into his mouth. She hoped he knew what he was doing.

She thought that four of the boys must be from the same group. They all had pudding-basin haircuts, Brooks Brothers shirts with high, button-down collars and thin ties, cream-coloured jackets with thin green and blue stripes on them, and maroon trousers. Everyone wore scuffed black high-heeled winkle-pickers. She noticed, in the corner, a very tall one wearing a short leather jacket and jeans. He looked more like a beatnik than the rest. His features while youthful were gaunt. He had his ear to his cherry-coloured guitar and kept plucking at the strings as if puzzled by something. He had a panatella sticking out of the corner of his mouth. Catherine thought he looked very romantic.

'Hello, Cath.' Jerry was merry. 'This is Brian – me old mate from school, remember? Ian. Bob. Pete.' She found it difficult to follow him, but she smiled at them all and they smiled at her. 'Nice to meet you,' she said.

'What a little darlin'!' said Brian appreciatively. He had a round, plump, cheeky face. 'How'd you fancy a big R-and-B star, Cathy?' Everyone laughed.

'The biggest he's ever been is two all-nighters in a row at the Flamingo,' said one of the boys in a cream jacket. 'Anyway, you don't know what R and B is. All you're interested in is bloody Muddy Waters and Leadbelly.'

Brian grinned, to reveal a missing middle tooth. 'Well, I've gone commercial, 'aven't I?'

'If three quid a week's commercial,' said another, 'we're really in the big time now. I'm gonna get me a *monster* Cadillac car an' drive off down Route 66, goin' nowhere!' His attempt at an

American accent seemed neither incongruous nor embarrassing, probably because of his enthusiasm.

'You'll be lucky.' Brian accepted the bottle. 'You told me you were behind with the payments on your Transit.'

Catherine began to enjoy the feeling of comradeship in the dressing room. She was reminded of old films she had seen, of soldiers or airmen in the mess, before they went on a mission. When Brian handed her the bottle, now almost empty, she took a swig. It was nice to be around people who were keen on what they were doing, who didn't seem to feel a need to justify it or rationalise it. She passed the bottle on and sat down next to the silent girl. 'Hello. Is your boyfriend in one of the groups?'

The girl seemed grateful for being spoken to. 'No. Me and Yvonne come from Haringey. We go to all the London gigs. We know Roy.'

'He's in The Moochers?'

'Yeah.'

'He's a friend of yours, is he?'

'Sort of, yeah.'

Somebody blundered past Catherine and fell against Yvonne. 'Sorry, darling.' He gave her breasts a squeeze. 'Co-ar!' He continued on his way, to speak to the gaunt guitarist in the corner. Catherine was surprised by the way Yvonne reacted. She looked at her friend as if she had scored a point, then turned. 'Do you mind?' she said.

'Not with you, darling. Any time,' said the boy absently, continuing to talk to the guitarist. 'What about it, then?'

'I wanted to start with "Mojo". You know, a good raver.'

'Yeah, but this way we build up to it.'

'I'd rather start with something easy.'

'Come off it, Paul. What's hard about "Memphis bloody Tennessee"?'

'Nothin'. But I like getting up on "Mojo". You know?'

'Okay, then.' As he stumbled back, he chucked Yvonne under the chin, 'See you later, darlin',' but he was looking speculatively at Catherine as he spoke.

The room had become very hot and the air was stale. Catherine could smell cigarette smoke, sweat and mould. She felt a bit dizzy. Nonetheless she had begun to enjoy herself.

The heavily built manager looked into the room. His voice was aggressive, offhand. 'Hurry it up, lads. You're on.' He spoke to no-one in particular. It was evident that he didn't know one of the groups from another. Four of the boys separated themselves from the rest and picked up their instruments. 'See you,' said Brian to Jerry. He grinned at Catherine. 'See *you*, too, eh?'

Catherine grinned back at him.

Jerry came over. 'Want to hear them? They're not bad.'

'Do they do the same sort of stuff as you?'

'R and B? Sort of.' He took her hand. 'Come on.'

She was glad to be out of the dressing room, into the comparatively fresh air. Peculiar whines and shrieks were coming from the stage. 'We can stand at the side,' said Jerry. They could see the stage now. The four young men were adjusting their instruments round their shoulders, kicking trailing leads clear of their feet, playing a few notes. The drummer kept thumping his bass drum and leaning down to adjust it. She saw one of them nod to the drummer who nodded back and immediately began a rapid roll around all the drums and cymbals in his kit. The noise was sudden and shook the floor as the guitars began to thump and scream out a fast eight-bar blues tune. She could clearly hear the words Brian was singing into the microphone. She craned her head to see the audience. Boys and girls were swaying on their feet, clapping inexpertly to the rhythm. The whole place was now packed, darkened.

> 'Come on baby, I'll show you how to dance,
> Let your hair down, baby, give me a chance,
> To show you the way to move.'

Brian began to play the mouth organ into the microphone. Though the noise threatened to give her a headache (Jerry was apparently not affected at all) she found its vitality and attack more thrilling than anything she had ever heard before.

'That's right, baby, you're learning so fast,
Gonna knock the future right back to the past.
Now show me how to move!'

Brian yelled and almost fell backwards as he struck at his guitar, possessed by a madness she could never have guessed at when he had been the cheeky, friendly little lad back in the dressing room. She felt as if she had witnessed some kind of religious transformation.

'That's right, baby, move it for me,
You got such hips, you shake 'em just for me.
Let's show 'em how to move.'

Brian was swinging his head from side to side so fast that it was a blur. 'Yeah! That's right!' he shouted. 'Oh, yeah! That's nice!'

The persistent beating of the bass, the high whining of the lead guitar, the swishing of the rhythm guitar, the rapping of the drums, produced in Catherine such a sense of joyful release that she wished now that she was in the audience, able to clap and sway with the others.

Without pausing, the group went into another number, a slower twelve-bar:

'I was driving down the highway minding my own mind,
Taking it easy and watchin' the signs,
'Cause I was goin' nowhere, I had plenty of time,
When I saw this little baby, she was jerkin' her thumb,
Hitchin' a ride, lookin' blue-eyed and dumb…'

Gradually her headache vanished. The music shuddered through her and every change was like a wave bearing her over a magical sea, and Brian's inexpert, wailing harmonica was like the cry of an exultant bird.

She stayed watching, even when Jerry returned to the dressing room, still amazed by Brian's transformation from cocky youth to authoritative high priest. It was as if she were privileged to perceive his whole being, all the secrets of a complex soul.

When they came off stage, Brian in front, they were sweating, and their eyes were blank. Brian didn't even see her as he padded to the dressing room. She had observed that particular kind of blankness only once before, in her own face, just after she had been beaten. She became alarmed.

'Aren't you going back in there for a drink?' The tall, gaunt guitarist was leaning over her. His face was as serious as ever. 'Terry's brought a bottle of rum.'

'Oh, I didn't see you there.' She smiled. 'You made me jump.'

'It's the sudden silence,' said Paul.

'Have you been watching them long?'

'No, just the last number. We do "Not Fade Away", too, but they do it better, I reckon.'

'You're the main act, aren't you?'

He nodded. 'Don't mean we're better, though, does it? We're just better-known. We're beginning to get a reputation, as they say.' He sniffed and rubbed his long nose. 'It's your brother, isn't it, who's one of the Blues Ensemble?'

'That's right. Jerry.'

'Yeah. They're not bad, either.'

'I don't really know. I haven't heard them play. I saw your group on telly that time. It didn't sound anything like this, though.'

'It wouldn't, would it? The BBC sound engineers are only happy if it's Gracie Fields or Alma Cogan. They don't know how to record an R-and-B group, so the sound always lacks power. They won't let you turn your amps right up in case it damages their equipment – and they balance out the bass until you can hardly hear it.'

'I didn't know that.'

'Yeah. If you want to hear any more, why don't you go out front and listen. It's better if you're in the middle. You get it all distorted from the side.' He smiled, tapping his ear. 'Like we do.'

'I enjoyed it, though.'

'Well, it's up to you.

'When are you on?'

'First set's about half nine, I suppose. You gonna watch?' His mouth was thin and tight, but his eyes were steady, mildly insistent. 'Eh?'

'I'd like to.'

'Good.' He picked up his guitar. 'I'll be playing for you, then.'

'Thank you.'

'Don't mention it.' For the first time his smile was open. 'And I hope you like it.'

'I'm sure I will.'

'If you do, come and have a meal with me between the sets.'

'All right. If I do.'

'You will.' He hefted the cherry-coloured guitar like a broadsword. 'You'll like this.'

As she watched him stride back into the darkness Catherine knew why those girls were prepared to spend so many hours hanging about in the dressing room. Before long, she thought, I'll be hanging about in there with them. But she knew better than to consider imitating their style.

17. In which Captain Persson and Major Nye consider the State of the Nation

'It's cold enough for snow,' said Major Nye, rubbing his thin blue-veined hands together. As he ushered her past the guards he hummed a few bars of 'White Christmas'. His offices, bare and poorly furnished, had, now that most of Whitehall was demolished, an uninterrupted view of St James's Park and the refugee camp in the bed of the drained ornamental lake. 'It's a great shame we can't get up some sort of entertainment this year. You know how much I enjoy your songs. *"There was I, waiting at the church..."*'

'I haven't done much singing lately.'

'And a great shame it is. Perhaps we could celebrate the season together?'

'I must be on my way, I'm afraid. I came to apologise.'

'You did your best, my dear. You always do. My regard for your courage and your determination remains as high as ever, Captain Persson.' His yellowed face broke into a trained smile. 'We cannot control this, any of us. The best we can hope for is to retain our personal,' he shrugged, 'integrity.'

'You think your people will stay in power here?'

'Power?' His smile became spontaneous. He attempted to straighten his stooped, thin shoulders. 'Oh, indeed. We'll try to keep things running, you know. There isn't anyone who wants the job. Not in London, at any rate.' There was no heating in the old suite and draughts seemed to blow from a dozen directions at once. He crossed a stretch of parquet flooring to close a connecting door. He wore his battledress, his balaclava helmet and a long grey scarf wound several times about his wrinkled throat. 'All we do is look after the refugees. The naked will has triumphed.

Civilisation is destroyed and most of those who would destroy it are now gone themselves. Their disciples scarcely know why they are still fighting. Who has the will to rebuild? I feared anarchy, but this apathy is much worse. They are sitting down to die. Out there!'

He waved at the window behind him. 'English men and women – sitting down to die!'

'Too tired to dream,' said Una. 'That is why someone who will do their dreaming for them has the means to move them to action, as a voodoo man controls his zombies. What about the fighting in the West?'

'Of course there's fighting still, but it's in the nature of a ritual. You'd be hard put to find any real anger. But they won't stop for a while – it's like an unconscious spasm, I suppose. It carries on under its own impetus, like an overshot bowling ball, eh? The jack has long since been missed.' He offered Una a copper-coloured tobacco tin containing small hand-rolled cigarettes. 'Smoke?'

She shook her head.

He lit one for himself. The tobacco smoke was sweet. He puffed as he sat down on the edge of his desk. 'Take the armchair.' He motioned.

She had not intended to talk, but she was tired. She had lost most of her initiative since her two abortive attempts to bring back order.

'In the twentieth century,' said Major Nye, 'free will has come to mean pure will. The juvenile imagination triumphs and the civil service can no longer maintain the balance – a thousand busy, conscientious rabbits are no match for one confident fox. This has been a century of reaction, Captain Persson. All that has come of our hopes, our attempts to bring great justice to the world, is that robber barons have become more powerful, better able to justify their huge, crude romantic ambitions, more able to convince once-rational men and women of the reality of their ludicrous visions. Bad poets, Captain Persson – bad romantic poets. It is awful, the power they held towards the end. Bards should be blinded, so that they can never become soldiers.' He rubbed his eyes. 'I'm rambling.'

'When I was a little girl,' said Una, 'I was convinced that God was German. Every night, out of respect, I used to begin my prayers "Dear Herr God", and if I did wrong I expected the Archangel Gabriel to turn up to punish me. He would be dressed in field-grey, wearing one of those spiked helmets. He had a waxed moustache, sometimes, too.'

'And if you were good?' Major Nye put his head on one side, his expression affectionate.

'Nothing,' she said. 'To some people authority can only punish. It can never reward. Perhaps if one has the kind of temperament which responds to praise from authority or expects rewards from authority, then it has no need for free will.'

'I see.' He re-lit his cigarette. 'Such a person has no interest, then, in the nature of that authority?'

'Not really. And one who trusts no authority is in the opposite position. Irrespective of the nature of the authority, he mistrusts it, must forever be in a posture of resistance. It is, perhaps, because it is so attractive. Probably that is why I admire only revolutionaries who are powerless.'

'I should have thought the problem more complicated than that.'

'Which is why you are a civil servant and I am a political activist, or was.'

'Oh dear, oh dear.' He shook his head from side to side. 'It could be part of the reason, I'll grant you. At any rate, you've helped us considerably. Don't we constitute some kind of authority?'

'You were losing,' she said. 'Weren't you?'

'Yet if we had won...?'

'I should have been on my way. Or joined your enemies. To keep the balance.'

'Perpetually in opposition.

'It's the easier rôle to play,' she said. 'Free will is the curse of the twentieth century. I can choose to be anything: wife, mother, businesswoman, poet, politician, soldier – all of them. And if I am successful in these rôles, all of them, have I any clearer sense of my own identity? Someone else might have, but not me. I refuse to relinquish that freedom, but I have no idea what to do with it. Not really. So many options confuse a person. You had the army and then the civil service. I had unspecific revolutionary fervour – a sympathy for the underdog, a romantic admiration for wild-eyed orators, a hatred of injustice. And I could choose to be so many things – helpmeet, partisan, leader.'

'Of course, it has been hard for women…'

'It is not only women who suffer from the burden of choice. So many of us, faced with free will, experience a huge desire towards enslavement. Any creed will do. The threat of freedom forces us to fling in with any passing flag, rather than be our own men and women. I have the same yearning, Major Nye – and I am not the only person to yearn for Robin Hood, an outlaw leader. We cry out for a commander. We pine for princes. And who is the leader who betrays us worst? The one who turns around and tells us that the power is in our hands, that we must tell him and his councillors what we want. What we want! As if we know! Lobkowitz was that sort. A traitor to his people. Him and his civil service! Oh, if I could only give myself up to slavery – to a cause, to another individual, to enmesh myself so deeply that I could blame all ills, all frustrations, on a specific government, a particular sex, a class, a phenomenon.' She spoke lightly, with self-mockery. 'Once, Major Nye, I had the theatre. It was perfect.'

'And so were you,' he murmured. They had first met at the theatre where she had been playing.

'It was a shallow world,' she said, 'A world of ghosts.'

'Aha.' He turned, significantly, to look out at the shanties in the park.

'This seemed more substantial.' She spoke almost with defiance. 'I had to keep trying.'

'But you, of all people, should have known that the result was inevitable.'

'I can't accept that. Besides, efforts I have made – in the past, as it were – have had better results. And who knows what good might eventually come from this complete collapse? You mourn only the civilisation which conditioned you, Major Nye. Society does not collapse, it modifies. In a generation or two, something magnificent could come crawling from that pit over there.'

'So you remain an optimist.'

'I have seen far too much, been involved in far too many failures, to be anything else.'

He replaced the remains of his cigarette in his tin. 'I've fought in four wars, served three political parties, and I can see little hope now for the future. Barbarism triumphs. We return to the Dark Ages.'

'I've fought in a thousand wars,' she said, 'and have served many individuals and have been as depressed to witness the behaviour of those individuals in periods of enlightenment as I have been impressed by the nobility of men and women during periods of darkness. I cannot believe that temperaments are changed by conditions, only that they are modified.'

'Very well. It is the same thing if those temperaments are radically modified, Captain Persson.' He seemed impatient. 'My forefathers were soldiers, scholars, politicians, all serving their society as best they could – my descendants will be savages, serving only their own ends.'

'You're simply talking about what you fear, Major Nye, not what you know to be true.'

'I'll grant you that.' He cleared his throat. 'I'm a bit off-colour this morning. My chest was affected by the smoke.'

'This would be a good time to give them up.'

'What?' He looked down at his cigarette tin. 'Oh, no. Not these. The smoke from the furnaces. We were burning papers. Files and so on. Mainly personal dossiers. There didn't seem much point in keeping them.'

'There never was,' she said. She got up. She was anxious to part from him amiably.

'Where are you off to now?' he asked.

'I had thought of leaving altogether, but I'm curious to follow things through for a bit.' She was, in fact, wondering if there might be a convergence before the century was out. 'You never know, do you? There could be a sudden reverse. Some new development nobody could anticipate.'

'So you'll stay in the country?'

'In England? Yes.'

'You could, in fairness, leave. I stay on because it's all I know. But you…'

'Oh, it's all I know, too.'

'There are parts of America, I hear…'

'Yes. There are little pockets of "order" in many parts of the globe. But the price of enjoying them is too great for me. At this moment, anyway. Civilisation involves too much self-deception for me, too much hypocrisy – at least, the sort of civilisation I am likely to find these days. I'll continue to take my chances amongst the savages for a while longer.'

'You remain a remarkable young woman.' They shook hands.

'And you are still a virtuous old man.' She smiled at him to disguise her sadness, her sympathy.

18. In which Catherine Cornelius enjoys her Silver Days and Golden Nights

'Well,' said Mrs Cornelius amiably, giving the huge cafeteria the once-over, 'I don't know abaht this.' The place was reserved for the performers, the journalists and photographers, for management. Outside, visible through the walls of transparent glass, was the empty asphalt of a car park. Around the fringes of the cordon could be seen knots of young people in Afghan coats, embroidered jeans, feather boas, long Indian skirts, floppy felt hats, beads, buttons and glowing skin-paint; the ones who were still hoping to get tickets. The people inside the cafeteria looked much like their would-be audiences, only the materials of their patched and embroidered velvets, silks and satins tended to be richer. Here and there were journalists in Burton and Cardin suits, managers and publicists in very clean jeans and tan jackets, cafeteria staff in black and white dresses and aprons.

'Where'd they race the dogs, then?' Mrs Cornelius clutched her port and lemon.

'That's the White City, Mum. This is Wembley.'

'Oh, the football.'

'That's right.' Catherine looked down as a three-year-old boy, in a patchwork jacket and tiny jeans, pulled at the fold of her scarlet skirt. 'Stop it, you little bugger.' She bent to give him her glass of wine. 'Want a drink, then?'

'Nah!' The boy glared at her as he backed off.

Terence Allen, the manager, appeared and kissed her on the cheek. 'Hello, Cathy, love. Seen Jack?' He had on a dark denim suit.

'He's in the dressing room,' she said. 'I couldn't stand it in there. Did you know Graham's turned up?'

Terence slapped his furrowed forehead. 'That's all I need. How many with him?'

'Only five or six.'

'Five or six will do it. I hate those fucking Angels.' He glanced around him to see if he had been overheard. 'Don't worry. I'll handle them. Who invited them?'

'Dunno,' said Catherine, though she knew it could have been Jack himself, in a euphoric moment. 'Probably nobody. You know what they're like.'

'Don't worry,' he said again. 'I'll handle it.' He sped off in the wrong direction and was almost immediately tackled by two angry roadies, with long, matted dark hair, who appeared to want him to settle a dispute they were having.

'Listen, Terence,' they kept saying.

'Don't worry!' Terence's voice was cracking.

''As it started, yet?' asked her mum.

'You'll hear it when it does.' At the moment it was just Jimi Hendrix records, played at the side of the stage by Mike, who travelled with the band as a permanent DJ, doing the warm-up before the live show actually got going.

'You goin' aht there?'

'Not me,' said Catherine. 'I've heard it before. I've brought my knitting, as usual.'

'Knitting? Really?' Mrs Cornelius was pleased.

'I always take my knitting to gigs,' Catherine told her. 'It's something to do. And Jack doesn't like it if I stay at home when they're playing in London. Besides,' she waved at a passing acquaintance, 'this is a special occasion, isn't it. Biggest gig of the year.'

Terence reappeared. 'We've sold out,' he said. 'There must be sixty thousand people out there.'

'Blimey!' Mrs Cornelius was impressed as she watched him scamper towards the dressing room. 'Sixty fahsand!'

'Say twenty and you'll be closer.' Catherine accepted a drink from a tray one of the waitresses offered her. 'He always doubles it, at least, by about this time. Since it's a big gig he'll have trebled it, probably.'

Mrs Cornelius didn't listen. She preferred Terence's estimate. 'Blimey!'

There were tables scattered about the cafeteria. Catherine sat down at one and pulled a chair towards it, for her mother. 'That's better,' said Mrs Cornelius. She peered contentedly around at the warpainted faces, the brocaded beauties, the worn-out boys in Texan boots and studded leather toreador pants whose pale chests were littered with silver crosses, swastikas, ankhs and medallions, whose flimsy shirts seemed fixed to their bodies only by the sweat of their backs and armpits, at the sharp-featured, gloomy girls whose eyes would become suddenly eager when they saw someone they recognised, at the fat teenagers in mou-mous who held babies in their arms and chatted good-naturedly to old friends with big belts and wistful smiles and long, lank, hennaed hair, who handed on joints or tiny containers made of silver foil. There was an enormous amount of movement, of people leaving tables, sitting briefly at tables, striding slowly about, while managers and roadies raced through the throngs. 'Have you seen Dave?' 'Have you seen Stoatsy?' 'Have you seen that bitch Beryl?' 'What's going on, then?' Nobody paid attention to them; they might have been noisy, playful dogs. Terence went by again, like the White Rabbit. 'There's going to be trouble. I know there's going to be trouble.' He vanished up a flight of stairs.

''Ullo, Cathy. Long time no see.' A familiar hand reached under her hair and fondled her neck. Long fingers pushed a joint between her lips, a head appeared to kiss her on the nose, dark drugged eyes regarded her from the depths of an almost fleshless skull. 'How are you love?' It was Zonk. She had been his chick for a couple of months before he had gone off to Wales on his own, to live on a farm, to get his head together.

'Oh, Zonk! I thought you were in the country!'

''Ad to come up for this, didn't I? Social event of the year.'

'This is my mum.'

He bowed. The action caused him to stumble and almost fall into Mrs Cornelius's lap. His body was even thinner than ever. He wore a green velvet waistcoat and muddy Levis, patched on the knees and seat. His arms were tattooed, with War on one arm and Peace on the other; they were as muscular as ever and hard as they gripped her round the shoulders, more for support than in affection.

'This is Zonk,' she said to her mother.

'Pleased ter meet yer.' Mrs Cornelius smiled up at the swaying newcomer.

'Yeah,' said Zonk. He nodded profoundly several times. 'Enjoying yourself, then?'

'Oo, yes!'

'That's great.' He fell towards her again, kissing and patting her jowls.

'This is so sudden,' giggled Mrs C. 'Are all your friends like this, Caff?'

'The best of them,' she said.

Steadying himself by means of the back of Mrs Cornelius's chair Zonk scratched himself with a blue fingernail. 'Seen Jack?' he said after a moment's thought.

'Probably in the dressing room,' said Cathy.

'You his old lady now, eh?'

'Well,' she said, 'I was before, wasn't I?'

'Oh, sure. Sure. No, that's good. Where is he?'

'Dressing room,' she said.

'Yeah. Right.' Zonk took a deep breath and shoved himself off into the crowd. 'See you, Cathy. Take care.'

'See you, Zonk.'

''E seemed a nice enough bloke,' said Mrs Cornelius. 'Sailor was 'e?'

Catherine took her knitting from her big denim bag.

'Wot you smokin'?' asked her mother.

'Oh.' She had been automatically drawing on the joint.

'Reefer, is it?'

'It's only…'

'Give us a puff,' said Mrs Cornelius adventurously.

Catherine handed the joint to her mother who drew on it deeply and coughed her heart out. 'Rough bloody stuff, innit?'

Catherine began to knit.

'Don't feel any different,' said Mrs Cornelius. ''Ere, ain't that the butcher's boy? 'Enry.' She pointed. 'You know, Caff. 'Is eldest.'

Catherine looked up. Her mother was indicating a group of Hell's Angels who were swaggering sheepishly towards the bar, their helmets and goggles under their arms. ''Enry! 'Enry! Yoo-oo!' One of the Angels turned, grinning with recognition. He came towards them, his mates following.

'Well, well, well,' he said, 'Mrs C! 'Ow you doin' then, love?'

'Pretty good. Ya know Caffy, doncher?'

'What 'o, Caff. Wouldn't a recognised ya in that gear.'

Catherine laughed. 'I wouldn't have recognised you in that gear, either, Henry. How long have you been with the Angels?'

'All me life,' he said seriously. 'We come up the M4 from Bristol this mornin'. Give us a drag, then, Mrs C.' He removed the joint from Mrs Cornelius's fingers. 'What is the older generation comin' to, eh? This is me brothers – Rotty, Bern, Carno and Swish. Old friends o' mine,' he explained to the other Angels, handing Swish the joint. 'Watch it. It's a bit manky. Well, well, well.' He fell into an awkward silence, shared by his brothers. 'So…'

'Shall we get that drink, then?' said Rotty.

'Yeah. Right, then. See ya later, maybe.' He raised his gauntleted hand in a clenched fist salute and led his friends once again in the direction of the bar.

''E must 'ave a motorbike now,' said Mrs Cornelius.

'Yes,' said Catherine, reaching the end of a row.

'*Is it tomorrow – or just the end of time?*' asked the late great Jimi Hendrix over the speakers.

Catherine began a new row.

She saw Jack striding through the crowds, scowling to keep the people at bay. His method of moving was to aim straight for the spot he wanted to get to, ignoring friends and strangers alike until he had arrived. Already journalists had sighted him and were beginning to circle, while acquaintances were left gasping 'Hello, Jack' in his wake.

Jack's black hair was damp with sweat, it curled around his swarthy, sullen face. He wore a Wrangler denim shirt and yellow velvet trousers. His feet were bare. As he approached their table, his scowl began to vanish and by the time he reached Cathy he was giving her a weary smile. 'You all right, then?'

'Fine,' she said. 'It got too crowded in the dressing room.'

''Alf of London's in there,' he said. 'Wotcher, Mrs C. Finding all this a bit strange, are you?'

'It's smashing,' said Catherine's mother. 'I'm glad I said I'd come. I could stay 'ere for ever. Everybody's so nice.'

Sighing, Jack sat between them. 'You seen what it's like out there?' He indicated the hall.

'Terence says there's sixty thousand.'

Jack was amused. 'What? Fleas?'

'It's packed out,' said Catherine.

'It'd 'ave to be, to pay for all the free booze Terence is givin' away.' Jack expected his career to collapse at any moment and he resented anything he considered unnecessary expense. He already had a fortune invested in property, but he continued to be as insecure as he had always been. He was the only member of Emerald City to take any interest at all in the book-keeping.

Already some journalist had arrived. He wore a black plastic windcheater and grey flannels, with a pink open-neck shirt, and his shortish fair hair was unkempt and greasy. The journalists were always the graceless ones. 'Have you got a moment, Jack? I don't want to break into a private party. But if we could get a photo. Is this the family?'

Jack ignored him, rubbing his left eye, his hand half-covering his face, his rings flashing on his fingers.

'How does it feel to be the greatest guitarist in the world?' the journalist went on.

Jack grabbed a handful of little sausages from a passing tray and began to cram them into his mouth. Journalists always made him act as crudely as possible. It was about his only protection.

'That's what our readers have just voted you. It was overwhelming. Did you see it?'

Jack had spent most of the morning laughing about it. He licked his fingers.

'Don't bother him now,' said Catherine. 'You know he won't speak to you.'

Catherine heard the journalist mutter to his photographer, even as the flashguns went off, blinding her. 'Arrogant sod. Manners of a pig.'

'I thought Terence said there wouldn't be any press people backstage.' Jack took the paper tissues Catherine handed him and began to wipe his fingers.

'He lets them in and you let the Angels in,' said Catherine. 'That's fair.'

Jack put his tongue in his cheek and smiled, relaxed again. 'I hadn't thought of it like that.' He cupped his strong hand behind her head and drew her to him for a kiss.

'Watch the bloody knitting,' she said.

'Bugger the knitting.' He whispered in her ear. 'I got a present for you.'

'Oh, thanks, Jack.' They shared a grin.

He sat, rocking his chair on its back legs, looking out at the crowd, whistling to himself. A couple of young girls approached holding pieces of paper and Biros. Without warning, perhaps not even conscious of their presence, he leapt up and set his face back into the scowl, heading for the dressing room, body stooped as if he pushed a plough. 'See ya.' He was gone.

'Cor!' Mrs Cornelius wheezed as she hunted in her bag for a cigarette. 'What 'appened to 'im?'

'It's all the fans,' Catherine explained. 'He gets embarrassed.'

'Go on! 'E enjoys it! 'Oo wouldn't?'

'I don't think he does, Mum. The more famous you get, the less you're sure of yourself. He hardly knows his own name sometimes.'

'Too many drugs.

'Maybe.'

'You gonna marry 'im?'

'Maybe.'

She continued with her knitting. She could guess what Jack's present would be. It was something to look forward to. She wished that she wasn't quite so tired, so that she would be able to enjoy it better tonight. Still, a short line of coke would solve that one.

She watched as two security guards entered and stood staring disapprovingly around them, arms folded. They wore white caps and navy-blue uniforms, with armbands printed in red: SECURITY. She became depressed. The two men talked together for a while and then moved off in different directions.

'I'll 'ave anuvver o' them, darlin'.' Mrs Cornelius reached for a drink. The waitress paused to let her take one from a tray. 'What abaht you, Caff?'

'I'll have a glass of red,' said Catherine.

The waitress's mouth tightened.

The music which began to come over the speakers was disorganised and unpleasant. Catherine realised that it must be live. The concert had begun, probably starting with Better Off Working, who were friends of Jack's. A high voice was singing. '*Sweet paranoia, well, it's melting my brain. Can't get away from that narcotic rain. Don't let it wash me right down the drain. Girl, won't you help me get back on my train...*'

Realising that she had missed a stitch, Catherine began to unravel the line.

Terence reappeared. 'I told them they should do a soundcheck. Oh, Jesus, it's horrible.'

'They always were horrible,' said Catherine. 'It was your idea to book them. Jack said you'd regret it.'

'Jack didn't say anything to me.'

'Well, he knows them, doesn't he?' Catherine reached for her wine. She had a headache. It might be worth going to the dressing room, now that the first band and its followers would have left, to get something to make her feel better. She put her knitting away. 'Will you be all right here for a bit, Mum?'

'Don't worry abaht me, love.'

Catherine stood up, shaking off her dizziness and trying to get on top of her depression. She drew a deep breath of the incensed air. It seemed cold, suddenly.

Reaching the corridor to the dressing rooms she was stopped by a middle-aged security guard. 'What d'you want, love?'

She looked beyond him, spotting one of the roadies chatting outside the door of Jack's room. 'Bob!'

The roadie saw her there and shouted, 'It's okay.' The guard let her through.

When she got into the room there were only five or six people there, sitting in the chairs or on the floor, all rolling joints. Jack sat on a table chatting to Zonk who appeared to have fallen against the wall and let himself slip to the ground. A very young girl, with long, straight, dark red hair, a beautiful oval face, wearing a dark blue sari, a headband, and little silver chains on her wrists, ankles and throat, stood close to Jack, looking at him as he spoke. She was lovely.

Jack saw Catherine enter but finished what he was saying before greeting her. 'It's better in here now,' he said. 'Cathy, this is Marijka.'

'Hello, Marijka.' Catherine admired her body.

'Hello.' She spoke with an accent.

'She's come all the way from Amsterdam to see us,' said Jack.

'Far out.'

Marijka moved a fraction closer to Jack. She was the loveliest present Catherine had ever had.

'You really ought to start another band, you know, Zonk,' Jack was saying reasonably. 'I mean, you're off the junk now. You'll be happier working.'

'No, man. I can't stand it,' Zonk mumbled. They had been together in the first band Jack had formed and Zonk had played bass in Red Harvest before it became Emerald City, but he hadn't been able to keep it going; mostly, then, it had been downers. They had wrecked his sense of rhythm.

Terence came in. 'Get these people out of here,' he said weakly. Nobody moved. 'Has Steve turned up yet, Jack?'

'No, man.'

'Then we won't have anybody to do the mixing, "man"!' Terence sounded almost triumphant. 'And you need someone to do the mixing. You really need someone. Have you seen the state Alan's in?' Alan was their keyboard player.

'Don't panic, Terence. It'll be all right.' Jack took a swig from a bottle of wine and made to hand it to Marijka, who shook her head. He reached under his dressing table and pulled a can of lager from a big cardboard box. The floor was littered with empty cans, bottles, roaches, cigarette packets.

'And you're not in any better condition,' continued Terence.

'Oh, fuck off, Terence.'

A young man in a pink leather suit covered in silver stars came in behind Terence. 'Evenin' all,' he said. He pushed past Terence. 'Evenin', Terry.'

'Piss off, Denny,' said Terence. 'There's a good lad.'

Denny's girlish features showed mock astonishment. 'What? What? When I've brought lovely goodies for everybody?' Denny was a dealer who attended most of Emerald City's Home Counties gigs, supplying good-quality drugs at moderate prices.

'What have you got?' asked Terence.

'Some genuine Nepalese Temple Dope,' Denny told him sensuously, spreading his hands to frame his face. '*Far* out!'

'Did you get those five grams, Denny?' asked Jack.

Denny put the tip of his left forefinger against the tip of his left thumb and winked. 'Almost a hundred per cent pure. You'll love it, man.'

'How much have you got?' asked Jack. 'Dope, I mean.'

'About four ounces.'

'I'll have the lot,' said Jack reaching into his back pocket.

Denny seemed disappointed. He was a dealer who loved to deal.

'You been in England before?' Catherine asked Marijka softly.

'Oh, yes, many times,' said Marijka. Plainly she did not want to be distracted from her contemplation of Jack.

Denny was handing over the coke. Five silver paper packets wrapped in a plastic bag. Catherine reached out and took it from Jack. 'I've got a rotten headache,' she said.

'This *is* for everybody,' Jack said, adding significantly: 'Marijka would probably like some, too. Why don't you two chicks go somewhere and have a quick snort?' He tended to be mean with his drugs. He snatched the packet back from her and separated one of the silver paper envelopes, handing it to her. 'Save some for later, eh?'

'I just want a little bit for now,' she said. 'Come on, love.'

Marijka looked at Jack.

He nodded. 'You go with her. Come back later. She'll give you some coke, mm?'

'Come on.' Catherine put her hand on Marijka's exposed right shoulder. 'Haven't you got lovely skin?'

Reluctantly, Marijka let Catherine lead her from the dressing room towards the lavatories at the end of the corridor. 'It'll be nice and private in here,' said Catherine, entering a cubicle and letting the plastic seat cover down. She put the cocaine on the seat and began to take her mirror, razor blade, spoon and straw from her bag.

Marijka watched passively, as she had watched Jack, while with the razor blade Catherine began to prepare two lines for them. She made her own line about twice as long as Marijka's. 'Shall I show you how to sniff it up?' she asked kindly.

Marijka, kneeling now, on the other side of the lavatory seat, nodded.

Catherine put the big glass straw into her left nostril and sniffed up half the first line. Denny had been right about the quality. As the stuff numbed her nose she got a fantastic buzz almost immediately. It seemed to open up the back of her head and let the headache out. She sighed with pleasure. 'Oh, great.'

She snorted the remainder of the line through her other nostril. 'Too much.'

She watched tenderly as Marijka imitated her. The girl had trouble getting the line up properly, but the coke brought her to life. Suddenly she was beaming at Catherine.

'It's wonderful.'

Catherine leaned over the seat and kissed her.

19. In which, once again, Captain Persson finds herself helping the wounded

There was thick, grey smoke rising over the tops of the tall rhododendron bushes. Una noticed that the red and purple flowers were blackened around the edges, as if, on its way past, something had singed them. She could think of no explanation as to the cause of this curious effect.

She had stayed in 1973 longer than she had needed to, but still she had not managed to get to Cambodia. She rather wished now that she had checked at a Time Centre before coming on to England in 1979. She wasn't used to horses. The big sorrel colt kept tossing its head back at her as if it had not been ridden for a while. She controlled it as best she could, yanking at the reins and clapping her heels against its flanks to make it go up the hill so that she could see what had happened on the other side of the rhododendrons. The colt's hoofs slipped in the wet, loamy earth and she thought they would both fall, but eventually the horse had reached the top and she could look out over what was left of the North Devon countryside. The smells were confusing – sweet, rich forest and bitter ash. It was an odd experience to come out of that oak wood to the sudden sight of such absolute devastation.

The trees were like the black bones of charred beasts, clearly defined, like specimens on white paper; the hillsides smoked and were also black, and where there were villages or houses a little flash of colour came from a red or yellow flame still guttering on, though it had been three days since the Brigante planes had been over. She had seen the jets, of course, since then; they were easily identifiable by the red and white roses they used for insignia. They had been heading back to their Pennine bases.

What disgusted her most was that this area had possessed

absolutely no anti-aircraft cover. The crashed C-130E she had seen earlier had come down purely as a result of inexpert flying (it had never been designed as a bomber in the first place) and she had regretted the waste of the four young crewmen – all with long blond braided hair and fair moustaches, all handsome – whose bodies she had found inside. She had gained something, however. She now possessed a good Polish-made AK-47 rifle (how it had come into Brigante hands she could not guess) which, because of its lightness and lack of kick, she had always preferred to longer-range assault rifles, and this one had the added advantage of the folding metal stock. It fitted neatly into the hand-tooled scabbard strapped to her saddle. She wore her old EM-3 on her back, together with a bag of scarce .28 cartridges which went with it. The AK-47 accepted the far more easily obtained standard 7.63 ammunition.

Una could not believe that anything survived in that landscape, but she had been told that Craven would meet her here and there was nothing for it but to take a deep breath of the relatively clean air and urge the colt forward. As she rode she checked the map she held in her free hand, trying to make out which of the ruined villages was Cattleford. She went slightly to the south-east and found the remains of a major road; the horse's hoofs skidded slightly on the asphalt, but it was easier than trying to ride over the burned scrub.

She was lucky. A sign for Cattleford, the metal singed and slightly warped, was still standing. She rode into a mess of masonry which had been so badly hit that there was scarcely a piece larger than the ragged straw sombrero she wore to protect her oversensitive eyes from the sun.

'Craven?' she called.

Something rose cautiously from what must have been a cellar; it stood there, its M16 held at the ready. The figure was tall and its gaunt features were covered in soot. It wore an old flying helmet which had been painted silver and it had a cracked leather jacket covered in patches bearing cryptic but not particularly interesting designs.

She knew Craven would not recognise her. He was, in turn, only a dim memory – something that was no longer real.

He was thinner than the men she normally found attractive and she wondered if he had changed physically, if it was merely the name that was the same.

'Craven?'

He smiled, still not sure if Una were an enemy or the courier he was expecting. 'Captain Persson?'

She nodded and dismounted. The sadness in his face attracted her. He seemed to be one of the few who had not been brutalised by this ferociously petty war. A weary veteran, an experienced fighter, like herself.

'Well.' Craven removed the flying helmet to reveal a shock of thick, red hair. 'We really don't need to know about reinforcements now.'

'So I see. How many of your people left?' He reminded her of a poet she had admired in her youth – Wilde, Swinburne, someone like that.

'Two,' he said. 'Both wounded. I had to shoot two others. The bastards were dropping nerve gas towards the end. They're lucky to have it to waste. The wounded ones are down there.' Craven jerked his head back at the pit from which he had just climbed. 'Have you any medical kit? Anything?'

She reached into the pannier on the left of her saddle and drew out a basic kit. 'There's morphine in here. Not as much as there should be. I used some last night on a civilian.'

'Seems a pity to waste it.' Craven made no other comment but stepped forward to take the kit. He replaced his helmet, slung the M16 over his shoulder and slid back into the hole. Una did not follow him. She stroked the nose of the horse, glancing around at the ruins, listening to the faint murmurings from the cellar.

Craven came back very quickly. He was shaking his head. 'One had died. I don't think the other will make it, but maybe we could get together some kind of stretcher. There's planks down there which didn't get too badly burned.'

Una sighed. 'You don't want to leave him?'

Craven shook his head. His smile was crooked, a trifle dishonest. 'This is the loser division, Captain Persson. We look after one another.'

While finding the statement a bit peculiar, Una's response was sympathetic. 'We'll use the horse, then. We could make some kind of travois.'

Craven frowned, momentarily abstracted. He looked at her and he smiled again. Then he straightened his back, his eyes becoming slightly hooded, making Una wonder what private rôle he was adopting to get him through this particular crisis. He was the first person she had met for some time who attracted her, whom she wanted to know better. He seemed to be a brave man, hiding a natural dignity behind what appeared to her to be something of a posture of dignity. Perhaps he was doing it for her. She glanced at the blasted ground so that he would not see the private humour in her eyes. This was no time to feel randy.

The deep stone cellar had, as Craven had claimed, hardly been touched by the fire-bombs. Through the gloom Una made out two figures, one moving faintly and muttering, the other quite still. Craven had already found two suitable planks and was clumsily trying to lash them together with a long piece of oily rope. Una put a hand on his shoulder.

'Let's get the bloke up first.'

Craven thought this over and nodded. He propped the planks against the wall and they toppled down, narrowly missing the wounded man. This time Una grinned openly and got her arms under the body of the soldier, through whose fresh bandages blood was already beginning to seep. He had been hit mainly in the right arm and leg, probably by shrapnel. Craven's bandaging had been almost completely useless.

'Take his legs,' said Una.

Craven followed her instructions and they made their way slowly up the slope formed by earth and rubble until they could lower the man to the ground. Craven went back for the planks and watched admiringly as Una, using the rope and her canvas cape, quickly built the travois. Then she re-bandaged the wounded man and they carried him to the travois, making him as comfortable as possible. He was grateful. His morphine-numbed lips formed a few words which Craven seemed to understand. He gave the man a thumbs-up sign.

'We'll be back in no time. There's a hospital in Taunton.'

Una felt that this was not the moment to mention what had happened to Taunton.

Later Una and Captain Craven lay in the shade of a large oak tree watching the horse cropping the grass near the grave which they had dug for the soldier, who had died five or six hours after they had set off. They were relaxing, smoking a joint, fairly sure that the CLF ground troops were nowhere nearby. Craven had removed his helmet and flying jacket and was stripped to the waist.

'So the Brigantes have occupied Leeds,' he said. 'Not bad. No wonder they suddenly started concentrating on the West Country. We really didn't expect that strike. We were sitting ducks. We hoped that the war might be over. It looks as if we can't count on a settlement now. We're finished, wouldn't you say?'

'We were finished years ago,' she said. 'It's the foreign interference that's kept everything going. I thought that when the French suddenly rediscovered their old Celtic affiliations it might create a fresh spurt of trouble but so far they don't seem to be supplying the Celtic Liberation Front with anything more than normal support. You should see their newspapers. Full of anti-Anglo-Saxon propaganda.'

Craven drew deeply on the joint. 'What about the Normans, then? Where do we fit?'

Una loosened the top buttons of her fatigue jacket. 'You're beginning to talk in their terms. That's never a very good sign. How did you come to get involved?'

'It was something to do. A cop-out, you could say. I used to be a writer. This, by and large, is a much easier life.'

'You must have been a very sentimental writer, if you can say that.'

'I don't think I was. Well, not about myself, at any rate. Maybe about technology. I was very interested in technology. That, too, is the attraction of the army. I originally applied to the air force, but I'd had a breakdown and apparently they think that's a bad qualification for a flyer but a good one for the infantry.'

Una accepted the joint as he handed it to her. It was Nepalese. She had rescued almost half a pound, along with the rifle, from the crashed C-130E.

'And what did you do before you joined up, Captain Persson?'

'A lot of things. Basically I was in the entertainment business. I took war pictures. I was on the stage for a while.' Una waved one of her beautiful hands. 'Boredom is what gets me.' She was surprised to find herself adopting a posture, perhaps in response to his.

'I can't think of anything much more boring than this fucking war,' he told her. 'It's a fantasy war. Who wants to fight it?'

'People who want to fight. Where did this one start? Perhaps in Belfast. The Irish problem. Of course, there wouldn't have been any Irish problem without England, would there?'

'Don't ask me. I've never had much of an interest in politics.'

'It's always been my weakness. We find our different forms of escape.'

'You like politicians?' He was not looking at her.

'It's glamour, you know, which keeps a woman going. Perhaps it's wrong, but that the truth of it. A dreadful instinct. Stronger than any sex drive, captain.'

His mind wasn't apparently on her words, but he turned his head politely back, his eyes half-closed, his fingers (longer even than hers) stroking the faded bracken. 'Sex drive?'

'Romance. Without it I doubt if the race would have gone on so long. Not if women had had anything to do with it, anyway.'

'Romance?' He smiled slowly at her and reached out to touch her cheek.

She lay back and watched as his face came towards her. There were little scars on the pale skin; there was a piece of tobacco on the upper lip; she noted one last flicker in the eyes before they shut and his lips breathed against hers and she shut her own eyes and put her arms around him so that her fingers closed on rib cage and muscle, on his lean shoulders; and she opened her lips to his teeth and his tongue, and she felt his tired legs against her own legs and she knew that almost certainly he would not be able to fuck her and, there and then, she loved him.

It had to be the uniform, she thought.

20. In which Catherine Cornelius enjoys a personal experience of Entropy

Catherine lay in bed listening to Trevor swearing in the next room. *If he slept an hour or two longer*, she thought, *he'd be a lot better off. And so would I*. But sleepers and tranquillisers rarely had much effect on him these days. He appeared in the doorway, glaring down at where she lay under the patchwork duvet. His hair was spikey. He had a towel around his thin waist. There was blood running along his neck from a small cut.

'You've been using my razor to shave your bloody legs again. You are a fucking sloppy bitch, aren't you?' When he raved like this he tended to spit.

She felt despondent. 'I haven't shaved my legs in weeks.' She pulled back the duvet and waved her right foot at him. 'Look.'

'Oh, fuck off. Anyway, somebody has been using my razor. Who was here while I was in Holland?'

With a shrug she put her leg back under the blanket. 'About three thousand friends of yours. People you said could crash here while you were away.'

He sneered. 'How many of them did you fuck?'

She remembered Richard. 'You think I'd fuck any of your manky friends? Bloody speed freaks, covered in sores?'

He wiped his neck with the towel. 'All you do is criticise. If I'm not good enough for you, if you don't like me or my friends, why don't you get out of here? I'm pissed off with supporting you. You just lie there all day doing bugger all. How long is it since you cooked me a breakfast?'

'You said you didn't like me doing domestic stuff.'

'Yeah. Well, you don't do anything else nowadays, do you?'

She began to get up. Her body ached with tension. 'I'll cook you a breakfast.'

'There isn't anything to eat.'

'You never eat breakfast, anyway.'

'I might. Shut up, for Christ's sake! I don't need your bloody sarcasm on top of everything else. I should have been at the studios by now. It'll be another bummer, thanks to you. I can't play after one of these scenes. You know that.'

'You ought to save yourself up. What's left of you. Why don't you stop making them?'

'I don't make them, darling. If this place was run a bit better – if I didn't find my bleeding razor fucked every morning – if you kept this place even reasonably tidy – maybe I wouldn't have to lose my temper. Think of that.'

She said: 'You used to accuse me of being too house-proud. Besides, I don't give a shit about your razor or this bloody flat. I came to stay with Mary, remember? You wanted me to. I didn't want to live with you. You asked me to, after Mary got killed. Remember?'

He turned away. 'Sure. I was a sucker.'

She sank back onto the pillows. 'I set out to ruin your life. To lead you on. To make a fool of you. Because I like it.'

'You're closer than you think, darling. I should have listened to Bob. He warned me about you. Why don't you piss off?'

'All right.'

'Oh, great. Now you're going to blackmail me.'

'Make up your mind.'

'It was fine, wasn't it, when I was in the money? When I brought plenty of chicks and drugs home. But it's not so good now, is it?'

'I told you to stop bringing anything home. I told you to get out of the band. Anyone could see Bob was ripping you off. I even told you not to sign that contract, and that was while I was still *with* Bob.'

'I told you so, I told you so. Thanks for nothing.'

'Do you want me to go out and get you something for breakfast?'

'Oh, fuck off.'

He left the room and she listened to him clattering about in the kitchen. She heard him muttering. She knew he was finishing off the rest of the formal accusations. She could no longer feel sorry for him; she could no longer feel guilty. She waited for the silence that usually came after a few minutes of this. Then she prepared herself for his re-entrance.

He came back holding a mug of tea.

'Want some tea?'

'Thanks,' she said.

'I'm sorry about that.'

She sipped the tea. It wasn't worth replying. He never seemed aware of the pattern himself and she couldn't bring herself to go through the ritual, even though it would mean a quieter life. Besides, this was probably only a pause, while he got his breath.

'Well, I am sorry,' he said.

'Good.'

'Well, it's shitty to find your razor fucked.'

'Yes.'

'I'm sorry.'

'Okay.'

'You understand?'

'Oh, sure.'

'You don't sound too convinced.'

She sighed.

'Oh, you fucking bitch!' He was off again. 'You lousy, sloppy, lazy cow! You –' He advanced to the bed and stood looking down at her. 'You bitch.'

'Hadn't you better get to the studio?'

He seized her naked shoulders. He leaned forward to try to kiss her. Instinctively she turned her head away.

'You bitch.' Half-heartedly he slapped her across the cheek. She wondered why she feared physical violence so much when it was accompanied by anger. He crossed the room to the mountain of giant cushions on which his jeans and shirt lay. He began to dress, pulling beads, bangles and medallions expertly over his head and wrists, adjusting his huge belt around his hips, pulling on his stackheel denim boots, one eye on the mirror. He always seemed to dress as if he were getting ready for the stage. 'You come on all lust and rolling eyes and you're really as frigid as a bloody nun.'

'You frighten me,' she said quietly.

'Baby, you frighten *me*.' He pointed a finger at her in much the way he had once pointed it at crowds of screaming thousands. 'You conned me, Catherine. What the fuck do I get out of this one? I lay bread on you, drugs on you, chicks on you, buy up the sex stores, and whenever I get home you're too tired or you're feeling funny or – I don't know!'

'I'll leave, then.'

'Don't threaten me.

'You don't love me.'

'I do love you.'

She hadn't the courage to say what she wanted to say, that she had never loved him, only felt sorry for him when Mary had been killed when the van hit a lorry head-on.

'When will you be back?' she asked.

'Day after tomorrow. If the roads are all right we're going straight on to Newcastle. We're doing a gig for the big base up there.' Most of his work was for the armed forces these days.

'I'll get your washing done for you,' she said.

'Look, there's no need to come on like a martyr, Cathy.'

'I said I'd do it.'

He sat down at the dressing table and began to pour cocaine from a plastic sachet onto the glass surface, carefully breaking down the white crystals with a razor blade. Through a rolled-up ten-pound note he sniffed the long line into his right nostril, a single snort. He held his nostrils together, still sniffing. He drew a deep breath. 'Nothing. This must be fifty per cent speed, twenty per cent soda, twenty per cent floor-sweepings and ten per cent coke.'

'It seemed all right to me,' she said.

'Maybe it was you cut it.'

'You only gave me about a hundredth of a gram.'

He was in better spirits. The coke was working, though he didn't know it. He went to get his coat and his guitars. He came back into the room, pulling on his Afghan coat. 'I'm sorry, Cathy. You know what I'm like when I'm going off early in the morning. I haven't had a lot of sleep.'

'You don't need to be there for a couple of hours,' she said.

'Yeah, I know, but I've got to score first, haven't I? Before we go, you know.'

'You'd think the army would supply you with that as well.'

He winked. 'They do, these days, but never enough. Those soldiers can keep going on less than a gram a day, some of 'em.' There was a rumour that the army was paying entertainers entirely in drugs, but that was probably the top acts who didn't need the bread.

He glanced around the bedroom. 'Try and tidy this place up a bit before I get back.'

He disappeared.

'Have a nice day,' she said.

'Bitch.' He went out of the front door and slammed it so that everything rattled.

Catherine turned over on her stomach and began to masturbate in the hope that it might relax her.

Later, she packed her things and went to see Richard. He acted as if he had expected her, kissed her and told her to put her things in the bedroom and get undressed. At least he was positive, she thought.

Richard came in and took some of his special gear from a drawer. 'All right?'

She nodded. She was remembering her first pair of high-heeled shoes. She had been fourteen. She remembered how difficult it had been to walk in them, how self-conscious and put-upon she had felt when, lipsticked and perfumed, she had tottered down the street on the way to the party at Sammy's. She had grinned, however, when the two boys on the corner had wolf-whistled her.

Then her mum had shaken her arm, telling her not to be so bloody vain. She supposed it was a silly thing to be thinking about, really, while Richard handcuffed her hands behind her naked back and told her what a disgusting whore she was and how he was going to fuck her sore. By and large, she reflected vaguely, he wasn't much of an improvement on Trevor. Richard wasn't even working now. He hadn't picked up his guitar in six months, Trevor had said, and before that he had only done a couple of sessions in a whole year.

The time passed slowly, but at last she was massaging Vaseline into her wrists while Richard held her shoulders in his manly left arm and told her how she was the only girl he had ever loved. She stared into the gloom of the basement room and wondered why the glittering rails of the brass bedstead reminded her of home. They had never had anything like a brass bedstead. She counted the bars. There were five. The knobs on the outer two had been replaced with glaring Chinese theatrical masks Richard had been given by some girlfriend. Richard's clothes hung over the top rail; brightly patched dirty Levis and a T-shirt that said Assassinate Frodo. She realised that she liked him even less than Trevor. It was probably this sentimentality which put her off him. Sadists were only worth living with if they were consistent. Her own clothes were folded, as usual, neatly on the chair. Richard reached over her and found his valium bottle. 'There's only about a hundred mills left.' He shook four of the yellow five-milligram tablets into his hand and swallowed them down. 'I'll have to get a new script tomorrow. Remind me, will you, Cath?'

She had decided not to stay, after all. 'Yes,' she agreed.

With Richard's history of breakdowns, he had had no difficulty scoring downers from the local GP. When they had first met she had told him that valium made you speedy and untogether and only calmed you down if you didn't do many drugs (it didn't always work, even then). As it was he had been living off mandies for years. He wouldn't accept her explanation that the reason he kept falling down and dropping things was not exhaustion, as he claimed, but the effects of the tranquillisers and sleeping pills.

He'd told her that she knew shit all about it and that valium was the only thing that kept him from going over the top, that if he didn't use it he would get violent.

She put the lid back on the Vaseline jar, turned on her side and tried to get comfortable on his constricting arm. The poor sod had served his time, she thought. He had been famous at nineteen. When he was twenty-one he had already been in two expensive mental hospitals. At twenty-two he had gone to the country to get himself together, had got bored one day and gone into Torquay where he had freaked out in a pub when four policemen had been called to ask him to stop talking to the barmaid because she had to go to bed and they wanted to close the pub. The police had brought on his anxiety with a vengeance and he had fought them for over twenty minutes before they got him into the car, into the nick, and from the nick to the local loony bin, where he had been filled up with largactyl and sent, after two weeks, into the world, knowing himself to be a fully accredited manic-depressive, because that was how they had classified him. After he had stopped the drugs they had prescribed and lived through the subsequent withdrawal, he had come back to London, joined two or three bands for a few gigs, started going up under his own steam and the euphoria of working again, had become so speedy that no-one had been able to stand him for more than an hour at a time, and his best friends had told him to go back on downers for his own sake. They hadn't made a lot of difference. He used more and more every day and every day got stranger, which proved to him that his manic depression was becoming increasingly difficult to control. He had given her as an illustration of his great self-control the fact that he never used speed because it made him worse, that he never, now, dropped acid because too many bummers had tipped him into his established madness, that he never did coke because it made him paranoid, junk made him only depressed, dope made him too self-aware. His point had been that he only used the valium and mogadon for keeping himself from doing harm to himself or others.

It was familiar drug-logic. Catherine had heard similar rationales a hundred times before. Some drugs worked for you; some didn't.

She smiled. They started out such nice guys. And so innocent, most of them. She wondered about the housewives and the politicians and soldiers and businessmen whose doctors were helpfully speeding them along through life, keeping them calm, active, happy while every single decision they made was made, as she made her decisions, as Richard made them, in what was rarely better than a semi-conscious condition, whatever it felt like at the time. About the only thing that could be said for the drug culture was that a lot of the people in it at least knew what was happening to them. Her brother, who had in the mid-sixties spent most of his time seeking out new drugs to try, had referred to the 'fantasy quotient'; he believed that the world was becoming less and less rational every day, that the increased reliance on the drug and electronics industries was like Rome relying on charms and omens when she could have been sorting out her economic problems. Nonetheless, she could have done with some coke. She was going to miss it a lot. It was the sort of drug that once enjoyed you missed for the rest of your life. She thought of it as a drug of invulnerability. It was the only substitute for sex she had ever found. She began to think of going back to Trevor, if only for the coke. She didn't know anyone else, these days, who could get hold of it easily. Maybe a soldier? She dismissed the idea. It had become so expensive, coke. It made up for a lot of things. She wondered why she had bothered to see Richard again. Her instincts were shot. She had an urge to return home. To see her mother. But she couldn't face the tension she would find. Perhaps she should get away from the rock scene. It had all gone sour, anyway. Everyone was dying or falling apart.

Richard gave his familiar, peculiar lurch against her buttocks. She relaxed as best she could, hoping that this would be his last effort of the evening to get it up and that, even if he failed, he would not begin one of his inquests. They always revolved around his efforts to give her the kind of sex-life she wanted (he had never accepted her claims that it had little, really, to do with sex). He always said at some stage, 'Well, it's what you want, isn't it, you bitch?' She wondered whether it was, perhaps, what she wanted now. It didn't give her the release she had come to expect. Maybe she had to be in love. Maybe she lacked self-respect.

Richard's hands clung to her breasts as if for support while his wasted body pushed desperately against her and then slowly, somewhat apologetically, she fell asleep.

21. In which Una Persson considers the problem of personal loyalty

'We're going to have to get out of England, Una,' said Craven. They had reached the Atlantic. They stood together on the cliff looking down towards Tintagel Bay, now an abandoned coastal installation. 'The Brigantes don't usually bother to collect heads. Apparently a warrior can win a lot of esteem if he brings in ours. Are you flattered?'

She was too introspective to bother to acknowledge this poor attempt at humour. Her original plan had been to steal one of the motor boats at Tintagel and head round the coast in the hope of contacting a friendly tribe. All the boats had gone.

Even in the sunshine Tintagel had a gloomy, seedy look, in common with many other once-glamorous places like Haight-Ashbury or Prague or Bangkok. The small beach and the sea of the bay below the castle ruins were spread with every sort of litter picked over by dirty gulls. Una was anxious to be on the move and she separated from Craven, plodding along the cliff edge, holding her long coat so that it would not be snagged by the rusting barbed wire. Soon it was possible to take note of the broader sweep of the ocean; it was blue and only slightly turbulent. The sun struck the cream of the surf and was reflected towards the land. A hint of a memory. She drew her brows together, shading her eyes.

Craven rejoined her. 'I don't think Arthur will be much help.' When she ignored him he added: 'You'd like to be shot of me, wouldn't you? I'm hampering you.'

'I don't think it's you,' she said.

He was displeased with her reply. He made a petulant sound. 'I thought you knew all the angles. You gave that impression.'

'I'm afraid inertia is taking over.'

'What are you looking at?' He was slightly short-sighted.

'It could be a ship.'

'Hadn't we better get off the cliffs before they spot us?'

'They've already seen us, if those flashes are from binoculars.'

'What sort of ship?'

'Not a warship. I've seen it before somewhere.'

'Friendly?'

'Possibly not. I can't remember.'

The ship was a fore-and-aft rigged steam yacht; a schooner, white-painted, its brasswork shining, its sails filled with wind. It approached in a curve, turned clear of the wind so that the sails went quite suddenly limp. She saw men furling canvas. She saw an anchor drop.

'Who the hell are they?' Craven started to laugh nervously. 'Pirates? Smugglers? The revenue men?'

Una nodded without listening to him. She saw the longboat go down, heard the clear sound of its engine starting. All the sailors were dressed in white, but the uniforms were not familiar. The longboat was heading for the bay.

She moved quickly, running back along the cliff. 'What's happening?' cried Craven. She shook her head. 'I don't know.' She found the broken concrete of the steps leading down the cliff. She controlled her haste and tested each step as she clambered down.

The longboat rounded the headland. She reached the beach, taking cover behind one of the weed-smeared bunkers. She watched the boat's approach. Craven skulked beside her now, his machine pistol in his hand. 'Would we have a chance,' he whispered, 'if we rushed them? We could steal the boat.'

'Wait.'

The longboat was beached. The sailors adjusted their clothes. They wore white baggy smocks, baggy trousers. At their throats and their wrists were huge red ruffs and instead of buttons there were red and blue pom-poms on their smocks, shoes and pointed hats. Only one of them had black and white pom-poms and black ruffs. He appeared to be the leader.

'Pierrots,' said Craven. 'This is ridiculous.'

As the pierrots drew the boat up the shingle Una could see the words on its side: *Tintagel Concert Party*.

The leading pierrot wore a black domino. He stood looking about him on the filthy beach, stripping off his mask. Una had already guessed who he might be. She was not entirely relieved; she continued to be suspicious, but she showed herself, wishing that her coat was not so tattered and muddy.

Jerry Cornelius seemed pensive. He screwed the domino in his left hand. 'There you are, Miss Persson. I thought we might be too late.'

'Not at all, colonel. You arrived just in time.'

Jerry regarded Craven with the cocked eye of a suspicious vulture. 'Who the fuck's this?'

'Craven. He's with me.'

'Any experience?'

'None.'

'Oh, sod. Why do you always have to introduce complications just when I think I've got everything neatly sussed…' He was not particularly querulous. 'We've no conditioning facilities on board the *Teddy Bear*. She's completely stripped down these days.'

'He'll have to risk it, then, won't he?'

'You've warned him? It's best to be prepared for an identity crisis.'

Craven began. 'Did you know all along about these people coming, Una? Hello, Jerry. A colonel now, are we?'

'I'm Gilbert the Filbert, didn't you know?' For Craven's benefit Jerry produced a silly smile. Craven missed the reference. It was obvious to Una that Jerry Cornelius didn't recognise Craven. Evidently he had been shifting about and his memory had been at least partially replaced.

One of the pierrots, a pale, anxious man, consulted a watch, the third in a row which stretched up his arm. Una had seen him once before at a Time Centre. 'We're behind schedule, Mr C. There's not much margin.'

Jerry acknowledged him. 'Okay. Everybody back in the boat.'

Craven showed reluctance. 'Are you sure this is wise, Una?'

She was already seating herself in the forward part of the long-boat, feeling better than she had done for a long while. There was something reassuring about Cornelius. It must be part of his attraction. 'Up to you,' she said. 'The only thing I can guarantee is that very shortly we'll be out of this zone altogether. I'm not saying the next zone will be any better. On a straight timeline, of course. Nothing fancy. No hopping about.' She looked to Cornelius for confirmation. He inclined his head.

'Zone?' Craven climbed in beside her. She did not elaborate. The pierrots unshipped the oars, to push the boat away from the shore. In the stern, Jerry started the engine. 'You'd forgotten how to get out, hadn't you?' he called to Una. 'It's been happening a lot lately. Everything's fragmenting, as usual.'

'I thought you liked it like that.' The noise of the engine half-drowned her voice.

'It depends what sort of shape you're in.' He ran a hand over his features, scratching at a faint stubble. 'And what shape they're in, too, of course.'

They left Tintagel behind and had soon reached the yacht. Una was surprised by the freshness of the air. The whole of England must be stinking of rot, she thought. Jerry helped her to climb the rope ladder up the white side. At the rail Shakey Mo Collier, clutching a huge sub-machine gun which dripped oil down his costume, awaited her. 'Glad to have you aboard, Captain Persson,' he said. She winked back at him. The little man still resembled a decadent Eskimo, his movements were still nervous, and excitement still burned in his eyes. He was the only one of the ship's company who sported a weapon.

Una was relieved now that she stood on the deck. She recognised a number of faces but could not name them. She looked around for her best friend.

'Catherine won't be with us on this shift.' Jerry spoke confidently. His spirits had improved considerably since their last encounter. He gave her hope as he put his arm around her, kissing her firmly on the forehead. 'But I expect we can find her, if you're keen. You're not looking well, Una.'

'I'm a bit tired,' she said. 'Were you hunting for me, then?'

'It was obvious you'd gone to pieces. How about the boyfriend?'

'Craven wants to escape. I couldn't leave him.'

'A bit clinging, is he?'

'You know what they're like.' She felt no guilt.

Craven lurched into earshot, swearing. He had lost his footing.

'Frank?' said Una.

'Below. Sulking as usual. He misses his mother.' Jerry watched his men swing the longboat aboard and fix it in its davits. 'Do you remember this yacht? I've probably had it cleaned a bit since you last saw it. It's fitted with my latest engines.'

Una looked back towards England. 'I shouldn't really have left it in that mess.'

'Well, it wasn't just your fault, you know. Everybody had a hand in it.'

'How many of the others are still in there?'

'Just a handful. They'll make their own way out.'

'I didn't.'

'They're not in such lousy shape.'

'Where are we going?' Craven demanded. 'Why is everyone being so bloody mysterious?'

'Because it's a mystery tour.' Jerry always adapted his jokes to his audience. 'Take it easy, Mr Craven. Just enjoy your holiday. It'll be over soon enough. What mysteries would you like to experience today?'

'Easy,' Una warned Jerry carelessly, 'I still have certain responsibilities.'

Jerry refused to listen. 'You're on holiday, too, Una. You can forget all about your responsibilities and relax for a while. I'm in charge. You'll find quite a lot of your old wardrobe in your cabin. Have a bath. There's a comfortable deckchair waiting for you as soon as you've changed.'

'What about me?' said Craven. 'Can I change, too?'

Jerry looked him over.

'I doubt it,' he said.

22. In which Catherine Cornelius bids farewell to ancient glories

'Few people,' said Constant, stroking Catherine's cheek as he moved his pawn, 'understand the trials and responsibilities of the committed sadist.' He pinched her earlobe in his nails.

Marius, his friend, scratched his long nose, glancing casually to where Catherine sat passively on the floor, her shoulder resting against Constant's worsted leg. He swept his queen the length of the board. 'Check,' he said.

Constant scowled and let go of her. His expression became boyish as he tugged at his little beard, studying his method of escape. He was Greek, with the weak, slightly furtive features of the typical antiquarian book-dealer. He was just what she had needed. He moved his king and put his hand against her face again.

'Good,' said Marius. He was a very old friend of Constant's. They had only recently met again, when Marius's regiment had been stationed in the Knightsbridge barracks. Their previous meeting had been in Rome, five years before. Marius hated wearing his uniform and was now dressed in a dark blue sweater and light grey slacks, but his grooming betrayed both his occupation and his race.

Catherine was glad to see that Constant was losing. It would give him the impetus to take his frustration out on her. While she enjoyed the waiting she was feeling a twinge or two of impatience.

The room was lit with dim lamps, mostly art nouveau oil lamps supported by draped Mucha nymphs in cast iron and bronze. Along one wall ran the locked, glass-fronted bookcases which held Constant's special collection. By taking one or two books from it a month he was able to live well. He believed that the collection and the other things he had locked in the trunk in the bedroom would provide an excellent income for the rest of his life. Marius was the only soldier who came to the house who was not a customer. Marius refused to be stimulated either by Constant's insinuating references or by the profusion of late-nineteenth- and early-twentieth-century erotica decorating walls, tables and mantelpieces. He showed a mild interest in Constant's Pre-Raphaelites, his Burne-Jones, his two Hunts, his late Millais, for he enjoyed collecting paintings, but his taste was more for Rembrandt and Hals.

'Check.'

Catherine took a keener interest in the game.

Constant said: 'It is weary work, wielding the whip.'

'Oh, true,' replied Marius. 'You should have my job, Constant.'

'They are not dissimilar, I suppose.'

Marius refused consensus.

Catherine, to relieve her boredom, kissed Constant's knee. He smiled affectionately down and slid his fingernail along her shoulder blade.

'I believe it's stalemate,' said Marius.

Constant fell back into his chair, caressing Catherine's face once more. 'Oh, very well.' He gave the appearance of magnanimity. 'My mind isn't on the game. This could go on all night.' He reached to grasp her left breast. 'And it would not be fair to keep this beautiful creature waiting.' He stood up. 'Let's call it a draw, shall we?'

Marius was amused. 'I have to phone Rome, anyway.' He was still nominally head of the family firm which specialised in canning luxury foods. 'It was a pleasant game. Thank you for the dinner. For the drinks.' He stared at Catherine as if he felt he should make some remark to her, perhaps to thank her for her decorative presence. He seemed to disapprove of her. Or perhaps, more likely, he disapproved of Constant's flaunting of his power over her. A man with as much personal power as Marius could afford to regard such displays as vulgar. He accepted the topcoat Constant handed him and began to button it up.

'Goodbye, colonel,' said Catherine sweetly.

But he was already in the hall. She heard Constant laugh and slap his thigh. She heard Marius clear his throat and murmur some remark.

Constant returned to her. 'Did you say something?'

'Only goodbye.'

He stood over her, his legs slightly apart. 'You can remove that dress now.' She wore the peasant frock he had found for her. Her own clothes were in the bedroom. She began to stand up. 'No,' he said, 'stay there.' She pulled the frock from her body, kneeling. Constant's breathing became deeper and his eyes, focused intensely on her body, had the sudden appearance of strength. 'Good girl,' he said. 'You are a good girl, aren't you, Catherine?'

'Yes,' she whispered, 'oh, yes.'

'And you want to please me?'

'Yes.'

'You shall.' He moved past her. She heard him enter the bedroom. 'Stay in exactly that position,' he told her.

She guessed that he was fetching one of his whips, but when he came into her field of vision again his hands were empty. He had changed into a kimono which reached to his knees, revealing his thin, hairy legs. He wore a pair of dark leather slippers on his feet. As he moved closer the kimono parted. He was naked. His penis was half-erect. She anticipated the effort needed to make it as stiff as possible. As a sadist he was excellent but, in common with most of those she had known, particularly the Greeks, he was never very far away from impotence.

'Take it in your lips,' he said.

Obediently she took his penis into her mouth, rolling her tongue around it, scraping it gently with her teeth, her body supported on her hands. 'Good,' he said. 'Slowly. Good.'

Deliberately, she tried to hold off his full arousal, even as his groin thrust against her face. She knew that he was unlikely to come, but tonight he might be satisfied only by this and she wanted more from him, for she had to leave early if she was to catch her plane. She pretended to cough, pulling free of him. For a moment he continued to move against her face. 'That wasn't right,' he said. 'You're wilful tonight.'

'I'm sorry,' she said. 'I think I've got a cold coming.'

'Hm.' He was mildly angry. 'Now, again.'

She accepted him for the second time and waited until his penis began to swell before she coughed. 'I'm sorry, Constant, really.'

'You are a bad girl, aren't you?' he said.

She bowed her head. 'Yes.'

Impatiently he put both hands under her chin and pushed his by now limp penis between her lips. Almost immediately she started to cough. He dragged her head back by the hair. He glowered down at her. 'Naughty child.'

'Yes.' She was beginning to get her lift. 'I'm sorry. I'm so sorry.' This time her cough was spontaneous. He slapped her across both cheeks. Her face glowed and she stopped coughing. 'Naughty little girl!'

She pretended that she was eager to try again. She bent towards his penis but he drew away. 'No. No more.'

'Please.' She crawled towards him.

'No.'

'I'll try not to –'

'Go into the bedroom,' he said sternly.

Again she began to get to her feet, but he pushed her down. 'No. Crawl.'

She crawled around the furniture, across the Persian carpet, into the gloom of the bedroom. It was lit by candles. 'Get onto the bed,' he said.

She obeyed, lying face forward, arms spread. She heard him open the lid of his trunk. There was a clatter as he took something out, closing the lid. Then he stood staring down at her.

'You have been a particularly bad child tonight,' he said. His accent grew thicker. 'Haven't you?'

She could only nod.

The tip of his whip touched her backbone. He drew it down to her bottom, he pushed the tip between her legs so that she felt it against her vagina before he moved it down the back of her legs, stroked her just behind the knees with it, caressed her calves with it, slid it around her feet and her ankles. By now she had lost her tiredness entirely and had become acutely conscious of her body, its smoothness, its beauty.

'There will be six strokes tonight,' he said, 'at least.' The whip hissed. Her buttocks flamed. She did not let him hear her groan. She held it from him. She owed him only a little generosity. He moved methodically down her bottom, placing each stroke expertly, one below the other. On the sixth stroke her whole body sang with white fire and, for her own pleasure, she screamed.

He had not finished. He fell on top of her, biting her neck, her shoulders, pinching the flesh of her waist, scratching her pubis, brutally clutching her clitoris. She groaned and, as methodically as he had whipped her, she began to recite a familiar litany, begging him to stop. He would not. He took her by the hair once again. He made her kneel on the floor while he sat on the edge of the bed with his legs spread.

'Now we will try again,' he said. 'Now you will not cough. You will do better, yes?'

She nodded. She was completely out of her head with pleasure. She sucked him hard, pretending desperation, she rubbed his penis against her cheek as she licked and nipped at his testicles, she took him into her mouth again, using her teeth so that now he groaned and shivered, tangling his fingers in her hair, until with a little feeble movement he ejaculated his drop of semen into her throat. She lay back on her heels, her eyes shut. She wiped her lips. He had collapsed onto the bed and was smoking one of his cheroots by the time she rejoined him, taking her own cigarettes and matches from the jet and mother-of-pearl table beside her. She found her watch. A few more minutes and she would have to be on her way. She hadn't told him of her plans. She became all at once aware of the welts on her bottom and again her whole body came alive. She would regret parting from Constant. He was about the best she had managed to find and had required little training.

He spoke unexpectedly. Usually he never spoke at this stage.

'You look very dignified tonight,' he said. He was praising himself as much as he praised her. 'So completely feminine.'

She smiled around her cigarette.

'And it has only just begun,' he added. She had left him thinking that he was the first; she had enjoyed the fantasy.

'For you,' she said.

She had puzzled him. Again his expression became boyish, petulant. 'What?'

'I've got to go in a moment,' she told him, as if in explanation.

'To your boyfriend?' He was contemptuous. 'To your rock-and-roll hero.'

'I'm leaving.' She was deliberately uncommunicative.

He said, as if to excuse her behaviour: 'Are you still taking drugs?'

'Oh, yes.' She gave in to her impulse. 'Would I be here, otherwise?' Before he could demand enlightenment, she continued: 'But I'm giving them up after tonight.'

'You are wise. You don't need them. You might think that you know what you are doing, but they could destroy you in the end.'

'True.' She sat up, straightening her fine back. She stretched. 'Ah!'

He said, not altogether seriously, 'I will be very angry with you if you go now.'

'You're tired.' She smiled. 'You've overdone it. You should sleep. Shall I get you a cup of cocoa before I leave?'

'No.' He was sulky. He didn't look at her.

She climbed into her underclothes. She pulled up her long golden skirt. She buttoned her shirt and over this she put her short, quilted jacket.

'You look lovely.' Either he had relented or he hoped to flatter her, to make her stay. She ran a brush over her hair. 'I feel wonderful.' She could give him that.

'You have your pride again.'

'Yes.'

'When shall I phone you?'

She hesitated, looking down at his odd body. She felt affection for him. She bent and kissed his little cock.

'When?' he said. She picked up her handbag.

'Whenever you like.'

'He won't be there for a while?'

She wondered, momentarily, if she should tell him that Viv would answer the phone to him, for she would have already left the country, if Marius's second in command was as good as his word. 'Don't worry,' she said. With a bouncing step she made for the exit.

'I won't phone.' He attempted firmness, but his desire had left him. 'You come here tomorrow. At seven o'clock.'

'Okay. See you then,' she said.

She reached the front door, opening it on its chains to peer outside. The best part of Smith Street consisted of neatly stacked rubble. Marius's men had cleared most of the roads soon after they had arrived. Up at the corner of King's Road she saw the dark outlines of a vehicle. It was waiting for her.

Closing Constant's door behind her, she began to stride up the street. She was whistling 'I'm Forever Blowing Bubbles'. It was almost her theme song, she thought.

23. In which Miss Una Persson witnesses at last the restoration of order

The man who had built the gibbet had taken pains with his work. It was an exact reproduction of the kind once seen in cowboy films. Against those wooden houses still standing in this section of Umeå the gibbet did not look out of place. Craven, on the other hand, hanging there in his flying jacket and silver helmet, looked incongruous. It was inevitable that he had tried to convince the soldiers that she had been involved in his stupid plot to steal the only seaworthy gunboat in the harbour. Una turned her back on her dead lover as the Finnish major cleared his throat to attract her attention. He was seated at a trestle table on which all the many papers were secured by a variety of heavy objects, including his Walther automatic pistol.

'Could we continue, Mademoiselle Persson?' He spoke Russian. 'A few more of these questions,' he tapped the documents, 'and you can go free. The pacification of Sweden is accomplished. They have already released most of the civilian prisoners in the south.' He was anxious to reassure her. 'A new autonomous parliament is in the process of being convened.' He studied the form, his felt-tip pen poised. Then he glanced up, his eyes amused. 'You agree to recognise the authority of the Emperor of Russia?'

She nodded.

'You are a Swedish national?'

'I have dual nationality. My father was Swedish. Mother was English.'

'They are resident in Sweden?'

'They are both dead.' A sad pout.

'Aha. Occupations?'

'He was a doctor, a missionary, an explorer. She became a

missionary, too. They met through the Church. Mother was very devout (although not without a sense of humour).'

'Natural causes? Or...?' He meant to ask if they had been killed in the fighting.

'They were killed some years ago.' Una lifted the collar of the mink. 'A ballooning accident in China. It was horrible. They were climbing aboard when the mooring ropes slipped too soon. Clinging to the ropes, they shot into the air. They could be seen trying to reach the basket, but it was improperly attached to the gasbag itself – Mother swung into it, it tipped sideways and down Mother fell, with the Peking ducks, the binoculars, the trunk of tropical clothing. Father remained. When he saw Mother go, he gave a shrug and released his hold on the rope, plunging after her...'

'Tragic.' The Finn wrote 'KILLED ABROAD' in neat Cyrillic capitals.

'Indeed!'

'Your occupation, mademoiselle?'

'I am an actress.'

'Last place of employment?'

She hesitated.

He tried to help her. 'Here, in Umeå?'

'I have been resting,' she told him.

His smile was sympathetic. 'Can you remember your last engagement?'

'Entertaining the troops in England.'

'That will do. A great shame about England. And yet it was inevitable.' He reached for a rubber stamp.

On the other side of the square a group of civilians were dragging a large handcart full of coarse red blankets. They all wore Russian army greatcoats and their breath was white in the sharp October air.

Apparently with relief he stamped a document and signed it. 'Here is your passport. You still intend to go on to St Petersburg?'

'I have friends there.'

'You are lucky.' He spoke without irony. For a moment his eyes rested on the hanging body of Craven. 'A few more hours and he would have been free, anyway.'

'Yes.'

'And next year the new century begins, or the old one ends. Nobody seems to be quite clear. It is strange how peace brutalises some people and ennobles others. It is the same with war. I wonder if there is actually any difference. Many people seem to feel more tranquil when they know there is nothing to do but fight.'

'I know what you mean, major.' She accepted the passport and tucked it into her ermine muff.

'You will be appearing on the stage in Petersburg?'

'I hope so.'

He stood up and saluted. 'I will come and see you.'

She inclined her head, the mink shako falling a little so that it almost covered her elaborately masacara'd left eye.

'You are a very beautiful woman. You will find many admirers in Petersburg.'

'Oh, certainly.' She laughed. She was touched by his innocent enthusiasm. 'It is a wonderful city in which to be admired.'

'You must come to Roveniemi some time. My home. The Paris of the North. The Gateway to Lapland!'

She knew the city. 'It is a lovely place,' she said. She felt uncomfortable. The handing over of the passport seemed to have reversed their positions. She was embarrassed. She would have preferred his condescension to his admiration. She turned to take one last look at Craven, her heavy furs swinging. It was odd, she thought, that now she had capitulated she had more power than she had ever possessed when she had been a fighter. The knowledge shocked her, as it always had done. She caught the heavy odour of her own perfume. This was no time for self-examination; she must let herself go, fall into her new rôle with all the old thoroughness. A good actress, she thought, is a contented woman. Too many rôle options and one became confused. It was much better to let oneself get typecast. And that, she reflected not for the first time, was the trouble with the twentieth century: there was far too much choice for comfort. Well, not any more. The war was over. The

Tsar ruled the world (what was left of it) and, with luck, would continue to do so for a long while. Perhaps Jerry had been right, after all, and one big war was preferable to a lot of small ones.

From somewhere the Finnish major had commandeered a hovercab. The driver wore one of Umeå's many municipal uniforms. He saluted self-consciously; the major opened the door for Una. The machine rocked slightly on its air cushion as she boarded. The door was shut.

'The airfield,' said the major in Swedish. 'Good luck, Miss Persson, and *bon voyage*.'

'Next year in St Petersburg.' She blew him a kiss. *A rôle is a rôle*, she thought. She was already remembering the old lines.

The taxi took the short, privileged route through the city and was soon in the suburbs, driving along streets lined with pines and birches, the timber houses of the rich, set back from the street, consciously built in the Swiss chalet style beloved of Edwardians who had settled in the English Lake District. These streets reminded her of New England and she felt a pang of loss.

The airport came in sight. She rubbed at the misted windows of the taxi. There were several gigantic airships moored there, most of them military craft, drifting at their masts in the wind. She saw the only civil vessel with its Cyrillic inscriptions, its black imperial eagles on their yellow backgrounds. In the semi-darkness its cabin lights were already glowing. Masses of lambent grey clouds swelled on the horizon. She anticipated the warmth and the luxury of the ship.

The taxi crossed the grass. Porters came forward to remove her trunks as the hovercab's engine stopped and the machine sighed to a halt. A loading derrick had been manoeuvred into position. The porters fitted her trunks onto its platform. An officer, in the dark green of the civil air service, politely took her papers. It was obvious that he had been expecting her, for he hardly looked at the documents before handing them back. He was quietly admiring. His nose wrinkled as her perfume reached him. 'We are honoured to have you with us on this flight, Mademoiselle Persson.'

'You are kind.' She gave him one of her endless smiles.

He led her to the passenger derrick. Unlike the other one, this was covered in sheets of aluminium, decorated with the insignia of the Swedish airline. She entered the lift. He pressed the button for her.

'You are holidaying in Russia?' he wanted to know.

'A little pleasure, a little work,' she told him.

The lift stopped and the door slid open. The short covered gangway between the derrick and the ship moved very slightly as she crossed it to be greeted by a steward in white-and-green livery. 'Good evening, ma'am.' He was English and seemed glad to welcome a fellow national.

The officer said: 'Will you show mademoiselle to her cabin?'

'With pleasure.' He led her along the narrow companionway. Tiny bulbs lit it, set into the slightly curved roof. With a key he opened a door about halfway along. He switched on a light for her. 'There is a bedroom through there,' he said. The cabin was quite small, but comfortably furnished. She would have been glad of a window in the far wall, but the only porthole looked out onto the companionway and the observation window beyond it. No airship cabins looked directly out into the sky.

She took her tiny purse from her muff and tipped the steward. He thanked her enthusiastically, showing her where she could find the service bell, the telephone if she wished the wireless operator to connect her with a number. When he had gone she shrugged off the furs and lay down on the wide bed, reading the standard literature, which was in Russian, smoking one of the cigarettes from the box the company had provided. She slid her hand over her silk dress, pulling the material up so that she could scratch her leg where her stocking met her suspender. She felt wonderful.

A little later she sensed the ship shudder as it freed itself from its mooring and turned slowly towards the east. By morning they would be over St Petersburg.

She undressed and got into her black pyjamas, putting on a matching cap to protect her elaborately waved hair, removing her make-up. Then she got into bed, put out the light and let the distant sound of the motors, the gentle swaying of the ship, send her to sleep.

She was awakened by a juddering, by gunfire. She ran to the porthole, seeing nothing but darkness on the other side of the observation windows. She put on her dressing gown, opened the cabin door, went out to peer downwards through the perspex. She heard the booming of big guns, saw their flashes below. Searchlights suddenly blinded her. Her steward ran up. 'Best get inside, ma'am.'

'This is horrible!' she complained, as if he was at fault. 'The war is over!'

'For most people, ma'am.'

'The airline should have warned us of any potential trouble.' She retreated and slumped on her bed. 'Oh, it's too bad!'

'Don't worry. We'll soon be out of range. We're making very good speed, with the wind behind us..'

'But we are losing height!'

'It'll be all right.'

She knew enough about the handling of airships to realise that his assurances were meaningless. The ship lurched. The steward fell against her, clutching the rail above the bed. 'Beg pardon, ma'am.' He tried to steady her with his free hand. She shook him off. 'Well,' he said, 'I'd better…' He staggered through the door and she slammed it behind him. She began to dress and make up. Her old instincts were coming back. If the ship did go down it was as well to be ready for whoever might have won her.

The cabin tilted from stem to stern. All her belongings slid along the floor into a heap against the wall. The ship righted herself slightly, but then came a terrifying scraping from below, a trembling bump. Quite suddenly all motion ceased. Una got her door open, swaying on high heels. The steward was still in the companionway. His head was bleeding. The perspex of the observation windows was smashed. They appeared to have crashed in a forest. She saw the outlines of pines. She saw figures moving amongst the trees. Riders appeared in the dawn light, their long hair blowing behind them. They were dressed in wolfskin and leather. They had rifles.

Una returned to her cabin and sat down miserably on her bed. She was far too tired for any more excitement.

There were no more shots, but she heard yells, screams, raised voices. She experienced a passing flash of déjà vu. She heard people in the companionway. She went outside.

The marauders who had brought down the ship were gently forcing the passengers back into the cabins. 'I'm sorry,' one of them said, 'we thought this was a warship. We'll do what we can for you.' All the marauders were female. All were good-looking. Some were very young, barely more than ten years old. They had fresh healthy faces. It was as if nuns and their pupils had become long-haired bandits overnight. They all had rifles slung on their backs and had thick fur jerkins, almost as a uniform.

'Don't you know the war is over?' Una asked one of the children. 'Didn't you know that?'

The girl looked at her uncomprehendingly. Una said in Russian: 'There is an amnesty for everyone. The war is finished.'

The girl smiled and touched her dress. 'You are very pretty.' She fingered Una between her legs.

'Oh!' Una was exasperated. 'Who is your commander? Where is he?' She half-suspected Cornelius.

The child pointed down the companionway. A girl, in black and white skins, was marching towards them, her face brightening as she recognised Una. 'Get the cargo off. Hurry, girls!' She was eating a piece of meat. 'Well, well, well. This is a turn up, eh, Una? Were you after this ship, too?'

'I just wanted to go to St Petersburg in peace.' Una realised she was still wearing her nightcap and snatched it off, patting at her hair. 'Are these your people, Catherine? What point is there in shooting us down?'

'We thought it was a military airship, honestly. I'm very sorry, Una. Aren't you pleased to see me?'

'Haven't you heard about the amnesty?'

'No. We're a bit cut off here, me and my gang.'

'Gang? You with a gang?'

'I used to have a gang, years ago. In Whitechapel. Before I got caught and improved.' Catherine was in a jolly mood. Her laughter was hearty. 'I haven't introduced us properly. Catherine Cornelius and her All Girl Guerrillas! Aren't you tickled?' She was as bad as her brother, when she felt like it.

But Una was in no state of mind to accept Catherine's levity. Her new way of life had cost her too much. 'You've ruined everything, Catherine. Playing at soldiers.'

'It runs in the family,' Catherine told her. 'Actually, I had a feeling I might be bumping into you soon.'

'How on earth did you turn up in this zone? In this god-forsaken place?'

'It suited me. I had to get away from it all.' Catherine studied her friend's face. 'You're not yourself today, are you, Una?'

'No, thanks to you, you silly bitch.' Una simply did not see any reason for disguising her feelings. She had never been more angry, yet already the intensity of her emotion was fading and when Catherine seized her head between her mittened hands and kissed her firmly, Una did not resist.

'I said I was sorry,' Catherine told her, nuzzling her ear. 'You're looking so lovely. And since we managed to hit the ship, we might as well loot it. My kids are starving.'

'Why did you bring them out here?'

'I didn't know there was an amnesty, did I? We'd blown up all these bridges, for one thing. And railways. And there was the garrison we massacred. We were trying to free the Ukraine.' Catherine swept her hair from her face. 'We got pushed back, of course. Oh, don't be so bloody pompous, Una. It's not like you!'

Una sulked on principle.

'Did you say you were going to St Petersburg?' asked Catherine.

'I had everything set up,' Una complained. 'The last thing I needed was another shambles. I'm tired. I want peace. Order. A quiet life with no responsibilities. Have you seen your brother?'

'No. I thought he was with you.'

'He's out. I was getting out. Frank's out. Even Major bloody Nye is out. But you're suddenly right in it, for the first time, doing God knows what damage!'

Catherine was hurt. 'I thought I was helping.'

'It's a fine fucking time to decide to become an activist, just when everything's settling down.'

'That's hardly my fault.'

'Oh, bugger off,' said Una. She returned to her cabin and sat on her bed again.

Catherine followed her in. 'I wanted to do something useful,' she said plaintively.

Una scowled at her.

'Look,' said Catherine, taking her friend's limp hand. 'What you need is a holiday.'

'I was just about to have one!'

'Let's have one together, then! Wouldn't you like that? Like old times?'

'Together? Riding about the frozen bloody forest shooting at airships?'

'If the war's over, there's nothing left for us to do. You and I'll go somewhere. I'll tell my girls about the amnesty. They'll be all right.'

Una sucked her lower lip as tenderly Catherine stroked her face. 'I'll look after you,' said Catherine. 'It seems as if things have been rough. I'll keep you safe and warm, Una.'

Una buried her head in Catherine's half-cured skins and began, contentedly, to sob.

Catherine raised her to her feet. 'Come on, then, love.' Una let Catherine lead her through the embarkation doors, down the metal stairway to the ground. A big roan stallion snorted as he recognised his mistress. His breath was white and warm. There was a smell of snow. Catherine climbed into her saddle and reached down to help her friend up. Una sat sideways on the horse in front of Catherine who kicked at the stallion's flanks. The sun was rising as the roan galloped through the frosty trees towards the east. Red light flooded the snow. 'New century soon,' said

Catherine, as if to comfort Una. 'By and large, I didn't think a lot of the last one.'

Una felt her spirits rising, for all that the jogging motion of the horse was making her slightly sick. She put her arms around Catherine's neck and kissed her. Catherine supported her back with a strong right hand. 'This won't take long. I've a jeep waiting in the valley.

'Where are we going?' Una asked. Like a damsel in distress she had been rescued and was reconciled.

'Somewhere nice,' Catherine promised.

'Not the future?'

'Of course not. Somewhere safe.'

The hard earth gave way to grass. The snow had almost melted here, for the proper winter had hardly begun. The horse slowed its pace as they descended towards a number of shacks in the valley below. 'That was our camp,' said Catherine. 'We were almost completely self-sufficient.'

'I've made such a balls-up of things,' said Una.

'Nonsense. I bet you've done wonders. You're the finest Elfberg of them all!'

Una stared up at her friend in astonishment. Then she kissed her firmly on the cheek.

Catherine pursed her lips in a confident whistle.

Part Three

Limping Home: The Problems Of Retirement

> So you thought silk stockings had had their day. Think again. Besides the male enthusiasts who bemoan the end of the suspender era they now have a new fan. None other than the fashion queen Mary Quant! She believes that 1976 will be The Year of the Sensual Woman and, to celebrate, she has produced a range of beautiful real silk stockings. Mary says: 'Not only will you feel like a lady, but you will have to be treated like one. Things like car doors will have to be opened for you, simply because you cannot afford to snag these stockings.'
>
> *Daily Mirror*, 3 November, 1975

24. In which our heroines, for the moment weary from their exploits in the world, enjoy the comforts of peacetime

It was 1939 on a warm summer day and Catherine Cornelius took Una Persson to tea in the roof garden of Derry & Toms. The garden had only been opened that year and it was to enjoy considerable vogue before the war came to make such places unfashionable. Both ladies were dressed to the nines in the styles they were favouring this summer, Catherine in her rather sporty tweed jacket and golfing skirt and Una in her pale green chiffon frock. Conscious of the other women sitting at the little white tables overlooking the ornamental ponds, Catherine was careful not to touch Una who was, as it happened, in one of her sensitive moods.

They chewed their cucumber sandwiches. They sipped weak tea. Around them came the sounds of lazy bees.

All day Catherine had been trying to amuse Una, to draw her out of her mood of sultry melancholy. 'You are looking so much better, dear,' she said now. 'Has your head gone?'

'It's still there.' Una languidly laid her sandwich upon its plate. 'But it's better.' She sighed.

'And the cinema? Do you still want to go?'

'I'm rather fatigued, after all the shopping.'

'Then we'll go straight home,' said Catherine. 'You can relax and I'll cook you a charming supper.'

'You are so good to me, my dear,' said Una raising a wide grey eye. 'If I were only healthier…' She uttered a delicate cough.

'You are an artist,' Catherine told her, 'and artists must be nurtured. Ah, look, here is Mr Koutrouboussis.' Mr Koutrouboussis was an impresario who had telephoned Una that morning to offer her the star part in his new West End production. 'Hello, Mr Koutrouboussis.'

The dignified old man sailed up to them, lifting his topper. 'Ladies. What pleasure! Ladies!'

'You will join us for a moment, Mr Koutrouboussis?'

'Oh, ladies! An honour.' He removed his hat and held it with his gloves and cane in his left hand, drawing forth a chair. He seated himself. 'You have had time to consider my suggestion, Miss Persson?'

'Not yet, I fear. Too soon. Too soon, Mr Koutrouboussis.'

'Aha. Of course.' He stroked his imperial beard as he contemplated the menu. 'Hm. Tea.'

'He…' Catherine hesitated, looking at Una through intense china-blue eyes. You…'

'Who?' Mr Koutrouboussis raised his own eyes above the level of the menu.

'Una. Una,' said Catherine. 'What's the part?'

'Today?'

'The play,' clarified Catherine.

'An excellent part,' said Mr Koutrouboussis. 'Perfect for Miss Persson. From *Victory*, you know. With music.'

'A musical comedy?' Catherine asked. 'How lovely.'

'Based on Conrad,' said Una, without inflection.

'Do you know Conrad, Miss Cornelius?' asked Mr Koutrouboussis.

'The name rings a bell,' said Catherine. 'Once, perhaps. Long ago.' She watched as a large, fat clergyman and his skinny daughter sat down at the next table and ordered pastries.

'He was a sweetie,' said Una. 'A sweetie.'

'All my life,' said Mr Koutrouboussis, 'I have admired his eye, exactitude, his sweep.'

'My brother,' said Catherine, 'has arrived, I gather, and is staying at Blenheim Crescent, while Mother…'

'He was abroad?' said Una.

'A postcard came. From Pom Pen. In China.'

'What was he doing there?' Una asked.

'Wasting time, as usual, I suppose.' She saw someone she

recognised, sitting on her own at a table in the far corner. She leaned forward to whisper to Una. 'Don't look now, but that's our old schoolteacher, Miss Brunner. Hasn't she *aged*!'

'Your brother's bête noire?'

'That's the one.' Catherine could not resist a second glance. Miss Brunner was being joined by another amazon. 'She's meeting our old *German* teacher here. Ho, ho! What can they be up to?'

'Very little, by the look of 'em,' said Una with some sudden animation. She relaxed again, studying Mr K. as he studied the menu. 'Hm.'

She produced a jade holder and fitted a cigarette. Mr Koutrouboussis hurried through his pockets and found a gold lighter. She puffed.

Catherine giggled to herself.

Una, with a glance at her tiny watch, rose. 'Well.'

Mr Koutrouboussis leapt to his feet.

'Please don't,' said Una. He descended.

Catherine began to gather up their parcels.

'A lift,' said Mr Koutrouboussis. 'Could I offer?'

'No,' said Una. 'Thank you. We have the car.'

'Oh, Una,' said Catherine as they paid at the till, 'you were so haughty.'

Una smiled.

When they arrived at the exit they saw that the sky had clouded. 'Wait here, darling,' Catherine put the parcels into the arms of a doorman. 'I'll fetch the car. It's turning chilly.'

With poise Una waited until Catherine drove up to the kerb. The doorman piled the parcels into the back of the car. Una sat beside Catherine.

They drove through the afternoon streets of Kensington and arrived at last at the house in Holland Park Avenue, borrowed from Catherine's brother. It was high and white. Catherine drove the car into the garage. They disembarked, carrying their parcels to the front door.

Their arrival had been observed. The door opened. Mrs Cornelius stood there, a cigarette in her carmine lips. She was expressionless.

'Well,' she said, 'you got 'ome all right, then.'

The Entropy Tango
by M. Moorcock
I. The Entropy Tango
At the Time Centre
The Birthplace of Harlequin.
2. Pierrot on the Moon
Harlequin's Courtship
Columbine's
3. Pierrot's Song of Positive Thinking
The Nature of the Catastrophe
Through the Megaflow
4. Every Gun Plays its own Tune
Pierrot in the Roof Garden
Harlequin and Columbine's Carol
5. Harlequin Transformed
Pierrot and Columbine's Reconciliation
Song of Entropy Tango (reprise)
Columbine's Lament.
Characters:
Nestor Makhno
Major Nye
Catherine
Jerry
Frank
Sebast
Shaky
Col.
Una Persson
Mrs Cornelius
Cornelius
Cornelius
Cornelius
Auchinek
Mo Collier
Pyat.
Hermann.
Kosinsky.
Der alte Moor.

The Entropy Tango

A Comic Romance

Pictures by Romain Slocombe

Lyrics by Michael Moorcock

Music by Michael Moorcock and Pete Pavli

For Pete Pavli
(who did most of the music)

Contents

List of Illustrations 254

1. INTRODUCTION 257

Chapter 1 For One Day Only: Two Mighty Empires Clash 263

2. DEVELOPMENT (A) 281

Chapter 2 The Kassandra Peninsula 289

3. DEVELOPMENT (B) 313

Chapter 3 Revolutions 317

4. RECAPITULATION 361

Chapter 4 The Minstrel Girl 369

5. CODA 385

Chapter 5 Harlequin's Lament 391

List of Illustrations

Endpapers: Canadian, British and Chinese soldiers of the counter-revolutionary army in Siberia – 1918; African soldier of the German army – Tanganyika 1914–1918

For one day only: two mighty empires clash 263
By the time Una got there Toronto had capitulated and Makhno's men were everywhere 270
Catherine Cornelius 276
Major Nye 279
The Kassandra Peninsula 289
It would mean a long wait while they radioed back to Kinshasha for instructions 295
'That Captain Cornelius, miss, 'e was 'ere before the real trouble started.' 296
Shakey Mo Collier 298
Miss Brunner 302
Mrs Cornelius 306
'Acute depression often follows a period of frenetic activity' 310
Revolutions 317
Colonel Pyat had addressed the soldiers as comrades and tried to appeal to their sense of liberty 321
Prinz Lobkowitz 324
Jerry Cornelius 329
Colonel Pyat 336
Mitzi Beesley 339
A green flag waved from a mast on the leading vehicle 341
Professor Hira 344

The DoX came in to land on the oily waters of the harbour 346
Pierrot 352
Jerry woke up 358
The minstrel girl 369
Maxime 374
The ship was commandeered by a South Korean gunboat 378
The images of demolished streets 382
Harlequin's lament 391
Mrs Persson would climb into her rickshaw 394
She was reminded of the old days, of Makhno and his riders 398
The Golden Gate Bridge sagged and squealed as the explosive took it out 400
Una Persson 404

1. Introduction

Entropy Tango

My pulse rate stood at zero
When I first saw my Pierrot
My temperature rose to ninety-nine
When I beheld my Columbine

Sigh, sigh, sigh…
For love that's oft denied
    Cry, cry, cry…
My lips remain unsatisfied
    I'm yearning so for my own Pierrot
As we dance the Entropy Tango!

I'll weep, weep, weep
Till he sweeps me off my feet
    My heart will beat, beat, beat,
And my body lose its heat
    Oh, life no longer seems so sweet
Since that sad Pierrot became my beau
    And taught me the Entropy Tango

So flow, flow, flow…
As the rains turn into snow
    And it's slow, slow, slow…
As the colours lose their glow…
    The Winds of Limbo no longer blow
For cold Columbine and her pale Pierrot
    As we dance the Entropy Tango!

At the Time Centre

Calling in and calling out
Crawling through the chronosphere
Will all members please report
To their own centuries
Where they will receive instructions
As to how to progress

This is an emergency signal
To all chrononauts and
Members of the Time Guild
Mrs Persson calls a conference
Code-name Pierrot – code-name Harlequin
Come in please – this is Columbine

Come in please, this is Columbine
Come in please, this is Columbine
Come in please, this is Columbine
Come in please, this is Columbine
Columbine calling,
Calling
Calling out…

The Birthplace of Harlequin

In this ancient time-fouled city discredited gods do brood
On all the imagined insults which down the aeons they've received
It is a place of graves and here dreams are destroyed
Dreams are brought from all the corners of the world
To be crushed or ripped or melted down
Into a healthy cynicism
Here are tricksters born
And fools divested of enchantment

This is where Pierrot is killed
And from his flesh Harlequin created
To race across the world, laughing at nothing,
Laughing at everything
Laughing at his pain,
Laughing at the tired gods who bore him
Here in this city, this city of shades,
This city of irony bereft of imagination
This city of suppression
This city of pragmatism
Where the jesters weep
And the tricksters scheme
Parading in motley
Too afraid to scream,
Too wary to acknowledge love
Unless love's made a game.
A game which they can win.

Here, in this city of swaggering fantasticos, of calculated gallantry
Was Harlequin the Trickster born, to go about the world, to win
To attract; to display an easy cleverness; to lie and to deceive
To show what shallow things are dreams, and promises impossible to keep
And should he meet with frankness, unashamed honesty
Back to this city Harlequin may flee
To be replenished, armed afresh by his weary masters,
The gorgeous gods of disharmony…

1. FOR ONE DAY ONLY: TWO MIGHTY EMPIRES CLASH

I

> Greta Garbo is here seen in the climax scene of 'Queen Christina' after she has forsaken her throne and is sailing away with her dead lover ... one of the greatest performances of her career, in a story and settings which are sombre and admirably suited to her strong dramatic powers.
>
> *Shots from Famous Films*, No. 19,
> issued by Gallagher Ltd, *c.* 1937

'I still breed and buy a little, but I rarely, these days, kill.' Balancing a pink gin in his thin hand Major Nye settled into the light blue plush, and pulled a photograph from his top pocket. Behind him was a wide observation window. He turned to glance through the clouds at what could be Transcarpathia below. There were only four passengers in the airship's lounge and two of them spoke no language known to him, so he was anxious to keep Mrs Persson nearby. As she approached, he said: 'What do you make of this couple?'

It was too hot. Una Persson regretted her Aran turtle-neck, and she tugged a little at the top so that her pearls clicked. 'Ukrainians.' She smiled at them. They were shy. 'They'll probably have Russian.'

'Russki.' The woman responded with an alacrity which dismayed her thickset husband. 'Da.' She wore a mixture of national dress (blouse and boots; a brown suit of the rather severe cut favoured east of Warsaw). He wore motley: a short red leather overcoat, tweed trousers, two-tone shoes.

'Then they're anarchists.' Major Nye looked curiously at the pair before finishing his gin. 'Do you think they'll last?'

Una was amused. They were probably rich emigrants. 'What's the alternative? Bolshevism?'

'Jolly good.' Major Nye was also feeling the heat. He adjusted the left sleeve of his uniform jacket. 'Do you hunt, Mrs Persson? At all?'

'Not seriously.'

Nodding at Una, perhaps embarrassed, the Ukrainians replaced their empty glasses on the bar. They offered a muted 'Dasvedanya' to the steward, and climbed up the open oak staircase to the main deck.

'Another half an hour and we'll be in Prague.' Major Nye was regretful. He had been glad to find an acquaintance aboard. 'Have you someone waiting for you? From the Consulate?'

'Do you know Prague?'

'Not since the war.' Major Nye smiled like a wistful conspirator. 'I change in Dublin for Toronto.' He had come from Hong Kong, with a Bradshaw's under his arm, hopping ships after he had missed the *Empress of Canada* on her weekly express run. By taking this flight via China and the Russian Republic he had actually saved himself several hours, since the *Empress* followed an All-Red Route established by seagoing vessels in the century's early years. Now, more than four decades later, big British airships might still moor at aerodromes built on sites of ancient coaling stations. But the Air Ship *Lady Charlotte Lever* belonged to E&A Lines who were concerned less with national prestige than with international competition. Built ten years before, in 1938, she had been one of the first so-called 'China clippers', lifting 31,000 tons and capable of almost 200 mph with a following wind. She stopped at only two British ports, making a six-day round-trip from Nagasaki, via Seoul, Peking, Samarkand, Tiflis, Kiev, Prague, Brussels and Liverpool, to Dublin; challenging the Russian, German and American lines who had previously dominated this territory. Major Nye felt unsafe in her. He preferred more stately, old-fashioned craft.

Mrs Persson sat on the opposite couch.

'I was hoping for a few days' leave.' Major Nye passed her the photograph. It showed an elderly grey being led from its stall by a smiling, plump young woman. 'That's my horse, Rhodes. My daughter, Elizabeth. She runs the stable now. Near Rye. Poor old chap. He's dying. I wanted to be with him.'

She was touched. She returned the photograph. 'A fine animal.'

'He was.' Major Nye stroked his white moustache with the tip of a nicotine-stained finger. 'Tempus fugit, eh? To the best of us.' His pale eyes stared hard out of the airship as if he willed back tears.

Una rose. 'I'll have to leave you, I'm afraid. Bags.'

'Of course.' He stood to attention. 'We'll doubtless meet again. That's the Service. Here today and gone tomorrow.'

'Or vice versa.' Una shook hands. She brushed the short chestnut hair from her face. 'Good luck in Canada.'

'Oh, it's nothing serious, I'm sure.'

When she had left he realised he still held Rhodes's photograph. He tucked it into a top pocket which he firmly buttoned. Moving between empty chairs, glass in hand, he straightened his jacket, looking behind the bland barman at the mirror. As he set his glass on mock tortoiseshell the ship gave one of those peculiar shudders which usually meant unexpected wind resistance and the glass clicked against a chrome railing before Major Nye's bony fingers could close on it. The lounge darkened. They sailed through heavy cloud and the sun and land had been completely obscured. The steward prepared a new drink.

'Not long now, sir, before we go down.'

2

> ESTONIA obtained her independence in 1918. The colours of her distinctive national flag, a horizontal tricolour: Blue for the sky, mutual confidence and fidelity, black for the nourishing soil and the dark past of the country; white for the winter, hope for the future...
>
> *National Flags and Arms*, No. 16,
> issued by John Player & Sons, *c.* 1937

'Can this, after all, be the Golden Age?' Una turned from the first-floor window and the bleak Notting Hill street. She had arrived in England less than three hours ago and had come directly here, hoping to find her lover Catherine, but only Catherine's mother had been in.

'I could do wiv a bit of it,' said Mrs Cornelius, mopping sweat, 'if, o' course, there's some ter spare.' She laughed and looked at the clock. 'Sovereigns.' On the wireless, briefly, an announcer spoke of chaos in the outskirts of Toronto, but Mrs Cornelius stretched a fat arm and turned the knob to find Ted Heath and His Music who were halfway through 'Little Man You've Had a Busy Day'. 'Thass an old one.' She was nostalgic. 'When did that come art? Four? Five years ago? Makes yer fink.' She returned to her horrible armchair and lowered herself into it, magazines and newspapers rising and falling around her as if she sank back into some polluted sea. 'Bin abroad agin, 'ave yer, love?'

'Here and there,' said Una equably. She felt both terror and affection for Catherine's mother. The woman seemed to maintain an ageless decrepitude, utterly at one with her preferred environment. The paint on her face might have been put on that day or ten years before and was flaking to exactly the same degree as the paint on her woodwork. 'Had a holiday this year, Mrs C?'

'Nothin' ter speak of. We went ter 'Astings, ther Kernewl an' me, fer Easter. It pissed darn.' She spoke of her boyfriend, 'the old Pole', who ran a second-hand clothes shop in Portobello Road. 'Spent the 'ole time on ther bleedin' pier. When we wasn't in ther pub.' She raised her tea to her lips. ''*E* was dead miserable, o' course. But *I* enjoyed meself.'

'That's the main thing.' Leaning against the damp draining board Una read the *Manchester Guardian* she had bought at Croydon. Makhno's 'insurgent army', consisting predominantly of Ukrainian settlers, Indians, Métis (pushed out of their homelands), and some disaffected Scots and French, had won control of rural Ontario. The main cities, including Ottawa and Toronto, were still in the hands of the RCMP. It was stalemate of sorts, since Makhno's army was defensive and would only respond to attacks, while the Mounties were unwilling to begin any action which would result in bloodshed. Una found this funny: Anarchism matched against Liberalism in a classic dilemma. But London was upset, which was why she had been ordered home from Prague.

The door opened. Catherine hurried in from the landing. 'Oh!' She was pleased. She wiped rain from her beautiful face and tugged off a headscarf to reveal curly blonde hair. 'How long have you got?'

'I have to be off tomorrow.'

After some hesitation, they embraced.

3

> The 'Riders of the Plains', hero-worshipped by readers of wild North-West literature as the 'Mounties', were formed in 1873 for the purpose of maintaining the law in sparsely populated parts of the Dominion. Recruiting was commenced in 1874, and early in their history their courage and integrity established order and respect in the Indian territory. Although tasks are less picturesque than in the bad old days, diverse activities still include punishment for wrongdoing and the enforcement of Federal Law throughout Canada.
>
> *Soldiers of the King*, No. 21,
> issued by Godfrey Phillips Ltd, *c.* 1939

By the time Una got there Toronto had capitulated and Makhno's people were everywhere, distributing characteristic anarchist leaflets, informing the citizens of their many rights. Confusingly, numbers of Makhnovischini wore red coats borrowed from disarmed Mounties and a few had even taken the full uniform, though usually with modifications. She went directly to the downtown offices of the Canadian Pacific Airship Company where Major Nye had the responsibility of processing applications from those who had elected to leave. The building was surprisingly quiet, though long lines of middle-aged men and women stood outside it. In the lobby soft-spoken Mounties patiently kept order,

manning desks formerly occupied by CPAC clerks. Una was shown straight through to Major Nye's office. It had been decorated in the clean, stripped-pine-and-hessian style favoured by most Canadian executives, while tasteful scenic paintings had been positioned along the walls at regular intervals.

The large window looked out over Lake Shore Avenue and the harbour beyond, where other refugees were crowding onto boats and ships which would take them to emergency immigration centres at Wilson on the American side. The United States had agreed

BY THE TIME UNA GOT THERE TOR-
ONTO HAD CAPITULATED AND MAKHNO'S
PEOPLE WERE EVERYWHERE

reluctantly to establish temporary camps, but already, Una knew, they were urging independent Ottawa and Britain to send military ships to the province, to oust the 'illegal anarchist government', as they insisted on terming it. Makhno and his insurgents evidently represented the popular interest and since the Mounties had made no attempt to defend the cities by force of arms (on instructions from London, who were anxious to negotiate with Makhno as soon as possible) there was technically no excuse to send either troops or aerial gunboats. The idea of a Commonwealth in which all were free and willing partners had to be maintained, London felt, above everything.

'I mean Britain has always been the guardian of liberal democracy,' said Major Nye, after he had offered her a chair and ordered some coffee. 'We can't resort to the methods of Frenchmen or Russians, can we? Or even Americans. We've an example to set. There hasn't been a serious clash of arms in the Empire for thirty years. Everything has been settled by discussion, arbitration, common sense. I can't see what they want with anarchism, can you? I mean, the difference seems so marginal!'

'They think,' said Una, 'of our democracy as Capital's last attempt to survive. In, as it were, disguise.'

'There'll always be conflicting interests.' He remained bewildered. 'Besides, there have been socialist governments for years!'

'Makhno's socialism is a trifle more extreme.' Una took the coffee cup with a smile of thanks to the girl who came in. 'They want me here, I gather, to parley with the Little Father.'

'Not many of our people have had much to do with him.' Major Nye returned his attention to the lines on the quays. 'You know him well, don't you?'

Una came to stand beside him. 'We're always looking out of windows, you and I, aren't we?'

He had not heard her. 'This is what comes of giving autonomy to Quebec,' he said. 'Canada simply isn't India.'

4

DRUMMOND. Motto 'Gang warily'. Badge, Wild Thyme. The ancestor is said to have been Maurice, a Hungarian, who accompanied Edgar Atheling into Scotland, and obtained from Malcolm III the lands of Drymen. This patriotic clan fought with distinguished bravery at Bannockburn.

Highland Clans, No. 3,
issued by John Player & Sons, *c.* 1920

Half Toronto seemed deserted now. Named like Ontario's towns and villages for their nostalgic associations with Britain, the quiet streets of the suburbs, with big shady trees and pleasant lawns, were almost wholly taken over by the insurgents to whom the references – Albion Road, Uxbridge Avenue, Ballantrae Drive – were all but meaningless. Certain self-conscious Métis and Indians, who occupied houses on their own farms, had pitched wigwams in the parks and were holding councils with local inhabitants. The smiling residents still found it hard not to be eagerly condescending to those now regarding them with cheerful contempt. The majority of Torontonians remaining behind were the same nationalist sympathisers who had elected the provincial government which had so quickly disappointed their hopes. In reaction, the rural people had made the ageing anarchist their spokesman.

The shirtsleeved driver of the Rolls landau pointed ahead to a large timber-built house at the end of the road and said in Ukrainian: 'Batko Makhno headquarters. See.' A black flag had been stuck in a chimney and was visible over the surrounding pines and birches. Una was delighted by the introduction of so much incongruity into this Home Counties dream of Utopia.

Makhno was leaning on the verandah frame as she walked up the crazy paving towards him. He was greyer and thinner than when she had last seen him during his successful campaigns against the Russian Republic in the thirties, but he had the same alert, sardonic eyes. He wore a jaunty astrakhan cap, a dragoon jacket in blue and gold, civilian jodhpurs and soft Ukrainian boots. Almost as a concession to his past he sported two large automatic pistols and a sabre. Although cured of TB he retained the slight flush often associated with the disease. He burst into laughter as they embraced. 'We've done it again. Only this time it was easier!'

'That's what I've come to see you about,' said Una.

They entered the cool open-plan interior, full of woollen scatter-rugs of Indian design, polished boards and low furniture in muted colours. A well-fed blonde Canadian girl with a smooth skin which needed to be tanned to look agreeable said brightly: 'Hi! I'm Nestor's new wife.'

'My twenty-first,' said Makhno. He put an arm about her upright shoulders. 'This,' he said of Una, 'is my oldest friend and closest enemy.'

'We've heard of you, Mrs Persson,' said the girl, 'even in Toronto.'

With a slightly studied display of carelessness, Makhno dropped into a beige armchair near the rough granite fireplace. 'Have you come to bargain, Una?'

'In a way. You know you've upset the Americans.'

'Certainly. Is that difficult? And the Russians. Our Alaska raid.'

'Exactly. Two airships. But London's under a lot of pressure.'

'We've already been promised autonomy. The same terms as agreed with Montreal. Everyone is happy.'

'The Russians are claiming that by recognising you Canada has violated the Alaskan treaty. Therefore they feel entitled to retaliate. The US would see such a move as the first step in an attempt by Russia to gain further North American territory.'

Makhno laughed. 'What are you suggesting? Some sort of second Great War?'

'You know there are tensions.'

'But no-one would risk so much over one tiny event!'

'They see it as the spread of anarchy. First the Ukraine. Then Andalusia. Argentina. Kwan Tung. You know what emotions are involved. Perhaps if you appeared initially to modify your programmes, give them a "liberal" slant...?'

The girl spoke, smiling earnestly, with self-conscious passion, as she tried to persuade Una to a point of view unfamiliar only to herself: 'You have to see, Mrs Persson, that this "liberalism" is the same sentiment people reserve for the beasts they keep for food. Their love of the masses is love for the lambs they shall one day slaughter! The impulse remains authoritarian, no matter what it pretends to be. Bolsheviks and capitalists. They're identical.'

The phone rang. Makhno went to it. He listened, his smile growing broader as his eyes became sad. He shrugged, replacing the receiver. 'There you are, Mrs Persson. British ships have been sighted over Winnipeg.' A large fleet. Evidently on their way here. It's the finish. Obviously. Is it my fault, do you think? Have I fallen into the trap I always warned you about? The fallacy of "history". The myth of "precedent"?'

'What shall you do?'

'Oh, I shall avoid bloodshed at all costs. I shall advise the army not to fight in cities, where civilians will be hurt. We shall have to do our fighting in the countryside.' He sighed. 'Where we belong.'

'But you'll continue to defend the revolution?'

'If people wish it. If not, I'll make a run for it. Not for the first time.'

The pale girl was confused. She squatted on her haunches in the middle of the room, holding her long hair away from her ears. 'Oh, my God. This is *Canada*! We've gone too far!'

Una was much harsher than Makhno. 'Your problem came when the Mounties changed their motto from *Mantien le Droit* to *Mea virtute me involvo*.'

Makhno interposed. 'If only it could have been *Omnia vincit amor, et nos cedamus amori*.' He looked regretfully down at the blonde. 'It'll be good to be on horseback again. I hate machines.'

'It's your one weakness, I'm afraid,' said Una.

The silence became uncertain.

5

CORONATION OF WILLIAM IV AND QUEEN ADELAIDE

> The Coronation of William IV took place on Sept. 8th, 1831, and was celebrated with less magnificence than usual on the ground of economy. The Queen's silver crown was set with jewels which were her own property, and were afterwards returned to her, as she desired that there should be no unnecessary expense incurred.
>
> *The Coronation Series*, No. 31,
> issued by W.D. & H.O. Wills, *c.* 1936

There was, it seemed, to be no consolation in England. Over tea in Derry & Toms roof garden ('their' place) Catherine told Una of her engagement to Mr Koutrouboussis, the ship-owner. 'His naturalisation came through last week and he popped the question.'

'You don't love him.' Una was bleak.

'I love what he represents.'

'Slavery!'

'Freedom. I shan't be his only interest.'

The sun shone on large mock silver cutlery, on sturdy china, on rock-cakes and scones. Beyond all this, in tiny artificial pools, marched fastidious pink flamingoes against a background of box and privet.

'And anyway,' Catherine continued, 'I need the security.'

'I'm giving up the Service.'

'I think you should.' She realised she had missed the implication and melted. 'You know how much I love you.'

'Going back into the profession,' Una said.

Catherine put a hand on Una's hand. 'You'd still be away a lot, dear. But now we can go on meeting – having lovely secret times. You already have more men friends than I do. That anarchist was one, wasn't he?'

It was true. Una removed her hand in order to open her bag.

'I really do think men are our superiors in almost every way,' said Catherine. She smiled. 'Of course, we are their superiors in one area – we can handle them without them realising it. But don't you feel the need to give yourself up to a man? To think you could die for him, if necessary? Oh, Una, there's nothing like self-sacrifice!'

'Jesus Christ,' said Una flatly. 'He's done it again.'

6

> MEADOW BROWN (*Epinephele ianira*). This species is the most abundant of all British Butterflies, occurring throughout the British Islands as far north as the Orkneys, and frequenting every meadow, lane, wood and waste land, from the middle of June until the middle of October. The Meadow Brown is one of the few butterflies that appear regardless of the weather, flying during dull stormy days, as well as in the hottest sunshine. At night it roosts amongst the foliage of trees, and also on low-growing plants. The life of the caterpillar of this butterfly extends over a period of about 250 days. Expanse of wings 2 inches.
>
> *British Butterflies*, No. 15,
> issued by W.D. & H.O. Wills, *c.* 1935

Exactly a week after she had had her meeting with Makhno, on Sunday, 27 June, 1948, Una Persson accepted Major Nye's invitation. She took a train to Rye and a cab from the station to the Jacobean house whose ornamental gardens had been almost entirely converted into fruit and vegetable beds and whose stables were now run as a commercial enterprise by Elizabeth Nye, one of the major's two daughters. His son was away at school. His wife had been confined to her rooms for three or four years.

It was a very hot day. Summer flowers, arranged in dense clusters and grown for profit, gave off a thick scent which brought Una a trace of euphoria as well as sad memories of Makhno's fall. The nurse who looked after Mrs Nye directed Una to the stables. Elizabeth had taken a group of children for a trek. Major Nye, in a worn tweed hacking jacket, darned pullover, moleskin trousers and old wellingtons, stood outside a stall over which the name 'Rhodes' had been engraved in pokerwork. He was feeding an ancient grey horse handfuls of grass from a bucket at his feet. The horse had watering, bloodshot eyes and its nostrils were encrusted with mucus. It laid its ears back as Una approached, causing Major Nye to turn.

'Mrs Persson! Wonderful! This is Rhodes.' The smell from the stall was strong, tinged with sickness.

Una, who had no special fondness for horses, stretched a hand to stroke its nose but it moved, refusing contact. 'I'm afraid he's a one-man horse. I'm so glad the Canadian business is over. Have you heard anything of our friend Makhno?'

Rather closer to self-pity than she would have liked, Una said: 'He's gone where the Southern cross the Yellow Dog.'

'Eh?'

'On his way to South America, I heard.'

'Best place for him. Plenty of room for political experiments there, eh?'

'Not according to everyone's thinking.'

'At least we avoided a Big One. You see I remember the Great War. I was at Geneva in 1910. Eighteen years old.' He smiled and patted Rhodes's nose. 'We don't want another, do we?'

'Perhaps the cost of peace has become a bit too high?'

'It's never too high, my dear. I speak as an army man.' He handed her the bucket. 'Rhodes can't graze for himself any more. Shaky on his pins. Come and help me pick some grass on that bit of lawn over there.' He reached down to pluck a muddy *Telegraph* from a pile near the stall's gate. 'Kneel on this. Have you got any older clothes?'

'Not with me.'

'We'll find you something. You're staying a week or two?'

'If that's all right.'

'All right for me.' He chuckled. She realised that she had never seen him happy before. 'They've allowed you some leave, have they? You've earned it. Makhno would never had given in to anyone else.'

'Possibly.' Una was reluctant to continue this line. 'But I'm not on holiday. I've resigned. I've decided to go back to the stage. I'm tired of diplomacy. It's a bit depressing. Or perhaps I'll try films.'

'Brave girl,' said Major Nye. 'You've sacrificed too much already.'

For a moment she rebelled, resenting his approval. Then she walked over to a lawn already practically bare, and began to tug up grass.

Major Nye joined her. He bent with difficulty. There was a tearing sound as he pulled roots and earth. 'They all say I should have him shot. But I can't do it, you know. I love him. Elizabeth,' he smiled with some pride, 'says he'll be the death of me.'

The shadow of an airship, going from Croydon to the continent, passed over them rapidly. They heard the distant drone of engines.

'It's the beginning of the end,' murmured Major Nye.

'It always is,' said Una.

2. Development (a)

Pierrot on the Moon

They didn't tell me
That breathing was so difficult.
I can't say I think
much
Of the scenery
I wish I was back
in my home again
– They've left me behind...

It seemed a good
idea at the time
Just me – Harlequin and
Columbine
– But they slipped off soon
And here I am
Stranded on the bloody
moon...

Next time things will be
different
And I'll know the score
I'll bring at least an
oxygen tent
And a good deal more
besides
Bacon, eggs and bread
And a telescope...

And I'll buy returns as well
There's no bloody ticket office
Or a gentleman's lavatory
Or a deckchair to be had
And every time I take a step –
I bounce…

They said it'd be just like
Brighton beach
Dodgems and roundabouts
Candyfloss and sticks of rock
Though not so many crowds
Try and get a donkey ride
That's all I've got to say…

Harlequin's Techniques of Courtship

If I let her see my love
Will she also see my pain
And flee from it
As I would flee?

And if I pulled my domino
From my eyes
Would she then know
How much of Pierrot's
Left in Harlequin?

And if I told her of my yearning
Would her body
Cease to burn for me
Instead would she give me
Only sympathy
And mistress turn to wife?

And if I swore eternal love
In anything but
A tone of insincerity
Would I alert her
To involvement
Turn her thoughts
Away from lust?

And if I wept upon her breast
And spoke of fears
Of ghosts and death
Would she withdraw
Her favours from me
Choosing silly Pierrot
For a husband
And shunning me?

No, I can only speak of bright lies
Offer only flattery
Tell her that there are no others
But let her think that many follow
That I may be gone tomorrow
Insecurity is all she wants
From me.
Madam, I present myself:
Sir Harlequin –
I bring you Sin…

Columbine Confused

On the banks of Time's river
Two lovers await me
As the flood takes me by
They reach out their hands
Pierrot and Harlequin
Weeping they greet me
The stream bears me onward
Future and Past…

Which shall I choose?
Oh, I am confused…
Often amused and
Constantly torn…
Down the long centuries
They have pursued me
Courted and cursed me
For what I am

Gravity holds me
In sweet indecision
Between Sun and Moon
To each I'm attracted
Pierrot and Harlequin
Loser and Trickster
Laughing they beckon
As the years flood away

Future and past
Future and past
Future and past
Future and past

As the years flood away
As the years flood away
As the years flood away
Future and past…

2. THE KASSANDRA PENINSULA

I

> In which his torment often was so great,
> That like a Lyon he would cry and rore,
> And rend his flesh, and his owne synewes eat.
> His owne deare Vna hearing euermore
> His ruefull shriekes and gronings, often tore
> Her guiltless garments, and her golden heare,
> For pitty of his paine and anguish sore;
> Yet all with patience wisely she did beare;
> For well she wist, his crime could else be neuer cleare.
>
> – Spenser,
> *The Faerie Queene*, I. x. 28

Una considered her compact. It was silver, with delicate enamel-work by Brule; one of his last pieces.

'Una.'

She shook her head. She refused his confession. His eyes were agony.

'Una.'

She replaced the compact, unused in her patent leather purse. His voice brought her the image of a dark, motionless sea. She drew breath. Makhno had gone on. It had been necessary. His success – what little he expected – depended on the speed of his strategies. Here there was only defeat.

'Una.'

He lay in the shadows, on straw. Through the barn door came the hard air of the New Hampshire winter. She could see across the deep, undulating snow the flat outline of a Dutch farmhouse, black against a near-white sky: the isolated birches, the clustering pines. She could hear the muffled sounds of work. It would be dawn in a moment. They would discover him soon. Freezing her face, Una forced herself to look at her ex-comrade. He had seemed so powerful.

'Una.' It was like the sound of a dying albatross she had heard on Midway Island in the early 1940s.

One of his hands moved a fraction. To stop her? To beg? She glanced beyond his head, at the disused harness, the rusty implements: mementoes of simpler days. She smoothed the silk of her skirt and swung the purse by its strap; then she placed it carefully on her shoulder. She battled against her particular curse, against mindless altruism. But was it a curse or merely her permanent dilemma?

'Una. They'll kill me.'

'No, Jerry.' He would probably be interned until after the primaries. She was close to offering reassurance when happily there came a scream from the sky and snow thudded from the roof of the barn as a pirate Concorde passed overhead, pursued by angry Freedom Fighters. It was so cold and she, like him, had no appropriate clothing. 'Montreal,' she said. 'Try to get to Montreal. I'll see you there.' She stepped in black, high-heeled court shoes into the snow. She shuddered. It had been stupid of them to trust the old Kamov.

2

> I'm ready when you are, señor…
>
> – Bob Dylan

'We begin with ambiguities and then we strive to reconcile them through the logic of Art,' said Prinz Lobkowitz. 'Though these chaps often begin with some simple idea and then try to achieve ambiguity through obfuscation. It won't do.' He threw the composition paper on the floor beside the piano and got up. 'I blame the academics.'

Something rumbled underfoot.

'Well,' she said, 'it's easy.'

She leaned back on the piano stool and swung round to peer at the half-built auditorium. She could see the night sky through the gaps in the tarpaulins covering the shattered glass of the dome; another publicist's broken dream. Lobkowitz, in evening dress, loped forward, tall and thin, looking less well than usual. His attempt, at the invitation of the United States' provisional government, to form a cabinet had failed, as he had predicted it would. As a result both he and Una were out of their jobs. She was relieved; he was contemplative. The meeting, which had been held earlier that evening, in the light of candles and oil lamps, had taken on the air of a funeral reception. Then, gradually, the distinguished old men had drifted away. All but a few of the lamps were out. It was a shame that the damp had affected the murals, from Mozart to Messiaen, on the hastily emulsioned walls. She appreciated the peculiarities of Gregg's style, with its muted colours and shadowy outlines. She had particularly liked the portrait of Schoenberg, on stage for *Pierrot Lunaire* in Berlin, 1912. Now, however, only the composer's raised hands were perceivable, as if he conducted the invisible crowd, here muting the antagonistic shouts, there bringing up the applause. Una wished she could explain her sudden feeling of well-being. She swung to smile at Lobkowitz who shrugged, grinning back at her.

'Ah, well.'

'We search so hard for these intense experiences. Then we reject them almost at once.

'Is it because we are frightened?'

3

There are jewels in the crown of England's Glory;
  And every jewel shines a thousand ways
Frankie Howerd and Noël Coward and Garden Gnomes
  Frankie Vaughan and Kenneth Horne and
    Sherlock Holmes
Monty and Biggles and Old King Cole, in the pink or
    on the dole
  Oliver Twist and Long John Silver, Captain
    Cook and Nellie Dean
Enid Blyton, Gilbert Harding, Malcolm Sargeant,
    Graham Greene
Gra-ham Gree--ne!

– Max Wall

Reluctantly she picked up the AK-47 as Petroff pushed pouches of ammunition across the table at her.

'It suits you,' he said. 'It's elegant, isn't it?' He lit a thin Danemann cheroot. 'You know the rifle?'

'Oh, yes.' She checked its action. 'I was hoping I'd never see one again.' The smoke from his cheroot made her feel sick.

'There's the M60…' He made a movement towards the rack.

'No, no.' She clipped the pouches to the webbing of her lightweight camouflage jacket. She wished that she did not feel quite so comfortable in the gear. It was suspicious. Another cloud of smoke reached her face. She turned away.

'You have everything else?' he asked. 'Plenty of mosquito oil?'

'Plenty. Can't you tell?' She wiped her fingers over the back of her greasy wrist.

He stood up.

'Una.'

'Oh, no you don't,' she said. Helping the wounded was no longer any part of her brief.

'It's you I'm thinking of.' He sat down again, staring beyond her at the veldt on the other side of the border. He brightened, pointing. 'Look. Vultures.'

She did not turn.

He was grinning. 'They're a protected species now!'

Carefully she closed the screen door behind her and stood on the verandah, looking up the road for her transport. It was already half an hour late. She wondered if something had happened to it. If so, it would mean a long wait while they radioed back to

" THAT CAPTAIN CORNELIUS, MISS, 'E WAS 'ERE BEFORE THE REAL TROUBLE STARTED."

Kinshasa for instructions. She glanced at her watch without reading it. She had never been overfond of Africa. Somehow, in spite of everything, they had continued to look to Europe for their models. Just like the Americans. And here she was, Britannia Encyclopaedia, returned for the shoot-out.

'You 'ave ter larf, don't yer, miss?' said the black Cockney corporal, holding up the water-can in which someone had shot two small holes. His heavy boots made the verandah shake as he went by, entering Petroff's office to request an order.

She sat down in a khaki deckchair, placing the rifle at her feet. She stretched her body. The corporal came out again. 'Seen anything o' that Captain Cornelius, miss?' he asked, to pass the time. ''E was 'ere before the real trouble started.'

She laughed.

'He usually is.'

4

In the event of a Sonic Attack, follow these rules:

– Hawkwind

As the river broadened, she became alert, releasing the safety catch, crouching in the front of the motor launch and studying the jungle.

She gave particular attention to the thicker clumps of reeds on both banks. Soon she had made out the funnels and the bridge of an old steamer which had been ambushed here two years before. *The Little Madam* had keeled over so that she was almost on her side; she was rusty and plants clung to her. As Una watched, a small crocodile emerged from one of the funnels and wriggled into the water. *The Little Madam* had been the last of her kind. She had been carrying missionaries back to the coast when a handful of Eritreans, lost and on the run, had mistaken her for a military vessel and used the rest of their mortars on her.

There was a horrible silence in the jungle, as if every bird and insect had been blown away. Yet the foliage itself was lusher than ever; fleshy and dark green. They approached a bend. A huge stretch of dirty detergent scum came swirling towards them and passed on both sides of the labouring launch.

In the stern Shakey Mo Collier, watched by a listless Makhno who had drunk at least twenty cans of local beer, was jumping up and down throwing carved wooden idols into the scum. 'Fuck you! Fuck you!' He drew the idols from a bulky sack, almost as large as himself. He had been upset to learn that his loot had become valueless since the falling off of the tourist trade.

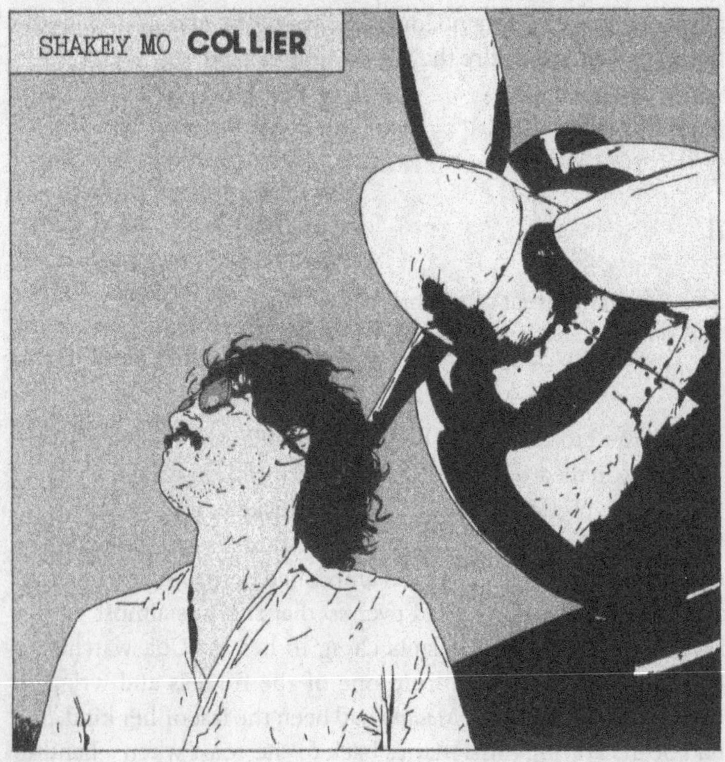

The jungle on the right bank ended suddenly, to be replaced by the great grey terraced complex of Durango Industries' protein processing plant. Una tried not to breathe any of the sweet air until they were past. Nearby were the white buildings of the hospital, identified by their red crosses, looking remarkably like reception buildings for the plant. It could have been one of the sleazier suburbs of Los Angeles, with huge, unhealthy palm trees growing all around. Workers on the roofs and gantries paused to watch the launch. Collier waved at them but lost interest when nobody waved back.

'Surly buggers.' He threw the last of his idols in their direction.

Makhno was asleep. Una was relieved. If he slept, there was not so much danger of his being sick over the seats. They were already slimy with a variety of filth.

Mo moved along the boat to stand beside her. He lit a papyrosa lifted from the tunic pocket of some fallen foe. 'There won't be trouble here, will there?'

'Unlikely.' She wiped her forehead. The worst is over. It seems we'll be slipping this shipment through, at least.'

'I'm making bloody sure I get my bonus in my hand next time.' Mo scowled. 'In gold.' He patted his belt pouch. It bulged. From under the tightly buttoned flap a few fair hairs emerged.

Una still marvelled at Mo's ability to adopt enthusiastically the ideals and ambitions of any employer. A day or so earlier she had asked him about this. He had replied: 'I enjoy being loyal.'

He had earned his high reputation. He had even earned his Russian scalps (he would pass them off, of course, as Rhodesian).

For all his awful habits, Una enjoyed his company and she would be sorry to part, but with the successful delivery of their cargo her mission would be over. She was glad the journey had been relatively swift. No amount of disinfectant or perfume could disguise the smell from the hold. It was the last time, she promised herself, that she took over one of Cornelius's jobs. He had only taken this one on so as not to lose face, to protect a reputation for ruthlessness which he had never really deserved.

Collier could continue with the load to Dubrovnik and get a plane home from there if he wanted to. But she would take her chances at the ports. She had had enough.

5

Isn't it delicious? There's a red sun in the sky! Every time we see it rise, another city dies…

– The Deep Fix

'Of course, I remember him from the early, carefree days,' said Miss Brunner, smiling up at the crystal ball which turned in the centre of the ceiling of Lionel Himmler's Blue Spot Bar. 'He was much better company, then.' She seemed to imply that that had been before he had met Una. There was nothing superficially attractive about the woman, in her severe suit; her awkward, almost self-conscious way of moving; but Una experienced a strong desire to make love to her, perhaps because she sensed no hint of resonance, no sympathy for Miss Brunner. She tried to suppress the desire; she had a good idea of any consequences resulting from even a brief affair. 'When he was still idealistic,' continued Miss Brunner. 'Weren't we all?'

'I still am,' said Una. 'It's silly, isn't it?' She was shocked at herself. That last remark was unlike her. She admired Miss Brunner's power to produce it.

Miss Brunner gave her a smile which might have been of sympathy or of triumph. 'When you're as old a campaigner as me, dear, you won't have time for that sort of thing.' She signed to the sour-faced Jewish waiter. As he approached, she pressed a coin in his hand. 'Bartók's *String Quartet No. 1*,' she said. She watched him shuffle towards the jukebox. It was her turn to display embarrassment. 'I'm feeling a bit reflective. You weren't about in the old days, of course.'

'It depends what you mean,' said Una.

'Our paths hadn't crossed, at any rate.'

'No.' Una wondered how, with so many wounds, the woman could continue to function.

Miss Brunner sipped her B&B. From the fur collar of her jacket came the smell of artificial hyacinths. 'It's nice to know someone's prepared to fill in for him.'

'I'm not exactly filling in,' said Una. 'I think you have the wrong impression.'

'That's what they told me at the Time Centre.'

'Auchinek?'

'No, the other one. Alvarez.'

'He only enjoyed working with Cornelius.'

'That's true.'

'Of course you move about more than any of us ever did, don't you?' Miss Brunner continued.

'I suppose I do.'

'I envy you your freedom. I'm afraid I'm very old-fashioned.'

Una was amused by the series of ploys. 'Oh, no,' she said.

'A terrible reactionary, eh?'

'Not at all.'

'I came out of a very different school.' Reminiscently Miss Brunner smacked her lips.

'It's just a question of temperaments,' said Una.

'Well we each of us see what we're looking for. Especially in a man. That's what "knowing" someone means, doesn't it?'

The waiter returned, just as the scratched record began to play.

'I hate Bartók.' Miss Brunner picked up the menu. 'I find him empty. Vivaldi's what I really like, but the selection's so limited here.' She peered savagely up at the waiter. 'I'll have the *moules* to begin.'

'They're Danish,' said the waiter.

'That's right. And then the jugged hare.'

'Just an omelette.' Una made no attempt to read the menu in the dim light. 'And some mineral water.'

'Plain omelette? Perrier?'

'Fine.'

'Anyway,' said Miss Brunner as she handed the menu to the waiter, 'Collier got through with that last consignment. Which about wraps Africa *and* South America up.'

'It's a relief.'

'It must be for you. I'll be going aback to Sweden tomorrow. It's where I live now.'

'Yes.'

'You know Sweden?'

'Oh, yes.'

'Kiruna?'

'Yes.'

'It's so peaceful.'

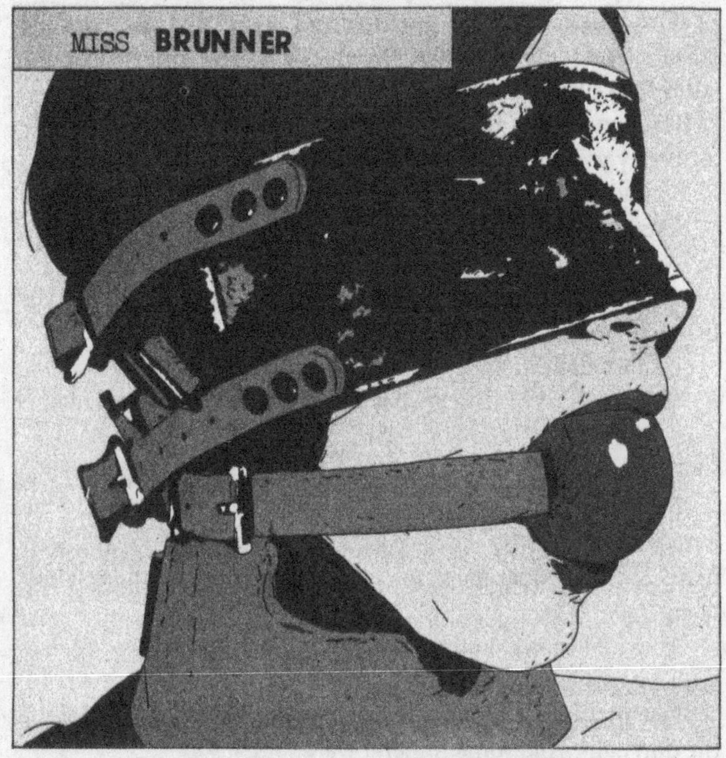

Una could not bring herself to confirm any of these desperate affirmations. As a result Miss Brunner became agitated and cast about for another weapon.

'He was never straightforward,' she said at length. 'That's what I couldn't stand.'

'Well, some of us need to create an atmosphere of ambiguity in which we can thrive.' Una hoped the response wasn't too evidently direct.

'I don't quite follow you, dear.' Miss Brunner had understood all too readily.

Una dispensed with caution. 'While others of course try to

resolve something from the ambiguity they sense around them. As I say, it's a matter of temperament.'

'It's obvious which kind of temperament meets with your approval.'

Una smiled. 'Yes.'

'Speaking for myself, all I want is a quiet life. You didn't get that with Cornelius. He'd foul anything up.'

'I probably didn't know him as well as you did.'

'Very few people could have done.'

Miss Brunner's mussels arrived. She bent her angry head over the bowl.

6

Their snakeskin suits packed with Detroit muscle...

– Bruce Springsteen

It was a relief to enter the car and stuff Ives's *Symphony No. 1* into the player. It wasn't that she had objected to the Bartók, but Himmler's ancient recordings, always too heavy on the bass and worn and scratched, made everything sound awful. Of course Himmler regarded even this as a concession. When he had opened the night-club there had been nothing but Phoenix records to play – a label devoted entirely to Hitler's speeches and National Socialist songs. It had been founded by Arnold Leese, best remembered for calling Mosley a 'Kosher Fascist'. This description was more appropriate to Himmler himself who had, in 1944, changed his name from Gutzmann. It was amazing, she thought, as the music began, how she was warming to America since it had rejected her.

She drove through a cleaned-out Soho, her body filled with sound from the quad speakers in the AMC Rambler Station Wagon she currently favoured. She had never been happy with non-automatics, and though this car had seen more exciting days it provided a secure environment in a world which, at present, she preferred for its chaos. The alternatives to chaos were all too suspect. With the volume as high as possible it was impossible to hear either the engine, the air-conditioning or the few other noises from the streets. This and her soundproofed flat helped her keep herself to herself. Just now, she had no time for civilians or casualties. The abandoned strip joints and casinos behind her, she made for Hyde Park as the second movement began. It was hard to believe that this was the conception of a seventeen-year-old. She yearned for her lost youth.

Studying her hands as they rested casually on the large steering wheel she almost crashed into the pack of dogs crossing the road in front of her. The dogs were the reason why it was now only safe to drive through the park. Mongrels, greyhounds, Alsatians, chows and poodles ran erratically, snapping at one another's necks and flanks, and disappeared into the shrubs. She turned out of the park into Bayswater Road, passed Notting Hill Gate and the ruins of the apartment buildings blocking Kensington Park Road, made a right into Ladbroke Grove, then, eventually, another right into Blenheim Crescent, stopping outside the seedy terraced house she feared so much, even though it sheltered at least one of the people she loved.

She disembarked from the car and locked it carefully, putting the keys into the pocket of her long black trench coat. She turned up her collar, mounted the cracked steps, found the appropriate bell and pressed it. She leaned on the door, watching the Co-op milkman as his van moved slowly down the other side of the street making deliveries. Una pressed the bell again, knowing that there was bound to be someone up. It was almost seven o'clock. There was no reply. The milkman came back along the other side of the road. Una pressed the bell for the third time. The milkman climbed the steps with five pints in his arms. He set them at her feet. 'You're up early,' he said. 'Who you after?'

'Cornelius,' she said.

He laughed, shaking his head as he went away.

Una found his attitude irritatingly mysterious and would have followed him to question him had not she heard a cautious movement on the other side of the door. She stepped out of view, huddling against the broken pillar of the porch. The door rattled. It opened a fraction. A red hand reached for the milk.

'Good morning,' said Una.

The hand withdrew, but the door did not shut.

'Mrs Cornelius?'

'Not in,' said an unmistakeable voice. 'Bugger orf.'

'It's Una Persson.'

The door opened wider and Mrs Cornelius stood there, in curlers, her woolly dressing gown drawn about her, her bleary eyes blinking. 'Ha!' she said. 'Thort you woz ther bleedin' milkman.' Now Una knew why he had laughed. It was why there had been no answer to the bell – the combination of bottles rattling and the doorbell ringing sent Mrs Cornelius automatically to cover. 'Wotcha want?'

'Actually I was looking for Catherine.'

'Actcherly, she ain't 'ere.'

Mrs Cornelius relented. 'Orl right, luv, come in.' She took two pints from the step, darted a look along the street, admitted Una, closed the door.

Una followed Mrs Cornelius, ascending stone stairs still bearing traces of broken linoleum; they reached a landing and a half-open door. She entered a room full of unattractive smells – cabbage, lavender water, beer, cigarette smoke. It was immediately evident that Catherine had been here recently, for the flat was tidier than usual. The piles of old weeklies were stacked neatly beside the sideboard which, though cluttered with Mrs Cornelius's cryptic souvenirs, lacked the bottles, cans and empty packages she allowed to accumulate while her daughter was not in residence. Mrs Cornelius made for the gas-stove in the far corner, picked up the dented kettle and filled it at the tap over the sink. Una could see through to Mrs Cornelius's small, dark bedroom, with its huge wardrobe, its walls covered with photographs, many of them cut from magazines and newspapers. The other door was shut. This was the door to Catherine's room.

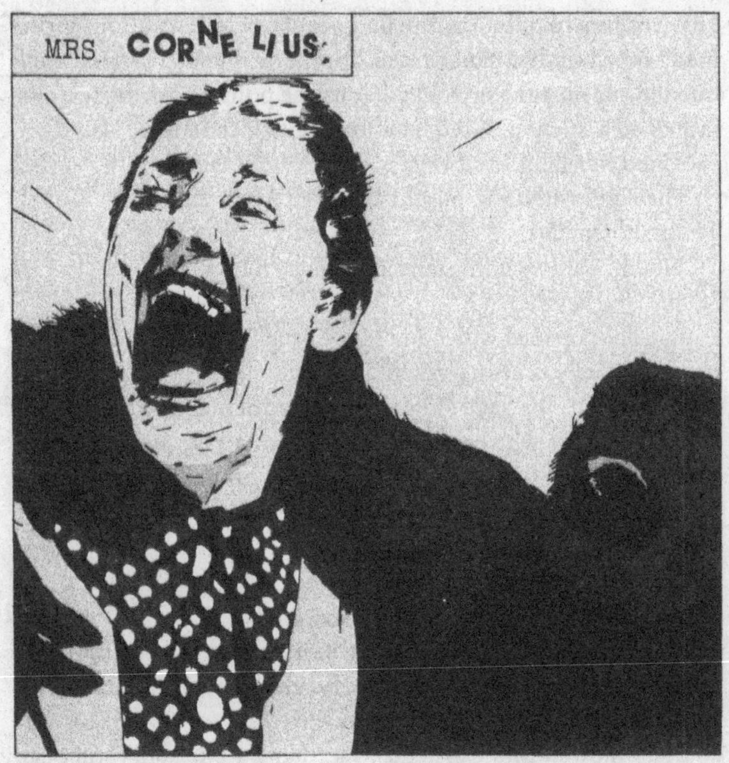

'She's not up yet, lazy bitch,' said Mrs Cornelius. 'Cuppa tea?' She relaxed and was friendly. Of her children's acquaintances Una was one of the few Mrs Cornelius actually liked. It did not stop Una being afraid of the woman as of nobody else.

'Thanks.' Una hated the prospect.

Mrs Cornelius shuffled to her daughter's door and hammered on it. 'Wakey, wakey, rise an' shine. 'Ere's yer mate fer yer!'

'What?' It was Catherine.

Mrs Cornelius laughed. 'It'd take the 'Orn o' Fate ter get 'er up!'

Suddenly the whole flat smelled of rose water. It was wonderful; a miracle.

'Bugger,' said Mrs Cornelius, picking up the fallen bottle.

7

In the heart of the city, where the alligator roams, I'm a little lost lamb. Ain't got no place to go…

– Nick Lowe

She found Lobkowitz where she had last met him, in the ruined auditorium. Through the speakers of an inefficient tannoy came the familiar last passages of the *Robert Browning Overture*. Then there was silence.

'Browning was a prose Wagner and so was Ives,' said the Prinz as he dusted down his tweed fishing suit.

'You've been seeing Cornelius. Is he back?'

'With a vengeance. Though not a very big one.'

'Anything I'd recognise.'

'You know his penchants…'

'I'm not surprised, though I felt he'd crack.'

Prinz Lobkowitz seemed to tire of this exchange. He leaned against the warped piano. 'There's rarely any danger of that. He just goes dormant.'

'I was right to trust my instincts, then?'

'Always, Una.'

'They're so hard to rationalise.'

'We waste too much time, trying to produce quick resolutions, when usually they're on the way and we don't know it.'

She was amused. 'The voice of experience!'

'I hope so.'

'Anyway, he's better?'

'Yes, he's better. The usual fever. We all suffer from that.'

She was not sure this was true of her, but she said: 'I was never any good at instant decisions.'

'Maybe because you had more to lose than anybody else.'

She shrugged.

'Anyway,' he continued wistfully, 'you received his message?'

'It was unmistakeable.'

'You didn't have to fulfil all his obligations. He was grateful when he heard.'

'There were other people involved. It wasn't his ego I was worried about. He was stupid to have tried for the Presidency. Then, of all times! He was never what you'd call a convinced republican, or a democrat, in the accepted sense.'

'Surely, though, that's why he tried?'

She nodded. 'I'm glad America's pulled a couple of decent chestnuts out of the fire.'

'You couldn't say they deserved it. But I'm sentimental about George Washington, too. Chile, Brazil, the Argentine – their worst crime was a kind of naïve complacency. Admittedly that attitude leads to excesses of brutality in the long run.' Lobkowitz yawned. 'I've never seen so much jungle on fire. And whole mountains. The apocalypse. I wish you'd been here.'

'I had to go back to England.'

'I know.' He was sympathetic. He put a white hand on her shoulder. 'Will you stay for a while now? In New England? You have a place in the Appalachians, haven't you?'

'A couple, at different ends. But there's a sub-tenant in one. He must have been there forty years or more. It would be interesting to see how he's getting on. I haven't aged that much. Not superficially.'

He shook his head. 'You can be very vague at times. Feminine, eh?'

'Is that what it is?' She bent to kiss his hand. 'Have you got the map? I'd better be going.'

8

She wants to be a bad girl. Good girl, bad girl. She needs to be a woman...

– The Deep Fix

'You're still looking ill.' She tried to disguise any hint of sympathy. She forced her mouth into disapproving lines.

'They don't treat you very well. But I'm grateful really. It kept me out of the war. I always wondered how I'd do it.'

'You thought you could stop it. You remember?'

He was bashful. 'Oh, yes. So thanks again.'

All his old charm had returned and it was hard for her not to warm to him, as she had first warmed, long ago. The self-pity was gone, for the moment, and he had a good deal of his old style. He fingered the collar of his black car coat, turning the lapels so that they framed his pale face. 'It's cold for spring.'

'The long range forecasts are predicting an Ice Age again.'

'Always a bad psychological sign. And the computers?'

'That we'll all be dead in a year or two.'

He grinned. 'Acute depression often follows a period of frenetic activity. You'll see – in a few months the weather forecasts will give us brilliant summers, plenty of rain for the crops, mild winters, and the computers will be going on about a Golden Age.' He put his arm around her shoulders. It was awful how quickly her resolution disappeared. Her struggle lasted less than a second. 'Stick with me, baby,' he promised, 'and it will always be a Golden Age somewhere.'

'That's not what you were saying the last time we spoke,' she reminded him.

'We all suffer from depression occasionally.' He dismissed the creature he had been. Probably he didn't remember. She began to think that his attitude was the healthiest.

She climbed into the driving seat of the Rambler. He sat beside

«ACUTE DEPRESSION OFTEN FOLLOWS
A PERIOD OF FRENETIC ACTIVITY.»

her, watching her with approval as she started the big car. 'It's a good thing petrol's cheap again. Where are we going? Concord?'

'Yes. First.' As she started the engine the tape she had been playing came on. He reached to remove it. 'Enough of that classical stuff,' he said. 'Let's have something romantic and jolly.' He sorted through the box of cartridges on the seat between them. 'Here we are.'

He slotted the *Holidays Symphony* into the player. 'Much better.'

He leaned back in the car as she drove it down the bumpy track to the empty highway.

'That's what I like about you, Una. You know how to relax.'

3. Development (b)

Pierrot's Song of Positive Thinking

I'm glad I'm not dead
I'm glad I'm not dead
I'm glad I'm not dead
I'm glad I'm not dead
I'm glad I'm not dead
I'm glad I'm not dead
I'm glad I'm not dead
I'm glad I'm not

The Nature of the Catastrophe

Can anyone suggest an explanation
Can anyone please suggest an explanation
Can anyone suggest an explanation

Through the Megaflow (Waltz)

Oh, Columbine
I'm lost in Time,
There ain't a sign
Of ho-o-ome...

Where is – where is –
My lovely Columbine?

She took a trip
On an old time ship
There was a slip
And now she's lost
Alone…

She could be
In Nine O Three
Or Twenty Million and Six
She told me
That she'd be free
But now she's lost her fix…

Oh, Columbine
Sweet love of mine
I missed you so
On the megaflow

Where is – where is –
My lovely Columbine?

She said we'd meet
In a place so neat
Say June of Fifty Seven,
But catastrophe
She could not beat
So maybe she's in Heaven…

Where is – where is –
My lovely Columbine?
Where is – where is –
My lovely Columbine?

3. REVOLUTIONS

I

Get Cracking on Kellogg's

Barnie stacks bricks as quick as some people talk, and he never drops them. 'Course it's simply a case of cause and effect. You see, his Missus knows that at least a quarter of a man's daily output of energy must come from his 8 o'clock intake of calories*. So she gives him Kellogg's Corn Flakes for energy and warmth. Food needn't be hot to warm you. Human beings take their fuel from energy-giving foods (chiefly carbohydrates) that are burned up in the body. Kellogg's are extremely rich in carbohydrates – so they give you energy and keep you warm.

* Calories are units of heat that measure the amount of energy different foods provide.

Ad, *Picture Post*, 1 March, 1952

'Those poor devils,' said Colonel Pyat, 'they cannot survive in the world of the imagination. They are afraid of it. They reject it as vulgar, or over-coloured or – what? And then they offer us their threadbare language, their worn-out images as –' he sniggered – 'poetry.'

'If I were you, colonel, I would be concentrating on the immediate problems.' Nestor Makhno shifted his weight as best he could. At least the truck was moving fairly rhythmically now and the swaying could be anticipated. They must be on one of the pieces of autobahn which had been extended into Bohemia in the days before the war. The men were tied to each wheel of a huge, old-fashioned 120mm field gun. 'I'm not impressed by your sudden discovery of the romantic agony.'

'Particularly since it was our money which helped you make

it.' In the corner, near the only place where the canopy was loose enough to let in a breeze and the occasional light from a passing vehicle's headlamps, Una Persson looked up from the rope which bound her hands. She had been trying to gnaw it but her mouth kept growing intolerably dry. She referred to the cocaine Colonel Pyat had brought with cash set aside for bribing their way out of Bohemia. At Passau, on the Danube, they had been changing trains with the other passengers when several militiamen had stopped them. At that time Colonel Pyat had been even more euphoric than now. He had addressed the soldiers as comrades and tried to appeal to their sense of liberty. Consequently he and the others had been searched and their weapons discovered. Now they were on their way back to Prague. Una knew that there was every possibility of treating with the new authorities and getting free again, but she was worried in case someone should link her name with that of Lobkowitz, who would be arriving on *The Kansas City Whirlwind* the next day, brought back, once more, from exile in America. Lobkowitz's peculiar mixture of anarcho-syndicalism and despotism had an appeal to all the factions involved in the Slavic Border Wars. Everyone was tired of the present cant, all of which denied authoritarianism and displayed it in every action. With a bit of luck the Czechs and Slovaks and Poles and Galiceans and Byelorussians and the rest would see some virtue in the example of the Ukraine, whose anarchism had given the country stability, relative wealth and security from outside attack, and had, since Istanbul had been razed by the so-called suicide fleet of Cypriot airships five years before, turned Kiev and Odessa into the most vital cultural centres of Europe or the Middle East. She turned her face against the cold stream of air and wet her lips. She was halfway through the rope and congratulated her captors for their contempt of her femininity when they had casually tied her hands in front of her. Makhno and Pyat were much more secure. If she used all her strength now, she might even snap the rope. But she continued to chew. In the meantime Nestor Makhno was rubbing fruitlessly, trying to find a suitably sharp place on the field gun, while Colonel Pyat's voice rose higher and higher as he

COLONEL PYAT HAD ADDRESSED THE SOLDIERS AS COMRADES AND TRIED TO APPEAL TO THEIR SEN-SE OF LIBERTY ...
7

elaborated his indignation, expressing cosmic disgust at their plight, offering cosmic solutions, the broadest of comforts.

Una sympathised with him. The tight, worried, stupid faces of the local authorities, who had sneered at them and sent them back to Prague, were still in her mind. There was nothing more depressing than those faces: men and women who, through expediency and fear, served a revolutionary cause they could not understand. She had seen so many of them. They continued to depress her. For some reason there were always more of them around railway stations than anywhere else. Perhaps the tracks and the timetables offered less ambiguity than the rest of the world. Wristwatches were important to them, too, she remembered. And tightly buckled coats. It was interesting to note how in the early, wild and enthusiastic days of the revolution the characteristic costume was a greatcoat flung open, a hat askew, a hand spread outwards; later the representations of leaders became identified with neatly buttoned uniforms, well-set caps and firm salutes, and only the Cossacks, as in Tsarist times, had been allowed to display a certain 'freedom', to represent the glories of irresponsibility. The new Tsars, in Muscovia, favoured the casual-bourgeois style of middle-aged German businessmen on holiday: cashmere pullovers, well-creased grey slacks, plaid sports jackets and straight-stemmed briar pipes. It was what they felt, Una assumed, the people wanted – middle-class monarchy, armchair imperialism. She feared those people almost as much as she feared the police-caste Pyat still raved against.

'They destroy so much in the name of safety. They destroy those who have enabled their kind to survive for millennia. Without us, they would die out!' Pyat continued.

Makhno was amused. 'Us? Your Zaporozhian Cossacks were not the most liberal and pacific of people.'

'The Cossacks held liberty to be their most prized possession!' Pyat had long since revealed, by his mistakes, that he had no Cossack background at all, but had been born in the slums of Minsk, probably of half-Jewish parents. He had fled the Ukraine in the uniform of a Zaporozhian Cossack colonel and for a while had benefited from the deception. But Makhno enjoyed pretending to believe the lie.

'And were prepared to kill every Jewish baby to defend their liberty!' The anarchist laughed.

'Don't blame the Cossacks for that!' said Pyat with heat. 'It was all the fault of the Polish landlords who leased their Russian lands to Jews. A lot of Jews said so themselves.'

'You mean the Jews blamed the Poles for letting them bleed Ukrainians?' Makhno flexed his arms. 'My God!'

'You're as anti-Semitic as the rest of them.' Pyat spoke in that peculiar, detached tone he always affected when the subject of Jews was raised. He thought the tone lofty. Sometimes it deceived and angered a less perceptive hearer. But it aroused Makhno's sympathy. The Ukrainian did his best to change the subject, in order to lose his temptation of baiting Pyat. 'I could do with a drink,' he said.

'You usually could.' Pyat disapproved of Makhno's habits.

Una was pleased with Makhno's self-control as he resisted any further mention of the twenty-five grams of cocaine found on Pyat while the militia was searching him. The soldiers had accepted his explanation that these were headache powders and had carefully set them aside, doubtless for their own use. Makhno and Una had been amused by such a turn of events but, for a while, just after they had been tied up in the truck, Pyat had wept. He still had some five grams hidden in the collar of his English shirt: just under his nose, as it were, but at this moment totally unattainable.

'The Cossacks aren't cowards, at least!' Pyat returned grumpily to the earlier point.

'No,' said Makhno. 'They seek out the highest possible authority and then fight for it to the death.' Actually, he shared a great deal of Pyat's romanticism where Cossack ideals were concerned. A number of renegades had fought with him at Ekaterinburg and elsewhere, though at least half his officers had been Jewish intellectuals who had recognised in him a tactician of almost preternatural genius. Because Makhno had objected to Grigorieff's pogroms the anarchist had shot down Grigorieff while the nationalist hetman's followers looked on. A little later he had gently disbanded the nationalist army as being of no use to him because it had 'absorbed inhumane habits of thought and action'. That had been the day before he had carried the black banner against the combined forces of Trotsky's reds and Krasnoff's Don Cossack whites, when the anarchist army, outnumbered four to one, had scattered its enemy so thinly along the banks of the Pripet, and later the Donets, that since then neither Reds nor Whites had ever considered a further strike against the Ukrainian heartland. Nowadays, of course, Makhno was *persona non grata* in Kiev. His sense of history gave him an ironic perspective on the situation. He had expected nothing else. For the past twenty-five years he had lent his energies to half a dozen successful

revolutions and a dozen failures, such as the recent ones in Canada, Yucatan and Somalia. It had only been to please Una, who had looked him up in Paris during one of his three-month benders, that he had become involved in supporting the Bohemian anarcho-communists who only a week before had threatened Prague under his leadership. But the whole army had been betrayed, in classic manner, by authoritarian socialists. Bolsheviks had all but destroyed the anarchists in an ambush in the Ruthenian Carpathians, near the Veretski Pass. There had been nothing for it but to try to take what was left of their light armour through Hungary and seek refuge in Vienna, but the Bolshevists had somehow found an air force and seven aerial cruisers and had bombed the rest of the army to bits. About fifty survivors had split up in order to cross the Austrian border, but Una, Pyat and Makhno had been recognised and turned back, having to take the train via Brno to Passau, where the Bolshevists, temporarily in control, had caught them. Una knew that their return to Prague as prisoners was bound to embarrass someone, so there was a chance that they would be 'lost' – shot or let go. It was a fifty-fifty chance. And if Lobkowitz was given the opportunity to save them, it would embarrass him and put him in an extremely difficult position, if he appeared to favour them.

Una freed herself at last. Lobkowitz hardly knew Makhno or Pyat and so their chances were better than hers. Travelling alone she would have more flexibility and therefore more hope of escape. She stood up. She spoke a little shakily as she peeled back the canopy, waiting for the truck to slow.

'Good luck.' She unhooked her tape player from her belt. She checked the batteries. It was still surprising that the militia had left the unfamiliar-looking machine with her. Perhaps they had decided it was a booby trap. She switched on. Richard Hell was singing 'You Gotta Lose'. 'It's painful unless it's loud,' she said. But she failed to get the volume very much higher. It served its purpose, however, drowning out Pyat's protests and causing the truck to slow.

She slipped through the curtain.

Time for a new temporary rôle, she thought.

2

Kitty-Kola: A Correction

Our attention has been drawn to an article entitled Sudan in Ferment in your issue of Dec. 29. In this article you refer to 'Egypt's plagiaristic Kitty-Cola.' We would point out that 'Kitty-Kola' has no connection whatever with Egypt. 'Kitty-Kola' is a speciality soft drink marketed by this company, and licences for its preparation and sale are granted to bottlers after their application has been approved. The Kitty-Kola Co. Ltd, of London, is associated with another English company which has now been established over 100 years and there is certainly no connection whatsoever with Egypt.

'Kitty-Kola' is a drink formulated here in England which is rapidly gaining acceptance on world markets. It is all part of this country's export drive and of our efforts to keep overseas markets which have been traditionally this country's for many, many years.

Letter to *Picture Post*, 1 March, 1952

It was 1952 according to Una's newspaper and 1976 according to Nick Lowe, who was singing 'Heart of the City' on her Vidor portable radio as she raised its lid and slid back in her deckchair, positioned to face Bognor's doubtful ocean. Jerry, that eternal spirit of seaside holidays past, came limping over the shingle towards her, his scrawny body bright red and peeling, his peculiar trunks threatening to slip over his hips.

'Blimey! Hot enough for you?'

Una pushed her sunglasses onto her forehead. 'You didn't get burned like that on any British beach. Not in May you didn't.'

'I'm not burned!' He was indignant. 'I'm tanning. What's that row?' He nodded at the Vidor.

She turned it off. 'The future. Do you want to get me an ice-cream? What flavours do they have?' She reached into her beach bag for her purse.

'Flavours? They might have strawberry. But it's probably only vanilla.'

'The newspaper was right.'

'Eh?'

'Get me a wafer, will you?'

He was glad to go. He returned with two hard blocks of ice-cream sandwiched between wafer biscuits. Austerity, she thought, took some getting into. She wished she was back in the Balkans where life, at least, was interesting. She looked to left and right at deckchairs and British bathers. This was Jerry's nightmare, not her own.

He kneeled beside her, licking the ice-cream, looking craftily out to sea.

'Well,' she said. 'What is it? You arranged to meet, don't forget.'

'Oh, yeah.' He was looking younger and weaker, as if time were running backwards in him and draining him as it did so. 'My mum said I ought to join the Home Guard.'

'You want me to get you out of some sort of domestic row? Or military service?'

'I'm stuck here, Una. I've lost all my old power. I don't think you realise...'

'I can't change the megaflow.'

The word was only dimly familiar to him. 'It's ever since Mum died.'

'Your mother's still alive. I saw her over near the entrance to the pier.'

'That's what's wrong.'

'Retrogressive tendencies, eh?' She shook her head. 'You always had them. But you never came this far back before – and not on this line. Do you know there's never been a Second World War here?'

He was disbelieving. 'Then why are we putting up with all this bloody austerity?'

'We never got over the General Strike. There's nothing much wrong with the economy. It's supporting the Empire. This is a sort of punishment on the working classes.'

'No!'

'There are pros and cons,' she told him.

'Cor!' He was impressed. 'What can you do to get me out of it?'

'I don't think you've got the moral rigour to do it,' she said. 'You're not even a force for Chaos any more. You've become a victim, Jerry. Once...'

He smirked.

It made her laugh. 'I'll do my best. Is your mate Collier around?'

'In London. His mum and dad aren't going anywhere this year.'

She closed the lid of the Vidor and fastened the catches, replacing it in her bag. She took out a strange Baedeker and turned to the timetables at the back.

3

Will the French Hold?

There is therefore grave danger that the French, losing every year the equivalent in officers of a complete promotion from their military college of Saint Cyr and 5,000 boys from every corner of France, deserted as they think by their natural allies, the British and the Americans, threatened as they think by a revived Wehrmacht, may pull out of Indo-China and bring their battle-trained divisions home to watch the Rhine. But if they do, Korea will look like a tactical exercise, and Malaya a piece of boy-scouting. Indo-China, as de Lattre told the Americans, is as important as the Battle of the Bulge in 1944. If it falls, Communism within a few short months could be battering at Suez and Australia. The Diggers might hold out: how about Farouk?

Article, *Picture Post*, 1 March, 1952

There had to be an alternative, thought Una, to Disco Fever on the one hand and the Red Army Ensemble on the other. She drove the hearse as fast as she dared; up past the West London Crematorium and round the corner into Ladbroke Grove. Behind her something in the elaborate coffin grumbled and squeaked. Jerry never travelled well, even when she was trying to help him through the early seventies and into the middle of that decade where, everything being equal, he could rest up for a bit. Most likely, she thought, he was objecting to the fact that the hearse was a converted Austin Princess and not the Daimler he had asked for. If he went on like this, however, she would have to give up all her promises and bury him in the country. Somewhere near Godalming, she thought viciously. But she hadn't the heart for it.

Or the sea, she thought. Not for the first time.

She groped on the seat beside her for her half-eaten apple. There was nothing harder, she reflected, as she speeded up past a

march of Radical Social Workers, for the imaginative person to imagine than an unimaginative person. Consequently the paranoid ascribed every Machiavellian motive to the dullest, least inventive people. Those least capable of subtle malice were those most often credited with it. The time dwellers had to learn such things early. Too often metaphysics got you and then you were lost. It was very much like a drug experience, she supposed. But that was more in Jerry's line than hers. She would have to ask him when he woke up.

She went past Ladbroke Grove Tube station, past the Kensington Palace Hotel on the one side and The Elgin on the other, past the new housing development standing on the site of the Convent of the Poor Clares, past Blenheim Crescent, where Jerry's mum had lived, and parked near the corner, just before Elgin Crescent. From the house opposite came Shakey Mo Collier and three of his ageless friends, in black leather, studs, silver, and street ephemera, members of the pop group Motörhead. In the lead, his features beaming with somewhat generalised good will behind mirror shades, was Lemmy. He pushed his hair back from his ears and lit a cigarette. 'Bloody hell,' he said. 'Is this it, then? Is it?'

'It's all yours.' Una found herself warming to the musician. He reminded her of Jerry. 'Is the hole ready?'

Mo interrupted. 'I dug it myself. Are you sure he won't – you know – cough it?'

'He can't,' said Una. 'Can he?'

4

Liner to Mars

We've seen how short-sighted these particular prophets were. Is the same story going to be repeated when, some time during the next fifty years, we begin the exploration of space? Most scientists who've made a serious study of 'astronautics' agree that we'll ultimately be able to build spaceships, but probably few consider that they'll be of much more than scientific value. We'll be able to send small expeditions to the Moon and planets, at very great expense – but as for large-scale space-flight and the colonisation of the planets, that belongs strictly to the realms of 'science fiction'. So say the pessimists – and we propose to ignore them. It may take a hundred years, it may take a thousand – but, ultimately, men will lift their commerce into space as they've lifted it into the air. The liners of the future, homeward bound from Mars or Venus, will link our Earth with the new worlds that now lie waiting for the first human footsteps.

– Arthur C. Clarke,
Picture Post, 1 March, 1952

'Every future we inhabit is someone else's past,' said Una as she and Catherine unpacked the picnic. 'God, how I yearn for the mindless present. When you were a kid. Do you remember?'

'Do you? I've got a lot of different memories. It's what happens to you.'

Una nodded and began to peel the sealing strip from the small jar of Beluga caviar they had brought, while Catherine buttered slices of Ryvita. They had parked their orange Mobylette-50s by the gate of this Cumbrian field and were seated in the long grass by the river. Overhead was a willow. To their left was a small stone bridge, thick with weeds and flowers and scarcely ever used. Behind them and ahead of them were rolling, varicoloured summer hills, their contours and buildings unchanged since the seventeenth century. The women took deep breaths of rich air and swatted at midges and wasps. As often happened in this part of England, summer had come early and would be short. They were making the most of it. It was one of the few parts of the world where both of them could feel completely at ease. Fifty miles or so away, on the coast, the great nuclear reactors seemed to guard their security, as timeless as the rest of the landscape. Una, so used to impermanence, to plastic vistas, to all kinds of physical and social permutations, found herself incapable of imagining any radical change to this world. They had built a six-lane motorway through it, and that had only enhanced it, added a dimension. She smiled to herself. She had thought the same of the Sussex downs, once, without realising that that was where she was. Was it a state of mind which imposed tranquillity upon a landscape, after all? Was it the only salve offered to the wounded romantic imagination? She had always preferred hills and mountains to valleys and plains. When she was in low country she always felt the urge to run off someone's cattle.

'There's an inevitability to linear thinking that sometimes brings me down a bit.' Catherine mused. 'Do you remember that time in Bombay? Or wherever. The future. No, it couldn't have been Bombay? Angkor Wat? Anuradhapura? One of those old cities. They had created a huge future and then it had deserted them. Is that what happened? A divergence of some kind? Where did they go? All these mysterious monuments scattered about the world. Monuments to literal-mindedness.'

'And the literal-minded, in turn, think that people from space built them.' Una was amused. 'There's an irony.'

'They'd never get it.' Catherine pulled back her blouse and bared her breasts to the sun. 'Ah. That's better. The only invasion from space I care about is the one that turns me nice and brown.'

'It's a very simple form of pragmatism,' said Una. She hitched up her summer frock and put her feet in the water. 'But that's fair enough. We are on holiday.'

'Which reminds me. How's Jerry?'

Una wished that Catherine hadn't raised the subject. 'Lying low.'

'In cold storage, is he? That makes a change.'

Una had forgotten how little disturbed Catherine could be where Jerry was concerned. Catherine believed Jerry to be immortal.

Her feet still in the water she turned at the waist and laid a lip on Catherine's nipple.

Catherine stroked Una's hair.

'You must be tired of playing Jerry's rôle,' she said sympathetically.

Una rolled onto her back. 'Shall we buy a place here? A retreat?'

'There's no such thing, love. Once you own it, it stops being a retreat. You know that as well as I do.' Catherine found her friend's hand. 'Sorry if I upset you. I didn't mean…'

'You don't understand,' said Una.

'Does one have to? I can't believe much in understanding. I do believe, though, in sympathy and comfort. In enthusiasm. What is understanding? It's translation. And you always lose something when you translate. Don't you?'

'But you have a rough idea of what I'm going through.'

'Sort of,' said Catherine. She laughed. 'No.'

Much to Una's own relief, she laughed in return.

5

'If Only My Name Was Denis'

To score double centuries, to man a frontier-post in Mexico, to pilot a Space-fleet to Mars – these are games popular with every boy of every age. And it is natural and right that this should be so. Tales of sport and adventure and excitement fire a boy's imagination; they help him to see the world in a fresh and vivid way; they enlarge his horizon, and inspire his ideals. Yet – it cannot be denied – a boy's longing for adventure and excitement may often cause great and reasonable anxiety. Adventurousness may be turned to violence, excitement to cruelty by a variety of vicious influences. And here cheap second-rate comic-strips are much to blame. They warp and distort a boy's sense of values and give him a false outlook on life; under their influence he fancies himself a hero, a superman; someone who escapes responsibility and seeks refuge in fantasy. It remains the prime object of EAGLE to change all that; and (adapting the famous phrase) to see that 'the Devil does not have all the exciting comics'. Here no creed of violence is preached; no tawdry morality or cheap sensationalism or worship of the superman ever appears. For EAGLE is edited by a Clergyman; and underlying the tales of Space Exploration, the exciting strip cartoons and articles on sport, the colourful features on Science and Nature and the World, there is a Christian philosophy of honesty and unselfishness. And in EAGLE it is shown in a form which every boy can understand and respect.

Ad, *Picture Post*, 1 March, 1952

Major Nye sat on a stool outside his shed, grunting as his daughter Elizabeth grew bright red and tugged at his left gumboot. 'Sorry about this,' he said.

Una and Catherine said in concert: 'Can I help?'

'It's okay,' said Elizabeth. 'Awkward buggers, wellies. Sorry, Dad.' She winked at her friends. 'He hates me swearing.'

'I shouldn't,' he said. 'Do enough of it myself.' He rose in his thin socks. 'What do you think of the patch now?' He regarded, with some satisfaction, his vegetable gardens. 'We're almost entirely self-sufficient, you know. Apart from tobacco. But that's not really any good for you, anyway, is it? Come the revolution, we'll be okay.'

Una remembered a thousand famines and gasped.

'You all right, Mrs P?' He put his hand on her arm. 'Trod on a stone? Put the kettle on, Liz, there's a good girl. We'll have some tea.'

Elizabeth shrugged. 'Come and help me, Cathy.'

Una and Major Nye stood alone in the garden. From an upstairs window a pale, forgotten face regarded them with miserable and imperfect knowledge. 'I had planned to retire completely,' said the major. 'But what with kids to educate and the wife's doctors, and the value of the pension going down every year…'

'We're the only ones Prinz Lobkowitz trusts,' said Una. 'If you can get Makhno out of prison in Australia I think it would do a lot of good. The charge was trumped up, wasn't it?'

'I wouldn't go as far as that. But I've looked at the file. A lot of circumstantial evidence, certainly. We could reopen the case.'

'And release him.'

'I think so.' Major Nye sat down on the stool again and put his feet into carpet slippers. He lifted a boot and began to bang it against a nearby step. 'I saved some radishes for you.'

'Lovely. The conference is to be held in September. In Trieste.'

'Best time of year for Trieste.' He began to roll himself a cigarette. 'I should think the Jugoslavs are happy about that. Not so far to go for them.'

'They're hardly playing an important rôle. They've been more or less neutral, along with the Ukraine. Lobkowitz hopes for a Pan-Slavic Treaty, to include the Russian states.'

'They've always been a bit stand-offish, haven't they?'

'But it isn't important. Makhno is still very much respected in the Ukraine, even if he isn't liked. He was never a natural politician.'

'That's obvious. Fancy trying to start an anarchist uprising in Queensland!' Major Nye lit his cigarette, puffing vigorously. 'That's what I call quixotic, Mrs P. Eh?'

'Well, optimistic, anyway.'

'I've heard that Makhno wasn't too pleased with you, however.' Major Nye squinted back at the house, but the face had withdrawn.

'Not Makhno. You're thinking of Pyat.'

'You know my nickname for that one?'

'No.'

'Squash.'

'Swede?'

'What? Oh, not the turnip sort. The game. Fives. Get it? Why does he call himself by a number? Is it an old code-name? Those Russians change their names at the drop of a hat.'

'I don't know what his real name is.' Una smiled. 'It's strange I never wondered. Colonel Five. Five what?'

'Five lives,' he said, 'at least.'

'Five lies, in his case. He's not a colonel, of course. I don't think he's ever served in a war. Not voluntarily, at any rate. He's from Kiev. An engineer or something. Born in Minsk. His family – his mother, at least, went to Tsaritsyn where he spent his early childhood. Later the pair of them turned up in Kiev. I think that's where he met Makhno.'

'A funny pair.'

'He doesn't like Makhno a bit. But he sticks close to him. Familiarity is a form of security, after all.'

'So Makhno is still friendly to you.'

'As always. That doesn't mean he listens to me. And I'm not going to represent you this time, major. I did it once, for reasons of my own.'

'Oh, quite. No. All I want you to do is brief him. I'm sure he'll support Lobkowitz. They're both anarchists.'

'Lobkowitz is a pacifist. Makhno isn't.'

'I suppose it was simple-minded of me to link them in that way.'

From the house Elizabeth called that tea was ready. Major Nye guided Una towards the side door, past the empty stables. 'You must come in June. It's the best time to see our place.'

'Maybe it's a diminutive,' she said. 'Of fifty. Pyatdyaset.'

'Why fifty?'

'No reason. It's just associations of my own. I'm rambling. Mozart sonatas. God, I hate the fifties.'

'You'll be out of them soon.' They reached the kitchen. 'Think of me. Stuck in 'em for God knows how long. Borderland years for me. For you they are merely the badlands. To be crossed quickly and forgotten about. They've done me in, Mrs Persson.' He reached to open the door into the sitting room. 'I assure you I don't like them any more than you.'

For the first time, she realised the extent of his dignity.

It was these old men she admired most. Those who had suffered so much and still kept their faith. They were braver than Makhno in many ways. But Makhno was one of them. And perhaps more attractive.

In the old couch Bishop Beesley leered at her.

'I don't believe you've met our vicar,' said Mrs Nye from her invalid chair.

6

S. Africa Seeking Leg Irons

> Tenders have been invited by the South African Police for the supply of 200 leg irons, apparently as the result of a ban imposed by the United States government last month on the export of 'torture' equipment to the republic. The exact specifications of what the police need are on file with the Director of State Purchases in Pretoria. They are to be marked 'SAP' – South African Police – and supplied with two keys. Emphasis is placed in the tender document on a 'secure system'.
>
> *Daily Telegraph*, 20 July, 1978

'The French can't help their Classicism any more than the Italians can control their Romanticism. Look at those poor French horror comics. Their sex magazines. Look at Le Drugstore! And so it is with politics. They must always embrace some classical, unambiguous cause. They become Marxists.' It was autumn in the Luxembourg Gardens and, as always, the only time they were at all atmospheric. A few leaves disgraced the orderly paths or lay, willy-nilly, on the gravel. Makhno stiffened his back to gain height, but he remained significantly shorter than Una. On the other hand, his girlfriend, Maxime, was diminutive. She wore her camelhair coat as if it were a uniform. Her small, fierce face peered at Una from beneath a defiant orange 'punk' coiffure. She gave exactly the same attention to Una as she did to Makhno. And she said nothing. Occasionally she would light a cigarette with an old-fashioned Polish petrol lighter, using energetic, economical movements. If Una smoked a cigarette, Maxime would light it. Makhno was smoking papyrosa cigarettes from a box inscribed with a representation of Ilya Moromyets and other Kievan legendary heroes. They were a commercial Russian brand called Vogatyr, made in Moscow. He was completely grey now and his face, although a little corroded from his drinking, was still humorous and attractive. He had the same sardonic manner, the same look of stocky integrity. He was nearly seventy, in exile in Paris again, having found the rôle of Bohemian diplomat too much at odds with ideals which, as he said, had become physical as well as mental habits, so that his very presence in conferences made other people uncomfortable. He wore an old-fashioned Norfolk jacket, plus fours and his favourite pair of English riding boots which he had picked up in some South American war. He held the tube of the Russian cigarette upwards and at an angle away from his hand. The smoke, drifting through the clear air, made Una feel at once nostalgic and wary. Her romance with the various Slav revolutions had brought her too much pain. It had been a century full of fire and she would look on it with nostalgia, if the memory lasted at all.

'Pure, classical Marxism,' murmured Makhno. 'Not the rough-edged vulgar Russian kind. Closer to the Chinese, of course, with whom the French have such an affinity. And they have made me a hero!' He dropped the cigarette. 'They have almost convinced me that I am "really" a Marxist. Poor old Kropotkin. He wasn't quite mad enough, was he?'

'You're becoming a racist,' said Una.

'I'm Ukrainian. All Ukrainians are racists. Racism is an honourable form of logic pre-dating psychology as a useful way of rationalising prejudice.'

Bishop Beesley, in gaiters and frock-coat, and Miss Brunner, in severe St Laurent tweed, approached them through the stiff, Parisian trees. The co-conspirators were arm in arm. They waved when they sighted Makhno's party.

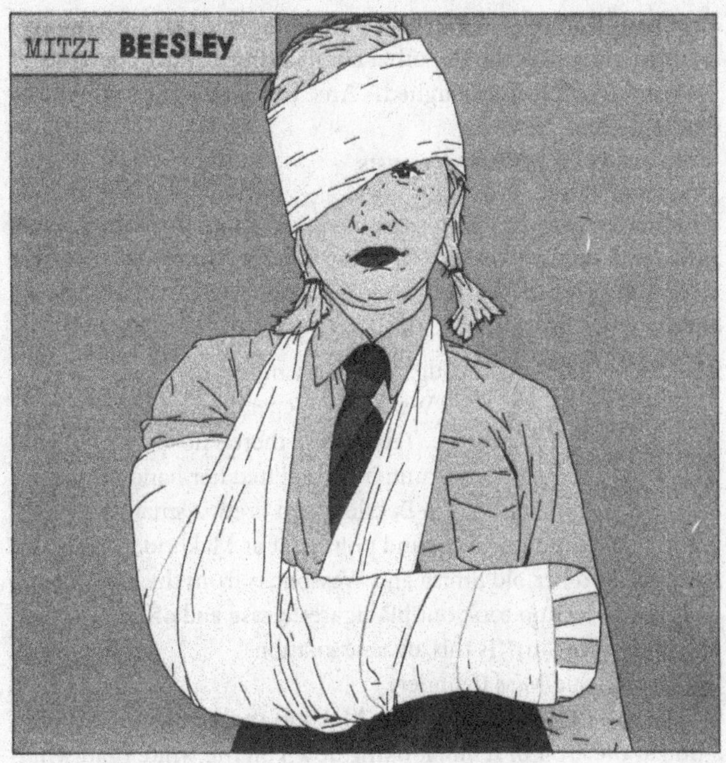

'Hi,' said the bishop, perhaps not sure where he was. 'How goes it?'

Maxime slowly turned her eyes on him. Then she regarded Miss Brunner. It was as if she absorbed their essence. Miss Brunner looked uncomfortable and then curious. She smiled at Maxime. 'Hello, dear. I don't know you, do I?'

Maxime looked to Makhno.

'This is Maxime,' he said. 'We are married.'

'Oh, congratulations.' Bishop Beesley put a fat hand towards the girl, who flinched. He looked at it, perhaps detecting a trace or two of chocolate on the pink flesh, and began to suck it before he drew a red and white spotted handkerchief from the pocket of his coat and wiped the hand carefully. Meanwhile Miss Brunner appeared to have sidled between Makhno and Una and threw a cloud of some Guerlain or other about them all. 'Darling Nestor!'

'What?' Makhno coughed. 'Are you emissaries from the Germans?'

'Certainly not. We are tourists.'

'Trapped,' added the bishop, 'like you.'

'We're not trapped.' Makhno grinned. 'We're communards, all of us.'

'Splendid,' said Miss Brunner. 'We were hoping you were.' She bit her lip, looking up as a flight of Prussian Starfighters came honking and wailing through the misty morning. 'Bombers?'

'They only observe us. We're an independent city. Technically, we're not even under siege. Technically, there's no German blockade.' Una watched Miss Brunner who hefted her handbag on her arm and glanced at Bishop Beesley who drew a small Browning automatic from his pocket and pointed it at Makhno. Miss Brunner produced her old Smith and Wesson .45 from the bag.

Nestor Makhno took out his cigarette case and offered a Vogatyr to the company. 'Is this an assassination?'

'Justice,' said Miss Brunner.

The scene fractured and Una, Makhno and a frowning Maxime stood at the crest of a hill, looking down on the white road winding across the yellow Ukrainian steppe. There were no houses to be seen. Behind them, three ponies, furnished for war, cropped at grass. Makhno returned his field glasses to their case. 'We had best make for the railway station,' he said. 'It's too far to ride.'

They mounted the ponies, but, even as they began to trot forward, the scene melted and became a town in flames. Nationalist bandits were looting it. It was the time of the retreat from Minsk. Makhno drew his revolver, firing into the air. 'Stop!' He moved round in his saddle and shot a looter wearing an army greatcoat and a sailor's cap. The man began to cough and searched for his own gun amongst the knives and swords and cartridge belts hung about his chest and waist. He fell on his knees and collapsed to one side before he had sorted through the collection and discovered that his holster had moved round to the small of his back.

A GREEN FLAG WAVED FROM A MAST ON THE LEADING VEHICLE

Two armoured cars moved through the smoke and the crowd. A green flag waved from a mast on the leading vehicle.

The street was mud. The noise of mortars and human beings mingled into one appalling scream. Una was about to wheel her mount when a silence fell and the ponies were plodding knee-deep through snow. Una shivered. The fracture had saved them from Miss Brunner and Bishop Beesley but it could have sent them into stasis. In this primordial snow they must soon freeze. It would mean the end of a whole cycle of consequences. She began to feel the familiar lethargy and prepared herself for the fate which must sooner or later befall all temporal adventurers.

'Mush!'

It was Jerry, driving a team of dogs, a corpse-shaped bundle before him on his sleigh. He was dressed in white furs and looking his most handsome. 'Want a lift?'

Makhno put fresh shells into his revolver. 'Where are you going?'

'Does it matter?' Una dismounted and plunged through the snow towards the sleigh which became a small boat in which Jerry and Catherine, dressed as seaside Pierrots, manned two sets of oars and at the same time stretched to where she stood waist-deep in the sea, trying to get to them. Una herself was dressed as Harlequin and her vision was impaired by her mask. She felt a strange, melancholy lust.

'Quick,' said Catherine. 'There's still time, Una. Quick.'

But Una was losing it. She knew. Memories dissipated. Identity failed. She was still in her Harlequin set as she stumbled up the yellow beach of some Indian Ocean island, weeping for rest. Desperate for consolation.

7

Computers Pick Likely 'Suicides'

> Computers can predict suicide attempts much more accurately than human therapists because they have no hesitation in asking blunt questions, according to a series of experiments by two psychiatrists at Wisconsin University Medical School. When hundreds of depressed patients were interviewed by a computer … three suicide attempts were accurately predicted. The two doctors had failed to predict any of them … In the first part of the interview, the computer would win their confidence with such morale-boosting remarks as: 'You're a pro at using the terminal.' Then it became blunter with such questions as: 'What are your chances of being dead from suicide one month from now?'
>
> *Daily Telegraph*, 20 July, 1978

'What are these new Americans who have made of tautology a substitute for literature? Who celebrate the euphuism as an art form? Who take crude peasant prejudice and elevate it, placing it on a par with Emerson or Paine? What are these babblers, so free to debase the Word? Who employ the corrupt terminology of the encounter group in all their dealings?' Professor Hira held the board against the window and reached for the hammer Una passed him. 'Eh?'

'I'm sure I don't know, darling. I'm not a great reader.'

'Do you have to be? You should wear something more practical.'

'I like satin. It's cool. Do you think the Dacoits will attack before help comes?' She adjusted a pink strap.

He scratched his hairline, just where his turban touched his forehead. 'We can't take chances. There is nothing worse than an Indo-Chinese pirate. You must shoot yourself, of course, if they land.' She turned back to look out to sea. The sails of the junks seemed no closer and the smoke of the white steam yacht which appeared to lead them was, if anything, closer to the horizon. The little Brahmin knocked an inexpert nail into the board and then made his way cautiously down the ladder. The main settlement of Rowe Island was below them: a group of stone and stucco buildings which had housed the mine-managers, their employees and the few traders who had found it worthwhile to set up shops and hotels here. Professor Hira's house had once been the control shack for the airship field. The steel, triangular mast was still there, but no ships had called in years, since the mining of phosphates had become unprofitable. The Malays and Chinese labourers had been the first to go. There had been some attempt by the mine-owners to turn the place into a resort, but it was too far from anywhere else in the world to attract more than a few of those who genuinely sought a remote haven. Now it was a sort of R&R base for members of the Guild, being away from all shipping routes. The one hotel was run by Olmeijer, the fat Dutchman, who for some reason found it convenient to serve Guild people, but Olmeijer had made his annual journey to Sarawak, to see one of his several families, and would not be back for two weeks. Hira and Una were presently the only inhabitants.

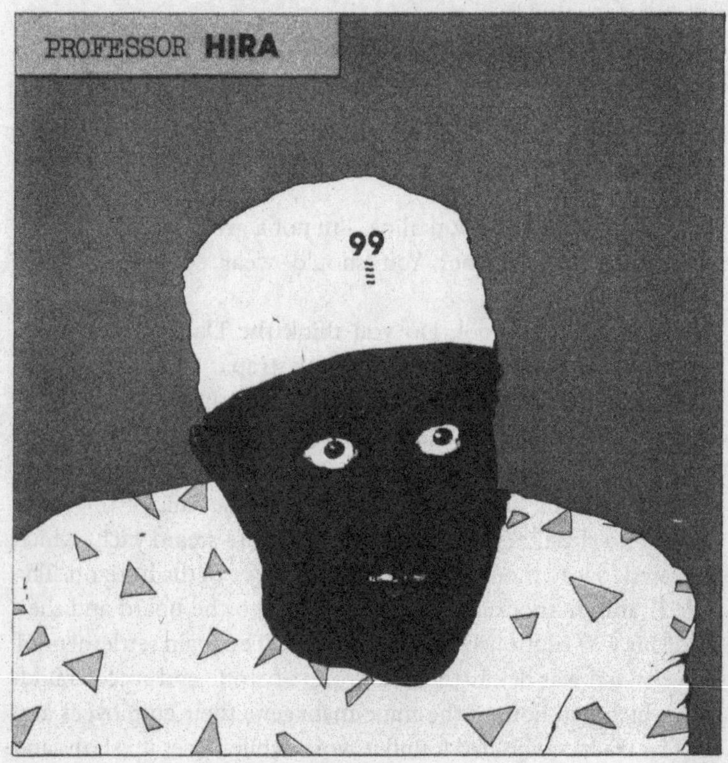

'There's nothing at all here for them.' Hira squinted out to sea. 'Could they be after us?'

'What would they want?'

'They could be linears, out to destroy our base. It wouldn't be the first time. Remember what happened in 1900, at the Centre?'

'It was one of the very first and oldest bases. We never made the same mistake. That Centre was shifted into the Palaeozoic. Or was it the Devonian?'

'Don't ask me. We have different terms for the time cycles. But they're about as vague as yours.' He heard a familiar coughing from the sky and looked up to point towards the silhouette of a cream-coloured Dornier DoX banking over the top of a cloud and heading clumsily towards the island. 'We all know who that must be.'

'I wish to god he'd get a better bloody plane.'

'It suits his sense of history.'

The huge white aircraft floundered lower, only half its engines firing at any one time. It had a grubby, underused look to it.

'I suppose,' said Una, hitching up her long dress, 'we'd better get down to the harbour before the pirates.' She had noticed that the yacht had picked up speed. She heard a distant rumble. 'They've got a Bofors. They're firing at the plane.'

It was impossible to tell if the plane were hit. From somewhere near its tail, a Browning M1917-A1 began to fire. The junks retaliated, with every kind of light weaponry, but principally, if Una's ear were in, with near-useless Ingram M10s.

'At least they're a bit more up to date,' said Una. They had reached the ramshackle outskirts of the settlement and were running over distorted flagstones towards the harbour. 'But at least we can be certain of one thing. We're in a fault of some sort. Maybe even a loop.'

'It's better than being frozen,' said the Brahmin.

Una's memory became vague again. At least she still knew enough to understand that there were no such things as paradoxes and that ambiguities sustained and enriched the basic fabric of human life; that Time was a notion and nothing more; and therefore could neither be challenged, nor overwhelmed: merely experienced.

Death, of course, was real enough, when it came. She looked nervously towards the yacht which appeared to be sporting a Hudson's Bay Company flag. She could easily spot the Dacoits on the deck. They were training the Bofors towards the harbour itself. She thought she saw the glint of a bishop's mitre on the bridge.

Whining and grunting intermittently, the DoX flew low overhead, its wings swaying, turned almost directly over the yacht and came in to land on the oily waters of the harbour, bouncing dangerously on its heavy floats. The engines continued to miss as a figure emerged from the cabin and stood on the float, signalling to them.

THE DOX CAME IN TO LAND ON THE OILY WATERS OF THE HARBOUR ...
DO-X

'We're going to have to swim for it,' said Professor Hira, removing his beautiful silk coat.

'Bugger,' said Una. She stripped off her pink satin evening dress and in nothing but her camisole returned gingerly to the water.

Shakey Mo Collier helped her crawl onto the float. His long hair fell about his yellow, seedy face. There was a black Burmese cheroot in one corner of his mouth. He wore huge mirror shades which gave him something of an insectile look. He was dressed as Captain Fracasse, although the costume was filthy and so torn as to be barely recognisable. 'We were on our way to

Australia,' he explained, 'when we got your call. Is that the *Teddy Bear* firing at us?'

'It must be,' said Una. 'The last time I was on it was for the concert party. Do you remember?' Dripping, she climbed into the cabin. Frank and Jerry, in identical flying gear, sat at the twin controls.

'Remember?' said Mo, reaching out a hand towards Professor Hira. 'I haven't had a moment to bloody change, have I?'

Frank looked round at her and licked chemically reddened lips. 'Cor! Me first,' he said appreciatively.

Jerry's voice was remote. 'No time.' An automatic arm stretched towards the throttle. 'Taking her up.' There was flak now, and spray, as shells struck the water near them. The plane lurched, bounced, slewed round and had to be straightened out. Then they were taking off, the sound of the inefficient engines drowning the sound of maniac gunfire which burst from every ship in the pirate fleet.

They were back in the political arena with a vengeance.

8

Six Life Sentences for Anti-Abortion Bomb Student

A 'brilliant' science student, who carried out fire bomb attacks on people whose pro-abortion views 'sickened' him, was given six concurrent life sentences when he appeared at the Old Bailey yesterday. [He] made 'lethal and beautifully designed bombs which, by the grace of God, did not kill anyone,' said the Recorder of London Mr James Miskin Q.C. 'He took the view that those who support abortion are wrong. He has exhibited no remorse or any concern for his intended victims...' In a workroom at his home police found 'a mass of bomb-making equipment' and a diary in which he recorded his crimes. He had written about his urge to 'purge the land of evil' and of his 'noble mission' against abortion. Of the bomb intended to maim Mrs Lord, he said: 'I laughed to think of my own cunning in constructing it ... I believe strongly that something should be done to remedy abortion. I am sickened by it and decided a campaign against those who preach the unwarranted murder of innocent children.'

Daily Telegraph, 20 July, 1978

'It only costs about £16.00 for the whole round trip,' said Una as she followed Catherine into the back of the Daimler limousine. 'Hardly any more than a taxi, these days.' She smiled at the chauffeur who had turned his head and was giving both of them the eye. She smoothed chiffon. 'Derry and Toms,' she said. 'In Kensington High Street. Do you know it?'

'Well…' He shrugged. 'I know what you mean.' He put the car into gear and drove round the corner into Campden Hill Road. 'Is that where you want to go? I mean, the only place?'

'And back,' said Una, 'when we've done some shopping and had our tea. Isn't it lovely today?'

'Lovely,' said the chauffeur.

'I'm so glad to be back.' Una giggled at Catherine. 'So much has happened!'

Catherine, looking a little wary, said: 'Yes?'

'You think I've changed?'

'Sort of.'

'I've given up everything. I've decided to be more feminine.'

'You're always deciding that,' said Catherine. She looked soberly at her own blonde frizz in the little mirror provided. Her make-up was fashionably extravagant: imitating the naïve almost as successfully as a Lowry, but with much more passion. She put her red lips together. 'And usually at the wrong time.'

Una's enthusiasm waned. She crossed her legs. 'It's the only escape they leave open.'

'They leave it open because they want you to take it.'

'Fine. I want to take it.'

'Fine.' Catherine spoke cheerfully, frustrating Una.

'Well, what else can I do? I need the rest.'

'You ought to find another way, dear. Or another chap.'

'He's lovely, Major Nye.'

'He's married to that poor old bag. And then there's Elizabeth. I mean, she'd be pissed off to say the least, if she found out. You can't screw fathers and daughters and get away with it.' Catherine laughed coarsely. 'Bloody hell!'

'It's not really like that.' Una was offended. She regretted suggesting the trip.

The Daimler reached Kensington High Street and turned left. 'I need to combine ideals with sex, that's my trouble.'

'It's because you're so puritanical.'

Una nodded.

'That's it,' said the chauffeur. 'Isn't it?'

'God help us!' Una was terrified as she stared out at the department store. 'I hoped I was safe!'

'It changed ages ago. To Biba's first. Then to this.' Catherine was sympathetic. 'I thought you knew. I thought you were being satirical.'

'How do you get to the roof garden?'

'You can't any more, I don't think. It's private.'

'Get anything in there these days,' said the chauffeur.

Una continued to stare in silence at the pale green, the faded gold, the new Marks & Spencer's.

9

Gift from Queen

Seven deer, two stags, and five hinds – the Queen's jubilee year gift to the Canadian province of Nova Scotia – will be flown from Heathrow today.

Daily Telegraph, 20 July, 1978

Beneath the grey Westway motorway, in the gloom of the half-ruined People's Theatre, peering out of the rain through wire netting, sat Jerry Cornelius, a crestfallen white linen Pierrot. He hugged his cold, thin body. He whimpered as, from another bay, further west, came the giggling and wheezing of his half-cut mum enjoying an afternoon gin with Bishop Beesley in some corner or other. He knew Una was standing at the back of the stage, behind him. She sniffed. The railway sleepers used for seats had been set on fire and partially burned. The theatre was useless, filthy, incredible. The Pierrot suit was wet, as if Jerry had tried to run home through the rain and then turned back. This Sunday they had all been due to make their appearance here, in a version of the rôle made famous by Sarah Bernhardt almost a century before, as *Pierrot Mort*. Jerry's white make-up had the flaky look of salt flats suddenly inundated. It made him look infinitely aged as he eventually turned reddish eyes to acknowledge her. 'I thought they'd turn up anyway,' he said. 'Did you bring your costume?'

'I left it at your mum's. Cathy's there.'

'I know. She wouldn't come.'

'She said.'

'Thought it wasn't worth it. There was no cancellation announced. I mean. Are we troopers or aren't we?'

'Troopers.' Una offered him a packet of Black Cats as she came towards him. 'Of some sort or other.'

'What's the point of doing a play to celebrate the spirit of the theatre and then showing none of that spirit yourself?' He took a cigarette.

'Do you want to put it on?'

'There were only about six people turned up and they went away when they saw what had happened. Bloody vandals. Who was it?'

'I think it was a rival political theatre group,' she said. 'That's what I heard. Marxists. They're very concerned about reaching the people in the correct way.'

'Bloody communists. Worse than the Church.'

'Well, so they say.'

'And they're bloody right.'

'Why can't they leave us alone?'

'It's not in their nature.'

'Sod them all.'

'No point in sulking, Jerry. Not if you're a trooper.'

'I'm not going to be brave about it. That's unhealthy. It's better if I sulk.'

She sat down at the hacked-about piano and played a chord. The sound was primeval; terrifying. She couldn't stop it. It grew in the bay; it echoed through all the other bays, right down to the end, in Ladbroke Grove. It joined the noise of the cars above, the trains of the Metropolitan Line to the south; there was a sense of eternal syncopation. Jerry's face cleared. Una shook the piano. The sound continued to swell from it.

'That's great,' said Jerry.

'It's cacophony.'

'No it's not. Listen.'

'I don't want to listen.'

'Everything intersects.'

'We all know that.'

'This is the music of the lines. Not the spheres. Like knitting. Like a vast cat's cradle. Can you hear it all, Una?'

'Nothing but a horrible noise.'

He sighed. 'Maybe you're right. All we have is imagination. And that lets you down so often. Everyone has a different explanation.'

'Can you suggest a universal one?'

'Music.'

'What?'

'Nothing.'

The smell of damp charcoal was getting to Una. 'Shall we go and have a cup of coffee in the Mountain Grill? We'll be under cover most of the way. You won't get much wetter.'

'If you like.' He had stopped sulking and had become artificially compliant. He got up at once and followed her through the gap in the wire, round the corner into Portobello Road. The windows of the Mountain Grill were steamed up from the inside. Within, the usual cast looked at the newcomers. There was a row of tables against either wall. Each row contained five tables. At the end of the café was the counter with the till on it. Behind the counter was the kitchen. In the kitchen were the Cypriot proprietor, his wife and his father. They were cooking the food. A little boy and a little girl, the proprietor's children, were serving it. There was a smell of boiling potatoes. It dominated all the other smells. At the furthest table on the left row sat Miss Brunner, Bishop Beesley, Karen von Krupp, Frank Cornelius. At the next table down sat Shakey Mo Collier, Nestor Makhno, Maxime, and Mrs Cornelius. At the third table were Major Nye, Elizabeth Nye, Pip Nye and Captain Nye. At the fourth were William Randolph Hearst, Orson Welles, Alfred Bester and Zenith the Albino, all in evening dress. The fifth was empty and Jerry and Una sat down at it, facing one another. On Una's right (her back was to the moist window) the tables were occupied thus:

Table One:	Nik Turner, Dave Brock, DikMik, Del Dettmar
Table Two:	Simon King, Bob Calvert, Lemmy, Martin Griffin
Table Three:	Pete Pavli, Adrian Shaw, Michael Moorcock, Simon House
Table Four:	Steve Gilmore, Douglas Smith, Wayne Bardel, Graham Charnock
Table Five:	Phil Taylor, Eddy Clarke, Catherine Cornelius, Harvey Bainbridge

'It's bloody full this afternoon,' said Jerry. 'It's a wonder there's any empty chairs at all.'

'They're for absent friends.'

'What is this? A private party?'

'We're just waiting for some transport.' Jerry began to feel a comforting sentimentality.

'You'd better get something inside you,' she said.

10

Viscount's Son 'Paid £70 for Child Sex'

A Viscount's son, on a 'fantasy bandwagon' fed by child pornography for several years, told Manchester Crown Court yesterday that he had paid £70 for an introduction to 'child prostitutes' at their mother's flat. [He] was giving evidence at the trial of a mother of three who is accused of inciting one of her daughters to commit gross indecency with him. [She] pleaded not guilty to three charges – encouraging an indecent assault on a girl under 16, indecent assault, with two men, on a girl under 13; and with a man, inciting a girl of 10 to commit gross indecency with [him]. [He] claimed that he was 'revolted and horrified' by the reality of seeking out child prostitutes and reaching the point where he actually saw 'these little girls' and went to bed with one aged 10 ... He had amassed a considerable quantity of 'child porn' over a number of years and 'a fantasy had been built up in my mind but it had not crashed at that time. That is why I went on.'

Daily Telegraph, 20 July, 1978

They were still in their uniforms as they left the tiny theatre and climbed into the back of the Ford Transit. Una crawled through to the driving seat and pulled off her Harlequin mask. Jerry and Catherine lay face forward on the mattress while Catherine unscrewed the top of a thermos. Una got the engine going and backed the van into the midnight street. Even as Catherine handed her the plastic cup of sweet tea Una said goodbye to Harrogate and took the A65, heading north. 'Never again,' she said.

'They were awful.' Jerry held out his own beaker and let it be filled. 'What did they expect?'

'Follies,' said Una. 'I knew it.'

'There's no audience for the traditional *commedia dell'arte*,' said Catherine dutifully, dabbing some tea-stains from her frothy costume. 'And Harrogate's where people retire. They're nostalgic for the seaside pierrots. That's what they were expecting. That's why they left, you know. They were disappointed, all those retired people. We have ourselves to blame.'

'Old farts,' said Jerry. 'You can keep bloody Harrogate. Where to next?' He remembered. 'Kendal?'

'We're booked in at the Community Hall, but I'm not sure we should carry on.' Una handed the cup behind her. 'London was okay because people are into that sort of thing now. But we're ahead of our time up here.'

'That's not hard.' Catherine was grim. 'I'm pissed off and no mistake. I never wanted any part of this pretentious crap. I thought it was going to be like those old people expected – songs and dances and that.' She had given up duty.

'There *are* songs and dances.' Una was aggrieved. It was she who had talked them both into the venture.

'Not proper ones.' Catherine turned over on her back and tried to get comfortable with her head on her suitcase. 'This is worse than rep.'

'It's what rep's all about.' Jerry, who had had less theatrical experience, still found the whole travelling part of it romantic.

'But it isn't rep. It's – God knows what!' Catherine sniffed and shut her eyes.

'It's how rep started. This.'

'It's self-conscious.' She opened her eyes again. 'Has anyone got a cigarette?'

Jerry went to his own grubby bag and found a tin. 'Only these rotten Russian ones.'

'They'll do.' She lit a papyrosa. 'I like 'em.' She was enjoying herself, testing her power. She knew that they were both trying to placate her. She continued her rôle. 'Couldn't we try to pep it up next time. With some more contemporary material – or at least some nostalgia stuff – vo-di-o-do – you know. This is so old nobody can feel nostalgic for it!'

'That's the point. It's genuine rediscovery of dramatic ideas disused for a couple of hundred years. Well, a hundred – if you count Debureau and Les Funambules –'

'Which I do,' said Catherine, taking an entirely different but equally aggressive tack.

'Some Good Companions we are,' said Jerry unhappily. 'This ain't rock and roll. It's Leonard Merrick.'

'Who?' they said.

He smiled smugly. He began to remove his make-up. He now seemed to be the only one who was enjoying himself.

They made their way into the Dales, down the dark, empty road towards Cumbria.

Somewhere beyond Ilkley, a Banning began to sound for a few seconds. Then the noise died.

Jerry was asleep. Catherine crawled into the passenger seat and handed Una one of her brother's Russian cigarettes already lit. 'Was that fighting?'

'There's an army near. Of some sort. But I don't think we should worry too much. I'm going to try to make for the old road, once we're past Kirkby. Get into safe country.'

Catherine nodded. 'Good idea.'

She began to doze.

She was wakened by the dawn and looked to see a disturbed, red-eyed Una, looking dreadfully pale in her red, green, blue and gold lozenge motley. 'What's the matter?'

'I can't find the bloody road. I've looked and looked. It's not blocked or anything. I just can't find it.'

They were on the motorway. 'But we're in it,' said Catherine. 'It's over there. And there.'

'We're going through it. But I can't get into it. I don't know what's wrong.'

'Where are we heading?'

'Where else?' said Una. 'The Lake District.'

They had reached Grasmere and had stopped in the deserted car park next to Dove Cottage before Jerry woke up, looked out of the back windows of the Transit, saw grey stone and turned pale. 'Oh, no.'

'Don't blame me,' said Una. 'All roads lead to Wordsworth.'

'What?'

'That's how it seems.'

'I hate this bloody place.'

'Why do you keep coming back to it then?' said Catherine sardonically. 'And you do, don't you?'

'Not voluntarily. I thought – Weren't we heading for Kendal? We've passed it.'

'By-passed it, actually,' said Una. She was grim. 'We can't go back and we don't want to stay here. Where shall we head for?'

Catherine said: 'Keswick's better than this.'

'Yeah,' said Jerry. 'Keswick.'

'Why not Scotland?' Una leaned on the steering wheel and peered at the ruins of the Prince Charles Hotel beside the lake. 'It's a free country, at least. And peaceful.'

'Sort of peaceful. Is your pal still there? The anarchist?'

'There are lots of anarchists in Scotland now,' said Una.

'You know the one I mean.'

'Makhno should still be there. I'd like to look him up. He's getting on now, you know. Must be at least eighty.'

'You wouldn't think it, would you?' said Catherine salaciously. The older they got the more she fancied them.

From the lake emerged a peculiar submersible vehicle. It paused on the bank, throbbing. Its conning tower turned as if to

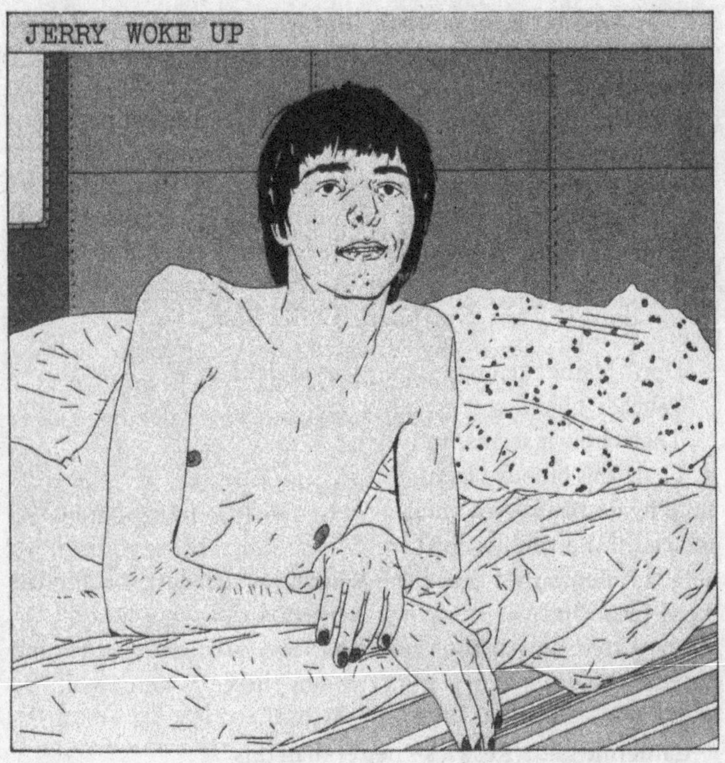

watch them. A Browning M2 .50 took their range. Una started the old engine. 'We can outrun that bastard if we're quick.'

'Better do it, then,' said Jerry. He unwrapped their only gun and wound down the side window even as he pushed Catherine into the back. The heavy Thompson .45 made him feel much better than it should have done.

The Transit lurched and Jerry fired a burst at the submersible more to startle it than anything else. The Browning did not fire back. Only when they were two hundred yards down the Scotland road did it begin to fire a few rounds, but it was evident that the crew – some kind of renegades – was conserving ammunition for defence rather than attack.

Jerry looked around him at ruined romance. The place had been the scene of five or six major battles between Black Watch divisions trying to establish themselves fresh territory since they had been driven out of Scotland and the local Cumbrian bandits who resented the incursion all the more since the Black Watch had little worth looting but their weapons.

By that afternoon they had crossed the border under the gaze of a small black patrol ship which had dropped to a few feet above their heads to inspect them and then risen swiftly as a sign that they could proceed.

By evening, after resting and eating, they could see sanctuary ahead as Glasgow's solid towers became visible above the mist.

'Shall we be staying?' asked Catherine of Una.

Una shook her head. 'Not for long. The war is endless, you know. Someone has to carry on.'

'You're sounding more like your old self,' said Catherine approvingly.

'Well, one of them, at least,' said Una.

Jerry rolled onto his side and began to snore.

4. Recapitulation

Every Gun Plays Its Own Tune

The Bishop and Mitzi
  Were on the rampage
She full of lust
  He full of rage
Looking for victims
  They hoped to convert
Stopped in the fifties
  And there found a cert

They got me again
They got me again
Oh, shit, they got me again
I was holed out in 'fifty
And having some fun
When I heard Mitzi coming
Caught the sound of her gun

Bang-bang-bang
Here come the gang
Bang-bang-bang-bang-bang!

The Bishop and Mitzi
  They found him at last
Stuck in a time-slip
  On his way to the past
He cried out for mercy
  But they only laughed
As they took him in
  To remind him of sin…

They got me again, etc.

Pierrot, poor Pierrot
Must become Harlequin
Learn about sin
Drugs, whisky and gin
Such a bad convert
That's the thing about him
He'll forget all his
Lessons in time…

They got me again, etc.
Bang-bang-bang, etc.

Pierrot in the Roof Garden

I've climbed so high
I can't climb higher
I've reached the top
And have to stop
Sitting on the steeple
Like a silly little fairy
Goodbye Tom and Goodbye Derry
Goodbye sahib, hello effendi
Biba's bust and I'm so trendy
Marx and Spencer's fails to send me
I've a hole in my trousers
And a boil on my nose
But they won't catch me
With my teeth round a rose
My time's run out
I'm a senile ghost
Run-down loony
Who never signed up
Music box
They can't wind up
You should see
What I had lined up
It was sweet
And it was tasty
Lost the lot
By being too hasty
I don't care
I've reached the limit
You can keep the world
There's nothing in it
I'll just sit here

And eat my spinach
Waiting for
The thing to finish
Up above the moon
Is shining
As I squat here
Quietly whining
For Columbine
I still am pining
My reel is spinning
But I can't get
The line in
So I think I'll just
Crawl under this bush.

Columbine's Carol

Sing for joy, we've met in time
Harlequin and Columbine
Praise the jolly myth of Yule
May good cheer forever rule
Fire doth blaze and snow doth fall
Peace on Earth for One and All
Holly shines and Ivy glows
Bunting from the roof-tops flows.
Sing for joy, we've met in time
Harlequin and Columbine.

In the bell-tower Pierrot kneels
Surrounded by the merry peals
Now they're singing ding-dong-dell
Send the sinners down to hell
Snow doth fall and fire doth blaze
Numbering poor Pierrot's days
Down the bell-rope he descends
Knowing he must face his end
Out into the graveyard white
Pierrot must embrace the night.

Sing for joy, we've met in time
Harlequin and Columbine
Sing for joy, we've met in time
Harlequin and Columbine

Surrounded by a Christmas throng
Pierrot sings a silent song
(Goodbye me and goodbye time
Goodbye lovely Columbine)
Falling snow and blazing fire
This is Pierrot's funeral pyre
Gone is laughter, gone is light
Pierrot must embrace the night.

Sing for joy, we've met in time
Harlequin and Columbine
Sing for joy, we've met in time
Harlequin and Columbine…

4. THE MINSTREL GIRL

I

Who Turned the Courtesy Car into a Hearse?

> ISIS provides accurate gyro-stabilised weapon-aiming for guns air-to-air and guns, rockets and bombs air-to-ground ... The D-282 has the added facility of airspeed computation in the air-to-ground strike role. A unique feature of this equipment is roll stabilisation of the aiming mark, reducing tracking time by 50%. Incorporated within the single optical lens system is a fixed cross standby sight. ISIS is also designed to integrate with laser rangefinders and inertial navigation systems.
>
> Ferranti

'Nuclear fusion will return our birthright to us. Melting our cities into the softer contours of our original hills; restoring our caves, our safe places, bringing back the radiant landscapes of the world before the Fall.' Jerry Cornelius stepped carefully over the huge blown-up photograph of the three murdered killers covering the middle of the studio's floor. It was black and white. He was a ghost. She was surprised that she could still see him.

'If you could only guarantee it,' she said. In the far corner of the studio Una shivered beside one of the old-fashioned flood-lamps. She extended her palms towards the warmth. She wore a military greatcoat, spangled tights. He, on the other hand, wore a huge black fur coat, some kind of shako, jackboots, as if he hoped that these rather more substantial clothes would hold him together long enough to do whatever it was he had come here for. Sinuously, with all that was left of his old self-conscious grace, he came to a stop beside a tank of developing fluid. He pushed back his coat and eased his needle gun into the heavy holster at his hip. The outline of the holster spoiled the otherwise perfect symmetry beneath the fur. 'Dusty roads,' he murmured nostalgically.

Her shoulders slumped. 'Why not?' Would he want her for his next victim?

There was a four-by-eight picture of a child pinned to the wall to her left; a naked blonde of about ten. He shrugged at it. 'We bring them into the world and then they die.'

She glanced at him in surprise. 'Die.'

He continued his approach. 'Love can be found nowhere, these days, except in the ruins.' His hands reached out.

'We're not there yet,' she said.

His hands fell.

As if to apologise she said: 'I cannot lose my belief in original sin. That is, I do think there are those who carry sin with them, who infect the rest.'

'What would you do with them?' He seemed to be sulking.

'Them? I suspect I'm talking about myself.'

'Why not.'

It was Twelfth Night and he was on his way, he had told her, to the Hunt Ball. He had a pair of antlers in the parcel he had left by the door as he had entered to rescue her. Through the glass roof she watched the sky grow cold, yellow, and then black. She thought of sex and sighed.

She sighed again, regretfully. She could see his body trembling beneath his clothes. They were worlds apart.

(The girl's face came closer. He saw the eyes narrow and the mouth twist. She began to weep. He backed away, raising his hands defensively and shaking his head from side to side. The music started and the dance went on.

Let the good times roll.)

2

Where Is the Killer Who Hated Redheads?

The Royal Air Force is currently undertaking studies on the use of the Hawk as a frontline operational aircraft in addition to its basic role as trainer. As Air Vice-Marshal Gilbert, Assistant

> Chief of Air Staff (Policy) put it to *Interavia*: 'We are well aware that the Hawk has an operational capability, in addition to training, and we are conducting studies to see to what extent the capability can be exploited under the operational conditions of the 1980s.' Among the tasks being looked at are ground attack, self-defence and air defence. A compact easily-maintained aircraft like the Hawk would clearly be an asset in any breakthrough situation in the NATO central region. It would be particularly effective against vehicles and thin-skinned armour columns which had advanced beyond the heavy anti-aircraft weapon support available in the existing front line.
>
> *Interavia*

'We do what we do. We are what we are.'

Maxime glanced up when she heard this. Her expression was one of amused irony. 'Your voice has altered. It's deeper. Almost negroid, hein?'

'Oh shut up.' Una freed herself from the grubby sheet and struggled towards the side of the vast Louis XIV bed. She reached it at last, rolled off, then crawled through the tangles of the sheepskin carpet to the mirrored wall to look at her seedy, youthful face. She stuck out her bruised red tongue and inspected the tiny sore on the tip. Naked, she turned and sat cross-legged with her back to the mirror, staring across the room to where Maxime, her faintly Asiatic face frozen in a frown, smoked a cigarette and smoothed her thin fringe down over her forehead. Behind the heavy yellow velvet curtains the dawn was breaking.

'Fuck!' said Una.

'Die,' sighed Maxime. She stretched her muscular arms. 'Is the world still there, this morning?'

Una got to her feet and, hunched with cold, padded for the door. 'I used to enjoy it all. I used to love it.'

Maxime's tight mouth smiled. 'First the romance goes, then the love, then the lust. The innocent! The gangster!'

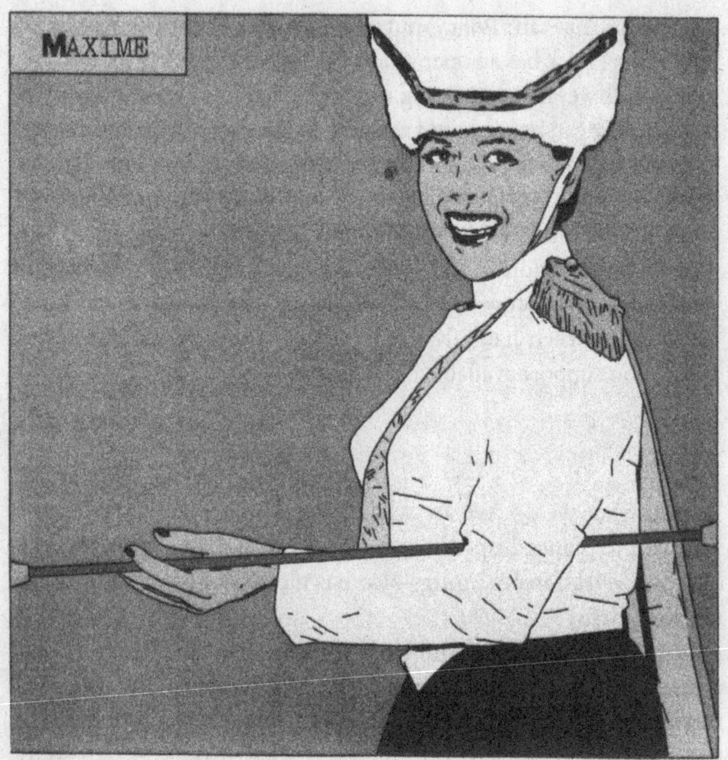

When the door closed, Maxime leapt from the bed and ran to the chair on which, last night, she had flung her party uniform.

Una watching her through the keyhole, experienced a faint stirring in the region of her pelvis. She had begun to develop a fear of individuals. Nowadays she could only embrace causes. She knew it was a weakness, but history was not, at present, on her side.

3

Can Too Much Sex Play Lead to Murder?

One of the largest potential military markets during the next decade will be that for subsonic trainer/ground attack aircraft. While estimates vary from source to source, a reasonable assessment of the demand is that about 6,000 aircraft will be needed to replace existing types in countries outside the United States and the East Bloc.

Interavia

'It is the disordered mind which detects order everywhere.' Prinz Lobkowitz held her tightly in his grey arms, looking down at her head through fine, fading irises as he stroked her hair. 'The schizoid brain seeks desperately for systems, the paranoid produces patterns from the most unlikely sources. The mad eye selects only what it wishes to see – proof of political plots, evidence of interstellar visitation, moral corruption in any given society. The evidence is not presented to us in linear form, you see, and cannot be read as we read lines of print. The secret is to make no specific selection.'

'And go mad,' said Una.

'No, no, no. And learn to love the world in all its aspects.'

'Even cancer?'

'Love and cancer are scarcely compatible. But you could say that what we call "cancer" has a perfect right to exist.'

'We'd all die,' she said. She broke away from him.

'Nonsense. We'd all experience miracle cures.' He was hurt by her action. He began to roll down his sleeves, glancing round him at the abandoned surgery in the hope that she would not see his tears.

She moved a step or two towards him. His body was stiffer than it had been, his tone was over-controlled. 'Shall I see you tonight, Una?'

'No,' she said. 'I can't come.'

The room shook. An explosion somewhere. The first for a long time. A tray of instruments tumbled to the floor. He picked up his jacket from the threadbare carpet, holding back a leaning screen with his other hand. She sat on the edge of the leatherette inspection couch and combed her hair. 'What about art?' she said. 'That orders things, surely? At best.'

'But at best it doesn't deny the rest of the evidence.' He buttoned his jacket and found his homburg where it had fallen behind the doctor's desk. The doctor's skeleton lay clean and slumped, skull back against the chair's headrest, resembling another piece of analytical equipment. 'You're staying here, then?'

'I said I'd meet a friend.'

'Cornelius?'

She blushed. 'No. His sister.'

'Aha.' He drew in his breath and headed for the door. 'The world's turned topsy-turvy!'

'That's only how you see it,' said Una. Then she regretted the irony. She had no wish to hurt him.

4

Is It True That the Secret of S.S.P. Had Turned Men into Gods and Can Show You How to Program and Receive Everything You've Ever Wanted in Just Seconds ... Including Riches, Luxurious Possessions, Power Over Others, and Even a Longer Life?

> In a deal worth £180 million, Iran has selected the 'tracked' version of the Rapier low-level air defence system which is based on the FMC M548 armoured carrier. Iran already operates the standard Rapier version.
>
> *Interavia*

Una and Catherine were completely out of ammunition by the time they hit the IBM building. They were disturbed to find that the building had not been defended at all and suspected a trap. They proceeded warily across the campus, but it seemed the remaining students had fallen back to the great hall. The two women ducked into the low concrete entrance and ran along the corridor, bursting in on the computer room. The machine filled all available wall space on four sides. But it was dead. None of its indicators flickered, none of its lights glowed and its tapes no longer rotated.

'We've been done,' said Catherine. She threw her carbine butt-first at a battleship-grey panel. It bounced back towards her so that she had to skip aside. It rattled across the floor. 'This bugger isn't controlling anything. There's no power.'

'I wonder why Maxime said she thought it was the centre of operations.' Una lit a thin brown cigarette.

'Because she couldn't bear the idea of being in any way responsible herself,' said Catherine spitefully. She patted at a blonde Marcel wave. 'What a cock-up eh? What a bloody waste of time!'

'That's the trouble with computers,' said Una. 'They do confuse things.'

'And take a lot of heat away from those who deserve to get it,' said Catherine. She bent down wearily to pick up her M16. 'Come on. Let's see if we can find any ammo outside.'

'Wait,' said Una. She opened her arms to her friend. 'I feel so lonely suddenly, don't you?'

Catherine shook her head, but she came to Una. 'Not here,' she said.

5

Will Your Job Be Next to Go?

Fixed armament on the General Dynamics F-16 consists of an internally mounted M61A1 Vulcan 20mm gun installed aft of the cockpit and avionics bays. External stores can be carried on nine stations: one central underfuselage, six underwing and two wingtip. A Pave Penny laser tracker pod hardpoint is also provided ... A potential world market for the F-16 is seen as 4,800 aircraft; the conservative programme basis is put at 1,500.

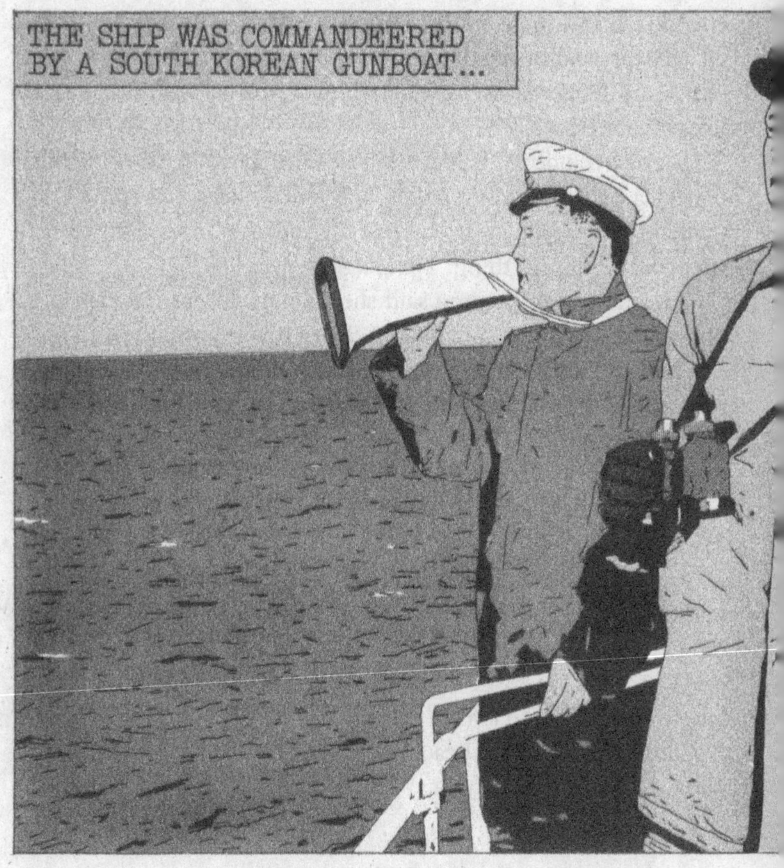
THE SHIP WAS COMMANDEERED
BY A SOUTH KOREAN GUNBOAT...

Based purely on the F-16 replacing the F-104. General Evans has said that there is a potential market for some 2,000 aircraft. (Almost 2,500 F-104s were built and over 2,200 of these were exported.)

Interavia

Catherine seemed to have settled down nicely so Una left her in Kiev and took the night train for Warsaw. From Warsaw she went

to Dubrovnik, a roundabout route but the safest (if her instincts were to be trusted). Large movements of men and equipment were taking place everywhere and she walked up the gangplank of the SS *Kao An* with a deep sense of relief. By the next morning they were making steam, heading for the less cluttered environments of Darwin and Sandakan. They had scarcely made it into the Timor Sea, however, before the ship was commandeered by a South Korean gunboat and Una and a selection of passengers were packed off back to the West with stamps on their passports forbidding them ever to cross beyond Lat. 30 or Long. 40 again. Paranoia was settling in all over, it seemed. Una had tried to make friends with one of the Korean officers, to find out what their complaint was. The man had struck her lightly across the mouth, refusing to speak English; he found that he had enjoyed hitting her and slapped her again until his commander had reprimanded him, not from any humane motive but, as Una interpreted it, because he would lose face.

Arriving in London, which had been 'cleaned up', she was subjected to an investigation into her movements over the past three years. Since she had begun to suffer from amnesia it was difficult for her to answer the questions but, knowing that they would be satisfied with any information so long as they could make it jell with their preconceptions, she invented a life story for herself which was not only acceptable to them but suited her. She regretted that it was fictional.

Prinz Lobkowitz, the new Minister for Controls, heard that she was in England and sent an invitation for her to join him for dinner, but she was too frightened to accept. She headed for the cotton-wool zone, eventually settling near Box Hill until one evening the telephone rang. Since it had never been connected at her request she saw this as a sign and returned to London and the Convent of the Poor Clares in Ladbroke Grove where a cell was held in readiness for this sort of emergency. She was convinced however that she was not going to escape. Her lovers were closing in on her.

She became desperate in her search for an ideal, a cause, a focus, but nothing presented itself to her. She refused to find what she wanted in an individual. She wanted, she said, something bigger. She regretted that her mind refused to manufacture fresh evidence for her researches.

Eventually, rather than face the more familiar dangers, she gave herself up to the nuns who had been begging to help her since her arrival.

6

The Strange Case of the Panty-Clad Coed and the Night-Riding Monster

> Financial restrictions are pushing Western aircraft development in one direction, while the East Bloc nations, spearheaded by the Soviet Union, are moving in another. The most remarkable point is that the latest Soviet aircraft display a sophistication that was almost unthinkable only a few years ago. During the 1950s and 1960s, the tendency was for all but the most specialised combat aircraft (e.g. reconnaissance and anti-submarine warfare) to be simple and robust, and produced in large numbers. The MiG-21, for example, was described by one Western analyst as a 'throw-away fighter', scarcely more than a piloted projectile.
>
> *Interavia*

Something was happening in the lower back section of the left-hand side of her brain. Memories of childhood disguised the deeper issues. She tried to trace the association. A flicker of hope. A few more cells began to die. She settled the expensive Koss headphones more comfortably over her ears and listened to the music with desperate concentration. Humour? Love? A sense of relish? The images of demolished streets and overgrown parks got in the way again. Perhaps if she adjusted the balance a fraction? She felt for the control, fingered it, moved it. Her face ached as she squeezed her eyes still tighter. All her heroes and heroines were dead. Those she had met had proved to be unworthy of what she had to give.

... I swear the moon turned to fire red. The night I was born...

She focused on the appropriate section of the cortex. Drugs could produce a terrible self-consciousness, particularly when coupled with psychiatric research. The brain scanned the brain, scanned the brain.

Surely it must be possible to awaken sections of the mind just

THE IMAGES OF DEMOLISHED STREETS ...

as one could sensitise areas of the body? She was right inside now. She slipped out. Her sense of yearning became even more painful. Inside again. Out. She increased the volume. Inside.

A question of proteins. They were being manufactured. But would they be the right ones?

The tempo of the drumbeats increased.

Inside.

The memories of childhood began to dim. Now she was sure something lay behind them. Deeper. She had isolated the cells at any rate.

The music stopped.

She screamed.

7
The Question Without an Answer

> The RBS70 missile system has been designed to provide extreme mobility and rapid deployment with a very short reaction time against high-speed aircraft flying at the lowest possible altitudes. The RBS70 missile system has recently been ordered by the Swedish Army, in an order worth nearly SKr-500 million. First deliveries, mostly of training equipment, will start in 1976, with series production by 1977. Bofors is also looking at future developments, including a possible nightfire version using electro-optical sensors for target detection. At the moment the visibility limitation on the use of the weapon is the ability of the crew to see the target. The laser guidance system is able to provide guidance under any conditions in which the target is visible.
>
> *Interavia*

Within the skull the universe was at war.

Maxime and Catherine, Jerry and Lobkowitz stood on each side of the white hospital bed, their eyes fixed on the tragic face.

'She was looking for love,' said Maxime.

'I loved her,' said Jerry a little shiftily.

'So did I,' said his sister.

'We all loved her,' said Lobkowitz. 'She was Life. She was Liberty. She was Hope.'

'She was Future,' said Jerry. 'Fusion and fission, the glowing, rolling obsidian ranges of the post-war landscape.' He sighed.

'But she was trying to love us, you see,' continued Lobkowitz. 'She wanted what we saw in her – she looked for the same things in us and could not find them. This is a good hospital. They will do what they can.'

Maxime nodded. 'Our people specialise in such complaints. *Tout cela vous honore / Lord Pierrot, mais encore?*'

Jerry glared a little resentfully at his rival.

'She thought she experienced it so many times,' said Catherine, 'but she was always disappointed. And yet she continued to seek that love, against all the odds.'

'She loved it all,' Maxime shrugged. 'All of it.'

'The data became confusing towards the end.' Lobkowitz was sad.

'I could have simplified it.' Jerry pouted. 'Only nobody would let me.' Then he laughed spontaneously. 'Too much!'

And for a moment the electrodes protruding from Una's skull quivered in sympathy with the sounds from her mouth.

5. Coda

Harlequin Transformed

3/4 (A sort of carousel tune)

Destroyed by a comedy I did not devise
I've reached the limit of my changes
Repeating tricks solely for my eyes
Now, at last, my legend ages
And reveals the structure of my lies...

And my body alters as I watch
Black mask fades
My skin is pale
The colour leaves my costume
And I'm no longer Harlequin
– I am defeated from within

4/4

Say goodbye to Harlequin
Poor Pierrot now replaces him...

3/4

By a legend I sustained
Sardonic gaze and vicious brain
By mythology I maintained
The posture that I feigned
Inevitably my pose dissolved
Entropy has left me cold
And Harlequin is slain –
Again...

4/4 (rep. tune Every Gun)

Drip, drip, drip, drip
Here comes the rain

(Plink, plink, plink, plink – plucked on violin) *Abrupt end.*

Pierrot and Columbine's Song of Reconciliation

Divided I love you
And united become you
Columbine, Columbine
We are one at last

Rejecting all armour
Thus we are conquered
Conquered, we vanquish
All that we fear

Pierrot and Columbine
(Harlequin with them)
Conquered, we vanquished
All that we feared...

(This leads into the tune of the Entropy Tango, acting as an introduction for the reprise, which is up-tempo, cheerful ...)

The Entropy Tango (Reprise – The Ensemble)

For a while at least it's all right
We're safe from Chaos and Old Night
The Cold of Space won't chill our veins
– We have danced the Entropy Tango...

So we'll love, love, love
One another like two doves…
And we'll hug, hug, hug
We can never have enough…
The power of love has won this throw
– We have danced the Entropy Tango…

And it's kiss, kiss, kiss
Fear and hate we have dismissed
And it's wish, wish, wish…
For a better world than this…
So say goodbye to pain and woe
– And we'll stop the Entropy Tango…

5. HARLEQUIN'S LAMENT

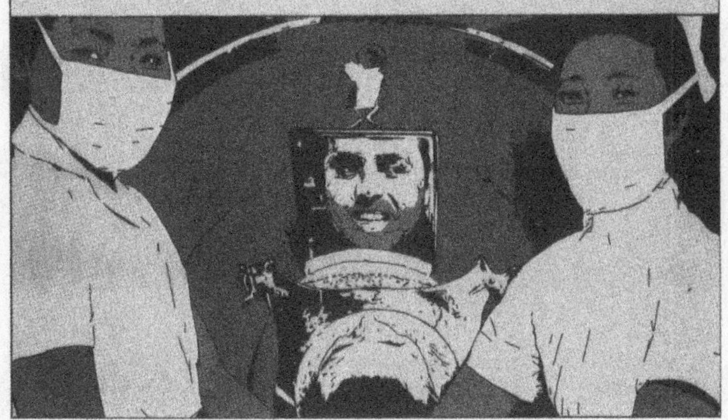

I

> This is the personal flag of the Sovereign, and a symbol of the tie which unites under one monarch the British Dominions throughout the world. The three golden lions represent England, the red lion rampant Scotland, while the golden harp stands for Ireland – the three states from which the Empire grew. Royal personages have the right to fly royal standards, members of the Royal Family having their particular standards. This flag should only be hoisted when H.M. the King is actually present, and ought never to be used for purposes of decoration.
>
> In the Royal Navy, by special privilege, the King's health is always drunk sitting.
>
> *Flags of the Empire*, No. 1,
> issued by W.D. & H.O. Wills, *c.* 1924

At sunset, when the beggars in Chowringhee settled themselves into doorways for the night and the kites and vultures on the lamp posts and telephone poles roosted, reconciled that they must wait for a fresh day to bring them their share of death and garbage, Mrs Persson would climb into her rickshaw and let the ageless coolie, in his turban and his loincloth, run with her to the Empire where she was starring as Diana Hunt in the musical comedy *Wonderful Woman*. She played a Greek goddess transported to 1930 (with hilarious misunderstandings) who eventually gives up all her powers to marry the hero and become an ordinary housewife. Una considered the rôle ideal. It was the sensation of Calcutta.

Through the mobs of cyclists, pedestrians, rickshaws; past the trams, bullock carts, limousines, trucks, taxis, buses which blared and flared in the twilight, darted Una and her coolie, until at last

MRS PERSSON WOULD CLIMB INTO HER RICKSHAW ...

they reached the marble face of the Empire (with her name in electric lights above its Graecian portico) round to the stage entrance, a little bit late as usual. Una got out and the rickshaw was off (she paid it weekly) and she, in silks and chiffon, in her Reynolds hat and veil, briskly went through, nodding to the Bengali stage-door keeper, who smiled and nodded at her. He was trusted by the management. He was one of the very few natives they employed at present. So many young Bengalis were anarchists and might be expected to attack the theatre.

Una got to her dressing room and became suddenly wary, for the door was open and voices emerged. She recomposed herself and entered. She vaguely recalled the couple who waited for her – the fat clergyman with his hat in his fingers, the thin bluestocking in pale linen. Her dresser began to speak rapidly in her lilting English. Una smiled. 'It's all right, Ranee. Bishop Beesley and –?'

'I'm Miss Brunner. We met, I believe, at Mrs Brightsett's garden party. Last week.'

'Oh, yes. And I promised you tickets!'

'No,' said Bishop Beesley. 'We are from the local Moral Rearmament Committee.'

'This play is objectionable? Surely not.'

'The play is fine. There's one scene, that's all.' Bishop Beesley brightened as Ranee offered him some of Una's Turkish Delight.

'Which one?'

'The –' he mumbled the confection – 'second act. Scene one.'

'Where I have my first drink?'

'Yes.' Miss Brunner spoke significantly.

'The audience love it. It's the funniest.'

'It's very good.' Miss Brunner seemed baffled. 'But we wondered if you could accommodate us. Accommodate the residents of the city, really. Anywhere else, I'm sure it would not be important – but there are Bengalis in the audience, and Anglo-Indians and so on, as well as English people.'

'Yes.'

'And we feel the scene could –' Bishop Beesley wiped sugary lips – 'corrupt some of them.'

'Because of me getting tipsy? I would have thought there was a moral there – not to drink.'

'You could see it as that,' Miss Brunner agreed, 'but when it is combined with your costume…'

'A bit flimsy?'

'Exactly,' said Bishop Beesley in relief.

'And the language,' said Miss Brunner. 'I mean – what you say.'

'What do I say?'

'Something about crime and anarchy?'

'Ah, yes: Here's to crime and here's to anarchy! I'm showing my frustration. I come round in the end.'

'Not the best-chosen line, given the current political climate.'

'I don't know anything about politics,' Una told them.

Ranee brought over some tea. 'Tea?' added Una.

'Thank you. Even you, Mrs Persson,' continued the bishop, 'must realise there have been bombings of white people almost daily. In the name of the anarchist cause.' He unrolled a copy of *The Englishman* and pointed out its headline: ANARCHY: A CHALLENGE TO THE EMPIRE. 'It's in the leading article. And you should read the Bengali papers. Full of such stuff.'

'What stuff?' asked Una.

'Anarchy,' said Miss Brunner, lifting her cup. 'They get it all from France, I believe.'

'Aha,' said Una. She sat down at her mirror and looked at her face. She gave herself a wink. 'Well, I'll bear it in mind, of course. Thanks for pointing the problem out.'

'You'll change your lines? And your costume?'

'I'll certainly give it some thought,' Una promised.

2

What man that sees the eur-whirling wheele
Of Change, the which all mortall things doth sway,
But that therby doth find, & plainly feele,
How MUTABILITY in them doth play
Her cruell sports, to many mens decay?
Which that to all may better yet appear,
I will rehearse that whylome I heard say,
How she at first her selfe began to reare,
Gainst all the Gods, and th'empire fought from them to beare.

– Spenser,
The Faerie Queene, 7. vi. 1

As the train pulled out of Odessa, leaving the warmth and the ocean behind, Una swayed on her feet, attempting to freshen her face in the mirror above the opposite seats. Her lipstick dropped from her hand and fell onto green plush. She said: 'Damn!' and bent to look for it just as the compartment door opened and a man holding a carpet bag entered and raised his straw hat. He wore rimless glasses and had the kind of goatee beard which hid nothing of his face, added no character and was perhaps a badge to make it clear that he was an intellectual. The casual Norfolk, the unpressed trousers, the peasant shirt, all proclaimed his chosen rôle and, of course, he addressed her in French rather than Russian. 'Excusez moi, mademoiselle.'

Una had recognised him. It was the old butcher himself. He couldn't see past her heavy make-up.

'Bronstein!' she laughed. 'Are you back in favour?'

He relaxed, at the same time displaying his embarrassment. 'It's you, comrade. Dressed up like a bourgeois whore. What are you doing? Going all the way?'

'Hoping to. Kiev?'

'I change there. I don't like this part of the world much. The people are lazy. Too rich, all of them.'

'All?'

'By my standards. What have you been up to?' He offered her a Sobranie which she accepted because she liked the feel of the gold tip on her mouth.

'I've been resting,' she said. 'I'm too tired, darling.'

'And why are you in Russia?'

'I'm not in Russia. I'm in the Ukraine.'

'You have a pass?' He pulled a card from his pocket. He seemed to be proud of the distinction. 'Like this? It's a special pass. Every-one must help me.'

'You're not posing as an anarchist now!'

'What's the difference? We're all socialists. I shall represent Kiev in Moscow and resume my position as head of the Bureau. In time.' He opened his bag and took out a large notebook. 'I have agreed to put the South Russian case.'

'They don't need it put. They're strong – and rich. You said so yourself.' The train began to move faster. They were in Odessa's new garden suburbs. The light was perfect. Una stared out of the window, back at the misty sea with all its ships, inland at the green

steppe ahead. 'You've conned them. You'll use their strength to help you get your job back! You cunning old bastard.'

Trotsky sniffed. 'I have a case to put. I must I have an effective power-base if I am to put it properly.'

'And Stalin?'

Trotsky pursed his lips and smiled. 'Didn't you know? He's dead.'

'I never understand politics.' Una looked out at golden fields and saw horsemen riding along the nearby white road. They were racing the train, waving their caps as they spurred their ponies. She was reminded of the old days, of Makhno and his riders. She waved back. They were past. She returned her attention to Trotsky. 'Maybe that's why I find them so eternally appealing.'

He leaned forward and put a familiar hand on her knee. 'Where have you been for the past five years? This time I want the truth.' He attempted joviality.

'You'll have it,' she said. 'But you'll never appreciate it.'

'Don't be mysterious.' He leaned back and picked up his book. He took a fountain pen from his inside pocket. 'It irritates me.'

'I can't be anything else. I'm Una. I'm the truth. Eh?'

'You're the very antithesis. You've gone back to acting, I see.'

'I had. But I've given it up again. I'm on my way to see a friend in Kiev.'

'Makhno, that hooligan?'

'No. Quite another hooligan. He's not fond of you.'

'Few are,' he said smugly. 'Who is it?'

'Jerry.'

'Cornelius. Bah! He's no threat at all. Except to himself. I thought he was liquidated. Or in a coma or something.'

'It's not his turn.'

He removed his glasses. The gesture was meant as a warning signal. He drew heavily on his cigarette as he leaned forward. 'Stop it! Una!' He wagged his finger. He was pretending to joke.

Una felt the familiar terror. She drew in a breath and was defiant. It was just what she had needed.

3

The River

> It is during the Diwali festival, when the darkest night in October is illumined by myriad bonfires, each symbolising a life sacrificed in the conflict between good and evil, that the girl, Harriet, falls in love with a young captain, lamed in the First World War. Lacking beauty, she hopes to win his heart by writing a poem for him about the legendary Radha, whose love for the god Krishna made her a goddess ... In India all rivers – symbols of Eternity – are sacred...
>
> Article, *Picture Post*, 1 March, 1952

Behind them, the Golden Gate Bridge sagged and squealed as the explosive took it out. It was dawn. There were fires all over San Francisco, particularly in the suburbs. From the harbour the pirate ships continued to shell the city. They were retreating now. On the bridge of the submarine liner *Seahorse* Una, her face blackened by smoke, her hand on the butt of her holstered revolver, looked at their hostages – almost all young men and women – totting up their value in her head. They would be ransomed.

The fleet, mainly a mixture of commercial and naval submarines stolen from half the countries in the world, had arrived at midnight, surfacing in the bay to begin its attack. It had fought off the few defending airships, and, in the time gained while Washington hesitated, had been able to loot the city of most of what they had come for.

Makhno, in a long leather coat and riding britches, an M60 in his left hand, joined her on the bridge. His men were hauling boxes aboard. 'There it is, Una. All the gold of Sacramento.'

She was a little dismayed at his tone. 'You sound like a bandit.'

'Don't be moralistic now you've had your fun. There's something Victorian about you, Una. Always washing your hands. I am a successful bandit!' He touched her arm gently. He was very old. The white hair was growing thin. His movements, however, were those of a ballet dancer – imitating youth from training and habit.

He went below, making some noise, and greeted the Pole, Captain Korzeniowski, who had inadvertently inspired this raid with his tales of gold and who had commanded the *Seahorse* ('For safety and comfort in troubled times, these luxurious hotels of the deep will get you where you want to go in the condition you'd wish to arrive!') before Makhno had requisitioned her. Korzeniowski was contemptuous. 'How many hundreds of innocents has your raid destroyed?'

'There are no innocents in this struggle.' Makhno spoke automatically and Una felt sad. The years had at last succeeded in coarsening him. It had been almost inevitable. She leaned down towards where the hostages still stood watching the gold being lowered into the special hatches. 'Let them go. Give them boats.' She told the guards. She would not take any more responsibility.

In a dinghy coming alongside from their own wrecked sub, Shakey Mo and Jerry called out to her. They were filthy and jubilant. Cornelius at least was drunk. It was always hard to tell with Mo what sort of condition he was in.

'Mrs P.' Jerry raised a bottle of wine in a salute. He began to get up but the rocking boat made him sit down again. 'Ready to leave when you are!

'Not long now,' she said. She searched the sky for dawn, but the flames obscured it.

'This is what I call effective political action,' said Mo. 'We need our course. We had the chart on the bridge when that bloody destroyer got us. Dropped a fucking great torpedo, didn't it?'

She had seen them leap into the sea just before the destroyer had, in turn, been blown out of the sky.

Could she hear screaming from the city? Smoke clogged her nostrils, stung her eyes. The suburbs were on fire, now. Many wooden houses were burning and they sweetened the otherwise acrid air.

Mo scrambled over the rail. 'Better than any earthquake,' he said. 'Better than any Indian raid. Where are we headed? My guess was Mexico.'

'You're not far out,' said Una. Mo clinked and looked embarrassed. 'What have you got this time?' she asked.

'Nothing much.' His grin was sheepish. He reached into one of his several sacks and pulled out a coin. 'Pieces of eight. Doubloons. And that…'

'Where on earth did you get them?'

'The museum. I always hit the museum first. You know me. An incurable bloody romantic. I love old things.'

She felt affection for him. More than she felt at that moment for the others.

'This did used to be called the Barbary Coast,' he said defensively.

'Wasn't that in Africa somewhere?'

'No,' he said. 'You're thinking of the Mountains of the Moon.' He vanished into the liner's enormous hull.

Una saw that Jerry was helping some of the girls into the boat he had abandoned. He looked as harmless as they did. He was being very gentle with them. She drew a deep breath and controlled her tears.

'It all seems a bit self-indulgent, really,' she said.

Fisherman's Wharf exploded suddenly and she was blinded.

4

Hooliganism on Soccer Terraces 'Harmless Ritual'

Soccer hooliganism provides a harmless outlet for aggression which could take more violent forms, says an Oxford psychologist in a book published today. Battles between rival groups on soccer terraces are an artificial form of violence rather than the real thing, and few people really get hurt, says Mr Peter Marsh, of the Oxford University Department of Experimental Psychology. In 'Aggro: the Illusion of Violence', he appeals to people to learn to live with 'aggro' – fights between rival gangs of youths at football matches, dance halls and public houses – rather than trying to stamp it out. 'By trying to eradicate aggro we end up with something far more sinister. Instead of social violence we get non-social violence that manifests itself in random, gratuitous injury ... By learning to live with aggro ... we begin to see that illusions of violence are much preferable to the very real violence which maims and kills...' Mr Marsh sees 'Aggro' between rival gangs as an equivalent of tribal warfare in less developed societies.

Daily Telegraph, 20 July, 1978

Although the hospital was virtually silent, it seemed to Una that there was a threat in the air. She tried to move her eyes a little further than they would comfortably go. The metal cage keeping her head in position (she had a broken neck) allowed her no flexibility. Major Nye was still there, holding her hand. He attempted to carry on the conversation where it had stopped, five minutes before. 'Yes,' he said. 'It's the vermin.'

'Rats?'

'Mainly.'

'Models, metaphors – even examples, I suppose.' Una was glad that they had taken the screen away and she could see at least part

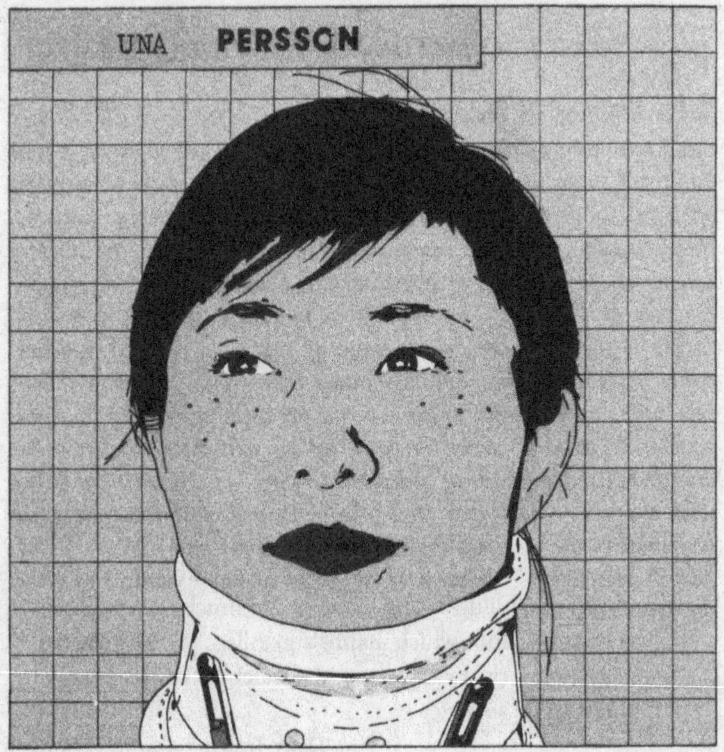

of the ward with its privileged beds. The hospital was run by nuns and was private. There was no vermin here to speak of.

'I see what you mean.' He smiled. 'You're too imaginative.'

'I live in a world of poetry,' she said. 'Or rather, of poetic images. Everything seems significant to me. Everything has meaning. It's what gets me into trouble. And I never listen. I only watch.'

He patted her hand.

She heard very soft sounds and thought at first that she was listening to his hand on hers, but they were footfalls. At the end of the bed stood Prinz Lobkowitz. 'They haven't moved you yet?'

'Not yet.' Major Nye answered for her. He got up and brought a chair to place next to his own. 'Sit down, old boy. You look very tired.'

Lobkowitz's back was stooped. His grey hair fell over his face. The skin of his face had become baggy with care. Una felt frustrated. She wished she could be of help.

'Makhno?' she said.

'Dead. The Americans caught him at last. He was electrocuted three days ago. In Oregon, I believe.'

'The Californians gave him up.'

'Californians are like Greeks. They talk themselves into things and then they talk themselves out of them again. It must be the sunshine. No, he's buried in some Portland cemetery. Shall I get you the details?'

'It's pointless,' she said. 'I'll be in this thing for six months.'

'Yes.'

'He made a name for himself, at least,' said Major Nye. 'There's no-one in the world hasn't heard of Nestor Makhno. He's a hero and a martyr in six continents. And his example lives on.' He was trying to console her, but he could not fail to register a little disapproval. She gripped his wrist.

'Don't worry,' she said. 'It's a victory for your sort of rationalism, major.'

'I've never much cared for my sort of rationalism. Not in isolation, anyway. I see myself as a balancing force – not as a positive one. Makhno represented all I envied. It was the same sort of balance which controlled the Empire for so long – we all admired the Bengalis, you know. And the Pathans. It's a terrible sort of paternalism, I suppose, but it had certain simple virtues.'

'Are you sure there are such things as simple virtues?' Prinz Lobkowitz's accent had grown a shade stronger. 'I would say that only vice was simple.'

Major Nye hadn't followed him. 'You sound as if you've come to preach the last rites,' he said. 'I don't think you'd make a very good clergyman, Prinz.'

'Oh, I'm not so sure!' He strove for levity and failed miserably.

'A couple of hundred years or so ago I could have filled the rôle you see as your own, major. A temporiser. Mm?'

'Church and State stuff. There's a fair bit to be said for the ideas of the Middle Ages. We've complicated them rather, haven't we, without improving on them.'

'I wouldn't say that,' said Una. She attempted to move and failed. The harness was firm.

'We're taking you by airship to the coast,' said Prinz Lobkowitz. 'And then, perhaps when you're whole again, a cruise.'

'I might have had enough of cruises.'

'We'll see.'

'Do you good,' said Major Nye with weary mindlessness.

'I'll happily take over.' Prinz Lobkowitz smiled at his old friend. 'You could do with some shut-eye, eh?'

'About as much as you.' Major Nye appreciated the thought. 'But I haven't any travelling in the morning. I'll carry on here.'

'You should both rest.' Una hoped they would not take her seriously. She was terrified of being left in the hospital. She needed one of them there at least, to comfort her.

'Well,' said Major Nye, 'perhaps you're right. Will you sleep now, Una?'

'Oh, yes. Of course.'

They rose; two tired ghosts. 'Goodbye.'

5

> But if he sees a sad face staring through the glamour of light, the face of a girl who is thinking of a lover who comes no more to her Christmas parties, of an old mother whose children have gone about their business in the world, Pierrot will go on tiptoe to them, and lay a hand lightly on their shoulders, and say, 'It is not good to remember too much. Play the game of life. I have suffered too; but listen to my laughter on this Christmas night. Come, play the fool with me. Why, there is little Columbine

who flouted me three hundred years ago! Bless her sweet heart; I will steal a kiss tonight.'

– Phillip Gibbs,
'The Spirit of Pierrot',
The Graphic, 27 November, 1911

The white steam yacht moved slowly through the drifts of ice. Steam curled from her deck as she gave her heat to the Arctic. The blue sky was like thin ice enclosing them. It was as if they sailed through the semi-fluid remains of some frozen confection, under glass. This was no place, thought Una as she pulled her huge white furs around her, for the *Teddy Bear*. It was no place for her, for that matter. She coughed and more heat escaped her to be absorbed by that unambiguous continent. The yacht bumped against a few small floes and the engines stalled for a second, then started up again, firmly pushing the ship on, heading closer and closer to the Pole.

From below came the sound of a piano, thin and brittle, and the applause of the guests. They had already had their turkey. They had opened their presents. Now the party was to begin with an entertainment.

Una turned from the tranquillity of endless ice and made her way to the louvred door which would lead her down. The ship, though strengthened in her hull, had been designed for warm-weather cruising.

In the saloon the audience had gathered. 'All our old chums,' as Bishop Beesley had said. He had handed over control of the ship only after he had been locked up for an afternoon without sweets. He was in the front row now, with a plate of cake and candy on his knees. Miss Brunner, wearing a paper hat on her violent red hair, sat next to him. She held a tiny piece of marzipan between the finger and thumb of her left hand. Her right hand rested against Maxime. The bishop's blonde daughter, Mitzi, glared at them from the other side of her corpulent dad.

Una removed her coat and revealed herself as Harlequin. She

put on her mask and her cap. She bowed and was cheered. Mrs Cornelius, behind the bishop, blew a friendly raspberry. Major Nye began to vamp a 4/4 tango. He looked a little incongruous in his clown costume. Columbine (played by Catherine) curtseyed on the tiny stage. Behind her, wistful as ever, stood Pierrot, pretending to play a guitar.

The audience began to clap in time to the music, so loudly that the words of the song could not be heard at all.

Outside, the ice grew thicker and it seemed it must soon stop the ship completely. The steam from the white decks was growing denser, almost hiding her from view, as the passengers put their hearts and souls into their enjoyment of the show.

A little faint music found an echo in the distant mountains; the ancient ice.

If it was to be a farewell performance, none of the actors had yet guessed. They sang louder and louder above the steady drumming of the applause, which took on the nature of a gigantic heartbeat. They sang as loud as they could. They sang with gusto. They sang for all the world.

THE END

Several early recordings now appear on The Entropy Tango & Gloriana Demo Sessions *CD, Noh Poetry Records, 2008*

M

The Great Rock 'n' Roll Swindle

For Nestor Makhno, the spirit of romantic, active anarchism. Although he might have been a trifle naïve in some of his hopes, I have a considerable soft spot for him. He died young, of consumption, in poverty and some despair, in Paris in 1936.

This is as much dedicated to the memory of Sid Vicious and all those others who have, in one way or another, been destroyed by their own simple dreams.

Lesson One
How To Manufacture Your Group

Designed by Huber & Pirsson, The Chelsea Hotel was opened in 1884 as one of the City's earliest co-operative apartment houses. It became a hotel about 1905. The florid cast iron balconies were made by the firm of J.B. & J.M. Cornell. Artists and writers who have lived here include Arthur B. Davies, James T. Farrell, Robert Flaherty, O. Henry, John Sloan, Dylan Thomas, Thomas Wolfe and Sid Vicious.

Plaque, The Chelsea Hotel, NY

'Well, it's not what I bloody corl a picture.' Mrs Cornelius waded across the foyer on old, flat feet and lowered her tray of Lyons Maids and Kia-Oras to the counter. 'I mean, in my day it was love an' adventure an' that, wannit.'

Tenpole lifted a crazed eye from behind the hot-dog warmer and opened a disturbed mouth. 'Who ...?' he began. But his attention was already wandering.

'Now it's all vomit an' screwin',' she continued. 'I wouldn't mind if it was Clark Gable doin' it. *An'* there's no bloody adventure, Tadpole. Wot you grinnin' at?'

'Who...?'

'Oh, shut up, you pore littel bugger. It's that Mrs Vicious I feel sorry for.'

'Killed...' said Tenpole.

'Too right.' Mrs C. heaved her tray around. 'Oh, well. Back into the effin' fray.'

Somebody Must Have the Money

On the screen an old robber, desperately clinging to the last vestiges of publicity (which he confused with dignity) pretended to play a guitar and wondered about the money. Something in his eyes showed that he really knew his credibility in South London was going down the drain.

'Then who the hell did get any satisfaction out of it?' Steve shifted Mary's head and felt about in his crotch for the popcorn he'd dropped.

'You got a complaint?' Her voice was muffled.

Steve sighed. 'Now's a fine time to start asking.'

Robbers cavorted on beaches. Robbers limbered up. Robbers made publishing deals and wondered why their victims went crazy.

Steve looked away from the screen. He sniffed. 'There's sulphate in the air-conditioning.'

'Is jussa keeps way,' said Mary.

'What?'

She raised her head again, impatiently. 'It's just to keep you awake.'

'Oh.'

The popcorn was running out.

A kilted figure came on screen and began to rationalise his own and others' despair. It was called hindsight.

'I think I'd better try to see what happened to it,' said Steve.

'What? The money?'

'Call it that, if you like. Unless you have a plot, see, you can't have the paranoia.'

Mary rested her head on his thigh. 'I don't think it *is* sulphate. It's something else.' She tasted the air. 'Is this an EMI cinema?'

But Steve was already backtracking.

New Recruits in the Psychic Wars

'As long as we all believe in the New Jerusalem,' said Helen of Troy, having trouble with her knickerbocker glory, 'we stay together. And as long as we stay together, we can all believe the same thing. And if we can all believe the same thing long enough, we can believe for a while that we've made it come true. We all have to be a bit over the top. But when some silly bastard goes well over the top, that rocks the boat. The trouble with Johnny, for instance, was that he wouldn't bloody well stay in uniform. And after Malcolm had gone to all that bother, too.'

'I wouldn't know abart any o' that, love.' Mrs Cornelius waved away the offer of a bit of jelly and ice-cream on a long spoon. 'Can't stand the stuff. I 'ave ter carry it arahnd orl bleedin' day, don't I?'

They sat together on red vinyl and chrome stools at the bar. Behind them was a big plate-glass window. Behind that was the traffic; the Beautiful People of the King's Road in their elegant bondagerie. Dandyism always degenerated into fashion.

Helen of Troy was having trouble getting to the bottom of her glory. Her arms were too short. Mrs C. tilted the glass. 'Poor fing. There you go.' She laughed. 'Didn't mean ter interfere, love.' She glanced out of the window.

From the direction of Sloane Square a mob was moving. It was difficult to make out what it consisted of.

'Skinheads,' said Mrs C. 'Or Mods, is it? Or them Rude Boys? Or is that ther same?'

'Divide and Rule,' said Helen of Troy. 'Divide and Rule. And *that's* the first lesson in the management of rock-and-roll bands.'

'Oh, well, they all do that, don't they.' Mrs C. squinted up the street. 'Blimey, it's a load of effin' actors. Innit?'

The mob was dressed in eighteenth-century costumes. ''Ighwaymen?'

'Nostalgia hasn't been such a positive force since the Romantic Revival.'

''Ippies, yer mean?'

'The Past and the Future – they'll get you every time.'

'I know wot you mean, love.' Mrs C. picked up her handbag. 'Stick to ther Present. I orlways said so, an' I bloody orlways will. I've met some funny bastards in me time. Lookin' backwards; lookin' bloody forwards. It's un'ealthy. Nar. Ther future's orl we fuckin' got, innit?'

'And it doesn't do you any harm.'

The mob was carrying effigies of four young men. Over loudspeakers came the sounds of Malcolm McLaren singing 'You Need Hands'. The mob began to growl in unison.

'I've seen 'em come an' I've seen 'em go.' Mrs C. shook her head. 'An' it'll end in tears every time. Wot good does it do?'

'It stops you getting bored,' said Helen of Troy. 'Some of the time, anyway.'

The effigies were being tossed on a tide of angry shoulders.

'You can get 'em attackin' anyfink, carn't yer.' Mrs C. was amused. 'Give 'em a slipper ter worry an' they won't bovver *you*.'

'The Sex Pistols were the best thing that ever happened for British politics at a very dodgy moment in their career.' Helen of Troy reached her money up to the girl at the till. 'Or so we like to think. But no bloody B.O.s or whatever they are for them. Divide and Rule, Mrs C. And up goes your ego.'

'I 'ope this doesn't mean they've stopped ther bloody buses again.' Mrs Cornelius looked at the clock over the bar. 'I'm due for work at one.'

'They still showin' that picture?'

'It's really good business.'

'I think Malcolm McLaren is the Sir Robert Boothby of his generation, don't you?' Helen got to the exit first and pushed on one of the doors.

'Well, 'e's no bloody Svengali, an' that's for sure.'

'He did identify with the product…'

''E should 'ave bought an Alsatian. They're easier ter train.'

A young man in a trilby and a dark trench coat went past them in a hurry.

'That's Steve.' Helen of Troy pulled on her jacket. 'He still thinks there's a solution to all this. Or at least a resolution.'

'It's one o' ther nice fings abart 'im.' Mrs C. directed a look of tolerant pity at his retreating back.

'The trouble with messed-up love affairs,' said Helen of Troy, 'is that you waste so much time going to the source of the pain and asking it to make you better.'

''E'll learn. You on'y got yerself ter blame in the end.' Mrs Cornelius saw that the mob had parted to allow a convoy of No. 11 buses through. 'I'd better 'op on one o' these while I've still got ther chance.'

'The ultimate business of management is not just to divide your group but to divide their minds. The more you fuck with their judgement, the more you control them. It's like being married, really.' Helen of Troy waved to Mrs C.'s lumbering figure as it launched itself towards the bus.

'Don't let 'em piss on yer, dear.' Mrs C. reached the platform. 'Just 'cos yore short.'

'You can only manage what you create yourself. The trouble with people is that they will keep breaking out. It almost cost poor Malcolm his health.'

The mob was beginning to split up. Fights were starting between different factions. Cocked hats flew.

'After all,' said Helen, deciding to shadow Steve, 'someone has to take the blame. But you can bet your chains we won't have anarchy in the UK in our lifetime. Just the usual bloody chaos.'

What Do You Need?

'Rôle models make Rolls-Royces. Kids pay for heroes. But it doesn't do to let either the audiences or the artists get out of control – or you stand to lose the profit. It's true in all forms of show business, but it's particularly important in the record industry.'

Frank Cornelius lay back in his Executive Comfort Mark VI leather swiveller and wondered if it would be going too far if he waved his unlit cigar.

'What can I do for you, Stevie?' His eyes, wasted by a thousand indulgences, moved like worms in his skull.

'I was wondering what happened to the money.' Steve unbuttoned his trench coat, looking around at the images of rock singers in various classic poses, emulating the stars of Westerns and War films except they had guitars instead of rifles.

'It hardly existed.' Frank put his cigar to his awful lips. 'Well, I mean, it's real enough in the *mind*. And I suppose that's the main thing. What are you selling me, Stevie? Thinking of going solo? This company's small, but it's keen. We really identify with the kids. Can you play your guitar yet? Don't worry if you can't. It's one of the easiest skills in the world to learn.'

'What happened to the money, Frank?'

'Don't look at me. Malcolm had it.'

'He says you had it.'

'I haven't made a penny, personally, in six months. It's all gone on expenses. Do you know how much it costs to keep an act on the road?'

'Where's the money?' Steve himself was beginning to lose his thread. Frank's responses were too familiar to keep anyone's attention for long, including his own.

'Gone in advances, probably. Ask Malcolm, not me. I only became a director towards the end. For legal reasons.'

'Where's Malcolm?'

'Who knows where Malcolm is? Does Malcolm know where Malcolm is? Is he Malcolm? What is Malcolm, anyway?'

Steve frowned. 'Give me an address, Frank.'

'You're not kipping on my floor again, Stevie. Not with your habits. Haven't you got a squat to go to?'

'Where?'

'You're too heavily into bread, Steve. That's your problem. You've really sold out, haven't you? I remember you when you didn't give a shit about money or anything else. What are you really after, Steve? Mummy and Daddy, is it? If you don't like the heat, you should stay out of the kitchen. I look after a lot of people, but I can't look after you all the time. It's killing me. I have to deal with all the hassles, cool out the managements of the venues, pay for the damage…'

He raised a suède arm. 'I haven't had more than twelve hours' sleep in a week. Profits? Do you think there are any profits in this business? If so, where are they? Show them to me!'

'They're up your nose, Frankie.'

There came a noise from Frank's throat like the sound of an

angry baby. Steve recognised it. It was called The Management Wail. It was time to leave.

Public Image

Identity Manipulation Associates (IMA = Whatever You Want Me To Be) had taken over the old Soho offices. Steve was beginning to feel a little flaky around the edges. He'd started off thinking this was a caper: a time-filler. Now, what with one thing and another, it was beginning to smell like an obsession.

'I've had enough of obsessions.' He felt the old call to retreat, to get some air. 'On the other hand, this might not be one. It could just be ordinary.'

He opened the door and went into the lobby. A young woman looked up at him from threatened brown eyes. 'Can I help you?'

'I was wondering about the money. Did Malcolm...?'

'We only do identities here. The money comes later.'

'Is there anyone I could see?'

'They're all in meetings. Are you a performer?'

'I...'

She became sympathetic and far less wary. Steve was no-one to be afraid of. She spoke softly. 'They won't be back this afternoon, love. What do you play?'

'I think it's Scrabble, but I'm not sure.'

'Magic!'

He was plodding off again.

Adapted for the Market: Finally It's the Movie

The permanently depressed tones of Malcolm McLaren, doing his best to make some sense of his impulses, could be heard on the other side of the doors.

Steve pushed his way through. There were no pictures, only a soundtrack. The little room was dark, but somewhere in it lawyers and accountants shuffled and whispered. 'Why is everybody so unhappy?'

'Sometimes it's all you've got left of your adolescent enthusiasm,' said Steve. He began to giggle.

'Were you ever talented?' Aggressive, self-protecting, attempting condescension, a lawyer spoke.

'Did you deliberately set out to shock?'

'I don't know,' said Steve. 'I don't read the papers any more.'

'Have you just come from Highgate?'

'That's an idea.'

'It's the image that's important, isn't it?' This was an upper-class woman's voice.

'So they say.'

Bodies were coming closer. 'Well, ta ta.'

'Ta ta.'

Swallowing Your Own Bullshit

Steve waded into the mud. He was not quite certain what lay on the other side of the vast building site. He wasn't sure why he was trying to get to South London. A helicopter came in low, seeming to be observing him. He looked up. 'Malcolm?'

A voice began to sing 'My Way' through a loud-hailer.

It was beginning to feel like victimisation, or a haunting. That energy was going. Or maybe it had already gone and that was what he was looking for.

All he'd wanted was a bit of this and that. Some peace and quiet. Some fun. Everybody was going crazy. He hated the lot of them. Why couldn't they leave him alone? Why couldn't he leave them alone?

He was dying for a crap.

He cast about for an anchor. About five feet away the back wheel of a new Honda could be seen, sticking out of the mud, as if the rider had tried to make it across this no man's land and failed.

Steve blinked. 'Sid?'

What the hell did it matter anyway?

Sulphate Heaven

The room was full of heavy metal. In one corner about fifteen old hippies were wondering where it had all gone, while in the opposite corner fifteen punks were wondering where it was all going. Steve stood in the middle.

'Anybody want a fight?'

A few eyes flickered, then faded again. Wired faces tried to move.

It was a musician's graveyard. They existed as far apart as Streatham and Kensal Rise. They had served their turn. Many of them had even shown a profit.

Helen of Troy came in. 'Blimey.' She rattled her box.

'Line up, lads,' said Steve. 'The lady's got the blues.'

'Been to Highgate yet?' she asked him.

'Is there any point?'

'Not a lot.'

'I'm on my way,' he said.

Lesson Two
Establish The Name

Johnny Rotten, the angelically malevolent Scaramouche, is a third-generation son of rock 'n' roll – the galvanic lead singer of the Sex Pistols. His band play at a hard heart-attacking, frantic pace. And they sing anti-love songs, cynical songs about suburbia and songs about repression, hate and aggression. They have shocked many people. But the band's music has always been true to life as they see it. Which is why they are so wildly popular. The fans love the Sex Pistols and identify with their songs because they know they are about their lives too.

Virgin Records publicity, 1977

'Sex and aggro are the best-selling commodities in the world. Everybody's frustrated or angry about something, particularly adolescents.'

Frank was having his hair redone to fit in with current trends. 'Easy on the Vicks, Mary. We don't want to go too far, do we?'

The phone rang. Mary picked it up. Her hand stank of camphor. 'Popcorn.'

She listened for a moment and giggled. She turned back to Frank. 'It's your mum.'

'Tell her I'm dead.'

'You're about the only one who isn't.'

Frank took the greasy receiver.

'Hello, Mum. How are you? What can I do for you, then?' He was patronising.

He listened for a while, his expression becoming devoutly earnest. 'Yeah.'

Mary began to pluck at his locks again, but he stopped her. 'Okay, Mum.'

He frowned.

'Okay, Mum. Yes. Yes. Look after yourself.' He handed the phone back to Mary. 'Well, well,' he said.

From the other side of his office door his dogs, a mixed pack of Irish wolfhounds and Alsatians, began to scratch and whine. He sometimes felt they were his only real security. Moved by some impulse he couldn't define, he placed a reluctant hand on Mary's bum.

Sentimental Journeys: The Other Side of the Coin

Steve had managed to reach Tooting. Autumn leaves fell onto the common. In the distance was what looked like a ruined Swimming Baths. He dipped into his tub of Sweet and Sour Pork and Chips. His fingers were already stained bright orange, as was his entire lower face. Over to his right the road was up. Drills were hammering. He was beginning to feel more relaxed. It was when they put you in the real country that you went to pieces.

Paul was waiting for him behind a large plane tree. 'I shouldn't really be talking to you, you cunt.'

'Divide and Rule,' said Steve. 'Aren't we part of the same faction any more?'

'What does Malcolm say?'

'Haven't seen him.'

'Or the record company.'

'They haven't released anything.'

'Then it could be okay.'

'It could be.' Steve offered Paul the tub. The drummer began to eat with eager, twitching fingers.

'I've been trying to make this deal with the devil all day,' he complained. 'Not a whisper. What you up to then, you bastard?'

'Very little, my son.'

'Got any money?'

Steve shook his head. 'How long you got to stay down here?'

'Another six months. Then I might get remission.'

'Play your cards right.'

'A bit of spit never hurt anybody. Are you in Tooting just to see me?'

'No. I'm looking for a train robber.'

'They're difficult to fence, trains.'

'You have to have a buyer set up already.'

'Things were simpler in the fifties, you know. The poor were poor and the rich were bloody rich. People knew where they stood. I blame it all on rock and roll.'

'It was the only way out. Now that doesn't work any more. You think it does. But it doesn't.'

'The mimic goes round and round.' Paul farted. 'And it comes out here.'

Rock Around the Clock

Mrs Cornelius flashed her torch around the cinema. 'It's filthy in 'ere. You fink they'd do somefing abart it.'

Customers began to complain at her. She switched off the torch. 'Please yerselves.'

She went back into the foyer.

With intense concentration, Tenpole was dissecting a hot-dog.

'Found anyfink?' she asked.

'Not a sausage.'

'Anybody ring fer me?'

'Ring?'

'Never mind.'

She'd done her best to warn Frank. Now it was up to him. Three guardsmen in heavy khaki and caps whose visors hid their eyes marched into the cinema and bought tickets. 'This had better be good,' said one of them threateningly to Tenpole.

'You can't go wrong with sex and pistols.' His mate began to guffaw. They had that smell of stale sweat and over-controlled violence common to most soldiers and policemen. It was probably something in the uniform.

Sonic Attack

'A little vomit is a dangerous thing.' Miss Brunner tried to smooth a lump in her satin trousers. Her thin hands were agitated, irritable. 'There's no point in going for that. Not unless you mean to do it properly. Vomit has to have some meaning, you know.'

'What about gobbing,' said her eager assistant, Sophie. 'Should that stay?'

'Well, it is associated with the band, after all.' She sniggered. 'Disgusting, really. But we have to get into disgust, don't we? Disgust equals the Pistols. Ugly times. You know?'

'But will people be disgusted enough?' This was the constant worry of the publicity department at the moment. 'I mean, it's important to associate Sex Pistols with nastiness. They should be synonymous in the public's view.'

'True.' Miss Brunner touched a finger to a blackened lid. 'Should we emphasise the urine angle?'

'Piss-stools,' said Sophie. She laughed a high-pitched, artificial laugh. 'Rebels with bladder problems?'

'Now you're being facetious. It won't do, Sophie. This is serious. We want the name in every paper by Thursday.'

'But the record isn't mixed yet.'

'The record, dear, is the least of our problems. We want the front page of *The Sun*. And the rest of them, if possible.'

Sophie put a pencil to her post office lips. 'Well, we'd better get busy, eh?'

'Our first problem,' said Miss Brunner, 'is to find a nicer word for gob.'

And Now, The Sex Pistols Controversy

Steve came out of Balham station and walked into the High Street. DIY shops and take-aways stretched in both directions.

'Nobody ever really hates you,' said Helen of Troy. 'It's more that they enjoy being threatened. You know, like throwing a baby up to the ceiling. You couldn't lose. It's just that you expected a different reaction. It's all fantasy. It happens every time.'

'You could kick 'em in the balls and they'd keep coming back for more. You've got to feel contempt for people like that.'

'I don't know why. They're only enjoying themselves. That's what they pay for. Better than funfairs. What you're asking them to do is to take you seriously, to believe you're real. But you're not real. You're a performer.'

They reached a high, corrugated iron fence.

'Here we are,' she said.

'Malcolm?'

'No.' She took a key from her pocket and undid a padlock, pushing open the creaking door.

It was a scrapyard. Piled on top of one another were dodgem cars, waltzers, chairoplanes, wooden horses and cockerels, roller coaster cars.

'See what I mean,' she said.

'What's the point of being here?'

'There's a fortune in scrap, Steve.'

Sex Pistols Chaos

Frank Cornelius zipped himself into his leather jacket while Mary added a few touches to his make-up. 'Why is everybody flying South?' he said.

'It's the way the bandwagon's going. Balham, Brazil, Brighton.'

'Get the car out. I'm going to Highgate.'

As they went down the stairs, he said: 'What we need is a few more novelty acts. They only have to think they're new, that's the main thing. As long as you *think* you're new, you *are* new. And the punters will think you're new, too. There's nothing new under the old limelights, Mary.'

'What about the spirit?'

'You mean the blood?'

He began to laugh. It was a hideous, strangled sound. 'New equals good. It's been going on for at least a hundred years. The

New Woman and all that. New equals vitality. New equals hope. One thing's for sure, Mary. New very rarely equals profit. Not at first, anyway. It has to be modified and represented before anyone will buy it in a hurry. That's the secret of the process. But it takes so much energy just to get a little bit of something happening that there are bound to be casualties. Look at poor Brian Epstein. It was the writing on the wall for management. It had to become us or them. We didn't want another manager coughing it, did we? How many A-and-R men do you know who've killed themselves recently?'

'I dunno.'

'None. It's the survival side of the business, my love.'

They arrived at the street. Ladbroke Grove was full of beaten-up American cars. Mary went round the corner to the mews to get Frank's Mercedes.

'It really is time we moved away from this neighbourhood,' he said. 'But it's where I've got my roots, you know.'

C'mon Everybody

'Your mistake was in cocking a snook at the queen, my lad.' Bishop Beesley unwrapped a Mars bar and began to peck at it like an overweight pigeon.

'Well, we took things more seriously at the time. We needed something.' Steve sat down in a battered dodgem. 'Do you really own all this?'

'Every bit. You must have a lot of money stashed away. How would you like to invest?' The bishop wiped his pudgy hands on his greasy black jacket. 'Americans buy it, you know. And people from Kensington and Chelsea. It's decorative. It's nostalgic. It's fun. Good times remembered.'

'If not exactly relived,' said Helen of Troy.

'You can't have everything, my dear. Junk, after all, has many functions and takes many forms. None of us is getting any younger.'

'Speak for yourself,' said Steve. 'This is an investigation.'

'Into what, my boy?'

'We haven't decided yet.'

'Anybody dead?' His chocolate-soaked eyes became speculative.

'You thinking of buying in?'

'I have an excellent wrecking crew, if you're interested. And we specialise in salvage, too. I mean salvation.' He grimaced and sought in his pockets for another Mars bar. 'We could be mutually useful to one another.'

Steve got up. A pile of Tunnel of Love boats began to creak and sway.

'We'll be in touch,' said Helen of Troy. From somewhere within the stacks came the sound of heavy breathing.

Bishop Beesley went back into his hut and locked the door.

Amateur Night at the Moscow Odeon

It was a mock Gothic complex. Frank signed in at the gatehouse and Mary drove through. The gates were electronically controlled and shut automatically behind them. Surrounding them now were tall brick walls topped with iron spikes. At intervals was a series of buildings once used to house Victorian painters. Now they were used for recording purposes.

The largest of the buildings was at the far end of the square. Mary parked in front of it.

Frank got out of the car, wheezing a little. 'I should never have had that last bottle of amyl.'

He mounted the steps and pressed a buzzer. A bouncer in a torn red T-shirt let him in. He descended to the basement.

The studio was deserted. In the booth a shadowy figure in a rubber bondage suit sat smoking a cigarette through an enema tube.

Frank said: 'Mr Big sent for me.'

'Not "Big", you stupid cunt, "Bug".' The voice was mysterious, slurred.

'Are you Mr Bug?'

'I represent his interests.'

'Somebody's on to us.'

'What's new?'

'My mother just told me.'

'So?'

'Hadn't we better start worrying?'

'Worrying? We're just about to make the real money.'

Frank was nervous. 'I can't see how…'

Mr Bug's representative began to unzip the front of his suit. 'In exposure, you fool. What do you think the *News of the World* is for?'

'I'm not entirely happy,' said Frank.

'That's the secret of success, isn't it?'

Frank began to sink.

The voice grew sympathetic.

'Come here, you poor old thing, and have a nibble on this.'

Frank crawled towards the booth.

Wotcha Gonna Do About It

The train from Balham was stuck on the bridge over the Thames. The bridge seemed to be swaying a lot. Steve felt tired. In the far corner of the compartment, Helen of Troy had curled herself on a seat and was asleep. Elsewhere came the sound of desultory vandalism, as if weary priests were performing a ritual whose point had been long since forgotten.

The train quivered and began to hum.

In the sunset, the Houses of Parliament gave the impression of being on fire. But it was only an illusion. The structure remained. A little graffiti on the sides made no real difference.

'Who's got the money?' Steve said again.

Helen opened her eyes. 'The people who had it in the first place. That's where it comes from and that's where it goes. How much did you spend at the pub last year?'

'About thirty thousand pounds.'

'Exactly.'

'What are you trying to say?'

She shook her head. 'What the bloody hell did you ever know about anarchy in the UK, Stevie? You gave all the power back, just like that. You gave all the money back, just as if you'd found it in the street and returned it to the police station.'

'Bollocks!'

She shrugged and closed her eyes again. 'What's in a name?'

From the luggage rack above them an old hippy said: 'Words are magic, man. They have power, you know.'

Helen glanced up at him. 'You've got to walk the walk as well as talking the talk, man.'

'I blame it all on nuclear energy,' he said.

'Well, you've got to blame something. It saves you a lot of worry.'

The train began to move again.

Helen began to sing a song to the tune of 'Woodstock'.

> 'We are wet; we are droopy
> And we simply love Peanuts and Snoopy…'

Hundreds of drab back gardens began to fill the windows. The train made a moaning noise.

Steve slid towards the door.

'A rose is a rose is a rose,' said the hippy.

Lesson Three
Sell The Swindle

Cries of 'Anarchy!' have always been associated with bored, middle class students who followed each other like sheep.

But the Pistols are spearheading, or hoping to, a backstreet backlash of working class kids who have never really had it hard, but are still put down.

'They try to ruin you from the start. They take away your soul. They destroy you. "Be a bank clerk" or "Join the Army" is what they give you at school.

'And if you do what they say you'll end up like the moron they want you to be. You have got to fight back or die.

'You have no future, nothing. You are made unequal. Most of the time the kids who fight back don't use their brains and it's wasted. Join a band is one way, or teach yourself is another. It doesn't take very much.'

Record Mirror, 11 December, 1976

Nestor Makhno, anarchist hero of the Ukraine, took another glass of absinthe and looked out onto deserted Rue Bonaparte. 'As far as I'm concerned,' he said, 'I died in the mid-thirties. But you can't believe anything you hear, can you?'

'I know what you mean,' said Sid.

Things were quiet, that evening, at the Café Hendrix. The romantic dead were all feeling generally low; though there was always a certain atmosphere of satisfaction when another young hero or heroine bit the dust.

'Besides,' said Brian Jones, 'there are all these second- and third-generation copycat deaths, aren't there, these days? You're not even sure if some of these people really are martyrs to the Cause.'

'What Cause is that?' Sid helped himself to a slice of pie.

'You know – Beautiful Losers – Dead Underdogs – Byronic Tragic figures. All that.' Jones was vague. It had been a long time since he had thought about it.

Sid was under the impression that Jones was simply upset. Maybe he thought his thunder had been stolen.

James Dean limped in and put his Michelob on the table. 'It's all bullshit. Boredom is what brought us to this, my friends. And little else.'

'That isn't what the fans say. They think we died for them.'

'Because of them, more likely.' One of the oldest inhabitants of the Café Hendrix (if this timeless gathering-place could be said to have an oldest inhabitant), Jesus Christ, offered them a twisted grin. 'Dead people are easier to believe in than live people. As soon as you're dead you can't stop the myth. That's what I found. They *want* you to die, mate.'

Several heads nodded. Several hands lifted drinks to pale lips.

'You always wind up doing what the public wants,' said Keith Moon, 'even if you don't do it deliberately. They expect violence, you give 'em violence. They expect a tragic death, well… Here we are.'

'That's show business,' said Makhno. 'The pressures get on top of you. You're carrying so many people's dreams. And all you wanted in the first place was a better life.'

'They expect you to do the same for them.'

Makhno was disapproving. 'That isn't anarchism. You can scream at them for years not to follow leaders and they'll say "Isn't he wonderful. He's right. Don't follow leaders". Then they come round and ask you what they should do with their lives.'

'They think anarchism means impulse or something. They don't realise it means self-determination, self-discipline and all of that. "Neither master nor slave". It serves us right for becoming heroes.' Mikhail Bakunin was on his usual hobby horse.

'Don't say you never liked it.' Makhno refilled his glass.

'Only sometimes. Anyway, how do you stop it once it starts?'

'Go into hiding and lead an unnatural life,' said Jesus. 'I wish to God I had. It wasn't any fun for me, I can tell you.'

'You didn't have so many bloody journalists in your day,' said Sid. 'And you had a high opinion of yourself. Admit it.'

'Well nobody was calling you the bloody Son of God.' Jesus tried to justify himself, but they could tell he was embarrassed.

'They called me the Antichrist,' said Makhno with some pride.

'Johnny called *himself* that,' said Sid.

Jesus sighed. 'It's all my damn fault.'

'You should be such a big man, to take the whole blame.' Brian Epstein sipped his orange juice. 'Do you think we're in Hell?'

'It was all a bloody con.' Marc Bolan adjusted his silk shirt. He was sulking again. Albert Camus, from behind his back, winked at the others.

'We just try to make death seem worth something. Like saying good comes out of pain. You can't blame people. And that's our job.'

'Dying young?' said Sid. He was still pretty new to the Café Hendrix.

'Making death seem romantic and noble.' Byron began to cough. 'How they can think that of me I don't know. Death is rotten and we shouldn't have to put up with it.'

In a far, dark corner of the café, Gene Vincent began to cry.

Nestor Makhno lifted his glass. 'Ah well, here's to another boring evening in eternity.'

'Fuck this,' said Sid. He went to the door and tried to open it.

'I'm afraid it's stuck, old chap,' said Shelley.

Sub-Mission

'Self-hatred makes excellent idealists. You tolerate yourself and you get to be able to tolerate almost anything. I suppose there's some good in that.' Helen of Troy stood on Steve's shoulders and climbed over the gate of the Gothic studios. 'What do you want me to say to him?'

'Just that I need to see him about me wages.'

'All right.' She scurried off into the darkness.

'I wish she'd stop bloody talking,' said Steve. He turned up the collar of his trench coat and lit a cigarette. 'This whole thing is ridiculous.'

A few lights went on in the farthest building. Then they went off again. He heard a car start up.

The gates opened outwards, forcing him backwards.

A Mercedes droned past. In it were Frank Cornelius, Mary and, trying to hide from him, Helen of Troy.

Steve shrugged and got through the gates before they closed again. He would do his own dirty work.

We're So Pretty

'You always think you must be in control,' said Frank, as the car turned towards Hampstead Heath, 'but it's usually other people's desperation that's operating for you. As soon as their desperation disappears, the scam stops working. That's why you have to keep as many people as desperate as possible. Look at me. I know what bloody desperation *means*.'

'But you should never let anyone know that,' said Helen of Troy. 'That's where you went wrong, Frank.'

'You were too honest,' said Mary.

'I couldn't keep all the balls in the air. When you drop one, you drop the lot.' Frank wiped his lips. 'Still, there's always tomorrow. I'm not finished, yet. Lick a few arses, suck a few cocks, and you're back on the strength again in no time.'

'You should have been rude to him,' said Mary.

'My morale's weak. After what Mum said.'

'Mums'll do it to you every time,' said Helen. 'Are you sure Steve will be all right in there?'

'He'll be better off than you or me,' said Frank. 'Little wanker. He deserves all he gets.'

I'm a Lonely Boy

'Every business is a compromise. You get into the business, you get into a compromise.' Mr Bug's representative stroked Steve's frightened head. The guitarist lay spreadeagled across a twenty-four track desk, his wrists and ankles secured by red leather bondage bracelets. Everything stank of warm rubber.

'Now what can I do for you, Steve?'

'Not this, my son.'

'You know you like it really. And you've got to do something for the money. Are you ticklish.'

'Blimey,' said Steve as the feather mop connected with his testicles. He added: 'But that's not where I'm dusty.'

'Are you a virgin, love?' The voice was greasy with sentiment.

'It depends where you mean.'

'Enjoy life while you can, darling. This whole place is due to go up in a few hours. Insurance.'

'Aren't the tapes all here?'

'Every single copy, my beauty.'

'They must be worth something.'

'They're worth more if they're destroyed. Didn't you ever realise that? The harder things are to get, the more valuable they are. If they don't exist at all, they become infinitely valuable.'

'Is that a fact? Tee hee.'

'There, darling. You *are* ticklish.'

'Tee hee.'

'Did you want to see Mr Bug?'

'Mr Bug anything like you?'

'I'm only his representative. I'm an amateur compared to him.'

'Then I'm not sure I want to see him. Can I go home now?'

'And where's home?'

'I suppose you've got a point.' Steve lay back on the desk. He might as well get the most out of this.

Mr Bug's representative's breath hissed within his mask. 'Now you're really going to make a record.'

He reached for a large jar of vapour rub.

Punk Disc Is Terrible Says EMI Chief

The black flag was flying over the Nashville Rooms. There must have been another temporary seizure of power. Outside in the street groups of hardcore punks, lookalikes for most of the Sex Pistols in their heyday, scrawled 'A' on every available surface. They weren't sure what it meant but they knew they had to do it.

Nestor Makhno rode up in his buggy. He had never been much of a horseman since his foot was wounded. His woolly hat was falling over his eyes. The rest of his anarchist Cossacks looked as worn-out as he did. Their ponies were old and hardly able to stand.

'I think we might be too late.' Makhno guided the buggy round to the side entrance. From inside came the sound of chanting. 'Is this what we fought Trotsky for?'

One of his lieutenants fired a ghostly pistol into the air. Its sound was faint, and drowned by the noise from within. 'Comrades!'

'They can't hear us,' said Makhno. 'Is this what we all died for?'

'It's an attack on the symptoms, not the disease,' cried a Cossack dutifully from the rear. 'Comrades, the disease lies within yourself, and so does the cure. Be free!'

With a shrug, Makhno tugged at the reins of the buggy and led his men away. 'Ah well. It was worth a try.'

'Where to now?' asked one of the Cossacks.

'Camden Town. We'll try the Music Machine.'

You Never Listen to a Word I Say

Something was collapsing.

Miss Brunner plucked at her hair and blouse.

'The more childish you are, the more you score. Throw enough tantrums and they'll pay anything to get rid of you.'

Frank looked wildly about. 'Are you sure this place is safe?'

'Safe enough.'

He lay tucked up in bed surrounded by Snow White and the

Seven Dwarfs wallpaper, Paddington Bear decals, Oz and Rupert books.

'I can hear a sort of breaking-up sound. Can't you?'

'It's in your mind,' she said. 'How much should we invest, do you think, in that new band?'

'We haven't got any money.'

'Neither have they.'

'Then it's all a bit in the air, isn't it?'

'Big money still exists, in big companies. It just takes a bit of winkling out.'

'No,' said Frank. 'No more. I've been warned off. I'm frightened. The City is involved. They can do things to you.'

'Mr Bug has scared the shit out of you, Frank.'

'How did you know about the shit?'

The Fucking Rotter

The former Johnny Rotten tried to focus on Nestor Makhno as best he could. The little Ukrainian was almost wholly transparent now.

'Don't you think we can do it through music?'

'Persuade the public,' said Makhno thinly. 'We had an education train. But do they ever know that the power rests in them?'

'They never seem to want it.

'They don't want responsibility.'

'And that's why managers exist.'

'I'll be seeing you…' said Makhno, fading.

'That's more than I can say for you.'

The former Johnny Rotten reached for his Kropotkin. Maybe it could still work. Maybe it was already working on some level.

Over the Top and Under the Bottom

Steve wriggled. 'What do you want me to say?'

Mr Bug's representative stroked the fronds of his cat-o'-nine-tails over his own rubber.

'Anything you like, sweetheart. Isn't this the way to relax? No personal responsibilities, no anxieties? Just lie back and enjoy yourself.'

'There must be other methods of relaxing.'

'Well, dearie, you could always join a rock-and-roll band.'

Steve began to scream.

Rolling in the Ruins

Bishop Beesley bit off half a Crunchie bar. Chocolate, like old blood, already stained his jowls. 'Why is everyone suddenly going South?' he asked.

Helen of Troy shook her head. 'Maybe it's winter.'

'Winter?' Frank Cornelius looked unblinkingly at the sun which was just visible over the heap of dodgems. 'Some winter of the mind, maybe.'

'Let's try and steer clear of abstractions, dear boy.' The bishop spoke with soft impatience. 'I have a meeting with the Prime Minister in just over an hour. What are we going to do about this, if anything? I mean is it a serious threat to authority?'

'I thought we were avoiding abstractions,' said Miss Brunner.

From within an abandoned Ghost Train car, Steve's weak voice said: 'I told them nothing.'

'You've nothing to tell them, you horrible little oik.' The bishop sighed. 'I think we're in a poor position, Mr Cornelius.'

'Somebody turned the power off,' said Steve vaguely.

The wind drummed against the hollow metal of the fairground débris.

City Lights

The Cossacks, by now hardly visible even to one another, had reached The Rainbow and were surrounding it. Their black flag had turned to a faint grey. They were getting despondent.

Determinedly, they rode their horses into the venue, able to pass through the audience as if they did not exist. On stage Queen were displaying the virtues of production over talent. Thousands of pounds' worth of equipment was manipulated to produce the desired effect. It was a tribute to technology.

Makhno cried into the empty megawatts: 'Brothers and Sisters! Brothers and Sisters!'

A young man with longish hair and a 'No Nukes' T-shirt turned, then raised his fist at the stage.

'Freedom!' he cried.

The volume began to rise.

Will the Sex Pistols Be Tomorrow's Beatles?

Back at the Café Hendrix Nestor Makhno took a long drink from his bottle of absinthe. He was shaking his head.

'Didn't you like any of the gigs?' asked Sid.

'I didn't see anything I liked. At first I'd hoped – you know, the audiences…' Makhno fell back in his chair. 'But there was nothing there for us to do.'

'Don't despair,' said Shelley, 'there's a rumour the Sex Pistols are going to reform. After all, they're more popular now than they ever were.'

Lesson Four
Do Not Play, Don't Give The Game Away

Says Johnny Rotten: 'Everyone is so fed up with the old way. We were constantly being dictated to by musical old farts out of university who've got rich parents. They look down on us and treat us like fools and expect us to pay POUNDS to see them while we entertain them and not the other way round. And people let it happen! But now they're not. Now there's a hell of a lot of new bands come up with exactly the opposite attitude. It's not condescending any more. It's plain honesty. If you don't like it – that's fine. You're not forced to like it through propaganda. People think we use propaganda. But we don't. We're not trying to be commercial. We're doing exactly what we want to do – what we've always done.'

But it hasn't been easy. Sceptics and cynics simply didn't want to believe what was happening. Quite unjustly The Sex Pistols were written off as musical incompetents. They were savagely criticised for daring to criticise society and the rock musician's role in it. They have been crucified by the uncaring national press – ever ready to ferret out a circulation boosting shock/horror story – and branded an unpleasant, highly reprehensible Great Media Hype.

Virgin Records publicity, 1977

The city was black. Through black smoke shone a dim, orange sun. The canal was still, smeared with flotsam. From Harrow Road came the sound of a single donkey engine, like a dying heartbeat. Overhead, on train bridge and motorway, carriages and trucks were unmoving. It seemed everything had stopped to watch the figure in the dark trench coat and trilby as he paused beside the canal and peered through the oily water as if through a glass.

A fly, ailing and lost, tried to buzz around his head. Slowly the traffic began to move again. From behind a pillar Helen of Troy emerged, hurrying on little legs towards him.

'You feeling any better, Steve?'

'You let me down, Helen.'

'I didn't have any choice.'

Steve did not resent her. 'How's that wanker Frank?'

'Going through a bit of a crisis, I gather.'

'He'd better look after his bloody kneecaps.'

'That's the least of his worries.'

Steve looked away from the water and back towards the half-built housing estate. 'It used to be all slums round here,' he said nostalgically. 'Now look at it.'

'You've got over your own spot of bother, then? You've stopped looking for the money.'

'I think so. But I'm still looking, anyway.'

'For what?'

'I dunno. A solution to the mystery.'

'The mystery goes on for ever. There's never a solution. There isn't even a cure.'

'We'll see.'

'Why are you here?'

'Said I'd meet someone.'

'Who?'

'Ever heard of the Old Survivor?'

'Well, there's a myth...'

'I'm seeing him here.'

'Lemmy of Motörhead?'

'He's doing me a favour.'

'Isn't he an old hippy fart?'

'His hair may be long, but underneath he's a white man, through and through.'

'Something's disturbed your brains, Steve. You need a rest.'

'I need help, that's for certain.'

Down the steps from the pedestrian bridge came a figure in black leather, festooned with Nazi badges, a bullet belt around his waist. His face, moulded in a thousand psychic adventures, was genial and distant, ageless. The Old Survivor laughed when he saw Steve and Helen standing together. 'You look fucking miserable. What's the matter?'

'I didn't think you'd come,' said Steve.

'Neither did I. But I was passing. On me way home. So here I am.'

'You're probably the only one left who can help me.' Steve was embarrassed.

'I haven't got any drugs,' said Lemmy.

'It's not that. But you'd know about the legend. Whether there's any truth in it or not.'

Lemmy frowned. 'I didn't realise you were a nutter.'

'I'm not. Well, I don't think I am. I'm desperate. Have you ever...?' Steve's voice dropped. Tactfully, Helen of Troy went to sit on the side of the canal and dip her boots in the liquid. 'What do you know about the Guild of Musician-Assassins?'

Lemmy began to chuckle. 'That hasn't come up in a long time.'

'But you were supposed...'

'It was ages ago. A different era. A different universe, probably.'

'Then there's some truth in it.'

Lemmy became cautious. 'I couldn't take a job like that. I've got enough to do as it is.'

'There's money...'

'It was never a question of money.' Lemmy drew a battered packet of Bensons from his top pocket and lit one. 'We soldier on, you know.'

'But what about the other one? The one who's supposed to be sleeping somewhere in Ladbroke Grove?'

'What about him?'

'You're in touch with him.'

'I see him occasionally, yeah.'

'Couldn't you ask him?'

'He gave it all up. He said there wasn't any point in it any more.'

'Does he really think that?'

'Well… He *has* been having second thoughts. He was round at his mum's the other day…'

'So he's not asleep.'

'It depends what you mean.' Lemmy was losing interest. He rubbed at his moustache and sighed.

'Could you put me in touch with him?'

'He's not working. I told you. None of us are. Bullshit-saturation does it to you in the end. Haven't you found that out yet?'

'Would his brother know…?'

'His brother doesn't know a fucking thing about anything. His brother spends his whole bloody life trying to work out what's going on. Whenever he thinks he's found it, he tries to exploit it. He's been doing it for years. But him and his mates seem to have won.' Lemmy looked up at the black buildings. 'They sort of linked hands and formed a vacuum.'

'It's important to me,' said Steve. 'I mean, I wouldn't be asking if I wasn't desperate…'

'You've only lost a battle, my son. We lost a war.'

'But the war's still going on, isn't it?'

'It's more like guerrilla tactics, these days.'

'All I want is a clue or two.'

'How do I know you're not working for Frank?'

'How do any of us know that?'

Lemmy took the point. 'I'll see what I can do,' he said. He returned to the steps, scratching his head and mumbling to himself.

'Shit!' said Steve, feeling ashamed. He reached out and tried to shove Helen of Troy into the canal. She resisted.

'Great,' she said. 'Let's take it out on each other.'

From the motorway, an empty oil-truck boomed.

I Love You with My Knife

The sea was pale and calm; a frozen blue. Steve walked out of the Dreamland enclosure and crossed the promenade in the peaceful Margate dawn. He wasn't sure, even now, if Lemmy hadn't tricked him into this trip. If the last of the musician-assassins had been sleeping under Ladbroke Grove, why had Steve been told to come to the seaside?

Near the horizon a seagull seemed to be wheeling. Then he heard the sound of an irregular drone. It was a plane.

It began to come in rapidly, heading straight for the beach. It was painted brilliant white and had wartime Luftwaffe markings. A huge biplane, with at least six engines, none of which was firing properly. The thing lurched in the air as it turned, the sunlight flashing on its floats. It was a Dornier DoX flying boat.

It landed on the water, almost keeling over, heading for the end of the pier. Steve began to run. He reached the turnstiles and climbed over them.

By the time he got to the edge, the flying boat had come to a stop and was bobbing on the surface of the sea like a waterlogged sponge.

A thin figure climbed out of the cockpit and stood shakily on the upper wing. 'Oh, Christ.' The figure began to vomit into the ocean. 'Oh, bloody hell.'

The figure was dressed in a long black jacket, black drainpipes, and wore black winkle-pickers. It removed its tattered flying helmet. 'I'm not up to this any more, you know.'

'Did Lemmy give you my message?'

The figure nodded. 'I didn't come all the bloody way from 1957 just to buy a stick of rock. What's going on?' The wasted, weary face regarded Steve through wiped-over eyes.

'I hoped you'd know.'

The figure coughed and spat again. 'I feel terrible. I've never known. I was just trying to cut out a bit of territory. But that fell through, too. Are you the one who wants to fly down to Rio?'

'If you think that's a good idea.'

'You'd better get in. Don't blame me, either, if we never make it. Got anyone to eat?'

Stepping Stone

'You said he could never be revived.' Frank was frightened. Even his grip on Helen's hair was weak.

Miss Brunner was at a loss. 'It's what we all understood. Why should he want to come back?'

'He's been resurrected.' Bishop Beesley spoke through mouthfuls of Maltesers. 'Before.'

'But never like this.' Frank helped himself to a few of the bishop's chocolate-covered valiums. 'We'd blanked out every bit of possible music. He has to have it, to recover at all. To sustain himself for any length of time. It's the one thing we were sure of.'

Miss Brunner pushed her red hair back from her forehead. 'Something got through to him. There's no point now in wondering how. Steve couldn't have done it. He didn't know anything, did he, Helen?'

'Ow,' said Helen. 'I'm getting tired of playing both ends against the middle. It hurts.'

'Did he?' Miss Brunner drew out her special razor.

'Not as far as I know.'

'He's a demon,' said Bishop Beesley. 'And he can never be completely exorcised, I'm certain of that now. Just when we thought we had everything under control.'

'Who got the music to him?' Frank let go of Helen. 'You?'

Helen of Troy shook her head.

'Lemmy?'

'Might have been.'

'Nothing came through on the detectors,' said Miss Brunner. 'There's always someone on duty. You know that.'

'We were squabbling amongst ourselves too much. It's that money problem.'

'A very real one,' said Bishop Beesley.

'I'll have the equipment checked.' Miss Brunner shrugged.

'Not that there's much point now. I could have sworn he was stuck in 1957 for the duration. Still, it's no use crying over spilt milk, is it?'

'The problem we have now,' said Bishop Beesley, 'is where he's got to. We found most of his bases and destroyed them. Any clues?'

'You'd better ask your mum,' suggested Helen of Troy.

Silence Is Golden

The blimp was drifting towards the coast of Brazil. The flying boat had been abandoned in Florida. The blimp was losing gas.

'I thought you were a fucking professional,' said Steve. He was unshaven. 'We've been in this bloody thing for days!'

The last of the musician-assassins blew his nose. 'I haven't been well. Anyway, all my equipment's old.'

'It was never anything else, as far as I can see.'

'I prefer stuff that doesn't work properly. I always did. How many bloody times do you think I've been resurrected? I'm coming apart all over the bloody place.'

Steve had got used to the self-pity by now, but the smell remained dreadful.

'Stand by,' said the last of the musician-assassins. The blimp bumped onto the beach. Blondes scattered, screaming. 'Here we are. I'll stay while you go and get the tapes I told you I needed.'

'I'm gonna be embarrassed.' Steve took off his coat and hat, revealing a T-shirt and shorts.

'Don't worry. They all talk English here.' The last of the musician-assassins frowned. 'Or is it German?'

'I don't mind about the Hendrix...'

'Well, just make it Hendrix, then. But hurry. You want help, squire, you'd better help me first. I never expected to pick up a bloody snob.'

Steve opened the door and put his big toe onto the warm sand. 'It's nice here, isn't it?'

Behind him, the pilot uttered a feeble sound. 'Get – the – fucking – music…'

Purple Haze

Miss Brunner studied the computer breakdowns. 'You were right about Hendrix,' she said. 'He always resorts to it in the final analysis. But there are other factors to consider. He seems to be finding boosters elsewhere, these days. Do you think that's what they're offering him?'

'Fresh energy?' Frank pushed the long sheets aside and looked blankly at the instruments.

She began to punch in a new programme. 'I've got a feeling it is. What's bothering me, however, is where they're getting through. I could have sworn we'd blocked every channel. And, moreover, that we'd got them to believe that that was what they wanted.'

Frank flicked an uninterested whip at the little body of Helen of Troy as she swung gently in her chains above the CRYPTIK VII computer. 'You can never afford to relax for a second. We'd become lazy, Miss Brunner.'

'What else did your mum say?'

'Nothing. He came to see her at her job, watched a bit of the film, had about fifteen bags of popcorn and ate all the hot-dogs, then left in his Duesenberg.'

'Which was found in?'

'Cromer.'

'We didn't know about Cromer.' She bit a nail.

'We're spread too thin,' he said. 'Those of us who are prepared to guard the borders. It's like the collapse of the Roman Empire. That's what I think, anyway. My own brother! When will he ever grow up?'

'He's got to be in Rio,' she said. 'Or, failing that, Maracaibo.'

'What's in Venezuela?'

'Airships.'

'And Brazil?'

'Failures. Exiles. The usual stuff he goes for. You'd better get someone to check all the record shops in Rio. After that, see what recording studios they have out there. It can't be much.'

'Has Steve given him his commission yet, do you think?'

'Nothing coming through on that.'

'And if so, who is it? Or how many of us?'

'I've got a feeling we're all going to be targets this time.'

From overhead, Helen's muffled titters phased in with the click of the CRYPTIK.

Cruel Fate

'Malcolm no more created the situation than Hitler started World War Two. But once it had happened he had to pretend it was deliberate.' Martin Bormann was closing up for the evening. 'Of course I didn't know him very well.'

'Hitler?'

'Nobody knew him very well. He tended to go with the tide. Do you know what I mean?'

'Not really,' said Steve, pocketing the tapes.

'Well, we were all heavily into mysticism in those days. How's my old mate Colin Wilson, by the way?'

'I think he lives in the country.'

Bormann nodded sympathetically. 'It's what happens to all of us. I envy you young lads, with your cities and your ruins. We never liked cities much. In the Party, I mean. I sometimes think the whole thing was an attempt to restore the virtues of village life. It's still going on, I suppose, but on a modified level. I blame the atom bomb. It's had the absolutely opposite effect it was meant to have. No wonder all those hippies are fed up with it. I had hopes...' His smile was sad. 'But there you go. I'm not complaining, really. Anything else you need?'

'I'm not sure.'

'That's the spirit.' Bormann patted Steve's shoulder. 'And not a word to anyone about this, eh?'

'All right.' Steve was puzzled.

'I wouldn't want people to think I was merely justifying my mistakes.'

As Steve walked up the street, looking for a tram to the beach, Bormann began to pull down the shutters.

It was a fine evening in the Lost City of the Amazon.

Lesson Five
How To Steal As Much Money As Possible From The Record Company Of Your Choice

> In October they signed with EMI. They released the hit single 'Anarchy In the UK' and they were all set for an extensive, triumphant tour of the country. Then they were invited onto the Today show. Bill Grundy got what he asked for – and the Nationals had a bean feast. The band who had been playing week after week all over the country for more than a year were suddenly front page news, branded 'filth' and made Public Enemies No. 1.
>
> All but five dates of the tour were hysterically banned and the band returned to London on Christmas Eve with the dramatic news that EMI was about to rescind their contract. In January EMI asked them to leave the label. Glen Matlock decided to form his own band called the Rich Kids. Sid Vicious replaced him. Everyone cheered when in March, it looked like the Pistols had found shelter at A&M.
>
> Virgin Records publicity, 1977

The last of the musician-assassins was looking a shade or two less wasted. He removed the headphones and signalled to Steve to turn up the volume. Steve was very bored, but he did as he was told. He was beginning to regret the whole idea. In front of the assassin was a collection of peculiar weaponry, most of it archaic: needle guns, vibraguns, light-pistols, a Rickenbacker 12-string.

The gondola of the little airship swayed and the hardware slid this way and that on the table. The assassin seemed oblivious. He took another pull from his Pernod bottle.

'Have a look out of the window,' he shouted. 'See if we're near Los Angeles yet.'

All Steve could see was silver mist.

Strange, garbled sounds began to issue from the assassin's lips.

Steve winced.

He had a feeling the assassin was singing the blues.

His colour was better, at any rate. His skin was changing from a sort of LED-green to near-white.

Old and Tired But Still Playing His Banjo

'If ants ever had an Ant of the Year competition,' said Miss Brunner disapprovingly, 'Branson would be the winner. It's the secret of his success.'

They were all uncomprehending. Only Mary said 'What?' and nobody listened to her.

Frank was biting his bullets to see if they were made of real silver. He began to load them into the clip. His hands were shaking terribly.

'Why don't we all go to Rio?' asked Bishop Beesley.

'Because you'd never squeeze into Concorde.' Miss Brunner checked the action of her Remington. 'Have you oiled your bazooka?'

'It doesn't need it.' He unwrapped a Twix and sulked in his own corner of the bunker. 'Did you try all the A-and-R men?'

'We can't get through to Virgin.'

'They've probably been used in the ritual sacrifice, ho, ho, ho.' Frank slid the clip into the Browning automatic he favoured.

'I said we weren't going to mention all that. It's poor publicity.'

Helen of Troy grinned to herself. She now had a Banning cannon all her own. 'When do we start to fight?' she asked.

'As soon as we run out of other choices,' Miss Brunner told her.

'You divided,' said Helen smugly, 'but they kept re-forming. It's just like real life now.'

'We'll be changing all that.' Bishop Beesley was no longer confident, however. He scraped ancient Cadbury's off his surplice and carefully carried the bits to his lips. 'I wish I'd stayed in the drug business now. You don't get this sort of trouble from junkies.'

'Do you mind?' said Frank, offended.

... Down the Drain and What She Found There

'That's not bloody Los Angeles,' said the assassin petulantly. 'That's Paris! Isn't it?'

'It's got to be.' Steve rubbed at his ear, which was hurting. 'Unless there's another Eiffel Tower.'

'Right. No harm done. I'll drop you off in Montmartre, if that's okay with you.'

'What are you going to do?'

'Well, you've told me all I need to know. I'll be in touch.' The assassin combed his lank hair with his fingers.

'You going to kill someone?'

'I'm going to kill everyone if I can get enough energy.' The thought seemed to revive the assassin. He cheered up.

He began to turn his steering wheel, cursing as the ship responded badly.

A little later he pushed open the door and started letting down a steel ladder.

'There you go. You should be able to get a taxi from here.'

Steve didn't like the look of the weather. He put on his trench coat and hat.

'What did you say to Mr Bugs?'

'Biggs,' corrected the assassin. 'Oh, I just needed a couple of addresses in South London and the name of his tailor.'

Steve lowered himself onto the swaying ladder. 'I hope you know what you're doing.'

'I never know what I'm doing until it's done. There's no point in working any other way in my business.'

It was raining over Montmartre now. It was cloudy. Steve became cautious. 'Are you sure this is the right district?'

'The district's fine. You should be worrying whether I've got the time right. For all we know it could be 1964 down there.'

'Stop trying to frighten me,' said Steve.

The assassin shrugged. 'They're all pretty much the same to me, these days. You should have tried the fifties, mate.' He began to shiver. 'Hurry up. I want to shut the door.'

Spirit of the Age

More data was coming through to the bunker. Miss Brunner pursed her lips as she studied the printouts.

'He's getting stronger. Five Virgin shops and the EMI shops in Oxford Street and Notting Hill have been raided and a significant list of records stolen. Three of the places were completely destroyed. And there's been a break-in at Glitterbest. That probably isn't him. But three recording studios have had master tapes taken. Seven managements have lost important demo tapes.'

'It might not mean anything,' said Frank. He was fixing himself a cocktail, drawing it into the syringe.

They ignored him.

Frank laid the syringe on the table and put his head in his hands. 'Oh, bloody hell. Who could have predicted this? I was *certain* it was all under control again. Bugger the Sex Pistols.'

'I told you so,' said Helen of Troy.

Miss Brunner pushed a pink phone towards her. 'Get in touch with Malcolm. Tell him we've got to stick together. He'll see sense. I'll try Branson again.'

Helen picked up the receiver. 'If you think it's worth it.'

They were all beginning to get on one another's nerves.

I Wanna Be Your Dog

Steve walked into the Princess Alexandra in Portobello Road. It had taken him ages to get from Paris and he had a feeling he was no further forward. All that he seemed to have done was start a lot a trouble he couldn't begin to understand.

The pub was full of black leather backs. He reached the bar and ordered a pint of bitter. The barman, for no good reason, was reluctant to serve him.

Various overtired musicians clocked him, but nobody really recognised him or he them. Lemmy was nowhere to be seen.

There was an atmosphere in the place, as if everybody was hanging about waiting for World War Three.

The talk was casual, yet Steve sensed that a great deal was not being said. Was the whole of London keeping something back from him? Was the revolution imminent? If so, what revolution was it? Whose revolution? Did he really feel up to a revolution?

He finished his pint. He was down to his last fifteen pence.

As he was leaving he thought he heard someone whispering behind him.

'Who killed Sid, then?'

'What?' He turned.

All the backs were towards him again.

Sleazy Slut of the Month

'They think they're heavily into manipulation, but really we just let them play at it.' Mr Bug's representative sat comfortably in the darkness of the limousine. 'Nobody who really believes they're manipulating things is safe. Sooner or later people lose patience. And people are very patient indeed. Most of you don't actually want to make anyone else do anything.'

'Live and let live,' said Helen of Troy. 'It's time I got back to the bunker.'

'I'm interested in human beings,' said Mr Bug's representative, squeaking a little as he moved in his rubber. 'I've studied them for years.'

'Do you understand them?'

'Not really, but I've learned a lot about what triggers to pull. And I know enough, too, not to think that I can keep too many balls in the air.'

'Have you seen Malcolm? That's who I was looking for, really.'

'We've all seen too much of Malcolm, haven't we?'

'Has he left your club?'

'You could try it. But hardly any of us go there any more.'

'Aliens?'

'Call us what you like. I prefer to think of myself as a student person. But I'm not sure I'm going to make the finals.'

Mr Bug's representative uttered a cheerful wheeze and opened the door so that Helen could step out.

'It's quite a nice morning, isn't it?' he said. 'It was Clapham Common you wanted?'

'It'll do,' said Helen.

'The malady lingers on.' Mr Bug's representative flicked his robot driver with his whip. 'We'll try Hampstead Heath again now.'

The driver's voice was feminine. 'What are we looking for, sir?'

Mr Bug's representative shrugged. 'Whatever they're looking for.'

'Do you think we'll find it, sir?'

'I'm not sure it matters. But it's something to pass the time. And we might meet some interesting people.'

'Are there any real people left in London, sir?'

'I take your point. The city seems to be filling up with nothing but the ghosts of old anarchists, these days. Not to mention Chartists and the like. Have you seen any of the Chartists?'

'Not recently, sir.'

'There's bound to be a few on Hampstead Heath. What London really lacks at present is a genuine, big, healthy Mob.'

Belsen Was a Gas

'Any news?'

Frank Cornelius looked anxiously at the CRYPTIK. It didn't seem a patch on some of Miss Brunner's other machines, but she put a great deal of faith in it.

'A few more record companies have been broken into. Tapes and records stolen. Some accounts. Majestic Studios have been blown up. Freerange have had a fire. Island's wiped out.'

'And the casualties?' asked Bishop Beesley, mopping his brow with an old Flake wrapper.

'They don't look significant. Everybody seems to be evacuating.'

'Mr Bug?'

'Not sure. No data.'

'Why are we sticking it out, then?' said Frank. 'Why should we be the only ones?'

'Because we know best, don't we?' Miss Brunner reached absently towards where Mary had been sitting. Now there was just a little pile of clothes. Mary had been absorbed some hours ago. 'Someone's going to have to go out for some food. I think it's you, Frank.'

'You're setting me up. If my brother finds me, you know what he'll do. He's got a nasty, vengeful nature. He's never forgiven me for Tony Blackburn, let alone anything else.'

'He's too busy at present.' She waved the printouts. 'Anyway, he hardly ever bothers you unless you've bothered him.'

'How do I know if I've bothered him or not?'

Miss Brunner became impatient. 'Frank! Go and get us someone to eat.'

'And some chocolate fudge, if possible,' said Bishop Beesley.

Frank put his Browning in the pocket of his mack. He sidled reluctantly towards the door.

'Hurry,' hissed Miss Brunner.

'Any special orders?'

'Anything tasty will suit me.' She returned her attention to the CRYPTIK. 'At this rate we'll be eating each other.'

This made her feel sick.

No Feelings

There was a bouncer on the door of the New Oldies Club as Steve tried to go through.

'No way, my son,' said the bouncer.

Steve blinked. 'You know me.'

'Never seen you before.'

'What's going on? Who's playing tonight.'

'Black Arabs.'

'Is Malcolm in there?'

'Not for me to say. Not for you to ask.'

'But I'm with the band.'

'What band?'

'What band do you want me to be with?'

'Off!' said the bouncer. 'Go on.'

'Ask Malcolm.'

'You, mate, are *persona non* bloody *grata*. Get it?'

'Is Malcolm in there?'

'You're a persistent little cunt, ain't ya.' The bouncer hit him.

'What you do that for?'

'Security.'

Steve nursed his lip. 'You shouldn't be afraid of me.'

'It's not you, chum. It's the people you're hanging around with.'

As Steve reached the street again, and began to walk in the general direction of Soho, he looked up. Over the rooftops was the outline of a small, sagging airship. It seemed to be drifting aimlessly on the wind.

To the north, quite close to the Post Office Tower, a fire was blazing.

United Artists, thought Steve absently.

Bodies

Mr Bug's representative said: 'Things look as if they're hotting up.'

They were crossing over Abbey Road. Police were making traffic detour around the ruins.

'All the old targets.' Mr Bug's representative lit a fresh cigarette and put it to his tube. 'Still, what new ones are there?'

The driver pressed the horn.

EMI Unlimited Edition

Steve leaned on the gates of Buckingham Palace and dragged the book from his inside pocket.

The book was called *Who Killed Bambi?* He opened it up. All the pages were blank. He was getting used to this sort of thing.

'Oh, there you are!' Helen of Troy came running over from St James's Park. 'We thought we'd lost you.'

'I don't trust you, Helen. You're with them now.'

'Why don't you join us?'

'What for?'

'There's safety in numbers.'

'So you say.'

'Anyway,' said Helen, 'you shouldn't be hanging about here, should you? Everyone's getting very security-conscious. They might arrest you.'

'Everything else has been arrested, by the look of it.'

'I'm worried about you, Steve.'

'Don't be.'

'We can help you.'

'That didn't work the last time.'

Army trucks were coming down the Mall. Garbled voices called through loudspeakers mounted on the tops of the trucks.

Steve decided to follow Helen round the corner into Buckingham Palace Road. She took his hand. 'Coming along then?'

'No,' he said. 'I think I'll catch a train from Victoria.'

Lesson Six
How To Become The World's Greatest Tourist Attraction

STEVE JONES: Twenty. Born in London. Lives in a one-room cold-water-only studio in Soho where the band rehearse. Ex-approved school. He was the lead singer with the Sex Pistols before he took up the guitar.

He has the reputation of being a man of a few words. But his sound intuition and low boredom threshold makes him great fun to be with. He's always looking for action. Of the four he probably had the most difficult childhood. His real father was a boxer whom he never knew. He never got on with his stepfather and since the family lived in one room only, this led to a very fraught home environment. The first record he remembers being impressed by was Jimi Hendrix's 'Purple Haze'. He always wanted to play electric guitar.

Virgin Records publicity, 1977

'Delusions of grandeur will get you a very long way in this world.' Martin Bormann leafed through his cut-price deletions. 'You just missed him, I'm afraid.'

Paul Cook handed him the album he'd selected. 'I'll have this, then. Do you know the times of the planes to New York?'

Bormann looked at his watch. 'There's one in an hour. You'd better hurry. It could be the last.'

God Save the Short and Stupid

'Ain't she fuckin' radiant, though?' Mrs C. studied the blue-and-white picture on her jubilee mug before putting it to her lips. 'Thassa nice cuppa tea, Frank. Wotcher want?'

'Jerry.' Frank was furtive. 'Mum, I haven't got much more margin. Have you seen him?'

'Yeah.'

'When?'

'Yesterday.'

'Where?'

'At work. 'E watched ther picture four times.'

'Why?'

'I fink 'e wanted a rest. 'E was asleep through most of 'em.'

'When he left, did he say where he was going?'

''E said 'e 'ad a few jobs ter do. Somefink abart pushin' a boat aht?'

Frank remained puzzled. 'That's all?'

'I fink so.' She puckered her brows. 'You know what 'e's like. Yer carn't fuckin' understand 'alf o' what 'e says.'

'Was he with anybody?'

'I dunno. Maybe wiv that bloke in a kilt. Like in ther film.'

Frank dropped his cup into the saucer. 'God almighty.'

'I didn't catch 'is name,' said Mrs Cornelius.

Sod the Sex Pistols

From where he stood on the Embankment, near the cannon, Steve could see the half-inflated airship tied to one of the spikes of Tower Bridge. Either the assassin was stranded, or he was becoming more catholic in his targets.

As he climbed up the steps to the bridge, he thought he saw a flash of tartan darting down the other side. He hesitated, not sure which lead to follow.

'Oh, bugger!'

It was the last of the musician-assassins, clambering unsteadily down his steel ladder, a Smith and Wesson Magnum held by its trigger guard in his teeth.

'You look a lot better,' said Steve.

'Feeling it, squire.' The assassin dusted off his black car coat and smoothed his hair. 'I've been eating better and getting more exercise. What's the time? My watch has stopped.'

Steve didn't know.

'It doesn't matter, really. We'll be all right. Come on.' The assassin took Steve's arm.

'Where are we going?'

'I had a nasty moment last night,' said the assassin obliviously. 'Somebody must have tried to slip some disco tapes into my feeder. Nearly blew my circuits. I think they're trying to get rid of me.' He strode rapidly in the direction of Butler's Wharf on the south side of the bridge.

'Where are we going?'

'1977.'

'What?'

'Nineteen bloody seventy-seven, mate. You've got a bloody gig to do. And this time you're going to do it properly.'

Abolishing the Future

Miss Brunner was white with rage. 'What on earth possessed you, Frank?'

A dozen dogs growled and grumbled as Frank tried to untangle their leads. 'I had nowhere else to bring them. And I need them.'

Bishop Beesley crouched in his corner munching handfuls of Poppets. 'This is a very small bunker, Mr Cornelius.'

'I've worked out what my brother's up to. He's made a tunnel into 1977.'

'Oh, no.' Miss Brunner began to punch spastically at her terminal. 'That was why he was doing all that stuff with record companies. To get the energy he needed.'

Frank nodded. The dogs began to pant. 'We're going to have to follow him. He's got that little wanker Jones with him and maybe the rest of them, I'm not sure.'

Bishop Beesley clambered to his feet. 'What are his plans?'

'To create an alternative, obviously. If he succeeds it means curtains for everything we've worked for.'

Miss Brunner was grim. 'We managed to abort it last time. We can do it again.'

Frank stroked the head of the nearest Dobermann. 'This could be the end of authority as we know it.'

'Aren't you being a trifle apocalyptic, Mr Cornelius?' Bishop Beesley reached a plump hand for the Walnut Whips on the steel table. 'I mean, what can he do with a couple of guitars and a drum kit?'

'You don't know him.' Frank unbuttoned his collar. 'He's reverting to type, just when it seemed he was getting more respectable at last.'

'He's fooled us before,' said Miss Brunner. 'And we should have known better.' Her hands were urgent now, as she fed in her programme. '1977 could have been a turning point.'

The CRYPTIK began to give her a printout. She grew whiter than ever. 'Oh, Jesus. It's worse than we thought.'

'What?' Frank's arm was yanked by a sudden movement of his dogs.

'I think he's trying to abolish the Future altogether. He's going for some kind of permanent Present.'

'He can't do it.' Bishop Beesley licked his fingers. 'Can he?'

'With help,' said Miss Brunner, 'he could.'

'How can a few illiterate and talentless rock and rollers be of any use?'

'It's what they represent,' she said. 'There's no getting away from it, gentlemen. He's playing for the highest stakes.'

'Can we stop him?' asked the bishop.

'We're under-strength. Half our usual allies are in stasis.'

'What will wake them up?'

'The Last Trump,' said Frank. He was panting now, in unison with his dogs.

Living in the Past

'Are you sure you know what you're doing?' said Steve, not for the first time.

The assassin was hurrying through the corridors of the vast warehouse. It had become very cold.

'I told you. I never know what I'm doing. I have to play it by ear. But I've got a Shifter Tunnel and I've got a fix and I'm bloody sure we can make it. After that it's up to all of us.'

'To do what?'

'The Jubilee gig, of course.'

'But we've done it.'

'You've *tried* it, you mean. Just think of that as a rehearsal.'

'I wish I'd never got in touch with you.'

'Well, you did.' The assassin was humming to himself. It seemed to be some sort of Walt Disney song.

Steve tried to pull back. 'I'm fed up with it all. I just want…'

'Satisfaction, squire,' said the assassin. 'And I'm going to give you your chance.'

'All I wanted was the booze and the birds,' said Steve weakly. 'I was enjoying meself.'

'And so you shall again, my son.' The last of the musician-assassins turned a crazed eye on the guitarist. 'Better than ever.'

The walls of the warehouse began to quiver. A silver mist engulfed them. From somewhere in the distance came the muffled sound of bells.

'We're through! We're through!' cackled the assassin.

He burst open a rotting door and they stood on the slime of a disused wharf. Beside the wharf was a large white schooner with a black flag waving on its topmast. The schooner seemed to be deserted. On the poop deck a drum kit had been set up and Steve noticed that there was PA all over the boat.

The assassin paused, checking his wrist. 'My watch's working again. That's good. We made it. The others should be along in a minute.'

'That equipment looks expensive.'

'It's the best there is,' said the assassin confidently. 'Megawatt upon megawatt, my son. Enough sound to shake the foundations of society to bits! Ho, ho, ho!'

'Will Malcolm be here with the money?' asked Steve.

'You won't need money if this works,' said the assassin.

'I haven't had any wages in months.' Steve set a wary foot on the gangplank.

'There are bigger things at stake,' said the last of the musician-assassins. 'More important things.'

'That's what they always seem to wind up saying.'

The white schooner rocked in the water. The assassin began to hurry about the decks, checking the sound system, following cables, adjusting mikes.

'Power,' he said. 'Power.'

'Wages,' said Steve. 'Wages.'

But he was already becoming infected. He could feel it in his veins.

Vomit to Glory

'Hurry up, bishop.' Miss Brunner was being dragged along by four of Frank's dogs. She had her Remington under her arm.

Frank was in the lead with six more dogs. The bishop, with two, rolled in the rear. It was dawn and Goldhawk Road was deserted apart from some red, white and blue bunting.

'If you ask me,' said Helen of Troy, catching up with Bishop Beesley, 'he's using all this for his own mad ends. All we wanted was a bit of publicity. Are you sure this is 1977?'

'Miss Brunner is never wrong about things like that. She's an expert on the Past. That's why I trust her.' Bishop Beesley set his mitre straight on his head with an expert prod of his crook. 'She stands for all the decent values.'

He wheezed a little.

'You haven't got a Tootsie Roll on you, or anything, I suppose?' he asked.

Helen shook her head.

They reached Shepherd's Bush. On the green people were beginning to set up marquees and stalls. Pictures of QEII were everywhere.

Miss Brunner paused, hauling at the leads. 'This could have achieved what the Festival of Britain was meant to achieve. A restoration of confidence.'

'In what?' asked Helen innocently.

'Don't be cynical, dear.'

They took the road to Hammersmith.

'It's just your interpretation I'm beginning to worry about,' said Helen.

The Management Fantasy

Everyone was on board. Nobody seemed absolutely certain why they were here. The assassin was checking his rocket launchers and grenade throwers, which lined the rails of the main deck.

'Hello, Sid,' said Paul. 'You're not looking well.'

Sid plucked at his bass. John cast a suspicious eye about the schooner. 'Ever get the feeling you're being trapped?'

'Used,' said Mary with relish, 'in a game of which we have no understanding.'

Automatically, Steve was tuning up. 'Has anybody seen Malcolm?' He thought he'd spotted a flutter of tartan on the yardarm.

The schooner was full of people now.

'Raise the anchor!' cried the assassin.

The band began to play.

Even they were astonished at the volume. The sound swelled and swelled, drowning the noise of the rocket launchers as the assassin took out first the bridge and then the White Tower. Stones crumbled. The whole embankment was coming down. Hundreds of sightseers were falling into the water, clutching at their ears.

Overhead, police helicopters developed metal fatigue and dropped like wounded bees.

On board the schooner everyone was cheering up no end.

Mrs Cornelius lifted her frock and began to dance. 'This is a bit o' fun, innit?'

Soon everyone was pogoing.

The assassin ran from launcher to launcher, from thrower to thrower, whispering and giggling to himself. On both sides of the river buildings were exploding and burning.

'No future! No future!' sang John.

London had never seemed brighter.

The schooner gathered speed. Down went Blackfriars Bridge. Down went Fleet Street. Down went the Law Courts. Down went the Savoy Hotel.

It wasn't World War Three, but it was better than nothing.

Number One in the Capital Hit Parade

Miss Brunner, Bishop Beesley and Frank Cornelius had managed to get through the crowds and reach Charing Cross. With the dogs gnashing and leaping, they stood in the middle of Hungerford Bridge, watching the devastation.

The schooner had dropped anchor in the middle of the river and the sound-waves were successfully driving back the variable-geometry Tornados as they attacked in close formation, trying to loose Skyflashes and Sidewinders into the sonic barrier.

'You have to fight fire with fire,' said Miss Brunner. 'Come on. We still have a chance of making it to the Festival Hall.'

They hurried on.

Helen let them go. She clambered over the railing of the bridge and dropped with a soft splash into the water. Then she struck out for the ship.

Behind her, the dogs had begun to howl.

The water had caught fire by the time she reached the side and was hauled aboard by the assassin himself. He was glowing with health now. 'What's Miss B. up to?'

'Festival Hall,' said Helen. 'They're going to try to broadcast a counter-offensive. Abba. Mike Oldfield. Rick Wakeman. Leonard Cohen. You name it.'

The assassin became alarmed for a moment. 'I'll have to boost the power,' he said.

'No future! No future! No future!'

From over on the South Bank the first sounds were getting through.

'They're fighting dirty,' said the assassin. 'That's the Eurovision Song Contest as I live and breathe. Look to your powder, Helen!'

He gave the National Theatre a broadside. Concrete blew apart. But the counter-offensive went on.

'We're never going to make it to the Houses of Parliament at this rate,' said the assassin. 'Keep playing, you cunts.'

It had grown dark. The fires burned everywhere. The volume rose and rose.

The schooner began to rock. Planes and helicopters wheeled overhead, hoping for a loophole in the defences.

'God Save the Queen!' sang the Sex Pistols.

'God Save the Queen!' sang the choir of what was left of St Paul's Cathedral.

Mrs Cornelius leaned to shout into Helen's ear. 'This is great, innit? Just like ther fuckin' Blitz.'

Another broadside took out the National Film Theatre. Celluloid crackled smartly.

The schooner creaked and swayed.

The assassin had begun to look worried. They were being hit from all sides by Radio 2.

Slowly, however, through the flames and the smoke, the schooner was making it under the bridge and heading for Vauxhall. There was still a chance.

Lesson Seven
Cultivate Hatred: It's Your Greatest Asset

> Malcolm first thought about the film when the group were banned. The idea was if they couldn't be seen playing, that they could be seen in a film. That was probably just after they got thrown off A&M in Spring 77.
>
> Obviously with 'God Save The Queen' and the kind of global attraction that the whole episode had, he began to think more seriously about it and he approached Russ Meyer in early Summer 77 and he went out to Hollywood and talked to him...
>
> I think [Meyer] intended it to be a Russ Meyer film using The Sex Pistols, whereas Malcolm obviously intended it to be a Sex Pistols film using Russ Meyer. So there was a basic conflict from the start. He thought it would be the film that would crown his career ... Meyer thought Malcolm was a mad Communist anti-American lunatic and he was demanding more money because the thing looked risky. Meyer was very, very angry when it fell through. Kept referring to Malcolm as Hitler. 'Sue Hitler's ass' and all this stuff.
>
> – Julien Temple,
> interview with John May,
> *New Musical Express*, October 1979

'We've lost a battle, but we haven't lost the war.' Petulantly, Miss Brunner switched off the equipment. Her face was smeared with soot. The dogs lay dead around her, bleeding from the ears.

Through a pair of battered binoculars Frank surveyed the ruins. 'They got the palace before they sank.'

'Did they all make it into the airship?'

'I think so.'

Bishop Beesley finished the last of his toasted marshmallows. 'They're a lot further forward,' he said. 'Aren't they?'

Miss Brunner glared at him.

Smoke from the gutted Houses of Parliament drifted towards them.

'It's a state of emergency all right,' said Frank.

'Somebody's got to teach the Sex Pistols a lesson.' Miss Brunner's lips were prim as, with a fastidious toe, she pushed aside a wolfhound.

'They have a lot of power now,' said Bishop Beesley.

She dismissed this. 'The secret there, bishop, is that childishly they don't want it. They'll give it up. They don't want it – but we do. Half the time all we have to do is wait.'

'I suppose so. They're not fond of responsibility, these young hooligans.' Bishop Beesley took off his dirty surplice. 'It makes you sick.'

Miss Brunner looked with horror at his paisley boxer shorts.

Hello, Julie

'You weren't breaking any ikons,' said Nestor Makhno. 'You were just drawing bits of graffiti over them. And helping the establishment make profits. You went about as far as Gilbert and Sullivan.'

It was a somewhat sour evening at the Café Hendrix.

'You have to go solo,' said Marc Bolan. 'It's the only way.'

'Don't give me any of your Stirnerist rationalisations.' The old anarchist poured himself another large shot of absinthe. '*The Ego and His Own*, eh?'

'*My* anarchists were always romantic leaders,' said Jules Verne, who had dropped over from The Mechaniste in the hope of finding his friend Meinhoff.

'Which is why they were never proper anarchists.' Makhno had had this argument before. He turned his back on the

Frenchman. 'It's all substitutes for religion, when you come down to it. I give up.'

'If you want my opinion, they should never have put a woman in charge.' Saint Paul, as usual, was lost in his own little world.

Big Money

Having failed to find what he needed at the Jolly Englishman public house, Steve put his disguise back on and went to Kings Cross. He was heading for the Cambridge Rapist Hotel.

He was sure, now that a few things had been settled along the embankment, Malcolm would want to talk.

The lady at the door recognised him. 'Go up to Room 12, dear,' she said. 'There'll be someone there in a minute.'

He didn't tell her what he was really after.

He got to the first landing and went directly to the cage room. This was where Malcolm had kept his special clients. It was empty apart from a miserable record company executive, who whined at him for a moment or two before he left. No information.

Other doors were locked. The ones which yielded showed him nothing he didn't already know. It was obvious, however, that Malcolm wasn't here.

Room 12 had been prepared for him. He suspected a trap. On the other hand the lady on the waterbed looked as if she could take his mind off his problems. He decided to risk it.

'You don't know where Malcolm is, I suppose,' he said, as he stripped.

She opened her oriental lips.

'Love me,' she said, 'you're so wonderful.'

'Oh, hell.' He gave up and flung himself onto the heaving rubber.

He hadn't got very far before the door opened. One of Mr Bug's representatives stood there. He seemed menacing. He had a wounded Alsatian with him. From beyond the window a car began to hoot. It was Paul. They had arranged to meet here.

Steve began to scramble out of the bed. As he made for the window he was certain he heard the dog say that Malcolm was on the 6.15 from Marylebone.

It was better than nothing. He plunged from the window and into Paul's car. 'Marylebone.'

I Need Your Tender Touch

'Monarchy's only a symbol,' said Mr Bug's representative to Helen of Troy as the car moved slowly through what remained of St James's Park, 'but then so are the Sex Pistols.'

Near the pond, groups of homeless civil servants were jollying each other along as they erected temporary shelters, prefabs and tents.

'I don't think anyone meant it to go this far,' said Helen. 'Could you hurry it up a bit? I've got a train to catch.'

'The assassin did. He likes a bit of chaos. It allows him more freedom of movement.'

'Malcolm has the same idea. Keep 'em fazed.'

Mr Bug's representative placed a rubber hand on her little knee. 'Instant gratification,' he said. 'Where are we going?'

'Marylebone.'

Mr Bug's representative tapped the chauffeur with his whip. 'Did you hear that?'

'Yes, sir.'

The car bumped up the path through the park towards Piccadilly. All the roads around the Palace were ruined.

'It's peaceful now, isn't it?' Helen wound down the window. 'I love the smell of smoke, don't you?'

'I can't smell a thing in this exoskeleton. My usual senses are cut off, you see.'

'I suppose that's the point of it.'

'Exactly. But it does allow one a certain kind of objectivity.'

'Like being a child?'

'Well, no. Like being an ant, really.'

Anarchy Dropped Out of the Top Twenty

'Missed it.' Steve and Paul stood panting on the platform watching the train as it pulled away.

'I saw him,' said Paul.

'Or someone like him.' Steve rubbed his nose. 'Should we find out where the train's going?'

'He could get off anywhere.'

'True.'

'You spent too long in that bloody hotel,' said Paul.

'You could have arrived a couple of minutes earlier,' said Steve.

'This is pointless. Let's give it up.'

'I want my wages.'

'He hasn't got them, though, has he? Or if he has, we're not going to get them now. What are you really after, Steve?'

'I need some answers, I told you.'

'Don't we all? But we never get them, do we?'

This Is the Receiver Speaking

Miss Brunner settled herself in the first-class compartment. 'We're going to have to deal with them.'

'I tried to get into the next carriage,' said Frank, 'but it seems to have been locked. I think there's some trouble going on.'

'It's locked at the other end as well.' Bishop Beesley wiped the sweet sweat from his cheeks. 'I think it could be part of the emergency regulations.'

He relished the phrase. It was like coming home.

The regular rhythm of the train was soothing them all.

'What are you going to offer him?' Frank asked her. 'I mean, what have we actually got?'

'Experience,' she said. 'Ambition. A sense of right and wrong. Everything you need to put things into proper order. Sooner or later the balloon will burst.'

'It seems to have burst already.'

'A pinprick. It'll be patched in no time.'

'I admire your resilience, Miss Brunner.' Bishop Beesley was feeling in his pockets for the remains of his chocolate digestives. 'I suppose you didn't notice if there was a buffet?'

'Not in this carriage,' Frank told him.

'They always come back to us.' Miss Brunner looked out at the windows. 'Cows,' she said.

Spreading False Rumours

The last of the musician-assassins put his vibragun into its holster. 'They'll be wanting a martyr,' he told Steve. 'A proper martyr to the seventies.'

'Well it isn't going to be poor old me. All I'm after is my wages and maybe a chance to do the odd gig. I should never have got mixed up with you.'

'You summoned me, remember?'

Steve shrugged. He sat hunched over his Bacon Burger in the Peckham Wimpy, watching the dirty rain on the windows. 'I've got a feeling I'm being used.'

'You keep saying that. I'm only doing what you said you wanted me to do.'

'There's always a snag about making deals. Particularly with old hippy demons.'

'Do you mind? I was around long before that.'

'Maybe that's your trouble. What are you trying to do? Recapture your lost youth.'

The assassin dipped into his Tastee-Freez. His whole attitude was self-pitying. 'Maybe. But probably I'm trying to recapture those few moments when I felt grown-up. Know what I mean? In charge of myself.'

'How did you lose it?'

'Equating action with inspiration, maybe. Or "energy", whatever that is.'

'You've done quite a lot. You're just feeling tired, probably.' Steve wondered how he came to be comforting the assassin.

The assassin gave a deep sigh. 'Bands start breaking up when they're faced with the implications of what they've started. When it threatens to turn into art, or something like it. Look at the problems the Dadaists had. Successful revolutions bring their own problems.'

Steve's attention was wavering. 'You really can be a boring old fart sometimes, can't you? Hippy or not.'

'I know,' said the assassin. 'It comes with analysing too much. But what else can I do these days? Imposition hasn't worked very well, has it? Analysis is all you're left with. Am I right or am I wrong?'

'Suit yourself.' Steve swivelled his red plastic seat round. 'You should do what you feel like doing.'

The assassin toyed with his Tastee-Freez. 'Look where that's got me.' He cast a miserable eye around him. 'The bloody Peckham Wimpy.'

Every Room Was a Dead End

'Isn't the train ever going to stop?' Miss Brunner couldn't recognise the countryside. 'Whose idea was this, anyway?'

'Yours,' said Frank. 'Or mine. I forget.' He was beginning to fugue a bit. 'Tra la la. Hi diddle de de. Ta ra a boom de ay.'

Bishop Beesley was of no use at all. He desperately needed a fix. His fat was turning a funny colour and the flesh was loosening even as she watched.

'We're out of control,' she said, 'and I don't like it.'

'I thought you said we knew what we were doing?' Frank wiped drool from his lips. 'Hic.'

'We do. But I didn't expect the corridors to be blocked. That little bastard has outmanoeuvred us.'

'But only for the moment, eh?' said Frank. He was being dutiful. 'What do you want me to say?'

'You're bloody useless!'

He winced.

'I have to do everything myself.'

Bishop Beesley mewled. 'A Milky Way would be all right.'

It became dark. The train had entered a tunnel. It stopped.

Miss Brunner thought she saw a white face press itself against the window for a second, but she was losing faith in her own judgement.

This realisation made her very angry.

She kicked Frank in the shin.

Frank began to giggle.

Holidays in the Sun

Mrs Cornelius had her sleeves rolled up. She was doling out soup from the specially erected canteen in Trafalgar Square.

'Hello, Mum.' The assassin held his tin cup to be filled.

'Oxtail,' she said, 'or Mulligatawny?'

'Oxtail, please.'

'You've done it this time,' she said. 'There's a lot of people pissed off wiv you. I told 'em it was just your way of celebratin'. But look wot you've caused. Pore ole Nelson's got 'alf 'is bleedin' body missin'. It's gonna take ages ter clear up ther mess.'

'Sorry, Mum.'

'No use bein' sorry now. You'd better keep yer 'ead down for a while. I thought you'd bloody learned yer lesson.'

'Lesson?'

'You 'eard me.'

'Can I have the key to the flat?'

'Oh, so ya fuckin' wanna come 'ome ter Mum now, do yer? Littel sod.' She softened. ''Ere y'are. Now move on. There's a lot more people waitin'.'

She watched him shuffle off, sipping at his soup. 'They just fuckin' use yer when they need yer. An' then they're fuckin' off again.'

But the crowd had recognised him. They were beginning to converge.

With a yelp of terror, the assassin scuttled towards the National Gallery.

Mrs Cornelius watched impassively. ''E'll be okay,' she said to herself. 'Unless they actually tear 'im ter pieces.'

She ladled Mulligatawny into the next outstretched cup.

When she looked again, the crowd was rushing through the doors of the gallery.

Ten minutes later they were all coming out again, like spectators whose team had lost.

She grinned to herself. 'Shifty littel bastard,' she said. 'At least 'e knows when ter scarper.'

I Killed a Cat

The train had begun to move again, but by now Bishop Beesley was catatonic and Frank Cornelius was completely gaga, dribbling and whistling to himself. Miss Brunner went into the corridor and tugged at the door. It wouldn't open. All the windows were jammed.

She ran along the corridor, looking for help. All the other compartments were filled with old rubber suits, as if Mr Bug's representatives had dematerialised.

'What's going on?' she cried. 'What's going on?'

The train groaned and clattered, as if in unison with her voice.

She clawed at the connecting door. It wouldn't budge.

'Somebody's going to pay for it.' She swore. 'I'm not used to treatment of this kind. Who's in charge? Who's in charge?'

The train grunted.

'Who's in charge?' Now her voice became pathetic. A tear appeared in her right eye. She adjusted her blouse. She whimpered.

The train was moving faster. It swayed wildly from side to side.

Miss Brunner began to scream.

Lesson Eight
How To Diversify Your Business

JULIEN TEMPLE (DIRECTOR)
Went to Cambridge University 'For the same reasons as one applies for an American Express Card'. Attended National Film School 'so that I didn't have to wait 20 years to be able to do something'. The Great Rock 'N' Roll Swindle was his graduation film. Since then he has made Punk Can Take It, featuring the UK Subs and narrated by John Snagge, who once declared the end of World War II on BBC Radio and ghosted for Churchill's speeches while it was still on.

Virgin Records publicity, 1980

The last of the musician-assassins was crawling along rooftops overlooking Portobello Road.

He was looking for his airship. He was certain he'd left it in the vicinity of Vernon's Yard.

'Bugger,' he muttered. 'Oh, bugger.'

He was not feeling at one with himself.

Every so often a demonic grin, a memory, crossed his poor, ravaged face.

'Why am I always getting mixed up with bloody bands? What's happened to my complicated vocabulary of ideas? Why do I prefer rock and roll?'

It was familiar stuff to him.

Flies clustered around a faded chimney stack, rising as he groped.

'Monica?' His mind cast about for any anchor. 'Mum?'

His cuban heels scraped slate. Something fell away from him and smashed in the street. The sun was rising.

He drew a scratched single from the pocket of his black car coat and put it close to his eyes, studying it as if it were a map.

He was crying.

The flies hissed rhythmically. A stuck needle. He held on to the chimney, pulling himself up, his feet slipping.

There had to be something better than this.

The Uncertain Ego

'Passion feeds passion and then we are left with a small death.' Mr Bug's representative was trying to comfort Miss Brunner.

She stared at the strangled corpse.

A young man in a trench coat and a trilby stepped backwards.

'Is anyone really dying?' she asked. 'Or are we all just very tired?'

'Some of you are really dying, I'm afraid.' Mr Bug's representative plucked at his mouth-tube. 'Time is Time, no matter how much you struggle against it.'

'Then we're done for.'

'I haven't come to any conclusions about that.' He was apologetic. 'I'm honestly only an observer.'

'You've interfered.'

'I've taken an interest. It's the best I can offer.'

Miss Brunner shrugged him away.

A whistle blew.

'I'm getting off this train,' she said.

Mr Bug's representative made a peculiar gesture with his right glove.

'There'll be another one along in a minute.'

Difficult Love

Very sluggishly, the airship was lifting.

The last of the musician-assassins lay spreadeagled on the floor of the gondola. A faint tape was playing 'Silly Thing'.

'It's what the public wanted,' murmured the assassin. 'Or at least some of them. I did my best. It was good while it lasted.'

The ship gently bumped against a church steeple. He pulled himself to a window. He recognised Powys Square. There was a bonfire.

Something bit at his groin.

He scratched.

Framed against the flames, a tartan-clad figure and a dwarf were dancing.

'I think I'm missing all the fun again,' said the assassin.

He switched on his engine.

It faltered. It was apologetic.

He tried again.

Something clicked.

The Laughing Policeman

'We're going to have to split up,' said Miss Brunner firmly. Her colleagues had revived enough to get off the train and sit, shaking, on the platform seat.

'I think I have already,' said Frank.

'You mean diversify, don't you?' Bishop Beesley wrenched a wrapper off a Mars.

'Disintegrate?' said Frank, thinking of himself as usual.

Miss Brunner had recovered a bit of her composure.

'McLaren is the only one who will know how to deal with all this. So much of it is his fault.'

'Oh, come on,' said Frank. 'We were partners. Malcolm's as decent as the rest of us underneath. He pretends to be a revolutionary, but he's really just an ordinary young man on the way up.'

Miss Brunner shook her head. 'In different ways, Mr Cornelius, you're as gullible as your brother. We're facing a genuine attempt to take power.'

'The Pistols.'

'Of course not, you idiot. You very rarely get that sort of trouble from the musicians. They want different things, most of them. Subtler things.'

'The Pistols want subtler things.' Bishop Beesley appeared to be trying to recondition his mind.

'That's hard to believe,' said Frank.

Miss Brunner yawned and glanced away. 'At least they're all good-looking.'

'I haven't been well,' said Frank. 'What's this about breaking up?'

'Diversifying,' said Bishop Beesley.

There was a peculiar lack of noise around the station. The train had long since pulled away.

'Splitting up,' she said. 'To find them.'

'Who?' said Frank. He watched a butterfly settle on the track.

'Anyone,' she said.

'Divide and Rule,' said Bishop Beesley. 'Where in hell are we, anyway?'

He began to snore.

Miss Brunner peered into the countryside. 'Is that real, do you think? It's such a long time since I've been anywhere.'

Familiar Air

'There must have been something in the marketing,' said Steve. He stood in the deserted office complex holding a phone without a lead. 'Badges and that. T-shirts.'

'There's a lot to be made from marketing,' agreed Helen of Troy. 'Posters. Programmes. People get a good profit off all that. Special books.'

'Masks. Sweets.'

'Tie up marketing and it's far less hassle than actually managing a band,' said Helen. She had seen it all. 'Often a better turnover. And there are no people to get in the way and spoil things.'

'Maybe the marketing company could pay me wages.'

'Ah, well. It's a separate organisation, you see. They would if they could. But they have their accounts.'

'Maybe I should look at their accounts.'

'Only accountants understand accounts. You need an accountant to check it for you.'

'A lawyer?'

'A lawyer and an accountant's what you need.'

'To keep an eye on the manager?'

'It isn't as simple as that, Steve.'

Dead Loyal

Mrs Cornelius stuck her neck through her strap. 'Ter tell yer the truth, Tadpole, I'm glad ter be back at me regular job. 'Ow's business?'

'Who?' said Tenpole.

'Not 'oo – wot.' She flashed her torch on and off. 'Somebody's got ter earn a livin'.'

She paused at the door of the auditorium. 'O' course, it's in troubled times like these, people see a good picture, don't they?'

'Killed,' said Tenpole.

'Oh, yeah. That, too.'

Before she could go through, Mr Bug's representative entered.

'Everything all right here?'

'Loverly,' she said. She had never liked the look of him.

'Plenty of stock?'

'Ask Tadpole.'

'Any more handcuffs? Whips? Lengths of chain?'

'We're orl right for most o' that, far as I know,' she said. 'But it's Tadpole does the stock, doncher, love?'

'We've got to look after the housewives,' said Mr Bug's representative. 'Can't have them getting bored, can we?'

Mrs Cornelius frowned at him. He seemed to be attempting a joke.

'Are you the usual fellah?' she asked.

'I'm filling in for him.'

'You 'aven't – I mean, it's not a takeover or nuffink?'

'Just a change of territory. It'll all settle back to normal soon. Are you sure you don't need any more gags?'

Mrs Cornelius tittered. 'Not if they're anyfink like ther last one.'

Mr Bug's representative didn't get it.

'What do you need?' he said. 'You must need some replacements.'

'New feet,' said Mrs Cornelius, 'would be nice.'

He looked at her shoes.

'Something elegant in rubber?'

She turned back towards the doors.

'I've got them in the car.'

'It's no good,' she told him. 'I 'ave ter rely on the National 'Ealth.'

'Business is bad all round at the moment, even in entertainment. I remember when you couldn't go wrong in entertainment, so long as there was plenty of crisis and stuff. Cash from Chaos, eh?'

'Chaos?'

'It's not the same as entropy. Not superficially, at any rate. Still, it's all the same in the end.'

'Wot the bloody 'ell you talkin' abart?'

'Stuff.' Mr Bug's representative felt about his person. 'I'm having a spot of trouble with my tubes. It's hard to remain attached. Do you find that?'

'Ask bleedin' Alice in bleedin' Wonderbloodyland,' said Mrs Cornelius. She sniffed. 'Blimey! You don't arf pong.'

'Ping,' said Tenpole.

Mr Bug's representative slouched away. 'Everything's rotting.'

'You could've fooled me. You're enough to give ther fuckin' 'ot-dogs a bad name. An' that's sayin' somefink.'

She backed through the doors with her tray. On the screen they were shooting extras.

Voices in the Night

The airship was drifting over the débris near the river. People had already set up stalls and were selling various souvenirs: bits of ship, parts of planes, twisted singles.

The assassin could hear their voices.

'Get yer genuine Prince Philip bandages.'

'Johnny Rotten's safety pins. All authentic.'

'Fresh Corgi!'

Not a lot had changed.

He watched the shadow of his own ship as it passed over the ruins, over the dirty water, over the collapsed bridges.

He was feeling more depressed than ever.

'I need…' he murmured. 'I need…'

But his memory was failing again. He had seen too many alternatives. All the directions were screwed up. All the pasts and all the futures. They rarely seemed to make a decent present, which was only what he'd been aiming for. A bit of relief. But Time resisted manipulation, finally.

'Time's a killer,' he said. He tried to turn up his volume, but the music remained a whisper.

With an effort he moved the wheel and set a course for what had once been Derry & Toms Famous Roof Garden. Now it was some sort of posh nightclub. He had relinquished his interest in 19—.

He had all but relinquished his interest in the twentieth century.

He checked his instruments.

'There's never a World War Three around when you need one.'

Please Leave the State in the Toilet in Which You Would Wish To Find It

Sid had lost another game of pool at the Café Hendrix. He went over to a window seat and looked out into the grey mist of eternity.

'I don't think it's going to clear up,' said Alfred, Lord Byron, arm in arm with Gene Vincent. They had been having a medical boot race. 'Don't mope, lad. You didn't do so badly. And think of all those Sid Is Innocent badges they won't be able to sell now.'

'What about all the Sid Still Lives badges they will be able to sell?'

'There's a lot more money in death, these days, than there was when I coughed it,' said Shelley. 'Although it didn't do any harm to the poetry sales. Just think what they could have done for me? I did get a funeral pyre, though, and all that. Shelley posters would have gone over a treat, don't you think? Shelley pens.'

Jesus came over, chewing on a toothpick. 'I've never had any problems,' he said. 'My marketing's been going strong for a couple of thousand years. Gets better all the time. But then none of you were crucified, were you.'

'Don't listen to him, the snob.' Oscar Wilde put his hand in Sid's lap. 'You still on for that game of skittles?'

'You have to aim for universal appeal,' said Jesus. 'And that means your middle classes, I'm afraid. Without them, you'll never do it.'

'Sid didn't understand that, did you Sid?' said Nestor Makhno. 'And neither did I. And neither would I want to.'

'I did it my way,' said Sid. 'I think.'

Grumbling Bums

Miss Brunner sighed with pleasure. 'What a terrible trip. I'm glad to be home.'

'We achieved nothing,' Frank complained.

'Not true, darling. We found out certain things by a process of elimination.'

'It was a wild-goose chase.'

'It was a field trip. Trust me, darling.' She stroked her CRYPTIK. 'We'll just feed in what we know and then run another complete programme. Be a good boy, Frank, and put the kettle on.'

Bishop Beesley said: 'You still think we might be able to get the concessions.'

'We've the experience and the know-how. Show me a product, bishop, and I'll show you a profit in a very short while. How have I managed to stay in business so long? We'll need a few ideas to show McLaren.'

'But we can't find him. No-one can find him.'

'Wait until he hears what we have to show him.'

'You're an incurable optimist, Miss Brunner,' said Bishop Beesley. He began to force a chocolate orange into his mouth.

Remixing

The assassin opened the door and manhandled the bomb out.

He watched it sail down towards the new estate opposite Rough Trade in Kensington Park Road.

It landed with a clang in the street. People began to come out of their doors and look at it.

Faces stared up at the last of the musician-assassins. He spread his hands.

'Sorry.'

'Is it a dud?' shouted the grocer.

'I was told it would go off.' The assassin shrugged. 'Win a few and lose a few, eh?'

When, a couple of seconds later, the bomb did explode and bits of the crowd were scattered in all directions, the assassin was struck in the face by the grocer's left hand.

He wiped the blood from his cheek.

'What a lovely bit of fragmentation.'

Lesson Nine
Taking Civilisation To The Barbarians

He violently dislikes Rotten because Rotten insulted him all the time. Rotten used to talk to him in words that he didn't understand, like English swear words. It was quite amusing to see Meyer trying to make sense of it.

Meyer took Rotten out to dinner and Rotten was incredibly rude and disgusting over his food. He was trying to alienate him because it was Malcolm's project. By that stage Rotten really didn't get on with Malcolm, so the film was one of the major causes of a rift in the group that led to the break up.

... Apparently they spent three days tracing down this deer until they found the right one, and Meyer shot it himself.

The focus puller was thrown off for being squeamish about the thing. Meyer wouldn't have anyone anti-American on his set.

– Julien Temple,
interview with John May,
NME, October 1979

'The fabric's wearing a bit thin, isn't it?' Mr Bug's representative sat in his static limo. People moved like ghosts through ghostly trees. 'Is there any way of compensating?'

'It's a write-off,' said the last of the musician-assassins sheepishly.

'You're losing your touch.'

'I haven't got the help I used to get.'

'True. You'd had hopes for the Pistols, then?'

'It isn't their fault.' Jerry shifted as far away from Mr Bug's representative as possible. He cleared his throat. 'Would you mind if we opened a window, squire?'

'Not at all. But the fumes…?'

'The fumes are fine. It's quite pleasant. The scent of dissipating dreams.'

'I'm afraid…'

'What?'

'I can't follow you.'

'Just as well, squire. I'm on my own. I have to be. People try to turn you into leaders. Do you find that?'

'Not exactly. I just tend to the sick. When I do anything at all.'

The car started up again and moved at less than ten miles an hour through the strangely faded part. Mr Bug's representative pointed at a distant outline. 'The Palace is springing back again. Isn't it?'

'Oh, I wouldn't be surprised, squire.'

A large mob, all greys and light browns, ran through the car, carrying torches. They wore eighteenth-century clothes. 'The Gordon Riots,' said Mr Bug's representative. 'But they seem to be burning the Pistols in effigy. Look over there.'

The assassin nodded. 'Everything's out of focus, at present. This happens when you mess about the way I was. Still, it might have jelled. You never know.'

'You manipulate Time?' Mr Bug's representative was impressed.

'I pretend to.'

'I pretend to manipulate people. On Mr Bug's behalf, of course.'

'Who is Mr Bug?' asked the assassin.

'Have a guess,' said Mr Bug's representative.

Boo-boo-boogaloo

The Cessna came in to land on the deserted airfield. Its wheels bumped on the broken tarmac and it narrowly avoided the collapsed remains of a small airship.

Mr Bug's representative and the last of the musician-assassins crouched behind a ruined wall and watched.

The assassin held his vibragun in a trembling hand.

'It's the Americans,' said Mr Bug's representative.

A figure in a red-and-blue diving suit emerged from the plane.

'Their technology's so sophisticated,' whispered Mr Bug's representative admiringly. 'You'd hardly know there was anyone inside would you?'

'I'm not even sure about you.' The assassin wet his lips.

Mr Bug's representative nodded in agreement. 'Yes.' His breathing became erratic. 'Yessss.'

The assassin had the feeling that, given half a chance, Mr Bug's representative would begin some kind of mating ritual with the American suit.

Tartan flashed in an abandoned control tower.

The assassin leaped from his cover.

'Not yet!' hissed Mr Bug's representative. But it was too late.

Aiming the vibragun, the assassin hit the American just as he was reaching the tower. The suit fell to the ground and began to thresh as the sonics shook him to death. Part of the tower broke away and crashed onto the corpse.

Tartan dodged from window to window as the vibragun swept the building. Concrete cracked. Glass shivered.

Mr Bug's representative grabbed the assassin's arm. 'Too sss-soon. Oh, dear!'

A helicopter swished into the sky.

'Bugger,' said the assassin.

'I'm not sure you have any understanding of anyone's best interests,' said Mr Bug's representative, walking with slow, sad steps towards the American corpse. 'It could be the culture gap, but I'm beginning to think you're past it. I must have a word with Mr Jones.'

'He wants his wages. I thought...'

A strange, high-pitched hiss came from Mr Bug's representative. It took the assassin a while to realise that he was whistling 'Dixie'.

Gather at the River

'Malcolm's in America, I'm afraid,' said Sophie on the phone. 'I'm sure he'll want to get in touch the minute he comes back.'

Steve replaced the receiver.

Helen of Troy said: 'I told you so. You ought to go there.'

'Why?'

'For the same reason he's gone. For the same reason everyone goes. Because you've run out of possibilities here. Desperate times require desperate journeys.'

'I never thought it would come to this.'

'Distance makes the bank grow fonder.'

'Do what?'

'Everyone else is going. You can bet your life on it.'

'This job involves a lot of travelling, doesn't it? And very little money.'

'Don't start whining.' Helen was in an unusually brisk mood. It probably meant that she was keen to go to America for her own reasons.

'I can't afford it.'

'I can get us a lift.'

'I could do with a lift,' he said feelingly.

'We'll have to hurry.'

'Where to?'

'Brighton,' she said.

'Brighton?'

'It's where the plane leaves from.'

Tragic Magic

'Americans always think British bands are setting out to shock, when half the time the band is just behaving normally,' said Frank. He had his new denim suit on.

'Like slobs, you mean,' said Miss Brunner. 'We have so many complaints from abroad.'

'They were right about Malcolm,' said Bishop Beesley. 'If not the band itself. But then Malcolm must be easily shocked himself.'

'He had his finger on the pulse of the public for a moment or two, I'll give him that.'

'He had his hands in their pockets, too,' said Frank. 'That's what I'm complaining about.'

'Times are hard,' she said. 'Everyone's got their hands in everyone else's pockets. Groping about for the pennies they're sure someone must have.'

'Disgusting,' said Bishop Beesley.

'Hurry up, bishop. Are you packed?'

He was trying to close the lid on a large suitcase full of Toffee Crunch and Milkybars.

'I have every admiration for American Management.' Frank became pious. 'They handle things so well over there.'

'They have nicer musicians, that's why.'

'Even the cowboys?'

'Hearts of gold, underneath.'

'Rough diamonds,' said Bishop Beesley sentimentally.

'Any kind would do me, right now.' Frank looked at his ticket. 'This had better work.'

'They love me,' she said. 'It's my accent.'

Touching Base

'Half the time you think you're flying,' said the assassin, fiddling with his controls, 'and when you get out you discover you've been in a Link Trainer the whole time.'

'Try and keep quiet and concentrate,' said Helen of Troy. They were all fed up with him. 'Are you sure you know this type of plane?'

'I love it,' he said. 'Therefore I know it.'

'A classic romantic delusion.' Mr Bug's representative wriggled in the navigator's chair.

'Get on with it, you stinking old has-been.' Steve sat with the rest of the group in the passenger seats. He lifted a bottle of Wild Turkey to his lips.

'Will we get to meet Bugs Bunny?' asked Paul. He was well out of things.

'I'm having a hard time,' said the assassin with characteristic self-pity.

'Getting them good times.' Only Helen was really looking forward to the trip.

The old Boeing Clipper lumbered through the water, its Wright Double Cyclone engines screaming and burping as they gave all they had left.

'You ought to be running a bloody transport museum,' said Steve. 'You're living in the past.'

'I think he simply wants the whole twentieth century at once,' said Mr Bug's representative. 'It's greed, really. And romance, of course.'

The assassin pulled down his goggles. 'I'm just heavily into technology,' he said.

'Well, I suppose I can't complain about that.' Mr Bug's representative crossed his legs (if they were legs). 'It's been my problem for years.'

The ancient Boeing heaved itself into the wild, blue yonder.

Helen clapped her little hands. 'Look out, Land of Opportunity, here we come!'

'If we're lucky,' said Steve sourly.

The assassin had a strange grin on his lips. 'Manifest Destiny! We'll be fine.'

'I think I'd feel safer in a bleedin' covered wagon,' said Johnny, waking up for a moment and not enjoying the experience.

Buddy, Can You Spare a Dime?

'Yanks,' said Mrs Cornelius reminiscently. 'I saw a lot of 'em durin' ther war.'

'War?' said Tenpole, rolling a hot-dog between his hands.

'Ther last one. Ther last big one, that is. Thass wot I liked. Mrs

Miniver, innit? Well, you wouldn't know abart any o' that. Yore too fuckin' young.'

'Who?'

'You.'

'Killed?'

'You, if ya don't fuckin' shut up. I'll tell yer one fing. I'm gettin' bleedin' bored wiv this picture, ain't you? I could do wiv a nice bit o' John Wayne.'

Ladies Love Outlaws

'Self-conscious, self-involved, chauvinistic and just downright bloody terrified.' Miss Brunner dragged Frank off the plane at LAX. 'Where's your sense of the International Brotherhood of Man, Mr Cornelius?'

'I've been here before.' Bishop Beesley wiped his brown lips.

'I never did like it.' Frank was miserable. 'It's hardly ever the way it is in the pictures.'

'A fact of life which your family has always failed to accept.' They moved towards the Immigration desks. 'And take that silly Stetson off.'

'Will they give us the money?' asked Bishop Beesley, in the rear as usual. 'In Los Angeles? Sunset Boulevard?'

'Sunset something,' she said. 'This could be the end of the line.'

Frank cheered up a little. 'You getting cold feet?'

'My feet are never hot, Mr Cornelius.'

She was sensitive about her inability to sweat.

Dead Puppies

They pushed Sid out first. He went down over the Bay, rolling and twisting in the air before his parachute opened.

'Go,' shouted the assassin, circling the Golden Gate Bridge. 'Go!'

One by one they jumped.

'At least it's sunny,' said Helen of Troy, passing Steve on the way down. 'It's amazing what a difference a bit of sunshine makes.'

'Have a nice day.' The Wild Turkey and crème de menthe hadn't mixed well. He began to vomit in the general direction of Haight-Ashbury.

They drifted over the city.

Mr Bug's representative hung limp in his harness. Stuff was oozing from his suit. 'Can this be a propaganda drop?'

'I've never tried them,' said Paul. He tugged at one of his ropes. 'This is all right, though, isn't it?'

One by one they hit the ocean.

The Boeing Clipper circled over the spreading blobs of silk.

The assassin was beginning to revive a trifle. He swung the plane out to sea and flipped a toggle. His vibracannon were now at Go.

He turned and headed back towards the city as fast as he could go. The tapes rolled, straight into the cannons' ammo-storage.

'Time for a little earthquake.'

He gave them 'Anarchy in the UK'. It seemed appropriate.

He whistled to himself as the buildings began to bounce.

Honky Tonk Masquerade

Helen of Troy stood dripping on the wharf while the cutters continued their search.

'Americans take everything so *seriously*. They're worse than the French.'

Mr Bug's representative was incapable of standing. Someone had tried to remove his suit but had stopped when they had seen what was inside. 'They're too polite. And when politeness fails, they're too violent.'

'There were at least four more went in.' The policewoman was staring wonderingly at the blasted city. 'What did they have to do that for?'

'Jealousy,' said Helen of Troy. 'Also revenge.'

'What for?'

'Oh, they're all looking for Malcolm. We thought he was here.'

'Malcolm X?'

'If you like.'

The Boeing Clipper had disappeared out to sea, pursued by helicopters and coastguard planes.

'Who's the pilot?' asked the policewoman. It was obvious that she still didn't believe what had happened.

'Just an old fart.'

Three familiar figures were picking their way over the tattered wood and concrete. 'Are we too late?' Miss Brunner wanted to know.

'Too late?' asked Frank and Bishop Beesley in unison.

'Too late,' agreed Helen.

'Poor lads.' Miss Brunner grinned like an ape. 'Will Malcolm be at the funeral?'

'There's got to be an inquest first,' said Helen.

'Questions are going to be asked, eh?' Frank prodded at the shoulder of Mr Bug's representative. It hissed back at him, a dying snake. 'Phew! He must have been dead for months.'

'It's what we're all beginning to realise.' Helen wandered off in the direction of Fisherman's Wharf. She was hoping she could still buy a postcard.

Lesson Ten
Who Killed Bambi?

Said Lydon in his statement: 'McLaren hoped that our record sales would be enhanced if the public were under the impression that we were banned from playing. That was certainly untrue. Some halls wouldn't have us, but others applied to Glitterbest for gigs during 1977 and were either refused or else received no replies.' In the end, he claimed, the Pistols resorted to doing three gigs under assumed names.

... Sid Vicious rang Lydon one morning at 5.00 am to inform him that McLaren had just visited him. McLaren had complained to Vicious about Lydon, and Vicious himself told Lydon that he had had enough of the Sex Pistols. 'Vicious sounded incoherent,' said Lydon's statement. 'I've since heard that he took an overdose of heroin shortly after McLaren's visit.' Subsequently, Wilmers claimed, Lydon and McLaren had a face to face showdown at which Lydon said he didn't like getting publicity out of a man who had left a train driver like a vegetable.

The judge asked whether Rotten had changed in view of his refusal to become involved with Biggs. 'The image projected is one in which violence is not opposed,' he commented.

Mr Wilmers said that Rotten did not approve of killing people.

NME, 24 February, 1979

Manager As Voyeur

'It was just another wank,' said Sid, picking at himself in the Café Hendrix.

'But a seminal wank, you must admit,' said Nancy. She had been allowed in on a visit. She had always been fond of bad jokes.

Nestor Makhno looked up from the next table, a spoonful of ruby-coloured borscht near his lips, his woolly hat slipping down over one eye. 'It's the politically illiterate who start revolutions. And it's the politically literate who lose them. You mustn't blame yourself.'

'I blame the Chelsea Hotel,' said Dylan Thomas. 'Have you ever stayed there? In the winter? Brrr. It brings you down, boyo.' Since arriving at the Café Hendrix he had adopted an appalling Welsh jocularity.

'What would you do?' asked Nancy. 'If they gave you the chance of a comeback?'

'Tell them to stuff it.'

'I know what I'd do,' said Nestor Makhno. 'I'd go all the way. Nihilism. I would have in the first place, I think, but the wife didn't like it.'

'Blow 'em all up,' said Bakunin cheerfully.

'Now there speaks a true wanker,' said Jesus. He went up to the counter to get another espresso. 'Who did you ever assassinate?'

'That's scarcely the point, is it?' Bakunin was hurt. But he knew he was talking to an ace.

Everyone was aware of it.

Sid winked at the pouting Russian. 'You can't compete with him. He's sent millions and millions off.

'It's a question of style.' Bakunin waved a gloved hand. 'Not of numbers killed.'

'You've probably got a point there.' Keats and Chatterton went by arm in arm. 'And Sid had a lot of style. A lot of potential.'

'Well, I might yet realise it,' said Sid. He was having a think.

Great Moments with the Immortals

'Maybe it's the Gulf Stream.' Paul and Steve were dragging themselves ashore at last. They had arrived on the beach at Rio.

'It's fate, lads!' Martin Bormann, wearing only red-and-black swimming trunks, a discreet swastika on his saluting arm, came marching up. 'I was only thinking about you this morning.'

'Have you seen Malcolm?' Steve asked.

'You've just missed him, I'm afraid. But Ronnie's about. He wants to join the group. I hear you're a couple of members short. I don't wish to push myself forward, but I used to be very fond of music...'

'We'll think about it,' said Paul.

'Pistols, pistols über alles,' sang Martin, striding along beside them. 'You look defeated. I know a great deal about defeat. You mustn't let it get you down.'

'You wouldn't happen to have seen an old Boeing Clipper about, would you?' Steve cast an eye on the sky.

'Oh, you know about that, do you?'

'Has one been here?'

'It's the plane Malcolm left on.'

'Betrayed!' said Steve.

'It's probably a coincidence,' said Paul.

'The entire German people betrayed me,' said Martin sympathetically. 'They weren't worthy of us, you see. But what do we actually mean by this word "betrayal"? Don't we in some ways betray only ourselves...?'

They hadn't time for his third-rate Nazi metaphysic. They began to run up the beach.

'We've got to earn some money, Steve,' said Paul.

Steve stopped.

'We'll have to do a few gigs.' He turned. 'Have you got any bookings, Martin?'

'Amazon, three nights starting from tomorrow. Then there's the Mardi Gras...'

'We'll take 'em,' said Paul.

Human Conditioner

Miss Brunner set the crudely printed invitation on top of her CRYPTIK and frowned at it.

'Maybe they're willing to deal at last?' said Frank. He had his areas of optimism.

'It could be a joke,' said Bishop Beesley.

She hovered over her keyboard, but nothing came to mind.

'A farewell gig, though,' said Frank. 'I thought they'd already done that.' He sniggered.

'Malcolm will be there.' Bishop Beesley waved an important Crunchie. 'And we need to raise some cash.'

'We'll make a few contacts.' Frank reached towards the invitation but had his wrist slapped away by Miss Brunner.

'It's another trap,' she said.

'What can they do to us? We've survived everything.'

'Your brother's involved. He's been resurrecting people again. You know what he's like.'

'Everyone who is everyone – or was anyone – will be there. Let's give it a go.' Frank stroked his hand. 'Please. My mum'll be there. She works at the venue. He wouldn't hurt our mum.'

Miss Brunner was letting him convince her. 'And I've never seen him live,' said Bishop Beesley. 'If live is the right word.'

'It'll be a relaxing night out.' Frank gave a stupid grin. 'Well, it'll make a change.'

'It'll make a change,' Miss Brunner agreed. 'Do we get to see the film as well?'

'It doesn't say.'

The CRYPTIK made a peculiar peeping noise.

'I think it's laughing,' she said.

The Mysteries

'I hope to God this is my final bloody comeback.' The last of the musician-assassins bit his mouldering lip and stared at his disintegrated fingers. 'There just isn't the energy around now.'

'It's because you've used it all up,' said Malcolm. 'Sue, where's the chequebook?'

'They took that as well.'

Malcolm began to look in the backs of his desk drawers, as if he hoped to find a little cash. 'This is silly.'

'What happened to the money?' asked the assassin.

'It was won in a dream and lost in a nightmare,' said Sue. She seemed to be quoting somebody.

'Where did it go?'

'Ask the bloody Official Receiver.'

'Isn't that what he's asking you?'

'Everybody's asking the wrong questions.' Sue glared at the assassin. 'Leave him alone. Can't you see he hasn't had any sleep in months?'

'That always happens when you try to make a dream come true, doesn't it?'

'I don't need you sitting there, rotting in my last good chair,' said Malcolm. 'Have all the invitations gone out, Sue?'

'I'm not moralising,' said the assassin defensively, 'exactly. I'm speaking from several lifetimes of experience.'

'All gone out,' said Sue.

'Isn't the dream better than what we've got?'

'Are you Mr Bug?'

'Let's just say I do his tailoring.'

'Where is he?'

'Where he always was. Zurich. Watching telly.'

'I never thought of Switzerland.' The assassin tried to recover a fingernail which had dropped onto the bare boards.

'Few people ever do.'

'It could just be the suit that's in Switzerland.'

'The suit is Mr Bug.' Malcolm paused in his search. 'I should know, shouldn't I?'

The assassin drew himself onto unsteady feet. He dusted a little light mould from his black car coat.

'Well, that clears everything up. Thanks. I'll see you at the gig.'

'See you there,' said Malcolm. He crossed the room and began to feel in the pockets of a pair of discarded bondage trousers.

The assassin paused by the door. 'Oh, by the way, who really did kill –?'

'Get off,' said Malcolm.

As the assassin went down the stairs, Sue came trotting after him. She whispered:

'It was Russ. But Malcolm set it up.'

The assassin had already forgotten the question.

When You Wish Upon a Star

The Concorde landed on schedule at Margaret Thatcher Airport.

'England looks very clean, these days,' said Martin Bormann with some satisfaction. 'I always knew there was a chance for her.'

An old robber, disguised as an ex-boxer, said through his balaclava: 'A return to proper standards. And about time.'

Steve settled his trilby on his head. 'As soon as I see Malcolm I'm going to...'

'Give it up,' said Paul. 'Just for a bit, eh?'

Martin Bormann was disappointed. 'I thought there'd be a crowd waiting for us. Like The Beatles.'

'Crowds need organising,' said Steve, 'and Malcolm's too busy for that. Besides, he's not managing us any more.'

'Are you sure?'

'Well, you can never be absolutely certain.'

Reaching the Market

'I'm glad I'm not dead. I'm glad I'm not dead,' mumbled the last of the musician-assassins to himself. He had put on his old Pierrot suit and had plastered his face with white make-up to hide the worst of the decay. 'You've got to think positive.'

He shuffled through the streets of North London. He was lost. He seemed to remember that he had been on his way to some kind of party. It was possible that he had missed it during one of his rests. It had started to rain. The silk suit began to stick to his skeleton as he turned into Finchley Road.

Everything was getting very hazy.

Requiem Mc2

'Two Rotten Bars, please.' Sue looked at her own little dolls on display in the foyer. She still thought she should get the bars free, but she paid for them anyway. Tenpole began to sing at her.

'You stop that, Tadpole.' Mrs Cornelius came round the corner. 'Don't let 'im bovver you, love. 'E wants ter be discovered. Will Malcolm be along later?'

'Discovered?'

'Like America.' She laughed heartily so that her goods in her tray bounced beneath her bouncing breasts. 'An' all them ovver bleedin' colonies.'

Sue went inside. She wanted to be sure of a good seat.

They were all beginning to arrive now. Nearly everybody was in some form of fancy dress. Mickie Most, in lugubrious and inappropriate corduroy, Jake Riviera, Tony Howard, Peter Jenner, Andrew Lloyd Webber, Martin Davis. A lot of denim and fur. A lot of vain leather.

Shuffling in and standing in the shadows, the half-collapsed pierrot looked at them going by. It was like a gathering of Mafia dons, old and new. Richard Branson, Michael Dempsey, Miles Copeland: some of them in modifications of demi-monde styles, some in grotesque parodies of dandyism. The Black Arabs arrived, singly or in couples, with their girlfriends.

The Pierrot noticed how comfortable they all were. It was probably because not a single punter had been on the invitation list. Some of them complained that they had to pay, but in the main they were not discontented.

Elton John, Rod Stewart, Olivia Newton-John, Cliff Richard and Barbra Streisand. Bishop Beesley, Miss Brunner, Anne Nightingale. Frank Cornelius didn't notice his brother. He was walking on air. He felt euphoric in the presence of cash. The slightly self-conscious members of the musical press, trying to look like musicians, and as usual never absolutely certain of their social status: their expressions changing constantly as they tried for an appropriate mode.

They were piling in, drawn by curiosity, greed, a wish not to be left out.

Music publishers, record company executives, the owners of studios; agents and managers.

'What a lot of controllers,' mumbled the last of the musician-assassins. 'What a lot of mortgages.'

Elegant cowboys, smoothed-up Hell's Angels, Beverly Hills punks. Nobody required any hope, only confirmation. They confirmed one another.

The Pierrot was reminded of a bunch of burghers going into church.

Steve and Paul wandered in. Steve's trench coat was covered in a variety of old food, vomit and semen. He had lost his hat. A bouncer appeared from nowhere. 'Sorry, you've got to have invitations.'

Ronnie Biggs and Martin Bormann said in chorus: 'It's all right. They're with us.'

'Johnny won't come,' said Steve to no-one in particular. He hadn't noticed the Pierrot in the shadows either.

Wasting It

'I've seen this before,' whispered Miss Brunner to Frank as the film came on.

'We've all seen it before,' said someone behind her. 'That doesn't mean we can't enjoy it.'

Steve was crawling between the seats, still looking for Malcolm.

He found a tartan knee. 'Malcolm? Wake up.'

'Give him a break,' said Sue. 'Can't you leave him alone for a minute?'

It was standing room only for the old pierrot. He held on tightly to the rail at the back, trying to focus fading eyes.

His mother popped in. 'Jerry. Yore lookin' terrible. There's a chap in the foyer. Sez 'es's Mr Bug's bailiff. Is it ther Receivers?'

'They're not playing tonight.'

'I'll tell 'im.' She disappeared.

'Mum...' He stretched out his wounded hand. 'My wiring's gone...' But she didn't hear him.

He could only dimly detect the soundtrack now. There was a lot of plummy laughter coming from the seats. The film was reassuring its audience while pretending to shock them; a perfect formula for success.

'It's sure to be a winner,' said Helen of Troy, slipping out for a pee.

The Pierrot gasped. Everything was going round and round.

Sometime later, as he desperately tried to revive his attention, he saw Sid at last. The operation had been a success. He wasn't absolutely sure by now if Sid was actually on stage or on film. He was singing 'My Way' with all his old style.

Steve crawled up and began to tug at the Pierrot's suit. Bits of it tore away in his hand. 'This is where I came in.'

He crawled on, towards the exit.

The volume rose higher and higher. There were a few murmurs of complaint.

The Pierrot felt a shade better. He managed an appreciative groan.

The song ended.

Gunfire began to sound in the auditorium.

The Pierrot sank to the dirty floor with a happy grunt. 'It worked, after all. We did it, Sid.'

The hall became filled with the sounds of terror. Blood and bits of flesh flew everywhere. The audience was tearing itself to pieces as it tried to escape. No-one did.

Eventually there was silence. A dark screen. A vacuum. An avenged ghost.

Mrs Cornelius opened the doors. She had an expression of resigned disgust on her face.

''Oo the bloody 'ell do they expect ter clear up this fuckin' mess, then?'

'Bambi?' said Tenpole behind her.

He began to sing again.

The Alchemist's Question

To all women at war

THE GUARDIAN

NEW • COMPACT MORE PAGES, SAME PRICE

Toronto — Tuesday May 20 1948

Crossman leads attack on Kremlin

By ROY KIPLING

There was still fierce fighting in the streets of Moscow today as General Sir Richard Crossman led a massive hovertank charge against the Kremlin where most of the Duma forces are now entrenched.

Earlier, a mixed division of British and Hungarian troops was able to reach Lubyanka Prison and release Emporer Michael and his family. They were unhurt. So far no press interviews have been granted. Much of the city is in ruins and already the outskirts are under military law. Meanwhile a minor sensation was created when a neutral Dutch war-correspondent, Jeremiah Cornelius, was discovered to be a double agent. He was shot this morning at the orders of the Israeli Commander Field Marshal Dayan. Israeli troops now occupy the whole of the southern section of the city and are proving, it is said, uncooperative with the other allied forces. In a statement issued yesterday evening, General Crossman said that he was confident that the Kremlin would fall by today.

(Victims of Ideology p.7)

German rift with soviet French

From OSWALD BASTABLE

Signs that the Franco-German Soviet Bloc is suffering internal disruptions were confirmed (say Versailles-watchers) by the announcement that Hugo Pyat had been replaced as leader of the Assembly by known hardliner Otto Lobkovitz. Lobkovitz, an Alsatian, is likely to have more success at reconciling differences between German and French members of the Assembly. These differences came to a head last month when the Ministry of Agriculture demanded that productivity on the Rhine collectives be doubled within three years. This was regarded by Germans as a French attempt to make up for their own poor agricultural returns in the past two years. While Lobkovitz may heal the rift within the Assembly concerning the agricultural issue, he will almost certainly bring up the Polish question at his first opportunity, with a consequent further increase in tension between the two factions.

Panthers speed on Berlin

The mood in Berlin today was, to say the least, gloomy as the news reached the Prussian capital of further Black Panther games in nearby towns. The remains of the Prussian army has retreated to Berlin and is now under the direct command of President-Emporer Manfred von Bismark. In a series of brilliant manoeuvres Black Panther armoured divisions have smashed through all other defences and are now moving rapidly on the capital. BP C-in-C General Seale claimed this morning that by tomorrow he would be 'dining in the Chancery'. The Prussian surrender is expected at any moment.

(Bohemia Next? Back Page)

British Jews face dole queues

JAMES COLVIN

If the new Alien Registration Bill becomes law after the House of Commons votes on Friday many British Jews will find themselves suddenly unemployed, said the Liberal Shadow Minister for Race Control, Dr Mark Bonham Carter, yesterday. In a speech to his constituency party at Haringay W, he told a packed hall that the Bill would not only control Jewish immigration into this country but would make it impossible for many British-born Jews to qualify for jobs. 'Unless the Bill is modified', he said, 'people who are entitled to regard themselves as British subjects will face the prospect of the doel queue or, at best, performing menial work when they have previously been practising in the professions or in the better-rewarded branches of trade and industry.' He said that Liberals were not opposed to the basic spirit of the Bill but would vote against it unless it was modified to protect British Nationals.

Iceland's military image left in ruins

By MEG ZETTERLING

Reykjavik, Monday

The ease with which a relatively small force of Swedish paratroopers were able to regain control of the country after Prime Minister Christiansen's announcement on Friday of his country's 'independence' has left Iceland's previously impressive military image in complete ruins. The hopes of various terrorist organisations in Norway, Denmark and Finland (so called 'Liberation Armies') must have been sadly dashed when it took the Swedes only a matter of hours to re-establish law and order throughout Iceland. Many had previously been of the opinion that the 'Swedish wolverine' had let its teeth decay, but Sunday's show of superior strength, speed and tactical ability will have squashed that impression for once and for all. This morning President Hellander told the Swedish Parliament that he was 'completely satisfied' with the manner in which the Icelandic 'uprising' had been dealt.

(Alan Brien, p.12)

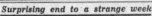

Surprising end to a strange week

Gandhi avenges his earlier torment

By HOPE DEMPSEY

In a week which saw three separate assassination attempts on the life of President Gandhi of Bantustan (formerly Cape Colony), and in which it seemed inevitable that the Indian-born dictator must surely fall, it has become obvious that the President is now even more firmly in control than before. The so called 'minority' parties have been declared illegal and yesterday a special court sentenced five 'minority' leaders to death for alleged treason. The five leaders are P W Waring (National Democrat), B J Vorster (Christian Republican), A Luthuli (Bantu Nationalist), K Mantamzima (South African Unity) and H Cornelius (Liberal). In some circles here Gandhi's severe sentences are seen as vengeance on the representatives of those who were originally responsible for his fifteen years of imprisonment, exile and, according to his own statements, torture while interned in the Capetown Correction Centre.

TV, radio—2

Arts	12	Overseas	2-4
Books	24, 25	Parliament	20
Business	17-19	Sport	25, 27
Ent'ments	20	Women	11
Home	5-8	X-words	23, 27
Horner	9		

Classified—9, 10, 21-23

I

England's Best Man

Sussex fast bowler Tony 'Lester' Pigott became a Test-hero instead of a husband in Christchurch early today. A last-minute SOS from injury-hit England forced Pigott to cancel his wedding plans. But there was no lack of celebrations as he put England firmly in the driving seat against New Zealand.

The Sun, 3 February, 1984

'I'm all speeded up again.' Fatalistically Jerry Cornelius checked his heat.

'Not as much as you should be, my son. Shakey Mo Collier was disapproving. It's getting so there's more speed in the coke than there is in the speed. I think it's immoral. And as for all this cheap EEC smack on the market, every bloody stockbroker can be a weekend junkie nowadays. It's not Mo's style, I know that.' Sighing he screwed up the empty paper. He placed it thoughtfully in his mouth and began to chew.

'It makes a nonsense of any attempt to gauge exponential decay,' said Miss Brunner.

They turned upon her the polite, puzzled eyes of recently awakened marmosets.

'$q(t) = De - \frac{\lambda}{t}$,' she added weakly. '$C(t) = \frac{D}{V} \frac{\lambda}{t}$.'

Mo sucked the last juice from his scrap of imitation art. 'Who sold you that?'

'A black man in the pub. He said it was pure.'

Mo became disgusted. 'We should never let you score for us.'

She took offence. 'There's not a lot wrong with my mathematics, Mr Collier. It tested out on the computer.' She removed a little speedometer from her bag. With a snap she placed it on the nearest console. Jerry picked it up. 'The batteries were probably a bit low.' He thought he should try to reduce the temperature.

Behind him a dozen brightly coloured graphs monitored Birmingham's shifty infrared emissions. Sergeant Alvarez tapped another series of flaky questions into the DUEL MX. The computer continued to answer with laconic, almost impatient negatives. A moment later all screens turned bright red and remained stable, flooding the Centre with their bloody glow. '$E = mc^2$,' said Mo with a happy grin.

Miss Brunner found his nursery humour tiresome. 'I was fond of Birmingham.'

'An' she don't even like curry!' Sputtering and slapping at himself, Mo applauded his wit.

Jerry was counting heartbeats. 'Too many,' he murmured. 'Too many.' He ran quivering white fingers through his antique hair, engulfed by nostalgia for those years when he had been the epitome, the chief troubleshooter, for the Simple Answer.

Perhaps in sluggish response to Alvarez's questioning, the screens began to show old newsreels of Adolf Hitler at Nuremberg, Hitler relaxing at home near the Austrian border, Hitler fondling little children. These were swiftly replaced with images of Kemal Atatürk smiling sternly at his modernised countrymen. Mussolini, Stalin, Trotsky, Lenin, Franco were played in a sequence culminating with a trembling still of Birmingham a few seconds before she was taken out.

Miss Brunner began to jot rapidly on her wrist-reckoner. 'If it's an equation it's deceptively crude.' She looked up, as if experiencing a brief revelation. 'Or is it just crude?'

Alvarez turned his head a degree or two to address her, but his eyes were all for his screens. 'Don't read too much into DUEL's original ideas,' he said. 'They're pretty primitive. It's like having to suffer the company of somebody's smart-ass kid.'

'I haven't the patience.'

'Who's complaining?' Jerry glared at the grime on his lace cuffs. 'That's why Alvarez is doing the job. You worrying about your slaves, general? I mean doctor. Do I?' He glanced up into furious eyes. Framed by its auburn perm, her face recalled an untranquil Mithras.

'It's a matter of responsibility,' she said. 'Who's for going under ground?'

Vaguely, Jerry wondered if she had decided to look for the entrance to the Hollow Earth again. Or did she just mean Lapland?

Alvarez sniffed. 'I'm thinking of packing it all in.'

'Greedy bastard.' Mo absently tracked a finger over the black trim of a printer then hopefully licked it. 'Bloody dust.'

'Malfunction. It's all I can come up with.' Alvarez was in his own world of dials and switches. 'There's got to be an alternative for Birmingham somewhere.'

'Well,' Miss Brunner dismissed their concerns, 'I have an appointment to keep.'

Alvarez, offended, whistled a snatch from a ditty popular in his youth. 'With the Devil?'

She twisted her lips. 'With a dentist.'

Jerry displayed a knowing wink. He had the satisfaction of a flame or two as she pressed the code to open the door. He had absolutely no idea what she had meant, but he knew how to make her tick.

The response had drained him. He sat with a deep sigh heavily on the nearest stool.

'Shit.' Alvarez gestured at his screens. 'Nothing but snow.'

For a second Mo brightened. His eyes became metallic with expectation then grew as suddenly dull.

'Time for me to fade,' said Jerry.

'Is this the winter of our disconnect?' Mo tittered. But he was full of unspecific anxiety. 'Fit. Fit. Hold it off. Keep it away.' His limbs copied the attitudes of athletes he had seen on television, just as they once fell almost automatically into the postures of his rock-and-roll heroes. 'You can't be too careful.' He cast about for Jerry. 'What should I identify with? Who?'

'Better ask Miss B.,' said Alvarez, wondering if his beard had turned much greyer. 'You can bet your life she'll be after recruits now. You're over-ripe for it, mate. Look at yourself!'

But Mo already was. He had caught a glimpse of his left calf in the blank lower monitor and was studying its reflection, flexing it this way and that. 'The answer's in yourself.' He only partially understood the old saw. He bent, peering at his gaunt features, pulling his lids to see how bloodshot his eyes were. 'Mo could do with a new haircut.'

'Who can you trust?' said Alvarez.

'Too right,' agreed Mo. 'My dad used to do the best job. You won't get Mo inside nothing Unisex.'

The engineer had lost him again. Alvarez opened a shutter and stared out at the only reality he had left. Strutting with bedraggled feathers across the damp leaves on the autumn lawn three peacocks and two peahens made their way through Holland Park's early-morning mist. Just as Alvarez made to return to his problem one of the peacocks uttered a honk of self-pity. The others neither replied nor gave it the attention it so plainly demanded. They disappeared into the rhododendron bushes. Observed only by Alvarez the peacock spread its tail. Alvarez closed the shutter. There had not been a glint of luminosity in the entire display; it had become merely a dusty fan.

Mo flexed the muscles of his left forearm.

'Fit.'

2

The Problem of Turkey

Between May 10th and May 30th one thousand two hundred of the most prominent Armenians and other Christians, denied confession, were seized in Diyarbekir and Mamouret-al-Aziz vilayets. It was said they would be taken to Mosul, but nothing further was heard of them. On May 30th six hundred and seventy four of these were placed in 13 Tigris barges on pretence of being taken to Mosul. The local governor's aide-de-camp, with fifty civil guardsmen, had responsibility for the convoy. Half the guards went onto the barges while the others rode on the bank. Shortly after the beginning of this journey the prisoners were forced to part with first their money (some £6,000 T.) and then their clothing. Next the prisoners were thrown in the river. The guards on the bank were ordered to let none escape. The clothing was sold in the Diyarbekir market.

Sonnenaufgang, Berlin, October 1915

Una Persson emerged from the sea shaking and refreshed. Her green wetsuit blended with the great ferns making her body almost invisible. 'How were things in Mandalay?'

'Dim.' Jerry sulked in his deckchair, pettish lips around a rainbow straw, his thin body unsunned and scarcely wholesome, as if exposure to light were actually draining it of colour. He scratched his chest. 'I made quite a good innings.'

Her smile attempted belief. 'What made you look me up?'

He giggled. 'I was hoping to find stable facilities.'

Her lovely hand presented the prehistoric landscape. 'This hardly ever changes.' The blue sluggish water and the high ferns, the beach of white shells, offered picture-book simplicity. 'I come here every year, given half a chance.'

'It would suit me.' Jerry eased one narrow buttock against the canvas. 'On a regular basis. A few slots and dippers would help it.' He stared blankly out, imagining how Frank, his brother, would have exploited the possibilities.

Una lit a Sherman's. There was some kind of faint, glittering mould on the white paper. Nobody with hay fever could tolerate this age for more than a few minutes at a time. 'And how's that friend of yours?'

'Mo?'

'Miss Brunner.'

'She's over the moon. She just found out about the nuclear winter.'

'I always said most of her problem was environmental.' Una coughed lightly and took a few sips of iced tea. 'Where do you go from here, Jerry?'

He nodded. 'Exactly.'

'You can't stay.' She was firm. 'I'm expecting company.'

He became self-pitying. 'What's she got that I haven't?'

'Charm.' Una put out her cigarette. 'And she can shimmy better. Shouldn't you be pulling yourself together?'

His grin was sickly. 'It's the "together" bit that always defeats me.' He rose slowly from the rainbow canvas. 'Give Catherine my love.'

'She's always had it, hasn't she?' Una softened. 'Or what you call love. You're getting feeble again. I had some hope of you in the sixties. Even the early seventies.'

'Well, I can still make it then, can't I?' His awkward attempt at machismo was awful. 'I think I'll hit Prague next.'

'Leave it out, Jerry. Instant gratification will be the death of you. Try growing up.'

'But I don't want to be a might-have-been.'

'Et tu Brut.' For a brief while they had shared a sentimental attachment to Barry.

He grew resentful. 'It isn't fair. I've been thrown out of the male conspiracy and left out of the female one.'

'Whose fault is that? You had more chances than most. When was the last time you made a decision on genuine moral grounds?'

'Morality explains expediency. I never bought it.'

'There's little else left, Jerry.'

He shrugged. 'I don't know which way the bloody wind's blowing now. I'm off then.'

'I didn't say you have to leave immediately.'

'It's okay. I've been disappointed in my expectation.' He stared about him as he picked up his antique finery, his collection of defunct weaponry and armour. He motioned with a purple bell-bottom. 'You can keep your sodding Palaeozoic.'

'Mesozoic.'

'The past's all one to me.' His braggadocio sounded foolish to his own ears. 'I may not know what's moral, Una, but I know what's fair.' His lip began to tremble. Then his whole body shook.

She was concerned. 'You look ghastly. What's up?'

'I can't seem to hold the energy.' He sat down again. 'Like a battery that won't recharge. I suppose it's exhaustion.'

'Drugs. You overdid it in the sixties. Since then you've been trying to live the same as you did then. How old are you now?'

He offered up a hollow, self-pitying laugh. 'Forty.'

She looked him over. 'It isn't entropy, Jerry, after all.'

'I know,' he said. 'It's Time. But isn't that the same? We learned to move about in it. We never beat it. When you realise that, you also realise you're bound to die. Really die, I mean. Not just fade away. A sense of mortality cramps your style. Well, it does mine. And it's hell on your judgement.' He climbed slowly to his feet and began to dress. 'I'm doing it all on durophet mostly. And I know for a fact Miss Brunner's got a whole case of benzedrine in her garage. But we soldier on, eh? Nomads of the bleeding time streams. Wandering jewels. Patching up chronology. Offering logic where none was ever needed or asked for.'

'You?' She was amused. 'Offering logic?'

'Of a sort, colonel. Someone has to be the servant of Chaos. Who better than Pierrot?'

'You'd better go and look for the moon.' She held out her hand. 'Congratulations. Forty! You must be about ready to make the great leap from adolescence to maturity.'

He took her hand, more it seemed for its warmth than its meaning. 'Oh, I made the leap all right. Unfortunately I fell somewhere in the middle. A gap between the steps. A hole in the stage. I'm always falling into something.' He bent to pick up a faded Mars bar wrapper. 'Hello! It must be a clue.' He looked expectantly into the primitive jungle as if he thought the owner might emerge.

'Don't jump to conclusions,' she said. She moved to kiss him but he had a flash of pride and stepped back into the Shifter before she could reach him.

Suddenly miserable, she watched his pathetic atoms flicker and disappear. Then she collected herself. 'It doesn't do to get emotional,' she said. 'I think.'

3

Wee Willie Winkie

At about 11pm, several hours after fences were shaken down and gates blockaded, 16 women got inside the perimeter fence and began cutting their way through a second barbed wire barricade. They were aiming for the missile silos near the Green gate. Soldiers then rushed towards the women, 'they were raving, kicking and shouting abuse,' said one of the 16 women this week. 'They rounded us up and made a little cage round us of barbed wire. One of the women was taken to a little hut 15 or 20 metres away. They were laying into her, kicking and shouting. By the time the police came the hole we'd got through in the fence had been blocked up with barbed wire. We were all standing cramped into the wire which cut through into some women's bodies. One of the soldiers had been staring at us very coldly. Suddenly he got his thing out, yanked it, and ejaculated immediately.'

City Limits, 10 February, 1984

Jerry had failed to reach the present. Prague looked too glossy to be post-war. He stood uncertainly in the dawn shadows of Neruda Street remembering a time in 1968 when he would pass through briefly as witness to the death of yet another reasonable dream. He headed away from the castle and down towards Malostronska Square, hoping to find the Old Town Bridge where he might get his bearings. The proliferation of ageing Gothic and overwrought Baroque was confusing him, as if he had found himself trapped in a Bach fugue. But he made it to the tram stop and caught a Number 17, full of workers in stale jackets and stained moleskins on their way to the ceramics factories on the other side of town. He had forgotten how much fussy old stone there was in Prague. He had, by the time he got off the tram, begun to brood on his conversation with Mrs Persson. 'I was androgynous before I was political.' He spoke aloud, doubtfully. 'Or, anyway, both together. I've been re-identified. Fuck their rotten poles.'

He was at last able to see the Lobkowitz Palace, a relatively clean-cut building with its curved wings veering on what was to him a far more comforting neo-classicism (though not without its share of urns and draperies). The eighteenth century of Mozart and Steele was, he romantically believed, his spiritual home. He remembered a time when you could choose what sex or race you wanted to represent and change when you felt like it. Now everything had hardened up again. It was the result of disappointed plans, he supposed. Almost everything like that was. He pulled the rope. From deep inside the Prinz's citadel came the clear echoes of a bell, but it was a while before a servant, apparently a Russian Jew, with reflective brown eyes and dark, fleshy good looks, arrived to ask him his business. The Jew was in his late thirties. You could read anything you liked in his eyes. Jerry wondered why he was wearing a Cossack uniform. He was familiar with the Brigade of St Basil. When he gave his name the servant seemed startled, but immediately unlocked the gate and admitted him. They crossed a short drive to the entrance hall where Jerry waited, staring up at the elaborate dome and arches of the ceiling. They seemed to be decorated with angels and various fruits. He frowned. He thought he remembered the Rape of the Sabine Women.

When Prinz Lobkowitz arrived he was smiling with pleasure. 'My dear old friend! How good to see you again in these moderately happy circumstances. You're pale. Have you been ill?'

'Just the end of an era.' Jerry was anxious to reassure him. 'Nothing serious.'

'Well, I suppose we're all a bit run-down. What are you doing in 1938?'

'Drifting. Or so it seems.'

'At loose ends, eh?' The diplomat waved a parchment hand towards Prague. 'I'm afraid I've done everything that needs to be done here. The race is lost.'

'And the Teutons?'

'On their way in again, it seems.'

'I forget what happens next.' Jerry spoke to himself.

'The usual.' Lobkowitz drew him through halls filled with heavy oils. 'When were you last in Bangladesh?'

'I'm not with you.'

Lobkowitz paused, looking from the shadows through a window into a lush, terraced garden crowded with greenery. 'Peasants, land, cities. The power élite is always by nature a combination of the most brutal and unimaginative elements in its society. That's why all this natural history, anthropology – what will they call it? Reductionism? – is both right and horribly wrong. Darwinism doesn't have a lot to do with moral order.'

'I thought Kropotkin was a naturalist.'

'Oh, no, he was always impeccably turned out. Something of a dandy, indeed. His subject was geography, you see.'

Jerry could not be sure what was going wrong with the conversation. It was possibly a semantic problem. Or things were slipping a bit, like loose or worn cogs. The outlines of the walls were indistinct. He blinked and tried to focus. 'Masters…' Sometimes he found it hard to see where these aristocratic anarchists were going. 'I know where you're coming from.' He had a vision of surf, a lonely mock Spanish castle on a hill where zebra and giraffe played. He wished he could get back to it.

'You must be freezing,' said Lobkowitz. 'Come, there's heat in the library.'

'I thought it was me.' He wondered why he had believed it to be summer. He could see, perfectly well, the remains of snow on distant roofs.

Walled by books, leather panels and old oak, they sat in high-backed chairs beside the fire. 'I've finished my history of Bohemian literature,' said Lobkowitz. 'The major work, of course, was on the nineteenth century. But it is the twentieth which shall provide the substantial stuff, I think. Much, of course, is still in German, like Kafka. Authors seek the largest and most profitable audience available to them. Eventually, everything may be in English. Would that be good or bad, I wonder?' He folded his long hands over the flames and stretched his arms. When he next looked directly at Jerry it was with kind-hearted concern. 'You're worn out. You've lost your bearings. What can I do for you?'

'I don't suppose there's anyone in Prague could help me get a fix?'

'Not yet. Not at present. This was once, you know, the Capital of Alchemy.' Lobkowitz glanced at the perpetual calendar set in the black marble clock on the mantel. 'All the most positive work was done in Prague. And much nonsense, too, naturally. I wouldn't advise you to wait here. Can't you get to a Time Centre?'

'They're closing down.'

'All of them?'

'There were some branches off Holland Park. We're drawing blanks. More every day. It's as if Time's run out. We can't tap in to any alternatives.'

'There are so many!'

'All gone. But maybe I've just forgotten the co-ordinates. My brother's dead.'

'I'm sorry.'

'I think he is, too.'

'But your sister's fine, I'm sure.'

'She ought to be. She's got it easy –' Jerry was suddenly astonished at his own resentment. Maybe Una was right. Not only was mortality catching up with him. He was also turning into a man.

He glared with alarm at those parts of his body visible to him. 'Bloody hell. What's the opposite of mutability?'

'Stagnation?' suggested the Prinz.

'Is that the same as death?'

4

Pierrot and Israeli Army Beat a Retreat

Then Pierrot appeared, in full Phalangist uniform, grinning from ear to ear, wearing the most fashionable sunglasses and speaking English to the Israelis with an accent that matured during his student days in Los Angeles. 'What's the problem?' he asked, as he walked over to Mr Shehayel and, quite incredibly, shook hands with him and smiled warmly.

It might have been high comedy had Pierrot's and Mr Shehayel's people not been cutting each other's throats – literally – in the Chouf mountains these past ten months. 'You heard what I said,' Mr Shehayel replied with some familiarity but not the slightest trace of hostility in his voice. 'You are bringing in reinforcements in these cars. We cannot let you through.'

Pierrot – the Phalange do not like surnames these days – tried his most winning smile. 'They are not reinforcements. They are just young men who have been on vacation and are going home.'

Mr Shehayel, who found this a likely story indeed, began to laugh. 'They are not,' he said bluntly. So we carried on standing there next to the Druze gunmen and the Israeli troops who were squinting down at this extraordinary scene from their half-tracks in the midday sun.

The Times, 3 August, 1983

'Mo's a victim of history, major. Well, of Time, any road.' Shakey Mo Collier smoothed at the beard and moustache, the oddly cut hair which, in his bizarre vanity, he thought would improve his looks. His muscular little body, also the result of concentrated effort rather than natural constitution, flexed itself almost to his surprise. 'Looks like the hand's healing up, though.' Of late he had come to refer to his limbs in this way. Increasingly he also spoke of himself in the third person. 'That's for Mo!' he would say, pointing to a coveted vehicle, or even 'Typical of Mo, eh?' He gave the Lake District a proprietorial once-over. Hundreds of feet below was the great spread of Derwent Water. 'This is Mo's cup of tea.'

Major Nye, in ragged fatigues, put dented brass binoculars to his pale blue eyes. The veins on his lean neck were so prominent they might have been stuck on his flesh for a joke. Mo's attention was caught by them. The old man, so anxious to do the right thing, so charitable to others, so fundamentally good-hearted, was a much better soldier than Mo, with his love of heavy hand weapons and spectacular delivery systems, could ever hope to be. Major Nye it appeared was not even slightly excited by violence. Mo was baffled.

They lay stretched in the bushes of a promontory overhanging the long cliff which fell in stages to the shores of the lake. Nearby one could hear the odd drip on the rocks of Lodore. It was a dry day, with occasional brilliant rays of sunshine piercing clouds to give the scene the exaggerated, apparently artificial, contrasts of a Victorian engraving. Below, on the unseen narrow road, a pack of wild dogs went by, whining and barking. 'Danes,' said Mo. A rhododendron leaf stuck itself to the sweat on his forehead. It was like a tribal mark.

Major Nye was studying the far shore of the lake. 'Those are our chaps.' They had their hands tied and were being pushed out of the woods into the shallows. The uniformed men, all Ghurkas, stood waist-deep in the water staring with hatred at their captors. The group of Australians had stuck Ghurka knives in their belts and were balancing the tiny hats on their huge blond heads. Armed with a collection of complicated French weapons in chrome and coloured plastic, the Australians disdained khaki and preferred what they called Cocktail Bar Camouflage (actually 'Cammies') the only common item of clothing being an Hawaiian shirt.

Mo accepted the glasses but returned them almost immediately.

He had seen the corpses of non-whites the Australians had left behind. 'On the other hand, Mo,' he told himself, 'the Ghurkas are no better.' Major Nye sat staring into the sky, listening to a peewit and the faint popping as the Australians finished their prisoners with explosive bullets and what they called 'missies': miniature guided missiles the French had used so effectively in their Alpine campaign during the war on the Swiss cantons in defence, they had said, of Catholic minorities.

'On the whole,' Major Nye remarked hopelessly, 'I think I prefer a jihad to genocide. At least where the parties can field similar strength. This sort of thing is so beastly unfair.'

'It doesn't do for Mo, major. He'd take the lot out with a handful of tacks.'

Major Nye turned, politely puzzled, and wiped earth from his eyes. 'Tax? Too late for civil measures now, I'd say. Or what? Drawing pins, Collier?'

'Tacticals, major. That would show the bastards what happens when they grab Shakey Mo Collier by the short and curlies. But it's too late to tell them now. We should have sent them back years ago!'

'The Pakistanis?' Major Nye was floundering.

'Of course not. They're on our side. I mean the bloody Anzacs and Canucks.'

'They think they're able to run things better. We've been telling them how vital they are for years. There wasn't much else to say. New blood, sort of thing. They were confident, too, like Texans. They knew they'd get support from Home. But God knows what they want from us. If it wasn't for their racialism I'd say they might as well have a crack at it. But there are some traditions not worth maintaining. It goes sour, doesn't it! We were all part of the same Empire once. Of course Amritsar wasn't the only incident. There were thousands of rotten injustices all over India. It would be wrong to forget that. But why perpetuate it?'

'It's easier to pick on the weak.' Mo saw no mystery. He added feelingly: 'Ask Mo Collier to tell you about it.' He threw a stone out towards the lake. 'Ka-boom! You could also ask him what's happened to bloody Mr Cornelius. He's let us all down.'

'Ask whom?' Major Nye emerged from his private world.

'Me,' said Mo and paused, sensing some discrepancy. 'Maybe it's the end of the world.'

'We'll know soon enough, old chap.

'They shouldn't have killed all those Armenians. It set a pattern.'

Major Nye returned to his reverie. 'There's a lie to be maintained, too. We're supposed to have struggled to achieve an enlightened future in the twentieth century. I doubt if things would be quite so bad if we at least admitted how we've gained nothing unless it's an extra level of self-deception. We're living in the Age of Hypocritical Barbarism. What could be worse?'

'Old Mo Collier could answer that one for you, major.' He passed familiar fingers down his left thigh. 'Mustn't complain. At least the tendon's on the mend.'

'I wonder what has actually happened to young Cornelius. He's frequently late, but rarely fails to turn up.'

'Maybe he's changed sides. People do when they pass forty. He looked funny the last time I saw him. All wrapped up in one of them silly foil space-blankets and going on about big tits. He was never a tit man.' Mo proudly recalled the old days. 'He was never a man, really. Not in that sense. Still, Mo's told nothing, is he?'

'Isn't he?' Major Nye toyed with the field glasses.

'He ain't.' He got up and leaned against a birch, lighting a fag-end. 'Maybe there's nothing for us. Maybe we've run out of everything.' He sniffed, remembering the doctor's surgery he had seen in Kirkby Lonsdale on the way up. With a bit of luck it would still be there when they retreated. 'Have you noticed how the granite's flaking?'

'Everything rots in this climate.' The major opened a metal map-case and withdrew a piece of stale Stilton, a miniature of Cockburn's Port. 'Can I tempt you, Collier?'

'Someone might tell old Mo what we're supposed to be looking for up here.' He waved away the feast.

'Intelligence.' Major Nye broke the seal off the port.

'A bit bloody vague, that.'

'Vague? Quite.'

'What do we tell 'em if we ever join up with the unit again? That Australians are slaughtering darkies wherever they find 'em. It's a farce, major.'

'Seems a bit of one, I agree.' He returned to his earlier line. 'Still, what isn't based on injustice of one form or another?'

'Mo knows.' A finger on the side of his nose.

Nye had not expected a reply.

'But he'd never tell.' Mo blinked. 'Sod this, the world's going barmy. Or is it me?'

A blundering form, virtually shapeless, came crashing through the undergrowth towards them. It wore at least two balaclava helmets, several sweaters, a couple of pairs of trousers and fisherman's waders. Over all this it had a green see-through cycling cape. Its voice was muffled.

'Sorry, old chap. I didn't catch that.' The major peered at the bundle's interior. 'Is it Cornelius?'

There came a stifled affirmative.

'What's up, then? Feeling the cold?' Major Nye was unnaturally bluff.

'It's over,' said the figure, gesticulating with heavy, much-gloved hands. 'All over.'

'The Civil War?'

'The lot.'

'I don't get it, old boy.'

But Mo Collier was collecting his kit, thinking of Kirkby Lonsdale. 'You will, major. You will.'

The figure mumbled complainingly and sat down on an empty ammunition chest.

'Do what?' Mo flicked at a Zippo he had just found. The bundle glowered through the holes in its balaclava, saying slowly and distinctly: 'Stage Two Limited Strike.'

'Then Europe's a write-off. How do we get out of this one, Mr C?'

His friend rambled on, with Mo listening carefully. Major Nye began to loosen the guy ropes of their small tent, somehow treating their conference as a private matter and doing his best to keep his distance. At length he saw the little man straighten up, stretching his arms on both sides of his body, flexing his fingers.

'Speak for yourself, mate. Mo's not the kind to sit anything out.' His face, however, contained a peculiar mixture of bafflement and blind aggression.

Seeing the look of surprise on Nye's face, Mo added: 'It's to do with integrity.' As if he had accidentally revealed some profound personal secret he let his face relax for a second into lines of utter terror.

5

UK Gets Six Hong Kongs

Britain is to get six free ports – 'mini Hong Kongs' – where firms can import, process and export raw goods duty free. They will be Belfast, Birmingham, Cardiff, Liverpool, Prestwich and Southampton.

The Sun, 3 February, 1984

Jerry shuffled into the bathing hut looking like a child's inept Guy or some badly stuffed home-made animal.

'Penny for your thoughts.' His voice was bland and distant. 'It's a zoo on the beach today. I suppose they reckon it's their last chance of a holiday before the holocaust.' The sound following this statement indicated agony or amusement.

Miss Brunner was not pleased to see him. 'I don't know why people of your type come to Jersey.'

'To avoid the tacks.' This time the accompanying sound had to be laughter. Only Jerry laughed louder than Mo at his own puns. He was clearly unaware of his lack of originality. 'Anyway, what's all this?' He indicated the row of old slot machines lining one wooden wall. 'It's like a cargo-cult Time Centre.' She had covered the existing decals and numbers with peculiar signs of her own, some of them apparently drawn from alchemy.

'It's beyond electronics, this. My calculations require something subtler than your home Apple. Something more in touch with the Earth.'

'Witchcraft.' He picked a piece of lint from his lips.

'I call it Female Science. As valid as Masculine Science – even compatible. But never acknowledged by the male orthodoxy.'

'It's amazing what use you can put a perfectly good political argument to.' He spoke more clearly since he had eased up the balaclava a little.

Miss Brunner was inexpertly pulling a chicken to pieces. 'This isn't necessarily going to be a bad thing after all.' She nodded to herself, full of enthusiasm, humming.

'What's not going to be so bad?'

'Nuclear war.' She turned, beaming. 'It's a blessing in disguise.'

'That's what I call making the best of things.' Jerry began shambling back to the door. 'Nil desperandum, Miss B. Better wrap up warm. I'm going North. You know where you are in the Arctic Circle.'

'It didn't do you much good last time.'

'More than it did you. Some marriages simply never work out.'

'I blame the genetic code. You're a fool, Mr Cornelius. My figures are immaculate.'

'It's the conception that's bothering me. Where did you pick up this bag of tricks?' Warmer, he grew more coherent, at least on some levels. His smell, however, reminded her of a neglected refrigerator.

'The man was very well dressed,' she said defensively. 'From Lagos. A physicist down on his luck, trying to get back home. It was all he had to sell, his thesis.'

'There are at least two hundred people in Portobello Road most days of the week selling either a Unified Field Theory or a map to the World Below. All with a convincing story, too. I used to do it myself.'

'This isn't what you'd expect,' she said.

Nothing now would be allowed to threaten her rationalisation. She, like the rest of them, was protecting the dream. Reality was beyond salvation. Surely this was the time to show tolerance. He folded lumpy arms and waited to listen.

But his movement distracted her. She became wary. 'That's not leprosy, is it? Or radiation, you know, stuff?'

'I don't get premature infections much. Or do I?' She had given him food for thought. He reassured her, however. 'I'm sound. Though I can't speak for the vision.'

'Well, so long as it isn't catching.'

He was upset. 'It might be. Could be a new style.'

'Don't you ever get sick of your fads?'

He refused her an answer. The question was ridiculous. 'Why are you talking about me all of a sudden?'

'You can't be too careful.'

The door creaked. In came Bishop Beesley. His massive bulk, black and purple, reached a sudden quivering halt when he observed Jerry. He took a fastidious step to one side. 'What's this?'

He stared in astonishment at the bundled-up creature as it picked through its layers of clothing to hand him at last an old Mars wrapper. 'Really!' He refused the offering and it dropped to the bare planks.

'They're funny about litter in the Mesozoic,' said Jerry. 'Though I must admit I can't see why they're bothering now.

'Perfectly understandable, I'm sure. Good afternoon, Mr Cornelius. But it is not, you see, my litter.' From his cassock he pulled a plastic bag full of neatly folded sweet wrappers. 'There's an offer on at present. It would not do to waste one.'

'What do you get?'

'First prize is a fortnight in the Alps at the new Mars plant, including all you can eat while there and all you can carry away in your arms. It's for two, moreover. So Mitzi will be able to help me.'

'Aren't the Alps restricted to VIPs now?'

'That's the beauty of it. A safe view of doomsday if we make the right contacts. There isn't a mountain left which hasn't been turned into luxury shelter complexes. Free air and parking. Security guards. Well, at any rate, it's worth trying for. And how's yourself?'

'Can't seem to get rid of this cold.'

'I have some excellent heroin, guaranteed to stop the snuffles and banish the blues.'

'I'll take the blues any time.'

'I don't approve of stimulants, as you're aware.' Unhurriedly he carefully peeled a 3 Musketeers. He had evidently been abroad recently. Noticing Jerry's eyes on the bar he motioned with it. 'Florida. Perhaps you should go to Miami?'

'There's a limit even to my pain, bishop. Where's Mitzi now?'

'I left her on the yacht. We're going to Torbay for a couple of days. Meanwhile don't hesitate to pull alongside whenever the spirit moves you.'

'Miss Brunner was about to explain how it's okay about World War Four.'

'These figures conclusively prove that the nuclear winter will set in almost instantaneously. That means the majority of the healthy and suitable survivors – say ten percent of the population, and who, after all, needs more? – will be frozen in their tracks, as it were. It's what we've been looking for, the bishop and I. A means of stopping the whole thing until we have a sane and ordered world again, where death and uncertainty are banished for good. There'll be work to do, of course, but we won't shirk that. This simplifies everything.'

Jerry was amazed: 'Yeah?'

'Wonderful! Nuclear bombs mean eternal life!' The bishop was ever one for the snappy slogan. They had got him where he was.

'Can't you see, Mr Cornelius?' Her expression was serene. 'It's the Cryogenic Winter we've all been waiting for. Everything will be held in Time until we choose to thaw it out!'

'I hope your professor made it back to Lagos.' Jerry could not disguise his disgust. He was surprised to be experiencing it. He had thought it lost for ever. It was not necessarily cause for celebration. He feared he was witnessing the return of sorrow and he could do without that at present. He walked out onto St Peter Port's unremarkable sands, taking particular note of the palm trees along the promenade. The only incongruous feature of the scene was himself. But he was too old to start looking for a thermal Pierrot suit.

He shuffled up the steps from beach to town. Children sniffed loudly as he passed and their parents said hurriedly: 'Now don't give him anything.'

It was as if Australia had fought the whole war simply to preserve this. Jerry was quite happy as a vagrant. He could not get over the idea that since he had reached forty all this end-of-the-world stuff had started to obsess him. Could it have something to do with transference? How many other children of the sixties were imposing their own fear of impending death on the planet at large? And how many had the power either to stop WWIV or, indeed, to start it? What sort of explanation was that? He suspected it was as desperate at Miss Brunner's discovery of a silver lining in the nuclear cloud. If his own body would stop malfunctioning he knew he'd feel all right. Why start worrying now? Nuclear wipe-out had always struck him as comic: the final punchline of the human farce. Did we deserve any better?

'Serves us bloody well right.' He spoke to a seagull which eyed him as if he might actually be a potentially tasty piece of offal. 'And you, mate. The triumph of the beast. The conquest of reason. The consequences of debased romanticism. Ragnarok. Chaos and Old Night. Fimbulwinter, by Christ. Well, it's neat enough.' He went back to the Salvation Army hostel where he had a cubicle and began checking schedules. He could be in Kiruna by tomorrow and hit the main tundra beyond Kvikjokk by the day after that. All he had to worry about was that Catherine would be there with the dog team.

6

No, No, Senor!

Argentine President Alfonsia suggests that the UN should send a peace keeping force to the Falklands.

Why?

There IS peace in the islands. It will stay that way if the Argentines abandon their aggressive designs.

Their new democratic president must accept that, having expelled one pack of foreigners by force, we are certainly not going to allow in another pack by the side-door.

The Sun, 3 February, 1984

Major Nye had made it to the Time Centre. He was disapproving when he noticed that someone, presumably Sergeant Alvarez, had pasted pin-ups of a particularly crude and grotesque nature over about half the monitor screens. 'What's this?'

Alvarez plucked at his greying beard as he swivelled in his chair to greet the major. His belly had grown. 'I'm afraid I went a bit crazy after all the screens had whited out. You know how I feel about cynicism. It's a disease. I had a dose…'

Irritated by Alvarez's small melodrama, Major Nye crossed to the central console. Everything was at zero. 'Good heavens.'

'Where's Collier?' asked the sergeant.

'The poor chap broke up. The stress of inactivity is my guess. Bit of a duodenal. You know how he likes to keep busy.'

'He's spent most of his life looking forward to the Big Bang. Maybe the actuality's too much for him.'

'We can't afford to think in terms of actuality, Sergeant Alvarez. It's still "possibility" when you're at the Time Centre.'

'Not according to these.' His hand swept to indicate his

impotent monitors. 'When there's no input there's nothing for them to show.'

'We must consider human error.'

'Isn't it a bit late for that, major? We've been leading up to this throughout the century. First the Turks in 1915, then Stalin, then the Germans and finally everyone wants a go at genocide. Since World War Two it looks as if there's been a real struggle between various powers looking for someone they can wipe off the face of the Earth. What do we call that but Armageddon?'

Nye could see the man was growing hysterical. 'The logic's been crude all along. The model's too simple. Surely you can come up with a couple of alternatives?'

'Every single observation is apocalyptical, major. They all amount to the same thing. Stopped Time, if you like. Sounds pleasantly abstract, eh? Frozen space. Or how about *kaput*?'

'Really, sergeant! This isn't the right moment for despair. Didn't Cornelius's father design the prototypes for most of our instruments? Perhaps Cornelius can come up with something?'

'His relationship with hardware is entirely romantic. Honestly, major, there's nothing we can do. If we'd wanted control we should have gone for it in the first place. But equilibrium's another matter. We've got it, all right. Don't they call it the equilibrium of death? Bloody liberal nonsense.'

As Alvarez grew steadily more rhetorical Major Nye's expression became sterner. He began to whistle snatches of 'When I'm Cleaning Windows' and 'A Little of What You Fancy Does You Good'. He was useless with electronics. And some of this stuff was not even that, but a more advanced system altogether, connected, he believed, with the sun and the motions of the planets. Mrs Persson, with her sophisticated understanding, had once sardonically referred to it as astrologistical. He looked at the screens still energised but blank. How could every possible alternative show an identical result? He refused to take so fatalistic a view of history or human nature. Somewhere, surely, a little reason had saved the day?

'Could anyone have bugged our instruments?'

'They're not computers, major. Not primarily. They present straightforward facts. What they see is what there is.'

'They make projections, too.'

'Naturally. That's what we're looking at now, after all.' Alvarez seemed to be taking pleasure in the doom of all possible worlds.

'Well,' Major Nye's voice was artificially calm, 'how do they receive the facts?'

Alvarez resisted hope. He had grown too morbid. It was what he was used to now. 'It's very clever stuff. My main job is to operate the consoles, not understand anything about the equipment. That's an engineer's job.'

'There must be someone who services it? Who understands it. I recall a Captain Maxwell. He was an engineer.'

'Killed accidentally by the Australians. He was trying some ridiculous SAS trick and had blacked up. Besides, I don't think he was that kind of engineer. Mo Collier claims certain skill, but it's plainly instinct and luck. He couldn't do anything radical to save his life. Catherine Cornelius was going off somewhere when I phoned. She said her abilities to make the subtler adjustments had probably been implanted by deep hypnosis before her father's death – or disappearance. Or Frank was responsible. She couldn't be sure. Frank certainly had a grasp of it, but he's dead, too. Jerry claims that his entire memory for technological facts was wiped out as a result of some trauma apparently involving a child. Mrs Persson seems the most consciously competent, but she wouldn't answer her beeper and now the sender isn't working. Battery's gone. Emergency generator's going. Miss Brunner hates the lot of it. Over-complicated in her view. She's of an earlier, mechanical age, I suppose. Babbage and batwing school. She's never been happy here, really.'

'She had disappointed expectations some years ago. Her own experiments in the field produced a lot of spectacular initial effects but in the main fizzled out. Damned upsetting for her, of course. I heard she was too impatient for results. Something wrong with the bases of her equations. Also she was working from someone else's research, wasn't she?'

'Old Man Cornelius's. My guess is she really thought she had the secret of the philosopher's stone in his microfilm. She's altered her ideas, if not her ambitions and attitudes, quite a bit since then. Who else?' Alvarez attempted to rally, but his heart was hardly in it. 'Mr Jagger? He's impossible to contact these days. Una could often find him. But she's doubtless buried herself in the distant past, sucking tits in some Arcadia or other…'

Major Nye was taken aback. 'I say!'

Alvarez, too, was puzzled by the remark. He had never said anything of the kind in his life. 'It's like being possessed.' He shivered.

'Can the past survive an absence of Future?' Major Nye hastily wondered.

'Beats me. I didn't mean to sound shitty about Mrs Persson. It's not like her to cop out in a crisis.'

'We must therefore assume there is no crisis. She must have a good reason for doing what she's opted for.'

Alvarez was frowning. 'Of course! What happens to all those cancelled futures? Do you know, major, I think you might have struck a clue. There's something fishy…'

'You mean we could really have been nobbled?'

'None of this is logical. Yet I was assuming a failure on our part to understand a higher logic – or at least a failure to provide an appropriate ontology.' He glared helplessly at his screens and dials. 'But there's still nothing I can do.'

'It even occurs to me, old chap, that if we have indeed been nobbled, someone has a big reason for doing it. Could we all be contributing, unknowingly, to that person's desired conclusion?'

'God in Heaven! I see what you mean. It's got to be that consortium of reactionaries. Or what's left of them. Von Krupp, Brunner, Beesley and the rest. Devil dentist!'

This was meaningless to the major.

'They could easily have got what they wanted out of Frank before he died,' Alvarez continued. 'He was always willing to work for them if he could do Jerry down.'

'It's only a theory.' Major Nye felt he had inspired too much hope in the sergeant. The man's moods were becoming disturbingly volatile. 'And I can't see we've any means of testing it.'

'Where's Catherine?'

'Helping her brother on his North Pole expedition. It looks like they're going to ground. Possibly looking for the Hollow World, too. Panic will do that, eh?'

Alvarez was descending. 'This one won't blow over. Not according to the readings. That's why he's gone. But what, with his hypothermia problems, made him go there?'

'Magical theory? Like curing like?' Major Nye had only the faintest grasp of such ideas. 'Homeopathy kind of business?'

'He knows something we don't. Cunning little shit.'

'Honestly, sergeant, it could be nothing more than animal instinct. A response to his own fear of death. He said as much.'

'Then we're stymied anyway. There's the mother, I suppose.' Alvarez hated Mrs Cornelius.

'I'm afraid she passed on.'

Alvarez raised an unsympathetic eyebrow. 'She had a man friend. Also some sort of scientist.'

'Pyat was an odd character. Emotionally, I suspect, in the mechanistic and reductionist camp. But I believe he died recently, too. Funny old chap. I met him in Constantinople years ago. Didn't see him again for an age.'

Alvarez stared at the silent instruments. 'So what do we do? Shut down?'

Major Nye sucked in his frail lips. 'We need something more positive. We need to prove there are options still available. We must refuse the logic of despair.'

'We'll never do it like this. I've tried everything. All I can pick up are fragments of the past, just a little of the present. Save for this specific zone. And even that's getting fainter all the time. It's as if someone has wiped an equation, or maybe removed a master component. No-one has ever really bothered to understand how the Centre works.' He hesitated, evidently feeling a return of his anxiety. 'Now I'm repeating myself. I hate loops. Even small, personal ones.'

'Sometimes,' said Major Nye, 'I can't help thinking that a Chinese might be of great help.' He brightened, for he had remembered Professor Hira. 'Much as I hate the thought of breaking the law, I'm afraid we might have to liberate someone from the Putney Common camp.'

'That's Pakistanis.'

'The authorities haven't made any distinction. Anyone from the sub-continent goes there. He's a Brahmin, actually. Someone who can think Hindu on a high level. I believe he is probably our only chance.'

'There aren't enough of us left to get him out. And he could easily be dead by now. The Australians have taken to calling them Long Roo. You know what that means.'

'I don't keep pets, luckily. Not since my horse died. Were you ever in India, Alvarez?'

'Not my cup of tea, major. The climate, the poverty, the perpetual social inequality.'

'To an observer the variety frequently makes up for a lot. We did our best. But, of course, we never had any business there after 1920. You could say sooner. From the time Ghandi returned from South Africa. A bad show all round. Now look what's happened to Afghanistan. I've fought those Pathans, too. I don't approve of the Russians, but I don't envy them, either.' He grew gloomy. 'Still, I think the phase of little, simple wars is over. World War Three must have been a disappointment to some people.'

'What if we can't liberate Hira?'

Major Nye collected himself. His face remained dreamy. 'I suppose I'd better check on all that. I still have a few Ministry contacts.'

Alvarez began to sweat. 'Didn't you say something about a Chinaman?'

Major Nye was superficially jaunty. 'Hira's even better. We speak the same language.'

'There's some rôle confusion here.' Sergeant Alvarez tapped his panels. 'We might be making a Great Leap Sideways.'

Major Nye had already picked up a phone. 'Are there any others? This one's dead.'

Alvarez shook his head. He grew doubtful about the old soldier's credibility. Physically, he even looked a bit like Don Quixote.

'Where's the nearest box?'

'Fox?' Alvarez tugged anxiously at his beard. 'Fox?'

Major Nye was on his way. 'Hold the fort, old chap. It's the last Charge of the Old Brigade!'

Alvarez collapsed against his lewd collage. 'The poor bugger's gone over the top.'

7

Alley Oops! French Give Boy George le Sex Test

... Boy George became Girl Geisha yesterday and had baffled French immigration men arguing over his sex. The culture clash came when George, dolled up as a Japanese handmaiden with a real-life oriental Miss in tow, landed at Nice airport. Officials did a double-take when they saw that the bizarre 'femme' had a passport in the name of an 'homme' – George O'Dowd. Culture Club's chameleon singer and his Japanese dancer friend were held up for three hours while the hopping mad Frogs decided whether to let them in.

The Sun, 3 February, 1984

'Not another Dance of Death, surely.' Miss Brunner peered from her hut into the rain. Along the beach, hand in hand, a group of teenagers in loose black overcoats were skipping and whooping. She was incapable of analysing their behaviour. She darted back and shut the door, returning to the security of her discoveries, her Eternal Life. Bishop Beesley's face peered from a mass of pink candyfloss. Beads of red sugar mingled with his sweat, so that he appeared to be suffering from some exotic disease. 'Are they after us?'

She was growing tired of his terrors. 'Of course not. We'll see to that.'

'I've no business being here, you know. How could Mitzi have sailed without me?'

'One can only think she misheard your orders. Bishop, nobody's betrayed you. At least, that's not the most obvious explanation.' She picked up the knuckle-bones of an ape, rattling them in her cupped hands.

'Cornelius is up to something.'

'He's up to nothing at present. He's on the run. Isn't it obvious? Looking for an entrance to the Inner World he never knew. That's my guess. Why should he succeed where everyone else has failed? We'll simply build better bunkers. We're in the strongest possible position.' She flipped a trigger and watched the steel ball roll round the broken circuit before dropping into a cup marked WIN. She had changed the lettering so that only one of the seven cups was now marked LOSE. 'There, you see. Have you written out your suggested selections yet?'

'I forgot the third category. There was Race and Colour, I know.' He put his hand on a sticky piece of quarto.

'It's the types we have to consider next. I think we should set sentiment aside and go entirely for white, don't you?'

'That's taken for granted.' He was making an effort but he remained horribly pathetic. She would have to write him off at this rate. 'Shall I just put down Anglo-Saxon?'

'I think it's open to some misinterpretation. What about "non-hybrid" for the moment. We don't want to create loopholes. On the other hand we can't be too rigid. Now let's consider Africa, shall we? According to the new chart we can expect a ninety per cent success rate.'

But he was immersed in his sweets again. From somewhere he had acquired an entire box of Torquay Rock.

She shrugged and unrolled a fresh map. 'You shouldn't let the zeitgeist get to you, bishop. After all, it might only be a simulation.'

His eyes were glazing. His red mouth was rounded about a huge pink stick. All he could do was nod.

8

White Heat

Fire engines raced to the White House in Washington yesterday after alarms were set off by smouldering wires in the basement.

The Sun, 3 February, 1984

Jerry and Catherine were on top of the world.

'It's nice to see you so cheerful again.' She took a small bite of hot duff. 'It's lovely here, isn't it?'

'Unspoiled.' Jerry stretched his relaxed body beneath the bloody rays of the midnight sun. 'Do you remember when Dad used to bring us here?'

'I'm too young.'

'I wouldn't say that.' He yawned and picked up one of his old copies of *Rainbow*. Tiger Tim and the Bruin Boys were at the seaside, making an elaborate sandcastle with buckets and spades. 'There was never any barbed wire on their beaches. Let's hope life begins at forty. It isn't easy, Cath, being a shadow of your former self.'

'Well, it's done you good, and that's the main thing.' Every day she sounded more like her mother. Mildly, she contemplated the plain of ice from horizon to shining horizon. 'Shouldn't we be getting back to the hotel?' Sky and ice were both pale blue, matching their eyes and the faint glow of their skins. When he had first appealed to her she had been suspicious. She knew he was jealous of Una and she had suspected a trick, but now she felt the sacrifice of her time had been worthwhile. Her own guess was that the deaths of Frank and their mother, coinciding roughly with his own sudden sense of mortality, affected him worse than he had realised. 'What will you do when you get home?'

'It might be an idea to look for a job. Not that anyone's interested in my skills.'

'You can handle a fairly complicated programme.'

'Nothing like the old days. But it's an idea. I could be an usherette. A posh one, I mean. At the National or somewhere like that.'

She felt sorry for him. It was almost a tragedy, this unadmitted loss of mutability. 'You could get any job you wanted.' She kissed his purple lips.

'I could do with some qualifications.' Gathering up his clothes and blankets he looked towards the Sno-Cat, yellow and black; then a silhouette against the huge sun.

'Too late for that.' Throwing pillows and hamper into the back she climbed up on the driving seat.

He began to dress as she started the engine. '$\frac{dg}{dt} = \lambda g(t)$ (when $\lambda = 0$),' he murmured uncertainly. '$g(t + \delta t) - g(t) = \lambda\delta t = g(t)$...'

'There!' She patted his woolly knee. 'You're feeling better already.'

9

Move to Patch It Up with Argies

Mrs Thatcher has made the first diplomatic move toward patching up Britain's relations with Argentina ... The British Government sent a message to Argentina last week suggesting how relations could be normalised – but no reply has been received yet ... Details of the ideas put forward have not been released.

The Sun, 3 February, 1984

Alvarez had passed from scepticism to resentment. The small Hindu, greyer and thinner since the horrors of Putney, pursed his lips and made a mental calculation. Alvarez said: 'Are you praying?'

'In a sense, old boy. A mixture, you'd say, of maths and mysticism. Faithful calculation, mm?'

Alvarez fell back in the face of this enthusiastic innocence. He stood with folded arms and watched Hira pull at another panel near the floor. The Brahmin crawled into the mass of conduits and wires and disappeared again.

'He's jolly brainy,' said Major Nye. 'And the only person I've ever met who came close to understanding the logical basis of old Cornelius's programmes.'

'Well, it all sounds like mumbo-jumbo to me. No better than Miss Brunner's nonsense.'

'I think the difference is in attitude. Faith, perhaps, as Professor Hira suggests. In oneself, rather than in the quest for power.'

'Well, I call it debased.'

'You're probably right in her case. Though,' Major Nye chuckled, 'she seems to be doing very well. The Australians trust her.'

Alvarez gave himself back to his old copies of *Forum* and *Libido*. He had not yet discovered an escape route, but he was sure he would find it in sex. One thing he was determined about: he would never return to the Catholic Church.

Meanwhile Major Nye replaced the headphones of his personal stereo over his ears and continued listening to radio bulletins relating to the coming crisis which everyone now regarded as inevitable. As yet, no missile had been fired. The race was as good as over. The runners lay exhausted in their millions, waiting for the relief of death. Between 1979 and 1984 something dreadful had happened to human morale. No amount of pep talk could rekindle the light of optimism. The world had given itself up to despair. It had even lost confidence in the power of its own greed.

Professor Hira re-emerged, covered in cobwebs, grinning. In his hand he held a circular object made of hair, straw and paper. 'A mouse's nest. Isn't it beautiful?'

'Could that be part of our problem?' Major Nye's voice was unnaturally loud.

'Oh, no, major. I think it's integral to one of the major functions. It must be a hundred years old at least. It's quite astonishing how much organic material was used. I suspect the symbolic structure will occur to me momentarily.' He beamed and carried the nest inside again.

'My God!' said Alvarez. He hunted frantically through his piles of *Bizarre*, *Rubber Fun*, *Spanking Times* and *Beastly Beauties*. Monstrous breasts and bondaged bottoms seemed to surround and engulf him. He felt his face being stifled by an enormous inner thigh bulging from vinyl knickers and he moaned once, falling heavily to the floor before his hand could reach his fly.

At the sound of the thump, Professor Hira re-emerged. 'That stuff will kill you, old chap, if you're not very careful.' He looked up at the major who was removing the headset. 'Could Miss B. have got at him in here?'

'Very possible. He's having trouble breathing.' Major Nye kneeled beside the sergeant. 'It's as if he's choking on something.'

Professor Hira glanced at the scattered magazines. 'It could be tangible evil.'

'Somebody will have to call a doctor.'

'But if it's a matter of possession…'

Alvarez opened his eyes. 'Please, not a priest.'

'Can you feel anything?'

'Not yet. I've been trying.'

Whistling Wagner, Hira returned to his maze.

Major Nye wondered if Alvarez would not have been better suited to the field. The staffing, he now realised, had been inadequate. Alvarez came round again. His pupils were tiny, his expression intense, yearning. 'Please! I can't get off.'

'Off?'

'Away. Out. It's not fair to leave me behind when you're all escaping.'

'Nonsense, nonsense. We're solving it, old son. Professor Hira's on the scent!'

Alvarez refused the frail hand and picked himself up. He swayed amongst the débris. 'I can't stand this. I need some C.'

'There's an excellent nursing home near Lyme Regis.'

'Why not?'

A screen on the top level, two from the left, came to life. Bright colours, clear geometrical shapes, something in Arabic. Then it was dead again.

'Voilà!' Major Nye tapped Alvarez on the arm. 'We've found a track.'

But Alvarez saw only danger, unreasoning hope. 'I'm going down to Torquay,' he said. 'She's there now, isn't she?' He began to stuff his porn into a worn leather attaché case.

Hira popped from a fresh hole. 'Please, Sergeant Alvarez, take that bag of samosas for the journey. They're vegetable. Very good!'

Alvarez gracelessly picked up the brown paper bag and added it to his cargo.

'Enjoy yourselves,' he said. 'Got a message for anyone down there?'

They stared at him in silence. He shrugged and left the Time Centre.

'It's madness,' said Hira. 'Has the chap gone to join the opposition?'

'If that's what it is, professor, I think so.'

Major Nye was surprised when Hira brightened. 'Excellent. Now we're establishing something like a balance.'

Major Nye reached wearily towards the floor and picked up a copy of *Restraints and Harness*. 'How extraordinary.' He had expected pictures of horses. Setting the magazine aside he craned to peer into the nearest cavity. Shadows curled like smoke. Mysterious lights seemed as distant as stars. There was a sense of extremes: weather, distances, time. Sounds reached his ears like the final echo of something far more substantial. He thought he heard water. 'How are you getting along, old chap?'

'I'm amazed, major, at the possibilities for manipulation which have been avoided here. It is sublime!'

'But are you any further forward?'

'That would depend a great deal on our definitions.' The Hindu giggled and was suddenly large as life under Nye's nose. But I'm pretty certain your guess was correct.'

'We've been nobbled, you mean?'

'Utterly, I'm afraid.'

The phone began to ring. Cautiously Major Nye placed the revived instrument against his ear.

After a while, he said: 'Torquay, I think.' He replaced the receiver. 'That was Mitzi Beesley. She's in the Atlantic. On her way from Annapolis where she's been recruiting new crew. She wondered where her father was. Well, at least you've got the phone working, old boy.'

10

Fantasy Manor

The Ultimate Sexual Fantasy starring Europe's No. 1 sex symbol ZETA, watch all your fantasies become reality.

Ad, Brightstar Adult Video Offers,
Daily Star, 3 February, 1984

Una Persson held up her black military coat and saw that the moths had eaten large holes in at least five places. This made her laugh. 'Well that'll have to be thrown away. What else is there?' She bent, naked, over the trunk Catherine and Jerry had picked up for her on their way back from the Pole. 'Did you have much trouble getting it out of him?'

'He charged us three pounds for storage.' Catherine was fascinated by the variety of clothing, all of it fouled and shredding now.

'Rags,' said Una.

'Experiential decay.' Jerry had not dared open his own boxes. As always, he admired her resolution. 'Goodbye, ladies. See you some time.'

'Where are you off to?'

'The government's sending me to Lan Tao Island. Administrative job in Hong Kong.'

'Isn't that where they keep the boatpeople?' Una dropped a mildewed Frye to the floor.

Jerry became cautious. 'Possibly.'

Catherine said: 'He needs security. But he also wanted to be socially useful. So the SS picked this out for him.'

'I thought they'd agreed to grant sovereignty to the Chinese.'

'His job will be unaffected.'

Jerry blinked. 'You're right, Una. A set-up.'

Catherine felt she had missed something. 'They said it was the best they could find. For someone his age. Good prospects.'

'Those bloody Australians!' Jerry rubbed hard at the side of his nose. 'And an old hand like me. What on earth's happening to my memory?'

'Self-induced senility, if you ask me.' Una hugged Catherine who by now was wondering if she had somehow betrayed her brother. 'You've still got a few choices open to you, Jerry.'

'They closed down the Time Centre,' he said. 'Hadn't you heard? Major Nye and Professor Hira are on the run. You need good contacts since Miss Brunner brought in her Prenuke Selection Programme. They've moved to Plymouth and taken over the Mecca Ballroom. Alvarez is working for her. Bishop Beesley's head of Gene Clearance. Mitzi's in charge of Ethnic Testing. They've a large Home Office budget.'

'I know,' said Una. 'And almost everyone else is wanted for questioning. Okay, maybe you should go to Hong Kong. I suppose you're lucky you're not in a camp.'

'Everybody's choosing sides.' Jerry was uncomfortable. 'What's happened to the individual?'

'Ask Plymouth.'

'How do you get so much news?' Catherine asked admiringly of her friend.

'I watch a lot of television.'

Jerry felt dimly that he was missing more than he was getting. He flexed his fingers. They were aching a little. Maybe he had the first twinges of arthritis. It would be as well to be out of the humid Mesozoic air. But where could he go? Death Valley sprang to mind.

'I think you can safely call it a write-off. Most of my own stuff was directly connected. Closing the Time Centre was Miss Brunner's greatest triumph. But I think she expects more of her new recruits than they can deliver. I'd hesitate before I'd employ disaffected radicals from the other side. Still, I suppose she deserves something for trying.' Una coughed suddenly. 'Spoors.' She moved away from her trunk.

'It's getting too sticky,' said Jerry. 'I used to have all these crutches.'

'You can't afford another cave-in.' Una pressed his cheek with her palm. He smelled exotic cream. 'You're better adapted than almost anyone to survive. Even now.'

'Who wants to survive Cryogenic Totalitarianism? What did happen to all those Armenians in 1915?'

'They were repatriated by the Turks. To the desert. Why are you worrying? What are you afraid of?'

'Becoming a minority.'

'You were, thank God, always that.'

He began to snarl. But it was self-imitation, without authority. His hand wandered to his cropped head, fell to touch the tweed of his jacket. 'What more can they do to me?'

'You're not even aware of what they've done already. They've reduced your options, destroyed your morale, robbed you of will and action. These are bleak times, Jerry. It suited them for you to be afraid. Just as it suited them to have everyone think it was the Bomb which was terrifying them. Actually the terror was more profound and immediate. It was the terror of knowing yourself to be entirely without even the power you possessed ten years ago.'

'Then we've all been nobbled?'

'Well nobbled. There was no way you could have won. It was a fixed event. That was why the Time Centre had to go. It was the only threat to their plot – for it still registered options. Miss Brunner and the rest will not allow alternatives. They have too much to control. Their investment is high and relentlessly linear. It's what passes for logic in troubled times. Most people will go for it like sheep through a gate.'

'Surely they won't put me on the dole?'

'Once you take the king's shilling, you follow the king's orders. That's the wonderful power of simple economics. It's not in their interest to have you rich again.'

'I thought I did it on my own.'

'Did what?'

'Everything, you know, that I used to do. That I achieved.'

'What was that?'

'Kept some openings available. And stuff. For everyone.'

'Your failure,' she said sadly, 'is obviously a failure of class.'

He was upset, shaking both his cuffs to show his white sleeves, the gold signet ring. 'What d'you mean? Class is my middle name.'

'They steered you wrong, Jerry.' She sighed. 'They were only after your energy. They don't need it now.'

'I can't fight them any more. I'm useless. I'm too old for it.'

'There's not much else open to you, Mr Cornelius.' She was firm. 'Unless you actually do want to die.'

He shuddered. He looked into her profound eyes. He saw the sole alternative there and it was unbearable.

'Not really.'

His expression was both pleading and apologetic. He seemed to be seeking her mercy. He had no clear notion as to why he responded as he did.

'Not yet.'

II

Shock for Maggie over Jobs

Britain's jobless jumped by 120,000 last month to just under 3.2 million … Ministers had been expecting the normal January increase of about 90,000.

The Sun, 3 February, 1984

The ghosts which had haunted his youth had given ground to a more commonplace sense of mortality. He had been born into an age in which manoeuvrability was apparently not only possible but encouraged. He liked to think he had manoeuvred with the best of them. Reality had been malleable, truth a question of individual definition. But at some point in the 1970s, around the time his mother had died, an attempt was made to restrict and contain possibility, to attack romance (in its fullest definition), even invade and annex the world of dreams. Eventually the attempt was successful. But he had never believed he would himself become enslaved by this new order. He had placed too much faith, he now realised, in the power of the imagination and had ignored the power of fear. At one point he felt that he, at least, had escaped or, if trapped, might escape again. But that was no longer possible. His actions, his very fantasies, were defined by this new authority, to which Law was equated with a tidy house and Justice was what kept the dust from rising.

'We're in this lifeboat together,' said Miss Brunner briskly. 'And can only survive if we accept the decisions of a captain and a steersman.'

Jerry was doing all he could to forget his doubts. Everyone had agreed his only course was to enrol in Miss Brunner's Retraining Scheme. He looked at the cracks in the pink marble walls, tracing them as if they would lead him to a clue, but they petered out. This kind of municipal architecture always defeated him.

'What I want to know is how we got in the lifeboat.'

'Mr Cornelius, I'm giving you far more time than you deserve. Unless you're serious, I can't help you.'

'The *Mary Celeste*,' he said. 'Something frightened the crew. But the ship was safe and sound, sailing under a fair stretch of canvas. How did you frighten the crew? And where the hell is the ship?'

'Don't be silly, Mr Cornelius. This is all we have. And we should be grateful for that. These are grim days.'

'Not for you. I've never seen you so satisfied. You got to everyone in the end. Now we're all acting according to your barmy logic. Where's the *Mary Celeste*, Miss Brunner?'

She shook her head. 'You're incorrigible. We'd hate to have to send you to Putney. But at this rate...'

'Rate? There isn't one. Or hardly anything to speak of. You've slowed us down nearly to zero. And when we hit zero, what? A Cryogenic Future? Eternal Life in the Nuclear Night? What do you hope to do when the dawn eventually breaks?'

'Initially there'll be some rationing of natural resources. That's the essence of sensible planning. Even you must see that.'

'Who'll deserve the sunlight and the air? Those who give up their minds to your miserable, hopeless, semi-literate equations? I think I'd rather...'

She was sweet. 'That's what your country would expect. Voluntary selection.'

'What if I jumped out of the lifeboat and tried to swim for it?'

'You'd find yourself in a swamp which is slowly freezing over.

'Is this –' he cast for the word – 'bad? Are you –' his breathing was laboured – 'wrong? Evil?'

'I think of you, Mr Cornelius, as an evil man. Self-indulgent, disloyal, irrational, ruthless. And so on. Society has been too lenient on you up to now. It has celebrated your type as a kind of jester, a lovable rogue. Well there's never much space for a lovable rogue in a lifeboat, not unless he mends his ways.'

Jerry heard the creak of timbers; but it might only have been something swinging on a gibbet. 'You're killing our children.'

'Oh, no, Mr Cornelius. We're going much further than that. This is the first time we've had the chance to make a clean sweep.'

'So it's true.' He saw a tree outside shed its leaves. 'You've invented the ultimate vacuum.' He felt something tug at his coat.

It was Mo Collier dressed in a spotless porter's uniform. 'Afternoon, sir. Mr C.' He touched the peak of his cap. 'I think it's time for you to go, sir.'

Miss Brunner had her back against Victorian marble, looking through heavy windows at the dull landscape beyond. She said nothing as he was escorted out. He followed Collier along green and brown corridors to the main steps. Something about the buildings surrounding the plaza, the dried-up fountain, reminded him of Liverpool. But it could be London. How had he arrived here?

Collier gave him a push from behind which sent him rapidly down a couple of steps. 'Piss off, you seedy little bastard. Next time don't even try to jump the queue.'

'I thought I'd been sent here.'

'You'll get your orders soon enough.'

This was such a familiar pattern of betrayal Jerry found himself immediately bored by it. Life in the Frozen Society held, by determined definition, no surprises.

12

Peace of Advice from Joan

Singing anti-war campaigner Joan Baez yesterday urged the Greenham Common peace women to be more peaceful. Sixties protester Joan, 43, said: 'They should be getting their message across by talking, singing and doing things gently. Instead they are invading military sites, rushing around creating a big noise and getting people's backs up. That might have worked in the sixties, but it's outdated now.' Joan, whose anti-war hits included *We Shall Overcome* and *Blowin' In the Wind*, will fly into Britain today and visit Greenham.

The Sun, 3 February, 1984

'Una won't come.' Catherine emerged from the darkness of the kitchen. There were old tins and bits of screwed-up paper everywhere; black bags of garbage, mouldering clothes, broken furniture. A little light came into the basement through the boarded-up windows. She added: 'I wish you'd picked somewhere else to meet. This place is horrible. Hadn't Frank told you he'd deal with it?'

'This must be what he meant.'

'You'd think the landlord would do something.'

'Don't you remember? It turned out Frank was mum's landlord. It stinks, doesn't it? I'm being looked for, Cath. I had twenty-four hours to report for the Retraining. I never made it. Not many people run into the ghetto to hide. It was all I could think of. Una can't have copped out. What's she up to?'

'I told you. She doesn't think she should have to be responsible for anyone else. Or for this.'

'No news from any other front? What can I do, Cath?' He squatted and began smoothing out some of the sheets of cheap notepaper. 'I've got enough suss back not to go along with Miss B., but no energy for anything else. Una was supposed to take over. I'm too old.'

'And she's too tired.'

'But she knows more than I do. At least she could let me have a bit of info.'

There was a soft engine in the sky. He craned to look through the slats. A 5000 series AI troop transport was hovering over Ladbroke Grove's ruined blocks. The airship was Australian-built; one of the latest Bond Corporation machines taken out of the private sector by government requisition. He had hoped it had come to rescue them. Now he watched cases of contaminated food falling from the main hatch. Another bloody symbol of his disappointed dreams. In the street outside a carton of corned beef exploded and a can struck the boards over the window.

'You're going to have to convince her, Cath. I can't handle it. Nothing works the way it used to. Don't you feel like that?'

'I haven't been trying, Jerry. Not so hard, anyway. I hate to see you this desperate.'

Two more boxes struck the pitted asphalt.

Jerry stopped himself from weeping. He was missing his mum. 'Cath? What can I offer her?'

'Una? I doubt she needs anything you have. Not yet. She's hardly judging you, Jerry. Her decision's personal.'

'She was never one to stay out of it for long.'

'Maybe she knows when she's beaten. You should have been content with getting your health and identity back. Why are you pushing on? You've no weapons, no information, no allies, no skills left. You've even forgotten your old style. You're an ordinary bloke, Jerry.'

'I have a duty,' he said, 'to honour my own memory.'

'It's a losing game.'

'Maybe. But it's the nearest thing I can find to courage.'

'This isn't an age which values anything much but decorum. And you always lacked that. I'm going back now, Jerry.'

'How long shall you be on holiday?'

'We're not on holiday. We've retired. What you're doing isn't realistic. It isn't even romantic.'

'I can't stand around and witness the end of everything I valued.'

She laughed. 'You should hear yourself. What did you ever value but your own appetites?'

He heard her go into the cellar. When he followed she was gone. He could find no exit.

13

Howe in Spy HQ Sackings Muddle

Foreign Secretary Sir Geoffrey Howe was last night at the centre of another major muddle over the Government's union ban at a spy centre. He claimed he knew nothing of a Minister's threat that Cheltenham HQ workers could be sacked without a penny if they refused to quit their union or move jobs. And he flatly contradicted a Commons written reply from Civil Service Minister Barney Hayhoe warning that staff would lose their jobs without compensation if they did not co-operate. Sir Geoffrey, who was questioned on ITV's TV Eye programme, said: 'I don't understand how that comes to be said.' And he pledged there would be an option of 'voluntary retirement on redundancy terms.'

Daily Star, 3 February, 1984

Major Nye regretted their decision to leave the river and try to strike overland. His regulation whites were stained with mud, pomegranate juice and tree-sap. Whereas Professor Hira remained, it seemed, immaculate in robes of pale cotton and a turban. The bearers, too, showed no discomfort for all that the equipment on their heads and backs was heavy and frequently difficult to manage.

'Surely we're across the Burmese border by now?' The major

squinted at bright, unlikely plumage. 'Shouldn't we pause and take some sort of fix?'

Professor Hira found this comical. 'My dear old chap, we can do all that at nightfall. Besides, we can't be sure we'll be in this neck of the woods from one hour to the next.'

It was true they kept breaking from one zone into another. Major Nye blamed that on their burden. They had started off from Shepperton and within a day had crossed part of Kenya in 1951, the outskirts of Famagusta in 1960, and negotiated a bayou in Louisiana some time in the 1920s. That was where they had almost lost the truck. It had collapsed completely in Chad in 1949 and it was here they had recruited their bearers. Proof that alternatives still existed, at least in some form, was not sufficient to cheer Major Nye more than a little. This trek was better than being captured or, indeed, forced to accept Miss Brunner's bleak logic. But he was frustrated. If they could get their load to a new site they could have a crack at rebuilding a temporary Time Centre.

They had entered a clearing. In the late-afternoon sunshine breaking through the higher terraces of giant trees Major Nye made out the structure of what at first he assumed was a ruined temple. Then it became apparent that the building was recent, resembling the control tower of a medium-sized airport. Leaving their bearers to follow at their own pace the two men approached the structure. 'Seems like a wartime effort,' said Major Nye. 'Something the Americans left behind, maybe.'

Hira shook his head. 'Japanese. Look at these.' He indicated oil-drums whose rust had not completely obscured some characters. 'Makes me feel almost nostalgic. I was their prisoner, you know, for about a week. Mistaken identity. Well, we can camp here for the night.'

Major Nye pressed with his remaining strength against a steel door. It creaked open. Small animals scuttled away. Some bats crawled into deeper shadow. 'Quite an elaborate set-up. I wonder what they planned.'

'Obviously they anticipated civil use after the military purpose was served. Not their usual thinking. What was the idea, do you suppose? To impress the locals that their South-East Asia Co-Prosperity Sphere actually had substance?'

'I'm always curious to come across the friendlier face of Imperialism. But where would the runway have been?'

'Possibly they never built one.'

'A very unusual way of going about things. I can hardly see the point. Yet here it is.' By the faint light from above and below they climbed metal stairs to the main control room, a relatively crude affair by 1980s standards. Radio equipment was everywhere, untouched, but most of the wiring was corroded and rubber housings bitten through. Only the steel, glass, brass and bakelite looked in reasonable shape.

'The Yanks never found this, evidently.' Major Nye could see, through smeared, ivy-grown windows, the deep green of the jungle, a glint of water beyond. Nocturnal monkeys were emerging from the foliage to swing softly from branch to branch. 'Nobody's been here for forty years. Seems odd to me. It's completely secret. Must be miles from anywhere.'

Professor Hira gave his attention to a faded wall chart. 'This wasn't a landing field as such, but an airship terminal. Some plan of the Japs and Germans. These are mooring instructions for a Zeppelin.'

Major Nye snorted. 'Oh, my lord!'

Professor Hira sat down on a table to contemplate the information. 'Well, at least your hope's confirmed again, major. We've struck an important series. A main vein. One Alvarez had thought totally wiped. So if there's one such, there are likely to be others.'

'Now all we have to do is get out of here and find young Cornelius. I'll call the bearers in. They can start setting up in the morning.' Major Nye drew a satisfied breath. 'This might even be the mother-lode.'

Professor Hira laughed appreciatively.

14

Mother Teresa Scandal

Mother Teresa of Calcutta has been cheated out of £200,000 in charity contributions. Money sent to help her care for millions of starving people was systematically plundered by a ruthless Asian Mafia. Much of the cash came from Britons, touched by the saintliness of the nun who last year received the Order of Merit from the Queen. Last night Mother Teresa's representative in London said: 'For God's sake don't send any more donations to Calcutta. So little of it has got through to the mission.'

Daily Star, 3 February, 1984

Prinz Lobkowitz retained something of a privileged position, largely because of the amount of foreign currency he was still able to earn for his translation work and his histories. He no longer kept the palace, but had a good-sized house near the Waldstein Gardens. He was delighted to see Jerry. 'You almost never come to Prague. How did you get an exit visa?'

'I didn't. I remembered a dormant identity in West Germany. It's still possible to travel to a limited extent within the EEC. But I had to leave England on a doctored passport, too. I'm a wanted traitor, you know. A spy and a saboteur. But you must be familiar with the story. Did you hear they'd given Mrs T. a public trial – and a public execution? It's Phase Two, coming right on schedule.'

'The Terror. That's due to disappointed expectations, of course, though God knows what else Miss Brunner wants. I thought the expectations had been reduced to nothing!'

'If I understand her programme she's aiming for full-scale nuclear war. To bring on the New Millennium. She has everything worked out in fine detail. But she's having more trouble than she thought convincing the Americans.'

'So you've come to warn us?'

'If you like. Don't they realise she's crazy?'

'On the contrary, old friend, our masters feel extremely comfortable with her. They understand reductionism. They're pleased they can now deal with someone who speaks with full authority a language they completely comprehend. Democratic leaders rarely can, you see. Do you think they're frightened of her? They've been committed to stasis as long as she has. Still, they'll be happy to make you a hero if you don't say too much. Have you come over officially?'

'I don't think so.'

'My advice is to delay all that as long as possible.' His thin, bloodless fingers shook as he poured amber vodka over ice.

Jerry thought he had never seen anyone who looked so old. The white hair and almost transparent skin, the frail body, were all healthy enough. But Lobkowitz looked two hundred if a day. How had he survived so many reverses and betrayals?

'What are you here for, Jerry? To learn the secret of serving under a no-option system? To find out why things scarcely improve once you abolish capitalism? Capitalism is a dreadful evil and is the cause of much injustice. Yet authoritarianism is worse. The two combined are an abomination. You have an abomination now, in England. And next it must be America, yes?'

'I'd hoped to avert that.'

'Alone?'

'My friends think it's stupid.'

Lobkowitz shook his head firmly. 'You can't. It's already in progress. The United States must be the hardest country in the world to simplify, yet they now have a plethora of examples.'

'Which means the world must end. As, I suppose, it deserves to. I'd hoped there were alternatives. The last reports from the Time Centre before it dissolved suggested there were none. I feel sorry for the Third World in all this.'

'I regret it's not my field. I couldn't speculate. All I know is that the USA can't last another year without accepting the logic of inevitable stasis. Then we shall have the nuclear missiles, then the Ice Age; the final goal of all their yearnings. Law and Order to the lowest common denominator. Everything at last easy to interpret. Better even than war itself. Justice is simply a question of which corpse is left frozen and which is thawed. But who will they blame for their troubles then?'

'I suppose it's all we've got to look forward to.'

'Well, we shan't see it, of course.' Lobkowitz made himself comfortable in a soft easy chair, spreading a heavy rug over his knees. 'You're welcome to stay here for the duration.'

Jerry bit his tongue by accident. 'Bugger.' They had got to Lobkowitz, too. 'Can you help me through to Madagascar?'

'My advice would be to calm down. You can scamper round and round the world until you're dizzy. But it won't change the situation.'

'Change is all I know.'

Lobkowitz found this embarrassing. He murmured that he would do what he could. 'But you must remember I am tolerated rather than respected. For the currency I bring in. I did take the precaution some years ago of joining our Writers' Union. It got me certain benefits.'

Depressed, Jerry excused himself and went to bed.

15

Girl, 15, in TV Porn Ordeal

Two men forced a pretty schoolgirl to watch a blue movie while they raped her, a court heard yesterday. And they acted out the porno video scenes flickering on the screen said Mr Roger Scott, prosecuting. 'They practised on her what they were seeing,' he told the jury.

Daily Star, 3 February, 1984

Professor Hira wondered if his wires were properly crossed. He looked towards the corner where Major Nye was dozing. The equipment had been carried in by the bearers and stacked on the low shelves which had held the radio and radar for the old mooring station. The tall, lanky men now spread themselves out over the clearing, playing an improvised game of cricket. In a little group on the left a family of gibbons formed an audience, occasionally applauding at random, to the annoyance of bowlers or batsmen.

The professor worked with leisurely good humour, content to solve what was a relatively simple problem now that he was no longer theoretically in the dark. He hardly dared consider the implications if he were successful in this relatively minor attempt.

A more puzzling mystery now was why this station had been abandoned. What was going on out there?

He watched with deep satisfaction as part of the jungle and two gibbons vanished for a second. He wished that one of the bearers was standing by. He was dying for a cup of tea.

Major Nye opened his weary eyes. 'How are we doing, old lad?'

'Very well, major. But it's all parlour-trick stuff so far.'

'Jolly good. Time we pushed on, eh?'

'Shouldn't be too long now, major. Reception's excellent but there are a few problems with transmission. Then we have to run proper tests.'

'It'll be a long time before they're up to that standard.' He lifted his head. 'Oh, well caught!' He became more animated, stretching, walking to one of the freshly cleaned observation windows. 'The jungle's at her best this time of the evening, don't you think?'

'We must hope that, at any rate.' Professor Hira cast about for the rusty screwdriver he had found. 'Keep your fingers together, major. Or is it your legs?'

Major Nye decided his friend was overworking.

16

Court Shocker!

A man appeared in court yesterday – for switching on a light. Michael Burke, a 37-year-old fitter, was accused of dishonestly using a quantity of electricity without authority.

Daily Star, 3 February, 1984

'Bondage is my way of liberating my true self.' Miss Brunner had come to be proud, these days, of her lack of originality. She insisted publicly on the virtues of what she called Inspired Similarity: The Aesthetics of Stasis. 'It was the only way to beat the Swiss to the thaw,' she told Jerry. Her voice was distorted by the Mickey Mouse gasmask she affected.

They had arrested him in Hungary and brought him home in the baggage compartment of an Aeroflot Ilyushin 808, an obvious copy of the Bond 48-seater. They had taken him directly to the Cotswolds. Only when he had recognised the tidy landscapes had he realised the seriousness of his plight. This was beyond Reclamation or Retraining. She had abandoned her recycling experiments and was now intent on nothing less than petrification. 'It looks as if we've reached worldwide agreement,' she told him.

'The big freeze without the big sneeze,' said Mo. He was hanging in a tangle of straps and crampons from what had once been an artificial climbing wall but was now a kind of specimen display. Miss Brunner's collection. Mo was an enthusiast for the system. He had told Jerry it was his tenth time up. 'I'm a veteran. It gets you a lot of status around the camp, believe me.'

Jerry felt a trace of his old salvation stirring in his wounded bones. His eyes flickered with a faint but distinctly feral spark. His remaining teeth nipped experimentally at the polished black vinyl in which Miss Brunner had suspended him.

'Old-fashioned virtues require old-fashioned support.' She tugged uncomfortably at her rubber corset. 'We have to sort out our priorities and give them proper emphasis.'

'Bloody hell.' Jerry drooped in his chains. 'Can't you come up with something fresher?'

'None of that "rotten fish" crap here.' Mo's warning was urgent, even hysterical.

Jerry turned his head. 'What's a pretty little capo like you doing in a web like this?'

'That's enough of the cheek,' said Miss Brunner tolerantly.

Jerry indicated Mo. 'Better concentrate, Miss B. Your fly's undone.'

Her eyes flew, coming to rest on his wasted frame, glaring. She flexed her crop. He was reminded by her plastic thigh boots of the last pantomime he had acted in. Her Prince Charming had possessed authority but had been lacking in dash. On the other hand his Buttons had, he thought, been only a fraction short of perfection. 'Cheer up, Cinders,' he said aloud, 'there's always tomorrow – and tomorrow's when rain turns to sunshine.' He began to hum the tune of his big song.

Miss Brunner swished her crop and brought it, with a hiss of painful fury, down on her gleaming black leg. 'Better not make that assumption, Mr Cornelius. The Future has not only been abolished. By six o'clock tonight it will be completely illegal. We have declared the Eternal Present.'

'Status Quo.' Mo spoke suddenly. He moaned, the contortions of his mouth mongoloid, his headphones at full volume. He was by now an old trusty with certain privileges. 'You've gotta keep your body fit. You've gotta keep your mind in shape. That's the only way to beat the Reaper.'

The words were unfamiliar to Jerry.

'I hope you'll come to understand how much we have your interests at heart,' she said. 'Indeed you could argue that generally speaking our interests are common ones.'

'Banal, certainly,' he agreed.

'You're over forty.' She tapped the crop in her hand. 'Don't you think it's time you grew up?'

'I'll have another try. But what will you be doing in the meantime?'

'Don't be facetious. Grow up!'

'I'll give it a crack of the whip if you will.'

'You're impossible.'

'You're all too likely.'

She formed her lips in a sinister pout. 'We'll educate you, yet, sonny jim. Eventually you'll accept the fact you've become a complete anachronism. That should bring you down to size if nothing else will, eh? You hate that, don't you? You trendy little wanker. Past your prime. Past your time. The only stinking fish around here will be the one that's out of water.'

Her insults became increasingly obscure as she worked herself up.

He tried to imitate her expression, knitting his brows, fixing his mouth, but Mickey Mouse kept getting in the way. He could not compete with a nose and ears that size.

He made one further appeal to Mo. 'How did she get you eating out of her bloody hand?'

Mo shrugged. 'Beats me.'

17

Liban: L'Heure de Chiites

Pour la première fois dans l'histoire du Liban, les chiites – la plus importante communauté du pays – jouent un rôle central: ils tiennant en main Beyrouth – ouest où leur dirigeant, Nubih Berri s'efforce de rétablir un minimum d'ordre.

Libération, 10 February, 1984

Sergeant Alvarez was content in his control box, producing the week's news for television. In some ways it was a more satisfying job, certainly more creative than a mere monitoring of actual events and possibilities. He had always been frustrated at the Time Centre. White City felt like a step up.

Mo Collier, flushed and tanned, in a new Nike tracksuit and expensive trainers, presented himself in the box. He handed the latest newstapes to his superior and saluted smartly. 'Here they are, sarge. All new, all fresh locations. The Second Festival of Britain, Rosegrowers Competition, Beaconsfield Morris Dancing, World Sport Looks To Britain, Biggest Crufts To Date, British Guts In The Ring. It's amazing how you keep coming up with them.'

'Did you ask Miss Brunner about another writer?'

'She's had your memo, that's all I know, sarge.'

'She had hopes of Cornelius. But once a pervert always an

apostate, as we say.' Alvarez slotted in the first tape and sank into a dream of England both Olde and Merrie. They were doing a great job. He wondered what madness had made him waste all those years at the Time Centre. In a sense he had to do better than many on account of his name. Since the abolition of foreign minorities a lot of Indians had tried to pass as descendants of Portuguese who had settled in Britain before 1933.

Miss Brunner was being interviewed against her new headquarters. Hever Castle never looked more solid. She was comparing herself to Mary Tudor ('only we, of course, are successful. The course of history is never irreversible. The river can be given a fresh direction – even turned completely back on itself. All it takes to turn that river into a tranquil lake is the will, the energy and, I admit, the technology. Britain has these in plenty. The treasures of our past, buried and forgotten beneath a flood of decadence and self-indulgence, are being rediscovered everywhere in our land. We are not retreating. We shall not retreat. We are standing our ground. Victorious and happy, we are the envy of all other nations').

Mo was almost violent in his applause. 'And we've got the Long Bow VDM, you bastards! Boom. Don't mess with Mo!'

'We're not supposed to mention that,' said Alvarez. 'Are we? Or has the directive been changed?'

'Slip of the tongue.' Mo was ashamed of himself. 'Sorry.'

'Nobody's perfect.'

'Amazing how secure it feels.' Mo flexed the muscles. 'The old Collier vitality's back. And the old Collier viability.' He displayed an uneasy pec. 'What's the opposite of hypochondria?' he asked thoughtfully. 'The instincts are... The back-brain's not coming through. The thought occurs...' He gave up. 'The calf's got a touch of cramp, that's all.'

'... Fools Paradise.' Jerry Cornelius looked older than forty now. Perhaps it was a deliberate ploy on the part of the studio. He appeared on the Channel 6 monitor, advertising Cocoa Pills, the Drink You Can Chew. They had slowed his voice slightly and put some extra bass on it, the suggestion of an echo.

Alvarez became alarmed. Mo reassured him. 'It's all pre-recorded. The old fart's no danger.'

'I'm suspicious. Why should he refuse a government post in favour of that stuff?'

'He's never been able to take responsibility. Ask Mo Collier what happened in the Panama Twist.'

'He went AWOL?'

'Took off. Took out Belize. Took Madagascar by the back door, then took a golden handshake from the Cabinet to abdicate in favour of King Alain. Those were the days, sarge. You should have seen Mo Collier all alone on the Old Mother Crag, minimum protection and a hurricane coming straight in from the north-east. Arse over tip under the Granny's Claw, hand-jamming in that rotten sandstone. The fingers were stripped raw. The feet were so numb it was like looking for holds with hobnailed boots. Meanwhile Cornelius sits in Mozambique playing old Hendrix records, eating crystallised fruit and surrounded by lilies while half a dozen naked women wait on him. For what? Mo was acting for a purpose, achieving something for himself. Jerry was looking after number one.'

'What were you doing on the crag?'

'I told you. The Twist.'

All at sea, Alvarez shrugged. 'It was just the tip of the iceberg, if you ask me. Who were you seconding?'

'Him! Or at least I thought so. He – Mo – I couldn't work out his route. It seemed random. Deliberately random, that is.'

'Well, we don't have random to worry about now. But I can't speak for the rest.' Alvarez watched the deck. It was two minutes before they went on the air.

Mo limped to the door. 'Everybody's doing it. What's bugging Collier, though, is why she's still preparing for the nuclear night.'

'Just a test run.'

It made sense to Mo. Carefully he opened the door.

There was something wrong suddenly with the monitors. Alvarez's short fingers moved frantically about on his board. 'Outside interference. I can't believe it.'

'Who –?' Mo was an alarmed owl.

'Not Cornelius. Someone altogether different.' He turned dials and slid knobs up and down. 'Not natural at all. It could scramble every transmission.'

'There isn't a power source in the country capable of that. Except ours, of course.'

Alvarez shook his head. 'It's gone. Probably just a fluke. An abandoned satellite bursting.'

'Feedback. There's not much Mo doesn't know about feedback. Better let him have a look at the generator, eh?'

The technician was adamant. 'I can deal with it.'

Offended, the rejected courier departed.

Alvarez announced the six o'clock news: The affirmation of a contented England.

18

Margaret's Lords Date

> Princess Margaret went to the House of Lords yesterday to see her friend Colin Tennant take his seat as the third Lord Glenconnor. She sat in a visitors' gallery with the new peer's wife, Lady Anne, as he took the oath. Lord Glenconnor owns the island of Mustique where she has a holiday home.
>
> *Daily Star*, 3 February, 1984

Una groaned in her sleep so loudly that she awakened herself. She was soaked. Her sheets and pillows were saturated. She could not remember her dream but when she called out for Catherine it was in Yiddish. She rubbed at her wet eyes. Only her mouth was dry.

Just tell me, baby, if you wanna little more speed
Said tell me, baby, if you wanna little more speed.
Just blow my whistle and I'll give you all you need.

She had no idea how the verse had come into her mind, but it stirred unwanted remembrance. Through the half-open door of the hut she could see the rail of her verandah and beyond that a green and tranquil tideless ocean teeming with the beginnings of sentience. All it needed was the right catalyst; then there would be no telling what might happen. She remained determined not to be the one to start it. Whatever else she was she had never been an Earth Mother. Clambering from her sweat-drenched bed she wiped salt from her lips and went out to the verandah.

'Catherine?'

Far away, beyond the waving fields of fern, yellow and black smoke rose against pure blue sky, forming what seemed a solid column. Una ran to the back of the hut. The jeep was gone.

In her horror, her panic, her vision of a wrecked vehicle in which Catherine's soft limbs slowly blistered and turned black, Una began to run towards the source of the smoke some two miles off. She was completely naked and without weapons. It was inconceivable that her retreat had been invaded. There had been an accident.

She was bruised and bleeding by the time she reached the fire, as if she had run a gauntlet of Turkish rods. The sun was high and irritated her eyes; she was exhausted. To her enormous relief she saw that the flames had their origin not in Catherine's jeep but in the gigantic skeleton of what she at first took to be a reptile and then realised was a dirigible; symbol of all the fine, failed dreams of the twentieth century. It was in its final death throes; as if it had sought the dignity of solitary extinction in the prehistoric past.

But Una knew something had let it through. Or sent it here. Or merely misdirected it. Nonetheless she chose to accept it as a personal omen, worthy of examination.

The aluminium structure began to collapse inwards. There was a stink of burning metal.

She could find no survivors.

Una made her way back to the sea. She reached the house in time to see Catherine driving the jeep along the beach from the west. Una ran down to try to wash off the worst of the dirt and blood before her friend got home.

Catherine waved from the shore as Una struck out. She turned over to float on her back, watching the thin streamers of blood running into the water. She waved a response.

'I've just seen three elephants!' Catherine was girlish with excitement.

Una went under.

When she came up again Catherine called: 'They don't have elephants, do they? Should they?'

Una pointed from the water. The smoke from the wrecked Zeppelin could still be made out, though it was much fainter.

'What is it?' called Catherine.

'A sign of the times,' said Una to herself.

'Eh?'

'The end of the world as we know it.' Una swam powerfully to the beach. 'We'd better start packing.'

Catherine was prepared for this. 'Any weapons?'

'Just on the off chance.' Una uttered a deep sigh, inspecting the welts and bruises on her arms. 'Put my MK14V in the case. And the Rickenbacker 12.'

'Blimey,' said Catherine. 'Who did that to you?'

'We'll be finding out shortly with a spot of luck.'

Whistling 'Dixie' (for she had been growing bored) Catherine Cornelius went to look for her thermal Union suit. Sooner or later she was bound to feel the cold.

Una, in Betty Jackson loose stripes, a wide-brimmed beige hat and matching jackboots, presented herself in front of the mirror while Catherine was still in the shower. Her more practical kit was permanently packed in two duffels. She was more nervous than usual. She was losing her confidence, maybe just because she had remained inactive for too long. After this, however, she planned to go to America and a house she had in Pennsylvania, 1933. She would rest before trying a long-term comeback.

Catherine picked the hairdryer from the rattan dressing table. She combed out her long hair and switched the machine on. It made a feeble purring noise then stopped altogether.

'That's funny. The electricity's gone.'

'Something's surging. An energy call-in. Probably by someone who's not entirely certain what they're doing.'

Suddenly the appliance buzzed violently. 'Thank God for that.' Catherine began to dry her hair. 'Could we be stuck here, then?'

'It's the energy keeping us here. The worst problem for us would be some sort of warp-out – thrown at random through the planes and zones to wind up almost anywhere. Doing it for fun's one thing. Getting stuck's another. One's a roller coaster ride; the other's a ride on a dozen streams which either never end or loop round and round for eternity.'

'Depressing, I should imagine.' Catherine tried to remember if it had ever happened to her.

'It's supposed to be good for the soul.'

'A maze without a map. Is that like, you know, the morality you were talking about? Before you came here?'

'All part of the same syndrome, dear.' Una laughed. 'You're a real Cornelius. I'll say that for you. Sometimes I forget.'

Since Una's tone was tolerant, even approving, Catherine made no attempt to understand what her friend was getting at. She was merely happy to enjoy the pleasure she always experienced when Una's spirits lifted.

It seemed, in contradiction of her statements, Una had been waiting for a call, like some questing knight spiritually preparing for a high crusade, perhaps for the Grail itself. As a little girl she had seen her brother Jerry in a similar light. She knew it was a weakness, but she still hoped he would one day fulfil her romantic dream of him. It was probably why she gave him so much of her time.

'Do you know anything about astrology?' Una was making up her mouth.

'No more than checking my horoscope in the paper.'

'Well, I've a horrible feeling we're going to be up to our eyes in it soon. Not to mention the bloody secret kingdom of – is it Shanhala? Maybe that's Glastonbury?'

'Layout lines!' Catherine remembered her girlhood in the sixties. 'I thought it was the same as stretch marks. Something to do with coke. Or is it coal?'

'Fertiliser!' Una snapped her fingers. 'Somerset's as good as anywhere.'

'Shit?'

'The Matter of Britain.' Una rubbed herself with scented cream. She was beginning to hum.

Blow your whistle baby if you want a little more speed.
I said blow your whistle baby if you want a little more speed.
'Cause I'm here to please you and give you just what you need.

Catherine, not knowing either the problem or the solution Una had apparently arrived at, took her friend by the waist and kissed her left lobe. 'Matter?'

'Time. Space. Oh, Christ. I need some on-line access. Morality. You're right, Cathy. Morality without Religion. Protestant Materialism. Scientific spirituality. There has to be some form of logic. It's what they've lost which can give us our answer. The Turks lost it, too. But not every Moslem did. Do you see?'

'Not a smidgeon. I'm just glad you're up again.'

'Was I so low?'

'I think so. Has all this something to do with hippies?'

'Mystical… No. A sense of mystery. A form of rationalism which is pragmatic only in the narrowest sense. And the appalling racism of the British. More objectionable, I think, than anyone's, frequently because it's so disguised.'

'Jerry says they killed all the Pakistanis and West Indians and voted themselves into the Union of Australian States. America wouldn't have them.'

'They're disgusting. At least they used to have a faith, a rhetoric of selfless service which a good many believed and even practised, no matter how barmy the base of it. Now they're merely cautious and greedy. It's not my job to save them from the consequences of their mediocrity and insularity.'

'For old time's sake.'

'Time had better start looking after itself. There's got to be change now and it must be radical.'

'Jerry said they're masterminding the Dawn of the Ice Age. Frank said it would automatically follow the Stoned Age.'

'He would. He was an active proponent, towards the end, of Firm But Cosy government. Remember it? A spin-off from what was left of the League of Afterdinner Novelists, the Festival of Light, the Empire Loyalists, Mrs Whitehouse, Mrs Thatcher and Miss Brunner.'

'Wasn't that the Twickenham Triumvirate? When? '84. The plot, I mean, to put that Canadian on the throne. The one who was married to a Kennedy. In *The Sun*. Or was it the *National Enquirer*?'

'It was all hushed up. Calmed down, they said. Those people are even more scared than me. Imitations of Man. They can't admit they're scared. Sex traitors. Gender finks.' Una laughed. 'They've sold out everything except their lunatic ambitions. Maintaining the status quo, from which their power derives, becomes their pseudo-ideal, by which they justify every betrayal, every cruelty, every act of greed and cowardice. They're worse than the men because they were not even conditioned to be that way. They imitated, learned it and by learning rejected their women's rights. The answer's there, I know. I've just got to frame the questions properly.'

'Like in that story. Greek or something.'

'Oracle's just another teletext these days. What am I trying to say?'

'It's obvious you're pissed off about something. Don't you want to save the world?'

'Which world? Maybe Miss Brunner's really done it and there's only one left to save. Your elephants, my Zeppelin, might be no more than bits of wreckage. It's not the world, Cathy. The Time Centre never had to bother about that. It's the proliferation of options. Choices. The bloody alternatives are what's important, not whether they're to our taste or not. That way there lies at least a chance of justice.'

'So it is to do with the Holy Grail?'

Now Una was brought up short. 'Come again?'

'It's my little fantasy. I've told you about it. In school. This teacher. She made us read it. Lancelot and that. But the earlier stuff more. Welsh?'

'It's not an – what are you saying?'

'I thought you might be looking for it. Some sort of pot. Or goblet.'

They were both almost packed. Catherine glanced down at the mirror resting in the palm of her hand. 'Ley lines! I remember.' She sniffed. 'But they weren't white. Flying saucers.'

'Cauldron, some say.'

'What? Like witches?'

'This is definitely drifting in the right general direction.' Una licked the mirror, breathed on it, watched closely, as if it were a screen which could reveal the substance of her notions. 'I think we can get a train from Paddington. The Goddess has no female evil adversary who is her equal. They tried to make Morgana that. The Church made war on women in those days. I'm still not sure what it was frightened of. Can you think of an equal? God has the Devil. The Goddess has only powerful male antagonists – warrior angels of unholy allegiance. But when women reject her who do they follow? God or Satan? Not much choice there, either.'

'Isn't this a bit, well, you know, like all that bullshit you hate? Peace and love stuff.'

'Desperate remedies.' Una was embarrassed. 'Anyway all I'm saying is that there's an inherent truth in any set of myths. The silly stuff doesn't interest me. But what's underneath? Jerry got hypothermia and went to the North Pole for a cure.'

'Was he trying to tell us something?'

'I doubt it. But he's a true survivor. He knows how to return to basics and trace a problem to its roots. He has a nose for the sources of almost every kind of logic. What's underneath?'

'Human misery and the need to believe in the value of our existence. I remember that's what you explained.' Catherine realised with a start that her memory, and with it her capacity to think and understand, was rapidly returning. 'Cor!'

'Something positive as well. It's been abused, I'd guess, for negative reasons. For escape rather than confrontation. Like any faith. But if we can work out the genuine logic it could destroy Miss Brunner and all she's achieved.'

'We don't really know what that is. Only what we've heard.' Catherine was still puzzled. 'You said it was merely a justification for women to go on knitting and having babies. You said it was a substitute for political power. You even thought Greenham was wet.'

'But it must have a positive quality. Things become debased. They have function. Only when their function is no longer needed or sometimes merely forgotten are they corrupted...'

Catherine was prepared to accept her friend's somewhat vague searching about for a solution. She had a rough idea of what was involved. 'So we don't take the firearms?'

'I see what you mean. Yes, that's in the logic too, isn't it? Okay, leave the guns and stuff behind.'

'I'm not used to this.' She knew a flash of anxiety.

'No. You're right. This time we have to go all the way. If we're going at all.'

'Is it the only answer?'

'The only one presenting itself. Better than nothing, my dear!'

Catherine glanced regretfully at her battledress where she had arranged it on the bed. 'I used to enjoy those adventures.'

'That's probably all they were.' Una was not critical, merely wistful. 'It was never really a revolution. Too much fun, maybe.'

They sat down, their heads resting against each other. Una, too, knew a sudden sense of loss. 'Not much of one, at any rate. We got carried away. A diversion.'

'They'll do it to you if they can. That's why they can take your power back any time they want to. We've got to establish a new base. A proper one. And the first thing to do is to get rid of the quasi-women and the pseudo-men. Then we're back to dealing with the devil we know. Our old kind of war.'

'We're virgins in all of this.' Una laughed. 'We've a lot to learn.'

'Maybe being virgins really is part of the strength. Maybe we know everything already and that's what we'll discover.'

'Let's not move too fast. We could easily fall into the trap of abstraction. And abstraction's the enemy of prosecution. We've got to realise all this bit by bit and deal with it as it comes. Don't you think?' Una kissed Catherine tenderly and with admiration. 'We're a better team than ever before.'

'We'll need allies, too.'

'You'll have to keep your brother out of this.'

'He used to bc my sister, too. It's just that he got in a rut. It's easy to do, you must admit, Una.'

'All that stuff's over for him. Bonding with Miss Brunner? How could they expect it to last? Then the cloning experiments! He might just as well have done it all with a bloke.'

'He meant well.'

'That's what they all say.'

'We were hoping to do it, you know.'

'Bond?'

'Sort of. He'd got hold of this book by that chap Browning did all the stuff about. You know, who invented centigrade. Paracelsus! Just after he broke completely with the Jesuits. That had a lot to do with cauldrons, too. And the philosopher's stone. You know.'

'How did he propose to achieve it with you?'

Catherine giggled. 'I suggested a big Robochef.'

'You need more than willpower.'

'I think the problem was financial. We lost everything, of course. Miss Brunner was always good with money. But originally, if it hadn't been for Frank, we might have made it.'

'Frank was jealous, wasn't he?'

'Murderously. The little bloody Judas.'

'Jerry was more confused than malevolent, I'll grant you that. But there's more to it than good intentions or even altered understanding. The motives have to change, too. That's why all he can do in a crisis is give up.'

'You did the same, Una.'

'For different reasons. Not better ones, I'll admit. Anyway my cop-outs don't justify Jerry's. Think what he could have done if he'd been just a little less self-indulgent. If it had been you in his position.'

'I was in his position sometimes.'

'You were, too. More than me. And you know what happened.'

'We blew it. I blame it on trench coats mainly.' She was self-mocking. 'I wanted to be Humphrey Bogart.'

'A feminine reading of heroes is always much more interesting than the actual thing. Jerry knew, at least, it was rôle-reversal. He'd tried it more consciously. But his motives were all fucked up. He did it for thrills. To get his rocks off.'

'Curiosity, more. It's his saving grace.'

'He could have done with a couple more. Grace!'

'I don't think he really achieved it, do you? Was there a moment?' She sighed for the brother she had wanted him to be. 'It's a shame.'

'We've got to look for it. He might know where to begin. It's something we'll have to give serious attention to.'

'We can't be passive – or even pacifists as such. It's not in our nature, Una. Not in yours, anyway.'

'Agreed. We need to find new weapons. Appropriate ones. We must have run across them before, even used them. In that respect Miss Brunner has less to answer for.'

'How do we get in touch with this goddess? This idea, then? And, Una, we must have allies. Miss Brunner would reduce the 7th Cavalry, or eat them, or blackmail them. I don't fancy that. I want to stay a virgin for a bit.'

'Exactly. Keep our power strong.' Una tapped her teeth. 'I suppose we'll have to use old colleagues. For their experience. But how many are there left? And of what sex?'

'Almost all men. But if we can make enough new female allies we'll be okay. Miss Brunner knows how to frighten women, of course. That's why they'll follow when she promises stability.'

'Let's assume we're stuck with Jerry and the others. They'll have to take direction. No interference. No power-games. They either accept our line or they don't come in.'

'I think they're terrified, too. If they haven't been completely swallowed up by Miss Brunner they'll agree to your terms.'

'And no bloody counter-revolutions, either. Or any how's your father.'

Catherine chuckled. 'I think they're all a bit too old for that.'

Una zipped her vanity bag. 'It's the old ones you've got to watch out for.' She winked.

When Catherine had chosen a blouse and skirt from her small collection they went arm in arm to the generator shed behind the main hut. Even as they entered, the overhead light flickered and faded to a dull orange. The generator's whine petered out.

Una held tightly to Catherine's hand. She felt a lurch which was neither the earth nor her own body but something far more powerful. It was profound. It filled her with terror. 'Oh, Catherine! All we need is a couple of minutes. Mother of God, just two minutes.' She began to reconnect wires and adjust switches on her old-fashioned board. 'Two minutes.'

Another shudder, as if the fabric of time and space were rupturing. Catherine grew dimmer. Una reached out to hold her. Their hands joined. Next the light blazed brighter. Now they were dazzled. 'Thirty seconds!' Una was praying.

She grabbed blindly for the car steering wheel she had once used so casually in her journeys out of tranquillity and into adventure. She moved it gently and carefully, two points to starboard, four to port. She knew her codes by heart. But everything had become so much harder. She was operating according to rules she only dimly perceived. Almost everything was new. Yet at the same time she had the clear feeling she was actually recollecting an inherited wisdom which she had once rejected as weakness. Catherine was radiant. Her eyes burned as if in the ecstasy of orgasm. Her smile when she looked briefly at Una across the bridge of their arms was intimate and glorious.

Prehistory was setting them free. Una continued to pray that she had calculated the co-ordinates correctly and they would arrive at a point where their faith and their wills, their enormous innocence could be most effective.

She felt miserably sick. Catherine glowed like the sun; shone like the moon. She had thrown back her lovely head. She was gasping, laughing, groaning. She was fiery silver.

They were together in a blue void. Marvelling at Catherine's sublime beauty, Una, for the first time in her confident, active life, felt fully at one with herself. Was this the reward of genuine Faith: an absolute trust in her own judgement? Religion or politics did not have to be mere escape or simplifications. But neither did Faith require their trappings; rationalisations, however noble, so quickly became tainted. Una gasped aloud. Then she was laughing. She had accepted her Goddess: Herself.

Buildings formed in a grey, damp morning. They were returning to their world of origin. They would probably never leave it again. Una no longer cared. She could die easy. She could face any danger without fear. It came to her that fear was not conquered by fear, nor fire fought by fire. There were no secondary rules, but in this instance she understood that those who sought to create the security of a false, idealised past might actually be countered by the realities from which they derived their rhetoric and yearnings: by the moral courage, the fierce, humane righteousness, the angry compassion, the recognition of mystery which had its source in the wisdom of her maternal ancestors.

London was colder and damper than she ever remembered. In their unsuitable clothes they waited an hour before the Paddington bus came. At least their money was good. With first-class tickets they headed west, shivering. Una relaxed as her clothing dried.

The train went through Didcot. The station was painted bright red; apparently decorated with glittering, multicoloured barbed wire, as if it were being prepared for some horrible, totalitarian festival. There was a touch of familiar humour in the scene and Una could only bring Auschwitz to mind, though the connection was obscure.

'I think we're travelling beyond fundamentalism.' She peered at the covered goods wagons in a siding, giving them an intense inspection which revealed nothing.

Her friend smiled and stretched a brave hand towards her.

19

May Day Fun

With the Kent Hooden Horse came the Mollie with her besom, in Wales the Mari Llwyd horse was accompanied by Judy who also carried a besom, while the broom-carrying she-male with the Old Tup players from the Sheffield area was called Our Old Lass. The Abbots Bromley Horn Dance she-male is now known as Maid Marian and her emblem of office is a ladle, while at the Horn Fair at Charlton any man could appear dressed in women's clothes. On May Day the London sweeps celebrated with the Lord and Lady, the Lady of course being a she-male, and on the Isle of Man in the May Day battle between the forces of the Queen of May and the Queen of Winter, the latter was also a she-male.

– Janet and Colin Bord,
Earth Rites, 1982

Major Nye tried once more with the makeshift connecting lever as Professor Hira hoarsely cried: 'Again!'

Outside, it was pitch dark. Earlier that day they had hidden while a war party of Dyaks went past, suggesting they were not in

Burma at all, but somewhere around the Malay Peninsula or the Islands. This had meant little to Hira, who babbled only equations now, but it had made sense to Major Nye. There was much more likelihood that someone would build (and abandon) an air-station on one of the smaller islands.

'We can't be far from Australia,' he had said. 'Or there's Rowe Island, too.' Comforted for a moment by the thought, he next remembered he was a wanted man, having fought on the Pakistani side during the war.

Professor Hira was much thinner. He settled himself on the floor and began to sing in a high lilting voice while still making adjustments to a circuit board resembling an almost perfect Star of David. 'Someone's coming through, I think.' He picked up a set of headphones, listening carefully. 'A definite beat. $C(b)-\frac{x}{g}=K\,(VG)+\frac{\text{ФГ}}{\text{МИ}}$ … At least one person. Splendid.'

'Any other zones yet, old boy?'

'Fading in and out. We're capable of receiving the entire chronosphere. The next step involves selecting and tracking specific zones. But without doubt the majority still exist. Whoever rigged the Time Centre did a thorough job. And a very clever one, major.'

'It was clearly Miss B.' Until now Major Nye had continued to hope her heart was in the right place.

'Motive, opportunity, technical understanding. Who else has the combinations? But does that matter?'

'I suppose it doesn't. Except that it's a sort of betrayal.' Major Nye drew air into his frail chest. 'Of course, she was never really part of the team. Not our team, anyway. She loved to interfere with people, you know. That's what she had in common with Beesley and the rest of them. It's like white and black magic, actually.' His brow cleared as if he had found an answer to a longtime problem. 'Not the power itself, as they say, but what you do with it.'

'And how has that lady used it, major?'

'Mm?'

Hira was back to his own quest. 'It's a kind of inversion. But at what point and how does it switch from positive to negative? And how does one reverse the process?'

'A lack of generosity, when all's said and done. That's what I think, old boy. A failure of imagination, perhaps. A solipsistic inability to recognise the individual needs of each member of the community and how that recognition also requires action.' He became embarrassed, out of his depth. 'Lack of sympathy? More than a lack: a positive hatred of other people's needs. Almost a fury that those people exist at all. Am I going too far? Certainly Miss Brunner gets into a terrible pet when we've refused to co-operate in her own gratification.' He looked at his military watch. It had stopped. He pursed his lips and whistled a bar or two of 'A Little of What You Fancy Does You Good'. 'Still, you can go too far the other way and never have an independent identity. A bit too oriental, that, for my taste. I thought anything was better than Hitler. Mad people need so desperately to have their view of the world confirmed by as many of us as possible. And if they don't get confirmation they demand silence. It's astonishing, isn't it? So many forms of tyranny reduced to so simple a formula. They win, I suppose, because of that forceful belief in the priority of their own needs.'

'Why do they lose, major? That's what we're looking for here.'

'I'm not sure I'm qualified to answer, old boy.'

Hira was more confident. 'They're forced to use more and more of their energy to support a fundamental lie. Everything's redirected to that end. First the self is rechristened and named "The Community", to draw on that greater power. Then the Community is gradually cannibalised. That is, it begins the process towards exhaustion very rapidly, feeding on its own substance even when it appears to be devouring others.'

'What becomes of the hunter who does not eat the beast he kills?' Major Nye was doing his best to recollect a conversation he had enjoyed in Calcutta more than fifty years before.

Hira was wriggling back into the tangle of cable. 'That's an old proverb!' He let his attention return to the circuits. 'What becomes of the woman who has a baby to save her marriage?'

'Baffles me,' said Major Nye politely. He was thinking of his dead wife, his lost children, his old horse.

20

Daily Star Birds

> Blonde Jackie Sharrock and the lovely Gina Nash make a stunning duo – even when they're toiling together at the kitchen sink. The two met on a glamour assignment and decided to pool their resources by sharing a 'bachelor girl' pad in London.
>
> *Daily Star*, 3 February, 1984

'Ask the fox!' Bishop Beesley looked with some satisfaction at the rubble of Westminster Abbey.

'What?' Mo lowered his Banning F7. It had taken him five rockets just to break up one of the western towers.

Beesley uttered a fat chuckle. 'If he enjoys it.' They watched the survivors running towards the bridge, unaware the middle had been taken out. They would soon be joining the other corpses in the grey Thames. 'That'll teach the perverts to claim sanctuary in one of our churches. I call it a nerve. They didn't seem to be aware, even, that the Lady Chapel was renamed years ago.' With a show of relish he unsheathed a Twix. 'Welsh scum!'

'I could do with a pie.' Mo felt wasted. In the old days he had always been exhilarated when provided with such wonderful firepower. He looked towards Parliament where the cross of St George flew in place of what Miss Brunner had lately called 'that hybrid, vulgar rag', the Union Jack. 'Shall we drop in at the canteen?'

Beesley began to plod towards the ranks of SAS who had helped in the Abbey's destruction. Beyond them workmen continued to lay out and roll the turf surrounding the Mother of Parliaments on three sides. 'We'll have it reproduced eventually,' he reassured Mo. 'But sometimes one must impress people with a thoroughly dramatic gesture. We had to prove we meant business, no matter what the cost. We can't afford sentiment.'

'Shit!' Mo had slipped on a piece of skin. He flung out his hand to grip Beesley's cassock and almost dragged him over.

'Easy does it. You'll have my bodyguards putting bullets in you if you're not careful.' The bishop found this amusing.

Mo had become depressed. Either the old thrills weren't working any more or there was something wrong with him. Maybe it was just the context. Or the company. He decided to skip his pie and go home.

As he climbed into a staff car he turned to look back at the ruins. For a moment it seemed as if the Abbey had restored herself, standing complete and solid, as she had been six hours earlier. Mo was surprised by the relief he felt. But it was only for a moment. Then the rubble, the broken corpses, the small, horrible fires, returned.

'Where to, colonel?' The driver was a cheeky New Zealander.

Mo could not get used to his promotion. It made him deeply uncomfortable. Miss Brunner had doubtless thought it would ensure his loyalty. Rather he was thinking of getting out of the army altogether, maybe defecting to some more attractive country, though as far as he could tell they were all on the same side now. How had he come to isolate himself so thoroughly? He had changed his mind but he had betrayed no-one. He was tired. He had seen sense. What was bad about that? It was realistic. Miss Brunner had said so. Pragmatism was their common language.

His house in Hyde Park Gate, small but smart, was furnished in the chintzy bad taste favoured by aristocrats who had looked to the Royal Family (now established in Sydney) for their style. It had belonged to a titled diplomat. Mo could never remember the man's name. He had been set upon and killed on Hampstead Heath while, it was rumoured, having intercourse with a black prostitute. The matter had either been hushed up, carefully obscured, or was a convenient lie. Miss Brunner had offered Mo the house shortly after she became Governor. Apparently Jerry, now a well-known TV personality, had turned it down as too modern. Jerry was living in one of Brixton's surviving Victorian red-brick houses. Brixton was now mostly replanted parkland. Mo only saw him these days on the telly. With his greying hair and the make-up he looked the picture of reassuring stability. Mo consoled himself. If he had sold out, Jerry had, too, body and soul. Mo had enjoyed the old days, but he had never known why.

He went straight up to bed. His bedroom was white and green with an elaborately moulded ceiling. Before he could get rid of his uniform the phone rang on the little Georgian-style table.

'Mo Collier's place,' he said. 'Who wants him?'

A whisper came down the line. At first all Mo could hear was the word 'Dope'. Then 'ounce'.

'Are you buying or selling?'

'Mo…' Or was it 'No'?

Now he felt he recognised the voice. 'Frank?'

'You bastard!'

'Jerry?'

The voice faded until Mo caught nothing but a hiss. At length he replaced the receiver. He felt he had been listening to an accusatory ghost.

'Some joker's playing a trick on old Mo.' He tried to imagine which of his friends it might be. Then he recalled he no longer had friends. He had lost or rejected them all. These days he had only peers and colleagues. Everyone had let him down. Nobody, in the end, had come up to scratch. He would follow a good leader anywhere, but he had to admire the person completely if they wanted him at his best. Once it had been 'Will it go?' These days it was 'Should I trust it?' They were all wankers or worse. 'The whole bloody world's let Mo down.' He had tried to learn the score. When that had not worked, he had attempted to invent some simple rules for himself As he understood it, that was what you were required to do. But only he had obeyed his rules and so they had proved pointless. He could scarcely even win self-approval. His brain congratulated his hands or some other part of his body when it did well, but that was not exactly the applause of the crowd. Along the line he had thrown something valuable away. He could not even go back to look for it, since he was not sure what it was. He had tried to find it once or twice in that grubby tangle of alleys and backstreets between Euston and Camden Town, then Miss Brunner had come along. She had had rules. She told him precisely what was required of him. And before he knew it he was a colonel in her personal guard. 'Teach me the game,' he had promised her, 'and I'll finish the job.' Yet, almost at once, he had begun to feel even more frustrated. He was more deeply suspicious of those around him than ever before.

When the phone rang again he was in the shower. He let a servant take a message.

Miss Brunner's secretary had called to congratulate him. He had been awarded a medal.

'Bugger.' Mo wrapped the towelling robe around his impeccable little body. 'What price Stirner now? Is this the old Mo Collier?'

In the vague belief that punishment brought, if not rewards, at least some form of consolation, he sent himself to bed without any supper.

21

The Airship Raid on London

The military airships made for London. Ample warning of their coming had been given, and the city was in deep darkness, save for the groping searchlights. The streets were full of people, whose curiosity mastered their prudence, and they were rewarded by one of the most marvellous spectacles which the war had yet seen. Two of the marauders were driven off by our gunfire, but one attempted to reach the city from the east. After midnight the sky was clear and star-strewn. The sound of the guns was heard and patches of bright light appeared in the heavens where our shells were bursting. Shortly after two o'clock on the morning of the 3rd, about 10,000 feet up in the air, an airship was seen moving south-westward. She dived and then climbed, as if to escape the shells, and for a moment seemed to be stationary. There came a burst of smoke which formed a screen around her and hid her from view, and then far above appeared little points of light. Suddenly the searchlights were shut off and the guns stopped. The next second the airship was visible like a glowing cigar, turning rapidly to a red and angry flame. She began to fall in a blazing wisp, lighting up the whole sky, so that country folk fifty miles off saw the portent. The spectators broke into

> wild cheering, for from some cause or other the raider had met its doom.
>
> – John Buchan,
> *History of the War*, Vol. XVII, Nelson, 1917

Jerry could not stop blinking. It had the effect of a stroboscope. Una and Catherine flickered about the room looking under his bed, behind his dressing table, searching, he supposed, for bugs. They had entered during the night and the visitation had frightened him. He had expected a heart attack. He was calmer now, but not completely at peace.

'What're you doing here?' His mouth was dry. The women's bodies seemed unnaturally bright to his eyes, accustomed to austerity and the slow seepage of colour which always prefigured a Freeze.

'We're going to bring you back to your senses.' Una folded her arms and looked down at him.

This alarmed him further. 'I don't want them any more. Dangerous.'

Catherine unrolled the bundle she had brought with her. An old black car coat, black trousers, black elastic-sided cuban boots, black waistcoat, black knitted tie and a white shirt with a button-down collar. He began to shiver uncontrollably. 'All gone. All gone. No!' He mewled and sought to fugue but his sister had anticipated him. She had a syringe ready. He felt it jab sharply through his pyjama sleeve into his arm. 'This'll halt the process,' he heard her say, 'but I'm not sure it will reverse it.'

Una murmured. 'How disgusting. He'd turned into his brother. Are they all possessed?'

'By Frank?'

'And the other dibbuks.'

A muscle spasm shook his body. His mouth drew back in a rictus, a dead man's grin. His skin had feeling for the first time in an age. His blood began to sing and there was an almost unbearable sharpening of the senses. 'What was it? Sulphate?'

'There's more where that came from,' Catherine promised.

'Tasty!' Jerry reordered his breathing and went to the bathroom. They heard him showering and brushing his teeth. When he emerged he was no longer greying and he had his old vulpine movements restored. He climbed expertly into the used clothes. 'Murder and mayhem time, is it, ladies?'

'I'm afraid not.' Una was almost embarrassed. 'The rules are changed a bit.'

'Say no more. Just point me in the right direction.'

Catherine knew this briskness would wear off soon enough, but she enjoyed the nostalgia of her brother's apparent return to the modes of his youth.

'You're following us, Jerry. No independent action. No sudden moves. No phasing. Nothing without consultation and confirmation.' Una was uncompromising.

'Suits me,' said Jerry. 'It's what I'm used to.'

'He's absolutely amoral,' Una said to Catherine as she watched Jerry clip a digital watch on either wrist.

'It was his decision.' Catherine was defensive.

Jerry had overheard them. 'That's right.' He winked. 'I'm merely a tool.'

'Let's say cog, shall we?' With a swift look to the ceiling Una led the way downstairs, stepping over the sleeping bodyguards. As they left the house they heard the phone ringing.

'How come you're dressed like Vestal Virgins?' Jerry crawled obligingly into the back seat of the old Citroën. 'All that loose white samite. Are we going to a party?'

'No more parties.' Una let off the handbrake and engaged the clutch. 'It's chastity, purity of thought, rectitude and courage for a while, I'm afraid. And valorous, unselfish action.'

'You've got the wrong man, then.' Jerry was amused. 'I'm no bleeding Parsifal.'

'You're all we've got, tiger.'

He shrugged. The effects of the drug were already fading a little. He slumped back in the padded leather. 'I gave up trying years ago, remember.'

'This isn't a holiday.'

Jerry, not wishing to hear any more, tried to change the subject. They were passing through Clapham. It was parks and commons now, all the way to Richmond and, beyond that, to Windsor. He had never seen so many maypoles. Yet they might also, he thought, be huge cricket pitches. Or airstrips. 'Miss B. will be furious when she finds out you've kidnapped me. She'd go through the roof. Millions watch me every day. I'm the symbol and the spirit of the nation.'

'That's why we're going to get you rinsed out and cleaned up.' Una tried to suppress her own ebullience. She must force herself to remember the new terms and not slip back into old habits, no matter how attractive.

The curfew was no problem. She had come by a special permit in Jerry's suit and used it when they reached Putney Bridge. The Civil Guard officer saluted Jerry who had begun to slump a little and they passed over to Fulham, not a quarter of a mile from the old Palace in Bishop's Park which Beesley had appropriated as his residence. He was now Archbishop of London and therefore head of the national Church. Turning into Fulham Palace Road Una made for Hammersmith and the old Odeon. The venue had been boarded up during the war and there had never been any reason to reopen it. Indeed half of Hammersmith, including the new town hall and shopping precinct, still lay in ruins from the fierce battle of King Street when the 2nd William Morris (Mixed) Battalion had made its last stand against mainly Australian tanks and mobile rocket launchers. Most of Hammersmith, between Dawes Road and Hammersmith Road, down to the river, was a Controlled Zone. Police and soldiers rarely went in but were content to contain the inhabitants in a ghetto slowly starving to death.

Leading the way through the stage door at the back, Una climbed a couple of concrete flights to the old dressing rooms. They had been decorated since Jerry had last seen them and were almost comfortable, with oil lamps, Bauhaus armchairs and even a portable gas heater. Jerry was startled to find Major Nye and

Professor Hira eating sandwiches and watching a tiny, battery-operated TV.

'Made it at last! Good show!' Major Nye pumped his hand. Professor Hira embraced him, kissing him on the cheek. 'Excuse my appearance, old chap. I've been working for days to get this sorted out.' He was covered in cobwebs, smears of oil, dust, mud and tree-bark.

'Five,' said Jerry dimly. 'Not a proper coven. Miss Brunner'll flush us.'

'Not if I'm right.' Una pushed back one long sleeve. 'Will you oblige, professor?'

In some excitement Professor Hira led the group along several dim corridors and into a larger room which Jerry seemed to recall had been used for projecting films, light shows and for sound-control. He grinned, yet he was growing weak. 'It's a sort of lashed-up Time Centre isn't it?'

'Even if she saw it with her own eyes she'd have a hard job believing it,' said Una.

The four of them moved to different sections of the equipment. The TV screens were of all different makes and sizes, but they were functioning; so were the boards.

'I must say we could use Alvarez as well.' Catherine puzzled over a junction box. 'He's the operator. The real expert.'

'He might despair, though, of my efforts.' Hira stroked his face then scratched under his turban.

'Better than anyone else's, professor.'

Jerry was upset. 'She told me it was all over. She proved that there were no alternatives left.'

'She's proved it to almost everyone.'

'We should try to get it across to the – to the – public…' Jerry sat down in a corner and began to dream.

'Is the poor old chap in shock again?' As always, Major Nye was sympathetic.

'He's easily brought round.' Una reassured him. 'What's Alvarez's address, Catherine?'

Catherine Cornelius consulted her notes. 'Royal Crescent,

Holland Park. Not too far from here. There's a strong chance he won't want to come in. He's jealous of the professor, I think. You know what technicians are like. Then there's Mo Collier.'

'No need to bother there. Elizabeth?'

'I'm afraid my daughter only survived her mother by a year.' Major Nye pulled at his cuff, as if in apology.

'Auchinek?'

'Concentration camp.' Hira spoke. 'He died somewhere in Somerset, I believe. And we know Pyat's gone, too. Bastable?'

'Resettled. Probably in a loop. We'd never find him in time. The same is true of Mr Jagger and all those others.'

'So we're six at most.'

'Probably,' said Una. 'Possibly.'

'We need one more. That's my sense of it. Three would be better. Preferably women. But we might have to take Mo, after all.'

'There's only so much time left if I'm any judge.' Hira looked exhausted. 'What do we mean to do exactly?'

'Pray,' Una told him. 'If you follow me.'

'I follow you, Mrs Persson. And the others?'

'They must learn.'

'It'll mean the death of variety.' Major Nye was chatting to Jerry whose eyes had opened suddenly. His glassy stare and odd skin made him look like a waxwork. 'No more Marie Lloyd. No more Max Wall. Television can't produce them. And variety's the spice of life, eh?'

'Space of what? Where am I?' said Jerry slowly.

'Where you always wanted to be.' His sister spoke to him as if he were senile. 'The Hammersmith Odeon. It's your chance of a fresh start.'

'Who –?' His mouth went slack.

Catherine looked despairingly towards Una.

'The walking wounded.' Una forced herself to remember her vows. 'This is getting too much like a McCarthy Western. And the next full moon is only two days away.'

Jerry began to drool. Tenderly Catherine gave him another shot.

22

Racial Extermination

Through an entire month corpses could be seen floating down the Euphrates, frequently bound together in groups. The male bodies were generally ferociously mutilated – with sexual organs cut off and with other wounds almost as terrible – while the female bodies were slit open. The Kaimakam of Djerablous, the Turkish military officer, has refused these corpses burial ... Dogs and vultures feed off those which lodge on the banks. Many Germans have witnessed this. A man working for the Baghdad Railway tells us the Biredjik prisons fill regularly every day and are disgorged every night – into the Euphrates ... Aleppo and Ourfa are the embarkation points for the Armenian exiles. An estimated 50,000 passed through from April to July 1915. The girls were abducted almost without exception by the soldiers and their Arab followers...

Sonnenaufgang, Berlin, October 1915

The ghosts (if they were ghosts) were becoming too much for Mo. Since both Jerry and Alvarez had disappeared he felt at once haunted and deserted by them. He needed to talk to them about his terrors, his longings for the days when they had travelled up the Amazon or rested in the Simla hills; when they had flown in white seaplanes over the Ukrainian steppe or conducted cryptic battles in the streets of a deserted Istanbul. Hourly the world he lived in became dimmer, greyer and yet he could discover no sign that it would get any better or that he might even be free of it. For the first time he considered suicide as a means of escape.

He was surprised when he received a message from Miss Brunner instructing him to be at Hampton Court for lunch.

They dined alone in the large Hall. From here they could

look out over the geometrically arranged hedges and flower beds, the neatly ordered nature so necessary to monarchs controlling their own instabilities of character. Miss Brunner, with her red hair in a sort of renaissance bouffant and wearing a long brocade dress, seemed to be making a conscious attempt to resemble Queen Mary Tudor. She was certainly supremely impressed by her own power, adopting that condescending air which she might have called 'gracious' (Mrs T. has possessed it before her) but which was actually the epitome of petit-bourgeois snobbery.

'Dear Colonel Collier, how very naice to see you.'

'Morning, ma'am. This is all a bit much for Mo Collier. And the knee's playing up a bit so if you don't mind he'll stretch the old leg out.' He grunted. 'Mo wouldn't have let things get that bad.' Yet he was somehow flattered by her attention, taking it as his due.

'Of course.' With a ladylike grimace she gestured for the *foie gras* to be served. 'Honourable wounds, colonel.' She was after something. He so longed for ordinary recognition of his achievements that he chose to ignore the evidence. 'Morocco,' he rubbed the calf, 'pinching oranges! Ho, ho, ho! What can I do for you?'

He was having a stab at the bluff old soldier.

She, however, did not recognise the rôle and was upset by his levity. She had become used to people responding to her the way she demanded – 'nicely' or 'courteously'. She saw a flash of the Mo she had thought to extinguish by promotion, drawing him apparently into her confidences.

'You can guess, I'm sure. I'll be frank, Colonel Collier…'

'Okay. And Mo'll be Jerry.'

She looked at him in horror. She tried to grin.

'Sorry, ma'am.' Mo resumed the manner due to his station. 'Old Colonel Collier's a bit light-headed. He's been seeing things lately. Could be malaria, I suppose.' Major Nye was his model now.

'Things?'

He shrugged. 'Ghosts and stuff.'

'Well, I'll get straight to the point, colonel. Both Mr Cornelius and Mr Alvarez have disappeared from their homes, as you know.'

'Too true,' he said. 'Ma'am.'

'I've decided to ask you to head the investigation.'

'Do what?' Mo gripped the arms of his chair.

'We believe you're the best qualified to find them. Before it's too late.'

Mo chewed his toast and goose liver. 'Mo's still in the dark. Why too late?'

'Colonel Collier. We are attempting to preserve civilisation. There's only one way to do that. Your old friends – our old friends – could harm everything we've done.'

'You mean they've gone AWOL.'

'They are more likely to have been kidnapped. I was certain of their loyalty. But we expect you to find that out. Did they confide in you?'

'Not sure. Those phone calls. Ghosts. Whispers. He's been freaking out.'

'Mr Cornelius?'

'He thought it was. Or Frank, like you said.'

'Who thought it was?'

'Mo!' He wondered if she were listening at all. 'Me. He's – I'm…' Mo concentrated fiercely on his food again. 'It's the ankle. The head. The ears. The eyes. The heart.'

'Is there something you're not telling me?'

'Don't ask Mo. He doesn't know. They started a few days ago. Jerry seemed in trouble. Maybe it was Alvarez. There was no way of telling. Just static and stuff half the time. Hissing. Faint voices. The past.'

'That's silly. You mustn't let yourself get fanciful. Concentrate on the realities. There are only a few. You know how to end your ordeal, don't you, colonel? Track down the source of your pain.

The government shall give you every assistance. And when the time comes for action, you'll have all the positive back-up we can supply.'

'Cruises?' Mo's face flashed with hope. 'Big stuff?'

Miss Brunner put a middle-class hand on his knee. He winced. She nodded.

'Big stuff.'

23

A Mission Is Proposed

'You are an intelligent fellow, and you will ask how a Polish adventurer, meaning Enver, and a collection of Jews and gipsies should have got control of a proud race. The ordinary man will tell you that it was German organisation backed up with German money and arms. You will inquire again how, since Turkey is primarily a religious power, Islam has played so small a part in it all. The Sheikh-ul-Islam is neglected, and though the Kaiser proclaims a Holy War and calls himself Hadji Mohammed Guilliamo, and says the Hohenzollerns are descended from the Prophet, that seems to have fallen pretty flat. The ordinary man will answer that Islam in Turkey is becoming a back number, and that Krupp guns are the new gods. Yet – I don't know. I do not quite believe in Islam becoming a back number ... There is a dry wind blowing through the East, and the parched grasses wait the spark. And the wind is blowing towards the Indian border. Whence comes that wind, think you?'

– John Buchan,
Greenmantle, 1916

Mitzi Beesley sat in the back of the mobile detector van fiddling with her Remington's mechanism, opening and closing the breech. The clip was beside her on the bench. Her father, wearing headphones which rose and fell to the rhythm of his munching, tried to get a fix on a suspicious radio source. 'Could be Barnes,' he reported. 'Or it could be Chiswick.' He spoke into a microphone, relaying his progress to Miss Brunner at HQ. He felt slighted. Someone in his position should not have to do this. But there were only four experts left since Karen von Krupp had been assassinated in Croydon the previous Christmas. Mo Collier was driving. Miss Brunner was monitoring. Their carefully marshalled reserves were falling faster than they had anticipated. This was entropy with a vengeance and not at all what they had planned.

Mo parked the van near the entrance to the M4. 'Even closer.' Beesley became excited. 'Look at these gauges, Mitzi.' She brushed back her quiff and peered. 'We're almost on top of them.'

Mitzi was bored. She did not respond. Her gun presenting no further attention she opened her compact and began to restore her mascara and pillar-box lipstick.

The graphics screen showed them a large church, the Tube station, a couple of office blocks, a cinema. The rest was ruins.

Mo got out of the van. 'Back in ten minutes. I'll check out the Odeon.'

'My guess is the church,' said Beesley.

Mo ignored him.

'Want me?' Mitzi was eager. Her little blue eyes were filled with a cold, forbidding lust.

'If you're needed you'll hear on the walkie-talkie.' Mo held up the instrument. He trod cautiously over broken slabs to the venue, raised his Banning and blew a hole in the front doors. He ran up the steps and disappeared through the smoking entrance.

Five minutes later Mitzi pushed open the van's rear doors. 'I'm going to find him. He could be in trouble.'

'Nonsense.' Beesley had made himself comfortable with a box of chocolate rabbits. 'He's in his element. We'd have heard something from his radio. That's odd.' Reluctantly he returned to the controls. 'Like a sort of seagull noise. Nothing there now.' A little chocolate came out of the corner of his lip and began to move down his chin. 'The fix. Everything. All gone.'

Mitzi ran from the van, fitting her clip into the rifle. The nearest stage door stood open and she entered, back against the wall, slowly mounting the unlit concrete stairs.

It took her over half an hour to search the Odeon. When she

returned to the van her father was dozing, his hand on a melted bunny. He yawned as she shook him. 'Any luck?'

'It's deserted. A fade-out, I could swear. They've flown the coop, and Mo with them!'

'That's not possible these days. Miss Brunner neutralised the Time Centre. It was the most important, most thoroughly accomplished stage of her plan. There isn't a Shifter which hasn't been closed. The shut-down was completely successful.'

Mitzi smiled. She for one was glad things might be hotting up again.

24

Christine Addresses the Ladies

Oh my ladies, flee, flee the foolish love they urge on you! Flee it, for God's sake, flee! For no good can come to you from it. Rather, rest assured that however deceptive their lures, their end is always to your detriment. And do not believe the contrary, for it cannot be otherwise. Remember, dear ladies, how these men call you frail, unserious, and easily influenced but yet try hard, using all kinds of strange and deceptive tricks, to catch you, just as one lays traps for wild animals. Flee, flee, my ladies, and avoid their company – under these smiles are hidden deadly and painful poisons.

– Christine de Pizan,
The Book of the City of Ladies, 1405

Prinz Lobkowitz, pale and so thin it seemed he must crumble like a mummy once he was exposed to the air, stepped out of the old Rolls and into the warmth of the little High Street inn. There was a fire in the inglenook, horse brasses glittering, old pictures whose glass reflected the polished oak. The black beams above threatened his snowy head, for he was still tall. He understood how artificially this was maintained, but he still found the Cotswold comfort attractive. His secret vice, he decided, though the anti-Semitism turned his stomach occasionally. He had studied dozens of books and films in an effort to discover an insight into the baffling logic of twentieth-century British mysticism and its links with the Christian ideals which somehow allowed the rise of Hitler. He had read *Goodbye, Mr Chips* more than *Lost Horizon*, *A Prince of the Captivity* more than *Mr Standfast*, while Dornford Yates, Warwick Deeping and Charles Morgan offered even less than H.E. Bates. He wondered if he were looking in the right places.

The Eagle and Child in Runford was one of the strangest symbols of this peculiar mixture of vice and virtue, of public-spirited, generous devotion and insular intolerance, even hatred, of everything which remained unconquered or foreign.

Prinz Lobkowitz crossed the dark lobby to the counter where Catherine Cornelius, in black and white, smiled affectionately but pretended she did not know him very well. 'How nice to see you again, sir. We received your telegram yesterday evening. How was your journey?'

'Rather tiring, but interesting.'

Two red-faced men at the bar detected his accent and looked briefly in his direction. Their expressions were non-committal. Lobkowitz knew an unwelcome frisson of familiarity. He removed his homburg and placed it neatly on the counter. Catherine offered him the book to sign.

'Thank you, Prince Michael,' she said, winking just for him. He smiled. She had confused them expertly.

Mo Collier came slowly through the door from where he had been serving in the public bar. 'Evening, sir.' Touching his forelock he picked up the prince's bag and led the way up the narrow staircase.

'We'll have a meal for you in the snug as soon as you want it.' Catherine returned her attention to the next day's luncheon menus.

It was only a moment before one of the men said cheerfully, 'Visitor's royal is 'e, then, miss?'

'Queen Victoria's great-nephew. From one of the oldest families in Europe. He can trace his bloodline back to before Roman times.'

'Bet 'e's worth a bit, then, eh?'

'Most of his fortune went to help British prisoners in the Balkans.' She referred to the BEF in support of the Turks in their abortive attempt to re-establish their old borders. They had been surprised by the Israeli push through Syria into Anatolia as far as the old NATO pipeline. At this, Britain had withdrawn due to conflict of interest.

'Decent old bloke by the look of 'im.'

'Decent as they come.' Catherine watched Mo descend. She was tense. Now everyone was here. She looked forward to closing time.

Major Nye was the first to call 'Drink up, gentlemen, please', from the private bar. He was the perfect picture of a retired Indian Army officer who had invested his savings here. The only problem they had had was with Jerry, who was well-known, sought-for, and only occasionally conscious, and Professor Hira, who was now completely out of place since hardly anyone of his colour still existed in England.

Alvarez, in striped apron and rolled shirtsleeves, closed the doors on the final customer and went immediately into the low-ceilinged shuttered dining room. Here Mrs Persson, in a loose-fitting, long-skirted suit, sat on a table waiting for the others. In the only leather easy chair Jerry Cornelius dreamed, his sister seated beside him on the arm. Major Nye and Professor Hira were followed in by Mo Collier escorting Prinz Lobkowitz.

'Well, here we all are,' said Alvarez. He was sour as usual, resenting the massive weight of habit which he refused to confuse with loyalty. He was a technician and his job, as he saw it, was to keep his mind as completely objective as possible. Only Mrs Persson's logic, he assured himself, had got him back into dickering with Professor Hira's lash-up which he regarded with a mixture of horrified awe and contempt, on one level unable to believe it could work at all and on another fascinated by a set of principles he could not really hope to comprehend. He avoided Hira's amiable eye.

Una said: 'It's time to pool whatever we have. We need to break up the walls Miss Brunner's erected. Then it will be much easier to build afresh. We need a good base; a new beginning. After that, things will spread in all directions again. The alternatives will be there to choose from. Others people will create for themselves. The centre – the core if you like – will, however, be run on female principles.'

'Quite so,' said Professor Hira. 'That's the secret.'

'How's it to be done?' Major Nye patted pockets in search of tobacco. 'We're so few.'

'Old-fashioned problems,' she said, 'demand old-fashioned remedies. They want Merrie England, King Arthur, jousting, maypoles, roasted ox and so on; the peasants in their place, the landlord secure and therefore, they argue, benign. Pageantry and armour. Chrétien de Troyes and the hard road to grace.'

'What? Where Elvis died?' Mo's hands had never shaken so violently.

'That was Memphis,' said Alvarez. 'And if we're talking about Christian mystery corrupted to justify human rapacity...'

'Don't pick on Memphis. We exported it there.' Mo looked about him. 'Didn't we? Like Cleopatra's needle.' Mo's sense of history was patchy but eager.

Prinz Lobkowitz was looking utterly baffled. He wondered if his command of English was all it should be. Too much reading in the past, perhaps?

'We don't have the time for this.' Una sucked her unlit Sherman's, turning to where Jerry lazed, a silly smile on his face as if he had just understood a joke made minutes earlier. 'Jerry's the one with the religious background. At least, he's the person who had a stab at following through, unlike you, Alvarez.'

'I never actually fancied those nuns.' Jerry was still defensive. 'Eh?' He blinked. 'It isn't my style. But I was fond of them.'

'She means the Jesuit stuff,' said Catherine gently.

'It was a phase I went through.'

'Some parts of it could be useful now.' As Una displayed impatience, Catherine curbed her urge to defend her brother. 'The basis, perhaps. You know how to reduce things.'

'It was because of the war.' He looked up in the hope of sympathy. 'Not just Martin Luther. There's nothing in that, really, except a kind of mental training. Some good brains, I think.' He smiled at her like a child suddenly struck by happiness.

'Oh, I get it! I could redeem myself, couldn't I? Become what I set out to be? And that.'

Una bit back a retort. She was trying hard to keep from making him leave, the habit was so strong. But she had no wish to return him to Miss Brunner. Moreover it had become obvious, since they had begun their experiments at The Eagle and Child, that Jerry actually was unique in certain important aspects.

'Miss Brunner and I were incompatible,' he told Una seriously. 'That's why we broke up.'

'We know all about that.'

'My father never intended to involve her. He didn't even know her. She came across his stuff. My mum knew best. But she's dead, of course.'

'Was your mother au fait with your father's work?' Professor Hira was surprised.

'She was his bloody inspiration.' Jerry's expression hardened. His shoulders began to straighten. 'She gave him all his ideas.'

'He doesn't mean the math,' said Catherine, herself puzzled by this apparent remission. 'He means the basics.'

'Never should have let Miss Brunner have anything to do with it. All that stupid fucking about in Lapland. It's been years, hasn't it? Years since we had our chance. Frank let me think you were dead, Cathy.

'I was dead,' she said. 'Sort of. As good as.'

'I was disguising my feelings a bit.' He became embarrassed as he realised there were so many witnesses to his confession. 'I didn't want to admit it couldn't go ahead. At the same time, I wasn't altogether myself. Self-pity, really. But I called it grief.'

'It might have been,' said Una. She was beginning to get his drift. 'You're talking about Lapland. That programme of Miss Brunner's?'

'Isn't that what you meant?'

'Partly.' Una became serious, leaving the table and walking carefully towards him as if she feared she might startle him into some form of retreat.

'I thought I was giving up everything,' he told her, dropping his voice, becoming intimate. 'I really did, Una. The ultimate sacrifice. But I think there was too much cynicism there. Can you get crucified in a crucible?' He laughed. 'It was all alchemy. Both of them – my father and Miss Brunner – used it as a foundation. But Miss Brunner dismissed my mother's importance, you see. And everything that went with it. Frank. Catherine. Jerry. Well, it makes sense. Threes and nines. That sort of sense, too. The knowledge was my father's. I'll grant you. But the wisdom was hers. Miss Brunner's not so different. She wants to be some sort of man, I suppose. She listens to men because she thinks they've got the secret. She dismisses women. I'm too weak…' He closed his eyes.

Catherine grinned. She had few fears for her brother's immediate future. 'Have we got an oracle, Una?'

'Good enough for our purposes.' Looking down at the old assassin Una shook her head. His body was limp again. His head fell to one side. He began to utter huge, ugly snores. 'How much more can he take?'

'Quite a bit, on record,' said his sister. 'Shall I give him another shot?'

Alvarez said petulantly from near the door. 'What I want to know is are we in business or are we not in business?'

'I think we are,' said Major Nye. His attention was on Jerry, whom he loved like a son.

'Well, then,' Collier spoke dourly, 'who's going to help old Mo shift this lot to Glastonbury?'

'To where?' Jerry had woken up on his own. 'To where?' He tried to wet his lips but failed. He was looking terrified again. Any trace of serenity had vanished. 'M = L = C. They're all the same. Oh, Christ! The Cretan Circuit problem. So that's why it's mixed up with Turkey!'

Una almost winced as she put her hand on Jerry's sweating head. 'He's got a vicious temperature. What can we do?'

'Sacrifice!' Jerry rolled his eyes. 'Mother!' Then he collapsed and was insensible once more.

'I blame the Convent,' said Alvarez unsympathetically. 'That's where you pick up ideas like that.'

'But why is he so scared?' Almost rudely, Major Nye pushed past Prinz Lobkowitz to get to Jerry's side. 'What are you planning to do with him?'

'Nothing he wasn't born for,' said the Prinz miserably.

'You didn't know those nuns.' Alvarez looked with deep self-pity at his past. 'The Jews were lucky they weren't running Sachsenburg.'

'Do you know South Africa, sergeant?' Major Nye was surprised.

'Never been within a sjambok's throw of the place.' Alvarez was cautious. 'I prefer colder climes.'

'You're safe enough here,' said Catherine.

'Well, anyway.' Mo Collier was growing impatient. 'Does he get his orders? Is someone going to lend a hand?'

'I'm sorry.' Una noted that Jerry seemed to be back to normal and was sleeping. 'I think there's more abstraction in this than I can take. I need a moment.'

Mo let off a disgusted fart.

25
Lost Gods

> It was a very young man's talk. I was about his own age but I had knocked about a bit and saw its crudity. Yet it most deeply impressed me. There were fire and poetry in it, and there was also a pleasant shrewdness. He had had his 'call' and was hastening to answer it. Henceforth his life was to be dedicated to one end, the building up of a British Equatoria, with the highlands of the East and South as the white man's base. It was to be both a white man's and black man's country, a new kingdom of Prester John. It was to link up South Africa with Egypt and the Sudan, and thereby complete Rhodes's plan. It was to be a magnet to attract our youth and a settlement ground for our surplus population. It was to carry with it a spiritual renaissance for England.
>
> – John Buchan,
> *The Isle of Sheep*, 1936

Miss Brunner's vision of Utopia was as powerful, she instructed herself, as ever. Taking it that an Ice Age was inevitable, no matter how it was created, it would still be possible to reconstruct the country as soon as the meltdown was achieved. But the preliminary work was important. She had laid the foundations thoroughly. Those serpents who had not fled her Eden had either been crushed or reformed. In castle and cottage, village and town, the British were free from strike and anxiety, from all those evils which had come to fruit in the twentieth century. It had been hard, bloody work, involving enormous sacrifice and causing terrible soul-searching. She had done her duty and begrudged nothing of what she had given. It had been for the good of the majority and she expected no reward, though she appreciated acknowledgement. But she still needed as much time as possible to continue her quest. This was for nothing less than the very soul of England. Now that the land was purified and purged, as Bishop Beesley had put it, it would soon emerge from the winter into the springtime, born again with a maypole on every green, a BBC to be proud of and a wholesome, decent younger generation with untainted ideals and an urgent desire to devote itself to public service. Slowly that great source of pride and responsibility of duty and devotion, which had taken on the nature of a genuine religion before the big wars of the twentieth century (the result chiefly of German jealousy) had knocked the stuffing out of people, the British Empire would flourish, a thing of permanence and a model to the rest of the world, as well as a reservoir of strength. The Australian solution was merely a stopgap, until matters could be righted.

Miss Brunner thought that anyone who opposed this vision was positively evil. Yet she pitied them their folly. It must be terrible to lead a life without meaning; a life devoted to destruction. She had never understood how any sane person could willingly set about the creation of anarchy. And the bizarre thing was that so many of these fanatics were women! They were a disgrace to their sex. They were truly perverted. Miss Brunner knew that self-sacrifice and discipline were always worth more in the end. Free will was a self-indulgent fallacy, a rationalisation for any form of wantonness or licence.

She stood on the battlements of Windsor Castle, her pale hand resting lightly on a Fender V2 howitzer, looking towards the town which, with neighbouring Eton, had become the chief gathering place of her great assembly of knights: the picked men whose chosen vocation was to defend the English way and seek the English Grail. Bishop Beesley and his daughter, dressed in the uniform of a major in the Household Cavalry, joined her. The sun was fading in a cold, blue sky. There were faint, elongated shadows in the Great Park. From the west a sudden flurry of wings set the branches of elms to waving like the hands of frightened matrons and a cloud of starlings rose against misty light from the river, then veered away into silence above red roofs.

'You are the reincarnation, dear lady, of our noblest rulers.' He bowed as far as his stomach would permit, keeping one hand on his wobbling mitre, the other on his crook. 'You are King Arthur in heart if not in body. And here, all round you, is Camelot restored again. Camelot before the armies of Mordred and Morgana le Fay rose against it. Here is our fortress against Darkness and Ignorance, our guarantee of permanence and true, unsullied tranquillity.'

She refused his proffered Bounty. She had never had much of a liking for nuts. 'I owe much of this to you, archbishop. While I have an understanding of our temporal needs, you provide profound knowledge of needs which are spiritual. Is there any further news of those few traitors who would destroy our cause?'

'None, marm. They are confined, I am ascertained, to dwelling beyond our borders. They have neither the strength of mind nor of character to threaten us much, and they surely lack strength of numbers.'

'Gods,' she said, palms against granite as she leaned forward to watch the barbed wire going up around the moat, 'if 'twere only fully confirmed. Must we yet do battle with them?'

'I think not, marm.'

'Good bishop!' She placed a grateful finger against his apron. 'Say so once more so I might rest easy in my bed this night.'

'Madam, we have taken away their weapons, exorcised their

spirits, banished them to the netherworld. Their very titles are forgot!'

She closed her eyes, saying in a whisper: 'I have not forgot them, my lord. Hourly their names are paraded through my skull. O, what a litany of evil! Would that they had been destroyed while we had them fully in our power.'

'We shall be sure next time, madam, if any live to be captured. But I think they'll not survive the Great Winter.'

'Let us pray so, archbishop. But let us also never forget they had recourse to demonic power.'

'That power is no more, madam!'

She let her long body in its rich costume lean against the battlement. From a field a trumpet sounded and horses trotted, rattling, towards a trough.

Bishop Beesley scratched under his mitre, looking sceptical. He enjoyed the spectacle of the striped pavilions, the standards, the crests, the bright bucklers with their ancient coats of arms, the blazons of a thousand knightly families; the cooking fires, the music of dulcimers and lyres, the hurrying squires, all seen against the lovely towers and spires of Eton. He was reminded, he told himself, of English chivalry on the eve of Poitiers; but actually it came to him that what he saw was the flower of the French aristocracy before Agincourt. He felt he had been a hair away from uttering heresy and gasped. This was pageantry; a tableau, no more. He turned his head. Then comfortable Windsor's Georgian and Victorian brick returned.

'Are we certain of our strategy?' He asked mildly, anxious not to attract her wrath.

'For the parade? The progress?'

'Aye, madam. For that.'

'Quite certain, my lord bishop.'

'All we need to know then,' Mitzi said, polishing her gorget with her glove, 'is where they'll choose to fight.'

'Fight?' Miss Brunner rounded on her well before the bishop's warning eye could prepare her. 'Is there some tournament arranged?'

'I thought a battle –'

'My daughter jests, Your Majesty.'

'I am not My Majesty, sir. Not yet.'

'There had been some talk of jousting.'

She pushed the red locks from her eyes, her ornamental sleeve brushing a golden leaf from the granite. 'What do you keep back, my lord? News of our enemies?'

'A rumour, my lady. No more.'

'Then out with this rumour, sir!'

'Our spies report a gathering of some kind. Near the town of Glastonbury. But we are by no means certain what it imports.'

'Imports? Why, sir, can you not guess?'

'It would be foolish to guess, madam.'

'Don't want to send the army off on a wild-goose chase,' said Mitzi. 'That'd be daft.' She was oblivious of her failure to get into the swing of things. 'I mean, think of the Battle of Hastings. We'd be marching all over the country and be exhausted by the time push came to shove.'

Miss Brunner looked at her with open dislike. She could scarcely believe that Bishop Beesley who was, admittedly, of the middle class, had not educated her better. Instead he had dragged her across the world with him, virtually turning her into a whore when it suited his ends. She yearned for better material. She knew it was out there, on the field, and that she would find it eventually. Meanwhile she must content herself with what she had. She felt that since she had made improvements where manners and deportment were concerned, the bishop might have done as much or, at least, ensured Mitzi was properly finished. But he lacked her resolve. He possessed a desire for the same things but not the will with which she had achieved them.

'But you think it's them,' she said. 'At Glastonbury.'

'The detectors suggest…' began Beesley.

'The old Arlekin troupe, eh?' She was frowning. 'It was inevitable. What would you prefer to do if you were they? Remain in limbo? They have no choice but to fight one last time. No choice.'

'No choice.' Mitzi became a military echo. Her small, rather greedy features had never looked more satisfied. She gripped her sabre hilt with her left hand, straightening the blade against her thigh.

'To fight,' said Miss Brunner softly, 'and to lose. I suppose I admire that. There is no way to win against me. Not now.'

'We'll have them where and when we want them,' said Mitzi. 'Our Commonwealth shall last a thousand – two thousand – three thousand...'

Bishop Beesley drew his daughter aside. 'Don't get over-excited, dear. I must say I was hoping to break the news a little less suddenly.'

'I didn't do anything wrong.' Mitzi shrugged away from him. 'She's as pleased as Punch.'

It did seem to the bishop his leader had grown more alert, but he was more concerned with Mitzi. He was unused to this attitude in his daughter. Pensively he felt in his pockets for his Smarties. He was not sure what had got into her but he secretly suspected Miss Brunner. Since she had formally renounced all previous treaties and compacts and declared a policy of armed neutrality she had grown more devious with her close colleagues. This displayed the beginnings, he believed, of extreme paranoia. In a way he was glad Mitzi had given herself so enthusiastically to the new rôle. They would, after this, have to be more than usually wary. When all external enemies were defeated Miss Brunner would inevitably turn on old friends. It was in the nature of things. He felt a cold touch on his cheek. He looked up. It was clouding over. A few snowflakes were falling.

26

Troubles in Syria

In the presence of the scenes of horror that are unfolding daily before our very eyes outside our school, our work as teachers becomes a challenge to humanity. How can we make our Armenian pupils read the story of *Snow White and the Seven Dwarfs*, how can we teach them to conjugate and decline, when in the yards next to the school their compatriots are dying of hunger? When almost naked girls, women and children, some lying on the ground, others huddled among the dying or the waiting coffins, are breathing their last breath?

Of the 2-3,000 peasants, women and girls from Upper Armenia brought here in good health, only 40 or 50 skeletal figures remain. The prettiest among them are victims of the lust of their guards. The ugly ones succumb to blows, hunger or thirst; for although they are lying beside the river they are not allowed to drink. Europeans are forbidden to distribute bread to the starving. Every day more than a hundred corpses are taken away from Aleppo. And all this is happening under the eyes of senior Turkish officials. 40 or 50 skeletal spectres are piled up in the courtyard opposite our school.

They are women driven crazy; they no longer know how to eat! When one offers them some bread, they throw it aside, and take no interest in it. They moan and wait to die. 'That', say the natives, 'is the *Ta-a-lim el Alman* (the teaching of the Germans).'

Letter to the German Minister of Foreign Affairs in Berlin from four teachers at the Realschüle, Aleppo, 8 October, 1915 (quoted in *The Armenians: From Genocide to Resistance*, 1983)

'Class war, too. The gods of the nobles are not the gods of the commons. The Celtic aristocracy knew Rhiannon, Mannanan and the rest, but perhaps the people only worshipped Brigantia. And out of the Goddess came forth witchcraft. And from that old knowledge, misunderstood, misused, the likes of Miss Brunner produce their hollow magic. They can create delusions but they are incapable of performing any true change. The grammar of the people is borrowed always in order to keep them in their place. We can't defeat Miss Brunner with her methods – besides, they're scarcely methods at all. But we can look back to the sources and from those sources tap the original power. We have the pride and anger of the frustrated masses, aching for some control over their own destiny, for knowledge and glamour, forever defeated by soft-tongued diplomats.' Prinz Lobkowitz smiled briefly. 'You have the source in your furious goddess. Your Brigantia. It stands to reason that some day she must be avenged.'

Una was beginning to wish she had never begun the conversation. As with most elderly men, Prinz Lobkowitz had become a bit of a droner, though he had not, apparently, lost his wits. How could she resist saying: 'On every man?' as she looked tenderly at her ex-lover?

'Sadly, I fear so. Perhaps only for a little while. I have no experience of her mercy.'

They had found the main chamber at the centre of the maze and watched in the dim gaslight as Mo and the others worked to set up the equipment. Part of the complex hollowed from the Tor had always been here but a good deal of it was restored or new. There had been some idea of using it as a base, perhaps a nuclear shelter, until a couple of minor cave-ins had changed the minds of whichever authority had sought to take the old hill over. There was also a rumour that, having reinforced the maze and developed it, they had lost too many staff in it, some of whom had never returned.

'Well, well, well.' Alvarez was almost cheerful. He came up to them, rubbing his oily hands. 'I suppose if we fail we can hope a bleeding flying saucer will come down and rescue us. Har, har, har.'

Una shared his contempt for the corruption but continued to find his general manner offensive. Her patience with most men, never considerable at the best of times, was shorter than ever. It made her work in some ways harder, in others easier. At least she did not experience the confusion she felt when she considered her enemies, Miss Brunner and Mitzi Beesley. They continued, in her eyes, to be both traitors and redeemable. Her emotions were therefore a good deal less trustworthy. Catherine, however, she trusted implicitly, almost as much as she trusted herself.

Major Nye had taken charge of Jerry's wheelchair. With the exception of Catherine, he seemed to be the only person who genuinely cared for the last male Cornelius. Having little left to do that was practical, he plainly felt happier looking after Jerry. 'Recognise all the boffinalia, old boy? They're turning it into some sort of big receiver now. For the duration, as it were. Tapping any spare energy we can find. Big show coming up in a day or two.'

Jerry mumbled a request. His skin had returned to the lifeless grey of former times.

'Certainly, old chap. Glad to oblige.' Major Nye began to sing 'Lily of Laguna' and followed it up with 'You're the Cream in My Coffee, You're the Milk in My Tea'. Unable to form words very well, Jerry crooned along as best he could.

Mo paused in his work to glare at the two as they went by. 'Bloody ligger, as usual. I thought we were all supposed to be pulling our weight, not our plonkers!'

'He's not ready to work yet.' Catherine handed him up a fresh circuit board.

'He's avoiding it, you mean.'

'If you knew what he knew, you'd be avoiding it as well.' She had gone off Mo since his final fart. She felt it was probably unwholesome to like so few people and to tolerate them only marginally, but she felt it did not much matter. Eventually she hoped to discover certain qualities of her brother's in herself. She must be patient.

Professor Hira was somewhere in the shadows of the rocky roof. She heard his voice calling out to Mo to bring up the circuit. Carefully Mo unhooked protection from his belt and began a slow ascent, as if he were climbing some two-thousand-foot slab in Yosemite.

Catherine took Una aside as soon as her friend had a spare second. 'Is it my imagination or are some of the men getting cruder and cruder?'

'I noticed the same thing. They're probably reverting, but it isn't serious. Resentment of that sort usually comes out in childish posturing, scatological jokes and so on. Apparently we only have Alvarez and Collier to worry about. The others seem surprisingly content with the situation.'

'Alvarez just described them as a bunch of poofters. Under his breath, to me.'

'I suppose we should be sympathetic.' Una laughed openly. 'We'd better get used to it. If this comes off we'll see a lot more like them in the future.'

'I still can't understand why Mo is quite content to work for Miss Brunner but doesn't like working for us.'

'We can't press the same buttons. That combination is what wins in the short term. A kind of ruthless willingness to use power in a masculine context but with the committed energy of a woman.' Una was growing bored with analysis since her long chat with Prinz Lobkowitz. 'Anyway, it impresses chaps like Mo. He understands the pecking order. The mistake we make is to appeal to parts of him which he either flatly denies exist or would rather forget about. He understands those characteristics as weakness because he believes them to be female. Poor bugger.'

Major Nye returned, pushing Jerry ahead of him. 'I gather we're almost ready. All hooked up for the final programme, eh?'

The joke was mysterious, but evidently he found it extremely amusing for he continued to laugh long after he had passed them. Then, very suddenly, his laughter stopped.

Catherine looked back. In the dim light she saw Jerry stand in his wheelchair and wave his arms. He stumbled forward while

Major Nye ran up, seeming to embrace him. 'The second – the new – coming. Coming!' Jerry stared wildly around him. 'They're coming. The whole bloody lot of them. And we're not finished!'

'Quite right, old son. Not finished by a long shot. We'll show 'em!' Major Nye was having trouble holding his charge. 'I say, could somebody give me a hand with him? I'm not as young as I used to be.'

Catherine ran forward. She helped the major get Jerry back into his wheelchair.

Jerry's voice was controlled and his eyes were steady when he looked at her next. 'They're on their way, Cath. It's Hello, Goodbye.' His smile was sweet.

Catherine began to cry.

Hira's voice was a vast boom from on high. 'Good show, Mr Collier. That should be the last component. Can you switch on, sergeant?'

Almost immediately the cavern was filled with music.

Jerry flexed his fingers and got out of the wheelchair. 'How are you now, old chap?' Major Nye was relieved. 'Feeling up to the mark again?'

'$N_2O_4(g) = 2NO_2(g)$.'

'What's that, old boy?'

'It's what the movement towards equilibrium must correspond to a decrease in,' said Jerry. 'You know, major, the free energy landscape. $G = H - TS$? $AG < 0$? 325K? Follow me?'

'I wish you'd try to find something better than the second law of thermodynamics, Jerry.' Una could not understand how his bloom had returned so rapidly. It was as if he fed off music. Was that a clue? 'It's the free energy minimum you should be concentrating on.'

'Then I'm on the right wavelength.'

'Don't be smug, Jerry.'

'I only sound smug,' he said. 'I was actually trying to be funny.'

'That's worse. Do you want to see what's going on outside?'

'Outside where? Is this Lapland?'

'It never was Lapland. Not in your father's stuff. My guess is

Miss Brunner misread the map. Or put the wrong two and two together. We're in Glastonbury Tor.'

'Oh, shit.' He looked afraid again. 'Well, I suppose I've had a good run.'

'I still wonder how much you always knew and refused to communicate. Or denied to yourself. Which was it?'

'I'm not the right person to ask, Una.' He was no longer facetious. He shivered. 'Can't they play anything other than Number Six?'

'Change the Beethoven.' Cathy spoke into the mike she was carrying. She looked to her brother. 'What to?'

'Anything else except Mahler's *Song of the Earth*. Oh, or the, you know, dead kids.' He followed Mrs Persson up the rickety wooden ladder into a misty gallery where TV screens displayed their immediate surroundings. 'We should get on with this quickly. I'm in danger of turning into a second-rate Doctor Who.'

'I've got news for you –' Una began, then changed her mind. She realised she had always believed him invulnerable. This was why his self-pity had always seemed especially ludicrous to her. She felt at last that he had some right to misery.

'We're completely surrounded.' Catherine waved at the screens. 'See.'

Banners flapped like the yards of windless clippers. Miss Brunner's pseudo-Arthurian arms, with a dragon dominant, were visible on flags, the sides of tanks and rocket launchers, her special cavalry. It was a massive army. Barely visible beyond it were Glastonbury's mellow towers. In a costume vaguely calling to mind both Mary and Elizabeth Tudor, Miss Brunner was seated on the turret of a Warwick Mk VII. They had made some sort of side-saddle for her. She had just given a speech. The men nearest her were cheering and waving their weapons. Jerry noticed not a single Australian present. He mentioned the fact to Catherine.

'Everyone seems to have decided this is a local affair and should be settled internally. I gather that's pretty much the entire British Army out there.'

'What happens if they beat us?'

'Death. God knows what horrors she'll resurrect. Public burning? Hanging, drawing and quartering?'

'And if we win?'

'Not a lot. The chance of a fresh start.'

'For me?' He was daring himself to ask the question.

'You don't really win either way, my dear. In terms of your ego, at any rate.'

'Are we going to get on with the show?'

'Not much longer.' She turned away, not trusting to keep to their agreed course if she had to watch him weep. 'You had some good ideas. They'll be used. But your methods were muddy. Imprecise. Tarnished.'

'And I shan't get to see the Grail?'

'You said it, Lancelot.'

'C = M = C = M = C.' His laughter was interrupted by a yawn. 'Sorry.'

'You could die with dignity,' she said. 'At least.'

'Bugger that. Mandala equals Circuit, equals Maze, equals Cell, equals Cauldron, equals Womb. I deserve to see the Grail.'

'Only women have that power as things stand. You could look, but you wouldn't see it. Don't you remember anything?'

Jerry's attention was drawn to a screen. The Beesley armoured staff car, a huge Mercedes, had rolled out of the main ranks and come to rest at the foot of the Tor. 'I think he wants to parley.'

'Is that a good sign for us?' asked Catherine.

'It doesn't mean a thing.' Una squinted at the television. 'Not when Beesley's involved.'

'Which one of us should go?' Catherine adjusted the left strap of her attack-suit. 'Me?'

'Major Nye's best suited for that.'

Catherine went to find the old soldier. Jerry recovered himself and was apparently relaxed. He put his hands deep in the pockets of his black car coat. 'So the labyrinth's complete again. This is its heart? Were you ever at Hampton Court?'

'Miss Brunner never invited me.'

'Before that. And what are you, Una? Mistress of the Maze?'

'I serve that mistress.'

He looked at her sharply, surprised by her seriousness. 'There's Miss Brunner and her witchcraft, her clumsy alchemy, and you going for a load of Jungian nonsense. I'm almost glad I'm doomed.'

'You're overstating things. All that will happen, if we're successful, is a replication of the same experiment you tried with Miss Brunner. You were incompatible then. This time we've licked all those problems! Our main worry is about the conditions we're working in. Did you say 325K?'

Dumbly he signalled his reluctant affirmation. 'We split up,' he said.

'It could never have worked. I was amazed to see it go on as long as it did.' She made a quick calculation on her wrist-computer. 'Everything else has been checked. Enzymes and so forth. We've had a full model operating for a month. This time, whatever other side effects, we won't be getting any unwanted pseudo-clones.'

'I was fond of them.'

'Perfectly understandable. But now all our eggs are in one basket. Only one chance.'

'How do we stop their guns?'

'We appeal to them. Sort of.'

'Appeal to those sweaty bastards? We might as well give up here and now.'

'Obviously we have to impress them first.'

He made a stab at retreating. 'Cnossos. Linear B. Womb.'

'You know as well as I do there's no going back.'

'Some rotten treacherous bloody Ariadne you turned out to be. You fooled me into thinking I was Perseus. Now you're saying I've got to be the Minotaur.'

'That's nonsense. This is a try at laying the Minotaur's ghost for good and all. Don't you feel a hint of memory, pleasure? Is it all buried? Were you ever really conscious?'

'Levels and kinds,' he said with a trace of his old self-confidence. 'Don't know mine, I won't knock yours. I thought we were a pool.'

She was shocked by his understanding. 'You're quite right.' A small breath. 'I was forgetting.'

'But what have you got to lose, I wonder, Una?'

'I'm not sure.' She turned away. This was no time to be angry with herself. 'My faith?'

'Hang on to it. There isn't a better catalyst. It'll set me a good example.'

She refused herself the luxury of embracing him.

27

Artois

In the famous Labyrinth, which by the middle of the month was practically in French hands, a murderous subterranean warfare endured for weeks. Tunnels ran thirty or forty feet below the ground, and that triangle between the Bethune and Lille roads was the scene of a struggle which for nightmarish horror can be paralleled only from the sack of some medieval city. The French, no longer moving freely in the open with flowers in their caps, as on the first day of the advance, fought from cellar to cellar, from sap-head to sap-head, hacking their way through partition walls. The only light came from the officers' electric torches. The enemy resisted stubbornly, and there, far below the earth, men fought at the closest quarters with picks and knives and bayonets – often like wild beasts with teeth and hands.

– John Buchan,
Nelson's History of the War, Vol. VIII, 1915

Major Nye picked his way carefully down the path until he reached the bottom of the Tor along the lane where Bishop Beesley waited. In the gold and black livery of a warrior-priest, his standard carried by a brocaded page, five men-at-arms (SAS) at his back, his daughter Mitzi, seated on a gelded chestnut, the white flag tied to her lance, on his right, the bishop sniffed. The late April air was sweet in his nostrils. Major Nye had been under ground so long he had forgotten how beautiful the Somerset countryside could be. From force of habit and from his natural amiability he offered his hand to the bishop who had to put fudge in pocket, transfer crook to plump left fist, and shake.

Major Nye was surprised to notice, discreet on the other side of the hedge, TV cameras taping the proceedings. 'Bit odd, that, isn't it?'

Bishop Beesley was conciliatory. A massive sigh of sympathy. 'Miss Brunner, in her wisdom, thought it best to treat the whole business as a sort of game. Seasonal fun, you know. The exact mixture of sport and pageantry which makes England such a jolly place to live in. I'm sure you'll agree there's no need to alarm the public.'

'Good god, man! What if there's bloodshed? Presumably those weapons are real. Your artillery won't be firing blanks will it?'

'That's the point, major. If you'll agree to our plan, that's exactly what they will be firing. And not a soul will be hurt. You'll have safe escort to the coast. A boat to any non-European destination you choose. All of you, I mean.'

'Even Jerry.' Mitzi motioned with a lance rather too heavy for her. 'Even those shitty turncoats Collier and Alvarez. Our quality of mercy's pretty high, wouldn't you say? Given that we out-weapon and outnumber you? But say the word, major! Our shells and rockets'll fall on your earthworks like the gentle bleeding rain from heaven. You've bugger all to hit back with. Certainly nothing nuclear. Our geigers would know.'

'You do seem, major, to be a bit up against it.' Bishop Beesley took a fresh handkerchief from his back pocket and handed it over. Major Nye began to wipe a sticky palm. 'Miss Brunner's not the whole hundred per cent stable. Between you and me. She might change her mind later.'

'Then your terms are worthless!' Major Nye was puzzled.

'Give 'em a shot! There's a good chap. Isn't it better than being wiped out on that miserable hill? The town would suffer, too. And the countryside. Please don't merely think of yourselves, major. I promise Mitzi and myself will do everything to ensure your safety.'

'I'll tell my colleagues. How long do we have to consider?'

'Until yonder orb has set and risen!' Mitzi leaned forward, the weight of her lance almost toppling her from the horse. 'If we've heard nothing by dawn, we waste no further time, sir! England's mighty armour shall hurl her weight upon you, crushing that hill. Crushing all the vermin that shelter in its horrid twittens.'

Major Nye blinked. 'Sorry?'

From beneath his surplice Bishop Beesley removed a large gold timepiece. 'Until lighting-up time tomorrow morning.' He regarded the cold sky. 'I have a feeling there'll be snow before then, don't you?' He wet his thick, grey lips. 'It's impossible to trust the weather.'

Major Nye felt they should be tossing a coin or inspecting the ground. 'A little late for snow, I'd say.'

'Never too late for snow.' The bishop was enjoying a private joke. 'Eh?'

The old soldier put his hands into the torn linings of his Norfolk. 'Frankly, I'm pretty thoroughly in the dark.'

'You're twenty-four hours ahead of yourself.' Mitzi grinned. It seemed to Major Nye she had sharpened her teeth to little points. Now he thought about it, there was something strangely barbaric in the whole display.

'I've a feeling,' he said, 'we'll decide to stick it out. From what you say, Miss Brunner is not easily reasoned with. You'll recall, moreover, this was our idea. We're not attempting to take your power.'

'Then why –?' Bishop Beesley was a trifle confounded. 'What do you want from us?'

'We want you to stop, old boy.'

Mitzi, with awkward ferocity, turned her horse's head in the direction of their grey pavilions. 'We fight for the soul of England, sir. For the lost Grail. For what we can salvage from the ruins. For what is best in us!'

Major Nye looked back at the top of the Tor where the stone remains of St Michael's Church, crenellated as if for defence, stood sharply out against the clouding sky.

As his daughter galloped back to the ranks, Bishop Beesley apologised. 'She's completely under Miss Brunner's spell, I'm afraid. I suppose you can't blame her. She's an impressionable child. Miss Brunner has an extremely forceful personality. Sometimes, even I...' He shrugged and searched for the fudge he had temporarily set aside. 'My advice, as a simple man of the cloth, is head for the Scillies tonight. Would you all fit in the same whirlybird?'

'Oh, easily.'

'Well.' Bishop Beesley popped confectionery into his maw and swallowed. 'You could go to America. There's still room for your sort there. Slip out of the country. Take the train to Penzance, say. Or even Portsmouth.' He chuckled uncertainly. 'Was that where the *Mayflower* sailed from?'

'We haven't a lot in common with the Pilgrim Fathers, old boy. Rather less than you.'

'This is no time to be splitting hairs, major.' A flurry of cold air captured his robes and banners. They flapped noisily. 'We'll both freeze to death standing here.' He dropped his voice, as if to make sure his hard men did not overhear. 'I give all this fifteen years before it crumbles completely. There'll be plenty of time after that to begin any new millennium you like. Play a waiting game, major. This is an era where cunning and patience are of greater value than displays of old-fashioned derring-do.'

'We're members of society, old boy. That involves moral responsibilities.'

'Naturally. I've said as much. So has Miss B.'

'Well, then, I suggest we follow our duty as we see it.'

Bishop Beesley frowned. 'My dear sir, I was simply pursuing a logical argument. Of course there remains room for compromise. That's why I'm here, eh? It was my idea, you know, to call this truce.'

Major Nye pointed. He was smiling slightly. 'Your white flag's gone back to camp. Technically I'm at your mercy.'

'That's been the case all along, I'm afraid. Still, I'm a reasonable chap. I'm sure you are, too.'

'You must believe we've something up our sleeve, archbishop. A trump?'

'Not at all. Have you?'

'It was never in our sleeves. Perhaps you simply didn't notice the card in the pack. Or discarded it.'

'Are you including the joker? Then we haven't been playing the same game.'

Major Nye nodded. 'I'm not a very imaginative chap. Yet that makes sense.'

Bishop Beesley was put out by this conversation. He seemed ready to motion his men-at-arms forward. But Major Nye was not attacked. Meanwhile they looked greedily at his body, like cowed ferrets.

'Bearing in mind what you've just told me, I'm sure Miss Brunner would be ready to bargain.'

'You've made your terms perfectly clear. I think I too have described our position as best I can.' Major Nye put out his palm to catch the first snowflake. 'You were spot on. Your weather sense is far superior to mine, old boy.' He turned to leave. 'A night-train to Penzance? Or what about Tintagel?'

Bishop Beesley grew nervous, placatory. 'I say, major. Hang on. If Miss Brunner continues with this, you must believe I disapprove of violence.' His men-at-arms looked sideways at him. Almost as one they straightened their berets on their heads. Their movements were precise but somehow spasmodic. He had upset them. Rapidly he added: 'But if violence is the name of the game...'

Major Nye reached the path, crossing the field at the bottom of the Tor. The April air, no longer clear, now carried a sharp, almost metallic smell. He hated snow. He was too old easily to bear the chill.

Bishop Beesley stood his ground. He watched the bent figure begin its climb slowly up the terraces, then vanish somewhere near the top of the south face. Beesley signalled.

One of the SAS boys went round the hedge at the double. TV

cameras still rolled. The boy started his jeep and drove it back through the hedge. He stopped only inches from his superior. He saluted. With some difficulty the Archbishop of London gathered his robes about him. He mounted the vehicle, handing his crook to one soldier, his plated mitre to another. His arms clanked on his polished brass breastplate as he tucked them in. As they screeched in a U-turn, roaring towards HQ, Bishop Beesley grew full of small doubts. He was not worried the battle would be lost. But he guessed it could involve more bloodshed than he had estimated. No matter how much Miss Brunner presented this final battle as a traditional ritual, it must eventually cause more public disquiet than she allowed for. He scarcely cared if Cornelius and his gang were wiped out (there were special squads waiting at all the south-western ports) or if they escaped. Now he desperately needed peace. Peace would be denied him if Miss Brunner's offer was not accepted. If the country disbelieved her lie. There was even a chance of a cult emerging which saw the gang as martyrs.

His jeep reached the outskirts of the main camp. It headed through muddy fields and requisitioned parks, for Miss Brunner's patriotically coloured tanks and trailers. In a long riding skirt she strode back and forth across the thin layer of snow. Her right hand held an ornamental sword which she would run occasionally along the side of a vehicle.

She did not acknowledge Bishop Beesley. He clambered from the jeep and limped towards her. 'Marm?'

At the window of one of the trailers a uniformed communications officer removed his headphones and snarled. 'We're getting something different. I can't identify it all.'

Going up to the window she snatched the cans. Holding one tight against her ear she listened carefully. She had still not acknowledged Bishop Beesley but she nodded when Mitzi emerged from the mobile toilet straightening her hair under a plumed helmet. 'Come here, my dear. What do you make of this?'

Taking the headphones Mitzi frowned. 'Sounds like early reggae, doesn't it. Dad?'

The bishop recognised the sound immediately. It took him back to his happiest days in Dixie. 'Good heavens!'

'Is it significant, my lord?' Miss Brunner pushed the tip of the blade into a surviving patch of turf.

'It's Ersel Hickey. "Bluebirds Over the Mountain".'

'But what year, my lord? What year?'

'Why, 1957. That's what's so odd. Cornelius hated the fifties. Ah, now it's 1958. Hickey again. More characteristic of his usual work. "Going Down That Road". In those days he rivalled Derrell Felts as a performer. Back when rock was rock and roll was roll.' His eyes dimmed with nostalgia for Hershey Bars, Tootsies and his favourite Oreos. 'I was originally ordained there, you know. Utica College of Divinity.'

'Do you think there's a message in it?'

'In 1957? This was before Bob Dylan, marm!'

'For you, my lord! For you!'

'Going down that road, feelin' kinda blue. Going down that road, feelin' kinda blue. And I got no word and I got no letter from you. Boom chicka boom ba ba. Boom chicka boom ba ba. Boom chicka boom ba ba,' sang the suddenly cheerful bishop. Mitzi stared at her father in outrage. She snatched the cans away and returned them to the officer.

'Father!'

Miss Brunner was satisfied. 'It's some kind of double slam. It can't be a coincidence.'

Mitzi slapped the bishop's jogging chops. 'Come back!'

He fell gasping to one knee. Behind him the sun began to set. The flakes were heavier now, turned pink and crimson by that light which cloud had not yet obscured. Miss Brunner looked down at her camp-table. All her maps were wet. She made a noise in her nose. 'What lies within that miserable domdaniel? My lord bishop, art thou thyself again?'

'Myself, madam, aye.' His eyes were glassy.

She turned on a heel to find comfort in her great army. 'They make use of murky magic, my lord. They have an oracle we cannot ourselves consult. Only heaven knows what further sorcery they command. We must attack them, my lord. We must destroy them.'

Bishop Beesley considered the tapes. They would be lost in an all-out fusillade. 'I gave them until dawn.'

'By what authority, my lord bishop, did you make this compact?'

'Why, by yours, madam. By your own word which you bade me carry to their envoy.'

'Then you misheard me, sir.'

'No, madam. I did not.'

'Aye, sir, you did. I said they would lie dead by dawn, lest they surrendered on the moment. Dost thou not recall my words?'

He downed his head. 'Aye, madam. I forgot.'

'Besides,' she said, 'who can trust the word of witches? It is burning they need and most rapidly. Theirs is a vile disease which can be carried on the slightest breeze.'

'It's changed again, ma'am.' The communications officer reached the 'phones towards her. Again, she listened.

Mitzi, helping her father to his feet, hardly saw anything in the snow. The twilight came, then darkness. She was surprised to see Miss Brunner transfixed, listening almost calmly to the music. Mitzi, searching her own memory for the worst that could be happening, wondered for a moment if they were broadcasting disco music. Leaving her father breathing heavily against the tank's massive treads, she approached her leader. 'Madam?' Receiving no response she looked enquiringly at the officer. He shrugged. 'I'm not an expert, but I think it's Gilbert and Sullivan.'

Mitzi pulled the headphones away. Miss Brunner screamed. Then she looked abstractedly at Mitzi. 'I wouldn't say you were the very model of a modern major-general.' But she was grateful. 'They have the means to reach into our deepest longings.' She told the officer to turn off his receiver. 'We'll learn no more from that source.'

'Flares,' said Mitzi. 'If we are to do our work tonight, my lady, we shall need to see.'

Miss Brunner shrugged. 'Their method is subtle. But 'tis no

more than defence. The morning will serve us well enough. Come, lad, help me to my tent.' She placed a thin arm about Mitzi's shoulders.

Bishop Beesley, breathing loudly, watched steam pour from his mouth and wondered if it were ectoplasm. He forced himself towards a likeness of optimism. The battle would be won, he was sure. However, it was to be a harder fight than he had guessed. His own alarm made him want to begin at once. He was convinced they were drawing strength from somewhere yet he had no means of anticipating either its form or its source.

He made for his own RV and spent the better part of the night with his Lion bars and his Linda Lovelace videos. He was surprised at about five o'clock by a thumping on his locked door. Outside, Mitzi's voice was urgent. 'We're getting ready, Dad.'

Hastily he switched off the confusing tangle of genitalia and let her in.

'You couldn't sleep, eh? Me, neither.' Her face had assumed an ugly paleness. 'You'd better wash the chocolate off. Why are you worried?'

He was shakier than he had realised; a little disconcerted by his daughter's apparent sympathy. 'The past catching up with me, I suppose.' His smile was a twisted request for further attention. But Mitzi had given him all she had. 'It'll be over in a couple of hours, Dad.'

'I'd forgotten all about Hickey. Curious how potent…'

'I'll meet you at Operations Control in fifteen minutes.'

When Beesley went to clean up he discovered that the water had frozen. He switched on his electric kettle but after ten minutes it had still not boiled what water was left from the previous evening. He was forced to lick Kleenex and get as much of the chocolate off as he could. By the time he had wriggled back into his finery he felt a little better. When he opened the door and saw how thick and solid the snow was he returned inside. Next time he emerged he had dragged a monstrous bearskin cloak around him. 'Body and mind,' he said to himself. 'Body and mind, Beesley.'

He walked through the camp, grateful that the snow had at

least stopped falling. He noted many soldiers heating up their vehicles with what appeared to be electric cattle-prods. *It must be the coldest May 1st in recorded history*. He wondered if the same conditions were evident all over the country. Or had Miss Brunner deliberately brought this about?

'Ah, here's the barley sugar man himself.' She wore ermine and sable over her armour and was plainly in a jovial mood. This eased his mind.

The sky was pewter gradually turning to silver. Glastonbury Tor stood out sharply and St Michael's on the brow was a black flat. Miss Brunner walked in a circle round her campaign table from which the snow had been cleared and on which now rested a fresh rolled-up map, a tray of tea and toast, a computer printout of the numbers of troops and their deployment, an old postcard of Ramsgate with an inscription in Jerry's handwriting, two or three bones, a heart-shaped locket containing some thick black hair, the sleeve of an early Elvis Costello album, part of a frilly cuff. Miss Brunner had evidently been having a stab at divination. She seemed satisfied with the result. Her speech was no longer so archaic. 'An historic day, archbishop. The start of the new millennium. How clean the snow is. It seems a shame to disturb it. Still, there'll be plenty more.'

'Some of the machinery's a bit sluggish.' Mitzi, disdaining fur, wore a heavy leather trench coat. 'You don't think they're getting help from Russia, do you?'

'Russia's on our side this time.'

'It's snowing all over the world?'

'It will be.' She spoke with quiet pride. 'Is the artillery standing by to give our cavalry cover?'

'Everyone's primed. A red flare's the signal.' Mitzi wondered if Cornelius and his gang were still there. 'Should we try a final parley?'

Miss Brunner caught her drift. 'I suppose so. We have to think of the viewers.'

'I'll bow out of this one.' The bishop unconsciously reached towards her biscuits. He caught himself. 'If I may, dear lady.'

'Help yourself, vicar.'

Thankfully, he munched, noticing that her tea had already turned to ice in the cup.

Mitzi called for a jeep. She did not wish to risk riding on the ice. She took her lance and her white flag. The jeep was forced to crawl, its driver cursing under his swaddling of wool. 'Language, lieutenant,' she said.

His dark eyes tried to show surprise. 'I was singing, ma'am.'

Mitzi found it hard to get the words of '(I Don't Want To Go To) Chelsea' out of her head. Miss Brunner had played it most frequently during the night. She saw it as a crucial part of whatever equation she sought to solve. 'Then sing it louder, soldier.'

With admirable quickness the lieutenant began 'Stand By Your Man' in the slurring, bar-room baritone common to most soldiers either on or off duty.

Eventually they got to the lane. It was almost blocked by snowdrifts. They stopped. A small, dark shape near a half-buried hedge caught Mitzi's attention. It was a dead wren. The hill was apparently deserted. There were few tracks and none of them was human. Mitzi waved her lance.

After about five minutes she saw figures emerge near the tower but it was impossible to identify them. A woman placed a long, home-made ladder against the wall. It reached almost to the crenellations.

Oblivious of his commander's concerns, the driver continued to sing. *'She's the Queen of the Silver Dollar and she rules a smoky kingdom...'* Apparently he was a C&W buff.

The ladder was taken down again. Mitzi had the impression it had been measured. Or was it a signal to her. Still nobody came down the hillside. She did not move. She had become curious.

With some difficulty, they were raising the ladder again. There seemed to be a figure strapped to it; something limp, like a Guy. A huge corn dolly? Mitzi smiled to herself. If they were reduced to that, then the battle would not be as hard as she had thought. She had no field glasses so could not distinguish much about the figure. It might be a totem; a message. She even thought, for a second, it might be some sort of conductor! It was pointing directly towards Miss Brunner's headquarters. Now they were securing the frame to the stone of the tower. At last she saw a person squat on what was plainly an improvised sled. The tobogganer began to bounce and slither rapidly down the Tor, following the route of one of the main paths. Near the hedge at the bottom the figure fell off. It emerged again, covered in snow, and walked towards her, banging snow from its bright, new yellow caggy. It pushed back its hood to reveal the oddly artificial haircut, the bright, terrier eyes of Shakey Mo Collier.

'Blimey!' said the soldier. 'The colonel.'

'They sent old Collier to tell you they're pretty much ready.' He removed a lump of snow from his elegant navy sweats. His attention was drawn to his arm. He flexed the fingers of his left hand. 'Bit of a bump back there.'

'You look healthier than the last time I saw you.'

He shook his head. 'Too much dope last night.'

She was incredulous. 'You really are slipping, aren't you?'

'Okay,' he said briskly, 'what's the score?'

'Nothing as yet. We haven't started, have we?'

Mo made a motion of his head towards the tower. 'Dunno 'bout you, but we have.'

'Are you hoping to draw our fire with that dummy?'

'It's not a bloody dummy. It's Cornelius.'

'I get it. You're making an offer.'

Mo sighed. 'It's more in the nature of a show of strength.'

'You're not going for any of this crap, are you, Mo?'

'It's the only crap I can take.' His cheek bulged as his tongue sought a tooth. 'Sorry.' He seemed to be apologising for his use of the personal pronoun. He plainly believed there was nothing wrong with self-reference so long as second or third person was employed, though second person sometimes involved a confusing degree of transference.

'You should really be on our side,' she said.

'That's been tried. Your arguments don't fit together properly.'

'And theirs?' She pointed at the sagging remains of the old assassin.

'Theirs can't be understood at all.'

'What? By any of them?' She offered her brandy-flask. He refused as if he suspected she tried to seduce him.

'Cornelius seems to understand it on some level. Mrs Persson understands it, she says. And Cathy. And Hira. And Lobkowitz. But Major Nye and Alvarez just go along with them.'

'And Mo?'

'Mo, too. Naturally.'

'Well, anyway, Miss Brunner thinks the omens are good so she'll be attacking shortly. This visit is just to make sure you're still here. We don't waste energy.'

Mo grinned at the ground. He expressed defiance rather than real amusement. 'They've got a goddess,' he said.

'Jesus! So it's not an invasion we're dealing with? Celtic shit. There's none of you with more than a drop of Irish blood. It's a retreat, eh?'

'That's for you to decide.'

'Just remember what happened to the Brigantes the last time they went up a hill in Yorkshire to make a last stand against the Romans. They waited for years. The Romans didn't notice they were there. In the end they trooped down again. Bet they felt silly.'

'That's your problem.'

Mitzi had the impression Mo attempted a crude form of verbal ju-jitsu. Who was schooling who? 'So what? You've got Brigantia up there, have you, in your silly imitation *sid*? Which one is Cathy playing? Macha? Morrigan? Baeve? All three?'

'Means bugger all to Mo. Anyway, the white flag's not you deciding to surrender, then? Okay.' He turned his back on her.

'Can't you see how ludicrous this is? What you've bought? Sentimental, mystical folk-remedies! Collier, have you seen our fire-power?'

By the twitch of his shoulders she could tell he was at least envious. He was possibly reconciled to martyrdom, like an old hero whose geisa had overtaken him. And was Cornelius trying to transform himself into some doomed Cu Chulain? Strapped to his pillar so that he would die without losing honour? A ridiculous, half-understood ritual of martyrdom: the mythologies of defeat.

Mitzi was almost surprised as the driver began to turn a careful wheel. *'Jesse James was a man, a friend of the poor. He had both a heart and a brain. But a dirty little coward shot Mr Howard, and laid Jesse James in his grave.'*

'Were you ever in Missouri, lieutenant?'

'No, ma'am. Never in the States at all. Too materialistic for me.'

'This stuff is powerful.' In a rare spirit of egalitarianism she handed him her flask. She was beginning to hope that Miss Brunner knew the rules. Or did rules matter when you had command of so many shells?

Meanwhile Mo Collier found his tin tray and put it under his arm, climbing carefully up the slope and wishing he had had the sense to bring at least one of his new French spikes. He had never known ground to freeze so quickly. But at least the air was clean and the task of returning was one he had trained himself for. He would rather be out here than stuck in some fuggy hole having to smell Mrs Persson's dreadful American gaspers. He was sweating by the time he reached the Tor's crowning ruin.

To Mo, Jerry was in his deepest fix of all. Although it was naked Jerry's body remained unaffected by the cold. It still glowed with a faint blue radiance. This effect was more in keeping with tropical decay than anything else Mo recognised. Was Jerry offering up his hard-won heat?

They were all waiting for him in the little keep. He shrugged to answer unasked questions. 'She just wanted to make sure we hadn't scarpered in the night. She probably thinks we're trying to turn Cornelius into a god or a martyr or something.'

'What did you tell her?' Catherine shivered in nothing but a blanket. She was comforted by Una's arm.

'There wasn't a lot to say.' Standing on one foot, Collier felt at the tendons of his left heel. 'At least the calf didn't get damaged.'

'Are we both playing for time?' Major Nye had not volunteered for a second confrontation. 'It's definitely dawn, now.'

'Casting their own runes, doubtless.' Prinz Lobkowitz, almost the colour of the snow outside, was virtually invisible in the semi-darkness. He had got himself up in some sort of uniform. 'How did Cornelius look to you as you came in?'

'Not bad, considering. Any more of those Diet Pepsis?'

'You had the last before you left. There's nothing but carrot juice, or something.' Alvarez hated missing breakfast. 'You should really start a day like this with a hot... But all the bloody power's been diverted, as usual. Are you hoping you'll distract them by putting him up there? A couple of near-misses would finish him off. They've every kind of explosive. A library of missiles. They can nuke us to kingdom come if they feel like it.' This was a variation on what was now a familiar theme. Yet he had made no sign he wished to leave. His fatalism, fed by his habit, kept him at his post. 'Sod it.'

Una was almost glad of his antipathy. Originally she had hoped he might come round. Now she realised his attitude helped her clarify her own thoughts. She was even amused when, leaning against the far wall, Mo Collier and Sergeant Alvarez enjoyed a surly joke or two at her expense. She trusted the others. She even trusted Cornelius. Anyway there was no looking back for him.

Major Nye had a telescope to his eye. It was poked through one of the narrow windows. A mixture of daylight and gaslight gave a Pre-Raphaelite quality to the colours within the tower.

Major Nye pointed his glass towards the horizon. Did the snow extend across the whole landscape? Had there perhaps already been a war? A war in heaven that shall be mirror'd by a war on earth... He was angry at himself. There was no room for idle speculation in this show. They were surrounded by the snouts of Miss Brunner's rank upon rank of artillery, of barrage racks, mobile launchers. He supposed they should be grateful the Australians had not allowed Miss B. an air force. Or perhaps, wishing to sustain the myth of the mock fight, she felt it unwise to deploy planes or larger missiles. Against the white ground their armour was garish, as were banners and uniforms; the yellow and black of their shelters was almost restful in comparison. Nonetheless the preponderance of primaries meant that he could not concentrate on them for long. A series of red flares suddenly lifted sluggishly into the sky. The whole scene became scarlet, as if drenched by the blood of some slaughtered monster.

'This is it!' Mo had seen the glow.

'We'd better hope your plan works, Mrs Persson.' Alvarez returned to his simplified monitors. The main stuff was still concentrated below. 'And they use Cornelius as their point of strike.'

'They've taken enough fixes off him before.' Alvarez guffawed and expertly flicked more switches than was absolutely necessary. He seemed less frightened by the coming battle than by what might happen should they win it.

'You'd better tell me when,' said Catherine softly.

'Drink the Coventina mixture now.' Three glasses stood on a little table, a kind of makeshift altar. 'And let's hope Maria the Jewess knew what she was talking about.'

'I'm chary of Byzantine alchemy.' Catherine drained the pearly liquid. She coughed and grinned. 'Blimey, it tastes like, I don't know, something…'

'Come.' Una led her to the doorway. The whole hill had begun to shake from the recoil of the guns below. Hundreds of shells rose into the air high above their heads and burst. They ducked back in as the shrapnel rained down. 'Either that was for effect or they haven't got our range yet.' From outside on the trellis came a faint shout of alarm. They went through the door again and round to where Jerry was tied. Pieces of red-hot metal lay everywhere, melting the snow. One had fallen onto the trellis itself and a rope was smouldering, but Jerry seemed unmarked.

'Hello, Cath.' He was terrified.

'Hello, Jerry. How does it feel to be top man on the totem pole?'

'You haven't got any of those chocolate biscuits left, have you, Una?'

'Not until afterwards, Jerry.'

'Easy for you to say.' When he moved his blue head waves of energy poured from it, like a halo. 'This is even cruder than the Lapland stuff.'

'Only on one level. Trust me.'

Dark smoke curled below and the armies of authority slowly re-deployed themselves. 'I think I'm picking something up,' he said. His gaze was sad. There came a further cannonade but this time the shells and rockets burst lower down, before they reached the Tor. Jerry, however, was impressed. 'Oh!'

Catherine's eyes were dreamy. The mixture she had drunk was affecting her. Increasingly, her attention was fixed on her brother. 'Can I join him yet?'

'Certainly not. I told you.'

The tanks and launchers were making a tighter circle now. They halted at the foot of the hill. Now they would be firing almost directly up at him.

Mo emerged. He was breathing rapidly. His fists were clenched. 'I wish we had something to throw back at them.'

'We don't need it,' said Una.

'Oh, no! Listen to old Mo and you'll learn something, lady.' He drew a pair of wraparound shades from within his costume and put them over his eyes. 'Do you still think you can do it all with mirrors?'

'Get back inside, you silly little bugger.'

Startled and with an expression of bemused respect on his features, Collier obeyed her.

Major Nye had overheard the exchange. 'She's right, old chap.'

'We shan't have won if we use the same methods as they're employing.' Professor Hira was smiling. In the darkness he looked like a Cheshire Cat, all teeth and eyes. 'Ironically enough, we can make use of the energy they expend on us. You surely see that now.'

'I'd bomb 'em back to the Stone Age if I could. Bunch of baboons. This isn't the sort of warfare I was trained for.'

'None of us was prepared exactly.' Prinz Lobkowitz looked reflectively at the two remaining glasses of liquid, one red and one blue. 'We were, I suppose, in danger of throwing out the baby with the bathwater. If we're successful it will be the end of alchemy and all the rest of it. Do you also find that ironic, Professor Hira?'

'In a merely literary sense, I suppose so. I'm inclined to see everything as serving a worthwhile purpose of some sort. My religious background, you see.'

'My God!' Major Nye was at the window again with his telescope. Livid lights played on the brass. 'She's sending up the cavalry, anyway. She suspected some sort of energy drain and had her alternative ready. But she can know nothing about – the poor damned beasts!'

At least a thousand horsemen had massed on the lower slopes. When they made some attempt at a charge their mounts failed to keep a grip on the ice and slid everywhere, bringing down those attempting to break through from behind. When the guns started up again there was immediate carnage. Major Nye turned away in disgusted misery. 'That was the best collection of mounts and riders I've ever seen.'

Alvarez took the glass from him,. 'Makes the Charge of the Light Brigade look like strategy, doesn't it?' He had never much liked horses.

Catherine came in alone. 'They can't reach us, it seems. Not up the terraces.' She was radiant. She was naked. Red-faced, Alvarez returned to peering at the death outside. Picking up the second glass, with the blue liquid, she drained it. 'Oh, it hurts.' She put her hand first to her throat, then to her breast, then to her stomach. Resolutely she turned and went back to where Una waited.

There was a dreadful shrieking and roaring from below. Red metal glinted where some of the riders had stabbed themselves or their mounts by accident. Una's features were white. Above, Jerry seemed to be sleeping. 'We are not the cause of this,' said Una. 'And as yet there's no help we can offer.' She was talking to herself. 'Did you drink it?'

'Oh, shit! Oh, shit! Get me down!' Jerry had woken up. 'Oh, shit!'

'Collect yourself, Mr C!'

He lifted his head in a vulpine howl.

'It's your rotten brother we've got to worry about. He's only got one way of winning. Look at his damned eyes.' They were crimson and so bright they spread their light over his shoulders as he swung his head from side to side. 'Vitriol! Vitriol!' he screamed. '*Visita interiora Terrae, rectificando, inveniens occultum lapidem! Intra muros! Intra muros! Inter arma silent leges!*'

'*Interdum stultus bene loquitur,*' said Una with dry humour.

Catherine was having a hard time following the Latin. A fresh burst of artillery-fire seemed closer. She dipped her head.

'Keep your cool.' Una was further amused by her own archaicisms. 'As long as we stick to our plan. They have no way now of getting through the maze. But we'll have to be quick before they think of incendiaries.'

Catherine looked at her flesh. 'I'm melting.'

'Not yet. Take up the catalyst now.'

Major Nye looked back from his telescope as Catherine came in. 'Mrs Persson seems to be right. Either that or we're facing the worst gunnery since the fourteenth century!' Mildly concerned for her he watched her pick up the final goblet and carry it carefully back to Una.

Prinz Lobkowitz was frowning. 'I hope they're not growing too hasty. The timing's of prime importance.'

Alvarez glanced up from his instruments. 'Looking good at this end.'

Jerry was now speaking rapid Hebrew, but incoherently. The entire hill had become surrounded by a wall of flame. Miss Brunner had ordered petrol poured on the dead and dying. The heat was designed to make it possible for tanks and infantry to mount the Tor.

'It stinks!' Jerry peered through creeping smoke. 'The whole farce stinks. I'll get down now.'

Major Nye had joined the party. 'Too late for that, old son.'

'I don't want to be the sacrifice.'

Una was disappointed by his deliberate obtuseness.

'Or a martyr,' he added. 'Or a symbol. Or…'

'You're our secret agent,' she said. 'And it's your wedding day.'

'The only marriages I'm interested in are chemical.'

'Then you're in luck, tiger.' She nodded to Catherine who, holding the full cup carefully in one hand, began slowly to climb towards her brother. Now both their skins gave off the same pale blue aura.

Catherine was only four or five steps from the ground when Mo Collier suddenly broke from the tower. Arms flailing, he ran then slithered down the hill, bumping from terrace to terrace. He was able to stop himself in the mud which spread like wax from the area of the flames. Shouting 'Fuck it! Fuck it!' and 'Bugger!' he scampered, a panicky beetle, around the circle, looking for an exit. Then he had vanished on the other side of the hill.

'It's to be fire, as we anticipated.' Major Nye waved at the fouled air.

Mo Collier had stopped thinking. He had not trusted his instincts for years. He knew instinct was the only way to get through this. He ran back a few yards. He rolled his body in the melting snow. When he was thoroughly soaked he shoved himself forward as fast as he could go, screaming at the top of his voice, his feet tangled in the harness of dead or dying men and horses, slipping in blood. He was choked by the horrible smell. The flames were so hot they represented something beyond pain. Then he was out of it, smouldering slightly, and glaring at the waiting army, at Miss Brunner, Mitzi Beesley, Bishop Beesley. They regarded him with bemused interest.

'I thought you were one of ours,' said the bishop. 'Have you come to surrender, old chap?'

'It's not a question of surrendering. It's a question of reason. Of logic. Nobody ever said Mo Collier was irrational.'

'But we've no use for you now, old chap. In an hour or two this whole hill will be going up. The moment for strategy of any other sort is well past.' The bishop's ruddy features were given an appearance of health by the leaping tongues.

'Do what? You can't say that to a man who's just risked his life to come over!'

'Say it in pidgin English.' Miss Brunner, too, was enjoying herself. She was going up on the destruction, forgetful of her original design. 'You feller Collier no good this place no more, savvy?'

'Oh, you bastards!'

The three of them watched impassively as Mo turned and walked sulkily back into the fire.

'I say,' cried Bishop Beesley suddenly. 'What do you think they're playing at? Some sort of witchcraft?'

'Chemical warfare.' Mo surrendered himself to something he had decided was purer than life.

Miss Brunner was suffering a sudden setback. 'My Lords of Telford and Widnes!' She glared this way and that. 'Who will rid me of this troublesome –?'

Bishop Beesley interrupted hastily. 'Tor!' he said. 'Or do you mean Cornelius? He used to be a Jesuit, I understand. Or attached. Or educated. Madam?'

Her lips drew back. He thought for one fascinated moment she intended to bite his throat out. Then she made a small, tidying movement at her back hair and breathed more evenly.

'Telford and Widnes were killed in the charge,' said Mitzi. She was having doubts about Miss Brunner's quality of leadership. She was sweating. 'We should have interrogated the little bastard. What's going on up there? Why are our shots missing?'

'The conjunction. The configuration. The arrangement of a maze. The positive power of the Horned God. The concrete. The physical manifestation...' Bishop Beesley devoted himself to his last Crunchie.

'Send the tanks through,' said Miss Brunner.

Uncertainly, Mitzi lifted her lance. She gave the signal.

As the first Lucan Mark Sevens rolled towards the flames, gushing extinguisher, Miss Brunner pulled tightly on the reins of her white stallion. 'This day will be remembered until the end of Time!'

'Not much longer now.' Bishop Beesley saw nothing through the clearing smoke. 'What did he mean about chemicals? Are we going to catch something?'

'Let the dog see the rabbit.' Mitzi murmured over her CB. The

Lucans' steady fusillade, although it was again possible to see the tower with the figures gathered outside, continued to miss.

'Two on the ladder now.' Beesley thought one reached a cup to the other's lips; some appalling parody of the sacrament? 'I knew there was witchcraft involved.'

''Twas what I told you all the while, my lord.' Miss Brunner held hard to her pommel. 'Some power I will admit they have. However, not for much longer will they stand against us. Their infamy and their insolence punished shall be.'

'Pardon, marm?'

'For them no pardon shall forthcoming be.'

Her inversions were fazing him more than usual. He recalled that the *Teddy Bear* still lay off Torquay and with a bit of luck he could be there before nightfall. It was not that he feared defeat; he feared her triumph and its aftermath. Would she insist that everyone talk, as it were, backwards? As an Englishman, it was all too Teutonic for him. He was becoming nostalgic for the Mississippi. It would not be difficult to find work in the Delta region.

Blinking, Beesley looked harder at the ladder. He was not completely certain he did see two figures. Perhaps it was only one? Maybe the light was playing tricks with his eyes?

At last, as if breaking through a barrier, the rockets and shells struck the tower. Swiftly the incendiary missiles engulfed everything. Soon the top of the Tor was burning as steadily as the ring of corpses at the bottom.

'*I fell into a burning rang of far*,' sang Mitzi's driver cheerfully, arriving with a message. 'Looks like it's curtains for the old Guy, eh, ma'am.'

Mitzi took the printout and held it close to her face.

Q: WHAT IS THE EXACT NATURE OF THE CATASTROPHE?

'Who sent this?'

'It came through on the bug, ma'am.'

Mitzi frowned at her father. He was sweating so badly she suspected there were diseases in the air. Pulling out a handkerchief she put it to her nose.

'We got the lot.' Miss Brunner was her old self again. Yet it was clear she could not believe her luck. 'Make sure this is all treated as a bit of a laugh!' she insisted to a camera crew roaring by in its jeep. She added, for her own ears: 'Ancient ceremonies revived in Somerset.' She felt obliged now to control every aspect of the operation, monitor every opinion throughout the country. As Mitzi had observed in Argentina and Vietnam, this was an unavoidable consequence of creating the myth of stability and competence. She was, like her father, beginning to see the writing on the wall. Surprised at the slowness of her reflexes, she realised why he was sweating. Usually she was quicker on the uptake. This time at least she would probably not have to leave him behind. Then she experienced something still more astonishing to her. She identified the emotion as affection for her father.

Mitzi looked at him again. How was it possible to love a creature as hopelessly wounded and vicious? It had to be fellow feeling. She must be transposing her own identity onto his. She was experiencing self-pity and self-preservation after all. It was the only credible explanation for her sensations. She realised they had been frozen, staring at each other, for a few seconds. Miss Brunner, anxious for the story to be right, was speaking rapidly to some press staff. 'Always bear it in mind. Get the image specific then the interpretation is no problem. The image, you see, always precedes the reality. The Corn Man knew that.'

'Ma'am?' A photographer looked up from where he was fumbling a new roll into his Kodak.

'Cornelius knew that. But from now on he will be referred to as the Glastonbury Corn Man. The sooner he's a legend the better.'

'Quite,' agreed a miserable captain. 'Do we explain the personnel losses, ma'am?'

'Best show a couple of healthy, smiling faces. Find a couple of salt-of-the-earth types with minor wounds. That will do to scotch the rumours. Most people would rather believe the best, don't you find?'

He was a fairly intelligent young man. 'I feel this is a crucial time, if you don't mind me speaking up, ma'am. It's important to maintain the country's morale. What if I organised a few of our blokes at the top? Dress 'em in funny clothes, as the opposition. Then we can show a picnic or something. Friends again after the bunfight?'

She was relieved. 'I thought I was being forced to provide all the creative input myself. Very good, captain. Report to me when I can look at some footage.'

He saluted.

Mitzi wondered if he knew how dangerous the game could get for him. 'Dad.' She spoke quietly to the trembling bishop. 'We've got to go up the hill before we can go over it.'

'I'm feeling funny. *Nolo episcopari*. *Teddy Bear* won't be there for ever. Numb.'

'Long enough, Dad. Trust me.'

His grin was hideous, but he obeyed her.

'Shouldn't we check just in case there are survivors?' Mitzi said loudly. 'My lady? Otherwise, embarrassment…'

Miss Brunner was adjusting her Tudorish garb. 'Eh?' She moved her lips as though attempting speech. Her eyes came slowly to life.

When Mitzi repeated her suggestion Miss Brunner said carefully: 'They're dead. All the king's horses and all the king's men won't put old Humpty together again. Not this time.' She tidied her beautiful red hair. 'No, No, General Beesley. You're perfectly right. Loyalty's the main thing now, dear. We must stick close. It's always darkest before the dawn. It should be smooth sailing from this moment on. But we must keep our wits about us. For England's sake, Mitzi. What did you say? This is a great victory, you know. Unification and centralisation will be our next step. But you understand that. I must have good friends. People who understand me. I don't have to spell it out to you, dear. Will you help me?'

'You're our leader.' Mitzi presented every sign of bafflement, as if there were no question in her mind. 'We have a duty to you. We need you now more than ever. You may rely on the Beesleys. Who could not believe you embody the true soul of England?'

'L'etat, c'est moi.'

'Quite,' said Mitzi. 'Your Majesty.'

'Follow me.' Miss Brunner strode in flaring divided skirts and glittering, smoke-patched armour towards her personal transport.

'Dad.' Mitzi took her father gently by the hand. 'England expects.'

The entire Tor was piled with tanks, launchers, half-tracks; it swarmed with infantry. There was scarcely a trace of snow or grass. Here and there the ring of dead men and horses continued to smoulder, but much had already been reduced to dull bones. Seated, with reasonable dignity on the special saddles fixed to the turret of the tank, Miss Brunner and her allies, a noble trinity of State, Church and Army, responded to the cheers of the camera-crews. The Lucan ground laboriously up the dilapidated terraces. St Michael's was flickering, smoking rubble. Mitzi grimaced. 'Humpty was really wasted today. I doubt if we'll find any bits.'

'From now on we use our greatest delicacy of judgement.' Miss Brunner released a gracious smile. Fire-hoses created arcs of extinguishing agents; strange rainbows. Vehicles were positioned everywhere at peculiar angles. Most had failed to make it to the top; others were pursuing erratic courses, as if following invisible roads. The Lucan began to judder and groan. Deciding it would make a better impression anyway, Miss Brunner allowed Bishop Beesley to help her to the ground. Saluting promiscuously, she made her way purposefully upward, using her sword as a cane, climbing with energetic precision: the perfect leader amongst her victorious men. But when she stopped at the ruins, slightly ahead of Mitzi and the bishop, her stance altered a little. She drew her brows together.

'What make you of this, my lords?' She pointed with her ceremonial blade.

Bishop Beesley, very pale now and wheezing, clutching at various parts of himself, came reluctantly to stand beside her.

'It's just a joke.' Mitzi was in no doubt. She sniffed. 'Meant to be, like, a dinosaur's egg, maybe. Tourist stuff.'

'Or one of those big Easter eggs they do.' Living, as always, in hope, her father licked his purple lips. 'That could be some sort of foil round it.'

'More like a glaze,' said Mitzi. 'I think it's ceramic.'

'It didn't get harmed by our rockets.' Miss Brunner cast a pathological eye over the bits of broken stone, the blackened rubble, the smouldering timber. 'It could even have been placed here afterwards. Methinks, my lords, we should be wary of this alien device.'

'I can't help thinking it's china. Very tough china.'

'Or very dense chocolate.' Bishop Beesley gasped and twitched. He seemed in pain. 'Mitzi?'

'Glazed,' she said firmly. 'You okay, Dad?'

The huge egg pulsed once: a faint, reddish light.

Then Miss Brunner was shouting suddenly for everyone to get back. She dropped her voice to address the Beesleys. 'It's a trap. A bomb. Canst thou not… Can't you tell? It's glowing! It's about to go off!'

'But it's ceramic.' Mitzi stepped closer. 'I'd swear.'

'Back to the town!' Miss Brunner called to her forces. They paused. Their amazement swiftly turned to fear, as if they had expected something terrible all along. 'Back! Back!' Again she hissed at her companions. 'It could easily be nuclear. They're fanatics.'

'We've established it's not chocolate.' The bishop was drifting off again. 'Not vegetable. Not animal. That only leaves mineral.'

The egg gave out a brief orange pulse. Mitzi giggled. 'Warmer.' She put her head close to his. 'It's our chance now, Dad. The schooner's waiting.'

But he was transfixed. 'Did I tell you about your mother?'

The glowing egg turned from pearly, translucent grey to misty blue, then to violet.

'I don't think it's a bomb,' Mitzi insisted. 'But it could be an infernal machine. Dad?'

'We must have a heart to heart.'

'On the boat.' She tugged at his sticky sleeve. 'We'll make the most of the confusion.'

At last she managed to get him moving. He plodded behind her, breathing like the minotaur, his feet dragging through melted snow and bloody mud. All round them the troops were moving out. They had panicked. By being unspecific, Miss Brunner had created a far greater terror in them. Mitzi found a jeep near the bottom and drove it back to the half-abandoned camp, telling him to wait in the passenger seat while she changed. She emerged from her caravan five minutes later. Her uniform discarded, she was disguised as a girl. 'We'll have that chat,' she promised, 'but in sunnier waters, calmer seas.' She wondered what her motive was for saving him. 'Maybe it was the – you know – philosophy stone?'

They went through Glastonbury. Save for a few military looters, the old town was deserted, evacuated on Miss Brunner's orders.

Soon they were bowling along the wide M5 towards Taunton. Bishop Beesley's head had fallen back and occasionally, over the engine, she could hear his snores. Only after they passed the Exeter turn-off did she realise he had died. In response to this fact, she accelerated, determined to get him to the steam yacht as she had promised. Then, just before the M5 joined the A380, she was forced to pull in to a lay-by. Her body became shaken by deep, convulsive sobs. But the bishop seemed at peace.

Meanwhile Miss Brunner's troops, convinced they had been defeated by witchcraft, spread over surrounding Somerset, getting rid of weapons and insignia, even battledress, when they could. Miss Brunner, hardly aware her army was scattering, stood in the peaceful grounds of the Abbey. She looked up towards the Tor and waited for the explosion. She had a walkie-talkie to her ear. It was playing marches by Walton and Bliss.

In their operations cavern, Una, Prinz Lobkowitz and Professor Hira stood leaning over Alvarez as he brought in the picture. They had left the tower by the tunnel, the entrance to the maze. This chamber was its centre. 'Are we somehow victorious?' Lobkowitz stroked his bruised left arm. They had escaped at the last possible minute before Jerry and Catherine were engulfed.

'We never knew what would happen.' Professor Hira reminded him. 'We could simply hope. But it looks pretty damn' good, don't you think so, Mrs P?'

She had not really heard him. 'I think we can go back now. But keep broadcasting that stuff, sergeant. It seems to work for us.'

Alvarez grunted. He was in at least two minds about almost everything. Nothing, as far as he was concerned, had gone as he had supposed it would. He simply could not bring himself to believe an operation could be such a hit-or-miss business. He required more clarity. He needed to be fairly certain of the outcome of any action they took. And here they were, still not sure if they had won or lost. They were a bunch of upper-class wankers and amateurs in his opinion. If there was another job to go to when all this was over he would find it. Moreover, he was upset at Mo's apparent suicide. Mo had been his only fellow spirit. Alvarez felt completely alone.

As soon as the others had left he leaned back on his stool and lit a cheroot, thinking about Mexico.

Una led the way through the unlikely turns of the passages. She carried a small Duracell torch as their only illumination. The walls were sometimes earth, sometimes a mixture of loose rocks, sometimes stone. There was a strong, almost uterine smell, so that sometimes Prinz Lobkowitz felt they moved in a medium that was almost liquid. Gradually they climbed upwards. Then Una stopped. By the dim light of the torch it was possible to see the steps and door to the tower blocked with rubble. They had expected this. They went on for a few yards. The smell of damp earth was giving way to the stink of the battlefield. Una paused. Then she pointed with her beam. Here, the wall was flat, grey stone. Professor Hira went forward and, picking up a flint, rapped as hard as he could. He was answered from the other side. Taking hold of an iron ring he pulled until the stone began to move, revealing daylight and Major Nye's weary, filthy face. 'Phew! Everything shipshape your end, professor?'

'Apparently. Yours, old boy?'

'I had a spot of weaving and dodging to do. Thought they'd

caught me a couple of times. Then the lot of them suddenly picked up their heels and scrammed. Do they know something we don't?'

'Could be.' Una wondered at the abandoned vehicles, the ring of corpses at the foot of the Tor. Then she noticed Major Nye's ragged, half-burned blazer and flannels. 'You've had a narrow squeak.'

'Cut things a bit fine. Did you scare 'em off, Mrs Persson?'

'I think it's something they swallowed.' Una with both large hands pushed her hair back from her face. 'Or maybe something they didn't. Whatever it was, it was in them. Maybe they saw a ghost?'

'This hill has plenty of those, I'd imagine.' Prinz Lobkowitz had witnessed worse destruction in his time, but there was something especially pathetic about the attitudes of the horses and riders heaped one on top of the other, their flesh black, blistered or burned to the bone. He looked to the east. The ravens were coming in. 'Something they swallowed?'

'A mickey in their duff, what?' The major showed them the path leading to what remained of the tower.

'It's an egg!' Hira was delighted. 'Just like something from mythology. Oh, this is wonderful. What a miracle! They've made an egg, Mrs P! Who would have guessed?'

Una laughed aloud. It was amazing what you could do when you gave up control; when you let matters take their own course. Although she had at times thrown herself upon the winds of fate, she had only risked her own identity, perhaps her life. This was a far more satisfying feeling. The egg was a kind of light orange but with swirling streaks of pink and veins of vermilion. Its shine was almost metallic. As she reached a hand towards its heat it rippled and became an even gold all over. The deep red-gold of the Celts. It was far too heavy, she discovered, to pick up. She pushed it with her foot. It hardly moved. 'The rebis,' she said. 'It was in Maier's book, I think. Join a brother with his sister and offer them the cup of love to drink. Mind you, the picture promised a bit more than this. Two heads, wings, plumed serpents, chalices, lions, eagles, three-headed dogs, sunflowers. Ah, well. That's the symbolism, I suppose, and this is the reality. A bit disappointing. Still, at least we got something. An egg.'

'From the union of opposites,' said Professor Hira, then paused. 'That's where all eggs come from.'

'Perhaps your eagle's in it,' said Major Nye, obscurely believing her to be disappointed. 'You could get a griffin or something out of an egg that size, I'd guess.'

'It might just be an accident.'

'Solid gold!' Una was laughing again. 'This is more what Miss Brunner would be after, eh? Maybe we shouldn't have let her be the final catalyst. It was the easiest way to find the sort of fast heat the recipe required.'

The egg appeared to be stable now.

'It's a bit of a paradox then, is it?' Major Nye wanted to know. He wished he could get rid of his feeling he had in some obscure way let the side down. It had been his job, after all, to stay outside, to look after whatever was left in the tower when the strike finished.

'There are no paradoxes in that egg.' Prinz Lobkowitz, who had read all the books on the subject, whose ancestors had been the patrons of scientists and astrologers from every corner of the world, could also see the funny side of it. He dare not look at Una for fear they would both begin giggling. 'There are no paradoxes, actually. We create them, do we not, by our impatience to rationalise the world too quickly? Have you read *The Golden Tract*, professor? When the king and queen made love the king's heart melted as a result of his passion and he collapsed into fragments. When the queen saw what had happened she, who loved him as completely as he loved her, began to weep. She wept so hard that at length the king's remains were entirely covered by her tears. Then, her sorrow unabated, she slew herself. When the alchemist, who had been charged to guard them, saw the one melted and the other dead he was reminded of Medea. She had brought a corpse back to life. With heat and vapour he was able to restore them, united, to life. Is that it? Hermaphroditus and

Salmacis? The philosopher's stone is called the "two that are one". It is not a paradox, surely, to be complete? Male and female, self-reproducing.'

'I'd expected a creature, though.' Una again tried to roll the egg. It moved a fraction in the rubble, then resumed its original position and stabilised. 'What are we going to do with it?'

'Frankly, I feel I've ballsed things up somehow.' Major Nye's fingers went to his singed moustache. 'Pardon my French.'

'There was nothing else you could have done,' she said. The other two nodded in agreement. 'We foolishly expected something more spectacular. Something livelier than an egg. What are we supposed to do with it? Sit on it?'

'And for how long?' Professor Hira shrugged. 'A *yuga*, a *manvantara*? This is pretty much where I came in. When shall the one become the many? What does Mademoiselle Coudert say about hermaphrodites drawing the individual beyond the everyday world of multiplicity to the transcendent point of origin where plurality vanishes in God? For God, as we know, is no more He than She, but all things combined in one. This, of course, is fundamental to the Celtic idea of the Mother Sea, in which we are all tiny bits of a single entity. If entity is quite the right word.'

They had all politely stopped listening to him and were giving their attention to the egg.

'Of course,' said Una, 'it might be an accident. A coincidence. It might be meaningless. Except we appear to have produced gold! Which, as everyone will tell you, is the corrupted use of the alchemical method. Have we gone wrong, in spite of doing our best? It wouldn't be surprising. And what would Catherine think? Not really worth the sacrifice, eh? I suppose we might have misinterpreted some of the Latin or the Greek. Even you, Prinz Lobkowitz, admitted your Hebrew was rusty. Is it back to the drawing board?' She stopped herself. She was falling into old habits. It was only fair to give the new ones a chance for a while. But she was stumped.

'What about Miss Brunner?' said Professor Hira. 'She, after all, believes in the value of material power. And as such she is representative of the would-be gold makers. The source of the heat is given so variously, in all the texts, yet never, of course, from weapons, as such. "In violent heat shall hermaphrodite be born" is perhaps the nearest. And Paracelsus tells us hardly anything. Either because he was too drunk or because he didn't know.'

'It's Cathy I'm worrying about,' said Una. Had her ego got the better of her, after all?

Major Nye cleared his throat. 'If there's nothing else I can do for the moment, I wouldn't mind cleaning up a bit.'

'I'm afraid I'm the only one who can lead you back,' said Una. She turned to the others. 'It's still rather cold. Shall you wait?'

'Happy to,' said Lobkowitz. Hira gravely bowed his agreement.

When Una and Major Nye were out of earshot, Hira said, 'I fear this is the constant lot of the experimental scientist. Perhaps Una will come to understand that.'

'She has lost her dearest companion,' said Lobkowitz. 'And she had hoped, as it were, to find her restored. She gave herself entirely to her faith. Now, naturally, she is assailed by every form of moral doubt.'

'Well,' said Hira, 'it's early days yet.'

Lobkowitz squatted in the ruins. He peered at the egg from a number of angles. 'I suppose we'll have to devise a way of getting it inside. What do you think, Hira?'

'Simple enough, I should say, if we put our heads together. I could go down to Glastonbury and try to borrow a wheelbarrow.'

'Worth a try! But I'll go, if you don't mind. I could do with the walk and it won't be so dangerous for me.

'Oh, my dear Prinz, surely that danger's passed?'

'We have no means of being certain. Not yet.'

Hira accepted this as reasonable. 'I'll stay and guard the egg.'

For a moment he watched Lobkowitz striding down the hill, then he, too, squatted. 'How are we doing?' he enquired of the egg. He would not have been surprised by a response. There was none.

Prinz Lobkowitz was glad to be stretching his long legs. The abandoned vehicles were of no great interest to him. He had strolled over more than one battlefield in his time. Sometimes it was impossible to tell what kind of mass hysteria seized a group of soldiers and made them flee. On the outskirts of the town he saw only a few signs of looting. Any deserters were gone. He wondered what Miss Brunner had done with the population. As he strolled up Chilkwell Street it occurred to him there might be a wheelbarrow somewhere in the Abbey grounds.

He had never been to the site before so was unprepared for the beauty of the Lady Chapel, roofless and somewhat battered, which seemed to Lobkowitz one of the best examples of late-twelfth- or early-thirteenth-century architecture. He began to walk around it, fascinated by the lovely angle turrets, the North Door with its elaborate stone carvings. He had seen their like only occasionally in Prague and once, through unusual good fortune, in Mirenburg. It was as he looked at the sculpture depicting the Massacre of the Innocents that he heard a small human groan from within the ruins.

He found Miss Brunner in the Galilee. Her knees were tucked under her chin and her face, though still lined from years of struggle, had a trace of innocence which suggested at once that her mind had snapped with the defection of her forces. Nonetheless he approached warily. Her only weapon seemed to be an elaborate sword, its hilt jewelled, its blade engraved with what he guessed were alchemical runes. 'Good morning.' He spoke softly.

She reached slowly for the blade and took it in both hands. With her head she indicated a khaki walkie-talkie. 'The battery went flat. Well, my lord? Are you come to carry me to the Tower?'

The reference escaped him. 'Your men destroyed it. Don't you remember?'

'A mirage. Is that what you call it, my lord? A glamour placed by your witchly allies upon our senses. We squandered our strength upon an illusion. Nothing clean defeated us. Black magic, my lord. Your supernatural chemistry was our downfall. We came with honest steel. It is harder to lose to a dishonourable enemy.'

She sighed, using the sword to get to her feet. She offered it to him, pommel first. 'Here is the symbol of your victory. I pray you, if you possess a dram of mercy, use it upon me, that I may not be vulgar entertainment for the Mob.'

'I assure you, madam, there is no plan to kill you, publicly or otherwise.'

'I could not bear long years of prison, sir.

He was at a loss. His diplomatic powers were scarcely up to the situation.

'Tell me, my lord, does Elizabeth already touch her weedy buttocks to the coronation throne?'

'You have no queen, I believe. Unless it's in Canada. Or possibly Australia. Britain has been a titular republic within the Commonwealth and under the jurisdiction of Sydney, I think. I've scarcely read a newspaper in weeks. Weren't you some sort of governor? A kind of tyrant?'

'I had hopes for England, my lord. An England brought back to grace.'

He rubbed his hands together, for they were beginning to freeze. 'Your vision, madam, could yet be realised.'

'Oh, no sir. My vision is ended with my capture.' She moved the sword insistently towards him. Awkwardly, he took it. 'I'm afraid…'

''Tis well to be so, sir. There's a great egg buried at the centre of the world. And when it hatches our globe shall be wrought asunder; hurled through the heavens like so many motes of dust. This is the end of our history, sir.'

'Madam, you are too desperate. Could it not be the beginning of another? Why, there are hopes for a Golden Age.'

'Such hopes died with our defeat, my lord. An Age of Ice must precede. And an Age of Iron, too. I tell you true, sir. The world ends with my death.'

It was such an ordinary point of view that Prinz Lobkowitz, balancing the sword with two fingers, again found himself unable to respond. 'Aha,' he said. Then: 'Did you have any ambition in the direction, if I may put it so, of an egg?'

'What, sir? You think I created it? I have devoted my life, my soul, my wisdom, to creating a world in which such an abomination could not possibly come into being. Sir, you do me great wrong. Would you have me be the mother of some grotesque? Progenitrix to a Phoenix? Slay me, my lord, I beg thee. Your words are not tolerable to my ears. I deserve more than casual insult. I near changed the very nature of this universe.'

'You feel no guilt?'

'Great guilt, sir, aye. Who could not? I failed. In the purity of winter I should have been both sire and dam to the Millennium. But I was betrayed. England betrayed me. My English were unworthy of me. I was deceived.'

'Think you, dear lady, that a little of that was self-delusion? Your army fled. I have seen armies in flight before. Frequently it is because the myth which sustains soldiers in their craft is suddenly perceived by them as false. The glamour falls from them almost in an instant.'

'The glamour, my lord, was the cause of our ruin. The work of that unholy coven. Those shape-changers are possessed of the Devil's power to vanish from one place and appear in another. What else is that but foul sorcery?'

'You are of an age which could see it as such.'

'It is so, my lord. There is no other interpretation.' Her old flare blazed on her face for an instant but was soon gone. She bowed her head. 'Are you here to try me, sir? To make me turn from Truth itself? Do you seek to make me lie, so that your murder of me and all my dreams shall be less unpalatable to your conscience? My lord, I'll not be party to my own dishonour. My pride remains. This body you see is my empire and until we are both extinguished I shall rule us honestly.'

Prinz Lobkowitz set the sword down on a worn block. 'As a matter of fact, Miss Brunner, I came here to find a wheelbarrow. Have you seen, possibly, a gardener's hut?'

She had discontinued the interview.

Sadly, he left the Lady Chapel. Eventually, on the far side of the Abbey, he discovered what he needed. It was a heavy, old-fashioned wheelbarrow and would take a good deal of his remaining strength to get it back to the top of the Tor, but he rather relished the task.

As he went back past the chapel he heard her gasp. Fearing she had fallen on her own sword, he hesitated. From a habit of discretion, he continued on his way.

Una and Major Nye had rejoined Hira by the time Prinz Lobkowitz, grinning and panting like an elderly sheepdog, eventually returned with his prize to the top.

'What an excellent idea.' Una fought against her melancholy. 'That should be just the job, Prinz Lobkowitz.'

'You look all in, old boy.' Major Nye was spruce again and had a jauntier air. 'You take it easy. We can carry on from here.'

Lobkowitz reported his encounter in the Lady Chapel, partly in the hope of relieving any loss of faith Una had in her judgement. 'The poor woman's mad as a hatter. But she's afraid of our egg. She says it will destroy the world.'

'I hope not.' Una bent to stroke the egg, treating it almost as a pet. 'I was merely hoping to destroy civilisation as we knew it.'

'That usually means much the same thing to the likes of Miss B.' Hira kept beaming, then, realising Una's dilemma, tried for attitudes less obviously cheerful. 'I suppose we'd better see if we can load our egg. Miss Brunner is such a silly goose, don't you find? Jolly difficult to sympathise with that type.' He was inclined clumsily to echo the snobbery of British India when attempting social compromise.

By manhandling the barrow so that its lip was under the egg, all four of them at last managed to get it aboard.

In the maze, as she led the way back, Una wondered, with a certain amount of need, if all this was merely an alternative; a minor event in the history of the multiverse? She would be glad to learn what was going on elsewhere. In his present mood, however, Alvarez would be reluctant to co-operate. She had even mourned for Collier. Now her concern was entirely for Catherine (was she actually part of the egg?). The egg could be a hoax. If Jerry had escaped, he might have left it simply to mystify everyone. The central chamber was warm and musty, a trifle damp. The egg, still in its wheelbarrow, was set in the middle of the floor.

'Is that it?' Alvarez was derisory. 'What was the idea? To put Britain back on the gold standard? How many of those can we make a week?'

'I would say our egg is unique.' Professor Hira spoke with soft disapproval. 'But we are not at all sure what to do with it, you see, old boy. Ha, ha!'

Una, clinging grimly to her faith, said: 'I'd guess we just leave it. It's all right here. For temperature and security and so on.'

'Like King Arthur sleeping in his cave.' Lobkowitz wondered if this were appropriate. 'Or Merlin?'

'Or Morgana,' she said.

'How are we going to get our stuff back to London?' Alvarez wanted to know. 'It'll be a bugger of a job.'

'We'll leave it. It was only intended for this.'

He was incredulous. 'There's some expensive gear here!' It was the last straw. 'Our egg's worth a king's ransom. We should at least have the place guarded!'

Shaking her head, Una drew several deep breaths. 'The maze guards it.'

'A wicked waste,' said Alvarez. 'Somebody should teach you lot the value of money. Do you know what it'll cost to finance a new Centre from scratch?'

'We don't plan to build one. This will do, should the need for it ever arise.' She smiled. 'It's a kind of schoolroom, really, isn't it?'

'It's not the Open bloody University.' Defiantly he lit another cheroot. 'This stuff is meant to function. We've hardly used it. I won't say it couldn't do with a bit of improvement and some of the systems are simply crazy, but I could get it all going in a couple of weeks.'

'Perhaps you'd rather stay behind,' she said. 'There's enough food, I'd imagine. I could fetch you later.'

'No need to get at me,' he said, 'just because your bloody

experiment failed. We now have to go out there and start trying to put the pieces back together. The country needs a stable government or she'll collapse.'

'A stable government's what it's had,' she said. 'Brigantia will be our only leader. She's perfect. She never interferes.'

'People are sick of women making a mess of things.' Alvarez, certain he had lost his job, was no longer cautious.

'I told you,' Una said. 'Those weren't women. They were fakes.'

'Blokes?' Alvarez was suddenly interested.

'Quasi-males,' said Una.

'Where's your power going to come from?'

'I'm not planning to rule anyone. My power comes from Brigantia.'

'You've gone potty, too, then.' He shrugged, moving a couple of marking pencils into a neater position on his mixing desk. 'Well, I can get a job in one of the emerging nations any time I like. I'll leave you to it.'

'You'll have a bit of company, I'd imagine, if the Goddess should inspire the country. It's going to be a woman's world, sergeant. I know it in my bones.'

'Sod you, then.' Alvarez now believed he had played a crucial part in producing this appalling change. If only he had thrown his weight on Miss Brunner's side things might have worked out far better. He puffed miserably on the cheroot. The end got soggier with every movement of his lips. 'Don't think I mind working for a woman. I've worked for women. I had a lot of respect for Miss Brunner. You haven't got what it takes, Una, if you don't mind me saying so, to command men. We've our pride, you know. Miss Brunner was different.'

Unable to resist responding to him, Una shook her head. 'Miss Brunner was sameness personified, sergeant. Sameness was her ideal.'

'I couldn't help feeling sorry for the poor woman.' Prinz Lobkowitz was disquieted by the tension. 'She believed she had the heart and stomach of a king. Would she want to be buried, do you think, in that graveyard down there?'

Alvarez would have left at that stage but only Una could lead them out. He opened his briefcase and found one of his remaining magazines. He gave *Pain Today* his sulky attention.

Major Nye and Professor Hira were still studying the egg. 'I can't say it looks at all organic.' Professor Hira ran a neat hand over the surface. 'So it's rather hard to believe it was created from something organic. We've run so much up the flagpole. It will be years before we're able to analyse all we've done in the past few weeks. Yet if we accept that an initial transmutation created the egg, I suppose further transmutations are possible. Since we have no way, as yet, of projecting likely results, we shall just have to wait and see. Meanwhile, I wonder what will happen to your island?'

Major Nye cleared his throat. 'People are pretty good at looking after themselves, you know. Given half a chance. My guess is some parts will be pretty awful while others thrive as jolly good places to live.'

'What's this, major?' Lobkowitz was jovial. 'Do I hear you putting in a good word for anarchy?'

'Never thought much of governments, top brass, that sort of thing. Have the women a chance?'

'They'll take it.'

'Then the threat of power struggles between rival warlords isn't nearly so great.'

Una joined them around the egg. 'A lot depends on what hatches. If anything. Or anyway what it comes to mean. But the men should –' She stopped herself. 'I believe we must have our turn, that's all. It's harder, of course, when the likes of Miss Brunner are discredited. She was a powerful enemy, you know. None stronger. She knew it. If she killed herself it was because there was no further prospect, in her eyes, of killing someone else. She was all she had left. Funny how that often happens.'

Only Prinz Lobkowitz had much sense of what the others took to be her private musings. 'So die all tyrants. It's a consolation. But is it true?'

Una's reluctance to leave had little to do with what she now faced outside. She continued to hope Catherine would appear. She felt that, having carefully avoided violence, she was somehow responsible for the murder of the human creature she had loved most. There were going to be some dark hours. The hardest struggle lay ahead. 'Will the last person out please switch off the main power?' She grew brisk. 'Just leave those little lights. They'll go on for ever.' Close to tears, she took old Major Nye's kindly, uncomprehending arm. 'They did do something positive,' he offered. 'It wasn't a useless sacrifice. The egg scared 'em off. I saw it. I saw them haring down the hill like kids who've spotted a ghost – or what they think is a ghost. Or a wasp's nest, too. Oh, I can't count the number of times I've been stung fooling about with those nests. Did you do that? As a girl? Poke a stick in to see what happens? Damn' fool thing to try. I suppose I was always a bit slow on the uptake.'

'But your heart's in the right place, major.'

Alvarez, followed by Professor Hira, took one last look at the equipment and swore under his breath. 'You should try to relax old chap,' said the Brahmin. 'The war's over, you know.'

'Is it ever? We'll see.'

Professor Hira pulled down the big switch. At first the whole centre seemed in darkness. Then he made out tiny emergency lights. Satisfied, he closed the door behind him. 'I wonder what it will be like in civvy street, after all these years,' he said.

'Australia,' said Alvarez. He was rapidly devising his own plans.

Hira paused. He thought he had heard a sound from inside the cavern. He opened the door again. He could just see the wheelbarrow and the egg. The egg appeared to be giving off a dim light of its own. Closing the door again Hira ran to catch up with the others.

Once they were out of the maze and the door had been freshly disguised, Alvarez felt better. 'Well, we didn't do badly, I suppose.'

Una could feel hope in her bones. She, too, cheered up a little.

'It's a woman's world,' she said. 'With a bit of luck it will stay one for a while. See over there! What a lovely day.'

Beyond the battlefield the snow had melted completely. Evaporating, it had given the landscape a soft, unreal quality. The sun was coming through.

Prinz Lobkowitz looked fondly towards their misty hills and woods. Perhaps they had at last discovered an acceptable form of immortality. He realised he was deeply content. Even happy.

The little troupe trailed Una down. Save for the flap and croak of ravens, the Tor was very still. They managed at last to get over the corpses. Once past the camp they all drew several deep breaths.

Major Nye and Una walked up the High Street arm in arm. 'D'you think poor Cornelius will become a tourist attraction too?' He sighed. 'And what about Catherine?'

'We'll see.' She was unable to speak at length.

'They're not dead, you know. I stayed out there, don't forget, though keeping to cover. I'd swear they merged. When they caught fire the ladder fell inwards. There's something incredibly enduring, you know, about them.'

Una shook her head. 'Jerry's dead, major. Gone for good. As Jerry, anyway. Catherine was always stronger.'

'Well, well. I suppose much still remains to be seen.'

She felt superstitious. She put out her hand to touch a thorn branch as she went by it. She was faintly surprised it was not yet blooming.

'Will you be staying in England long?' Professor Hira addressed Prinz Lobkowitz as they paused to look in a bookshop full of Ashe, Caine and Graves.

'I'm due in Prague fairly soon. We've no idea how long things will take to spread. I hope to be back in time for the start of the new millennium.'

'It will be that long at least. I don't envy Mrs P. her task. What do you feel about her ambitions?'

'I've told her what I think. Who enjoys giving up power? Particularly if it's a kind one uses casually. You know my relish for multiplicity and variety, professor. There's only one moral position, however, where Una's work is concerned.'

He patted the frowning Brahmin's back. 'Come on, old man! We've nothing to lose but our smugness!'

'And nothing to gain but your chains.' Alvarez was at last openly contemptuous. He wondered which was the best way to get to Australia. Then he recalled his morning tape. The *Teddy Bear* was in Torquay. If he got there quickly he must easily soon be captain of his own ship. 'And master of my own bleedin' fate,' he said to himself. As he began to try car door handles the distance between him and the others grew.

At the top of the High Street, Una waited for Hira and Lobkowitz to catch her up. The little brown scientist and the etiolated pale diplomat were like cartoon characters from an old *Comic Cuts*.

'Come on, Alvarez!' shouted Hira in a strained display of comradeship. 'We're going to Hyde Park Corner and Trafalgar Square and the Post Office Tower. We're disciples now, I think. We're spreading the word.'

'Pommy bastards.' To his profound satisfaction, Alvarez felt the door of a Mercedes 350SL yield to his questing thumb. 'Oh, Christ! It's my lucky day.' The keys were not in the ignition. He was delighted by this: a chance to doctor the wires, test his old skills, get his judgement back. The drive to Torquay would be one of his life's happiest moments. The technician whistled as he worked. 'Va va voom, sexy bombshell! Your sarge has copped himself a Mercky.'

By the time the others paused outside St Benedict's Church Alvarez offered them a satisfied wave before becoming a red blur. He vanished.

Una yawned. She still wondered why she felt so much better.

Looking back she saw that the mist around the Tor was thicker, mixing with what remained of the smoke. Confident they had found paradise, ravens hopped from one delicious Tommy Atkins to the next.

Deep at the Tor's core the egg, still apparently of dense gold, gave a beat. An hour later the beat was repeated: The heart of a hibernating fabulous monster. Little lights around the cavern's roof twinkled like stars in the damp heat. There was a faint smell of ozone.

It took six months however for the egg to speak.

'It's a tasty world,' she said.

The Final Programme

Opening pages, 1991/'92, previously unpublished, from an aborted graphic adaptation by Mark Reeve of *The Final Programme*

preliminary data
bully for her

THE YEAR IS 196 . JERRY CORNELIUS IS DRESSED INCONGRUOUSLY FOR THE PLACE AND CLIMATE, AND EVEN IN THE WEST HIS CLOTHES WOULD HAVE A SLIGHTLY OLD-FASHIONED LOOK ABOUT THEM. THE HIGH HEELED ELASTIC SIDED BOOTS FOR INSTANCE, ARE NOT AT ALL IN STYLE NOR HAVE THEY BEEN FOR SEVERAL YEARS.

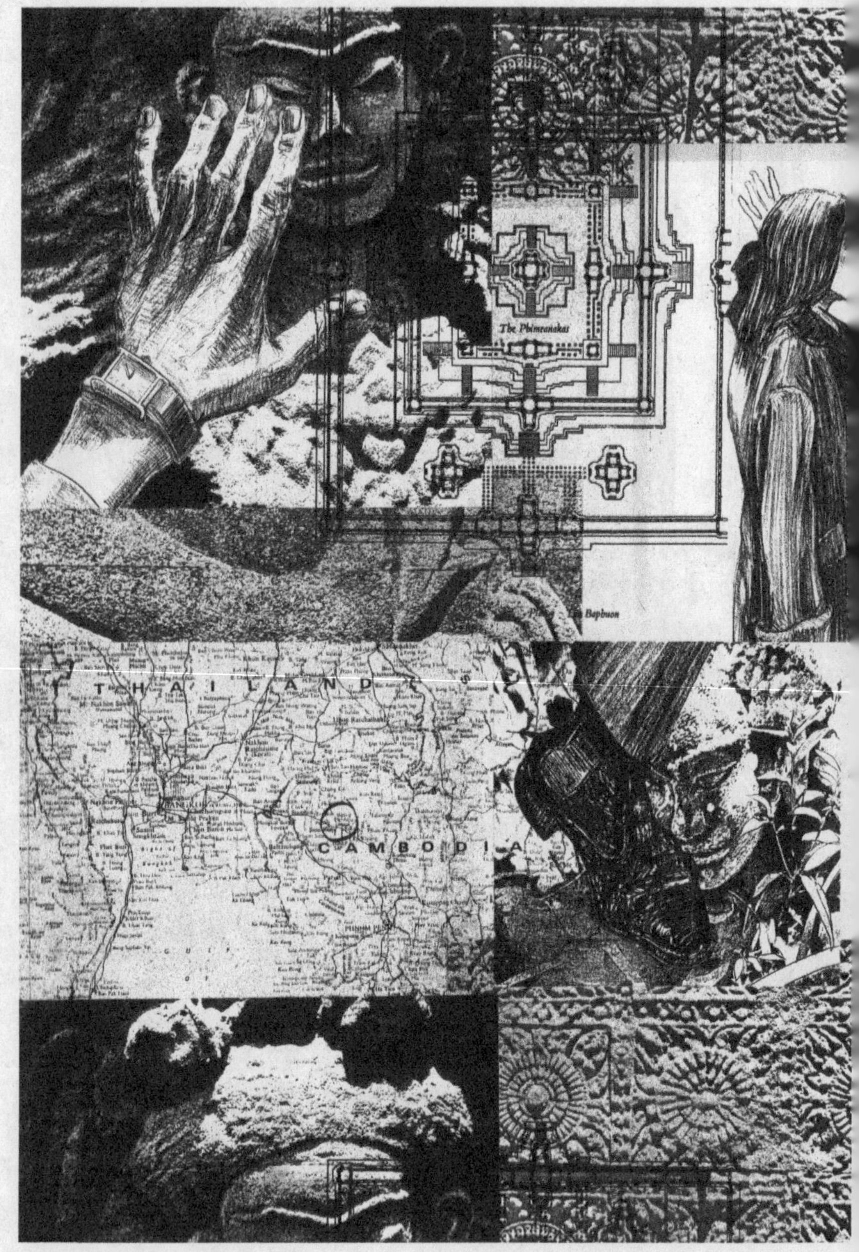
The Phimeanakas
T H A I L A N D
C A M B O D I A

ELIUS IS ON HIS WAY
EEPADATE.

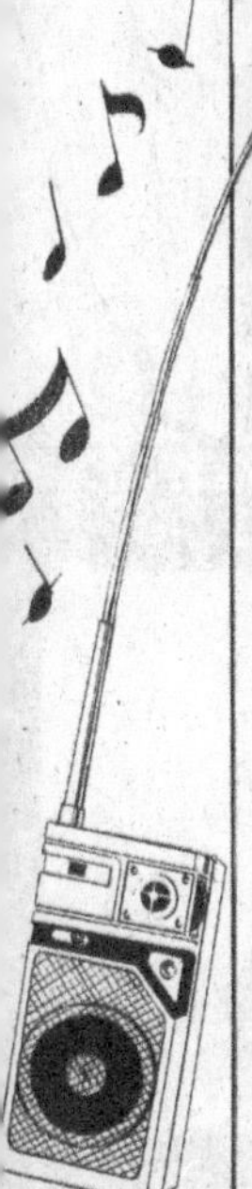

SERENE AND CARVED IN ANCIENT ROCK, THE FACES OF BUDDHAS AND THE THREE ASPECTS OF ISHWARA LOOK FROM TERRACE AND ARCHWAYS; HUGE STATUES BAS-RELIEFS — PROBABLY THE GREATEST CLUTTER OF DEITIES AND DEVILS EVER ASSEMBLED IN ONE PLACE. BENEATH AN EXTRAVAGANTLY BLOATED REPRESENTATION OF VISHNU THE DESTROYER, ONE OF ISH-WARA'S THREE ASPECTS, A TINY TRANSISTOR RADIO IS PLAYING. IT IS CORNELIUS'S RADIO. THE TUNE IS 'ZOOTS SUITE' BY ZOOT MONEY'S BIG ROLL BAND. BESIDE THE RADIO, IN THE GREEN-GOLD EARLY AFTERNOON SUNSHINE, A MAN SITS AT LEISURE WHILE MOSQUITOES BUZZ AND GIBBONS CHATTER * * * * * * * * *

A BUDDHIST PRIEST PASSES BY, SHAVEN AND SAFFRONED, AND A GROUP OF BROWN CHILDREN PLAY AMONG THE MASSIVE STATUES OF FORGOTTEN HEROES. IT IS A PLEASANT AFTERNOON, WITH A SLIGHT BREEZE FANNING THE JUNGLE. A GOOD TIME FOR IDLE SPECULATION THINKS CORNELIUS SITTING DOWN BESIDE THE MAN AND SHAKING HANDS.

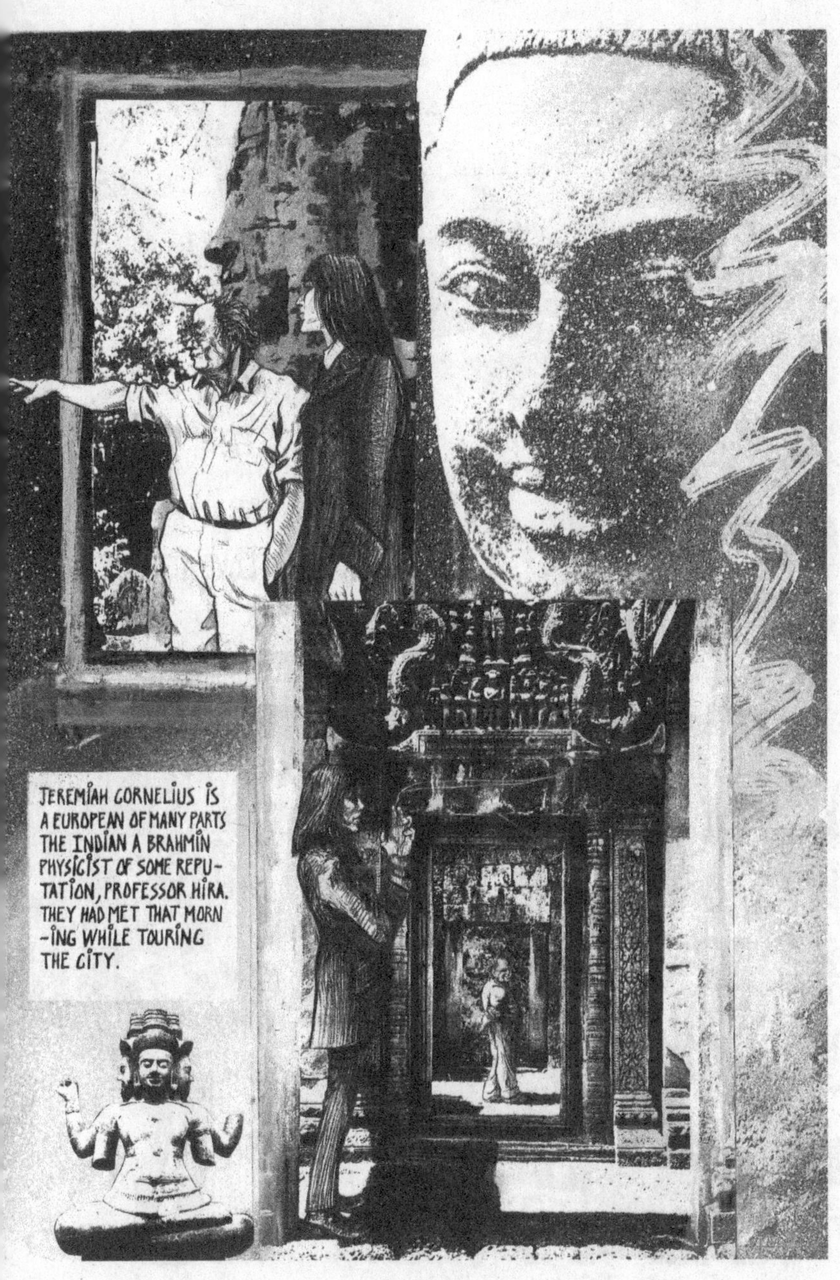
JEREMIAH CORNELIUS IS
A EUROPEAN OF MANY PARTS
THE INDIAN A BRAHMIN
PHYSICIST OF SOME REPU-
TATION, PROFESSOR HIRA.
THEY HAD MET THAT MORN
-ING WHILE TOURING
THE CITY.

Plan 4 Angkor Wat (central part)
Plan 5 The Bayon
Plan 6 Preah Khan
IT HAD BEEN LOVE AT FIRST SIGHT.

THE GNOSTICS POSSESSED A COSMOLOGY VERY SIMILAR, IN MANY WAYS, TO THE HINDU AND BUDDHIST. INTERPRETATIONS VARIED, OF COURSE, BUT THE FIGURES WERE VERY CLOSE.
WHAT FIGURES EXACTLY?
WELL, FOR INSTANCE, THE COSMIC HISTORY CYCLE — WE CALL IT *manvantara* IN SANSKRIT. BOTH HINDUS AND GNOSTICS GIVE THE FIGURE AS 432,000^{10} YEARS. THAT IS AN INTERESTING COINCIDENCE FROM ANY POINT OF VIEW, EH?
T ABOUT THE *Kalpa*? I THOUGHT THAT WAS YOUR WORD FOR A TIME CYCLE.
ND, THAT IS A DAY AND IGHT OF BRAHMA; 20 MILLION YEARS.
AS LITTLE AS THAT?
E *manvantara* IS DIVIDED INTO FOUR YUGAS, OR AGES. THE CURRENT CYCLE IS ARING ITS END. THE PRESENT AGE IS THE LAST OF FOUR.
ND WHAT ARE THEY?
OH LET ME THINK.... THE *satya yuga*, THE GOLDEN AGE THAT ACCOUNTED FOR THE FIRST FOUR-TENTHS OF THE CYCLE. THEN WE HAD THE *Dwapara yuga*, THE SECOND AGE. THAT TOOK CARE OF ANOTHER 864,000 YEARS. THE THIRD AGE — THE *Tretya yuga* — CAN YOU HEAR THE ECHOES OF AN ANCIENT COMMON LANGUAGE? — LASTED FOR ONLY TWO-TENTHS OF THE WHOLE CYCLE. THE *Kali yuga*, OF COURSE, IS THE CURRENT AGE. IT BEGAN, AS I RECALL ON FEBRUARY 18, 3102 B.C.
AND WHAT IS THE *Kali Yuga*?

THE DARK AGE, MR. CORNELIUS. HA! HA!
HOW LONG IS THAT SUPPOSED TO LAST?
JUST ONE-TENTH OF THE *mahayuga*.
THAT GIVES US PLENTY OF TIME
THEN AT THE END OF THE *manvantara* THE WHOLE CYCLE REPEATS ITSELF DOES IT? THE WHOLE OF HISTORY ALL OVER AGAIN!
SOME BELIEVE SO. OTHERS THINK THAT THE CYCLES VARY SLIGHTLY. IT IS BASICALLY AN EXTENSION OF OUR CONVICTIONS CONCERNING REINCARNATION. THE STRANGE THING IS THAT MODERN PHYSICS BEGINS TO CONFIRM THESE FIGURES — IN TERMS OF THE COMPLETE REVOLUTION OF THE GALAXY AND SO ON. I MUST ADMIT THAT THE MORE I READ OF THE PAPERS PUBLISHED THESE DAYS, THE MORE CONFUSED I BECOME BETWEEN WHAT I WAS TAUGHT AS A HINDU AND WHAT I HAVE LEARNED AS A PHYSICIST. IT REQUIRES INCREASING SELF-DISCIPLINE TO SEPARATE THEM IN MY MIND.
WHY DO YOU BOTHER, PROFESSOR?

YET THE COSMOLOGIES MINGLE AND ABSORB ONE ANOTHER. THERE ARE PEOPLE IN EUROPE WHO BELIEVE THAT THE Vedas DESCRIBE A PRE-HISTORIC CIVILIZATION AS ADVANCED, OR MORE SO, AS OUR OWN THAT WOULD TIE IN WITH YOUR FIRST AGE, WOULDN'T IT?
SOME OF MY FRIENDS HAVE WONDERED ABOUT THAT, TOO. IT IS POSSIBLE, NATURALLY, BUT NOT LIKELY. EXQUISITE PARABLES, MR. CORNELIUS, BUT NOTHING MORE. NOT THE MYTHICAL VESTIGES OF A GREAT SCIENCE I FEAR. THE EMBROIDERED REMNANTS OF A GREAT PHILOSOPHY, PERHAPS.
PLEASANT EMBROIDERY.
YOU ARE KIND TO THINK SO; BUT YOU HAVE STUDIED THE VEDAS? IT SEEMS THAT MORE WESTERNERS STUDY SANSKRIT THAN WE. AND WE READ EINSTEIN.
SO DO WE.
YOU HAVE MORE TIME FOR EVERYTHING OVER THERE OLD MAN. YOU ARE AT THE END OF YOUR manvantara, EH? WE HAVE BEGUN A NEW ONE.
I WONDER
I DO NOT SPEAK SERIOUSLY — AS A HINDU — BUT THERE ARE SHORTER CYCLES WITHIN THE AGES. SEVERAL OF MY MORE METAPHYSICALLY INCLINED ACQUAINTANCES HAVE PREDICTED THAT WE ARE AT THE END OF SUCH A CYCLE.

BUT OUR AFFAIRS DIMINISH IN SIGNIFICANCE COMPARED WITH A SPAN OF EVEN 432,000 YEARS.
THAT'S A WESTERN IDEA, MR. CORNELIUS. WHAT IS TIME? HOW LONG IS A MILLISECOND OR A MILLENIUM? IF THE OLD HINDUS WERE RIGHT, THEN WE HAVE MET IN ANGKOR BEFORE AND SHALL AGAIN — AND THE DATE WILL ALWAYS BE TODAY'S, OCTOBER 31, 196 WILL ANYTHING HAVE CHANGED, I WONDER, IN THE NEXT manvantara? WILL GODS WALK THE EARTH? WILL MAN BE —?
WHO KNOWS? LET'S COMPARE NOTES THEN. I'LL BE SEEING YOU PROFESSOR.
THIS TIME NEXT manvantara?
IF YOU LIKE.
WHERE ARE YOU OFF TO NOW?
THANKS. I'M GOING TO Phnom Penh AIRPORT AND THEN TO LONDON. I WANT TO ORDER A GUITAR.
YOU'RE AT THE ANGKOR HILTON TOO, AREN'T YOU? WHY NOT STAY ONE MORE NIGHT AT THE HOTEL?
WELL, ALL RIGHT.

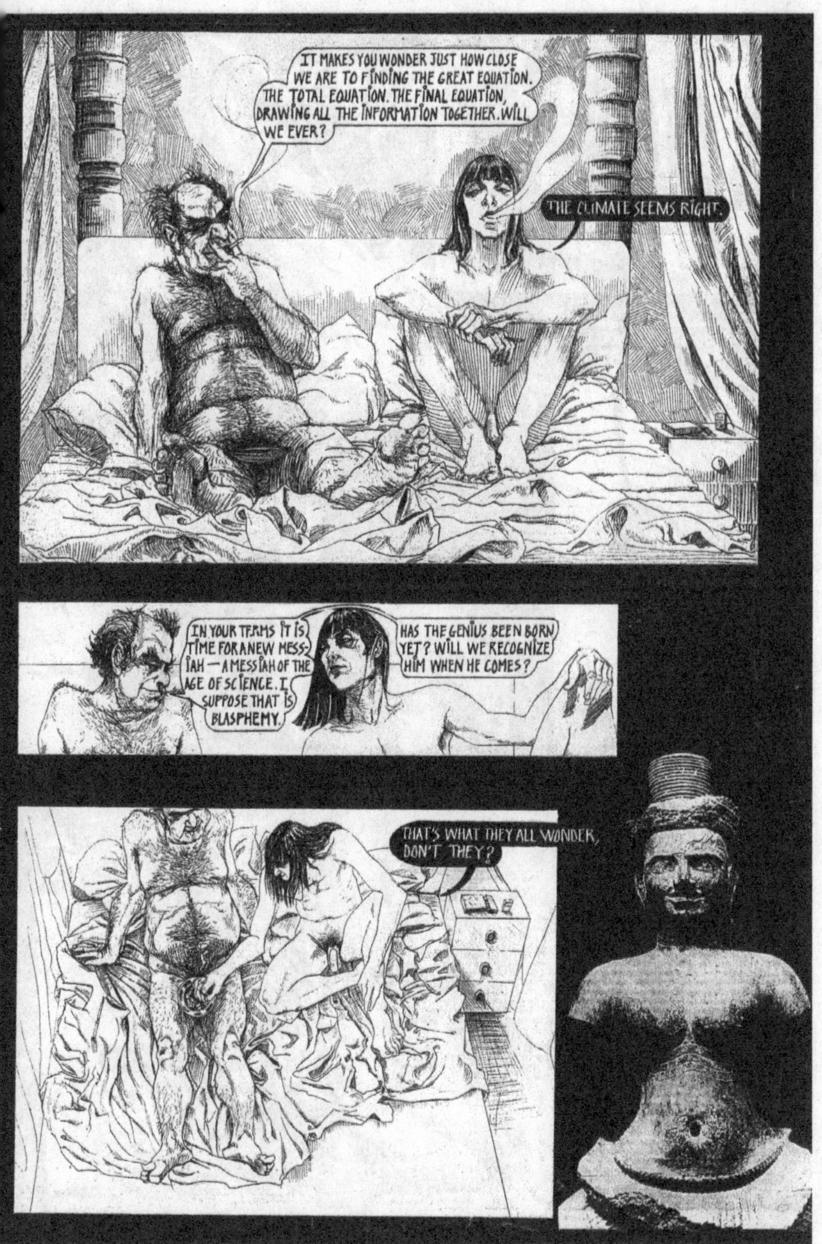
IT MAKES YOU WONDER JUST HOW CLOSE WE ARE TO FINDING THE GREAT EQUATION. THE TOTAL EQUATION. THE FINAL EQUATION, DRAWING ALL THE INFORMATION TOGETHER. WILL WE EVER?
THE CLIMATE SEEMS RIGHT.
IN YOUR TERMS IT IS TIME FOR A NEW MESS-IAH — A MESSIAH OF THE AGE OF SCIENCE. I SUPPOSE THAT IS BLASPHEMY.
HAS THE GENIUS BEEN BORN YET? WILL WE RECOGNIZE HIM WHEN HE COMES?
THAT'S WHAT THEY ALL WONDER, DON'T THEY?

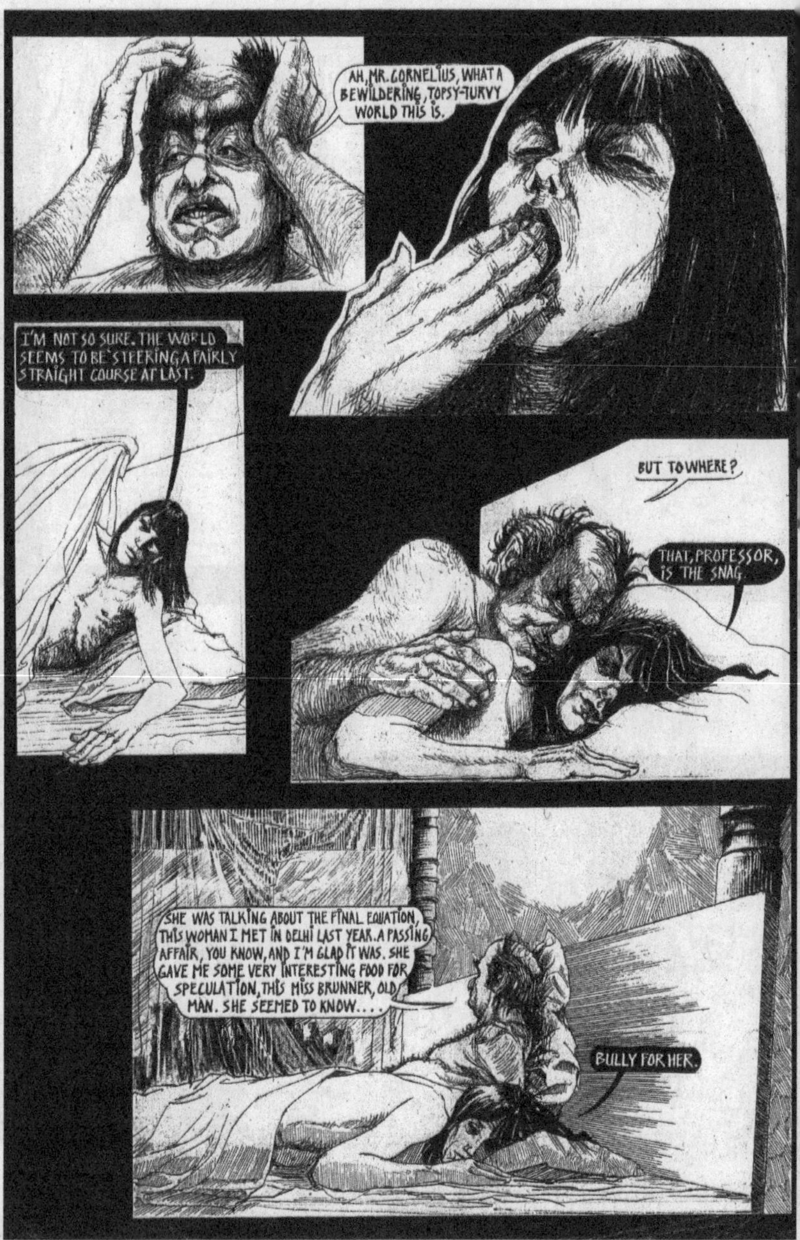
AH, MR. CORNELIUS, WHAT A BEWILDERING, TOPSY-TURVY WORLD THIS IS.
I'M NOT SO SURE. THE WORLD SEEMS TO BE STEERING A FAIRLY STRAIGHT COURSE AT LAST.
BUT TO WHERE?
THAT, PROFESSOR, IS THE SNAG.
SHE WAS TALKING ABOUT THE FINAL EQUATION, THIS WOMAN I MET IN DELHI LAST YEAR. A PASSING AFFAIR, YOU KNOW, AND I'M GLAD IT WAS. SHE GAVE ME SOME VERY INTERESTING FOOD FOR SPECULATION, THIS MISS BRUNNER, OLD MAN. SHE SEEMED TO KNOW...
BULLY FOR HER.

jerry
CORNELIUS
the second coming

Firing the Cathedral

To Iain Sinclair,
Partner in Time.

Heavy Fighting in Jerusalem

Jerusalem, Saturday
The heaviest fighting for over three weeks broke out in Jerusalem tonight when Jews using mortars, opened fire on the Arab area of Katamon.

Two big explosions shook the city as the attackers blew up Arab houses, which they claimed were snipers' nests and operational headquarters.

Firing then broke out in other quarters of the city. Army bren carriers moved up to vantage points and fired into the fighting areas, gradually bring the situation under control and quietening the city.

News of the World, 14 March, 1948

Nothing Heard from Air Liner Six Minutes After Leaving Calcutta

COMET MISSING
A Comet jet air-liner with 43 people – including 10 women, a child, and a baby – on board was missing last night on its flight from Singapore to London.

The Comet, owned by BOAC, left Dum Dum Airport, Calcutta, just before 11 a.m. for its three-hour flight to New Delhi. Six minutes later the Comet made its routine report 'Climbing on track.' Then there was silence.

Sunday Dispatch, 3 May, 1953

Stormbringer

Upon the 10th inst., we began the storm; and after some hot dispute we entered, the enemy disputing it very stiffly with us. Our men that stormed the breaches were forced to recoil; they made a second attempt and became masters both of their retrenchments and the Church. Divers of the Enemy retreated into the Mill-Mount; a place very strong and difficult of access. The Governor, Sir Arthur Ashton, and divers considerable officers being there, our men getting up to them, were ordered by me to put them all to the sword: and indeed, being in the heat of action, I forbade them to spare any that were in arms in the town: and, I think, that night they put to the sword about 2000 men; about 100 of them possessing St Peter's Church-steeple whereupon I ordered it to be fired, when one of them was heard to say in the midst of the flames: 'God damn me, God confound me; I burn, I burn.'

The next day, the other two Towers were summoned. When they submitted, their officers were knocked on the head; and every tenth man of the soldiers killed; and the rest shipped for the Barbadoes. I am persuaded that this is a righteous judgement of God upon these barbarous wretches, who have imbrued their hands in so much innocent blood; and that it will tend to prevent the effusion of blood for the future, which are satisfactory grounds to such actions, which otherwise cannot but work remorse and regret.

– Oliver Cromwell on the Massacre at Lenthall,
17 September, 1649

This Axis of Evil.

– David Frum (speechwriter for G.W. Bush)

I

Buffalo Soldiers

Jerusalem: This is where it all began.
This is where it will all end.

CNN, 16 January, 2002

It is true that whenever difficulties arose with awkward Governments of backward oil areas, they were always worsened when the Great Powers intervened. Of course, as soon as the first World War had demonstrated that oil was the most important of all war materials, the Great Powers never stopped interfering. In *The Oil Trusts and Anglo-American Relations*, a book which I wrote in 1923, I revealed some of the undignified squabbling between the victorious Allies which had been raging over the oil of the Middle East … The unseemly commotion was sufficient to put the Governments of the backward oil countries wise to the politics of international oil.

– Nicholas Davenport,
'Oily Spectacles',
New Statesman and Nation, 6 October, 1951

The business of America is business.

– Calvin Coolidge,
17 January, 1925

'Aha, young patriot! And what do you desire the Gandalf to bring you for July 4th?'

In his faded grey cassock, puffing on a churchwarden and wearing a patriotic pointed hat instead of his mitre, Bishop Beesley was doing his seasonal job at the WTC Memorial Mall. He had a small living in St James's, John Street, so it wasn't far to walk. He did Uncle Santa or Sam Claus from September 11th to December 25th, took a break until Easter, then started the Gandalf job again around the middle of May. 'A moveable feast?' Shakey Mo Collier twitched up the bishop's cassock with his MK51, sniffing critically at the sweet smoke. 'Know what I mean, Dennis? Is that your own beard?'

'Bugger off at once, you cheeky young sprig,' boomed the Gandalf, 'or you'll feel my sandal on your sitmedown. Mark my words, young hobnob, I am old and wise. I know better than anyone. While I appear to make ill-considered decisions on the spur of the moment, I am, just like our president and all his sages, actually behaving according to a carefully pre-arranged plan. *White men in grey this world shall rule, Till justice come to Kent State School.*' He cast a benign eye down the line of kids and handlers waiting to have their wishes granted. They were all security-tagged and lightly tranked. The mall was a haven. It was a paradise. 'I wonder if you would be interested in the leg of Saint George, a genuine relic, with full provenance. A fake went on eBay for over a million dollars last week. Pickled, but considering the age…?'

'Dragon's Claw?' Mo hated buying dope from the clergy. He couldn't help it. He came from a time before consumerology. As an anachronism, he now had a mysterious and unexpected power. He liked the taste of it. The economics defeated him but the idea of the blood feud provided a deep sense of security. Reagan and Thatcher should have been made king and queen of the world. You knew where you were with them. A tooth for a tooth. But the liberals had done their usual meddling and now war was endless, which was some consolation.

The Gandalf felt about inside his robe. He seemed to be listening for an emergency warning. He dropped his voice. 'Cash only. Mill a lid.' He caught a movement through the pseudo-glass and cast a nervous eye out at the ragged New York skyline. 'Azrael?'

From a stylish, queerly stained flak jacket Mo pulled a big wad. His meaning frown settled on the National Guardsmen looking after the crowd. They were soft-faced college footballers, drafted for the season and glad of the extra money. They checked their watches. 'Coffee break.' Zonked on Afghani black they had been chilling through most of the century. The heavy tar had got to their blood and their arteries were hardening so fast they moved towards the *Syrup Dog* concession like tin men who had lost their oil can. Mo sighed deeply. He was free of any immediate anxieties. A Golden Age like this normally lasted at least a year.

Wasn't it time Jerry turned up? It didn't seem fair otherwise. He'd been on ice for too long.

The Gandalf slipped into his plastic cave for a moment. He came out fast, holding the remains of a Mars bar. Aware of his watching customers, he fussily adjusted his points. But he was all over the place. His nose lifting with disgust, he slipped the lid into Mo's blackened hand. 'Some little oik's wanking over the hobbit costumes. Where's a policeman when you need him?' The Nats were still enjoying their Caramel Corn Dogs, watching the adventures of Sweet Doggy on the overhead screen. Seizing his chance, Mo dived inside to see what pleasure he could get from the situation.

Bishop Beesley smoothed his grey smock and used the diversion to recover himself. He cleared his throat. 'Ho, ho, ho, ho…'

Slowly he began to beam. He had some brief sense of authority. He turned back to his customers. From the tent, they heard a dull thump and a squeak, some muffled grunting.

The Gandalf discreetly settled on his stool. The moment was now Mo's.

The whole mall was silent for ten minutes, awaiting the inevitable gunshot.

2

Tell Me There's a Heaven

> I want to bite the hand that feeds me.
> I want to bite that hand so badly.
>
> – Elvis Costello,
> 'Radio, Radio'

> A new George W. Bush last Tuesday addressed a transformed country, wholly unlike the one he campaigned in, and as not quite the man who campaigned ... He leads a country in which the political terrain has been utterly altered, with old constraints leveled, and new possibilities revealed. It is too early to tell what these may lead to. But not to describe what they are.
>
> – Noemie Emery,
> *Weekly Standard*, 11 February, 2002

> He has no soul.
>
> – George W. Bush,
> Fox TV, 18 December, 2001

Jerry Cornelius had popped into Graucho's for a swift tequila sunset. He moved through the chattering crowd, a little underdressed for the evening, reached the bar and looked for service. He had shredded his retro threads in Houston and now wore a bum-freezer suit in style since 1960. It made him look bit of a mod, a movie crook, an eastender. The sunglasses were the final touch. There was nothing like the comforts of convention. Sunglasses were a classic. He never listened to anyone's advice. He had weak eyes, these days.

They couldn't fault the whistle, though. 'There's always

authority in a nice plain suit,' his brother assured him. 'A short haircut, a touch of gold and plenty of cuff. It speaks volumes.'

Jerry still wasn't too sure about the head-shave. He couldn't help being reminded of electric chairs and Jews. He was on his way to Princelet Street now. In spite of his disgust with the heritage industry, Taffy still sometimes used the synagogue as a rendezvous. He had some last message tapes to hand over, he said. They needed an honest broker. He had examined all he was interested in. The Home Office pathologist had developed a special research study of the final words of the dying. He knew there was a truth eluding him. Ever since Jerry had known him Sir Taffy Sinclair had been up to something. Jerry still didn't know what it was. Sinclair had helped him out of the eighties and stayed with him through the nineties, so Jerry owed him. That had been a deadly dull twenty years with almost nothing to show for it but the *Belgrano* and the Basra Road. Sinclair had been more than decent. He had delivered Jerry to some nice holiday spots in the Middle East. There had been no shortage of skirmishes, but very little to get your teeth into. So when Sinclair sent a message, the old assassin was going to come through. But the trail back wasn't always easy, these days. Every second brought a thousand choices. Surely it wasn't only the fault of information technology?

When the old troupe effectively split up, Jerry had looked forward to spending some time in the Cairo pyramid he'd bought from the Egyptians when property values sank so suddenly in 2001. He had spent a fortune on restorations. He always got delusions of grandeur on holiday. It hadn't been long before he had returned to London. The coming collapse of New York made him realise he only felt thoroughly easy in a big city. But he had kept a low profile. You knew when your age was over. You just had to wait and hope that you'd get another chance. It was a turning world, at least for now.

'And when all's said and done,' he told Mitzi, behind the bar, 'London's the place to be.'

She enjoyed this. 'Not many places left,' she said. 'Not big ones. Just bits. And little ones.'

They were old friends. Mitzi flirted at him. She was only a bishop's daughter but she knew how to juice up a Jesuit. 'You can't beat a police bike. You can't match the classic Royal Albert.' Her gorgeous mascara fell like blue junk onto the damp bar and bonded with the rest of her ashy droppings. An unlikely grin broke through her lip-rouge. It defied her powdered cheeks, it cracked her neck and blacked her eyes. It brought back something Jerry hadn't seen since the early seventies. 'Your dad doing all right?' he asked.

'Well, he's working regularly. He's got a job in the States. They spent a fortune on reproducing The Two Towers. Then someone took out the Empire State. So tourism's up again. They want him for his accent. They love us over there. They think we're on their side.' She turned to dust at her picture of Margaret Thatcher in its red, white and blue frame. 'But things aren't the same, are they? I was going to move to Hastings. Or Worthing? What do you think?'

'My mum preferred Worthing,' said Jerry. 'She liked the minstrels at the Delaware Pavilion. Or was that Bexhill?' It was all South London-on-Sea now, which made everything simpler. Indian restaurants and racist raffles. It was a matter of time before the yardies took over Hove.

Almost his old self, he lit a triumphant Sherman's. He was back on home territory. This was the real thing. The big finish. He was enjoying it no end. 'I'm getting myself a little place in the Lakes after this. I've had enough of international tourism. It's my last Smoke Opera.' At her look of discomfort he added: 'Well, naturally I'll be home to die. To become one with the concrete from which I was conceived. From concrete we come and to concrete we return. The only place you're allowed to grow old and die without a lot of fuss being made about it is a proper city. And, when all's said and done, there is no more proper city than London.'

She was used to his self-pity. 'Well, at least you haven't changed much. You back in the seminary?' She tasted her own lips with her tongue, staring a little critically at his shaven scalp. 'It doesn't make you any younger, you know. Have you see those sculptures of Bedlam loonies at the V and A, is it? You look like an eighteenth-century murderer.'

Jerry accepted the criticism. 'That's where it started for me,' he said, 'One crap, half-baked revolution after another, then seventeen seventy-six and every sodding thing went pear-shaped. Revolutions are about people either trying to keep things the same or restore a Golden Age. The Americans were successful in holding back the march of time for over two hundred years. They're a bigger version of late-eighteenth-century Britain – hangings, harsh prisons and disgustingly rich autocrats above the law.'

'They can't help it.' Mitzi relaxed into a reminiscent smile. 'They're a very unvolatile people. They're mostly krauts, aren't they?'

'Well, they all blew their bloody revolutions. Trust Cromwell to fuck everything up. All this stuff could have been thrashed out over a table in ten minutes. But they got too scared. People really hate liberty. First sniff they get of it and they dive back into their familiar captivity. They fight to the death to keep those chains.'

Mitzi snorted. Various essences clouded the air around her head. 'Tom Paine, eh? And *Common Sense*. If you ask me the Canadians are the ones who had the common sense.'

Jerry looked up at the clock. 'Is that the right time?'

3
Oliver's Army

The Christians had gathered for Sunday services and the disciples expressed an interest in seeing the services, and the Master agreed. As they entered the building, the priest and the congregation recognised them and went over to greet them. There was so much joy that everyone began to experience an uplifting spiritual state. Several Sufi singers in the Master's group asked permission to chant verses from the Qur'an and the priests granted it.

The joy of receiving our Master, combined with the singers' praise of the Lord, brought an ecstatic state to those present. Many were in rapture. When the signing was finished and Abu Sai'd prepared to leave, one of his disciples exclaimed enthusiastically, 'If the Master wills and mentions it, many Christians here will abandon their garments of Christianity and put on the robe of Islam.'

The master retorted, 'We did not put their garment on them in the first place that we should presume to take it off.'

– Ibn Munawwar,
Asrar at-Tawhid, ed. Shafi-Kadkani, 1210

They get a white bucket for emergency squirts, while they are instructed to hold two fingers up for the alternative. At that time, a guard shackles them and takes them to the port-o-loo. While the military has spared no expense in construction costs (in three weeks, they built a completely operational field hospital staffed by 160 medical personnel – two more than there are prisoners), they've saved a fortune in toilet paper. It's the detainees' cultural preference not to use any. 'We don't shake hands,' says one camp guard.

– Matt Labash,
'Guantanamo's Unhappy Campers, The only abuse
the detainees are experiencing is self-inflicted',
Weekly Standard, 11 February, 2002

'All American soldiers are left-handed,' said Jerry. 'I read it in a magazine.'

'I can't look at CNN without thinking of my poor, silly son,' With a broad smile, Abu Sai'd stretched his rule from shoulder blades to thigh. 'You've put on a little length since we last had business. But you could do with fattening up. I'll take you home with me tonight. We are, God willing, having a good dinner.'

'What was that you were saying about sheep?' Jerry reached for his jacket.

'I was talking about sheepdogs. I've known some funny sheepdogs. I admire your collies, of course. Who couldn't? I always made a point of catching the trials on the telly.' He had come home to Jelalabad when things started to get tricky in Tipton.

'Ever known one that killed sheep?' Jerry lifted his arms. Abu Sai'd read off numbers to his palmtop.

'Never. There's a lot of wolf to a good sheepdog, as anyone will tell you, but there's something in them, just like there is in a lot of humans, that just won't let them do it. What sort of wolf is that, Monsignor Cornelius?'

'A fairly ineffective wolf.'

'But a very effective sheepdog.'

'You must get a bad cross, every so often. They can't all be naturally good.'

'Oh, perhaps.' Abu Sai'd retracted his measure. 'Are you familiar with Camus? I have been re-reading *Le Mythe de Sisyphe*. Constant striving. Constant disappointment. Constant joy. Always a consolation in times like these.'

Jerry was uncomfortable with this posture of acquiescence. 'When did the world's leaders learn the trick of talking aggressively and putting civilians in the front line? It saves a fortune in military spending.' He slid his right index finger down the silk swathe his companion offered him. 'As smooth as oil. You'd hardly know what it was.'

'No, but it's worms as usual.' The tailor indicated big bolts of cloth racked along the three walls of the shop not facing the street. 'The rest is oil. Man-made, as they say. Think of that one – that gauzy pale green up there for instance – starting somewhere in the desert, under ground.' His amused brown eyes looked hard into Jerry's face. 'You were speaking of the Rif. Abd'-al-Krim, I think his name was. Didn't he die of tuberculosis in Paris? They usually do. Are you still called the Raven in the Maghreb?'

'You're thinking of Texas. A different, more complicated age,' said Jerry. 'They could have called me the Red Shadow and put on the same show.'

'*Men of toil and danger, would you serve a stranger, and bow down to Burgundy? Fight, fight, fight for liberty*,' sang Abu Sai'd inexpertly. He couldn't help adding classical Egyptian flourishes. 'Why are you so interested in that shitty little country?' He shook his head and took out a pack of Camels, offering them to Jerry. 'Smoke?'

'It keeps us forging ahead.' Jerry fished a battered cigarette from the pack and very gently placed it to his lips, as if he tasted the paper. He felt the ghost of memory. 'It keeps us happy.'

'"Ah," said Christ, brushing at his tears with bloody hands, "would you re-crucify me?"' Abu Sai'd drew a breath for a further quote then became alert. He sniffed the air. 'Can you smell it too? That's a wolf. I thought the Jews had killed them all.' He got up hastily, knocking over his dummy, opened the little door in the back and ran through the house, taking down a long switch from the rack and going outside to check his sheep pens.

Jerry followed him. On the dark horizon were the outlines of Bethlehem. The sleeping sheep began to rise, blinking in the glare of Abu Sai'd's sweeping flashlight.

Jerry sniffed the wind.

'Is something burning?'

4

Pig Alley Blues

> You've grown up in a world that says you don't belong to it. So you make one you *can* belong to. But it takes a bit of nerve to go to Selfridge's dressed as Boadicea.
>
> – Boy George,
> BBC Radio 4, 16 January, 2002

> Captain Marvel Battles THE AXIS OF EVIL!
>
> *Captain Marvel Adventures*, January 1945

Islam means peace.

– George W. Bush, September 2001

'Eat pork, mother-coverers!'

Trixie Brunner was getting it on at the VR arcade. There were dozens of great new games. She had her name down for *Daisy-cutter Panic* and *Towelhead Run*. Meanwhile she was playing *Imam Hunt* with one hand and *American Terrorist* with the other. It improved her sense of balance. '*Frum, frum, frum...*'

Trixie's prim foxy face was bright with carmine and turquoise. She wore a little red dress and five-inch black spikes. With her pale skin and platinum rinse she looked like a Nazi poster. Her mother, waking from one of her long reveries, was convinced Trixie sported a false bottom. 'It doesn't suit you,' she said. It was a pathetic stab at regaining power and Trixie, feeling sentimental, didn't respond. Her mother soon drifted off again. The junk Trixie was giving her kept her comfortable.

The baroness had been almost all gangrene before they operated. Now she was mostly mouth. Trixie was using her own old stroller to take her mum for her weekly spin to the arcade. She had given up the bingo. Her mother kept insisting the numbers on her card were all winners. She would shout 'Bingo!' in the middle of a game. Her fellow players had turned against her.

'She's a bit of an archosaur, I'm so sorry.' Trixie apologised to Mo Collier who scratched his stubble and grunted agreeably. The idea of a prosthetic arse was turning him on.

With uneasy grace he offered Trixie's dam one of the Mars bars he'd taken off the vicar. 'Would she like to mumble something?'

'Better not,' said Trixie. 'It goes all over her.'

'Anyway,' Mo carried on where he'd left off. 'You know, I was thinking if you fancied a, you know, bit of fun.'

'I'm having a bit of fun,' Trixie pointed out. 'If it's you, I'd rather bang than bonk. But I don't mind doing a VR double-up. Want a round of *Screw You*?'

Mo's pride threatened his lust, but eventually he agreed. 'How much is it?'

Trixie shouted into her drooling mum's ear. 'Hear that, Mum? He's learning.'

It was too much for Mo. He swung his MK800-50 off his shoulder and threw a small, showy, irritable needle-burst into the machine's slot. The tiny heart-searchers clattered about for a while. Finding nothing organic, they settled down to wait. They had an active life-span of twenty hours.

This gesture interested Trixie. 'What are you doing for Christmas?' she asked absently, leaning back to straighten the seam of her stocking, her bottom bending awkwardly. 'Or are you invited down?'

Mo's juices began to rise.

5

On the Beach

> Frodo: 'I wish none of this had happened.'
>
> Gandalf: 'So do all who live to see such times, but that is not for them to decide. All we have to decide is what to do with the time that is given us.'
>
> New Line Cinema ad, December 2001

> For all the talk about the country moving on from Sept. 11, one group isn't quite ready, and that's the nation's marketers.
>
> *Wall Street Journal*, 5 February, 2002

> This smug, self-righteous, ignorant and aggressive people, whose myths are supported by self-deception and self-serving lies, have been breaking treaties since their history began. They have habitually invaded and settled territories guaranteed to others and,

ultimately, driven those inhabitants to violence as a last resort. This violence, then condemned as savage and unprovoked, they punished with vicious, genocidal and horrific intensity. In the languages of those they invade they are called The Treaty Breakers, but they call themselves the Chosen People, whose manifest destiny is to occupy the lands promised to them by God. They have used their scriptures to justify all the crimes they have committed against their own Biblical commandments.

– Lobkowitz,
The Monotheists: A Trail of Tears, 1952

Bishop Beesley had reverted to his richer robes and mitre. 'Boston?' His golden crook was blotchy with chocolate. He licked at his fingers with what was almost sensuality. 'There's much to be said to falling back into the old routines. The cardinal virtues. And, of course, the cardinal sins. Still, I shall miss dear old Hobbes.' Beesley reluctantly offered a bonbon. He was relieved when Jerry refused. He began to gush.

'Dear colleague!' He indicated a chair.

Jerry walked towards the bookshelves.

Beesley had been glad to get this job after that awful Russian affair. He turned to his hi-fi shelf. He took up the arm of his record player and lowered it onto the record. 'Jazz, okay? Italian-American? I'm secretly a bit of a rebel, as you've no doubt guessed. You've probably never seen my soft-shoe shuffle. This is *Abyssinian Stomp*. Do you know it?'

'I heard it in Rome once.' Jerry sighed as the cleric began his awkward jive. 'It never did much over here.'

The light through the stained-glass windows gave the Gothic room the detailed richness of an early Pre-Raphaelite. The light reflecting from copper, brass, silver and gold. The old books, the iconography, the boxes with the logos of Mars and Smucker's blended well with other muted colours. The rest of the shelves were stacked with Utilitarian pamphlets. In some surprise, Jerry fished out an early copy of *The Newgate Calendar*. 'Did you read this?'

'My illiterate daughter / thought / it had something / to do with / nougat.' The bishop was still shaking his stuff. A dance to set the earth vibrating on her axis; but for the moment the aftershocks were confined to the untrustworthy towers of Oxford. Jerry turned to the window. Outside, a steeple gasped and fell languidly to the rubble. Beesley was celebrating his return to the Anglican church. He called it a reconciliation and received what was left of the parish in return. All his entrepreneurial attempts to found a new proselytising sect had come to nothing with the legalisation of Class A drugs.

Still, there wasn't much more mileage in the Oxford Movement. To Bishop Beesley, Muscular Christianity seemed something of a contradiction in terms. His maiden sermon had been called 'Keep It Sweet' and had gone down a treat in the ruins of Christ Church. You wouldn't get too many customers, these days, with a pile of gloom.

The spring of the gramophone had begun to run down. Beesley boogied faster and faster, as if to compensate for the record's melodic groan.

'You're not worried about a heart attack?' Jerry picked up the arm and replaced it on the rest.

'Oh, we're not likely to have another for a while. I think they've made enough of an example of Oxford, don't you?' The bishop subsided, reaching for a Snickers.

'You can still get batteries, you know.' Jerry turned the handle of the instrument. 'You don't have to use springs and clockwork. You'll rediscover steam next. This is real life, not some kind of exotic urban fantasy.'

The bishop sat down suddenly, panting and crimson. 'Are you trying to wind me up? I've been ordered to do this by the quack. He suggested Soul, but Dixieland's the furthest I'll go. Weren't you here on business?'

'I'm back with the Jesuits,' said Jerry. 'I was sent to suggest an alliance.'

Bishop Beesley calmed his jowls with a grubby pink hand. Suddenly his ambition had returned. He was only one conversion away from being the next Pope.

'This is from where?' He straightened his mitre and picked up his crook. 'Vatican?'

'Via Westminster.'

'Westminster? I thought the survivors were snorting the dust! Blowing in the wind, monsignor.' He uttered a small, reflective fart. He was determined not to seem a walkover. 'Who are you really with?'

Jerry showed his fake badge. Bishop Beesley admired it. 'So who are you really with, then?'

'The Society.' Jerry laughed. 'The old Co-op.'

Beesley was clearly convinced, but he had to be absolutely sure. He reached for an instrument.

'What's your number?'

'Four nine four oh six.' Jerry displayed the brass tag on his watch-chain. It was well-used. Bent and battered. It looked like a Roman coin.

The atmosphere became suddenly cheerful.

Beesley thoughtfully peeled a Yorkie. 'So how's old Poppa?'

6

What's Your Movie?

Skinner's Horse, 1st Duke of York's Own Cavalry (India)
This fine cavalry regiment dates its history back to 1803-14; it is an amalgamation of Skinner's Horse and 3rd Skinner's Horse. The present designation was given in 1927. 'Captain Skinner's Corps of Irregular Horse' was raised from a body of horse who came over to the British after the battle of Delhi; at one time they were called '1st Bengal Irregular Cavalry'. The 3rds were originally styled 'Second Corps of Lt.-Colonel Skinner's Irregular Horse'. Composition is Hindustani Musalmans

and Musalman Rajputs (Ranghars), Rajputs (U.P. and Eastern Punjab) and Jats.

Soldiers of the King, No. 25,
issued by Godfrey Phillips Ltd, *c.* 1939

When I get into a lift full of businessmen when I'm wearing full make-up, you can tell by the way they behave whether much has changed or not.

– Boy George,
BBC Radio 4, 16 January, 2002

Maximus Minor

As America's victory in Afghanistan unfolds, what keeps coming up for me are the opening scenes of the movie 'Gladiator'. The barbarians, dressed in skins, have thrown the decapitated head of the Roman peace negotiator at the Romans' feet, and are jumping up and down in maniacal, murderous frenzy. The Roman General, Maximus, calmly reaffirms with his commanders their most cherished values – 'strength and honor' – and then quietly orders: 'At my signal, unleash hell.' In the war on Moslem terrorism being waged today, George W. Bush has become America's Maximus.

– Jack Wheeler,
Soldier of Fortune, March 2002

'The clowns have taken over the circus.' Major Nye was driving Una Persson down to the coast where she had six weeks in *Oh, What a Lovely War!* live on Brighton pier where it had all originally happened.

'Have you heard the news today? I suppose it was inevitable. I wasn't so worried when they were simply running politics. But the circus! I used to love the circus. We had a big one come through every year when I was a lad.'

The old administrator was showing his age. His pale blue eyes were bright in his weather-faded face. His handsome skull was almost fleshless. His thin grey hair was smartly combed but his moustache lacked its old bristle. In a dark suit a couple of sizes too large for him, he looked as he had when a young man, coming back from the Burma Road and being handed his civvies.

On the black wheel, his pale, lightly veined hands stuck out of his gloves like picked bones. 'Billy Smart, I think. Or Lord George Sanger was it? They were great rivals at one time. Then there started to be these visiting acts from Russia and France and so on. Very chic, I suppose. Not my taste. Elephants and clowns is what I call a circus. Lion tamers. Equestriennes. White ponies. Sharpshooters. My uncle met Buffalo Bill, you know, at Earls Court. I would love to have seen Buffalo Bill. And what about Annie Oakley! Was she Jewish, do you think?'

Gearing expertly, he swerved to avoid the potholes created by a cluster bomb blast across the M25. 'Bloody American gunnery. Makes you wonder about the actual prowess of the outlaws and the riflemen and all that. I suppose that was true once, but you know how dangerous it is to rest on your own military or political laurels. I think they got used to easy shots. Instead of putting men in the field, they spent their money on gadgets. They all learn in arcades, you know. Virtual experience. Virtual authority. You can't blame them for wanting to simplify everything.'

'It's grids,' said Una. 'They can't get enough of them. Once they've got it in a grid and named it, they think it's theirs.'

'They were already very insecure before this started. Their lack of education was beginning to dawn on them.' A straight stretch coming up, he sought his smokes in the top pocket of his boiler suit, flipped the top open with his thumb and fished a thin roll-up into his lips. 'Forty years ago, when I was first dealing with the CIA it was full of smart, humorous young men who knew a thing or two. They had decent degrees. A few languages. Good manners. Sporting attitude. They were like Foreign Office johnnies.

The best of them tended to go native, of course, but always remembered their duty in the end. Like Lawrence and Samson. Nowadays, it's a bunch of smart-alec apparatchiks installed by the Busch gestapo.

'Business isn't much good at running business, let alone nations. Soldiers are no good at politics. It's business, not politics, builds empires. They can't help themselves. What was it Marx said about stupidity?'

Una was growing a little irritated with this litany. 'We're all USUKs now, Major Nye.'

The old soldier was unrelenting. 'Look what happened when we let them get in on the last German war. First they backed Hitler and Mussolini with great enthusiasm and cash. Then it soon became obvious their bets were barking barmy and losing seriously. So they sent us all those poor, badly trained boys for cannon fodder, and used Wall Street money to install their own awful glory-seeking generals who, as now, threw away lives faster than Kitchener and made enough blunders to extend the fighting in Europe by a year.'

Major Nye cleared his throat.

Una tried to arouse herself long enough to interrupt him. Too late.

'They then make films claiming our victories. Thieves as well as incompetents. But I suppose that's what happens when you draw your labour force from Middle European peasants. You get the crusades all over again. Thank God for Oppenheimer, various Hungarians and the A-bomb or we'd still be fighting the Japs.'

This woke her enough to stir and speak.

'What's up with you, major?' She pushed her dark hair back from her eyes. She needed a hairdresser. She was amused. 'I thought you admired Woodrow Wilson. You always rather liked the Yanks.'

'I still do. I just don't think they're any good at wars or politics. They have no proper experience. They didn't have to work for a Magna Carta or a Bill of Rights, you see. They got them imposed by Jefferson and Co. Entirely different approach. Easy victories.

Most of them just started out wanting a reasonable tax break, a bit of respect. Badly handled. Easy victories usually mean a long war. Johnny Turk discovered that after he took Constantinople.'

He braked a bit sharply to avoid a crater.

'Do what?' Una was paying attention to the road.

'It's their Achilles' heel, really. Easy victories over under-equipped enemies made us complacent, too.'

He did his best to see the truth. Too many of his beliefs had been successfully challenged and he was a conscientious bureaucrat at home and abroad.

'They always get back at you somehow and you always get stretched too thin. We did the same. The problem is they have never known true shame.'

'Shame,' said Una. 'Shame.'

She began to brighten.

'Ah, look – the road's still there. We should be in Hove by lunchtime.'

Privately she thought the Americans had saved her life. Without the GI audiences tonight she'd have been playing to one old lady and a deaf dog.

7

Shorty Says

RAF's Missiles on Alert in Far East

Britain's Bloodhound missiles in Singapore are ready to fire in defence of the city, now threatened by Indonesia's trouble-mongering President Sukarno.

An RAF announcement in Singapore said yesterday: 'The missile systems have been activated and are fully operational.'

The 25-foot long Bloodhounds are 'purely defensive anti-aircraft weapons' said an RAF spokesman.

They home on to their targets by radar.

Activating involves tests of the guidance and firing systems to ensure that the rockets are ready for launching.

Rocket firing Hunters yesterday attacked jungle hideouts in South-Central Malaya, flushing out five more of the Indonesian paratroops dropped there eleven days ago.

Sunday Mirror, 13 September, 1964

I made peace with all the people in the world, resolving never to wage war on anyone, and I waged war against my self and have never since made peace with it.

– Kharqani in 'Attar,
Tadhkirat

Jerry met Mo coming out of the rather flashy and over-cleaned Arndale *Kebabarama*. It was doing well since the trams had stopped coming into central Manchester. Mo widened his mouth and took a large bite of his lamb-burger. The rich curry sauce ran down through his stubble like a flood in the desert. 'Wotcher, Mr C. If you want another of these, don't bother. They just ran out of meat.'

Jerry looked up and down the street outside the deserted complex. It was a big brutalist anachronism. These days, people were building down, rather than up. All the show was on the inside. 'You were supposed to be looking after Taffy.'

'Bugger!' With unconscious ease, Mo transferred his guilt into a belligerent glare. 'He said he wanted fish and chips. There's supposed to be a chippy in Deansgate. What a bastard that geezer is. Going on about jam tarts.' He peered nostalgically about him, at the huge tower block, the spanking clean shops. In his memory he drew in the dust of his ancestry. 'It was all ruins round here once.'

An eastern breeze carried the faint chords of George Harrison's ukelele as he did his famous Formby imitations. *Tee hee missus...*

'Oh, come on.' Jerry's instincts were buzzing. He holstered his heat and ran with long, economical strides towards Deansgate. 'The old Savoy farts. He'll be sniffing out the ghosts of departed jailbirds. He's only interested in something once it's compost for his own necromantic art. I know exactly where to start.' This was too boring to be a trap.

Mo opened up a manhole cover. He couldn't help himself. He shouldered his clumsy MK907-243 and began to descend. 'I'll meet you in the basement.'

His caution served him well.

Taking the corner by the looted car showroom, Jerry ran headlong into a squadron of 'Cossacks'. These mounted Bengalis sported long lances from which fluttered the various pennants of their clans. They had found an old Jew in the street. As the Jew ran towards him, clutching at a straw, Jerry hesitated.

The heavily bearded and turbaned lancers reined in their miscellaneous mounts, waiting to see what Jerry would do.

He turned to the terrified septuagenarian. 'I suppose it's too late to talk?'

From up the street he heard a burst of celebratory gunfire. The Bengalis turned their horses and galloped towards the source. It was their instinct. If there was a gun, they would charge it.

Jerry relaxed. Mo would deal with them.

He peered into the twitching face of the man they had been going to murder. 'Didn't you used to be a bloke called Auchinek.'

Auchinek was grateful for any recognition. 'I was a promoter,' he said. 'One of the best. I had no enemies. At least to speak of. Then all this had to happen. Is there still time to get to Jerusalem?'

'Not now,' said Jerry.

'What about London? The West End?'

Jerry didn't know what to tell him.

They strolled slowly after the disappearing Bengalis. 'It's a musical,' said Auchinek. He was cheering up in his own hangdog way. 'It will run for ever, believe me. I was hoping to get the backing in Israel. Do you have any idea of the current political climate? I've been in a cellar for a week.'

'Well,' said Jerry, 'someone's got to tell you, so I'm going to. There's been a reality shift. The world turned upside down. Things are still settling at the moment.'

'A perfect time for a new musical.' Auchinek beamed. He was pleased with himself. There had been a period when he had only been able to do this on prozac. 'Remind me to buy you a drink. This will be a natural for Broadway.'

'That's what I'm trying to say,' said Jerry.

8

Black, Brown and White

> If I'd arrived in Esfahan first, I kept thinking, instead of Tehran, I would have had a whole different first impression of the Islamic Republic. Iran, as personified by its *chador*-cloaked women, would have seemed much more impenetrable to me ... The chador the Esfahani women taught me, was not just a swathe of black fabric but rather a formidable garment to be reckoned with.
>
> – Christiane Bird,
> *Neither East Nor West*, 2001

> It's not surprising that a Republican governor should take a dim view of children's health insurance. It was Perry's predecessor, George W. Bush, who unsuccessfully fought expansion of the CHIP program in the 1999 Legislature, even as he was campaigning for president with a promise to 'leave no child behind'.
>
> – Michael King,
> *Austin Chronicle*, 15 February, 2002

EVERY WEDNESDAY! **ASIAN NIGHT!**
TOPLESS FEMALE SUMO WRESTLING! ASIAN
BEER, SUSHI AND SAKE SPECIALS!

Ad, Penthouse Austin,
Austin Chronicle, 15 February, 2002

TOTALLY EXPOSED. **OIL WRESTLING.**
WEDNESDAY FEBRUARY 20TH

Ad, The Show Palace,
Austin Chronicle, 15 February, 2002

'What sort of time do you call this, then?' Taffy was distant with irritability. In his loose, green suit he issued from the shadows of the Princelet Street synagogue and closed the doors behind him, a lofty Norman abbot.

'Bloody hell,' said Jerry. 'Do you know how many Ainsworth diversions it took to get from Manchester –'

The Home Office pathologist hated tech talk. He brushed past his visitor and, lighting the way with an early bicycle lamp, climbed the wormy stairs to the weaving loft. Below, the creaks and groans of the wood echoed the cries of long-dead patients, of dismantled looms. The shrieks and wails of sawn bones.

'Lord, the pain.' Taffy had recovered himself. With an habitual air of resolution, he opened his bag, took out his gloves and slipped them on. 'Once a pathologist…'

He was all that was left of the Home Office. He would be retiring soon, to St Leonards-on-Sea where he had a lease on a small sweet and tobacconist's. His wife didn't like his idea of having a second-hand book section, or even some sort of lending library, where the videos would normally go. She had scotched his grave, sub-Morrisian scheme to re-install newspaper deliveries and possibly a milk round. 'Sometimes,' he had told Jerry, 'she loathes my nostalgia and I must admit it's not the nicest side of my nature.'

He scratched suddenly at his cheek. He was ferociously clean-shaven. A Roman patrician, an Iroquois sachem. A Benedictine reformer. A puritan, like Milton, with a devilish soul, an unprincipled curiosity. His stern spectacles glared in the dawn light, biting through the dust of the transom. 'This is where they operated,' he said. 'No anaesthetic of course. Just speed and a spot of luck.' He cocked his ear to the light. 'Was that a voice?'

'Gus Elen,' said Jerry, 'or probably George Formby.' His tears fell like rain.

A clear, sweet soprano, too Gertie Lawrence for the real music hall, began to sing with brisk self-mockery:

I finks a cove sh'd fink afore 'e talks abaht th' woar,
There's blokes wot talks as dunno wot they mean,
But yer tumble as yer 'umble knows a bit abaht th' Boar –
W'en they calls me nibs 'The Bore of Bef'nal Green'

It was Una, of course, waiting for them in the eaves, dressed as a West End masher, a collapsing topper under her elegant arm, hand in pocket, the other hand sporting a cigarette holder, a smouldering Gitane. 'Nobody remembers the good old days.' She winked. 'There's more money in murders and villains. *Sweeney Todd* always did better than *Nell of Old Drury*. In the provinces at least. When I refer to good old Jack, I'm talking Buchanan.'

A little below Jerry's height, she slipped elegantly towards him, embracing him. 'Oh, I just don't know what it is about you. You lovely little wanker.' She remembered her manners, stepping back. 'Sorry, Colonel Sinclair.' She went to pick up her swordstick. She left Jerry still trying to work out what this had to do with *Greenmantle*. 'Business as usual, I'm afraid.'

Sinclair despised that kind of formality. He judged people by it. 'No need,' he said. 'Honestly.' He was firm. A strong-minded bishop, driven by the truth.

'Shalom,' said Jerry. 'Shalom. Shalom.'

Una smiled. 'What I tell you three times will be true.' She popped her hat open, to disguise her despair.

'Pain.' Sinclair sucked at his suicide tooth and then remembered his manners. 'Pain will do it.'

Through the house's groaning frame, her uneasy boards, came a sudden prayer, a distant chorus. 'Haunted,' said Una. 'Haunted as hell.'

'Pain.' Sinclair was firm.

Hastily Jerry sought his reflection in the dusty windows and was relieved when he found it. 'It's amazing none of them are broken,' he said. 'What would they have had originally, do you think?'

Sinclair looked at his watch. 'I think I've done pretty much all I can do here. I'd better be off.'

'Taxi?' Una produced her mobile phone.

Sinclair shook his head. 'I drove myself in.'

Jerry was growing uneasy. 'I think we should all probably get out of here. Don't you?'

In some disgust, he looked down at his hands and feet and recoiled from the blood. 'Oh, shit. Here of all places.'

Una sighed. 'I suppose we can't ask you for a lift in this state?'

The pathologist shrugged. 'Don't worry, I have some old polythene in the boot.'

9

When Will I Get to Be Called a Man?

> *BEGINS TO-DAY. No. 1 of a great bunch of stories about the No. 1 man of the North-West Frontier of India* – *THE WOLF OF KABUL*
>
> The Afghans, the Pathans, the Kurds, the Afridis, and all the bandits from Baluchistan, on the coast of the Arabian Sea, to far Kashmir and the borders of forbidden Tibet, live in dread of The Wolf of Kabul, the man who can make them or break them.
>
> *The Wizard*, September 1930

A society which punishes those who do not agree that it is perfect, can never, of course, progress. It will, however, grow increasingly aggressive even as it inevitably corrodes from within.

– Lobkowitz,
Time and Meaning, 1938

Keep from me God, all forms of certainty.

Moslem prayer

Prinz Lobkowitz was doing his best to pull his weight. But his palsy was growing worse. He held his arms to his sides, trying to stop the shaking. There was something wrong with this brain, he insisted. He was subtly out of sync. He had no previous experience of the condition.

'If time is a field, Monsignor Cornelius, and space but a dimension of time, the few dimensions we are able to conceptualise are surely a comment upon our paucity of invention, rather than our boasted Prometheanism?'

Jerry Cornelius was beginning to regret falling back on religion. He'd always known there was a flaw in this escape plan. But Prinz Lobkowitz was his only wholly trustworthy ally. Mrs Persson was probably on the square, but you could never be sure of her overall game plan. Lady Luck was sometimes his only hope. The cards built houses wherever they fell.

His long-term memory was improving. He remembered the Medrasim in Cairo and Marrakech, the years of meditation in the retreats of Oom and Cádiz. All in order to take a few extra steps in the never-ending Dance of Time. It was so easy for Mrs Persson. He didn't have the mental discipline. He had paid a high price, not being able to follow her when her skills had surpassed his own. He was still paying it. *'I sometimes feel I lived my life like a candle up your qui –'*

'Ladies present,' warned Lobkowitz, who hated vulgarity.

Jerry paused to lock the door of the church. Prinz Lobkowitz had come to take him down to the village, where there was still a reasonably good tea shop which could tell the difference between a teacake and a muffin. 'Ladies?'

Too late, he sniffed the air.

'Oh, thank God, monsignor, there you are!' The self-pitying shriek of her threatened species.

It was Trixie Brunner from the manor. She was distraught. 'I, as you know, have not one racist bone in my whole body. Yet why I have to pay taxes at eight billion pounds in the pound just to keep a bunch of greasy little oiks from God knows where when my whole family has lived and farmed and had businesses in these parts for years. Well, where *are* they from, monsignor? And don't tell me all my chickens committed suicide.'

Jerry was recalling his schooldays. 'I'm so sorry, Miss Brunner? Was it the Jews?'

'Oh, no.' She was genuinely disgusted. 'These aren't intellectuals at all. I'm talking about asylum seekers.' She frowned. Something had just occurred to her. 'Who on earth would wish to live in an asylum?'

Steadying his shakes, Lobkowitz stood to attention and when he was introduced he clicked his heels and kissed her trembling hand. She was immediately reassured.

The old diplomat had lost none of his graceful trickery. 'We in Europe long for your English freedoms,' he said. 'That is why it is so important for you to join us in this alliance of nations. You have so much to teach us.'

'Well the first thing I'd do is abolish Brussels. Not exactly the farmer's friend, are they.' She had found the remains of a constituency in the Country Sidereal Alliance. She was doing what she could to fit in. Her awkwardly slung buttocks proclaimed her a horsewoman, but all her life she'd had an aversion to getting close to any living thing even a few inches larger than herself. The faux denier swung like panniers on a camel, reminding Jerry that when he had last seen her she had been reluctantly returning from a trans-Saharan expedition, commanded in the name of her mother, attempting to discover a Middle Eastern route to the past. She had not wanted to tell him what she had found. When she eventually let her mother know, it had nearly knocked her off her throne.

'We have our own pipeline now, you know.' She spoke brightly, attempting to impress Prinz Lobkowitz. 'You can adopt a length. But we're funding a whole line through Afghanistan. It's the patriotic thing to do.' She tugged off her headscarf.

Jerry stopped by the Prinz's new Lexus pickup. It was the only working vehicle in the car park.

Lobkowitz drew on his driving coat. 'Can we drop you anywhere?'

10

Joe Turner Blues

> As part of Operation Plumbbob tests conducted in 1957, the Atomic Energy Commission hung nuclear weapons as large as 74 kilotons beneath blimps. The nuclear balloon era came to a close in 1963 after a pair of freak accidents destroyed the AEC's two airships on two consecutive days.
>
> *Popular Mechanics*, March 2002

> There is a remote human reflex known, to those who witness it most often, as the 'flashpoint'. This is when a calm person moves suddenly into hysteria. A 999 operator learns that it can be triggered by as little as the words, 'Hello, ambulance service.' Even the coolest emergency caller has trouble coping with the question 'Are they still breathing?'
>
> – Emma Brockes,
> *Guardian*, 6 February, 2002

George Bush's budget is not for the faint-hearted. His $2.13 trillion spending plans for 2003 include a 14% increase in the defence budget, the biggest rise since Ronald Reagan, as well as doubling of spending on homeland security. It is bold. By keeping overall government spending outside defence and homeland security to a 2% rise next year (compared with a recent annual average of more than 7%) Mr Bush is proposing a dramatic shift in America's spending priorities.

And it is brazen. Far from trimming his tax cuts to help pay for more guns, Mr Bush reinforces, nay increases, his proposed tax cuts by almost $600 billion over the next decade…

The result is a dramatic turnaround in America's fiscal outlook. Far from using the Social Security surplus to pay down debt or restructure America's pension system – a goal both parties claimed to be overriding only nine months ago – Mr Bush's budget uses the surplus to pay for defence spending and, particularly, tax cuts.

Economist, 9 February, 2002

Wrong-Way Lindbergh turned his mild, expectant blue eyes drunkenly on Jerry. He patted vaguely at his own bottom, looking for a back pocket, a pint. 'I was expecting Captain Ewell. He was bringing me something.'

'Fancy a drink, general?' Jerry slipped a slender flask from inside his black car coat. 'I hope you don't mind. It's Armagnac and it might be on the turn. It's Napoleon.' He wore his long hair Jacobin style and, with his full lapels, had the look of a romantic Deputy in the days before the Terror.

Mrs Persson reflected that it was good to see him in youthful good spirits again. He had been taking his work too seriously.

'So old "Four Eyes" Ewell isn't here yet?' The general stroked his almost hairless head.

'Well, it's my fault, I think. I'm pretty bad at the rituals.'

Continuing to pedal his exercise bike, General Lindbergh

studied the full-length mirror. He was still not satisfied with the rake of his cap which had originally been worn by Sterling Hayden in *Doctor Strangelove*. Lindbergh had always coveted it. The guys at the last base he commanded had, at his suggestion, clubbed together to buy it for him. There wasn't much he could have said to them without choking, so he had saluted them instead. They had returned his salute with their own.

'Any kind of politics.' He concentrated on the mirror. 'I'm no friend of politics. We could have finished this job in ten seconds. But all we got was interference. We could have taken out the whole lot of them.'

'On one card, I bet.' Trixie Brunner gushed. 'I love Americans. I love your generosity. Why can't we all be Americans? I'm so jealous of your wonderful optimism.'

He nodded agreeably, his eyes still on the mirror. He tipped the cap a little further to the right. 'Guess who?'

The door behind them opened revealing a tall black man in a fatigue jacket from which the insignia had been ripped. He was clearly in poor spirits. 'Sir?'

'How's the war going, captain?'

'Sir, until we realise we are over-confident, under-informed and over there, we are not going to move forward. Sooner or later we must conclude the obvious. We sound good but we are crap at real life. Every boast we have made, we have been unable to deliver on. I suggest we waste no further time. I further suggest we do not compound our mistakes. We have been living a fantasy. Sir.'

'Well-spoken, Corporal Ewell. You can tell them I'll be down for my photo opportunity in a couple, okay?'

'Sir.' The black man closed the door slowly.

Wrong-Way shared a confidence with Trixie. 'He lost it. He's a screamer. You know what I mean, don't you, sweetheart? Poor bastard. He was doing so well until he started wetting his panties. A tribute to his race. But that's war for you.' He paused in his pumping and looked around for his cigar.

Jerry felt the phone vibrating in his back pocket. He fished it out while Mrs Persson got Wrong-Way by the goolies and hauled him off the bike. 'Pentagon Emergency Room,' he said.

'Where is this?' he asked the grimacing general. 'Approximately?'

'You're asking me?' Wrong-Way was beginning to relax into familiar discomforts as Mrs Persson gave him another squeeze. He winked at her. 'I've always been attractive to strong women. It's the uniform, isn't it? What do you think of the cap?'

Jerry went to find a window.

He met Trixie sorting through the ruined office. 'What a mess. You'd think someone had let off a bomb in here.' She was depressed. 'I'd expected something a little more, well, expensive.'

'This is the twelfth Penta-cabin they've built. They were supposed to fool the enemy, but they made them too big. It was a matter of prestige, apparently. You can't really have a *tiny* Pentagon. It would send out the wrong signals.'

Wrong-Way was sweating and giggling. 'Is this a bust?'

'Or is it a bust,' Trixie agreed. She had found a player and was hooking it up to the computer. 'Here we go-go.' The Pet Shop Boys were soon strutting their stuff over the microwaves.

She was living out the life her mother had missed.

'I say, Jerry.' She began to bop. 'Did you ever see Freddie Mercury at the Flamingo?'

'Only as I was leaving.' Jerry closed his eyes and took a grip. It was time to order a pizza. He reached for his phone again.

It was missing.

Trixie waved it as she left, anxious to catch up with Corporal Ewell, who was walking slowly, with shoulders slumped, down the porta-passage. 'Sorry. Force of habit.' With an apologetic shrug, she popped it in her purse.

Jerry went to see if there was still a fridge. The way things were going, he'd be perfectly happy with a Coke and a pretzel.

11

Digging My Potatoes

> Over 23,000 American steel workers have lost their jobs because of unfair foreign trade practices.
>
> The US Department of Commerce calls it 'the thirty-year history of repeated unfair trade actions' … Foreign countries dump their subsidised steel in US markets. It destroys American jobs and devastates communities. Since 1998 alone, 29 steel companies have gone bankrupt and over 23,000 workers have lost their jobs. The International Trade Commission ruled that surging imports have seriously injured the US steel industry.
>
> It's time to level the playing field for American steel workers. Under Section 201 of the Trade Act of 1974, the President can institute a strong remedy that gives workers in America's steel companies a fair chance to compete. Urge the President to implement strong 201 trade relief.
>
> Ad, Minimill 201 Coalition,
> *Representing America's 21st Century Steel Companies*

> The effects are also touching Wall Street. In the past few weeks, investors have shifted their attention to other companies, making a frenzied search for any dodgy accounting that might reveal the next Enron … This week shares in Elan, an Irish-based drug maker, were pummelled by worries over its accounting policies … All this might create the impression that corporate financial reports, the quality of company profits and the standard of auditing in America have suddenly and simultaneously deteriorated. Yet that would be wide of the mark: the deterioration has actually been apparent for many years.
>
> *Economist*, 9 February, 2002

'It was probably a bit short-sighted making the States autonomous, although that was the thinking of the day.' Professor Hira embraced his favourite occidental. 'You have to admit the idea has merits. But as the states divided, the corporations united. Oh, Jerry, you are looking so fit and chipper. You were so beautiful when you were young.' It was very warm. There was a smell of new-mown grass. Somewhere, over on the other side of the cholera ditch, a game was still going on.

Jerry leaned his bat against a yim-yum tree and stooped to remove his pads. He knew that his whites were tightening over his bottom, distracting the physicist. He also knew how good his thighs and buttocks looked again. He wanted something out of Hira and he knew he had to use every possible device.

Hira was blooming, too. The little Brahmin radiated good health. 'Weren't we right to start with, all those years ago? But can this be the beginning of the end? So soon? Something will follow us, surely?'

'Well, it's Hobbes eat Hobbes round here at the moment,' said Jerry. 'Worse than usual. The problem with the imperial leviathan, as you know, is feeding him. If we are going to make anything to last, we'd better get busy.'

'I have always had control of the juggernaut. I needed your engine.' Professor Hira beamed. He passed a plump, delicate hand over Jerry's left cheek, arm and hip. 'Your energy is high. I hope you are wiser than the first time we met.'

Jerry grinned.

The Hindu was surprised. 'Have you been filing your teeth? Have you had trouble with your meat?'

'No,' said Jerry. 'I've been living in France.'

Professor Hira followed Jerry gingerly into the big double hammock. It took him a moment to stop swinging. 'I always said that's where you'd end up.'

'We resist the inner voice,' said Jerry. 'It is our destiny.'

'*Nous verrons…*'

Professor Hira took some long, deep breaths. He sat up carefully, removed his crumpled linen jacket and threw it towards the table where they had taken their drinks. 'Isn't it astonishing how possession of the atomic bomb immediately robs one of moral authority?'

For a time there was silence. In the distance there still could be heard the clip of leather on willow, the cheering, the clapping. After some years, Kashmir was once again playing Bengal. It had taken a while to build back the teams. But there was unlikely to be much violence, now. Sometimes people took a game altogether too seriously.

Jerry swung out of the hammock and went to find his cigarettes. The dirty glasses had been removed. The collapsible card table was new. A fresh bottle was in the ice-bucket. Two glasses on a side table.

Hira approached on weakened legs, tucking in his shirt. He squinted against the sun. Jerry offered him a Sullivan's.

'Do you need moral authority, once you have the bomb?' Jerry sat down opposite him at the dark green baize. He took a fresh pack of cards from the side box, broke the seals and spread the deck before him, shuffled, spread, shuffled again. He put the deck in the middle of the baize. Hira picked it back up and began to shuffle left to right.

He admitted to feeling a little uneasy if his various gods were not treated with proper respect. Even though he was a rational man. 'There is a certain authority demanded by even the smallest household god,' he said. 'I'm not sure that's our best model. But pantheism must always be preferable, surely, to monotheism? You lived in a world which promised choice but denied it at the most fundamental levels! A complete perversion of the ideals, the enthusiasm which it harnessed. Thank the great Lord Ganesh that it's over. Look at the awful trouble you get into by cutting your road straight, no matter what the nature of the landscape. It's a mind-set which, to say the least, leads swiftly to a cul-de-sac.'

'Oh, it's just communications and demographics.' Jerry was determined not to get into anything too heavy. 'News travels faster, ages come and go faster, one generation swiftly succeeds another. *Ovem lupo committere.*' It was odd how his Latin was coming back.

He fingered the elegant cut of his vestments. He was getting used to this reversal in his fortunes. He had been the underdog for too long.

Jerry was to be the first Catholic governor of Kashmir. He looked across the lawn at his wonderful palace, white filigree like carved ivory in the evening sunlight. The Society had been persuaded to pay for the building. Locals were only impressed by lavish lifestyles. They respected you for it. Most of all, as he had explained to the Pope, they admired a religion which could afford such extensive building work. India had been fine under the nabobs. It was the bureaucrats who spoiled everything.

This job was really a sort of retirement. He had been removed from the active list. The locals looked after the paperwork and saw any would-be converts. There were fewer and fewer these days, as the Moslem population dwindled. There had been only two conversions to Hinduism. It would have been graceless to point this out to Hira. Christianity had a way of turning its aggressions into effective instruments. It must have something. He had never been able to stand outside his culture as much as he would have liked.

Without speaking, they sat staring at their hands. Temporarily, they appeared to have forgotten the game they were playing. 'What a shame our religions have so little in common.' Professor Hira frowned. 'Was it always so?'

'You once argued that physics and Hinduism moved in the same direction to the same end.'

'Oh, that was a very long time ago. I was so optimistic about everything. A very twisted tiny twig on the great multiversal tree. We have come a long way, Monsignor Cornelius. We have learned something fundamental about the nature of Time. Such a very, very long way. Now we are closer to discovering what Time actually is, we are almost free of the concrete. Don't you feel your load lightening, your feet walking on air?'

Jerry wasn't sure.

Reaching across the table, Professor Hira smoothed Jerry's hair. 'It is a terrific responsibility, old boy. Am I supposed to represent courage, temperance, justice and practical wisdom? And, if so, how? It's a bit of a stumbler, that one.'

Greeks, now, was it? Jerry was beginning to wonder what he had ever seen in his little buddy.

12

Lively Up Yourself

> Perhaps the most common observation at the annual meeting last week in New York of the World Economic Forum, that feast of self-congratulation by the business and political elite, was that most businessmen are gloomier about America's economic prospects than most economists are ... corporate America fears a rather weak recovery.
>
> *Economist*, 9 February, 2001

> **Sudan Defence Forces**
> The Sudan Defence Forces consist of a Cavalry Corps, Camel Corps, Eastern Arab Corps, Sudanese Machine Gun battery, Western Corps, as well as engineer troops and various departmental corps; a typical member of the Camel Corps is shown. With the exception of one regular battalion the units are made up of irregulars who enlist for three years. The force is jointly officered by British and native officers, and consists of approximately half Arabs and half Sudanese and Equatorial Africans; the language used is Arabic. A private is known as a 'Nafar', a lieutenant 'Mulazim Awal' and the commandant of the force 'Kaid El 'Amm.'
>
> *Soldiers of the King*, No. 36,
> issued by Godfrey Phillips Ltd, *c.* 1939

FREEDOM IS BEING THERE

> The freedom to go where you want to go, when you want to go, is a precious liberty. And with government and industry taking important steps to ensure your comfort and safety, the nation's skyways are once again ready to help you make the most of that freedom.
>
> Ad, Boeing,
> *Forever New Frontiers*

The Scottish Special Forces were pulling out of Nova New Washington when Jerry and Taffy turned up. It had been a dodgy journey from Hollywood. Their ancient Westland Whirlwind had barely made the journey. It needed oil. It had been under wraps in the Long Beach Spruce Goose Aviation Museum until they found it.

Captain Hamish 'Flash' Gordon came up over the rubble on sturdy legs, his sporran swinging. He saluted Taffy Sinclair. He adjusted his cap on his orange hair. He was sternly freckled. 'Not much for you, sir. We've found most of the mines. Those bastards must have been digging for years. Guy bloody Fawkes, sir, if you don't mind. All over again. But it's not safe.'

'Oh, it's all right, captain.' Sinclair took off his leather gloves. Underneath he wore another pair, made from medical rubber. 'I just want a souvenir, really. Anybody hurt?'

'Not a scratch, sir. A bit of collateral damage, but I don't think we'll get many complaints.' Overhead a squadron of black F117s flew in irregular formation towards the north. 'That's our lads finishing off the job. Those Dutchies will find it was a mistake to take out Glasgow.'

Sinclair shrugged. 'Call them Dutchies if you like, captain, but they are Americans. Our allies. This is a bit of an embarrassment.'

'If they're not Dutchies, sir, why do they all have German names?'

'They're more comfortable with them. I think they sound more warlike. They've always admired the old Germans. It's the new ones they have trouble with.'

'Well, they'll settle down again as soon as we get a railway built.' Captain Gordon was an engineer by nature. 'There's nothing like a good bit of track and a couple of sturdy locomotives to pull a people together. Didn't these Dutchies invade Canada once, too?'

'They're not famous for learning anything.' Fastidiously Sinclair leaned down and picked up a small, bloody door handle. 'What's this off, do you think?'

The men had prisoners. Hooded and handcuffed, they were being bundled towards a helicopter. Jerry recognised the muffled voice of General Lindbergh. The tone of his threats was not confident. Wasn't Una supposed to be looking after him? He wondered if one of the others was Corporal Ewell. He would find out soon. He might never have been sure it was Wrong-Way but for the cap he clasped in his chained hands.

Easy come, easy go.

Jerry looked around for his sergeant. He was enjoying all this authority. He felt he'd earned it. The simple euphoria of optionless violence.

He kicked at some limbs sticking out of the concrete. 'I thought you said you'd cleared up.'

Taffy Sinclair was grateful. He kneeled on the broken slabs to get his samples. 'These will be invaluable to future generations.'

He was taking a keen interest in maggots. 'It's amazing how the blowfly finds corpses so quickly. Any decay, really.' He was having to pretend to collect DNA samples. Until the Scots established order, he had worked unofficially for the FBI. Of course, the world was running out of manpower. The new cadet corps might help. Meanwhile the local gasmen were striking, claiming that their civil rights were threatened by the Federal people having sexier uniforms. They also wanted their breathing equipment redesigned along more fashionable lines.

'Monsignor Cornelius. I'm told I have you to thank for my release.' General Ewell, his uniform brilliant with the symbols of his redemption and Trixie tripping happily in tow, clambered manfully over the ruins to shake Jerry's hands. 'You are a saint, sir.

Jerry nodded absently. He was, in fact, several saints. Meanwhile he had to get this awful smell of white smoke out of his nose.

'We're talking tidal waves here,' General Ewell was saying to Trixie. 'Massive waves which could hit the coast of Texas and sweep all the way inland to Dallas.'

'I know,' she said. 'I'm so pleased they gave you your uniform back, aren't you? Do they zip or button?'

Spontaneously this veteran of the psychic wars put his arm around her. 'Hold on there, young lady. I'm a married guy.' He laughed easily, full of the comfort of her flattery. 'At least I think I still am!' His eyes had the steady, unflinching gaze of a man who had been through hell, humiliation and high water and had come out the other side stronger, wiser and even more determined to fight the forces of evil. Trixie sighed with wonder at her good fortune.

13

No Love at All

WHERE 'GSVT' SPELLS 'GORILLA'

Rwanda is now a Guaranteed Secure Vacation Territory

Fly on Air France High Security Jet Liners to your glorious holiday amongst the gorillas of Rwanda's famous hill country. Visit this beautiful region's historic sights and shop in the newest mall concepts, including the Jungle River, Deep Congo and Heart of Darkness, all situated within convenient high security compounds.

Ad, *Port Sabatini Advertiser*, July 2002

OUR KINDA HISTORY – EGYPT AND THE HOLY LAND!

Open for Business.

Ibid.

DO THE DUNES
ARABIAN STYLE

Lands of Two Thousand and Two Delights
Do the Dunes Saudi Style
A big Saudi hug awaits you in Arabia's friendliest state.

Ibid.

Africa was developing nicely. Services, security and surveillance – the famous Triple 'S' option of the World Tourist Organisation – had never been higher. The smart money was in Nature Reserves, Safaris and Marine Expeditions. Burundi, the seventieth state to join the union, was flying the Stars and Stripes over the Federal Capital of Washingwood, a city of light, a city of ethereal towers and splendid armament, the centre of a glorious sisterhood of emergent nations and entertainment capital of the free world.

Jerry was glad to be back from Europe. He just couldn't take the cold, these days. Still, sooner or later he would have to go and get his sister out of her drawer. Their Ice Age had come so suddenly, it had caught them napping. It was more like a slow avalanche, taking roads, railways, tunnels and burying them under tons of rapidly hardening snow. Global warming was just the second law of thermodynamics doing exactly what he had hoped it would in his optimistic, entropic youth. Energy dissipating rapidly. Everything speeding up. Get the whole farce over with and enjoy it as much as possible. The universe moving faster and faster into the great sphincter, the black hole which might or might not be its own. Rapid heat: rapid cool. Even Rwanda was cooler than this, but they hadn't installed their AC yet.

'Lord, lord,' said President Ewell. He was putting on weight. His faux *gravitas* had given way to a film of vulgar self-confidence. 'This is just the right place to hang out and plan our strategy. It's perfect. Thank you, colonel.'

Colonel Frank Cornelius cracked an adoring smile which

worked in unison with his perfect salute, which seemed to click his heels together. Jerry was proud of his brother. He should have been dead. Nobody had ever made a comeback from so many different overdoses. Frank had been diligent. He had studied German clockwork toys for years. He had wanted only the source. The model. The inspiration.

'Now, Your Holiness, how about a run-down on these European girlies. They still getting a touch of the vapours?' President Ewell clenched his massive, well-kept teeth around a vast cigar. By his slightly surprised expression it appeared he had found, in his mind's eye at least, true love.

Jerry wondered how he had ever worried about his feminine side. He flicked at his boot with his dog-whip. He was here as Papa Beesley's personal bodyguard. These were to be very high-level talks. They had to be, of course, since so much of the rest of the world was uncertainly flooded. You could never tell where the next wave or downpour was coming from. That was what made life such a pleasure. You could run a book on whether it would be Iowa or Indonesia which would go under next. He couldn't help grinning, remembering those ludicrous conversations Mitzi and Trixie once had at every dinner party about how the sea levels wouldn't rise higher than Bognor or Atlantic City. But, as he'd tried to point out, the sun also rises.

He gave his leg a celebratory tap. Africa was climatically more stable and that meant a lot these days. Especially to the surviving Africans. Political stabilisation had taken a few months, but all that was behind them now. Africa, Trixie had announced to the fashionable world, was the new United States. It had all the old features and was scarcely developed. A brand ready for reinvestment. The continental US was too unstable, too old-fashioned, too saturated. In the end the Constitution and the Bill of Rights had become embarrassing. When the time came, the Land of Liberty could re-launch herself as the Fjord of a Thousand Islands. It wouldn't take long. Even now the water was hiding a lot of very unattractive ruins. They would improve when the barnacles and coral had begun their work. People's romantic imaginations would do the rest. But this still wasn't the right time to be buying fjords, not until they settled down a bit. Canada, as usual, had the moral high ground, as well as the high physical ground, and had missed much of the southern ice rush.

They crossed the helipad and entered the gorgeous security lobby of the G.W. Bush Memorial Pentagonican, the elevator bearing them rapidly down below ground level, to the deep, safe bunkers where calm-faced young creatures busied themselves with security assignments. Jerry rather liked it. He was reminded of the Vatican. He didn't mind one of the boys relieving him of his heat, but he insisted he keep his shades. While one young man kneeled to pat his leg, Jerry rather ostentatiously blessed him, then unzipped. 'Better check inside,' he said.

There was a strong smell of popcorn. General-President Ewell slipped his arm around the intoxicated Trixie. 'Ah. They have the Chief's favourite snack ready and waiting. Who loves popcorn?' His brown eyes brightened and focused on the door marked DEN. He strode forward.

Jerry felt a hand teasing his penis. He had forgotten to rezip. He smiled amiably and winked at Trixie. He didn't mind her coaxing up a little extra support. Mrs General Ewell had not taken quietly to the annulment of her marriage, the bastardisation of her children, and the loss of her Lexus Strongbow. There were some podunk little broadcasters who were giving her publicity in urban Rangoon, but that was about all it was worth. Nonetheless, Trixie had to do what a girl had to do and Monsignor Cornelius could only applaud her prudence. This did, unfortunately, bring him back to thoughts of his sister. She was still in her drawer in the cellars of the Convent of the Poor Clares, Ladbroke Grove, 1971. He couldn't find his notes about the exact dates. But it had been traumatic and he had to get back there somehow. He had a bunch of dogs to feed.

President Ewell snapped his fingers and at this signal a ring of hand-picked young marines surrounded him. He gave them all a manly punch, a manly hug. Some of them blushed to the roots of their crew-cuts. A hug from President Ewell meant more than meat and drink to these unflinching patriots. This was where the war against the Death Star Terrorists and all other rogue nations would begin and there was no doubt who would be attracting the tourists next season. For the DST, there would be no 'next season'.

His triumph, his luck in surviving, gave his hips the swing of a high-class pimp. 'I love it here,' he told Jerry. 'I love it. It's my roots, you know. It gets to my soul. You don't know what it did to me when that bastard took out Jerusalem. That's stupid. Get rid of the problem by getting rid of the disputed territory? It'll take years to reproduce. It was one of the most valuable heritage sites in the world.'

Trixie spoke significantly to Jerry, her eyes urgently enigmatic. 'Well, we all thought it looked okay in the rehearsals and nobody bothers to listen to those projections any more.'

'Run by a bunch of little novice nunnies, monsignor, if you'll forgive the reference.' President Ewell flung himself into his big easy chair and reached for his remote. 'But in those days we didn't know any better. New Jerusalem seemed just the idea to stop Britain bumping along the bottom. We owed that to our allies, at least, what was left of them. Oh, Jesus, was that a waste of time and money!' He laughed and lit his cigar. It was a massive blunt. The glorious smell of Pakistani Mountain began to ease through the corridors of power. Almost every passive smoker was pleased the president was home.

'Fucking bagpipe fuckers.' While his guests settled themselves about the room, the president snapped on his control. Road runners and cartoon mice raced back and forth in awesome clarity. 'My mother named me after the Lord of Loch Awe, you know. We had ties with the Scots. And that's what they did to us.' A tiny screen appeared in the main picture. Smoke and rubble, but there was no way of knowing exactly where.

'It confounded the futurologists, anyway,' said Trixie. 'Just shows you what their warnings were worth. Scottish independence all the way! I blame that awful Blurr.'

Scotland was the latest rogue state. Parachuting in and firing a few shots, the Black Watch had raised the cross of St Andrew over the Great Temple. Their Sikh and Pashtoon allies had secured the Great Mosque and they thought it politic to let the Covenanters bring the Church under Christian control.

Britain conquered, it was a Race to Nova Nova Washington, which the Scots, with their battle blimps, won easily, wiping out most of the opposition. The president had opened the prisons and armed the inmates in a desperate rearguard action, but the prisoners had fallen on one another, settling old scores, and again the Scots needed to do little but watch. Given enough time, Americans would always wipe one another out. The miserable climate cheered the Scots up. Flash Gordon was never more ebullient. He exposed a sturdy groin for the camera.

'But we're already working out how to get back what's left of our native real estate.' Trixie nodded confidently.

For some reason President Ewell remembered Jerry as an ally at one of the old pentagons when he was, as he had put it himself, going through his baptism of shit which had turned him into the man of steel they saw before them. He liked to keep Jerry around, he said, even though he would be forced to shoot his brother. Sometimes he needed a little spiritual consolation. The dandy priest was no threat and he made an ideal bodyguard, a perfect mouthpiece. He was a great all-rounder.

Jerry murmured something ecclesiastical and went to pour himself a glass of wine.

'Back in the saddle are we, Jerry?'

It was Una. She was as friendly as ever. Still a little disconcerting. But they were lovers again, at least when it suited her, and the sex was almost as good as home-made.

'Where's Catherine?' Una wanted to know. It was clear, too, that she was enjoying herself. You could tell from her clothes. She was wearing her long, tailored coat, her high boots, her black silk scarf, her black bearskin hat. Given the heat of the den, with its massive home-entertainment centre, she seemed overdressed. And yet when she spoke, her breath steamed.

'They took all my weapons at the door. Even my little Swiss

Army knife. I use that for my nails.' She stopped to cough. More white vapour came out of her mouth. It was like ectoplasm. This disconcerted him. He moved to embrace her.

'Oh, darling,' she said. 'It's been hideous without you.'

14

Ghost Riders in the Sky

> In the early, emotionally charged days after 11 September, I am told, Bush gave the go-ahead to the CIA and the US military to use torture against captives; this I suspect, could return to haunt him.
>
> Not with the American public, who in their current mood would heartily support Bush and endorse not only torture, but slow death by strangulation and molten iron if they could. But such visible unravelling and official wrongdoing, if exposed, would certainly give the rest of the world a 'bad case of the vapours'. And the US will have found that, in its enthusiasm, it has burnt bridges to overseas which, it will turn out – perhaps before too long – Americans need desperately.
>
> – Andrew Stephen,
> *New Statesman*, 25 February, 2002

They had tracked down the GB Oil Gang, or what was left of it. Ewsuck had been forced in the end to give them up. There were one or two small-time oil lords still at large, but most of the organisation's high-ranking members were all accounted for. It was now just a formality to declare their former homeland a terrorist state and send in the daisy cutters.

Someone had clearly warned the Barbecue Kid. The Kid had created a diversion and escaped. There wasn't much left of Houston or Dallas. Every so often he issued a video.

President-General Ewell was still reassuring his economists.

'This is like the Hundred Years War. Out of that came a stronger Germany. It paved the way for Bismarck. And whereas it took them generations, we can do it in a week. That's the wonder of modern IT technology. Don't worry. I'm looking out for any fräuleins wearing dynamite vests.'

He glanced at them for their approval. They nodded. He returned his attention to the TV.

His captured predecessor was munching pretzels and watching reruns of college football games. He still didn't know he was under arrest. He gasped and pointed and waved his fists in the air.

They sat in his tower, looking out over the campus of the University of Texas, at Austin. The city was virtually untouched. Her parks and lakes were tranquil in the afternoon sun. She had been collaterally cleansed with a new kind of audio weapon. When they had arrived, only the Kid's soft-eyed fighters patrolled the streets. These had been quietly taken out by some Ghurkas who had jokingly cut their heads off and then stuck them back again the wrong way round. From hiding they had watched as other fighters had discovered their comrades. Much of the time it looked as if they themselves had inadvertently knocked their colleagues' heads off. Usually the Ghurkas gave themselves away by giggling.

Now they were mopping up. It was mostly blood. It would take the usual three days, but there wasn't much left of any value. From where he sat with his advisors, General-President Ewell pointed up suddenly. He could see the full moon through his window. 'Isn't that perfect. Wouldn't you call that perfect?'

His prisoner took another chocolate brownie from the piled plate beside him. 'Make yourselves at home, my friends. Presumably you want to talk about peace terms. Well you won't wriggle out of the consequences of your action quite so easily. You've run up a big bill there.' He turned squinting, vacant eyes on them. 'It's going to have to be paid.'

They ignored him. He returned his attention to the television.

'I was never sure of those chaps whose eyes were too close together. Say what you like, Roy Rogers was untrustworthy.' Una handed Jerry a barbecued French bean. 'Could I ask you for some spiritual advice?'

'Always open for business for you, dear Mrs Persson.' His beautiful white and gold vestments rose and fell as he sat down on the edge of a floral sofa. 'But I hope we're not plotting. You know how I prefer to put the pieces together later.'

'What would that gain us? A perpetual Byzantium?'

'Which was a hectic place for most of the time. A Greek Empire should have been our goal, not some awful second-hand Rome.'

'Did you know the Caliphates despised Rome?' She cracked a carrot. 'They weren't interested in anything about them. You could call it rivalrous, but I honestly believe they saw Romans as barbarians, just as the Egyptians saw the Saudis.'

'Well, they were right about the Saudis. The last bunch of Egyptians I saw were stripped to the waist and working on the roads. But it is very difficult to revitalise a nation without the resources of the outlaw economies. When will we be getting the oil through, do you think?' She felt about in a salad for some bacon.

'We don't need oil any more.' Jerry took her greasy hand. 'It's all wind-power, these days.'

The Prisoner-President had heard that. His frown deepened. He raised his voice. 'There are some things I don't want to hear on my watch, gentlemen.' He rose up, magnificent in his special Indian set. 'Let's remember our language. There is a lady present.' With a geeky gesture, he stooped to kiss her hand, but she withdrew it fastidiously. She had a feeling he was after her Rolex. 'Why are you all obsessed with watches.'

'Watches are responsibility,' he told her. 'And time is money.'

'I hate to break into your last big wank,' she said, 'but did you know you're under arrest?'

'I never put my own family interests ahead of this great nation's.' He had become a rich, dark plum colour. 'Because my family interests are the fucking country. You know what – there's guys out there want me to be king. King George sounds a lot better than King Ko-leen. That ain't a monarch, it's a country song.

How does that sound? Ko-leen? Studies have shown this. Many studies. They have shown it. That's what you socialistic assholes fail to determinate.' Without his autoprompt, he was losing his inhibitions.

'I don't have to apologise to anyone in the world.'

'There's nothing to apologise for,' said Jerry, cocking his shooter. 'Turn him over, Mrs P. We might as well finish the job right here. It's what his inner man would have wanted.'

She took a step back. She had never approved of Jerry's taste in torture. Or revenge. Or, in this case, what could be sex.

Averting her eyes, she handed him the tube of KY.

15

Who Is That Man?

> It is on George Tenet's watch, after all, that the CIA was unable to penetrate al-Qaeda in order to determine its capabilities, and more important, the terrorists organization's intentions, prior to September 11.
>
> It is on George Tenet's watch that the CIA allowed the bombing of the Chinese embassy in Belgrade because it didn't have the right maps.
>
> It is under George Tenet's watch that the Khobar Towers and U.S.S. Cole bombing investigations have been botched.
>
> And it is under George Tenet's watch that the Counterterrorism Center was in the words of J., a former CTC official, 'eviscertated'.
>
> –John Weisman,
>
> *Soldier of Fortune*, March 2002

Fourth came what is universally seen here as the 'victory' of the war in Afghanistan by an invincible military, despite its failure to apprehend Osama Bin Laden, or virtually any of the rest of the top al-Qaeda leadership, or even the pathetic Mullah Omar.

This has led to what the late Senator J. William Fulbright called the 'arrogance of power' here. Even Colin Powell has rudely and condescendingly turned on America's European critics.

– Andrew Stephen,
New Statesman, 25 February, 2002

Jodhpur Lancers
Jodhpur, or Marwar, is the largest Indian State in the Rajputana Agency, and the State Forces include a regiment of lancers, an infantry battalion, and a transport corps. These troops are maintained by the Maharaja – who has a salute of seventeen guns – and placed at the service of the Empire in case of great emergency. The Jodhpur Lancers upheld all their ancient glory and tradition when they fought side by side with other units of Indian cavalry in France and Palestine during the Great War of 1914-1918. Jodhpur was taken under British protection in 1818.

Soldiers of the King, No. 31,
issued by Godfrey Phillips Ltd, *c*. 1939

HITLER PLANS TO REINFORCE FRANCO
Germans in Spain Claim Five Divisions May Join Rebels

Warning from Army Chiefs ignored.

News Chronicle, 21 December, 1936

Almost diffidently, Taffy came into the cell. 'How are they looking after you?' His white coat made him look like a Smithfield trader. The old pig pens under the market had been adapted to a jail. Mo, of course, was an obvious suspect and had been caught red-handed in the basement of Bertram Rota's, desperately trying to find a first edition of *Out on the Pampas* by G.A. Henty. Someone had told him he was mentioned in it.

Mo was reconciled now. He knew the locals were hoping for a hanging. Through the little barred window, not far away, came the sound of merriment as they played curling and quoits on the Thames ice above Blackfriars. Taffy had, in fact, just returned from a curling match in which the Home Office played the Foreign Office. He had never met the Foreign Office before who had remarked on his excellent Welsh.

'Very well,' said Mo. 'Oh, very well, indeed. I mean, this is luxury. Though they won't let me have my gun. Other than that, perfect. Very good. And they haven't touched me. Universal human rights and all that. Impeccable. But boring. My only serious complaint. I've tried everything to wind them up, but they're Mormons, you know, or Seventh Day Adventists, and it's not altogether sporting. The drugs are excellent. I've no complaints, guv'nor. That's why I'm not complaining.' His arms and hands were covered with small, bloody cracks. As if they had split suddenly and then healed.

Taffy was looking at the marks. 'I've never seen stigmata like them. What happened?'

'It's a long story,' said Mo. 'It started in Carthage. The date was well BC, but I couldn't tell you exactly how long ago. Not me, you understand. Someone I know. You can pass this stuff on. It can stay dormant in the blood for centuries. He didn't know it. I never bothered. Then, about a year ago, I saw the prison doctor.'

Taffy smiled to himself. 'I am the prison doctor. The only one they need.'

'Don't worry, doc.' Mo rolled up his sleeves. 'I won't tell them, if you don't.' He offered loyalty as a matter of course. He loved being loyal. He loved a good cause. 'How's that fine lady of yours.' He rolled down his sleeves. 'What about some Iron Maiden?' He snapped a CD into its player.

'Not now,' said Taffy. 'I've come to take blood. And spot of DNA, if that's okay. We're eliminating today.'

Mo wasn't sure if they were joking. 'Not in my cell you don't. What's happened? Lost your enema machine again? My guess is the Yanks have got it.'

'But you don't know about Brick Lane.' Taffy began to prepare the syringe. 'Not about what happened at Number Eighteen?'

'When was this?' Mo hopefully eyed the syringe. 'Few months ago, or longer? Number Eighteen? Is that the top end or the bottom end? We did a lot of houses that day. Straight through the walls, Israeli-style. Those guys are hard, right?'

Taffy pressed the 'record' button of his old-fashioned tape player. 'And when did you discover they were hard?'

'Not long after it started. I was watching the news and eating an apple. I always used to eat an apple in those days. Of course they weren't organic. Do you think that could have done it, doc? Turned me stupid, like that?'

'I don't know. They still want to get you for murder, if they can.'

Mo began to laugh spontaneously. 'I haven't killed anyone in weeks. That's not murder, that's enemy crossfire. You know you can't afford a bunch of prisoners when you're going in. There's only one thing you can do for them. I wasn't in the SAS for my health, doc. Although, I have to admit, I picked up some healthy habits. Never lost them. They were like brothers to me, those guys. I could have wept when they busted up the unit. I loved those guys. We had a bond.' He brushed away a manly tear.

'How did they do it?'

'Oh, some sort of fragmentation device. They had no idea what they were using. I was pissed off. I could have done a lot more with it. But that's sodding American gunnery for you. Worst in the world, after the Turks. And the Turks have an excuse. Most of their guns are about five hundred years old. Great while they lasted, I have to admit.'

'So how were you captured?'

'Captured?' Mo began to laugh. 'I wasn't captured. I walked all the way here from Watford and signed myself in. I know the Yeomen of the Guard, see. Then I went to find my book.' He brandished the handsome three-decker. 'And they came and picked me up when they were ready. Not much left around Piccadilly, eh? It wasn't a bad walk. Nothing left of Leicester Square, of course. Funny fires. Very fatty. Buggers your nose up.'

'What?' said Taffy, who had been fiddling with his tape recorder. 'All the way through?'

16

Get Yourself Another Fool

> *AS TERRORISM GROWS, THE MORE VITAL BATTLE BLIMPS BECOME*
>
> 'A lot of NASA Helios technology has found its way into what we are doing,' Charles K. Lavan Jr. tells *POPULAR MECHANICS*. He is the principal engineer for advanced programs at Lockheed Martin Naval Electronics and Surveillance Systems in Akron. The company has designed a high-altitude airship that can carry telephone- and internet-switching equipment. Lavan heads a team that comes up with a design that uses nacelle-mounted, brushless DC motors to keep a blimp 'on station'. Hydrogen and oxygen are stored in hollow tail-structure tubes – and there will be plenty to store.
>
> – Jim Wilson,
> *Popular Mechanics*, March 2002

'We're Back in a Nightmare of Aggression'

> 'We are in a menacing world, but we're British, we'll pull it off,' declared Mr Herbert Morrison at Birmingham last night.
>
> Mr Morrison said that before we had really had time to grasp the balance of payments crisis the bad news from Prague came as another blow in the rear. 'In fact on top of all our economic

troubles we find ourselves back in the same sort of nightmare of aggression we thought we had banished by disposing of Hitler.'

News of the World, 14 March, 1948

The action taken by Washington on August 20, 1998, continues to deprive the people of Sudan of needed medicine.

Germany's Ambassador to Sudan writes that 'It is difficult to assess how many people in this poor African country died as a consequence of the destruction of the Al-Shida factory, but several tens of thousands seems a reasonable guess.'

– Noam Chomsky,
9-11, Seven Stories Press,
New York, October 2001

The End of Sterling Imperialism

This country is not strong enough to face such a war without the wholehearted and immediate support of the United States. There was never the slightest chance that the United States, which by established tradition expects its capitalists to take care of themselves, would pluck Anglo-Iranian's chestnuts out of the fire for Mr Attlee or Mr Churchill or any other combination of British Interests. The Americans might indeed have been dragged in eventually, but only if Abadan had become the Sarajevo of 1951. The morality is equally simple. If the world is to have a chance of making progress towards freedom and peace, it can only be by recognising that commercial enterprises in backward countries must no longer be backed by guns. The rule of law means the end of sterling imperialism; and Britain accepted that doctrine as binding in subscribing to the Charter of the United Nations.

New Statesman and Nation, 6 October, 1951

'Are you sure this is the appropriate time to be escaping?' Una held the co-pilot's controls as Jerry stripped off his heavy djellabah. The C-Class Empire flying boat flew with her usual steady grace. Kept in good order, she would last until the end of Time. Jerry drew a deep, relaxing breath, enjoying the familiar finishes of his instrument panels, the purist aesthetic of his deco passenger quarters.

'You don't know what this means to me,' he said. 'I was just beginning to slip away again. I couldn't have lasted. Didn't you see me thinning out?'

'My guess is, you're looking for your mum.'

'God knows, Mrs P. I'm in this for the fun.'

'Well, I'll believe you when I see the run.'

'Annie Get Your Effing Gun?'

A little pettishly, Jerry took the controls. The aircraft dipped and recovered. Judging by the smoke, they were still somewhere over Kashmir. Jerry turned right towards the sea.

'Steady on!' cried Major Nye from the starboard toilet. 'Having a bit of trouble in here, as it is.'

Side by side in the comfortable seats, Taffy Sinclair and Mo Collier were going through an old cigarette card collection they had found in a locker. 'Look at this one!' Mo showed it to his new friend. 'Fifty Famous Chickens.'

'See,' said Jerry, setting the automatic pilot and accepting a Russian Tea from Mitzi Beesley, who had found the bar and was loving the retro implements. She had mixed far too many cocktails already and was running out of glasses.

Jerry sipped his tea. 'How did we go from living like this, to living like that?'

'It has to do with how we trade.' Una got up and smoothed down her skirt. 'But you know me. Economics was always my Achilles' heel.' She went to look at the drinks, gently vibrating on the bar. 'What's that pink one, Mitzi?'

'It's meant to be a Shirley Temple, but I forgot not to add the gin. It's a bit sweet.'

Una placed her fingers firmly round the glass. Sipping, she

grimaced and looked down through a window. 'Oh, that's so beautiful. The turquoise water. Where is that?'

'Well, it was Bengal.' Major Nye came out of the toilet. His hair was freshly brushed and he had spruced his moustache. 'Very little of her left now, poor bastards. I was stationed there once, as a young man. Not a rich country. But the tigers were magnificent.'

He went to look for his Singapore Sling.

'What happens next?' asked Mitzi happily. 'Do the tigers all evolve into fish?' Her sense of evolutionary time was derived entirely from half-hour Nature documentaries. 'I expect the people will do some beautiful fish farms. You know how they can make anything gorgeous from a few fronds and a rock. And they're *so* spiritual.'

When Mitzi had wiggled into the loo, Mrs Persson pulled the shutters and closed her eyes, trying to see a way forward. All she could make out was a tangle of highways, twisted into unnavigable shapes by some astonishingly malevolent force. Was she at last about to confront Satan?

She was kicking herself for letting Jerry talk her into this. She had fallen for his charm all over again. Well, it was too late for regrets. Besides, she was by and large having a very good time. Just as some people were designed for untroubled rural peace or constant love affairs, others were designed for crisis. They needed almost constant adrenaline surges or they could not feel properly alive. She was beginning to remember who she was. She was recollecting the subtle flavours of different livers.

'Tasty,' she said.

Jerry put on his headphones. From his skull came the faint tones of Mose Allison's 'Everybody's Cryin' Mercy'. The plane flew gracefully over the water, disturbing herons and other waterbirds. He reached his hand towards the bank of toggles and began to flick them on and off in rapid, coded sequences. Then he turned up his headphones until he could hear only the music.

As soon as she was back, Major Nye rejoined Mitzi at the little bar. 'Same again, my dear, if you please.' He glanced at his watch. 'We should be there soon, with a spot of luck.'

17

Last Train to San Fernando

Former vice-president Al Gore said tonight there should be a 'final reckoning' with Iraqi President Saddam Hussein's regime in the war on terrorism…

Washington Post, 12 February, 2002

'This is going to be a war of attrition,' Mr Davis said of the Republicans' strategy against Democrats nationwide in a meeting with one of his recruits, 'and we have more tanks, more helicopters, more troops than they do.'

– Rep. Thos. M. Davis III,
Chairman of the Republican
Congressional Campaign Committee,
New York Times, 3 March, 2001

Unlike in Afghanistan, there is no obliging opposition to do the dirty work.

There is little hope that the elite Republican guard … will turn traitor. That leaves the prospect of a ground war involving up to 200,000 US troops, and deplored by every section of Mr Bush's crumbling alliance…

Mr Bush's motives are more murky. They are about oil, naturally. (Iran's 'evilness', for instance, rests on its democratic tendency's wish to exploit its energy reserves with other partners) … They are about imposing a Pax America from Georgia to the Philippines. They are about double standards.

– Mary Riddell,
Observer, 3 March, 2002

As the flying boat circled over the lagoons and waterways of High Calcutta, Professor Hira came from the back of the plane to sit in the navigator's chair, behind Jerry. 'Is that the marina?' he asked.

Jerry banked for a landing.

'The whole place looks abandoned,' said Una. 'Who was it responded to your phone call?'

'I didn't ask,' said Jerry, checking his instruments. 'But it sounded like an elephant. Would that be Ganesh?'

'Not likely,' Hira said. 'Not after the big one. But it was a deep voice, eh?'

'It had to be a demigod, the way the whole phone shook. Didn't they build this place?'

'Well, they had the vision, but their worshippers did the grunt work. I'm really not happy with all this myths-and-legends stuff. I blame Hollywood. It's just revived the worst regressive aspects of everyone's DNA.'

Una put a placatory hand on Professor Hira's sleeve. He had turned his eyes to the floor. He had lost touch with his own metaphysics and he wasn't sure he could get back. Einsteinian logic had meant so much to him. But now everything he had placed his faith in was proving to be as disappointing as everything he thought he had escaped. Oppenheimer had known what was going on. But it was not in his nature to complain.

'It was nobody's fault,' he said. 'All the punters moved to Nanking.'

They were coming down fast.

Jerry lifted his nose and felt the floats touch smooth water, slowly taking purchase as he cut the engine and lifted the ailerons. The plane swung a little on the surface, then he switched on again and began to taxi towards the huge white marble quay.

The quayside was completely deserted. The signs, the stores, the few office buildings, had all received the worst of the recent hurricane. The last Hindu Nationalist government had built these massive marble sea walls and monumental quays, each dedicated to a major deity. But the huge brass statues had been lost to the elements as their pedestals crumbled into the aggressive ocean. Above the water poked the massive head of Ganesh, part of an ear, an eye and a tusk, encrusted with algae and nameless flotsam.

'He doesn't look at all happy,' said Jerry. Jerry himself was full of high spirits.

He cut the engine and let the flying boat float towards the steps. The place had a morbid, sinister air.

They bumped gently against the quay.

Professor Hira was first off the plane and running up the steps with a mooring rope. He wound several turns around the broken capstan. Then he waved to them and, beneath wide, grey skies, trotted towards the flattened remains of the Customs House. Una Persson stepped down onto the float and with some elegance reached towards an iron ring, putting her foot onto the sea-stairs. Rapidly, followed by Jerry and Major Nye, she began to climb.

A damp wind blew across the deserted quays and Una turned up the collar of her black, military coat. Overhead wave after wave of grey cloud rolled. Jerry pushed his hands deeper into his pockets. 'Parky,' he said. Was this really the end of Empire?

'Who'd have thought it? Brought low by a few heavy showers?' The Americans had fought a war on too many fronts, yet they had good domestic reasons to know that nobody beats the weather. The English had understood that for centuries. Especially where Ireland was concerned.

Major Nye looked behind him. 'All ashore that's going ashore!' He was almost jovial now.

Back in the tiny kinema, Mitzi and Mo Collier were snuggled up watching a Seaton Begg thriller, *The Terror of Tangier*. For Mo a new Seaton Begg movie was a sort of epiphany. In other lives, the stars had been close acquaintances of his.

Gloria Cornish had never been more sexy and sophisticated than when she played the infamous adventuress Mademoiselle Roxanne, G.H. Teed's finest character. Mo had read the book and didn't think it was a very good adaptation but was enjoying this scene. Shackled in his cell, guarded by sinister Arabs, Seaton Begg's assistant Tozer hasn't a chance, but, disguised as a dancing girl, Roxanne sneaks in to his rescue.

Gloria Cornish played the dashing Frenchwoman and Sir Seaton Begg was, as usual, played by debonair Max Peters. Mitzi never tired of Mo's boasting of his acquaintance with the stars. It was one of his most attractive features.

18

Not Dark Yet

Law Enforcement Products
For
Law Enforcement Professionals
Smith & Wesson
American Made American Owned
* Handguns * Handcuffs * Bicycles *
Smith & Wesson

Ad, *Guns & Weapons for Law Enforcement*,
April 2002

The phrase 'business as usual', which we make a show of trotting out whenever we suffer a terrorist attack here, seems to have no resonance on the other side of the Atlantic.

– Simon Heffer,
Spectator, 9 February, 2002

AMMO AS STREET-READY AS THE OFFICER CARRYING IT

Law Enforcement professionals face a greater variety of tactical situations than ever before. That's why TAP™ ammunition from Hornady is quickly becoming the standard by which all ammo is measured.

Hornady has developed a complete line of rifle, handgun and shotgun ammunition that delivers reliability, incredible accuracy, and hard-hitting terminal performance.

Ad, *Guns & Weapons*, April, 2002

Colonel Pyat had never looked younger to Jerry. He wore his fur cap on the side of his head, sported a fancy silk dark green coat with light green frogging, his baggy trousers tucked into soft riding boots. Belts of ammunition were over both shoulders and hanging from his saddle. He had a sabre in his right hand, a pair of Webley .45s on his hips, a Martini carbine in the holster on his saddle. From his belt hung a long black-and-silver Cossack dagger.

Pyat had risen swiftly in the Canadian hetman's ranks and by the time the Cossacks reached Boston's lagoons he was in command of five squadrons and a number of flying machine-gun carts, drawn by sturdy Arab horses, ridden bareback by the careless boys who took them into battle. The method of temporary causeways developed by the Cossacks' Bengali engineers was ingenious.

The colonel's massive moustache made him look like Josef Stalin, but his dark brown eyes were full of a life Stalin's had never known.

He saluted as he rode up on his stocky steppe pony. He resheathed his sabre, staring over the waterlogged landscape. The well-trained pony scarcely moved. 'My dear Monsignor Cornelius? You are very welcome. As you know, you have co-religionists here in New Ukraine, though most of us prefer the more ancient resonances of the Orthodox Church. Still, many of our lads are dutiful Catholics and would welcome a little confessing, I'm sure.' He had become more tolerant as his military successes increased. 'I have friends in both Rome and Venice. You?'

'Well, I did have.' Jerry was a little baffled. 'Rome, Mecca and Jerusalem were all taken out. It was President Giuliani's big initiative. When they banned the Old Testament? Tough on terrorism. Tough on the causes of terrorism.'

'I wonder why everyone was so tolerant towards Poland.' Colonel Pyat was not one to give up on old grudges.

'Religion is the gunpowder of the masses,' said Archbishop Beesley, heavy in his new Greek vestments and sporting a false black beard several sizes too big for him. It was attached around the mouth by what his acquaintances knew to be chocolate.

'Well, the flintlock at least.' Mrs Persson was a good horsewoman but she was not fond of horses. She sat her mount with disdainful detachment. This appeared to depress the horse.

'The more advanced forms seem to leave them a bit cold.'

'Turkey,' said the bishop. 'Now there's a problem. How do we peel them out of the alliance?'

'Oh, that won't be any trouble.' Mrs Persson flipped up her mobile. 'Their leadership is riddled with fanatical zealots who have sworn on the gun and the Qur'an to spill the blood of Christian babies. I'll just let New New Nova Washington know.'

Bishop Beesley uttered a small, appreciative belch. He frowned in some dismay. 'I appear to have singed my beard. It's all this foreign food I'm being forced to eat.' Gloomily he took a tin of crystallised figs from beneath his cassock. 'Still, it's a sacrifice one makes for Mother Church.'

'I used to love her chicken.' Shakey Mo Collier, almost invisible beneath an arsenal of assault rifles and rocket launchers, led his horse to join the group. He spoke with some reluctance. 'Could someone give me a hand. I can't seem to get up into the stirrup.'

Jerry cast an eye over the swamp. He had a feeling this was going to be the easiest part of the campaign.

For as far as he could see, on any little hillock or grassy knoll, the combined Cossack horde was beginning to set up its fires and tents. They were living off the land and their nickname for themselves was 'the locusts'. Certainly there was very little left behind in Wendy's and Whataburger after they had been through, but generally speaking they tended to leave Taco Bell and Jack in the Box alone. Jerry Cornelius wondered how long their triumph would last. He had no argument with Major Nye. Flying cavalry was the answer to high-flying bombers, most of which had no bombs left anyway and helicopters were no trouble to sideline. But what happened when they got to the serious wetlands? It wouldn't be long, after all, before this lot was completely under. They didn't need to do a sweep to the sea. The sea was doing a sweep to them.

At this rate it would take centuries to build an infrastructure good enough to supply his particular needs. The movie industry was already reduced to defending an enclave swiftly retreating to Sherman Hills and Fort Davy Crockett. Given Crockett's history, Jerry wasn't entirely sure he'd feel safe in any fort named after him.

He shook his head as he spurred forward to have a word with Major Nye. The signs were all pointing south and he had a feeling it was time they let the Cossack momentum carry itself to the beaches while they peeled off to seek more settled political climates. He didn't care what the others thought, but he was heading down to Texas and wouldn't stop until he had crossed the Rio Grande.

Mrs Persson reined in beside him. She could probably read his mind. 'Don't they still call you the Raven there?'

'It's just the clothes,' he said. '*Sartor Resartus*, eh? I was just rereading it.'

She was tolerant, but she found his references to the old days too self-pitying for her taste. Any moment now he would reach into his saddlebag and slip on a stetson.

'I'll come with you as far as Laredo,' she said. 'I have someone I'd like to see out there. Then I'll head for Mexico City and fly down to Rio. A little Portuguese is what I need after all this excitement.'

Major Nye pulled at his moustache. Since seeing Bishop Beesley's beard, he had become self-conscious about his own facial hair and was afraid he had caught some food in it. 'I only need to get down to Belize, so I'll turn right as soon as I need to. I'll be perfectly comfortable, there. It's still more or less British.'

Jerry steadied his antsy pony. 'We always thought the South would rise again.'

'Funny about the weather.' Major Nye was nostalgic for his old monsoons. 'Mosquitoes bothering you?'

Jerry turned, miserably searching for the source of a familiar voice. But it had only been his mother he had heard. He suppressed anger which he had distilled so rapidly from his self-pity.

'Funny about the weather,' he said. 'It was the same with the Spanish Armada and the Luftwaffe invasion of Britain. Just as you think you're buggered, along comes a bit of wind or rain, and Bob's your uncle. Sometimes you even have to think there's a bit of justice in the universe. Or God really is an Englishman. Those who live by the Big Engine get run over by the Big Engine.'

They all looked at him with a mixture of disgust and bewilderment.

'Not turning preachy on us, are you, old boy?' asked Major Nye. In his father's day their village had seen off four vicars who tried to introduce an unwelcome gravity into their sermons.

'Just something I read in the *Telegraph*.' Jerry knew by now how to get out of an English foxhole in a hurry. But he could tell he was still a bit rusty or he wouldn't have fallen in at all.

None of this would have happened if he had read more modernist fiction as a boy.

'Don't mind him.' Mrs Persson was surprised to find herself coming to his defence. She laid a hand on his arm as he lifted his toe for another bash at his leg. 'He's shell-shocked. Or has been. He has his mother's eyes. I'll have an export pale. Six letters and it's not "wanker".'

While they were considering this, she took his horse by the bridle and led it away.

'Come on,' she said. 'There's nowhere else.'

Jerry relaxed. From a saddlebag he retrieved his little ukelele. It would take him a while to tune it up.

At last they began to see cactus. This caused Shakey Mo some excitement. He had to shoot a couple to be sure they were real. His horse was covered with pale green pulp. Bishop Beesley, who had lost his hat but was stuck with his false beard, put his plump hands over his ears. 'Oh, dear!'

Major Nye rode in beside him. 'Too noisy for you, vicar?' He turned to Jerry. 'Come on, old boy. Help us out with a sing-song! "A Four Legged Friend".'

It would be a week before they found the old Chisholm Trail.

By the time they left Oklahoma, Mrs Persson had grown a little tired of 'South of the Border' and 'Happy Trails', especially after Jerry lost his G-string, but even that was better than Major Nye's nostalgic rendering of the Moore and Burgess Minstrels' favourite 'I'm My Own Grandpa':

And I have no hesitation, when I make this declaration,
Not a nation in creation, can produce another man,
In this trying situation, of relation complication,
I invite investigation, introduce him if you can...

A shadow went by swiftly overhead. She looked up. She saw a hint of something already merging with the line of hills on the horizon.

'Azrael,' she said.

19

Roll On Texas Moon

FOR TRANS-OCEAN TRAVEL...

The SR.45 long range flying boat

FOR MARITIME DEFENCE...

The SR/A1 fighter flying boat

The 80-120 passenger SR/45 flying boats, now under construction, redesigned to lead the world in safe, comfortable and economic long distance travel.

The SR/A1, the world's first jet propelled fighter flying boat, performs all the functions of a land based fighter, with the added advantages of operating from easily camouflaged bases and runways that cannot be made unserviceable by enemy action.

In all parts of the world Nature provides suitable operating bases for both these types of aircraft.

SAUNDERS-ROE

Ad, *London Mystery Magazine*, No. 1, January 1950

British-based Price Western Leather may not be a familiar household name in the United States, but in many of the world's hotspots PWL holsters are held in high regard as equipment that can be counted on. Americans can now purchase this high quality gear as PWL-USA has opened its doors down in Georgia. USA sales representative Ron Bunch recently sent me a sampling of PWL gear and I've found it to be outstanding.

MODEL 120TS

This is the original PWL covert holster and it has been in constant production since 1976.

– Dave Spaulding,
Guns & Weapons for Law Enforcement, April 2002

The showdown at Abadan has arrived. The British Government, rather than landing troops to sustain our commercial interests by force, has appealed to the Security Council and by implication accepted for the moment Dr Moussadek's notice to quit. By now the last of the British oil men has left Persia. No Government can expect to escape criticism in such a situation by soberly choosing to obey the law rather than resorting to some flashy gesture of defiance or retaliation … an unworthy, and probably ephemeral, emotion.

New Statesman and Nation, 6 October, 1951

In the middle of the song two young hipsters scraped their chairs as they left. I could not contain my fury. Big Bill took me

> aside. 'Why blame those kids? What do they know about a mule? They never had a mule die on them … When I visited Europe after WWII, I saw where all the bombs fell and destroyed all the people. What do I know about a bomb? I never had no bomb fall on me. The only bomb I saw was in the movies. Same thing with those kids and the mule.'
>
> 'Bill, are you telling me that we must experience horror such as war in order to understand it?' Bill nodded. 'I am afraid that's so, unless we learn something from the past.'
>
> – Studs Terkel,
> edited liner quote for *Big Bill Broonzy, Trouble in Mind*,
> November 1999

'I'd forgotten about those multiple orgasms.' Mrs Persson rolled towards the blind and opened a chink. Jerry lit two Shermans. The smell of their juices had intoxicated him all over again. He ran his hand up her soft inner thigh. It was good to get away from those muggy New Mexican swamps. Even better to get away from what Texas had become. The rainfall and rising tides had been a catalyst for the vast areas of chemical, nuclear and human waste, one of Texas's main money-spinners in the good old days, and something unlikely was being born there. He whistled a few bars of 'Maybe It's Because I'm a Londoner', realising what a fool he had been to move out in the first place. He handed her the Sherman's. She inhaled its rich, unadulterated smoke.

From somewhere in the far northern part of Ladbroke Grove came the familiar whine of a Banning cannon. He had been wondering when the New Alliance would revive that one. They had been banned under the Geneva Convention and, of course, it was a typical irony that Geneva, ultimately, had been the first to be shaken out by a Banning.

The Banning's relentless vibrations were so familiar that it relaxed them, like the sound of the sea. Bass and drums. They could hear the buildings falling with regular precision. There was plenty of time. Soon the Banning would stop and whoever was using it would have to do some mopping up while the weapon recharged.

Jerry checked his watches.

'Where to next?'

She went into the bathroom and tried the shower. It was still working. She tested the water for serious pollutants. 'I'm thinking,' she said. She got in.

Jerry pulled on his fatigues. He was longing for some R&R, a little peace time, so he could get back into something elegant again. He remembered he had forgotten to check his answering service.

The first message. 'The war is endless. The most we can hope for is an occasional pause in the conflict.'

It was a pre-recorded solicitation and sounded familiar. But Jerry couldn't work out what they were selling. There was only one other message and again there was something familiar about it. It could also have been a sales pitch. Another obscure reference in a voice so lugubrious Jerry thought they must be selling suicide packages:

My 'Azrael'

Every few hours now,
Mostly in the day,
I'll spot the shade
I name my 'Azrael'.
'You hint at death,' I say,
'Your darkness tenders me
A taste of resolution,
So I'll call you 'Azrael'.
I'll call you 'Azrael'
To translate my terror
Into something else.
So, 'Azrael', I'd look
You in the eye to
Maybe catch some clue
About my future, 'Azrael',
Before I die.'

'A friend of yours?' Una knew enough not to spend too long in a shower. She was towelling herself robustly. She, too, was curious about who had left the message.

Jerry thought he recognised the voice. It wasn't Taffy Sinclair, was it? Someone older. 'I haven't been called the Angel of Death for a quarter of a century, at least. It's a bit flattering. Do you think it's accusatory?'

'Oh, I'm not sure.' She reached for the repeat button, then changed her mind. 'It might be a warning. Or a threat.' Jerry thought she sounded jealous. 'I mean if that's meant to be poetry, it's crap.'

Jerry had no opinion. The Banning had stopped. 'We'd better get it together,' he said. 'Can't you imagine the kind of pain those things cause? They shake you inside out. You can even live like that for a little while, with your face where your brain should be and your guts unravelling onto the carpet.'

'You don't have to tell me.' Sighing with her usual distaste at his vulgarity, she started zipping up her battle rubbers. 'I was at Mecca *and* Seattle.' She pulled the protective helmet down over her head and zipped it at her neck. Now she would hear nothing until her receivers were switched on. She let her breathers rest against her chest while she stepped over the empty cartons to give him an affectionate kiss.

'I never expected an ending as good as this,' she said.

He was getting edgy. 'What's that?' He cocked his head.

She sniffed and crossed to the French windows at the back of the abandoned apartment. They looked out into a large communal square, with trees and playgrounds. 'They're having some fun out there. They're burning the Straw Jack. You can hear it squealing, that's all. Sounds almost human, doesn't it?' Through the dusty gloom of the morning, she watched the local savages dancing around the manikin as it bounced, jerked and cackled in the heat. Their rituals and language had become increasingly primitive and desperate as their certainties collapsed.

Una plugged in her communications. Jerry winked at her as he pulled down his goggles.

They took the basement exit, climbed the area stairs, checked for any movement in Elgin Crescent, then began to run towards the guns.

Life had never been sweeter. Jerry was his old self again.

20

I Shot the Sheriff

£1,000-a-year Plan for Life Peers

There May Be 100 New Barons
It is now fairly certain that when official information is available about the progress of talks on the reform of the House of Lords it will be disclosed that an entirely new class of peers will be created. These will be chosen as life peers, and they will number 100, possibly 150. They will be created for the express purpose of bringing into the Second Chamber a cross-section of the community which would not otherwise have the means or background to justify an hereditary peerage. These talks have gone on at the highest level, and it is understood that the King has been kept informed of the progress made.

The question of salary for life peers has been raised, and the figure I have heard mentioned as gaining most support is £1,000 a year – the same as that received by a Member of the House of Commons.

News of the World, 14 March, 1948

What Next in Korea?

A massive demonstration by the American people that they are fed up with the Korean war was the true significance of the vote in the Presidential election. This is clear from the enormous rally to Eisenhower himself and the comparative failure of his Republican Party.

Daily Mirror, 7 November, 1952

A Feeble Argument

The Prime Minister gains in political stature week by week. Why? Because he is honest, intelligent and entirely devoid of self-seeking personal ambition. Those are the qualities the British admire. It was therefore disappointing to find Mr Attlee taking refuge behind a smoke-screen of a somewhat murky character when he answered Mr Crossman's question as to whether or not we were still engaged in military collaboration with the USA.

Leader Magazine, 7 December, 1946

Mo Collier was in poor spirits. It had taken him days to reach London and when he got there most of the South Bank was down. He'd been promised a go in the demolition and had been working out how he could collapse the Queen Elizabeth Hall with four well-placed charges. In his view this was not a level playing field. 'Bannings just aren't bloody sporting,' he complained. 'Otherwise there would have been no point in banning them.' Actually named for the California town where it had been invented, the Banning had shaken the buildings to dust. There wasn't even so much left as a miniature London Wheel.

'They told me there was a seventy-five-year cycle on this sector. I was sure I had at least another five years. It's hard to take, Mr C., I'll be frank with you. At this rate you're going to find increasing backing for linear time and that'll fuck up your plans, eh?'

'I haven't got any opinion, at the moment.'

Mo swung his empty MK2000. '*Ak – ak – ak – frum – frum – frum…*'

'Oh, god, can't you keep a bit of respect?' Julia Barnes, the transsexual novelist, straightened her Dusty Springfield wig with prim dignity. She was regretting accepting his invitation. This was beyond slumming. She cast an unseeing eye over the few remaining ruins. 'Of course there's no way to deal with this. Not yet. Not in fiction. I haven't absorbed what it means to me. You know, I haven't taken it in. Maybe, I could have one of my characters walking by and seeing it... This is such a difficult art, isn't it?'

'Not when you got the right equipment, Julie, mate.' Mo winked and admired her pearls. 'Are those real?'

'Naturally,' she said. 'This costume's pure *Salammbô*, Mr Collier, not some bit of sub-Lotian oriental tat. I resent that implied criticism.'

Jerry had to admit she was beautifully dressed in a whole variety of Liberty's silks and feathers. She might have been a character in an early Melvyn Bragg movie. 'Is that a parrot in your bosom, or are you just pleased to see me?'

Automatically, Julia glanced down. She was self-conscious about these things.

'I just don't think they should have done it.' Mitzi Beesley was close to tears. 'I loved this place. I grew up with it. I had a subscription to the National Film Theatre when I was a student and everything.'

'But you have to admit it was crap,' said Julia. 'I mean, it was crap, right? I mean crap architecture, right? Ideas inherited from the Bauhausers. Or am I wrong here?' She had seen Mo's other clip and was doing her best to fit in. 'Is that live?'

'I'm not going to waste it, if that's what you mean.' Mo kicked at the vibrated dust. 'That concrete was all imported. Otherwise, I'd have minded more. You want some respect for your ancestors, right? Or am I wrong here?'

'I don't think so,' said Julia. She hated her thing for little men. 'What was that song you were singing?'

'It's an old one.' He knew what was happening and had begun to strut around her. 'Goes back hundreds of years. *I've got gangrene, jolly, jolly gangrene. I've got gangrene to take away my life. I've got gangrene that black's and gangrene that's green but some gangrene's a funny shade of white.* My dad got it off his granddad who got it off someone who was in the Crimea and they got it off some Russian geezer who said he got it off his granddad, who was French. So there you have it.' He spoke carefully, accenting his vowels and consonants, almost one at a time, in a way he thought was posh.

Responding in her own half-Cockney, Julia carefully inspected her bosom while he faced the river. She began to make small adjustments to her silks. 'Blimey! Goes back a bit, then.'

'Oh, yes.' Mo nodded slowly. 'It's very antique. I prefer the antique to the modern, any day, by and large.' This was his effort at social chit-chat.

He looked across to where the House of Commons clock tower still stood, saved at the eleventh hour by a band of heritage salvagers flying in with massive battle-blimps to throw up an electronic net which made a Banning even more dangerous to the user.

The Americans, driven back by bouncing vibes, had taken to the river. Like Rif clans on a *harka*, they preferred to avoid major conflicts and simply massacre the nearest *mellah* before going home. The Rangers planned to finish the job they should have finished in Oxford the first time around. There were old scores to settle. It had only been an hour or so since the sound of their squealing merrimac engines had died away.

Mo offered his free arm to Julia Barnes. 'If you've seen enough, I'll take you back to the motor.'

21
Sermonette

HAIFA
Haifa Women in Black are now at
Shederot Ben-Gurion and Hagefen
Friday, 1-2 p.m.
Contact: Dalia Sachs
Men are Welcome
JERUSALEM
Women in Black
Hagar (Paris) Square and junction of King George,
Gaza, Ramban, Keren Hayesod, and Agron.
Friday, 1-2 p.m.
Contact: Judy Blanc

Nixon's Vision of Peace

It is in the most unlikely times that Richard Nixon's hopes for peace shine through most strongly. With the Mideast in torment and Vietnam still a bleeding sore, there is more talk than ever in the back corridors of the White House and the State Department about what is seen as the approaching era of negotiation.

Nixon's persistent vision, that he will usher in a generation of world peace, illumines his often dark Washington days and gives him reason for cautioning his men to avoid petty political and bureaucratic squabbles. 'Always look beyond these things,' he told one group. 'There's a bigger picture.'

Life, 25 September, 1970

The Spirit of America

On Sept. 11, our lives and our nation were changed forever. We are now engaged in a struggle for civilization itself. We did not seek this conflict. But we will win it. And we will win it in a way that is consistent with our values. More than anything else, America values its freedom – the freedom to worship, the freedom to assemble, and the freedom to pursue our dreams. These are the freedoms that make America great and good.

– George W. Bush,
100 Years of Popular Mechanics, March 2002

'Fuck me with a small priest!' President Ewell was checking his co-ordinates. 'We've gained almost a mile. That can't be bad, can it?'

'Well.' Jerry read the corrupted screens. 'If they're right, you've extended the borders of the USA almost as far inland as Rhode Island.'

'It's a beginning,' said President Ewell. He was not looking young. His face had taken on a peculiar patchy greyness, like thin coffee. Jerry was beginning to wonder if it was some form of leprosy. There had been a huge increase of sufferers in South New York. During the brief period when one of the warlords had been in control, there had been some attempt to bring in doctors, but the drugs had turned out to be fakes. 'Washington didn't do it in a day.'

Or, Jerry wondered suddenly, had the Old Man been bleaching his skin. Personally, he couldn't see the point of it now. There were, after all, seventeen black self-proclaimed Presidents of the United States, along with another forty or so Latinos, Euros and Asians, most of whom were controlling various small island regions roughly the size of the Isle of Wight. He looked up as Prinz Lobkowitz pushed back the tent flap and came into the Portapent. 'Cheerful news, eh?'

'We've pushed them back for at least a mile and are about ready to retake New Jersey.' President Ewell's skin was slowly changing colour even as Jerry watched. It was a phenomenon he hadn't witnessed since the early seventies. 'At this rate, we'll be in Pittsburgh by Easter and will be sitting down to our turkey dinners in Baltimore by Thanksgiving.'

'Isn't that a little optimistic?'

'Not when you have a Banning.' Ewell lit a fresh blank.

'You have a Banning?'

'On the way.' Ewell looked at Jerry and winked. 'If that clever brother of yours comes through, eh, Jerry?'

Prinz Lobkowitz pursed his lips. Jerry knew when his old friend was losing his self-control. 'The president was telling me how Alfred the Great started with similar setbacks, burning the cakes and everything, but eventually went on to found the British Empire.'

'There's a lot to be said for starting from the bottom,' Lobkowitz agreed.

Jerry smirked.

A small explosion, quite close.

As soon as President Ewell had found his cane, they walked outside. A shell had landed in a lagoon and splattered even more mud over the quonset huts and canvas-sheltered ruins of the presidential compound.

'Damn.' Ewell carefully put out his cigar. 'So who the hell is this?'

Jerry pointed out across the lake. At first he had thought it was the steeple of the church sticking above the waterline, but this was moving towards them and growing taller. Then, with a rush and a roar of her jury-rigged nukes, the submarine began to rise, shedding plastic bottles, old milk cartons, broken computer parts and all the usual detritus which normally lay undisturbed upon the surface of the American waters.

President Ewell grinned. He saw the two Bannings bolted to the top of the conning tower. They didn't have to be covered. That wasn't how they worked.

'I think your brother made it, Jerry!'

Jerry said nothing. He waited until the submarine had settled. As the hatch began to hiss open, he sighed. He had already recognised the scent of lavender.

Major Nye clambered unsteadily through the hatch and came to stand on the deck. He held tightly to a rail as he waved his white handkerchief. 'Sorry about the shell. This old girl's a bit quirky. We thought we were stopping engines. Lost the manual overboard while I was trying to see how the periscope came up. Nobody hurt, I hope?'

Prinz Lobkowitz walked down the beach until he stood at the water's edge. 'I trust Her Majesty is in good health.'

'Well, old boy, between you and me, she was never a great sailor.' Behind him, the electronic flagstaff was rising jerkily. There was a reluctant click and the rust-proof Union flag appeared, like a souvenir tea tray. 'Presumably you are the diplomatic representative here? Good afternoon, Monsignor Cornelius. Good afternoon, President Ewell. You no doubt understand that I am reclaiming this territory in the name of its rightful ruler, our good queen, Gloriana the Second and must ask you to refrain from using any weapons or giving any hindrance to Her Majesty's representatives.' He frowned, going over the points to himself. 'I think that's everything. Are there just the three of you?'

'Three here – and ten thousand coming up from Georgia armed to the gunnels with Bannings and convies. Seventeen merrimacs should be enough to blow *you* out of the water, Johnny Redcoat.'

'I imagine they would, sir.'

Jerry never ceased to admire American virtuality. They really did believe if they spoke strongly enough and used enough willpower what they wanted to happen would happen. Even now he found himself being persuaded by Ewell's total conviction.

'Meanwhile,' said Major Nye almost apologetically, 'I wonder if you would mind coming aboard. We have to do a little Banning work on those ruins. No point in building anything until you've established some good foundations.'

'It's been a long time since I heard so much common sense.' President Ewell made an elaborate bow. He also recognised lethal reality when it was offered. 'And my people have always remembered that Great Britain outlawed slavery fifty years before the United States.'

Then, keeping his hands dry, he began to wade into the water towards the hull. Jerry was puzzled. The hull was painted khaki, but the disfiguring patches were identical in colour to those on the ex-president's skin.

'I think I would feel much more at ease with myself if I were perhaps merely the governor of a small colony. I do have certain British honours, as you know. I would imagine they would count for something.'

'Oh, no doubt about it, old boy.' Major Nye was decently reassuring. 'It's not as if you were ever a rebel or anything.'

Though glad that the farce had ended so happily, Jerry could not help keeping an eye on the horizon.

There was always a chance that Frank would outwit them all and keep his word.

President Ewell was swimming strongly now towards the sub. Major Nye threw out a rope to him. He looked up at the others. 'Won't you join us, gentlemen. It could get very buzzy here.'

Jerry shook his head. 'This is the last pair of decent boots I own. And you have to look after the threads, these days, don't you?'

Prinz Lobkowitz shrugged and began to tramp back to the other side of the little island. 'We can probably get the merrimac far enough away in time.'

As Jerry turned to join him, Trixie Brunner appeared in the conning tower.

'Not coming with us, Jerry?'

The old assassin shook his head. He had never been interested in power for its own sake. And nowadays there wasn't anything interesting you could do with it.

Prinz Lobkowitz had started the engine by the time Jerry got down to the beach. 'If we're lucky, we can make it back across the Atlantic in a couple of days. It'll have to be sandwiches, I'm afraid. The microwave's on the blink.' As soon as they were settled in their chairs, Lobkowitz closed the silver-platinum canopy. 'These little jobs are expensive, but they were built to last. Are they French?'

'Originally,' said Jerry, starting the rotor. 'But this one's Chinese, I think. Let's get busy, Prinz. The faster she warms, the sooner she cools.'

He stretched and yawned. 'Good to be back on the old entropy wagon, again. It's where I belong, really.'

Prinz Lobkowitz hit the 'Heidegger' button. 'You've always been a romantic, monsignor.'

22
On the Road Again

IT'S TIME TO FIGHT BACK!

It's the crime that plagues the town – and we are giving you the chance to fight back...

Today we launch our DON'T campaign which gives you the readers the opportunity to hit back against the car thieves who cause misery to thousands of us each year. Each week we will carry a series of stories and features highlighting what you can do to make sure you are not a victim. It will also give you the chance to help bring the criminals to justice.

Hastings & St Leonards Observer, 25 January, 2002

Wherever mullahs are not around, it's there
That paradise can be found. Where mullahs' ire
And crazed rage and delirious fits do not
Exist, there heaven's own land is found to be.
From mullah fury and mullah zeal may
The world all be set free, so none again
Take heed of fatwas and mullah's mad decrees!

– Dara Shikuh in Hasrat,
Dara Shikuh, 139

Dhu'l-Nun was asked: 'What causes a devotee to be worthy of entrance to paradise?'

He said: 'One merits entrance to paradise by five things: unwavering constancy, unflagging effort, meditation in God in solitude and society, anticipating death by preparing provision for the hereafter, and bringing oneself to account before one is brought to judgement.'

– Attar,
Tadhkirat, 156

'Notwithstanding what vicissitudes the world visits upon us,' Bishop Beesley dipped his ring-heavy fingers into a bag of Maltesers, 'we need never again fear slipping back into ruin. To maintain our economies it is necessary to be rich. Almost everyone alive today is rich. There are so few of us. So our needs are fewer. But we still have satellites and decent dishes. Disposable wealth. Our lifestyle, those of us who survive, is threatened only by the unpredictable. The lunches might not be entirely free, Mrs Persson, but at least we don't have to pick up the bill.'

'Not yet,' said Una Persson. 'Not until I've had a chance to chill with my friend.'

Beesley chuckled. When his face had settled, he said: 'Never, one hopes.'

The British Ice Age not entirely over, Catherine Cornelius was still a bit blue. Every so often her teeth chattered tunefully. It sounded to Una like 'Mother of a Thousand Dead' but she had never been an uncritical Crass fan. With an aggressive gesture, Cathy poked back her pale hair. 'Could you turn the heat up? Or not?' She embraced the mug of tea Una handed her. 'Is Jerry still here? Not that it awfully matters.'

'Of course it matters.' Ecstatically reunited with her baffled friend, Una took off her military coat and put it over Catherine's shoulders. She wore the remains of her old battle suit. She apologised for her appearance.

'I think it looks romantic. Especially the burn marks.' Mitzi popped out of the little mini-sphere marked *Office*. It vaguely resembled Santa's Grotto. She had been working for Beesley at the Grasmere Boating Mall ever since she had returned to the Lake District. The climate-controlled William Wordsworth Dome still attracted a fair number of customers, especially during the season. She herself wore a Cinders Claus outfit. A fetching elfette in a tastefully torn ragged cheerleader skirt.

Catherine felt an artery begin to warm in her right leg. The blood flowed with increasing enthusiasm. She took a breath. With some relief, she heard a thin, tuneful whistle. Another vein pulsed rapidly in her left leg. She knew who was whistling McCartney's 'Give Ireland Back to the Irish'. It made a change from 'Oliver's Army', which she had to hear over and over again ever since they had left the Ice Age. Even the dogs had begun to complain.

Una looked up optimistically at the newcomer, but it was, as Cathy knew, Jerry. He had slipped through on a Universal Access card he had won in a quiz show and was picking his way elegantly across the little wooden bridge to join them. The walls of the dome were tinted against whatever it was created such a glare on the wide delta water. Bishop Beesley was trying to make adjustments with his hand control. He had been certain he had put a filter on the gate. 'How did you find us?'

Jerry winked at Cathy. The atmosphere was already improving. 'I hope you don't mind. I left the dogs outside. Have you got some sort of electronic fence up?' He unzipped his massive parka. 'Hot enough for you?' He turned to give the thumb to a group of air-masked and goggled punters waiting on the other side of the bridge. Hesitantly they began to cross. Mitzi rushed to distribute brochures.

Bishop Beesley was disturbed by this turn of events, but he had a job to do. 'I didn't object when you asked if your sister could take a go at our heating unit,' he said, unwrapping a Mighty Mars, 'but we closed to regular customers at three.'

Mitzi pressed forward in a haze of hairspray and cologne. 'Congratulations,' she chirruped. 'Brave souls searching for freedom. May I say first how I applaud your courage in deciding to risk the undoubted terrors of our rather mercurial weather. But now you're here, you'll find it worthwhile, believe me.'

'Climate choice is the next big freedom.' Mitzi cracked a monster smile. 'Any bubble you like. Personal vacation. Security. Seashore. Golf-side. We are in direct contact with the manufacturer and can personally guarantee every level of workmanship, from plumbing to sky-toning. This is what makes our prices so competitive. It's perfectly safe, by the way, to get rid of that breathing- and seeing-apparatus. In our domes, there is no chance of a leak. That is also personally guaranteed.' The bishop coughed on his Mars. Mitzi guided the customers on. 'Now why don't we go and enjoy the hydroponic herb garden to get us all in the mood. Everyone's aware, I'm sure, of the great precursors of our domic movement. After the Dome of Discovery there was the Millennium Dome which did so much for London, in the end, and the EnviroDome in Cornwall which, until the collapse, had become such an important part of our countryside heritage.' She led them past the row of mud-and-wattle cottages where they could stay if they decided. 'These are what we call jokingly "the Hovels", but of course they are thoroughly modernised.'

'Azrael,' said Una brightly, looking up. 'Azrael!'

'No need for that kind of unpatriotic talk, young lady.' Beesley adjusted his beard. Red, white and blue didn't really suit him.

'Let's remember where we are, shall we? The great privileges we have in our womblike comfort: this securisphere, this hemisphere, this sceptred sphere set in a spherical sea. No longer need we fear the elements. No longer will the future be uncertain. We have, out of confusion, found Paradise.'

The bishop cocked his top-hatted head. He jigged his gaitered leg. 'A globe is for ever. No longer need you worry about it raining on your parade or waterlogging your fête. Global warming?

Global cooling? These aren't important when you're safe inside your heavenly sphere, where the skies are as sunny or grey as you demand. For it is in today's natural climate, dear co-religionists, that the social and economic reflect. And we must be sure ours is a brand which says "Reflect", which lets us see ourselves full length in the best possible light.'

The bishop cast a slightly anxious eye over the wide water. It was clear that he and his daughter were not entirely reconciled.

From nearby she was turning up the volume of her PA. He glared, grinning, towards the demonstration tent.

She was bright, warm, sympathetic. 'The personal dome is the ultimate in freedom and personal security. And long, arduous trips are a thing of the past. Snow at Christmas, sunshine for July 4th. For the more gregarious amongst you, we also do a metrodome, large enough to protect most small cities. But frankly, my friends, the day of the city is done. Today is the day of the dome. A noble day. A day by which we remember all victims of terrorism and show our conviction that such a thing shall never happen again. The future of our uncertain hemisphere is the thoroughly predictable hemisphere. By blurr and boosh our world's restored, so on your knees and thank the Lord. Floods and storms might roar and rain, but you'll be snug as a rat up a drain.'

'That's terrible,' said Catherine.

'It's a hymn,' she apologised. 'You need to hear the music. An organ gives it more dignity. More resonance.'

'Depending on the organ,' Jerry said. He was embracing his sister. Slowly, Cathy was coming back to a normal colour. 'I used to have one of those Hamptons when I was with the Deep Fix, but I never really got the hang of it. Too many consoles for my taste. You know how I like to keep things simple.'

'That's the reason they always get so complicated,' said Catherine, swinging her arms. One last puff of icy air emerged from her mouth and hung there for a moment like a speech balloon. 'You're always trying to reduce everything down to something you can understand. As a kid you were constantly obsessed with pi. Do you remember? Dad used to tell us it would be pi today, possibly pi tomorrow, but pi had no prolonged future. And you proved him wrong, as you've been doing ever since. But does that make you right, Jerry?'

'I'm not interested in being right. I'm interested in what happens. Like with the test tubes.'

'A little of this and a little of that. You blew up two of my dolly stoves and broke the windows.'

'But I found out what happened.' He raised a reminiscent finger to his face, tracing the lines of his re-grown eyebrows. 'Most people try to stop things happening. I try to make them happen quicker. Then we can get on to the next thing.'

'You're not worried about the human cost?'

'You mean taxes?' said Jerry. 'They're a thing of the past. It's mutuality we go for these days. Anarchism in action. Green solutions. Co-operation. Call me a radical. Call me a visionary. But the way I see it, if you get a grip on the future, you might as well bring it along as quickly as possible.'

'I prefer,' said Bishop Beesley, 'to preserve the best and embrace the worst.' He frowned. He was sure he had just seen Mo Collier go by outside in a speedboat, heading for Huddersfield. So that was where the little bastard was buying his ammo.

Una put her arm around Cathy, who was shivering again. 'You were doing 45 rpm when you should have been doing at least 100. I thought you were just getting old or something had gone wrong with your roots. For a while everything was in stasis there. Talk about dodgy ground. What a snotty score of years that turned out to be. After 1980 I thought the sodding century would never end.'

They turned to look out at the blossoming islands, like so many large, transparent eggs.

'Still, it's all right now,' said Jerry. 'I mean the worst is over, isn't it? Soon it will be safe to head for London.' He breathed against the wall, rubbing a clean spot on the curved, transparent shield. A cackle from overhead as a flock of gulls settled high on the surface. They might have been doves. He began to whistle. The world was altogether brighter.

He had never felt fresher.

Musical references to Peter Keane; Willie Nelson; Chris Rea; Mose Allison; Elvis Costello; Big Bill Broonzy; Lambert, Hendricks & Ross; Bob Marley.

The Wisdom of Sufism *compiled by Leonard Lewisohn is published by Oneworld of Wisdom, Oxford, UK.*

Modem Times 2.0

For Terry Bisson

Miniature phones you carry in your pocket and that use satellite tracking technology to pinpoint your location to just a few centimetres; itty-bitty tags that supermarkets use to track their products; bus passes that simultaneously monitor your body temperature to find out how often you are having sex...

– James Harkin,
New Statesman, 15 January, 2007

Mother Goose: Youth, why despair?
The girl thou shalt obtain
This present shall her guardian's sanction gain
The GOOSE *appears*
Nay doubt not, while she's kindly used, she'll lay
A golden egg on each succeeding day;
You served me – no reply – there lies your way.

– Thomas Dibdin,
Harlequin and Mother Goose; or, The Golden Egg
first performance, Theatre Royal, Covent Garden,
29 December, 1806

Living Off The Market

I

A Mystery in Motley

> GALKAYO, Somalia – Beyond clan rivalry and Islamic fervor, an entirely different motive is helping fuel the chaos in Somalia: profit. A whole class of opportunists – from squatter landlords to teenage gunmen for hire to vendors of out-of-date baby formula – have been feeding off the anarchy in Somalia for so long that they refuse to let go.
>
> *New York Times*, 25 April, 2007

> Madness has been the instigator of so much suffering and destruction in the world throughout the ages that it is vitally important to uncover its mechanisms.
>
> Publisher's ad, *Schizophrenia: The Bearded Lady Disease*

The smell of pine and blood and sweet mincemeat, cakes and pies and printing ink, a touch of ice in the air, a golden aura from shops and stalls. Apples and oranges; fresh fruit, chipolata sausages. 'Come on girls, get another turkey for a neighbour. Buy a ten pounder, get another ten pounder with it. Give me a fiver. Twenty-five pounds – give us a fiver, love. Come on, ladies, buy a pound and I'll throw in another pound with it. *Absolutely free.*' Flash business as the hour comes round. No space in the cold room for all that meat. No cold room at all for that fruit and veg.

The decorations and fancies have to be gone before the season changes. 'Two boxes of crackers, love, look at these fancy paper plates. I'll tell you what, I'll throw in a tablecloth. Give us a quid for the lot. Give us a quid thank you, sir. Thanks, love. That lady there, Alf. Thank you, love. Merry Christmas. Merry Christmas.'

'I hate the way they commercialise everything these days.'

'That's right, love. A couple of chickens, there you go, love – and I'll tell you what – here's a pound of chipos for nothing. Merry Christmas! Merry Christmas! Merry Christmas! Seven pound sacks. Two bob. No. Two sacks for half a dollar. Half a dollar for two, love. Last you the rest of the year. Stand up, darling. Here, Bob, hold the fort, I'm dying for a slash. Dolly mixtures, two bags for a shilling. Two for a shilling, love. That's it, darling! Genuine Airfix they are, sir. All the same price. Those little boys are going to wake up laughing when they see what Santa's brought them. Go on, sir, try it out. I'll throw in the batteries. Give it a go, sir. No, it's all right, son. Not your fault. It went off the curb. I saw it happen. Go on, no damage. I'll tell you what, give me ten bob for the two. Tanner each, missis. You'll pay three and six for one in Woolworth's. I'll tell you what. Go in and have a look. If I'm wrong I'll give you both of 'em free. Hot doughnuts! Hot doughnuts. Watch out, young lady, that fat's boiling. How many do you want? Don't do that, lad, if you're not buying it. Get some cocoa. Over here, Jack. This lady wants some cocoa, don't you, darling? Brussels. Brussels. Five pounds a shilling. Come on, darling – keep 'em out on the step. You don't need a fridge in this weather.'

Now as the sky darkens over the uneven roofs of the road, there's a touch of silver in the air. It's rain at first, then sleet, then snow. It *is* snow. Softly falling snow. They lift their heads, warm under hoods and hats, their faces framed by scarves and turned-up collars. (Harlequin goes flitting past, dark blue cloak over chequered suit, heading for the Panto and late, dark footprints left behind before they fill up again.) A new murmur. Snow. It's snow. 'Merry Christmas, my love! Merry Christmas.' Deep-chested laughter. Sounds like Santa's about. The students stop to watch the snow. The men with their children point up into the drawing night. 'Merry Christmas! Merry Christmas!' It's a miracle. Proof that all the disappointments of the past year are disappearing and all the promises are really going to be kept. 'Happy Christmas, darling. Happy Christmas!' The Salvation Army stops on the corner of Latimer Road. The tuba player takes out his vacuum of tea, sips, blows an experimental blast. Glowing gold flows from the pub and onto the cracked and littered pavement. A sudden roar before the door closes again. 'Merry Christmas!'

A boy of about seven holds his younger sister's hand, laughing at the flakes falling on their upturned faces. His cheeks are bright from cold and warm grease. His thin face frowns in happy concentration.

'Here you go, darling. Shove it in your oven. Of course it'll go. Have it for a quid.' All the canny last-minute shoppers picking up their bargains, choosing what they can from what's too big or too small or too much, what's left over or can't be sold tomorrow or next week. It has to be sold tonight. 'I'll tell you what, love. Give us a pony for the lot.' *Merry Christmas. Merry Christmas* – sparking toys – little windmills, tanks and miniature artillery – glittering foil, tinsel and trinkets. Clattering, clicking, nattering, chattering, clanking, whizzing, hissing, swishing, splashing the street with cascades of tiny lights. Multicoloured bulbs winking and shivering, red, white, blue, green and silver.

Stacks of tightly bound trees, already shedding ripples of needles, some rootless, freshly sawn, some still with their roots. The smell of fresh sawdust, of earth… The smell of a distant forest. The boy knows he has to get a big one and it has to have roots. 'Five bob, son. That's bigger than you, that is. Give us four. Six foot if it's an inch. Beautiful roots. What you going to do with it after? Plant it in the garden? That'll grow nicely for next year. Never buy another tree. That'll last you a lifetime, that will.'

Jerry holds his money tight in his fist, shoved down between his woollen glove and his hot flesh. He has his list. He knows what his mum has to have. Some brussels. Some potatoes. Parsnips. Onions. Chipolatas. The biggest turkey they'll let him have for two quid. Looks like he'll get a huge one for that. And in his other glove is the tree money. He must buy some more candle-holders if he sees them. And a few decorations if he has anything left over. And some sweets. He knows how to get the bargains. She trusts him, Mum does. She knows what Cathy's like. Cathy, his sister, would hold out the money for the first turkey offered, but Jerry goes up to Portwine's to the chuckling ruby-faced giant who fancies his mum. Nothing makes a fat old-fashioned butcher happier than being kind to a kid at Christmas. He looks down over his swollen belly, his bloodied apron. ('Wotcher, young Jerry. What can I do you for?') *Turkeys! Turkeys! Come on love. Best in the market. Go on, have two.* ('Ten bob to you, Jerry.')

There's a row of huge unclaimed turkeys hanging like felons on hooks in the window. Blood-red prices slashed. Jerry knows he can come back. Cathy smiles at Mr Portwine. The little flirt. She's learning. That smile's worth a bird all by itself. Down towards Blenheim Crescent. Dewhurst's doing a good few, too. Down further, on both sides of the road. Plenty of turkeys, chickens, geese, pheasants. 'Fowl a-plenty,' he says to himself with relish. Down all the way to Oxford Gardens, to the cheap end where already every vegetable is half the price it is at the top. The snow settles on their heads and shoulders, and through the busy, joyful business of the noisy market comes the syncopated clatter of a barrel organ. 'God Rest Ye, Merry Gentlemen', 'The First Noël', 'The Holly and the Ivy' cycle out at the same manic pace as the organ grinder turns his handle and holds out his black velvet bag.

'Merry Christmas! Merry Christmas!' His hat is covered in melting snow but his arm moves the crank with the same disciplined regularity it's turned for forty years or more. 'Away in a Manger'. 'Good King Wenzslaslas'. 'O, Tannenbaum. O, Tannenbaum'. 'Silent Night'. 'Rudolph the Red-Nosed Reindeer'. Cathy puts a halfpenny in his hat for luck, but Jerry's never known his luck to change one way or another from giving anything to the barrel organ man. He pulls Cathy's hand for fear her generosity will beggar them. 'Come on. We'll do that butcher right at the top. Then we'll work our way down.' There's no such thing as a frozen turkey here. Not in any Portobello butcher's worth the name, and all the veg is fresh from Covent Garden. All the fruit is there for the handling, though the stall-holders affect shocked disgust when the middle-class women, copying French models, reach to feel. 'No need for that, love. It's all fresh. Don't worry, darling, it won't get any harder if you squeeze it.' Dirty laughter does the trick. 'Ha, ha, ha!' Gin and best bitter add nuance to the innuendo. Panatella smoke drifts from the warm pubs. Chestnuts roast and pop on red-hot oil-drum braziers.

And Jerry looks behind him. 'It was all true,' he says. 'It really was. Every Christmas after the Blitz.'

'Well, possibly.' Miss Brunner's attention was on the present. The box was big enough at any rate, in red, gold and green shining paper and a spotted black-and-white bow. 'Nothing beats Christmas for horrible colour combinations.'

'Of course, it couldn't last.' Jerry contemplated the best way of opening the present without messing up the wrapping. 'The snow, I mean. Turned to sleet almost immediately. By the time we got to our place at eighty-seven Ladbroke Grove, with the turkey, it was pelting down rain. I had to go back for the tree. At least I could hold it over my head on the way home.' He'd opened it. The brown cardboard box was revealed, covered in black and blue printed legends and specifications. Automatically, neatly, he folded the wrapping. He beamed his appreciation, his fingers caressing the familiar sans serif brand name in bars of red, white and blue. 'Oh, *blimey*! A new Banning.'

Shakey Mo Collier grinned through his scrubby beard. 'I got another for myself at the same time. Joe's Guns had a two-for-one.'

Using a Mackintosh chair she'd found, Miss Brunner had built a blaze in the ornamental grate. Smoke and cinders were blowing everywhere. 'There's nothing like a fire on Christmas morning.' She drew back the heavy Morris curtains. There was a touch of grey in the black sky. Somewhere a motor grunted and shuffled. 'Don't worry,' she said. 'I think it's dead.'

Carefully, Jerry peeled the scotch tape from the box. The number in big letters was beside a picture of the gun itself: BM-152A. He reached in and drew out a ziploc full of heavy clips. 'Oh,

God! Ammo included.' His eyes were touched with silver. 'I don't deserve friends like you.'

'Shall we get started?' Miss Brunner smoothed the skirt of her tweed two-piece, indicating the three identical gent's Royal Albert bicycles she'd brought up from the basement. 'We're running out of time.'

'Back to good old sixty-two.' Mo smacked his lips. 'Even earlier, if we pedal fast enough. Okay, me old mucker. Strap that thing on and let's go go go!'

They wheeled their bikes out through the side door of the V&A into Exhibition Road. White flakes settled on the shoulders of Jerry's black car coat. He knew yet another thrill of delight. 'Snow!'

'Don't be silly,' she said. 'Ash.'

With a certain sadness Jerry swung the Banning on his back then threw his leg over the saddle. He was happy to be leaving the future.

2

When Did Sunnis Start Fighting Shiites?

> Scanning your brain while you watch horror movies might hold the key to making them even more frightening. The findings could reshape the way scary movies – perhaps all movies – are filmed.
>
> *Popular Science*, June 2010

The holidays over, Jerry Cornelius stepped off the Darfur jet and set his watch for 1962. Time to go home. At least this wouldn't be as hairy as last time. He'd had a close shave on the plane. His head was altogether smoother now.

Shakey Mo and Major Nye met him at the check-out. Shakey rattled his new keys. 'Where to, chief?' He was already getting into character.

Major Nye wasn't comfortable with the Hummer. It was ostentatious and far too strange for the times. He might as well be driving a Model T, he got so much attention.

'I hate it,' said Jerry. 'And not in a good way.'

Resignedly, Major Nye let Mo take the Westway exit. 'A military vehicle should be just that. A civilian vehicle should be suitable for civilian roads. This is a kind of jeep, what?' He had never liked jeeps for some reason. Even Land-Rovers weren't his cup of tea. He had enjoyed the old Duesenberg or the green Lagonda. To disguise his disapproval he sang fragments of his favourite music hall songs. '*A little of what you fancy does you good... My old man said follow the van... Don't you think my dress is a little bit, just a little bit, not too much of it... With a pair of opera glasses, you could see to Hackney Marshes, if it wasn't for the houses in between...*'

'So how was the genocide, boss?' Mo was well pleased, as if the years of isolation had never been. He patted his big Mark Eight on the seat beside him and rearranged the ammo pods. 'Going well?'

'A bit disappointing.' Jerry looked out at grey London roofs. He smiled, remembering his mum. All he needed was a touch of drizzle.

'*Heaven, I'm in heaven...*' began Major Nye, shifting into Fred Astaire. 'Oh Bugger!' Mo started inching into the new Shepherd's Bush turn-off. The major would be glad to see this American heap returned to the garage so he could start dusting off the yellow Commer as soon as Mr Trux came back from his holidays. Thank God it was only rented. Mo, of course, had wanted to buy one. Over in the next century Karl Lagerfeld was selling his. A sure sign the vehicles were out of fashion. They drove between the dull brick piles of the Notting Dale housing estates whose architecture was designed to soak up all the city's misery and reflect it. Major Nye glanced at Jerry. With his sixties car coat and knitted white scarf, his shaven head, Jerry resembled a released French convict, some Vautrin back from the past to claim his revenge. Actually, of course, he was returning to the past to pay what remained of his dues. He'd had enough of revenge. He had appeared, it was said, in West London in 1960, the offspring of a Notting Hill Gate greengrocer and a South London music-hall performer. But who really knew? He had spent almost his whole existence as a self-invented myth.

Major Nye knew for certain that Mrs Cornelius had died at a ripe age in a Blenheim Crescent basement in 1976. At least, it might have been 1976. Possibly '77. Her 'boyfriend', as she called him, Pyat, the old Polish second-hand clothes dealer, had died in the same year. A heart attack. It had been a bit of a tragic time, all in all. Four years later, Jerry had left, been killed and resurrected countless times, went missing. After that, Nye had stopped visiting London. He was glad he had spent most of his life in the country. The climate was much healthier.

As Mo steered into the mews the major approvingly noted that the cobbles were back. Half the little cul-de-sac was still stables with Dutch doors. Mo got out to undo the lock-up where they had arranged to leave the car. Nye could tell from the general condition of the place, with its flaking nondescript paint and stink of mould and manure, that they were already as good as home. From somewhere in the back of the totters' yard came the rasp of old Cockney, the stink of drunkard's sweat. It had to be Jerry's Uncle Edmond. That cawing might be the distant *kar-har-kaa* of crows or an old man's familiar cough.

Major Nye could not be sure he was actually home but it was clear that the others were certain. This was their natural environment. From somewhere came the aroma of vinegar-soaked newspaper, limp chips.

3

Captain Marvel Battles His Own Conscience!!!!!

Knowing that we are slaves of our virtual histories, the soldiers play dice beneath the cross. A bloody spear leans against the base. A goblet and a piece of good cloth are to be won. 'What's that?' says a soldier, hearing a groan overhead. 'Nothing.' His companion rattles the dice in his cupped hands. 'Something about his father.'

– Michel LeBriard,
Les Nihilists

'Up to your old tricks, eh, Mr Cornelius?' Miss Brunner adjusted her costume. 'Well, they won't work here.'

'They never did work. You just had the illusion of effect. But you said it yourself, Miss B. – *follow the money*. You can't change the economics. You can just arrange the window dressing a bit.'

'Sez you!' Shakey Mo fingered his gun's elaborate instrumentation. 'There's a bullet in here with your address on it.'

Birmingham had started to burn. The reflected flames gave a certain liveliness to Miss Brunner's features. 'Now look what you've done!'

'It doesn't matter.' Jerry rubbed at his itching skull. 'They'll never make anything out of it. I must be off.'

She sniffed. 'Yes. That explains everything.'

She wobbled a little on her ultra-high heels as she reboarded the chopper. 'Where to next?'

4
Ecce Rumpo

All Nazis fear The Yellow Star,
Who leaves his card upon the bar.
And 'scaping from their railroad car
He's gone again, the Yellow Star!

– Lafarge and Taylor,
The Adventures of the Yellow Star, 1941

Jerry was surprised to see his dad's faux Le Corbusier château in such good shape, considering the beating it had taken over the years. Obviously someone had kept it up. In spite of the driving rain and the mud, the place looked almost welcoming.

Mo took a proprietorial pleasure in watching Jerry's face. 'Maintenance is what I've always been into. Everything that isn't original is a perfect repro. Even those psychedelic towers your dad was so keen on. He was ahead of his time, your dad. He practically invented acid. Not to mention acid rain. And we all know how far ahead of his time he was with computers.' Mo sighed. 'He was a baby badly waiting for the microchip. If he'd lived.' He blinked reflectively and studied the curved metal casings of his Banning, fingering the ammo clips and running the flat of his hand over the long, tapering barrel. 'He understood machinery, your dad. He lived for it. The Leo IV was his love. He built that house for machinery.'

'And these days all he'd need for the same thing would be a speck or two of dandruff.' Miss Brunner passed her hand through her tight perm and then looked suspiciously at her nails. 'Can we go in?' She sat down on the chopper's platform and started pulling her thick wellies up her leg.

High above them, against the dark beauty of the night, a rocket streaked, its intense red tail burning like a ruby.

Jerry laughed. 'I thought all that was over.'

'Nothing's over.' She sighed. 'Nothing's ever bloody over.'

Mo remembered why he disliked her.

They began to trudge through the clutching mud which oozed around them. Melting chocolate.

'Bloody global warming,' said Jerry.

'You should have concentrated harder, Mr C.'

He didn't hear her. In his mind he was eyeless in Gaza at the doors of perception.

5

The Wanton of Argos

> People claim that Portugal is an island. They say that you can't get there without wetting your feet. They say all those tales concerning dusty border roads into Spain are mere fables.
>
> – Geert Mak,
> *In Europe*, 2004

Up at the far end of the hall Miss Brunner was enjoying an Abu Ghraib moment. The screams were getting on all their nerves. Jerry turned up 'Pidgin English' by Elvis Costello but nothing worked the way it should any more. He had systematically searched his father's house while Miss Brunner applied electrodes to his brother Frank's tackle. 'Was this really what the sixties were all about?' he mused.

'Oh, God,' said Frank. 'Oh, bloody hell.' He'd never looked very good naked. Too pale. Too skinny. But ready to talk:

'You think you're going to find the secret of the sixties in a fake French modernist villa built by a barmy lapsed papist romantic Jew who went through World War Two in a trench coat and winceyette pyjamas fucking every sixty-a-day bereaved or would-be bereaved middle-class Englishwoman who ever got a first at Cambridge, who was fucked by a communist and who claimed that deddy had never wanted her to be heppy? Not exactly rock and roll, is it, Jerry. You'd be better off questioning your old mum. The Spirit of the bloody Blitz.' He sniffed. 'Is that Bar-B-Q?'

'They all had the jazz habit.' Jerry was defensive. 'They all knew the blues.'

'Oh, quite.' Miss Brunner was disgusted. 'Jack Parnell and his Gentleman Jazzers at the Café de Paris. Or was it Chris Barber and his Skiffling Sidemen?'

'Skiffle,' said Jerry, casting around for his washboard. 'The Blue

Men. The Square Men. The Quarry Men. The Green Horns. The Black Labels. The Red Barrels.'

'You ought to be ashamed of yourself,' said Mo. He was rifling through the débris, looking for some antique ammo clips. 'Someone went to a lot of trouble to bring this place over, stone by stone, to Ladbroke Grove. Though, I agree, it's a shame about the Hearst Castle.'

'It was always more suitable for Hastings.' Miss Brunner stared furiously at Jerry's elastic-sided cubans. 'You're going to ruin those shoes, if you're not careful.'

'It's not cool to be careful,' he said. 'Remember, this is the sixties. You haven't won yet. Careful is the eighties. Entirely different.'

'Is this the Gibson?' Mo had found the guitar behind a mould-grown library desk.

Miss Brunner went back to working on Frank.

'The Gibson?' Jerry spoke hopefully. But when he checked, it was the wrong number.

'Can I have it, then?' asked Mo.

Jerry shrugged.

6

William's Crowded Hour

> ... and does anyone know what 'the flip side' was? It was from the days when gramophone records were double-sided. You played your 78rpm or your 33¹/₃ or your 45 and then you turned it over and played the other side. Only nostalgia dealers and vinyl freaks remember that stuff now.
>
> – Maurice Little,
> *Down the Portobello*, 2007

Christmas 1962, snow still falling. Reports said there was no end in sight. Someone on the Third Programme even suggested a new Ice

Age had started. At dawn, Jerry left his flat in Lancaster Gate, awakened by the tolling of bells from the church tower almost directly in line with his window, and went out into Hyde Park. His were the first footprints in the snow. It felt like sacrilege. Above him, crows circled. He told himself they were calling to him. He knew them all by name. They were reluctant to land, but then he saw their black claw prints as he got closer to the Serpentine. The prints were beginning to fill up. He wondered if the birds would follow him again. He planned to go over to Ladbroke Grove and take the presents to his mum and the others. But first he had to visit Mrs Pash and listen to the player piano for old times' sake. They always got their Schoenberg rolls out for Christmas Day.

A crone appeared from behind a large chestnut. She wore a big red coat with a hood, trimmed in white, and she carried a basket. Jerry recognised her; but, to humour her, he pretended to be surprised as she approached.

'Good luck, dear,' she said. 'You've got almost seven years left. And seven's a lucky number, isn't it?' She wrapped her lilac chiffon round her scrawny throat. Ersatz syrup. Somewhere drums and motorcycle engines began to beat. 'Seven years!'

Jerry knew better. 'Twenty-two years and some months according to the SS. Owning your misery is the quickest way of getting out from under. What will happen to individualism under the law?'

'Obama will change all that, darling. Great lawyers are coming. They will change corporations into individuals. Cross my palm with silver and I'll tell you the future. Cross it with gold and I'll explain the present.'

Checking his watches, Jerry smiled and turned up the collar of his black car coat. He put one gloved hand on the Roller's gearstick, another on the wheel. He was still searching for his Dornier DoX seaplane. Last he'd looked Catherine had been aboard.

'What's the time? My watches have stopped.'

7

How to Get Your Free State $2 Bills

> When asked to imagine the Earth in 2040, many scientists describe a grim scenario, a landscape so bare and dry it's almost uninhabitable. But that's not what Willem van Cottem sees. 'It will be a green world,' says van Cottem, a Belgian scientist turned social entrepreneur. 'Tropical fruit can grow wherever it's warm. You still need water, but not much. A brief splash of rain every once in a while is enough. And voila – from sandy soil, lush gardens grow. The secret is hydrogels, powerfully absorbent polymers that can suck up hundreds of times their weight in water. Hydrogels have many applications today, from food processing to mopping up oil spills, but they are most familiar as the magic ingredient in disposable diapers.
>
> *Popular Science*, July 2010

'Belonging, Jerry, is very important to me.' Colonel Pyat glanced up and down the deserted Portobello. Crows were hopping about in the gutters. Old newspapers, scraps of lettuce, squashed tomatoes, ruined apples. Even the scavengers, their ragged forms moving methodically up and down the street, rejected them.

Jerry looked over at the cinema. The Essoldo was showing three pictures for 1/6d. *Mrs Miniver*, *The Winslow Boy* and *Brief Encounter*.

'Heppy deddy?' he asked no-one in particular.

'There you are!' The colonel was triumphant. 'You can speak perfectly properly if you want to!'

Jerry was disappointed. He had expected a different triple feature. He had been told it would be *Epic Hero and the Beast*, *First Spaceship on Venus* and *Forbidden Planet*.

'Rets!' he said.

8

A Game of Patience

> Art, which should be the unique preoccupation of the privileged few, has become a general rule … A fashion … A furor … artism!
>
> – Felix Pyat

'There's always a bridge somewhere.' Mo paced up and down the levee like a neurotic dog. Every few minutes he licked his lips with his long red tongue. At other times he stood stock-still staring inland, upriver. From the gloom came the sound of a riverboat's groaning wail, and an exchange of shouts between pilots over their bullhorns. Heavy waves of black liquid crashed against hulls. The words were impossible to make out, like cops ordering traffic, but nobody cared what they were saying. Further downriver, from what remained of the city, came the mock carousel music inviting visitors to a showboat whose paddles, splashing like the vanes of a ruined windmill, stuck high out of filthy brown water full of empty Evian and Ozarka bottles.

Further upstream, scavengers with empty cans were trying to skim thick oil off the surface.

Jerry called up from the water. He had found a raft and was poling it slowly to the gently curving concrete level. 'Mo. Throw down a rope!'

'The Pope? We haven't got a pope.' Mo was confused.

'A rope!'

'We going to hang him?'

Jerry gave up and let the raft drift back into midstream. He sat down in the centre, his gun stuck up between his spread legs.

'You going to town?' Mo wanted to know.

When Jerry didn't answer, he began to pad slowly along the levee, following the creak of the raft in the water, the shadow that he guessed to be his friend's. From somewhere in the region of Jackson Square vivid red, white and blue neon flickered on and off before it was again extinguished. Then the sun set, turning the water a beautiful, bloody crimson. The broken towers along St Charles Street appeared in deep silhouette for a few moments and disappeared in the general darkness. The voices of the pilots stopped suddenly and all Mo could hear was the sullen lapping of the river.

'Jerry?'

Later, Mo was relieved at the familiar razz – a kazoo playing a version of 'Alexander's Ragtime Band'. He looked up and down. 'Is that you?'

Jerry had always been fond of Berlin.

9

Pakistan – The Taliban Takeover

A mysterious young man met at luncheon
Said 'My jaws are so big I can munch on
A horse and a pig and a ship in full rig
And my member's the size of a truncheon.'

– Maurice LeB, 1907

Monstrous hovering battle-cruisers cast black shadows over half a mile in all directions when Jerry finally reached the field, his armoured Lotus HMV VII's batteries all but exhausted. He would have to abandon the vehicle and hope to get back to Exeter with the cavalry, assuming there was still a chance to make peace and assuming there still was an Exeter. He leapt from the vehicle and ran towards the tent where the Cornish commander had set up his headquarters.

The cool air moaned with the soft noise of idling motors. Cornish forces, including Breton and Basque allies, covered the moors on four sides of the Doone valley, the sound of their vast camp all but silenced by its understanding of the force brought against it. Imperial Germany, Burgundy and Catalonia had joined Hannover to crush this final attempt to restore Tudor power and return the British capital to Cardiff.

Even as Jerry reached the royal tent, Queen Eva stepped out, a vision in mirrored steel, acknowledging his deep bow. Her captains crowded behind her, anxious for information.

'Do you, my lord, bring news from Poole?' She was pale, straight-backed, ever beautiful. He cared as much for her extraordinary posture as any of her other qualities. Were they still lovers?

'Poole has fallen, Your Majesty, while the Isle of Wight lies smouldering and extinguished. Even Barnstaple's great shipyards are destroyed. We reckoned, my lady, without the unsentimental severity of Hannover's fleet. We have only cavalry and infantry remaining.'

'Your own family?'

'Your Majesty, I sent them to sanctuary in the Scillies.'

She turned away, hiding her expression from him.

Her voice was steady when it addressed her commanders. 'Gentlemen, you may return to your homes. The day is already lost and I would not see you die in vain.' She turned to Jerry, murmuring: 'And what of Gloucester?'

'The same, my lady.'

A tear showed now in her calm, beautiful eyes. Yet her voice remained steady. 'Then we are all defeated. I'll spill no more senseless blood. Tell Hannover I will come to London by July's end. Take this to him.' Slowly, with firm hands, she unbuckled her sword.

10

The Epic Search for a Tech Hero

> The penalties in France will be much higher than in Belgium. The fine for a first offence will be €150. And a man who is found to have forced a woman to wear a full-length veil will be punished with a fine of €15,000 and face imprisonment. The crackdown on the veil has come from the very top of the political establishment, with President Sarkozy declaring that the burqa is 'not welcome' in France and denouncing it as a symbol of female 'subservience and debasement.'
>
> *New Statesman*, 31 May, 2010

Maria Amis, Julia Barnes and Iona MacEwan, the greatest lady novelists of their day, were taking tea at Liberty one afternoon in the summer of 2011. They had all been close friends at Girton in the same class and had shared many adventures. As time passed their fortunes prospered and their interests changed, to such a degree, in fact, that on occasion they had 'had words' and spent almost a decade out of direct communication; but now, in middle years, they were reconciled. *Love's Arrow* had won the Netta Muskett Award; *The Lime Sofa* the Ouida Prize and *Under Alum Chine* the Barbara Cartland Memorial Prize. All regularly topped the bestseller lists.

In their expensive but unshowy summer frocks and hats, they were a vision of civilised femininity.

The tea rooms had recently been redecorated in William Morris 'Willow Pattern', and brought a refreshing lightness to their surroundings. The lady novelists enjoyed a sense of secure content which they had not known since their Cambridge days.

The satisfaction of this cosy moment was only a little spoiled by the presence of a young man with bright shoulder-length black hair, dark blue eyes, long, regular features and a rather athletic physique, wearing a white shirt, black car coat and narrow, dark grey trousers, with pointed cuban elastic-sided boots, who sat in the corner nearest to the door. Occasionally, he would look up from his teacakes and Darjeeling and offer them a friendly, knowing wink.

'And should we feel concern for the Irish?' Iona determinedly asked the table. She had always nursed an interest in politics.

'Cherchez l'argent,' reflected Maria.

Thinking this vulgar, Julia looked for the waitress.

II

Les Faux Monnayeurs

> Things were happening as we motored into Ypres. When were they not? A cannonade of sorts behind the roofless ruins, perhaps outside of town; nobody seems to know or care; only an air-fight for our benefit. We crane our necks and train our glasses. Nothing whatever to be seen.
>
> – E.W. Hornung,
> *New Statesman*, 30 June, 1917

> The buying power of the proletariat's gone down
> Our money's getting shallow and weak.
>
> – Bob Dylan,
> *Modern Times*, 2006

Jerry's head turned on the massive white pillow and he saw something new in his sister's trust even as she slipped into his arms, her soft comfort warming him. 'You'll be leaving, then?' she asked.

'I catch the evening packet from Canterbury. By tonight I'll be in Paris. There's still time to think again.'

'I must stay here.' Her breathing became more rapid. 'But I

promise I'll join you if the cryogenics…' Her voice broke. 'By Christmas. Oh, Jesus, Jerry. It's tragic. I love you.'

His expression puzzled her, he knew. He had dreamed of her lying in her coffin while an elaborate funeral went on around her. He remembered her in both centuries. Image after image came back to him, confusing in their intensity and clarity. It was almost unbearable. Why had he always loved her with such passion? Such complete commitment? That old feeling. Of course, she had not been the only woman he had loved so unselfconsciously, so deeply, but she was the only one to reciprocate with the same depth and commitment. The only one to last his lifetime. The texture of her short, brown hair reminded him of Jenny. Of Jenny's friend, Eve. Of the pleasures the three of them had shared through much of the seventies when Catherine was away with Una Persson…

Looking over Eve's head through copper-hot eyes as her friend moved her beautiful full lips over his penis, Jenny's face bore that expression of strong affection which was the nearest she came to love. His fingers clung deep in Eve's long dark hair, his mouth on Jenny's as she frigged herself. The subtle differences of skin shades; their eye colours. The graceful movements. That extraordinary passion. Jenny's lips parted and small delicious grunts came from her mouth. This was almost the last of what the sixties had brought them and which most other generations could never enjoy: pleasure without conflict or fear of serious consequences; the most exquisite form of lust. Meanwhile, taking such deep humane pleasure in the love of the moment, Jerry could not know (though he had begun to guess) what the future would bring. And were his actions, which felt so innocent, the cause of the horror which would within two decades begin to fill the whole world?

'Was it my fault?' he asked her.

She sat up, smiling. 'Look at the time!'

12

Home Alone Five

> I learned from Taguba that the first wave of materials included descriptions of the sexual humiliation of a father with his son, who were both detainees. Several of these images, including one of an Iraqi woman detainee baring her breasts, have since surfaced; others have not. (Taguba's report noted that photographs and videos were being held by the CID because of ongoing criminal investigations and their 'extremely sensitive nature.') Taguba said that he saw 'a video of a male American soldier in uniform sodomising a female detainee.' The video was not made public in any of the subsequent court proceedings, nor has there been any public government mention of it. Such images would have added an even more inflammatory element to the outcry over Abu Ghraib. 'It's bad enough that there were photographs of Arab men wearing women's panties,' Taguba said.
>
> – Seymour M. Hersh,
'The General's Report',
New Yorker, 25 June, 2007

Portobello Road, deserted except for a few stall-holders setting up before dawn, had kept its familiar Friday morning atmosphere. As Jerry approached the Westway, one hand deep in the pocket of his black car coat, the other still in its black glove resting on the handlebars of his gent's Royal Albert bicycle, he glanced at the big neon *New Worlds* Millennium clock, in vivid red and blue, erected to celebrate the magazine's fifty-fifth birthday. Two doors closer to the bridge, and not yet open, were the *Frendz* offices and nearby were *Time Out*, Rough Trade, Stiff Records International, Riviera Management, Mac's Music, Trux Transportation, Stone's Antiquarian Books, Pash's Instruments, The Mountain Grill, Brock and Turner, The Mandrake, Smilin' Mike's Club; all the great names which had made the Grove famous and given the area its enduring character.

'I remember when I used to be a denizen round here. Glad to see the old neighbourhood has kept going.' Jerry spoke to his friend, Professor Hira, who had remained behind when the others had gone away.

'Only by a whisker,' said the plump Brahmin, shaking his head. 'By a lot of hard work and visionary thinking on the part of those of us who didn't leave.'

Jerry began to smile; clearly Hira was overpraising himself and being slightly judgemental at the same time. But Hira was serious: 'Believe me, old boy, I'm not blaming you for going. You had a different destiny. But you don't know what it's like out there any more. North Kensington is all that remains of the free world. Roughly east of Queensway, north of Harrow Road, south of Holland Park Avenue, west of Wood Lane, a new kind of tyranny triumphs.'

'It can't be much worse than it was!'

'Oh, that's what we all thought in 1975 or so. We hadn't, even then, begun to realise what Fate – or anyway The City – had in store for us. Ladbroke Grove is the only part of Britain which managed to resist the march of the Whiteshirts from out of the suburbs. We keep the night alive with our signs. That's a battle we're constantly fighting. Thank God we still have a few people with money *and* conscience. All the work we did in the sixties and seventies, to maintain the freeholds and rents successfully, kept the Grove in the hands of the original inhabitants, so that, at worst, we are a living museum of the Golden Age. At our best, we have slowed Time long enough for people to take stock, not to be panicked or threatened by the Whiteshirts. Here, the wealth is still evenly distributed, continuing the progress made between 1920 and 1970. And through the insistence of our ancient charters, the Grove, along with Brookgate in the east, like London's ancient Alsacia, has managed to keep her status as an independent state, a sanctuary.'

'Ruritania, eh? I thought the air smelled a bit stale.'

'Well, we've developed recycling to a bit of a fine art. Out there in the rest of the country, as in the USA, where the majority of the wealth was encouraged by Thatcher and her colleagues to flow back to Capital, things of course are considerably worse for the greater middle class. Thatcher and her kind used all the power put into their hands by short-sighted unions and their far-sighted opponents. Every threat. Every technique. Those who resisted made themselves helpless by refusing to change their rhetoric and so were also unable to change their strategies. It's true, old boy. For thirty years the outside world has collapsed into cynicism as the international conglomerates became big enough to challenge, then control and finally replace elected governments. You're lucky you were brought back here, Mr C. Outside, it's pretty unpleasant, I can tell you. Most Londoners can't afford to live where they were born. *Colons* from the suburbs or worse, the country, have flooded in, taking over our houses, our businesses, our restaurants and shops. Of course, it was starting in your time: George Melly and stripped-pine shops. But now the working class is strictly confined to its ghettoes, distracted by drugs, lifestyle magazines and reality TV. The middle class has been trained to compete tooth and nail for the advantages they once took for granted, and the rich do whatever they like, including murder, thanks to their obscene amounts of moolah.' Even Hira's language appeared to have been frozen in the period of his dog years. 'At least the middle class learned to value what they had taken for granted, even if it's too late to do anything about it now!'

'Bloody hell,' said Jerry. 'It looks like I was better off in that other future, after all. And now I've burned my bridges. Who's Thatcher?'

'We call her the Goddess Miggea. Most of them worship her today, though she was the one who formulated the language used to place the middle class in its present unhappy position. She was a sort of quisling for the Whiteshirts. She's the main symbol of middle-class downfall, yet they still think she saved them, the way the Yanks think Reagan got them out of trouble. Amazing, isn't it? You said yourself that the secret of successful feudalism is to make the peasants believe it's the best of all possible worlds. Blair and

Bush thought they could reproduce those successes with a brief war against a weak nation, but they miscalculated rather badly. Too late now. The personalities have changed. Remember the old scenario for nuclear war which put Pakistan at the centre of the picture? Well, it's not far off. Religion's back with a vengeance. I'd return to India, only things aren't much better there. You probably haven't heard of Hindu Nationalism, either. Or the Mumbai Tiger. The rich are so much richer and the poor are so much poorer. The rich have no sense of charity or *gravitas*. They enjoy the power and the extravagance of eighteenth-century French aristocrats. They distract themselves with all kinds of speculative adventures, including wars, which make Vietnam seem idealistic. How the people of Eastern Europe mourn the fall of the old Soviet empire, nostalgic for the return of the certainties of tyranny! Am I boring you, Mr Cornelius?'

'Sorry.' Jerry was admiring a massive plasma TV in an electrical shop's display window. 'Wow! The future's got everything we hoped it would have! The Soviet Union's fallen?'

'I forget. I suppose that in your day so much of this seemed impossible, or at least unlikely. Thirty-five years ago you were talking about zero population growth and the problem of leisure. Here we are at the new Smaller Business Bureau. Lovely, isn't it? Yes, I know, it smells like Amsterdam. I work here now.' Carefully, he opened the doors of Reception.

13

Offshore Operations

> 'Carbon neutral' sounds pretty straightforward – simply remove as much carbon from the atmosphere as you put in. The trouble is civilization began emitting CO2 when humans burned the first lump of coal about 4,000 years ago.
>
> *Popular Science*, July 2010

'I thought you were an ally.' Jerry tucked his shirt into his chinos and swung down from the examination couch. 'No?'

Dr Didi Dee looked up from beneath furious brows. 'Why should I be now?' She assumed a frozen defence. 'Now I'm a missionary? A Christian?'

Jerry's mum heard this. She had forced him to keep this appointment and almost forced him to come. She was looking tired, even for her age. 'But you were a Christian before, weren't you, dear? Before poor ol' Obarmy, I mean.'

'Don't refer to our president like that.'

'Sorry, love. I forgot what gods yer always puttin' up, you Yanks. No offence. Personally I don't know wot yer see in 'im, long streak a piss.'

'It's all right, Mum.' Jerry didn't like her timing. 'It's just authority. They love it. They're even pre-Biblical sometimes. Poor old Moses. Talk about idolatry.'

'Now you're being spiteful.' Dr Didi Dee was grim again. 'I'm the one with the prescription pad. Are you going to do as I tell you or not?'

'It's the German influence, I fink.' Mrs Cornelius was trying out the umbrella she had brought with her from Sri Lanka. 'It's not 'cos you're black, dearie, is it? I 'ad a friend like you. Well, not as pretty, admittedly. But not in this day an' age, surely?'

'Get her out of here.' Didi Dee folded her arms under her breasts. 'And I'd get out of town, if I were you.'

'Oh, bugger.' Jerry rubbed at a small scab on his wrist. 'I thought this was too good to be true. So what's it about?'

'It's abaht Obarmy, dear, innit? We're all disappointed. It's not just you.'

Mrs Cornelius had become a little spiteful since her recent resurrection, thought Jerry. There were subtleties to American society mysterious to most Europeans. They thought they knew what was going on, but really they had absolutely no idea. They mocked Americans for not knowing where Prague was and didn't know how to pronounce Houston. Jerry wondered if the country would be any better if the French had beaten the British. Or if

Tom Paine's Parliament had been permitted. Well, there was no point in going to Mississippi now: now that he knew Cathy/Colinda wasn't there. Maybe Louisiana? And then Texas? He'd like to see the Gulf again, if only to take a gamble on the boats, risk his all at the Terminal Café. *La mer d'huile Mes jolies, mes corazoa, deux pieds assayez langue du gringo, meyenherren.* How can we stop all this?

He began to laugh at last.

14
Chasing a Cure

> When it comes to internal rules for the U.S. military, the Obama administration is not going to be wishy-washy. The armed forces will be given, well, marching orders.
>
> *Northeast Mississippi Daily Journal: A Locally Owned Newspaper Dedicated to the Service of God and Mankind,* 15 June, 2010

It won't be long, Major Nye thought of telling his captors, before the public become confused and bewildered and that's when they got to be radical activists. So which came first, the golden egg or Mother Goose? But he saw no point in voicing this question. The kidnappers had been courteous to a fault and he had no wish to trouble them with his own problems. Nonetheless, he was beginning to wonder if he shouldn't have taken them to a French farce first.

The orchestra grew louder, anticipating the coming scenes. Clown crept comically across the stage, a long string of sausages trailing from his pocket, the huge golden egg clutched to his splendid chest. Alerted by the music, he stared nervously around him, trying to stuff the egg into his pocket, to hide the sausages.

Where was Columbine? Could she save him again?

The limelight found Harlequin, following him as he danced across the stage, admired himself in the mirror, then dived through it, discovering with amazement the fantastic world of the future where mounted highwaymen held up trams on Hampstead Heath and were pursued by Bow Street Runners.

15

A Night to Remember

> Artificial clouds, flocks of jet packs, carbon emissions turned back into gasoline – it all sounds a little crazy, but the people behind these ideas are the bold thinkers who could save the planet. Plus: not everyone can be a visionary.
>
> *Popular Science*, July 2010

How sad to be back in Simla as the rainy season ended, and an Ice Age was yet to begin. Jerry looked for his old nanny, his governess, his uncle in his gorgeous uniform but they appeared to have gone ahead. He watched a lazy flotilla of civil airships bringing holidaymakers back from Nepal and Ever Rest.

'Goodbye.' He straightened his panama on his raven waves. It would be strange to see the old place taken over by developers. Major Nye had been close to tears, but Jerry had nothing to feel nostalgia for, not really. Just race memory he supposed of Victorian novels, Sexton Blake stories, John Ford movies and all that Jewel in the Skull romancery. He had never wanted it back but he had wanted to retain the fiction, the escape. Major Nye had been its finest creation. The visionary patriarch who saw Modern India rising from the ruins of religion and barbaric tradition. Thank God the major wasn't in the position of the many poor devils stranded between India A&M missing the power and the swagger of it all.

Didi looked glamorous in her scarlet-and-yellow sari, and she had mellowed a bit, gliding her long fingers between his arm and his torso, coupling. Jerry wasn't too easy with this. He let her fingers curl onto his arm but his body withdrew somehow. 'You must miss it,' she whispered.

'Not this time,' he promised. 'This time I'll hit it.'

A black Oriental cat, tail erect, rubbed itself against his leg. He bent to pick it up.

She was weeping. She felt around in her purse and found a handkerchief, a bottle of smelling salts, some Kleenex.

'Bloody allergies.' It was a request. 'I'd forgotten all about that.'

He raised the cat in his arms, stroking it. 'What?'

She shuddered at his cruelty. 'Obedient girls.'

He winked.

'You're addicted to the dosh, aren't you? Is that why you joined the Baptists?'

16

Biggles: The Limited Editions

> Sixty years after the famous outdoor writer Nash Buckingham lost his beloved shotgun after a duck hunt in Arkansas, a highly-anticipated auction delivers the beautiful Fox 12-gauge to its final resting place.
>
> *Garden & Gun*, June/July 2010

Jerry was back in panto playing Clown to his brother Frank's Harlequin. As usual, Cathy was Columbine. Jerry had Grimaldi's vegetable monster routine pretty much perfected. The orchestra struck up, all drums, cymbals and brass, as Harlequin drew his slapstick and chopped the monster to bits before Clown's widening eyes.

But Sadler's Wells wasn't the place it had been, thought Major

Nye, who hoped he was offering moral support by coming to this dress rehearsal. He had persuaded his captors to make the exchange here. He hated breaking promises and, as old-school mobsmen, they respected that.

The scenery was perhaps too familiar. The big trick numbers, the magic and transformation business, all had a bit of a tawdry look. Major Nye had an idea that the public recognised what that revealed but kept coming anyway, missing the richness of shades and forms still unrecognised by an academia preferring a macrocosm and simplicity rather than complexity. It won't be long, he had told his captors, before the public became confused and bewildered and that's when they produced radical activists. Of course, even the Cornelius family, as old as the Grimaldis, the Lupinos and the Lanes, were hardly aware of the deep tradition they reflected.

'We're running late.' The big, old wrestler, a Greek, put gentle fingers on Major Nye's arm. He had the ransom money in a brown paper carrier bag. 'We'll be on our way, major. You won't mind us not standing on ceremony, will you? We were expected back in Bayswater half an hour ago.'

'Not a bit, old boy. Mind how you drive.' The major tried to stand but he was numb all over.

The Greek shook his head, gesturing for him to remain seated.

For the first time Major Nye noticed that the two heavy, somewhat overdressed men were sweating.

He felt grateful to them and a little proud that at his age he could still fetch a good price.

The limelight fell on Jerry stepping to the front of the stage to reprise his tribute to Joey Grimaldi:

> 'Lastly, be jolly, be alive, be light,
> Twitch, flirt and caper, tumble, fall and throw,
> Grow up right ugly in thy father's sight,
> And be an "absolute Joseph", like old Joe.'

Katrina, Katrina!

> It fell to Neville Chamberlain in one of the supreme crises of the world to be contradicted by events, to be disappointed in his hopes, and to be deceived and cheated by a wicked man. But what were these hopes in which he was disappointed? What were these wishes in which he was frustrated? What was the faith that was abused? They were among the most noble instincts of the human heart – the love of peace, the strife for peace, the pursuit of peace, even at great peril and certainly to the utter disdain of popularity or clamour.
>
> – Winston Churchill to Parliament,
> 12 November, 1940

I

Why You Should Fear President Giuliani

> Parts of rural China are seeing a burgeoning market for female corpses, the result of the reappearance of a strange custom called 'ghost marriages'. Chinese tradition demands that husbands and wives always share a grave. Sometimes when a man died unmarried, his parents would procure the body of a woman, hold a 'wedding', and bury the couple together.
>
> *Economist*, 28 July, 2007

'There are no more sanctuaries, m'sieu. You are probably too young even to dream of such things. But I grew up with the idea that, I don't know, you could retire to a little cottage in the country or find a deserted beach somewhere or a cabin in the mountains.

Now we're lucky if we can get an apartment in Nice, enough equity in it to pay for the extra healthcare we'll need.' Monsieur Pardon stood upright in the barge as it emerged from under the bridge on Canal St Martin. 'And we French increasingly have to find jobs overseas. Who knows? Am I destined for a condo in Florida? This is my stop. I live in Rue Oberkampf. And you?'

'This will do for me, too.' Jerry got ready to disembark. 'How long have you lived in Paris?'

'Only for a couple of years. Before that I was a professional autoharp player in Nantes. But the work dried up. I'm currently looking for a job.'

They had reached the bank and stood together beside a newspaper kiosk. Jerry took down a copy of the *Herald Tribune* and paid with a three-euro piece.

'You seem lost, m'sieu. Can I help?'

'Thank you. I'm just trying to follow a story. I wonder. May I ask? What makes you cry, Monsieur Pardon?'

The neatly dressed rather serious young man fingered his waxed moustache. He looked down at his pale grey suit, patting his pockets. 'Eh?'

'Well, for instance, I cry at almost any example of empathy I encounter. Pretty much any observation of sympathetic imagination. And music. I cry in response to music. Or a generous act. Or a sentimental movie.'

M. Pardon smiled. 'Well, yes. I am a terrible sentimentalist. I cry, I suppose, when I hear of some evil deed. Or an innocent soul suffering some terrible misfortune.'

Jerry nodded, almost to himself. 'I understand.'

Together, they turned the corner in Rue Oberkampf.

'So it is imagination that moves you to tears?'

'Not exactly. Some forms of imagination merely bore me.'

2

South Rampart Street Parade

> Presidential hopeful Rudy Giuliani recently fumbled one of the dumbest questions asked since 'boxers or briefs?' Campaigning in Alabama, he was asked, 'What is the price of a gallon of milk?' He was off by a buck or two, thus failing a tiresome common-citizen test. But far more important questions need to be posed. Let's start with asking our future leaders about how affordable PCs, broadband internet connectivity, and other information technologies are transforming the lives of every American.
>
> – Dan Costa,
> *PC Magazine*, 7 August, 2007

'Angry, Mr Cornelius?' Miss Brunner unpacked her case. Reluctantly, he had brought her from St Pancras. Mist was still lifting from St James's Park. He stood by the window, trying to identify a duck. From this height, it was difficult.

'I'm never angry.' He turned as she was hanging a piece of complicated lingerie on a hanger. 'You know me.'

'A man of action.'

'If nothing else.' He grew aware of a smell he didn't like. Anaesthetic? Some sort of spray? Was it coming from her case?

'When did you arrive?'

'You met me at Eurostar.'

'I meant in Paris. From New Orleans?' That was it. The perfume used to disguise the smell of mould. Her clothes had that specific iridescence. They'd been looted.

'Saks,' he said.

'You can't see the label from there, can you? You wouldn't believe how cheap they were.'

'*Laissez les bon temps roulez.*' Jerry had begun to cheer up.

'I'm so tired of the English.'

3

Pompier Paris

> Meet TOPIO.3, the ping-pong playing robot. Made by Vietnam's first ever robotics firm, TOSY, the bipedal humanoid uses two 200-fps cameras to detect the ball…
>
> *Popular Science*, March 2010

'Hot enough for you? Everyone's leaving for the country.' Jerry and Bishop Beesley disembarked from the taxi at the corner of Elgin Crescent and Portobello Road. All the old familiar shops were gone. The pubs had become wine bars and restaurants. Tables and chairs stood outside fake bistros stretching into the middle distance. The fruit and veg on the market stalls had the look of mock organics. Heritage tomatoes. The air was filled with braying aggression. If the heat got any worse there might be a Whiteshirt riot. Jerry could imagine nothing worse than watching the *nouveaux riches* taking it out on what remained of the *anciens pauvres*. The people in the council flats must be getting nervous.

'*Après moi, le frisson nouveau.*'

'Do what?' Bishop Beesley was distracted. He had spotted one of his former parishioners stumbling dazedly out of Finch's. The poor bugger had tripped into a time warp but brightened when he saw the bishop. Sidling up, he mumbled a familiar mantra and forced a handful of old fivers into Beesley's sweating fist. Reluctantly, the bishop took something from under his surplice in exchange. Watching the decrepit speed freak stumble away, he said apologetically, 'They're still my flock. But of course there's been a massive falling off compared to the numbers I used to serve. Once, you could rely on an active congregation west of Portobello, but these days everything left is mostly in Kilburn. Not my parish, you see.'

Jerry whistled sympathetically.

Beesley stopped to admire one of the newly decorated stalls. The owner, wearing a fresh white overall and a pearly cap, recognised him. 'You lost weight, your worship?'

'Sadly…' The bishop fingered the stock. 'I've never seen brussels as big.'

'Bugger me.' Jerry stared in astonishment at a fawn bottom rolling towards Colville Terrace. Who needed jodhpurs and green wellies to drive a Range-Rover to the Ladbroke Grove Sainsbury's? 'Trixie?' Wasn't it Miss Brunner's little girl, all grown up? Distracted, Jerry looked for a hand of long branches that used to hide a sign he remembered on the other side of the Midland Bank. The bank was now an HSBC. Who on earth would want to erase his childhood? He remembered how he used to have a thing against the past. Maybe it was generational.

'Are you okay?' His hand moving restlessly in his pocket, Bishop Beesley looked yearningly across the road at a new sweet and tobacconist's called Yummy Puffs. 'Would you mind?'

Jerry watched him cross the road and emerge shortly afterwards with his arms full of bags of M&Ms Where, he wondered absently, were the chocolate bars of yesterday? The Five Boys? He could taste the Fry's peppermint cream on his tongue. Dairy Milk. Those Quakers had known how to make chocolate. As a lad he had wondered why the old Underground vending machines, the Terry's, the Rowntree's, the Cadbury's, were always empty, painted up, like poorly made props meant only to be glimpsed as the backgrounds of Ealing comedies. The heavy cast-iron machines had been sprayed post office red or municipal green, and there was nothing behind the glass panels, no way of opening the sliding dispensers. They had slots for pennies. Signs calling for 2*d*. They had been empty since the war, he learned from his mum. When chocolate had been rationed and prices had risen. Yet the machines had remained on Tube train platforms well into the late 1950s, awaiting new hope; serving to make the Underground mysterious, a tunnel into the past, a labyrinth of memory, where people had once sought sanctuary from bombs. Escalators to heaven and hell. The trains, the ticket machines, the vast escalators, the massive lift cages had all functioned as well as they ever had, but the chocolate machines had become museum pieces, offering a clue to a certain state of mind, a stoicism that perceived them as mere self-indulgence, at odds with the serious business of survival. Not even the most beautiful, desirable machines survived such puritanism. How many times as a little boy had he hoped that one sharp kick would reward him with an Aero bar, or even a couple of overlooked pennies? And then one day, in the name of modernisation, they were carried off, never to be replaced. It was just as well. They had vanished before they could be turned into nostalgic *features*.

Brands meant familiarity and familiarity meant repeated experience and repetition meant security. Once. Now Londoners had achieved the semblance of security, at the very moment when real protection from the fruits of their greed was needed. The Underground had been a false shelter, too, of course. They had poured down there to avoid the bombs, to be drowned and buried. Yet he had loved the atmosphere, the friendship, as he had played with his toy AA gun, his little battery-powered searchlight hunting the dusty arches for a miniature enemy. Portobello began to fill with the yap of *colons* settling their laptops and unfolding their *Independents*, pushing up their sweater sleeves as they sauntered into the pubs, as familiar with their favourite spots as the Germans who had so affectionately occupied Paris.

'They defeated the Underground,' Jerry said. 'Captured our most potent memories and converted them to cashpoints. They're blowing up everything they don't like. And anything they don't understand, they don't like.'

Beesley was looking at him with a certain concern, his lower face pasted with chocolate so that he resembled some Afghan commando. With a plump, dainty finger he dabbed at the corner of his mouth. 'Ready?'

Mournfully, Jerry whistled 'La Marseillaise'.

4

Les Boudins Noirs

> Blood-spurting martyrs, biblical parables, ascendant doves – most church windows feature the same preachy images that have awed parishioners for centuries. But a new stained-glass window in Germany's Cologne Cathedral, to be completed in August, evokes technology and science, not religion and the divine.
>
> *Wired*, August 2007

'Are you familiar with torture, Herr Cornelius?' Karen von Krupp hitched up her black leather miniskirt and adjusted his blindfold, but over the top he could still see her square, pink face, surrounded by its thick blonde perm, her peachy neck ascending above her swollen breasts. When she reached to pull the mask up he was grateful for the sudden blindness.

'How do you mean, "familiar"?'

'Have you done much of it?'

'It depends a bit on how you define it.' He giggled as he heard her crack her little whip. 'I used to be able to get into it. Between consenting adults. In more innocent days, you know.'

'Oh!' She seemed impatient. Frustrated. 'Consent? You mean obedience? Obedient girls?'

Jerry was beginning to understand why he was back in her dentist chair after so many years. 'It's Poland all over again, isn't it?'

He heard her light a cigarette, smelled the smoke. A Sullivan's.

She said, 'I believe I ask the questions.'

'And I respect your beliefs. Did you know that the largest number of immigrants to the US were German? That's why they love Christmas and why they have Easter bunnies, marching bands and think black cats are unlucky.' He settled into his bonds. It was going to be a long night.

'Of course. But now I want you to tell me something I don't know.'

'I can still see some light.'

'We'll soon put a stop to that.' Again, she cracked the whip.

'Are we on TV?'

'Should we be?'

'These days, everyone's on TV. Even miners. And riggers. Don't you watch the Guantánamo Dailies? Or is it too boring?'

'We don't have cable. Just remember this, Herr Cornelius. There's more than one way of gassing a canary.'

5

Les Boudins Blancs

> The railway from Nairobi to Mombasa is a Victorian relic. But it's the best way to see Kenya.
>
> *New Statesman*, 25 June, 2007

'I got these rules, see.' Shakey Mo looked carefully into the mirror. 'That's how I keep on top of things. You can't survive, these days, without rules. Set yourself goals, yeah? Draw up a flow chart. A yearly planner. And then you stick to it. Okay? Religiously. Rules is rules. It's survival. It's Mo's survival, anyway.' He had begun talking about himself in the third person again. Jerry guessed he was in a bad way.

'Fun?' Jerry stared at the cabinets on the walls. He had to admit Mo kept a neat ship. Each cabinet held a different gun, with its clips, its ammunition, its instruction manual, the date it was acquired, whom it had shot and when.

'Clubbing,' Mo told him. 'Whenever you get the chance. Blimey, Jerry, where have you been?'

'Rules.' Jerry wiped his lovely lips. 'The jugged hare seemed a bit bland today. Out of season, maybe? Frozen?'

'There aren't any seasons, these days, Jerry. Just seasoning. Man, you're so retro!' Mo rearranged his hair again. He guffawed. 'That's the nineties for you. You need a more fashionable lexicon. You want *au naturel*, you gotta pay for it.'

'It wasn't always like this.'

'We were young and stupid. We almost lost it. Went too far. That costs, if you're lucky enough to survive. AIDS and the abolition of controlled rents. A high price to pay.'

Jerry regarded his shaking hands. 'If this is the price of a misspent youth, I'll take a dozen.'

Mo wasn't listening. He had found still another reflection. 'I think Mo needs a new stylist.'

6

How to Deal with a Shrinking Population

> There's a lot of hot air wafting around the Venice Biennale. But one thing is for sure: the art world can party.
>
> *New Statesman*, 25 June, 2007

'Hi, hi, American pie chart.' Jerry sniffed. A miasma was creeping across the world. He'd read about it, heard about it, been warned about it. A cloud born of the dreadful dust of conflict, greed and power addiction, according to old Major Nye. It rose from Auschwitz, London, Hiroshima, Seoul, Jerusalem, Rwanda, New York and Baghdad. But Jerry wasn't sure. He remarked on it.

Max Pardon buttoned his elegant grey overcoat, nodding emphatically: *'D'accord.'* He resorted to his own language. 'We inhale the dust of the dead with every breath. The deeper the breath, the greater the number of others' memories we take to ourselves. Those wind-borne lives bring horror into our hearts, and every dream we have, every anxiety we feel, is a result of all those fires, all those explosions, all those devastations. Out of that miasma shapes are formed. Those shapes achieve substance resembling bone, blood, flesh and skin, creating monsters, some of them in human form.

'That was how monsters procreated in the heat and destruction of Dachau, the Blitz and the Gaza strip; from massive bombs dropped on the innocent; from massacre and the thick, oily smoke of burning flesh. The miasma accumulated mass as more bombs were dropped and bodies burned. The monsters created from this mass, born of shed blood and human fright, bestrode the ruins of our sanctuaries and savoured our fear like connoisseurs: Here is the Belsen '44; taste the subtle flavours of a Kent State '68 or the nutty sweetness of an Abu Ghraib '04, the amusing lightness of a Madrid '04, a London '05. What good years they were! Perfect conditions. These New York '01s are so much more full-bodied than the Belfast '98s. The monsters sit at table, relishing their feast. They stink of satiation. Their farts expel the sucked-dry husks of human souls: Judge Dredd, Lord Horror, Stuporman. Praise the great miasma wherever it creeps. Into TV sets, computer games, the language of sport, of advertising. The language of politics, infected by the lexicon of war. The language of war wrapped up in the vocabularies of candy-salesmen, toilet sanitisers, room sprays. That filth on our feet isn't dog shit. That city film on our skins is the physical manifestation of human greed. You feel it as soon as you smell New Orleans, Montgomery or Biloxi.

'That whimpering you heard was the sound of cowards finding it harder and harder to discover sanctuary.

'Where can you hide? The Bahamas? Grand Cayman? The BVAs? The Isle of Man or Monaco? Not now that you've stopped burying treasure, melted the icebergs, called up the tsunamis and made the oceans rise. All that's left is Switzerland with her melting glaciers and strengthened boundaries. The monsters respond by playing dead. This is their moment of weakness when they can be slain, but it takes a special hero to cut off their heads and dispose of their bodies so that they can't rise again. Some Charlemagne, perhaps? Some doomed champion? There can be no sequels. Only remakes. Only remakes. But, because we have exhausted a few of the monsters, that doesn't mean they no longer move amongst us, sampling our souls, watching us scamper in fear at the first signs of their return. We are thoroughly poisoned. We have inhaled the despairing dust of Burundi and Baghdad.'

'Well, that was a mouthful.' The three of them had crossed the Seine from the Isle St Louis. It began to get chilly. Jerry pulled on his old car coat and checked his heat. His resurrected needle gun, primed and charged, was ready to start stitching up the enemy. 'Shall we go?'

'You know what my French is like.' Mo stared with some curiosity at Max Pardon. A small, neatly wrapped figure wearing an English tweed cap, Pardon had exhausted himself and stood with his back to a gilded statue. 'What's he saying?'

'That his taxes are too high,' said Jerry.

7

Pump Up Your Network

Daran habe ich gar nicht gedacht!

– Albert Einstein

'Now look here, Mr Cornelius, you can't come in here with your insults and your threats. What will happen to the poor beggars who depend on their corps for their healthcare and their massive mortgages? Would you care to have negative equity and be unemployed?' Rupert Fox spread his gnarled Antipodean hands, then mournfully fingered the folds of his features, leaning into the mirror-cam. This facelift had not taken as well as he had hoped. He looked like a poorly re-hydrated peach. 'Platitudes *are* news, old boy.' He exposed his expensive teeth to the window overlooking Green Park. In the distance, the six flags of Texas waved all the way up the Mall to Buckingham Palace. 'We give them reality in other ways. The reality the public wants. Swelp me. I should know. I've got God. What do you have? A bunch of idols.'

'I thought idolatry was your stock-in-trade.'

'Trade makes the world go round.'

'The great idolater, eh? All those beads swapped with the natives. All those presents.'

'I don't have to listen to this crap.' Rupert Fox made a show of good humour. 'You enjoy yourself with your fantasies, while I get on with my realities, sport. You can't live in the past for ever. Our empire has to grow and change.' He motioned towards his office's outer door. 'William will show you to the elevator.'

8

Is He the Greatest Fantasy Player of All Time?

> One of the keys to being seen as a great leader is to be seen as a commander-in-chief ... My father had all this political capital built up when he drove the Iraqis out of Kuwait and he wasted it. If I have a chance to invade ... if I had that much capital, I'm not going to waste it...
>
> – George W. Bush
> to Mickey Herskowitz, 1999

Banning never really changed. Jerry parked the Corniche in the disabled parking space and got out. A block to the east, I-10 roared and shook like a disturbed beast. A block to the west, and the town spread to merge with the scrub of semi-desert, its single-storey houses decaying before his eyes. But here, outside Grandma's Kitchen, he knew he was home and dry. He was going to get the best country cooking between Santa Monica and Palm Springs. The restaurant was alone amongst the concessions and chains of Main Street. It might change owners now and again, but never its cooks or waitresses. Never its well-advertised politics, patriotism and faith. Grandma's was the only place worth eating in a thousand miles. He took off his wide-brimmed panama and wiped his neck and forehead. It had to be a hundred and ten. The rain, roaring down from Canada and up from the Gulf of Mexico, had not yet reached California. When it did, it would not stop. Somewhere out there, in the heavily irrigated fields, wetbacks were desperately working to bring in the crops before they were swamped. From now on, they would grow rice, like the rest of the country.

Jerry pushed open the door and walked past the display of flags, crosses, fish and Support Our Troops signs. There was a Christmas theme, too. Every sign and icon had fake snow sprayed over it. Santa and his sleigh and reindeers swung from all available parts of the roof. A big artificial tree in the middle of the main dining room dropped tinsel around its base so that it seemed to be emerging from a sparkling pool. Christmas songs played over the speakers. A few rednecks looked up at him, nodding a greeting. A woman in a red felt elf hat, who might have been the original Grandma, led him through the wealth of red-and-white chequered tablecloths and wagonwheel-backed chairs to an empty place in the corner. 'How about a nice big glass of ice tea, son?'

'Unsweetened. Thanks, ma'am. I'm waiting for a friend.'

'I can recommend the Turkey Special,' she said.

Twenty minutes went by before Max Pardon came in, removing his own hat and looking around him in delight. 'Jerry! This is perfect. A cultural miracle.' The natty Frenchman had shaved his moustache. He had been stationed out here for a couple of months. Banning had once owed a certain prosperity, or at least her existence, to oil. Now she was a dormitory extension for the casinos. You could have bought the whole place for the price of a mid-sized Pasadena apartment. M. Pardon had actually been thinking of doing just that. He ordered his food and gave the waitress one of his sad, charming smiles. She responded by calling him 'Darling'.

When their meals arrived, he picked up his knife and fork and shrugged. 'Don't feel too sorry for me, Jerry. It's healthy enough, once you get back and lose those old interstate habits. You know LA.' He spoke idiomatic American. He leaned forward over his turkey dinner to murmur. 'I think I've found the guns.'

Gladly Jerry grinned.

As if in response to M. Pardon's information, from somewhere out in the scrubland came the sound of rapid shooting. 'That's not the Indians,' he said. 'The locals do that about this time every day.'

'You'll manage to get the guns to the Diné on schedule?'

'Sure.' Tasting the fowl, Max raised his eyebrows. 'You bet.'

Grandma brought them condiments. She turned up her hearing aid, cocking her head. 'This'll put Banning on the map.' She spoke with cheerful satisfaction. 'Just in time to celebrate the season.'

Jerry sipped his tea.

Max Pardon always knew how to make the most of Christmas. By the time the Diné arrived, Banning would be a serious bargain.

9

They Want to Make Firearms Ownership a Burden – Not a Freedom!

> In August most upscale Parisians head north for Deauville for the polo and the racing or to the cool woods of their country estates in the Loire or Bordeaux ... Paris's most prestigious hotel at that time of the year is crawling with camera-toting tourists and rubberneckers.
>
> – Tina Brown,
> *The Diana Chronicles*, 2007

'*Welcome to the Hotel California,*' Jerry sang into his Bluetooth. In his long, dark hair the beautiful violet light winked in time as the ruins sped past on either side of I-10: wounded houses, shops, shacks, filling stations, churches, all covered in Dayglo blue PVC, stacks of fallen trunks, piles of reclaimed planks, leaning firehouses, collapsed trees lying where the hurricane had thrown them, overturned cars and trucks, collapsed barns, flattened billboards, flooded strip malls, mountains of torn foliage, state and federal direction signs twisted into tattered scrap, smashed motels and roadside restaurants, mile upon mile of detritus growing more plentiful the closer they got to the coast.

In the identical midnight-blue Corniche beside him, connected by her own Bluetooth, Cathy joined in the chorus. The twin cars headed over cypress swamps, bayous and swollen rivers on the way to where the Mississippi met the city.

Standing in the still, swollen ponds on either side of the long bridges, egrets and storks regarded them with cool, incurious eyes. Families of crows hopped along the roadside, pecking at miscellaneous corpses; buzzards cruised overhead. It looked like rain again.

Here and there, massive cracks and gaps in the concrete had been filled in with tar like black holes in a flat grey vacuum. Handmade signs offered the services of motel chains or burger concessions, and every few miles they were told how much closer they were to Prejean's or Michaux's where the music was still good and the gumbo even tastier. The fish had been enjoying a more varied diet. Zydeco and Cajun, crawfish and boudin. Oo-oo. Oo-oo. Still having fon on the bayou… Everything still for sale. The Louisiana heritage.

'*Them Houston gals done got ma soul!*' crooned Cathy. 'Nearly home.'

10

Pirates of the Underseas

> At places where two road networks cross, a vertical interchange of bridges and tunnels will separate the traffic systems, and Palestinians from Israelis.
>
> – Eyal Weizman,
> *Hollow Land: Israel's Architecture of Occupation*, 2007

'Christmas won't be Christmas without presents,' grumbled Mo, lying on the rug. He got up to sit down again at his keyboard. 'Sorry, but that's my experience.' He was writing about the authenticity of rules in the game of *Risk*. 'I mean you have to give it a chance, don't you? Or you'll never know who you are.' He cast an absent-minded glance about the lab. He was in a world of his own.

Miss Brunner came in wearing a white coat. 'The kids called. They won't be here until Boxing Day.'

'Bugger,' said Mo. 'Don't they want to finish this bloody game?' He was suspicious. Had her snobbery motivated her to dissuade them, perhaps subtly, from coming? He already had her down as a social climber. Still, a climber was a climber. 'Why didn't you let them talk to me?'

'You were out of it,' she said. 'Or cycling or something. They thought you might be dead.'

He shook his head. 'There's days I wonder about you.'

Catherine Cornelius decided to step in. He was clearly at the end of his rope. 'Can I ask a question, Mo?'

Mo took a breath and began to comb his hair. 'Be my guest.'

'What's this word?' She had been looking at Jerry's notes. 'Is this holes, hoes or holds?'

'I think it's ladies,' said Mo.

'Oh, of course.' She brightened. 'Little women. Concord, yes? The dangers of the unexamined life?'

11

Rebooting the Body

> We could hear the Americans counting money and saying to the Pakistanis: 'Each person is $5,000. Five persons, $25,000. Seven persons, $35,000.'
>
> – Laurel Fletcher and Eric Stover, *The Guantánamo Effect: Exposing the Consequences of U.S. Detention and Interrogation Practices*

He had built up his identity with the help of toy soldiers, cigarette cards, foreign stamps, all those books from the tuppenny lending library with their wonderful bright jackets preserved in sticky plastic. Netta Muskett was his mum's favourite and he went for P.G. Wodehouse, Edgar Rice Burroughs, P.C. Wren, Baroness Orczy and the rest. They were still printed in hundreds of thousands then. Thrillers, comedies, fantastic adventure, historical adventure. Rafael Sabatini. What a disappointing picture of him that was in *Lilliput* magazine, wearing waders, holding a rod, caught bending in midstream, an old gent. It came to us all.

Didi Dee seemed to feel more comfortable without her clothes, nodding to herself as she looked at his books. Was she confirming something? He sat in the big Morris library chair and watched her, dark as the mahogany, reflecting the light.

'I wasn't exactly a virgin. My dad started fucking me when I was twelve.' She turned to study his reaction. 'Does that shock you?'

Jerry laughed. 'What? Me? I'm a moralist, I know, but I'm not a petty moralist. You think a spot of finger-wagging is what Jesus would have done. So I should be saying "Bloody hell! The fucking bastard"?'

She came back into the bedroom and started snapping on her kit. 'It was all right. He got it over with quickly and then he was guilty as hell and I could go out all night and do what and whom I liked without his saying a word because he was scared I'd tell the cops and my mum would find out, though really I think she knew and didn't care. Gave her a quiet life. So by day I was doing my mock A-levels at St Paul's and by night I was having all the fun of the fair.' She blinked reminiscently. 'Or thought I was. It took me a bit of time to find out what I liked. What I was like. When I met you I'd just turned twenty-one. I thought I was ready to settle down.'

He didn't make the obvious response. He licked the smell of her cunt off his upper lip. He needed a shave. Maybe he'd teach her how to use the straight razor on his face. She required training. She'd said so herself. 'What a waste.' He thought of those lost nine years.

Suddenly her face opened up into one of those old cheeky grins. A lot better than nothing but it made him want to pee. No, he wasn't really getting that old feeling. She showed him her perfect ass. So this is where nostalgia got you. She lay down next to him. A coquette. 'I trust you,' she said.

This puzzled him even more. He had once understood her, even if she didn't like him much. Her passivity was her power. It gave her what she wanted or at least it had done so up to now.

He changed the subject a little. 'Why are you so cruel to the dead?'

'Because they betrayed me by dying.'

'And who will you betray by dying?'

'Who will you betray?'

A no-brainer. 'Nobody,' he said. 'Why?' He suspected one of those boring little traps Christians set for you. Of course God loved him, but he didn't feel very special in this near-infinity of planes that was the multiverse. He was as big as the multiverse, as small as God. It wasn't always this hard to understand. Space is a dimension of time. Light speed varied enormously. There was a black tide running.

'A black tide running.' He tucked her head into his shoulder.

She tensed. 'Is that another dig at Obama?'

'What?' He had fallen asleep suddenly. 'What about him? Has he betrayed you?'

'That isn't the point. Electing him was what it was about.'

'Sure, he's doing such a lot for black pride.' Jerry rolled over and found a half-smoked box of Sullivans. He lit one. 'God knows what poor old Mandela thinks.'

'The Labour Party's trying to find one just like him.'

'Hardly worth blacking up for.'

From outside came a shout of glee. They both recognised it. Mo was jumping on his prey. He must have caught a kid.

12

Popsci's Guide to Summer Sci-Tech Movies

> Staring at the vast military history section of the airport shop, I had a choice: the derring-do of psychopaths or scholarly tomes with their illicit devotion to the cult of organized killing. There was nothing I recognized from reporting war. Nothing on the spectacle of children's limbs hanging in trees and nothing on the burden of shit in your trousers. War is a good read. War is fun. More war, please.
>
> – John Pilger
>
> *New Statesman*, 10 May, 2010

Mo wasn't having any and neither, he remarked happily, had he been getting any. But there was this little yellow lady to the west of Katmandu and the crew had come to know her just as 'Belle'. They were banging on the wedding gongs and decorating dresses, and they were praying that she didn't go to hell, because Mo he was a white man and not the best at that and they didn't want their girl to wear his band. They consoled themselves, however, that they needn't curse the moon for poor Belle would be a widow pretty soon. So they smiled at Mo and offered him the best seat in the house until

Belle herself, she said, could smell a rat. And they put their heads together and they made a little plan to see her married by some other means or man. Really, Mo thought, he was probably a goner.

'Mo?'

He turned. He had been on his feet long enough to understand his bit as he fell onto the carpet. Buggered.

He could still hear. 'Of course it's not curaré.'

Jerry was wistful as he watched Mitzi Beesley drag the little fellow into the hedge. 'But then again it's not chocolate, either!'

'I wouldn't personally be talking about sweets,' Didi Dee murmured. She had become shy. Flirtatious. Weak. Self-righteous. Religious.

Why was she searching out his contempt?

This whole thing was altogether too retro for Jerry. He cleared his throat, spat on the ground. Where was his 1954? Surely earlier? What numbers had she offered him?

Should he get into the spirit of the times? Feeling guilty. Finding places to hide. Telling lies? You needed a voice. He couldn't muster a voice on top of everything else.

Somewhere up there in the diminishing hills he heard an engine. Jimmy van Doren's awful old Rolls-Royce.

Time to be shunting along. He kissed Didi on her dimpled cheek. 'Tee tee eff en.'

The Wheels Of Chance

I

Guns is Guns

> Everyone will be wealthy, living like a lord,
> Getting plenty of things today they can't afford
> But when's it going to happen? When? Just by and by!
> Oh, everything will be lovely, when the pigs begin to fly!
>
> – Charles Lambourne,
> *Everything Will Be Lovely*, c. 1860

During the tour you will visit many of the key sites connected to these infamous 'Whitechapel Murders.' You will retrace the footsteps of Jack The Ripper and discover, when, where and how his five unfortunate victims lived and died. You will also discover why the Ripper was never caught and what life was really like for people living in the London's notorious East End.

FREE Jack The Ripper starts and finishes at Mary Jane's, named after the Ripper's fifth and final victim, Mary Jane Kelly, where from 6pm you have access to 2-4-1 house cocktails, 2-4-1 bottles of Kronenbourg, £8.90 bottles of house wine, £8.90 cocktail jugs and 3-4-2 on all small plates of food … what a killer offer!!!

Celebrity & Pop Culture Tours of the Planet,
Celebrity Planet, 2010

'I admire a man who can look cool on a camel.' Bessy Burroughs presented Jerry with her perfectly rounded vowels. Born in Kansas, she had been educated in Sussex, near Brighton. Regular vowels, her dad had always said, were the key to success, no matter what your calling. 'God! Is it always this hot in Cairo?'

'It used to be lovely in the winter.' Jerry jumped down from his kneeling beast and came to help Bessy dismount. Only Karen von Krupp preferred to remain in her saddle. Shielding her eyes against the rising sun, she peered disdainfully at a distant clump of palms.

Bessy had none of her father Bunny's lean, lunatic wit. Her full name was Timobeth, a combination of those her parents had chosen for a girl or a boy. Bunny believed that old-fashioned names were an insult to the future. They pandered to history. Her parents still hated history. A sense of the past was but a step on the road to nostalgia and nostalgia, as Bunny was fond of saying, was a vice that corrupts and distorts.

Jerry remembered his lazy lunches at Rules. Bunny had loved Rules. But he had come to hate the heritage industry as 'a brothel disguised as a church'. Jerry wasn't sure what he meant and had never had a chance to find out. If he turned up, as promised, by the Sphinx, perhaps this would be a good time to ask him.

'Dad loves it out here.' Pulling her veil from her hat to her face, Bessy began to follow him across the hard sand towards the big pyramid. 'Apart from the old stuff. He hates the old stuff. But he loves the beach. The old stuff can crumble to dust for all he cares.' She paused to wipe her massive cheeks and forehead. That last box of Turkish Delight was beginning to tell on her. She had been raised, by some trick of fate, by Bishop Beesley as his own daughter until Mitzi had finally objected and Bunny had been recalled from Tangier to perform his paternal duties.

'You don't like to be connected to the past?' asked Karen von Krupp, bringing up a lascivious leer and with a curious-looking whip thwacking her 'Charlie' on its rump. 'I love history. So romantic.'

'Hate it. Loathe it. History disgusts me. Hello! Who's this type, I wonder?'

'Good god!' Suddenly fully awake, Jerry pushed back his hat. 'Talk about history! It's Major Nye.'

Major Nye, in the full uniform of Skinner's Horse, rode up at a clip and brought his grey to a skidding stop in the sand.

'Morning, major.'

'Morning, Cornelius. Where's that hotel gone?'

'I gather it had its day, major. Demolished. I can't imagine what's going up in its place.' His knees were cramping.

'I can.' With a complacent hand, Bessy patted a brochure she produced from a saddlebag. 'It's going to be like The Pyramid. That's why I asked you all here. Only three times bigger. And in two buildings. You'll be able to get up in the morning and look down on all that.' She waved vaguely in the direction of the pyramids. 'It'll be a knockout. It will knock you *unconscious*! Really!' She nodded vigorously, inviting them, by her example, to smile. 'It did me. I daren't ask what diverting the Nile's going to cost. But it's guaranteed terrorist-free.'

'Gosh,' said Jerry. Major Nye peered gravely down at his horse's mane.

'We are born unconscious and we die unconscious.' Karen von Krupp gestured with her whip. 'In between we suffer precisely because we are conscious, whereas the other creatures with whom we share this unhappy planet are unconscious for ever, no? I was not. I am. I shall not be. Is this the past, present and future? Is this what we desire from Time?'

'Rather.' Bessy nodded for good luck, approval and physical power. All the things deprived her in her childhood. Massive tears of self-pity ran rhythmically down her face. 'This heat! These allergies!'

'I must apologise, dear lady. I'm not following you, I fear.'

'This hotel I'm talking about. Two big pyramids. Sheraton are interested already.'

'Ah, but the security.' Karen von Krupp laid her whip against her beautiful leg and arranged her pleated skirt. 'These days. What can you guarantee?'

'No problem. Indonesians. Germans. French. British. The cream of the crop.'

'I prefer Nubians,' said Jerry.

'These will be as stated. No Saudis or Pashtoon, either. That's non-negotiable.'

Jerry looked up. From the far horizon came the steady thump of helicopter engines, then the sharper thwacking of their blades. He had a feeling about this. 'Nubians or nothing,' he said. And began to run back towards his camel.

Almost at ground level, rising and falling with the dunes, eight engines roaring in a terrible, shrill chorus, the massive, two-tiered monster of mankind's miserable imagination, the Dornier DoX flying boat appeared over the oasis and attempted to land on the brackish water from which their camels were now shying. Their clothing and harnesses were whipped by the wind from its propellers. As soon as she had made a pass or two over the watering hole and failed, the Dornier lumbered up into the air and out of sight, still seeking to complete the round-the-world-flight she had begun to break when she set out from the Bavarian lakes four and a half years ago.

'What I can't work out,' said Jerry, 'is how it took them so long to get the power–weight ratio right.'

He cocked his head, listening for the plane's return.

'I wonder who's flying her this evening.'

2

The Brandy and Seltzer Boys

According to quantum theory, a card perfectly balanced on its edge will fall down in what is known as a 'superposition' – the card really is in two places at once. If a gambler bets money on the queen landing face up, the gambler's own state changes to become a superposition of two possible outcomes – winning

> or losing the bet in either of these parallel worlds, the gambler is unaware of the other outcome and feels as if the card fell randomly.
>
> *Nature*, 5 July, 2007

'We need rituals, Jerry. We need repetition. We need music and mythology and the constant reassurance that at certain times of the day we can visit the waterhole in safety. Without ritual, we are worthless. That's what the torturer knows when he takes away even the consistent repetition of our torment.' Bunny Burroughs ordered another beer. There were still a few minutes to curtain-up. This was to be the first time Gloria Cornish and Una Persson had appeared on the same stage. A revival. *The Arcadians*.

'These are on me.' Jerry signed for the bill. 'Repetition is a kind of death. It's what hopeless people do – what loonies do – sitting and rocking and muttering the same meaningless mantras over and over again. That's not conscious life.'

'We don't *want* conscious life.' Miss Brunner, coming in late, gave her coat to Bishop Beesley to take to the cloakroom. 'Have I got time for a quick G and T? We don't want real variety. From the catchphrase of the comedian to the reiteration of familiar opinions, they're the beating of a mother's heart, the breathing of a sleeping father.'

'Maybe we've at last dispossessed ourselves of the past. We name our children after bathroom products, fantasy characters, drugs, diseases and candy bars. We used to name them after saints or popular politicians…' Jerry finished his beer. A bell began to ring.

'That's just a different kind of continuity. The trusted brand has taken over from the trusted saint.' Miss B. picked up her programme. 'We're still desperate for the familiar. We try to discard it in favour of novelty, but it isn't really novelty, it's just another kind of familiarity. We tell ourselves of our self-expression and self-assertion. When I was a girl, my days were counted in terms of food. Sunday was a hot joint. Tuesday was cold sliced meat, potatoes and a vegetable. Wednesday was shepherd's pie. Thursday was cauliflower cheese. Friday was fish. Saturday, we had a mixed grill. With chips. Just as lessons came and went at school, we attended the Saturday matinée, Sunday at a museum. Something uplifting, anyway, on Sunday. We move forward by means of rituals. We just try to find the means of keeping the carousel turning. We sing work-songs as we build roads. Music allows a semblance of progression, but it isn't real progression. Real progress leads where? To the grave, if we're lucky? Our stories are the same, with minor variations. We're comfortable, with minor variations, in the same clothes. The sun comes up and sets at the same time and we welcome the rise and fall of the workman's hammer, the beat of the drum. If we really wanted to cut our ties with the past we would do the only logical thing. We would kill ourselves.'

'Isn't that just as boring?'

'Oh, I guess so, Mr Cornelius.' Bunny petted at his face and put down his empty glass.

As they walked towards their box, the overture was striking up.

3

From Clue to Clue

> The theme of the Wandering Jew has a history of centuries behind it, and many are the romances which that sinister and melancholy figure has flitted through. In this story you will see how the coming of the mythical Wanderer was a direct threat to the existence of our Empire, and how, when he, as the figurehead of revolt faded out of the picture, Sexton Blake tackled the real causes behind it.
>
> 'The Case of the Wandering Jew',
> *Sexton Blake Annual*, 1940

'I'm running out of memory.' Jerry put his head on one side, like a parrot. 'Or at best storage. I'm forgetting things. I think I might have something.'

'Oh, God, don't give it to us.' Miss Brunner became contemplative. 'Is it catching? Like Alzheimer's?'

'I don't remember.' Jerry took an A-to-Z from the pocket of his black car coat. 'It depends whether it's the past or the present. Or the future. I remember where Berwick Street is in Soho and I could locate Decatur Street. I'm not losing my bearings any worse than usual. Why is everyone trying to forget?'

'It wasn't part of the plan. I'm a bit new to this.' Bunny Burroughs glanced hopefully at Miss Brunner. 'I think.'

Now Jerry really was baffled. 'Plan?'

'The plan for America. Remember Reagan?'

'Vaguely,' said Jerry. He pointed ahead of him. 'If that's not a mirage, we've found an oasis.'

'He's all turned around, poor thing,' said Miss von Krupp.

4

The New XJ – Luxury Transformed by Design

> Freighter captains avoid them as potential catastrophes, climate scientists see them as a bellwether of global warming. But now marine biologists have a more positive take on the thousands of icebergs that have broken free from Antarctica in recent years. These frigid, starkly beautiful mountains of floating ice turn out to be bubbling hot spots of biological activity. And in theory at least they could help counteract the buildup of greenhouse gases that are heating the planet.
>
> – Michael D. Lemonick,
> *Time*, 6 August, 2007

'They've been in Trinity churchyard digging up the famous. I can't tell you how much they got for Audubon.' Jerry sipped his chicory and coffee. The Café du Monde wasn't what it had been but they'd taken the worst of the rust off the chairs, and the joss sticks helped. From somewhere down by the river came the broken sound of a riverboat bell. Then he began to smile at his friend across the table. 'That was you, wasn't it?'

Max Pardon shrugged. 'We were downsized. What can I say? We have to make a living as best we can. The bottom dropped out of real estate. I'm a bone broker, these days, Mr Cornelius. It's an honest job. Some of us still have an interest in our heritage. Monsieur Audubon was a very great man. He made his living, you could say, as a resurrectionist. Mostly. He killed that poor, mad, golden eagle. Do I do anything worse?'

Jerry took a deep breath and regretted it.

The oil had not proved the blessing some had predicted.

5

The Floods That Really Matter Are Composed of Migrant Labour

> Intimate talk about loving your age, finding true joy, and the three words that can change your life.
>
> *Good Housekeeping*, June 2005

In Islamabad, Jerry traded his Banning for an antique Lee-Enfield .303 with a telescopic sight. He had come all the way by aerial cruiser, the guest of Major Nye, with the intention of seeing, if he could do it secretly, his natural son Hussein, who was almost ten. Slipping the beautifully embellished rifle into his cricket bag, he made for an address on Kabul Street, ridding himself of two sets of 'shadows'. The most recent Islamic government was highly suspicious of all Europeans, even though Jerry's Turkish passport gave his religion as Moslem. He wore a beautifully cut coat in two shades of light blue silk, with a set of silver buttons and a turban in darker blue. To the casual eye he resembled a prosperous young stockbroker, perhaps from Singapore.

Arriving at Number Eight, Jerry made his way through a beautiful courtyard to a shaded staircase, which he climbed rapidly after a glance behind him to see if he was followed. On the third floor about halfway down the landing he stopped and knocked. Almost immediately the recently painted door was opened and Bunny Burroughs let him in, his thin lips twisting as he recognised the cricket bag.

'Your fifth attempt, I understand, Jerry. Did you have a safe trip? And will you be playing your usual game this Sunday?'

'If I can find some whites.' Jerry set the bag down and removed his rifle. With his silk handkerchief he dabbed at his sleeve. 'Oil. Virgin. Is the boy over there?'

'With his nanny. The mother, as I told you, is visiting her uncle.'

Jerry peered through the slats of a blind. Across the courtyard, at a tall window, a young woman in a sari was mixing a glass of diluted lemon juice and sugar. Behind her the blue screen of a TV was showing an old Humphrey Bogart movie.

'*Casablanca*,' murmured Bunny.

'*The Big Sleep*.' Jerry lifted the rifle to his shoulder and put his eye close to the sight.

He would never know another sound like that which followed his pulling of the trigger and the bang the gun made.

He had done the best he could. That at least he understood.

Was that a mosquito? He slapped his face.

6

The Phantom of the Towers

International trade in great white sharks now will be regulated, which is especially important for fish who range far beyond the shelter of regional protection. The humphead or Napoleon wrasse – worth tens of thousands of dollars on the market – also received protections, in turn saving coral reefs from the cyanide used to capture them.

Animal Update, Winter 2005

Hubert Lane and Violet Elizabeth Bott were waiting on the corner for Jerry as soon as he reached the outskirts of the village. He had driven over from Hadley to see old Mr Brown. Hubert smirked when he saw Jerry's Phantom IV. 'You've done a lot better for yourself than anyone would have guessed a few years ago.'

Jerry ignored him.

'Hewwo, Jewwy,' lisped Violet Elizabeth, rather grotesquely coy for her age. 'Wovely to see you.'

Jerry scowled. He was already regretting his decision but he opened the gate and began to walk up the surprisingly overgrown path. The Browns clearly hadn't kept their gardener on. Things had deteriorated rather a lot since 1978. The front door of the double-fronted Tudor-style detached house could do with a lick of paint. The brass needed a polish, too. He lifted the knocker.

The door was opened by a woman in uniform.

'Mr "Cornelius"?'

'That's right.'

'Mr Brown said you were coming. He's upstairs. I'm the District Nurse. I hung on specially. This way.'

She moved her full lips in a thin, professional smile and took him straight upstairs. The house smelled familiar and the wallpaper hadn't changed since his last visit. Mrs Brown had been alive then. The older children, Ethel and Robert, had been home from America and Australia respectively.

'They're expected any time,' said the nurse when he asked. She opened the bedroom door. Now the medicinal smell overwhelmed everything else. Old Mr Brown was completely bald. His face was much thinner. Jerry no longer had any idea of his age. He looked a hundred.

'Hello, boy.' Mr Brown's voice was surprisingly vibrant. 'Nice of you to drop in.' His smile broadened. 'Hoping for a tip, were you?'

'Crumbs!' said Jerry.

7

A Game of Patience

> The new centre-right government in UK unveiled on Tuesday the first of its series of measures to curb immigration, saying Indians must now pass English tests if they wanted to marry a British citizen.
>
> *The Times of India*, 9 June, 2010

Banning behind him, Mo put the Humvee in gear and set off across a desert which reminded him of Marilyn Monroe, Charles Manson and Clark Gable. Tumbleweed, red dust, the occasional cactus, yucca, jasper trees. He was heading west and south, trying to avoid the highways. Eventually he saw mountains.

A couple of days later, he woke Jerry who had been asleep in the back since Banning.

'Here we are, Mr C.'

Jerry stretched out on the old rug covering the floor of the vehicle. 'Christmas should be Christmas now we've presents.' He blinked out of the window at a butte. There were faces in every rock. This was the Southwest as he preferred it.

Mo was dragging his gun behind him as he squeezed into a narrow fissure, one of several in the massive rockface. According to legend, a hunted Indian army had made this its last retreat. Somewhere within, there was water, grass, even corn. The countless variegated shades of red and brown offered some hint of logic, at least symmetry, swirling across the outcrops and natural walls as if painted by a New York expressionist. They reminded

Jerry of those ochre Barsoomian Dead Sea bottoms he had loved in his youth. He had been born in London, but he had been raised on Mars. He could imagine the steady movement of waves overhead. He looked up.

Zuni knifewings had been carved at intervals around the entrance of the canyon; between each pair was a swastika.

'I wonder what they had against the Jews,' said Mo. He paused to take a swig from his canteen.

Jerry shrugged. 'You'd have thought there was a lot in common.'

Now Mo disappeared into the fissure. His voice echoed. 'It's huge in here. Amazing. I'll start placing the charges, shall I?'

Jerry began to have second thoughts. 'This doesn't feel like Christmas any more.'

Behind them, on the horizon, a Diné or Apache warband sat on ponies so still they might have been carved from the same ancient rock.

Jerry sighed. 'Or bloody Kansas!' He started to set up his Banning. He was getting tired of this. It had turned out to be much harder work than they'd suggested.

8

A City Slicker Emailed in the Sticks

> Tony Blair claims that one of his many achievements in office was not to repeal the employment laws passed by Margaret Thatcher's government to weaken trade union power. But Blair, as a young and politically ambitious barrister, was a staunch supporter of trade union rights.
>
> *New Statesman*, 25 June, 2007

'I know where you're coming from, Jerry.' Bunny Burroughs closed his laptop. Of course he didn't. He had only the vaguest idea. Jerry didn't even bother to tell him about *The Magnet*, Sexton

Blake or George Formby. They certainly had some memories in common, but even those were filtered through a mix of singular cultural references that changed the simplest meaning. Bunny's baseball and Cornelius's cricket: the list was endless. Yet somehow exile brought out the best in them. They would always have Paris.

Jerry sniffed. 'Are you still selling that stuff?'

'Virtual vapour? It's very popular. While thousands die in Rwanda, millions watch TV and concern themselves with the fate of the mountain gorilla whose time in the world is actually less limited. Assuming zoos continue to do their stuff.' He held up a can. 'Want a sniff?' He peered round at the others. 'Anybody?'

'If I had a shilling for every year I've thought about the future, I'd be a rich man today.' Bishop Beesley hesitated before slipping a Heath bar between his lips and breathing in the soft scent of chocolate and burned sugar. 'Sweet!' He let a sentimental smile drift across his lips. 'I know it's a weakness, but which of us isn't weak somewhere? I live to forget. I mean forgive. I've a parish in South London now. Did you know?'

'I think you told me.'

'No,' said Bunny.

'No? It's only across the river. We could.'

'No.' Jerry continued to look for a channel. 'I don't cross running water if I can help it. And I don't do snow.'

'It's really not as cold as people say it is. Even Norbury's warmer than you'd guess. Kingsley Amis grew up there. And Edwy Searles Brooks. Brooks was the most famous person to come from Norbury. St Franks? Waldo the Wonderman? And Frank Bellamy. You know. In *The Eagle*. Not to mention rock and roll. Martin Stone, England's greatest electric guitarist –'

Jerry shuddered. He'd be hearing about the wonders of Wimbledon next. Tactfully he asked if Beesley knew a second-hand tyre shop easily reached.

'There's even a beach of sorts.' The bishop breathed impatience. 'Where Tooting Common used to be. The water's invigorating, I'm told. Though they haven't axed the chestnut trees.'

'They must be borders,' suggested Bunny.

'Still plenty for the little 'uns.'

'Plenty?'

'Conkers.' The bishop put a knowing hand on Jerry's arm. 'Don't worry. No ward of mine has ever come to harm.'

'Conkers? No, you're barmy. Bonkers.' Jerry shook him off, swiftly walking to the outside door.

'Pop in. Anytime. You've not forgotten how to pray?' The bishop's voice was muffled, full of half-masticated Heath.

Jerry paused, trying to think of a retort.

Bunny Burroughs stood up, his thin body awkward beneath the cloth of his loose, charcoal-grey suit. 'I am a gloomy man, Mr Cornelius. I have a vision. Follow me. Of the appalling filth of this world, I am frequently unobservant. Once I revelled in it, you could fairly say. Now it disgusts me. I am no longer a lover of shit. I came on the streetcar. That's what I like about Europe, the streetcars. Environment-friendly and everything. They have a narrative value you don't run into much any more. Certainly not in America. My mother was German. Studied eugenics, I think. On the evidence. But I'm English on my father's side. I fought on my father's side.'

He turned to look out of the window. 'The slaveships threw over the dead and dying. Typhoon coming on.' He picked up the laptop. 'Trained octopi drove those trams, they say.'

Jerry said, 'Okay. I give up. When can you get me connected?'

'It depends.' Burroughs frowned, either making a calculation or pretending to make one. 'It depends how much memory you want. Four to seven days?' His long, sad face contemplated some invisible chart. His thin fingers played air computer. 'Any options?'

Jerry had become impatient. 'Only connect,' he said. God, how he yearned for a taste of the real world. The world he had been sure he knew. Even Norbury.

The old trees they knew as the 'Manor' grew in ground surrounding the Barclay's Bank and were more or less public until the cricket club became more conscious of its privacy. The egalitarian spirit disappeared rapidly with the success of the first post-war Conservative government.

The best woods lay on top of Biggin Hill where one of wartime Britain's most active airfields had lain in the flat delta where two valleys met. Croydon had been another. Then Norbury Cross, carved out of Mitcham Common and restored, when Jerry first went back, to a replica of its pre-war appearance.

It didn't do to get sentimental. Jerry felt cold again. His breath was thick on the rapidly cooling air. But he had spent too many years finding this place to risk losing it completely.

High elms where the rooks nested making the sharpness of an autumn evening, the smell of wood-smoke, the red and orange skies on the horizon, the noise of the returning birds. Like laughter. Sneering, quarrelsome laughter.

Once real wealth came into the equation, the seeds of fresh class warfare were sewn as the salaries grew farther apart and bonuses became a kind of Danegeld to dissuade directors from taking their strength elsewhere. Most of that strength lay in guilty secrets.

'What the bloody 'ell d'yer fink you're doin' sittin' there dreamin', yer silly-lookin' toad! Go an' get us some fish an' chips.'

'Yes, Mum.' He climbed out of the sheet under which he'd been hiding to frighten his brother Frank.

'Can yer smell pee?' she asked anxiously as he went out through the front door. 'Tell me if yer can smell it when yer come in, love.'

9

The Most Fuel Efficient Auto Company in America

> BRUSSELS: A Belgian high school today sacked a Muslim maths teacher after she insisted she would continue to wear the burqa while taking classes.
>
> *The Times of India*, 9 June, 2010

'What I can't understand about you, Mr Cornelius,' Miss Brunner said, opening a cornflower-blue sunshade only slightly wider than her royal-blue Gainsborough hat, 'is why so many of your mentors are gay. Or Catholic. Or both.'

'Or Jewish,' said Jerry. 'You can't forget the Jews. It's probably the guilt.'

'You? Guilt? Have you ever felt guilt?'

'That's not the point.' He found himself thinking again of Alexander, his unborn son. Invisibly, he collected himself. 'I reflect it.'

'That's gilt. Not guilt.'

'Oh, believe me. They're often the same thing.'

From somewhere beyond the crowd a gun cracked.

She brightened, quickening her high-heeled trot. 'They're off!'

Jerry tripped behind her. There was something about Surrey he was never going to like.

10

The Sleep You've Been Dreaming Of

> The creator of the Segway is one of the most successful and admired inventors in the world. He leads a team of 300 scientists and engineers devoted to making things that better mankind. But Dean Kamen won't feel satisfied until he achieves his greatest goal: reinventing us.
>
> *Popular Mechanics*, June 2010

Back in Islamabad Jerry read the news from New Orleans. He wondered if the French were going to regret their decision to buy it back. How could they possibly make it pay? The clean-up alone had already bankrupted BP. It hadn't been a great couple of years for the oligarchs. Of course, it did give France the refineries and a means of getting their tankers up to Memphis, but how would the American public take to the reintroduction of the minstrels on the showboats?

'People who are free, who live in a real republic, are never offended, Jerry. At best they are a little irritated. They should be able to take a joke by now. In context.'

'Wait till they burn *your* bloody car.' Jerry was still upset about what had happened in Marseilles.

'They are citizens. They have the same rights and responsibilities as me.' Max Pardon swung his legs on his stool. He had rewaxed his moustache. Possibly with cocoa butter.

Jerry lit a long, black Sherman's. 'At least you've brought back smoking.'

'That's the Republic, Jerry.'

Max Pardon raised his hat to a passing Bedouin. 'God bless the man who discovered sand-power.' Overhead the last of the great aerial steamers made its stately way into the sunrise just as the muezzin began to call the faithful to prayer. Monsieur Pardon unrolled his mat and kneeled. 'If you'll forgive me.'

II

Why I Love Metal

> It's what you've been craving. Peaceful sleep without a struggle. That's what LUNESTA© is all about: helping most people fall asleep quickly, and stay asleep all through the night. It's not only non-narcotic; it's approved for long-term use.
>
> Ad for eszopiclone,
> *Time*, 6 August, 2007

'I am sick of people who can't distinguish the taste of sugar from the taste of fruit, who can't tell salt from cheese, who think watching CNN makes them into intellectuals and believe that *Big*

Brother and *The Bachelor* is real life. The richest, most powerful country in the world is about as removed from reality as Oz is from Kansas or Kansas is from Kabul or Obama is from Kenya.' Major Nye was in a rare mood as he leaned over the rail of *The Empress of India* searching with his binoculars for his old station. His long, ancient fingers with their thin tanned skin resembled the claws of an albino crow he had once kept at the station. 'Which half knows Africa best? Bleeding Africa…'

From somewhere among the bleak rolling downs, puffs of smoke showed the positions of the Pashtoon.

'I remember all the times the British tried to invade and hold Afghanistan. What surprises me is why these Yanks think they are somehow better at it, when they've never won a war by themselves since the Mexicans decided to let them have California. Every few years they start another bloody campaign and refuse to listen to their own military chaps and go swaggering in to get their bottoms kicked for the umpteenth time. Then they turn on the French and the Italians whom they consider inferior warriors to themselves. The Europeans learned their lessons. They knew how easy it was to start a war and how difficult it was to finish one. The Americans learned an unfortunate lesson from their successes against the Indians, such as they were. If you ask me, they would have done better to have taken a leaf from Custer's book.'

'Education's never been their strength.' Holding her hat with her left hand, Miss Brunner waved and smiled at someone in the observation gallery. 'It's windy out here, don't you think?'

'Better than that fug in there.' Major Nye indicated the smoking room. With a gesture close to impatience, he threw his cigarette over the side.

As if in answer, another rifle-shot echoed below.

Miss Brunner looked down disapprovingly. 'There should be more public shootings, if you ask me. Why are the decent ones always the first to be taken? They should just be more selective.' She looked up, directing a frigid smile at Mitzi Beesley, who came out to join them. Mitzi was wearing a borrowed flying helmet, a short, pink divided skirt, a flounced white blouse, a knitted bolero jacket.

Mitzi was going through her radical phase. 'That's exactly what the YCFA says. You pinched that from the Left.'

'Oh, we pinched a lot from the Left. Just as the Right pinched from us. When the Left have become Centre Right and the Right has become reactionary, you know exactly where you stand, eh? Exactly. How many times in the last century did you see that?' Miss Brunner laughed happily. 'Oh, I do love old times, don't you? And the one-party system.'

Jerry remembered her closing the gate of her Hampstead Garden Village bijou cottage, as she left him in charge for a week. That had been the last time they had met. She was no longer speaking to him. He went back into the bar and closed the door. It seemed almost silent here; just the soft hum of the giant electric motors. He accepted a pint of Black Velvet. He had a rat buttoned inside his coat. Its nose tickled his chest and he gave an involuntary twitch. Mitzi still didn't know he had rescued 'Sweety' from the fire. He had grown attached to the little animal and felt Mitzi was an imperfect owner.

The Bengali barman polished a glass. 'Life's a bloody tragedy, isn't it, sir? Same again?'

Outside, the rain began to drum on the canopy. Major Nye and the women came running in. 'I for one will be glad to get back to Casablanca,' said Miss Brunner.

12

Obama, Barbour Meet on Coast

> Until recently, criticisms of the BBC were helpful, and attacks upon it harmless; indeed it provided, among other blessings, a happy grumbling ground for the sedentary, where they could release their superfluous force ... and if not much good was done there was anyhow no harm ... Unfortunately, [the BBC's] dignity

is only superficial. It does yield to criticism, and to bad criticism, and it yields in advance – the most pernicious of surrenders.

– E.M. Forster
New Statesman, 4 April, 1931

Jerry had showered and was getting into his regular clothes when Professor Hira came into the changing rooms.

'You were superb today, Mr Cornelius. Especially under the circumstances.'

Jerry accepted his handshake. 'Oh, you know, it's not as if they got the whole of London.'

'Hampstead, Islington, Camden! The Heath is a pit of ash. We saw the cloud on TV. Red and black. The blood! The smoke. Of course, we know that our bombs, for instance, are much more powerful. But Hampstead Garden Village! My home was there for over four years. The Beesleys' too. And so many other dear neighbours.'

'You think it was their target?'

'No doubt about it. And next time it will be Hyde Park or Wimbledon Common. Even Victoria Park. They are easy to home in on, you see.'

'Another park is where they'll strike next?'

'Or, heaven forbid, Lords. Or the Oval.'

'Good God. They'll keep the ashes for ever!'

'Our fear exactly.' Professor Hira took Jerry's other hand. 'You plan, I hope, to stay in Mumbai for a bit? We could do with a good all-rounder.'

Jerry considered this. It was quite a while since he'd been to the pictures. 'It depends what's on, I suppose.' He bent and picked up his cricket bag. 'And I'm sure it's still possible to get a game or two in before things become too hot.'

'Oh, at least. And, Mr Cornelius, it will never be too hot for you in India. Pakistan has far too many distractions, what with the Americans and their own religeuses.'

Jerry scratched his head. Reluctant as he was to leave, he thought it was time he got back home again.

13

The Tears I Shared with Laura Bush

> The most ambitious weapons program in Army history calls for a whole new arsenal of connected gear, from helicopter drones to GPS-guided missiles. But what happens if the network that links it all isn't ready?
>
> *Popular Science*, May 2009

The bats were rising over Austin as usual. Mo had at last given up trying to count them and was eating a hot-dog. He was resentful. He had been told that Texas was the most gun-friendly state in the Union, but had been stopped four times from carrying his Banning into the Capitol. 'Fucking hypocrites.'

'Sir, I must really ask you again to watch your language.'

Mo recognised the Texas Ranger. Jerry caught him in time. The bats rose in a long lazy curve against the dark blue evening sky. It was time to get back to the desert. Jerry had had enough of culture.

He had only come here to get himself a real cowboy hat.

He explained this to the Ranger. 'I suppose you couldn't sell me yours? I think we're about the same head size.'

But he hadn't distracted the Ranger long enough.

'Were you fucking talking to me?' Mo came gleefully forward.

Jerry sighed. He had a feeling they weren't going to be leaving as quietly as he'd hoped. He took out his mobile and dialled Didi Dee. He hated to cancel dinner so close to the time.

He looked at his wrists.

'What's the time? My watches have stopped.'

14

Betrayal in Iraq

MEN LOVE POWER. Why? Ever see what happens when something gets in the way of a tornado? Exactly. That's the thinking behind the Chevy Vortec™ Max powertrain – create a ferocious vortex inside the combustion chamber, along with a high compression ratio, to generate formidable power. And the 345-hp Vortec™ Max, available on the 2006 Silverado, is no exception … **CHEVY SILVERADO: AN AMERICAN REVOLUTION.**

Chevrolet ad, *Texas Monthly*, December 2005

Christmas 1962. Snow was still falling just after dawn when Jerry sprung the gate into Ladbroke Grove/Elgin Gardens and walked onto the path, leaving black pointed prints and tiny heel marks. He had never made a cooler trail. Slipping between the gaps in the netting, he crossed the tennis court and stopped to look back. The marks might have been those of an exotic animal. Nobody coming behind him would know a human had made them. Yet they were already filling up again.

He would never be sure he had deceived anyone. He darted into the nearest back garden. From the French windows came the sound of a Schoenberg piano roll. The snow was a foot deep against the brick wall, on the small lawn. Yellow light fell from the window above. He heard a woman's voice not unlike his mother's. 'Go back to bed, love. It's not time yet.' He recognised Mrs Pash.

Her grandchildren were up early, pedalling the piano. He caught a glimpse of the tree through the half-drawn curtains.

Jerry stepped softly out of the little garden. A blind moved on the first floor in the corner house. The colonel and his wife were looking at him. Another minute and they'd call the police. Their hangovers always made them doubly suspicious. He bowed and went back the way he had come, back into Ladbroke Grove, back across to Blenheim Crescent, past the Convent of the Poor Clares, on his left, to 51, where his mother still lived.

Humming to himself, Jerry went down the slippery area steps to let himself in with his key. Nobody was up. He unshipped the sack from his shoulder and checked out the row of stockings hanging over the black, greasy kitchen range from which a few wisps of smoke escaped. He opened the stove's top and shovelled in more coke. His mum had put the turkey in to cook overnight. There wasn't a tastier smell in the whole world. Then, carefully, he began to fill the stockings from his sack.

Upstairs, he thought he heard someone stirring. He could imagine what the tree looked like, how delighted Catherine and Frank would be when they came down to see their presents.

Outside, the snow still fell, softening the morning. He found the radio set and turned it on. Christmas carols sounded. The noises upstairs grew louder.

Travel certainly made you appreciate the simple things of life, he thought. His eyes filled with happy tears. He went to the kitchen cupboard and took out the bottle of Hine he had put there the night before. Frank hadn't found it. The seal was unbroken. Jerry helped himself to a little nip.

Mrs Cornelius came thumping downstairs in her old carpet slippers. She wore a bright red-and-green dressing gown, her hair still in curlers, last night's make-up still smeared across her face. She rubbed her eyes, staring with approval at the lumpy stockings hanging over the stove. Behind her peered bleary Frank, Catherine's huge blue eyes, suspicious Colonel Pyat.

'Cor,' she said. 'Merry Christmas, love.'

'Merry Christmas, Mum.' He leaned to kiss her. 'God help us, one and all.'

Parts of this story originally appeared in *Nature*, *Planet Stories*, *The New Statesman*, *Time*, *The Spectator*, *Garden & Gun*, *Fantasy Spots*, *PC World*, *Wired*, *The Happy Mag*, *Boys' Friend Library*, *Schoolboys' Own Library*, *Popular Science*, *The Magnet*, *Nelson Lee Library*, *Sexton Blake Library*, *Union Jack Library*, *Good Housekeeping*, *Sports Illustrated*, *Texas Monthly*, *Harper's*, *The New Yorker*, *The New York Times*, *The Guardian*, *Novae Terrae* and others.

REEVE

MICHAEL MOORCOCK (1939–) is one of the most important figures in British SF and Fantasy literature. The author of many literary novels and stories in practically every genre, he has won and been shortlisted for numerous awards including the Hugo, Nebula, World Fantasy, Whitbread and Guardian Fiction Prize. He is also a musician who performed in the seventies with his own band, the Deep Fix; and, as a member of the space-rock band, Hawkwind, won a platinum disc. His tenure as editor of NEW WORLDS magazine in the sixties and seventies is seen as the high watermark of SF editorship in the UK, and was crucial in the development of the SF New Wave. Michael Moorcock's literary creations include Hawkmoon, Corum, Von Bek, Jerry Cornelius and, of course, his most famous character, Elric. He has been compared to, among others, Balzac, Dumas, Dickens, James Joyce, Ian Fleming, J.R.R. Tolkien and Robert E. Howard. Although born in London, he now splits his time between homes in Texas and Paris.

For a more detailed biography, please see Michael Moorcock's entry in *The Encyclopedia of Science Fiction* at: http://www.sf-encyclopedia.com/

For further information about Michael Moorcock and his work, please visit www.multiverse.org, or send S.A.E. to The Nomads Of The Time Streams, Mo Dhachaidh, Loch Awe, Dalmally, Argyll, PA33 1AQ, Scotland, or P.O. Box 385716, Waikoloa, HI 96738, USA.